**Four
Five
and Six
by Tey**

# Four
# Five
# and Six
# by Tey

*The Singing Sands*
*A Shilling for Candles*
*The Daughter of Time*

by Josephine Tey

THE MACMILLAN COMPANY
New York
*A Murder Revisited Classic*

# The
# Singing
# Sands

# 1

IT WAS SIX O'CLOCK of a March morning, and still dark. The long train came sidling through the scattered lights of the yard, clicking gently over the points. Into the glow of the signal cabin and out again. Under the solitary emerald among the rubies on the signal bridge. On towards the empty grey waste of platform that waited under the arcs.

The London Mail at the end of its journey.

Five hundred miles of track lay behind it in the darkness all the way to Euston and last night. Five hundred miles of moonlit fields and sleeping villages; of black towns and unsleeping furnaces; rain, fog, and frost; snow flurry and flood; tunnel and viaduct. Now, in the six o'clock bleakness of a March morning the hills had risen round it and it was coming, casual-seeming and quiet, to rest after its long urgency. And only one person in all its crowded length did not sigh with relief at the realisation.

Of those who sighed, two at least sighed with a gladness that bordered on passion. One of these was a passenger, and the other was a railway employee. The passenger was Alan Grant, and the railway employee was Murdo Gallacher.

Murdo Gallacher was a sleeping-car attendant, and the best-hated living creature between Thurso and Torquay. For twenty years Murdo had browbeaten the travelling public into acquiescence and blackmailed them into tribute. Monetary tribute, that is. Their vocal tribute was voluntary. To first-class passengers far and wide he was known as Yoghourt. (Oh, God, it's Old Yoghourt! they would say as his sour face became visible through the steamy gloom of Euston.) The third-class passengers called him a variety of things, both frank and descriptive. What his colleagues called him is nobody's business. Only three people had ever got the better of Murdo: a cowhand from Texas, a lance-corporal of the Queen's Own Cameron Highlanders, and an unknown little cockney woman in the third-class who had threatened to beat him over his bald head with a lemonade bottle. Neither rank nor achievement impressed Murdo: he hated one and resented the other; but he was greatly afraid of physical pain.

For twenty years Murdo Gallacher had done the absolute minimum. He had been bored by the job before he had been a week at it, but he had found it a rich lode and he had stayed to mine it. If you got morning tea from Murdo, the tea would be weak, the biscuit soft, the sugar dirty, the tray slopped, and the spoon missing; but when Murdo came to collect the tray the protests which you had been rehearsing died on your lips. Now and then an Admiral of the Fleet or something like that would venture an opinion that it was damned awful tea, but the ruck smiled and paid up. For twenty years they had paid up, weary and browbeaten and blackmailed. And Murdo had collected. He was now the owner of a villa at Dunoon, a string of fried-fish shops in Glasgow, and a very nice bank balance. He might have retired years ago but he could not bear the thought of losing his full pension; so he endured the boredom a little longer and evened things up by not bothering with early-morning teas unless passengers suggested the thing themselves; and sometimes, if he was very sleepy, forgetting about the order anyway. He hailed the end of each journey with the relief of a man who is working out his sentence and has only a short time left.

Alan Grant, watching the lights of the yard float past beyond the steamed-up window and listening to the gentle sound of the wheels clicking over the points, was glad because the end of the journey was the end of a night's suffering. Grant had spent the night trying not to open the door into the corridor. Wide awake, he had lain on his expensive pallet and sweated by the hour. He had sweated not because the compartment was too hot—the air-conditioning worked to a marvel—but because (O Misery! O Shame! O Mortification!) the compartment represented A Small Enclosed Space. To the normal eye the compartment was just a neat little room with a bunk, a wash-basin, a mirror, luggage racks in assorted sizes, shelves that appeared or disappeared as bidden, a fine little drawer for one's hypothetical valuables, and a hook for one's presumably unhocked watch. But to the initiate, the sad and haunted initiate, it was A Small Enclosed Space.

Overwork, the doctor called it.

"Sit back and browse for a little," the doctor had said, crossing one elegant Wimpole Street leg over the other and admiring the hang of it.

Grant could not imagine himself sitting back, and he considered browsing a loathsome word and a contemptible occupation. Browsing. A fattening-up for the table. A mindless satisfaction of animal desires. Browse, indeed! The very sound of the word was an offence. A snore.

"Have you any hobbies?" the doctor had asked, his admiring glance going on to his shoes.

"No," Grant had said shortly.

"What do you do when you go on holiday?"

"I fish."

"You fish?" said the psychologist, seduced from his Narcissian gazing. "And you don't consider that a hobby?"

"Certainly not."

"What is it, then, would you say?"

"Something between a sport and a religion."

And at that Wimpole Street had smiled and had looked quite human, and assured him that his cure was only a matter of time. Time and relaxation.

Well, at least he had managed not to open the door last night. But the triumph had been dearly bought. He was drained and empty, a walking nothingness. "Don't fight it," the doctor had said. "If you want to be in the open, go into the open." But to have opened that door last night would have meant a defeat so mortal that he felt there would be no recovery. It would have been an unconditional surrender to the forces of Unreason. So he had lain and sweated. And the door had stayed closed.

But now, in the unrewarding dark of early morning, in the bleak, anonymous dark, he was as without virtue as if he had lost. "I suppose this is how women feel after long labour," he thought, with that fundamental detachment which Wimpole Street had noted and approved. "But at least they have a brat to show for it. What have I got?"

His pride, he supposed. Pride that he had not opened a door that there was no reason to open. Oh, God!

He opened the door now. Reluctantly, and appreciating the irony of that reluctance. Loath to face the morning and life. Wishing that he could throw himself back on the rumpled couch and sleep and sleep and sleep.

He picked up the two suitcases which Yoghourt had not offered to do anything about, tucked the bundle of unread periodicals under his arm, and went out into the corridor. The little vestibule at the end of it was blocked almost to the roof with the luggage of the more lavish tippers, so that the door was nearly invisible; and Grant moved on into the second of the first-class coaches. The forward end of that too was stacked waist-deep with privileged obstacles, and he began to walk down the corridor towards the door at the rear end. As he did so Yoghourt himself came from his cubby-hole at the far end to make sure that Number B Seven was aware that they were nearly at the terminus. It was the acknowledged right of Number B Seven, or of any Number whatever, to leave the train at his leisure after arrival; but Yoghourt had of course no intention of hanging round while someone had his sleep out. So he knocked loudly on the door of B Seven and went in.

As Grant came level with the open door, Yoghourt was shaking B Seven, who was lying fully dressed on the bunk, by the cloth of his sleeve and saying in choked exasperation: "Come on, sir, come on! We're practically in."

He looked up as Grant's shadow darkened the door and said disgustedly, "Tight as an owl!"

The compartment was so solid with the reek of whisky that you could stand a walking-stick in it, Grant noticed. Automatically he picked up the newspaper that Yoghourt's shaking had dislodged on to the compartment floor, and straightened the man's jacket.

"Can't you recognise a dead man when you see one?" he said. Through the haze of his tiredness he heard his own voice say it: Can't you recognise a dead man when you see one? As if it were a thing of no moment. Can't you recognise a primrose when you see one? Can't you recognise a Rubens when you see one? Can't you recognise the Albert Memorial when—

"Dead!" said Yoghourt in a kind of howl. "He can't be! I'm due to go off."

That, Grant noted from his far-away stance, was all that it meant to Mr. Blast His Soul Gallacher. Someone had taken leave of life, had gone out from warmth and feeling and perception to nothingness, and all it meant to Damn His Eyes Gallacher was that he would be late in getting off duty.

"What'll I do?" said Yoghourt. "How was I to know anyone was drinking themselves to death in my coach! What'll I do?"

"Report to the police, of course," Grant said, and for the first time he was conscious of life again as a place where one might have pleasure. It gave him a twisted, macabre pleasure that Yoghourt had at last met his match: the man who would get out of tipping him; and that that man should be the one to put him to more inconvenience than anyone had succeeded in doing in all his twenty years in the railway service.

He looked again at the young face under the rumpled dark hair, and went away down the corridor. Dead men were not his responsibility. He had had his fill of dead men in his time, and although he had never quite lost a heart-contraction at its irrevocability death had no longer power to shock him.

The wheels ceased their clicking, and instead came the long low hollow sound that a train makes coming into a railway station. Grant lowered the window and watched the grey ribbon of the platform run past. The cold struck him like a blow in the face, and he began to shiver uncontrollably.

He dropped the two suitcases on the platform and stood there (chattering like a blasted monkey, he thought resentfully) and wished that it were possible to die temporarily. In some last dim recess of his mind he knew that to dither with cold and nerves on a station platform at six of a winter morning was in the final resort a privilege, a corollary to being alive; but oh, how wonderful it would be to achieve temporary death and pick up life again at some happier moment.

"To the hotel, sir?" the porter said. "Yes, I'll take them over when I've seen to this barrow-load."

He stumbled up the steps and across the bridge. The wood sounded drum-like and hollow under his tread; great bursts of steam billowed up round him from below; noises clanged and echoed from the dark vault about him. They were all wrong about hell, he thought. Hell wasn't a nice cosy place where you fried. Hell was a great cold echoing cave where there was neither past nor future; a black, echoing desolation. Hell was concentrated essence of a winter morning after a sleepless night of self-distaste.

He stepped out into the empty courtyard, and the sudden quiet soothed him. The darkness was cold but clean. A hint of greyness in its quality spoke of morning, and a breath of snow in its cleanness spoke of the "high tops." Presently, when it was daylight, Tommy would come to the hotel and pick him up and they would drive away into the great clean Highland country; away into the wide, unchanging, undemanding Highland world where people died only in their beds and no one bothered to shut a door anyhow because it was too much trouble.

In the hotel dining-room the lights were on only at one end, and into the gloom of the unlit spaces marched ranks of naked baize-topped tables. He had never before, now he came to think of it, seen restaurant tables undressed. They were really very humble shabby things stripped of their white armour. Like waiters without their shirt-fronts.

A child in a black uniform dress and a green jersey coat embroidered with flowers poked her head round a screen and seemed startled to see him. He asked what he might have for breakfast. She took a cruet from the sideboard and set it on the cloth in front of him with an air of ringing the curtain up. "I'll send Mary to you," she said kindly, and went away behind the screen.

Service, he thought, had lost its starch and its high glaze. It had become what housewives call rough-dried. But now and then a promise to send Mary to one made up for embroidered jerseys and similar infelicities.

Mary was a plump calm creature who would inevitably have been a Nannie if Nannies were not out of fashion, and under her ministrations Grant felt himself relaxing as a child does in the presence of a benevolent authority. It was a fine state of affairs, he thought bitterly, when he needed reassurance so badly that a fat hotel waitress could provide it.

But he ate what she put in front of him and began to feel better. Presently she came back, removed the slices of cut bread, and put in their place a plate of morning rolls.

"Here's the baps to you," she said. "They've just this minute come. They're poor things nowadays. No chew in them at all. But they're better than that bread."

She pushed the marmalade nearer to his hand, looked to see if he needed more milk, and went away again. Grant, who had had no intention of eating any more, buttered a bap and reached for one of the unread papers from last night's store. What came to his hand was a London evening paper, and he looked at it with a puzzled lack of recognition. Had he bought an evening paper? Surely he had read the evening paper at the normal hour of four o'clock in the afternoon. Why buy another at seven o'clock in the evening? Had buying an evening paper become a reflex action, as automatic as brushing one's teeth? Lighted bookstall: evening paper. Was that the way it worked?

The paper was a *Signal*, the afternoon voice of the morning *Clarion*. Grant looked again at the headlines which he had absorbed yesterday afternoon and thought how constant in kind they were. It was yesterday's paper, but it might equally be last year's or next month's. The headlines would for ever be the ones that he was looking at now: the Cabinet row, the dead body of the blonde in Maida Vale, the Customs prosecution, the hold-up, the arrival of an American actor, the street accident. He pushed the thing away from him, but as he reached out a hand for the next roll in the pile he noticed that the blank space for the Stop Press news bore scribblings in pencil. He turned the paper round so that he could see what someone had been calculating. But it seemed that the scribble was not, after all, some newsboy's hasty reckoning of the odds. It was someone's attempt at verse. That it was an original work and not an attempt to remember some verse already known was apparent in the desultory writing and in the fact that the writer had filled the two missing lines by ticking in the required number of feet, a trick that Grant himself had used in the days when he had been the best sonnet-writer in the sixth form.

But this time the poem was none of his.

And suddenly he knew where the paper had come from. He had acquired it by an action much more automatic than buying an evening paper. He had put it under his arm with the others when he picked it up as it slipped to the floor of compartment B Seven. His conscious mind—or as much of it as was conscious after last night—was concerned with the disarray that Yoghourt was making of a helpless man. His only deliberate action had been his reproof to Yoghourt in his straightening of the man's jacket, and for that he had needed a hand, and so the paper had gone under his arm with the rest.

So the young man with the tumbled black hair and the reckless eyebrows had been a poet, had he?

Grant looked with interest at the pencilled words. The writer had designed his effort in eight lines, it seemed, but he had not been able to think of the fifth and sixth, so that the scribble read:

> *The beasts that talk,*
> *The streams that stand,*
> *The stones that walk,*
> *The singing sand,*
> . . . . . . . . . . . .
> . . . . . . . . . . . .
> *That guard the way*
> *To Paradise.*

Well, it was odd enough, in all conscience. The beginnings of delirium tremens?

It was understandable that the owner of that very individual face would see nothing so ordinary in his alcoholic dreams as pink rats. Nature itself would turn cartwheels for the young man with the reckless eyebrows. What was the Paradise that was guarded by so terrifying a strangeness? Oblivion? Why had he needed oblivion so badly that it represented Paradise to him? That he had been prepared to run the known horror of the approaches to it?

Grant ate the fine fresh bap that there was "no chew in" and considered the matter. The writing was unformed but not at all shaky; it looked the writing of an adult who wrote an unformed hand not because his co-ordination was bad but because he had never quite grown up. Because in essentials he was still the schoolboy who had originally written that way. This theory was confirmed by the shape of the capital letters, which were made in pure copy-book form. Odd that so individual a creature had had no desire to impress his individuality on the form of his letters. Very few people indeed did not adapt the copy-book form to their own liking, to their own unconscious need.

One of Grant's milder interests had for years been the business of hand-writing; and in his work he had found the results of his long observation greatly useful. Now and then, of course, he was shaken out of any com-placency about his deductions—a multiple murderer who dissolved his victims in acid turned out to have handwriting remarkable only for its extreme logic, which after all was perhaps appropriate enough—but in general, handwriting provided a very good index to a man. And in general a man who continued to use the schoolboy form for his letters did so for one of two reasons: either he was unintelligent, or he wrote so little that the writing had had no chance of absorbing his personality.

Considering the high degree of intelligence that had put into words that nightmare hazard at the gates of Paradise, it was obvious that it was not lack of personality that had kept the young man's writing adolescent. His per-sonality—his vitality and interest—had gone into something else.

Into what?

Something active, something extrovert. Something in which writing was used for messages like: "Meet me Cumberland bar, 6.45, Tony," or for filling up a log.

But he was introvert enough to have analysed and put into words that country-of-the-moon on the way to his Paradise. Introvert enough to have stood apart and looked at it, to have wanted to record it.

Grant sat in a pleasant warm daze, chewing and considering. He noted the tightly joined tops of the *n*s and *m*s. A liar? Or just secretive? A curiously cautious trait to appear in the writing of a man with those eyebrows. It was a strange thing how much the meaning of a countenance depended on eye-brows. One change of degree in the angle this way or that, and the whole effect was different. Film magnates took nice little girls from Balham and Muswell Hill and rubbed out their eyebrows and painted in other ones and they became straightway mysterious creatures from Omsk and Tomsk. He had once been told by Trabb, the cartoonist, that it was his eyebrows that had lost Ernie Price his chance of being Prime Minister. "They didn't like his eyebrows," Trabb had said, blinking owlishly over his beer. "Why? Don't ask me. I just draw. Because they looked bad-tempered, perhaps. They don't like a bad-tempered man. Don't trust him. But that's what lost him his chance, take it from me. His eyebrows. They didn't like 'em." Bad-tempered eye-brows, supercilious eyebrows, calm eyebrows, worried eyebrows—it was the eyebrows that gave a face its keynote. And it was the slant of the black eyebrows that had given that thin white face on the pillow its reckless look even in death.

Well, the man had been sober when he wrote those words, that at least was clear. That toper's oblivion in compartment B Seven—the fugged air, the rucked blankets, the empty bottle rolling about on the floor, the overturned glass on the shelf—may have been the Paradise he sought, but he was sober when he blueprinted the way to it.

The singing sand.

Uncanny but somehow attractive.

Singing sand. Surely there actually were singing sands somewhere? It had a vaguely familiar sound. Singing sands. They cried out under your feet as you walked. Or the wind did it, or something. A man's forearm in a checked tweed sleeve reached in front of him and took a bap from the plate.

"You seem to be doing yourself very well," Tommy said, pulling out a chair and sitting down. He split the bap and buttered it. "There's no chew in these things at all nowadays. When I was a boy you sank your teeth in them and pulled. It was evens which came away first, your teeth or the bit of bap. But if your teeth won, you really had something worth having. A nice floury, yeasty mouthful that would last you for a couple of minutes. They don't taste of anything nowadays, and you could fold them in two and put the whole thing in your mouth without any danger of choking yourself."

Grant looked at him in silence and with affection. There was no intimacy so close, he thought, as the intimacy that bound you to a man with whom you'd shared a prep-school dorm. They had shared their public school days too, but it was prep school that he remembered each time he encountered Tommy anew. Perhaps because in all essentials that fresh pinky-brown face with the round, ingenuous blue eyes was the same face that used to appear above a crookedly buttoned maroon blazer. Tommy had always buttoned his blazer with a fine insouciance.

It was so like Tommy not to waste time or vitality on conventional inquiries as to his journey and his health. Neither would Laura, of course. They would accept him as he stood, as if he had been there for some time; as if he had never gone away at all but was still on his previous visit. It was an extraordinarily restful atmosphere to sink back into.

"How is Laura?"

"Never better. Putting on a bit of weight. At least that's what she says. Don't see it myself. I never liked skinny women."

There had been a time, when they were both about twenty, when Grant had thought of marrying his cousin Laura; and she, he had been sure, had had thoughts of marrying him. But before any word had been said, the magic had faded and they were back on the old friendly footing. The magic had been part of the long intoxication of a Highland summer. Part of hill mornings smelling of pine needles, and of endless twilights sweet with the scent of clover. For Grant his cousin Laura had always been part of the happiness of summer holidays; they had graduated together from burn-paddling to their first fishing-rods, and together they had first walked the Larig and together had stood for the first time on the top of Braeriach. But it was not until that summer at the end of their adolescence that the happiness had crystallised into Laura herself; that the whole of summer was focused into the person of Laura Grant. He still had a slight lifting of the heart when he thought of that summer. It had the light perfection, the iridescence, of a bubble. And because no word had been said, the bubble would never now be broken. It stayed light and perfect and iridescent and poised, where they had left it. They had both gone on to other things, to other people. Laura, indeed, had skipped from one person to the next one with the bright indifference of a child playing hop-scotch. And then he had taken her to that Old Boys' dance. And she had met Tommy Rankin. And that had been that.

"What's the fuss at the station?" Tommy asked. "Ambulances and things."

"A man died on the train. I expect it is that."

"Oh," said Tommy, dismissing it. "Not your funeral this time," he added in a congratulatory way.

"No. Not my funeral, thank Heaven."

"They'll miss you on the Embankment."

"I doubt it."

"Mary," said Tommy, "I could do with a pot of good strong tea." He flicked the plate that held the baps with a contemptuous forefinger. "And another couple of these poor bargains." He turned his serious childlike gaze on Grant and said: "They'll have to miss you. They'll be one short, won't they?"

Grant expelled his breath in the nearest he had come to a laugh for months. Tommy had been commiserating with Headquarters, not on the loss of his genius, but on the lack of his presence. His "family" attitude had been almost identical with the professional reaction of his Chief. "Sick leave!" Bryce had said, his little elephant eyes running over Grant's healthy looking frame and coming back to his face with disgust. "Well, well! What is the Force coming to! In my young days you stayed on duty until you fell over. And you went on writing up your notes until the ambulance carted you away off the floor." It had not been easy to tell Bryce what the doctor had said, and Bryce had not made it any easier. Bryce had never had a nerve of any sort in his body; he was mere physical force animated by a shrewd if limited brain. There had been neither comprehension nor sympathy in his reception of Grant's news. Indeed, there had been a subtle suggestion, a mere whiff of an implication, that Grant was malingering; that this so-strange breakdown that left him so markedly well and fit in appearance had something to do with the spring run in Highland rivers; that he had already arranged his fishing flies before going to Wimpole Street.

"What will they do to fill the gap?" Tommy asked.

"Promote Sergeant Williams, probably. His promotion is long overdue anyhow."

It had been no easier to tell the faithful Williams. When your subordinate has openly hero-worshipped you for years, it is not pleasant to have to appear before him as a poor nerve-ridden creature at the mercy of non-existent demons. Williams, too, had never had a nerve in his body. He took everything as it came, placid and unquestioning. It had not been easy to tell Williams and see the admiration change to concern. To—pity?

"Push over the marmalade," Tommy said.

# 2

THE PEACE INDUCED by Tommy's matter-of-fact acceptance of him deepened as they drove into the hills. These two accepted him; standing around in a detached benevolence, watching him come in a familiar quiet. It was a grey morning, and still. The landscape was tidy and bare. Tidy grey walls round bare fields, bare fences along the tidy ditches. Nothing had begun to grow yet in the waiting countryside. Only a willow here and there by a culvert side showed live and green in the half-shades.

It was going to be all right. This was what he had needed, this wide silence, this space, this serenity. He had forgotten how benevolent the place was, how satisfying. The near hills were round and green and kind; beyond them were farther ones, stained blue by the distance. And behind all stood the long rampart of the Highland line, white and remote against the calm sky.

"The river is very low, isn't it?" he said, as they came down into the valley of the Turlie. And was invaded by panic.

That was the way it always happened. One moment a sane, free, self-possessed human being, and the next a helpless creature in the grip of unreason. He pressed his hands together to keep himself from flinging the door open and tried to listen to what Tommy was saying. No rain for weeks. They had had no rain for weeks. Let him think about the lack of rain. It was important, the lack of rain. It spoiled the fishing. It was to fish he had come to Clune. If they didn't have rain, there would be no run of fish. No water for them. Oh, God, help me not to make Tommy stop! No water. Think intelligently about fishing. If they had had no rain for weeks, then rain must be due, mustn't it? Why could you ask a friend to stop the car and let you be sick and yet not ask him to stop the car so that you could get out of its small shut-in-ness? Look at the river. *Look* at it. Remember things about it. That was where you caught your best fish last year. That was where Pat slipped down when he was sitting on the rock and was left hanging by the seat of his pants.

"As nice a clean-run fish as ever you saw," Tommy was saying.

The hazels by the river made a bright mauve smudge in the grey-green of the moor. Presently, when it was summer-time, the cold clattering of their leaves would make an obbligato to the river's song, but just now they stood in a pink, silent huddle along the bank.

Tommy, looking at the state of the water, also noticed the bare hazel twigs, but being a parent he was not moved to think of summer afternoons. "Pat has discovered that he is a diviner," he said.

That was better. Think about Pat. Talk about Pat.

"The house is strewn with twigs of all shapes and sizes."

"Has he discovered anything?" If he could keep his mind on Pat, it might be all right.

"He has discovered gold under the sitting-room hearth, a body under the what-you-may-call-'em in the downstairs bathroom, and two wells."

"Where are the wells?" It couldn't be so very long now. Five miles to the head of the glen and Clune.

"One under the dining-room floor and one under the kitchen passage."

"I take it that you haven't dug up the sitting-room hearth." The window was wide open. What was there to worry about? It wasn't really a closed space, not a closed space at all.

"We have not. He is very peeved about that. Said I was a once-born."

"Once-born?"

"Yes. It's his latest word. It ranks just one degree below a stinker, I understand."

"Where did he get the word?" He would hang on till they got to that birch wood at the corner. Then he would ask Tommy to stop.

"Don't know. From some Theosophist woman who talked to the W.R.I. last autumn, I should think."

Why should he mind Tommy's knowing? There was nothing shameful about it. If he were a paralysed syphilitic, he would accept Tommy's help and sympathy. Why should he want to keep from Tommy's knowledge the fact that he was sweating with terror because of something that didn't exist? Perhaps he could cheat? Perhaps he could just ask Tommy to stop for a little while he admired the view?

Here was the birch wood. At least he had lasted that far.

He would make it the bit of road level with the bend of the river. He would make the excuse of having a look at the water. Much more plausible than looking at the view. Tommy would look with alacrity at a river and only with passive protest at a view.

About fifty seconds more. One, two, three, four . . .

Now.

"We lost two sheep in that pool this winter," Tommy said, sweeping past the bend.

Too late.

What other excuse could he make? He was too near Clune now for excuses to be easy to find.

He could not even light a cigarette for fear his hands were shaking too much.

Perhaps if he did something, however trivial . . .

He took the bundle of papers from the seat by his side, rearranging them, shuffling them busily and without point. He noticed that the *Signal* was not among them. He had meant to take it with him because of the odd little tentative verse in the Stop Press, but he must have left it in the hotel dining-room. Oh, well. It didn't matter. It had served its turn in giving interest to his breakfast. And the owner certainly would not want it again. He had achieved his Paradise, his oblivion; if that was what he had wanted. Not for him the privilege of uncontrolled hands and sweating skin. The privilege of wrestling with demons. Not for him the clean morning, the kind earth, the loveliness of the Highland line against the sky.

For the first time it occurred to him to wonder what had brought the young man to the North.

He had not, presumably, engaged a first-class sleeping compartment just to drink himself insensible in. He had had an intended destination. He had had business and desire. A purpose.

Why had he come to the North at this bleak, unfashionable season? To fish? To climb? The compartment as he remembered it had given an impression of bareness, but the heavy luggage might have been under the bunk. Or, indeed, in the van. Apart from sport what was there?

Official business?

Not with that face, no.

An actor? An artist? Just possibly.

A sailor going to join his ship? Going to some naval base beyond Inverness? That was possible. The face would look very well on the bridge of a ship. A small ship; very fast; and hellish in any kind of sea.

What else was there? What would bring a dark, thin young man with reckless eyebrows and a passion for alcohol to the Highlands at the beginning of March? Unless in these days of whisky shortage he had had thoughts of starting an illicit still?

It was a pleasant idea, at that. How easy would it be? Not as easy as in Ireland, because the will to lawlessness was lacking; but once you had achieved it the whisky would be a great deal better. He almost wished that he could have put the idea to the young man. Could have sat opposite him at dinner last night, perhaps, and watched the gleam come into his eye at the thought of such delicious flouting of the Law. He wished that he could have talked to him anyway; exchanged ideas with him; found out about him. If someone had talked with him last night, he might now be part of this living morning, of this fine gracious world with its gifts and its promise, instead of—

"And gaffed him in the pool below the footbridge," said Tommy, finishing a story.

Grant looked down at his hands, and found that they were still.

The dead young man, who could not save himself, had saved him.

He looked up and saw in front of him the white house of Clune. It lay in the green cup of the hill, alone except for its attendant slab of sheltering fir-wood stuck like some dark green wool-work on the bare landscape. A blue curl of smoke rose up from the chimney into the still air. It was the fine essence of peace.

As they drove up the sandy track from the road, he saw Laura come out of the door and stand waiting for them. She waved to them, and as her arm came down from its wave she tucked in the strand of hair that fell on to her forehead. The familiar gesture warmed his chilled being. Just so she used to be waiting on the little Badenoch platform for him when she was a child, with just that wave and that tucking-in of a strand of hair. The same strand of hair.

"Damn," said Tommy, "I forgot to post her letters. Don't mention it unless she asks."

Laura kissed him on both cheeks, took one look at him, and said:

"I have a lovely bird for your lunch, but you look as if a good long sleep would do you more good. So go straight up and have it and forget about food until you waken. We have weeks to gossip in, so we don't have to start right now."

Only Laura, he thought, would have streamlined her hostess rôle to a guest's need so neatly. No subtle touting of the beautifully planned luncheon, no concealed blackmail. She did not even ply one with unwanted cups of tea, nor pointedly recommend her fine hot bath-water. She did not even demand the small-chat of arrival, the polite hanging around. She supplied without question and without hesitation the thing that he needed. A pillow.

He wondered whether it was that he looked a wreck or whether it was just that Laura knew him so well. It occurred to him that he would not mind Laura's knowing about his bondage of fear. It was odd that where he had shrunk from exhibiting his weakness to Tommy he should not care that Laura might learn about it. It should have been the other way about.

"I have put you in the other bedroom this time," she said, preceding him up the stairs, "because the west one has been done up and it still stinks a bit."

She was in truth putting on weight a little, he noticed; but her ankles were as good as ever. And then, with that native detachment that never quite deserted him, he realised that his lack of any desire to conceal from Laura his childish fits of panic was proof that no small remote part of him was still in love with her. The need of the male to look well in the eyes of the beloved one was no part of his relation with Laura.

"People always say about east bedrooms that they get the morning sun," she said, standing in the middle of the east bedroom and looking at it as if she had never seen it before. "As if it were a recommendation. I think myself it's much nicer to be able to look out on a sunny landscape. Which you can't do with the sun in your eyes." She stuck her thumbs in her waistband and eased the belt that was growing too tight. "But the west room will be habitable in a day or two, so you can change over then if you want to. How is my dear Sergeant Williams?"

"Pink and clean."

He had an instant picture of Williams, sitting solid and shy at the tea-table in the lounge of the Westmorland. He had been on his way out after a session with the manager and had come across Laura and Grant having tea, and had been persuaded to join them. He had made a great success with Laura.

"You know, whenever this country is in one of its periodic messes, I think of Sergeant Williams and am quite sure on the instant that everything is going to be all right."

"I suppose *I* don't reassure you at all," Grant said, busy unstrapping luggage.

"Not noticeably. Not that way, anyway. You'd only be a comfort if everything *wasn't* going to be all right." With which cryptic statement she left him. "Don't come down until you want to. Don't come down at all, if it comes to that. Just ring when you waken."

Her footsteps went away down the passage, and the silence flooded in behind her.

He stripped off his clothes and without bothering to pull a curtain over the light he fell into bed. Presently he thought: I'd better draw those curtains or the light may waken me too soon. He opened his eyes reluctantly, to gauge the degree of light, and found that the light was no longer coming in at the window at all. It was lying on the out-of-doors instead. He lifted his head from the pillow to consider this oddity, and realised that it was late afternoon.

Relaxed and amused, he turned on to his back and lay listening to the quiet. The immemorial quiet. He savored it, and luxuriated in his long reprieve. Not an enclosed space between this and the Pentland Firth. Between this and the North Pole, if it came to that. Through the wide-open window he could see the evening sky, still grey but faintly luminous and streaked with level cloud. No rain in that sky; only an echo of the peace that held the world in this contented quiet. Oh, well, if he could not fish he could walk. If the worst came to the worst, he could shoot rabbits.

He watched the level clouds darken against their background and wondered whom Laura would have got for him to marry this time. It was an extraordinary thing how all married women were banded together against the state of singleness in man. If the women were happily married, like Laura, they considered marriage the only satisfactory state for an adult not suffering from any marked incapacity or relevant hindrance. If they were unhappily yoked, then they were filled with resentment of anyone who had escaped such punishment. Each time that he came to Clune, Laura was in the habit of producing some carefully vetted female for his consideration. Nothing was ever said about their desirable qualities, of course; they were just trotted up and down in front of him so that he might view their paces. Nor, when he showed no particular interest in a candidate, was there any overt regret in the atmosphere, any suggestion of reproof. All that happened was that next time Laura had a new idea.

Somewhere, far away, was a sound that was either the lazy clucking of a hen or the clash of teacups being assembled. He listened for a little, hoping that it was a hen, but decided with regret that it was tea in preparation. He must get up. Pat would be home from school, and Bridget awake from her afternoon nap. It was quite typically Laura that she should not even have demanded from him a due admiration of her daughter; that he had not been asked to exclaim over her growth in the last year, her intelligence, her looks. Bridget had not been mentioned at all. She was merely a young creature somewhere out of sight, like the rest of the farm animals.

He got up and went to have a bath. And twenty minutes later he went downstairs conscious that he was hungry for the first time for months.

The family picture upon which the sitting-room door opened was pure Zoffany, he thought. The sitting-room at Clune occupied almost the whole of what had been the original farmhouse and was now a small wing to the main building. Because it had once been several rooms instead of one, it had more windows than are usual in its kind; because it had thick walls it was warm and safe-feeling; and because it had a south-west outlook it was brighter than most. All the traffic of the house was concentrated there, as in the hall of some medieval manor. Only at luncheon and supper was any other room used by the family. A large round table by the fire ensured the comforts of "dining-room" meals at tea and breakfast, and the rest of the room was a fine free mixture of office, drawing-room, music-room, schoolroom and greenhouse. Johan, Grant thought, would not have had to alter one detail. It was all there already, even to the cadging terrier at the table and Bridget splay-legged on the hearthrug.

Bridget was a blonde, silent child of three who spent her days endlessly rearranging the same few objects into new patterns. "I can't make up my mind whether she is mentally deficient or a genius," Laura said. But Grant thought that the two-second glance with which Bridget favoured him on introduction entirely justified the cheerfulness of Laura's tone; there was nothing wrong with the intelligence of The Child, as Patrick called her. This epithet as used by Pat had no sense of opprobrium, nor even any marked condescension; it merely emphasised his own inclusion in the adult group, to which his six years of seniority in his own estimation entitled him.

Pat had red hair, and a bleak and intimidating grey eye. He was wearing a tattered green tartan kilt, smoke-blue stockings, and a much-darned grey jersey. His greeting to Grant was offhand but reassuringly uncouth. Pat spoke from choice what his mother called "clotted Perthshire," his bosom friend at the village school being the shepherd's son, who hailed from Killin. He could, of course, when he had a mind, speak faultless English, but it was always a bad sign. When Pat was "not speaking" to you, he was always not speaking in the best English.

Over tea, Grant asked him if he had yet made up his mind what he was going to be, Pat's invariable answer to the question from the age of four having been, "A'm taking it into avizandum." A phrase borrowed from his J.P. father.

"Ay," said Pat, spreading jam with a liberal hand. "A've made up muh mind."

"You have? That's fine. What are you going to be?"

"A revolutionary."

"I hope I never have to arrest you."

"Yu couldna," said Pat simply.

"Why not?"

"A'll be *good,* man," said Pat, dipping the spoon again.

"I'm sure that's the sense Queen Victoria used the word in," Laura said, removing the jam from her son's possession.

It was for that sort of thing that he had loved her. The odd glinting detachment that shot the texture of her maternalism.

"I have a fish for you," Pat said, scraping the jam to one side of the slice of bread so that it would, over at least half the surface, achieve the required depth. (What he actually said was, "Ah hiv a fush forrya," but Pat's phonetics are no pleasanter to the eye than they are on the ear, and may be left to the imagination.) "Under the ledge in the Cuddy Pool. You can have a len' of my fly, if you like."

Since Pat possessed a large tin box full of assorted invitations to slaughter, "my fly" in the singular could only mean "the fly I have invented."

"What is Pat's lure like?" Grant asked when Pat had taken himself off.

"Actionable, I should say," said his mother. "A fearsome object."

"Does he catch anything with it?"

"Oddly enough, yes," Tommy said. "I suppose there are suckers in the fish world just the same as in any other."

"The poor things just gape with astonishment at sight of it," Laura said, "and before they have time to shut their mouths the current has swept it in. Tomorrow's Saturday, so you can see it in operation. But I don't think that anything, even Pat's unholy creation, will lure that six-pounder in the Cuddy Pool to the surface with the water the way it is just now."

And of course Laura was right. Saturday morning was bright and rainless, and the six-pounder in the Cuddy Pool was far too dismayed by his imprisonment, far too obsessed with his desire to go higher up the river, to be interested in surface distractions. So it was suggested that Grant should go trout fishing in the loch, with Pat as gillie. The loch was two miles away in the hills, a flat pool on a bleak bit of moor. When it was windy on Lochan Dhu, the gale took your line out of the water at right angles and held it stiff as a telephone wire. When it was calm the midges made a meal of you while the trout came to the surface and openly laughed. But if trout fishing was not Grant's idea of the perfect occupation, being gillie was obviously Patrick's idea of heaven. There was nothing, from riding the black bull down at Dalmore to demanding three-pence-worth of sweets from Mrs. Mair at the post-office with the aid of a ha'penny and menaces, that Pat was not capable of. But the joy of messing about in a boat was still something that he could not provide for himself. The boat at the loch was padlocked.

So Grant set off up the sandy path through the dry heather, with Pat at his side and one pace in the rear like a gun dog on its best behaviour. And as he went he was conscious of his own reluctance, and wondered at it.

Why should there be any qualification in his pleasure this morning, in his delight in going fishing? Brown trout might not be his idea of a sporting contest, but he was glad enough to be spending the day with a rod in his hand even if he caught nothing whatever. He was supremely glad to be out in the open, alive and at leisure, with the familiar spring of peaty turf under his feet, and the hills before him. Why the small unwillingness at the back of his mind? Why, instead of taking a boat out for the day on Lochan Dhu, did he want to hang round the farm?

They had walked for a mile before he had flushed the reason from the cover of his subconscious. He had wanted to stay at Clune today so that he could see the daily paper when it arrived.

He had wanted to find out about B Seven.

His conscious mind had dropped B Seven behind, with the tribulations of the journey and the memory of his humiliation. He had not consciously remembered him from the moment when he fell into bed on arrival until now, nearly twenty-four hours later. But B Seven was still with him, it would seem.

"When does the daily paper arrive at Clune these days?" he asked Pat, still silent and on his best behaviour one pace in the rear.

"If it's Johnny it comes at twelve, but if it's Kenny it's often near one before it comes." And Pat added, as if glad to have conversation introduced into the expeditionary routine, "Kenny stops to have a cup at Dalmore, east the road. He's gone on the MacFadyean's Kirsty."

A world where the news of the nations' clamour waited while Kenny had a cup from the MacFadyean's Kirsty was a very pleasant one, Grant thought. In the days before radio it must have bordered on Paradise.

*"That guard the way to Paradise."*

The singing sands.

*The beasts that talk,*
*The streams that stand,*
*The stones that walk,*
*The singing sand . . .*

What had it stood for? *Was* it just a country of the mind?

Out here in the open, in this elemental land, it had an appropriateness that somehow lessened its strangeness. It was quite possible to believe this morning that there were places on this earth where stones might walk. Were there not places, known places, even in the Highlands, where a man alone in the bright sunlight of a summer day could be invaded by the knowledge of unseen watchers, so that he was filled with a great fear and ran panic-stricken from the place? Yes, and without any previous interviews in Wimpole Street, either. In the "old" places anything was possible. Even beasts that talked.

Where had B Seven got his idea of strangeness?

They launched the light boat from its wooden runway, and Grant pulled out into the loch and made for the windward end. It was much too bright, but there was a breath of air that might lift to a breeze strong enough to put a ripple on the surface. He watched Pat put his rod together and bend a fly on the line, and thought that if he could not have the felicity of possessing a son then a small redheaded cousin made a very good substitute.

"Did you ever present a bouquet, Alan?" asked Pat, busy with the fly. He called it a "bookey."

"Not that I can remember," Grant said carefully. "Why?"

"They're at me to present a bookey to a Viscountess that's coming to open the Dalmore hall."

"Hall?"

"That shed place at the cross-roads," Pat said bitterly. He was silent a moment, evidently mulling it over. "It's an awful jessie-like thing to present a bookey."

Grant, bound in duty to the absent Laura, searched his mind. "It's a great honour," he said.

"Then let The Child have the honour."

"She is a little young yet for such responsibility."

"Well, if she's too young for such responsibility I'm too old for such capers. So they'll have to get some other family to do it. It's all havers anyway. The hall's been open for months."

To this disillusioned contempt for adult pretence Grant had no answer.

They fished turn-about, in a fine male amity, Grant flicking his line with a lazy indifference, Pat with the incurable optimism of his kind. By noon they had drifted back to a point level with the little jetty, and they turned inshore to make tea on the primus in the little bothy. As Grant was paddling the last few yards, he saw Pat's eye fixed on something along the shore, and turned to see what occasioned such marked distaste. Having looked at the advancing figure with its shoggly body and inappropriate magnificence, he asked who that might be.

"That's Wee Archie," said Pat.

Wee Archie was wielding a shepherd's crook that, as Tommy remarked later, no shepherd would be found dead with, and he was wearing a kilt that no Highlander would dream of being found alive in. The crook stood nearly two feet above his head, and the kilt hung down at the back from his non-existent hips like a draggled petticoat. But it was obvious that the wearer was conscious of no lack. The tartan of his sad little skirt screamed like a peacock, raucous and alien against the moor. His small dark eel's head was crowned by a pale blue Balmoral with a diced band, the bonnet being pulled down side-ways at such a dashing angle that the slack covered his right ear. On the upper side a large piece of vegetation sprouted from the crest on the band. The socks on the hairpin legs were a brilliant blue, and so hairy in texture that they gave the effect of some unfortunate growth. Round the meagre ankles the thongs of the brogues were cross-gartered with a verve that even Malvolio had never achieved.

"What is he doing round here?" Grant asked, fascinated.

"He lives at the inn at Moymore."

"Oh. What does he do?"

"He's a revolutionary."

"Really? Is that the same revolution as yours?"

"Nah!" said Pat in great scorn. "Oh, I'm not saying maybe he didn't put the idea in my head. But no one would take heed of the likes of him. He writes pomes."

"I take it that he is a once-born."

"Him! He's not born at all, man. He's a—a—a *egg*."

Grant concluded that the word Pat had sought was amoeba, but that knowledge had not reached so far. The lowest form of life he knew of was the egg.

The "egg" came blithely towards them along the stony beach, swinging the tail of his deplorable petticoat with a fine swagger that went ill with his hirpling movement over the stones. Grant was suddenly convinced that he had corns. Corns on thin pink feet that sweated easily. The kind of feet people were always writing to medical columns in the Press about. (Wash every evening without fail and dry thoroughly, especially between the toes. Dust well with talcum powder and put on fresh socks each morning.)

"*Cia mar tha si?*" he called as he came within hailing distance.

Was it just chance, Grant wondered, that all cranky people had that thin bodiless voice? Or was it that thin bodiless voices belonged to the failures and the frustrated and that frustration and failure bred the desire to repudiate the herd?

He had not heard that Gaelic phrase since he was a child, and the affec-tation of it cooled his welcome. He bade the man good-morning.

"Patrick should have told you that it was too bright to fish today," he said, swinging up to them. Grant did not know which displeased him more: the vile Glasgow speech or the unwarranted patronage.

The freckles on Pat's fair skin were lost in a red tide. Speech trembled on his lips.

"I expect he didn't want to do me out of my pleasure," Grant said smoothly, and watched the tide recede and a slow appreciation dawn. Pat had discovered that there were more effective ways of dealing with folly than direct attack. It was a quite new idea, and he was trying the taste of it, rolling it on his tongue.

"You've come ashore for your elevenses, I take it," Wee Archie said brightly. "I'll be glad to join you if you've no objection."

So they made tea for Wee Archie, glum and polite. He produced his own sandwiches, and while they ate he lectured them on the glory of Scotland, its mighty past and dazzling future. He had not asked Grant's name and was betrayed by his speech into taking him for an Englishman. Surprised, Grant heard of England's iniquities to a captive and helpless Scotland. (Anything less captive or less helpless than the Scotland he had known would be difficult to imagine.) England, it seemed, was a bloodsucker, a vampire, draining the good blood of Scotland and leaving her limp and white. Scotland had groaned under the foreign yoke; she had come staggering behind the conqueror's chariot; she had paid tribute and prostituted her talents to the tyrant's needs. But she was about to throw off the yoke, to unloose the bands; the fiery cross was about to be sent out once more, and soon the heather would be alight. There was no cliché that Wee Archie spared them.

Grant watched him with the interest one accords to a new exhibit in a collection. He decided that the man was older than he had thought. Forty-five at least; probably nearer fifty. Too old to be curable. Whatever success he had coveted had passed him by; there would never be anything for him but his pitiable fancy-dress and his clichés.

He looked across to see what effect this perversion of patriotism was having on Young Scotland, and rejoiced in his heart. Young Scotland was sitting facing the loch, as if even the sight of Wee Archie was too much for him. He was chewing in a dogged detachment, and his eye reminded Grant of Flurry Knox: "an eye like a stone wall with broken glass on top." The revolutionaries would want heavier guns than Archie to make any impression on their countrymen.

Grant wondered what the creature lived on. "Pomes" did not provide a living. Nor did free-lance journalism; or, rather, the kind of journalism that Archie was likely to write. Perhaps he scraped a living from "criticism." It was from the ranks of the ineffective that the minor critics were recruited. There was always the chance, of course, that he was subsidised; if not by some native malcontent with a thirst for power, then by some foreign agency with an interest in trouble-making. He was of a type very familiar to the Special Branch: the failure, sick of a curdled vanity.

Grant, still hankering after the midday newspaper that Johnny or Kenny was due to deliver at Clune, had had thoughts of suggesting to Pat that they call it a day, and give up enticing fish that had no intention of biting. But if they went now they would have to walk back in Wee Archie's company, and that was something to be avoided. He prepared to resume his idle flicking of the loch water.

But Archie, it seemed, was anxious to make one of the fishing party. If there was room in the boat for a third passenger, he said, he would be glad to accompany them.

Again speech trembled on Pat's lips.

"Yes," said Grant, "do come. You can help to bale."

"Bale?" said the saviour of Scotland, blenching.

"Yes. Her seams are not too good. She makes a lot of water."

On second thoughts Archie decided that perhaps after all it was time that he was wending his way (Archie never went anywhere, he always wended his way) towards Moymore. The post would be in, and there would be his mail to deal with. And then, lest it might cross their minds that he was un-used to boats, he told them how good he was in a boat. It was thanks only to his skill in a boat that he and four others had reached a Hebridean beach alive last summer. He told the tale with a growing verve that gave rise to a base suspicion that he was making it up as he went along, and having finished he switched hastily from the subject, as if afraid of questions, and asked if Grant knew the islands.

Grant, locking up the bothy and pocketing the key, said that he did not. Whereupon Archie made him free of them with a proprietor's generosity: the herring fleets of Lewis, the cliffs of Mingulay, the songs of Barra, the hills of Harris, the wild flowers of Benbecula, and the sands, the endless won-derful white sand, of Berneray.

"The sands don't sing, I suppose," Grant said, putting bounds to the boasting. He stepped into the boat, and pushed off.

"No," said Wee Archie, "no. They're in Cladda."

"What are?" asked Grant, startled.

"The singing sands. Well, good fishing to you, but it's not a day for fishing, you know. Much too bright."

And with this kindly pat on the head he re-erected his shepherd's crook, and swung away along the shore towards Moymore and his letters. Grant stood motionless in the boat, watching him go. When he was nearly beyond earshot he called to him suddenly:

"Are there any walking stones on Cladda?"

"What?" said Archie's inadequate pipe.

"Are there *any walking stones on Cladda?*"

"No. They're in Lewis."

And the dragonfly creature with its mosquito voice went away into the brown distance.

# 3

THEY CAME HOME at teatime with five unimpressive-looking trout and large appetites. Pat, excusing the thin trout, pointed out that on such a day you couldn't expect to catch any but what he called "the sillies"; the respect-worthy fish had more sense than to be caught in such weather. They came down the last half-mile to Clune like homing horses, Pat skipping from turf to turf like a young goat, and as voluble as he had been silent on the way out. The world and London River seemed the width of stellar space away, and Grant would not have called the King his cousin.

But as they scraped their shoes at the flagged doorway of Clune, he became aware of his unreasonable impatience to see the newspaper. And since he resented unreason in anyone and abominated it in himself, he carefully scraped his shoes all over a second time.

"Man, you're awfully particular," said Pat, giving his footgear a rudimentary wipe on the twin scraper.

"It's a boorish thing to go into a house with mud on one's shoes."

"Boorish?" asked Pat, who, as Grant suspected, held it a "jessie-like" thing to be clean.

"Yes. Slovenly and un-grown-up."

"Huh," said Pat, and surreptitiously scraped his shoes again. "It's a poor house that can't stand a few dollops of mud," he said, reasserting his independence, and went storming into the sitting-room like an invading army.

In the sitting-room Tommy was dripping honey on to a hot scone, Laura was pouring tea, Bridget was arranging a new set of objects in a design on the floor, and the terrier was on the make round the table. Except that sunlight had been added to firelight, it was the same picture as last night. With one difference. Somewhere in the room there was a daily paper that mattered.

Laura, seeing his searching eye, asked him if he was looking for something.

"Yes, the daily paper."

"Oh, Bella has it." Bella was the cook. "I'll get it from her after tea if you want to see it."

He had a moment of stinging impatience with her. She was far too complacent. She was far too happy, here in her fastness, with her laden tea-table, and her little roll of fat above the belt, and her healthy children, and her nice Tommy, and her security. It would do her good to have some demons to fight, to be swung out in space and held over some bottomless pit now and then. But his own absurdity rescued him, and he knew that it was not so. There was no complacence in Laura's happiness, nor was Clune any refuge from the realities. The two young sheep-dogs who had welcomed them at the road gate in a swirl of black-and-white bodies and lashing tails would once upon a time have been called Moss or Glen or Trim or something like that. Today, he had noticed, they answered to Tong and Zang. The waters of the Chindwin had long ago flowed into the Turlie. There were no Ivory Towers any more.

"There is *The Times,* of course," Laura said; "but it is always yesterday's, so you will have seen it."

"Who is Wee Archie?" he asked, sitting down at the table.

"So you've met Archie Brown, have you?" Tommy said, clapping the top half on his hot scone, and licking the honey that oozed from it.

"Is that his name?"

"It used to be. Since he elected himself the champion of Gaeldom, he calls himself Gilleasbuig Mac-a'-Bruithainn. He's frightfully unpopular at hotels."

"Why?"

"How would *you* like to page someone called Gilleasbuig Mac-a'-Bruithainn?"

"I wouldn't like to have him under my roof at all. What is he doing here?"

"He's writing an epic poem in Gaelic, so he says. He didn't know any Gaelic until about two years ago, so I don't think the poem can be up to much. He used to belong to the cleesh-clavers-clatter school. You know, the Lowland-Scots boys. He was one of them for years. But he didn't get anywhere very much. The competition was too keen. So he decided that Lowland Scots was just debased English and very reprehensible, and that there was nothing like a return to the 'old tongue,' to a real language. So he 'sat under' a bank clerk in Glasgow, a chap from Uist, and swotted up some Gaelic. He comes to the back door and talks to Bella now and then, but she says she doesn't understand a word. She thinks he's 'not right in the head.' "

"There's nothing wrong with Archie Brown's head," Laura said tartly. "If he hadn't had the wit to think up this rôle for himself, he would be teaching school in some God forsaken backwater and even the school inspector wouldn't have known his name."

"He's very conspicuous on a moor, anyhow," Grant said.

"He's even worse on a platform. Like one of those awful souvenir dolls that tourists take home, and just about as Scottish."

"Isn't he Scots?"

"No. He hasn't a drop of Scottish blood in him. His father came from Liverpool and his mother was an O'Hanrahan."

"Odd how all the most bigoted patriots are Auslanders," Grant said. "I don't think he'll get very far with those xenophobes, the Gaels."

"He has a much worse handicap than that," Laura said.

"What is that?"

"His Glasgow accent."

"Yes. It is pretty repellent."

"I didn't mean that. I mean, every time he opens his mouth his audience is reminded of the possibility of being ruled from Glasgow: a fate worse than death."

"When he was talking about the beauty of the Islands, he mentioned some sands that 'sing.' Do you know anything about them?"

"I seem to," said Tommy, not interested. "On Barra or Berneray or somewhere."

"On Cladda, he said."

"Yes, perhaps it's Cladda. Do you think that boat at Lochan Dhu will last a season or two yet?"

"Can I go and get the *Clarion* from Bella now?" asked Pat, having wolfed four scones and a slab of cake with the neat speed of a sheep-dog consuming a stolen titbit.

"If she has finished with it," his mother said.

"Uch, she'll have finished with it this long time," Pat said. "She only reads the bits about the stars."

"Stars?" said Grant, as the door closed behind Pat. "Film stars?"

"No," Laura said, "the Great Bear and Co."

"Oh. The day as arranged by Sirius, Vega, and Capella."

"Yes. In Lewis they have to wait for the second-sight, she says. It's a fine convenient thing to have the future in the paper every day."

"What does Pat want with the *Clarion?*"

"The strip, of course. Two objects called Tolly and Snib. I can't remember whether they are ducks or rabbits."

So Grant had to wait until Pat had finished with Tolly and Snib, and by that time both Laura and Tommy had taken themselves off, the one to the kitchen and the other to out-of-doors, so that he was left alone with the silent child on the mat, endlessly rearranging her treasures. He took the tidily folded paper from Pat ceremoniously, and as Pat went away he unfolded it with controlled interest. It was a Scottish edition, and apart from the "middles" the paper was crammed with the most parochial of news, but there seemed to be nothing about yesterday's railway event in it. To and fro he went, through the jungle of unimportances, like a terrier routing through bracken, and at last he came on it: a tiny paragraph at the bottom of a column, down among the bicycle accidents and the centenarians. MAN DIES IN TRAIN, said the inconspicuous heading. And under the heading was a succinct statement:

> On the arrival of the *Flying Highlander* at its destination yesterday morning it was found that one of the passengers, a young Frenchman, Charles Martin, had died during the night. It is understood that the death was due to natural causes, but since the death occurred in England, the body is being returned to London for an inquest.

*"French!"* he said aloud, and Bridget looked up from her playthings to watch him.

French? Surely not! Surely not?

The face, yes. Perhaps. The face quite likely. But not that writing. That very English, schoolboy writing.

Had the paper not belonged to B Seven at all?

Had he just picked it up? In a restaurant where he was having a meal before boarding the train, perhaps. The chairs of station dining-rooms were habitually strewn with the discarded papers of those who had eaten there. Or in his home, for that matter; or his rooms or wherever he lived. He might have come by the paper in a score of casual ways.

Or, of course, he might be a Frenchman who was educated in England, so that the round untidy script was substituted for the slanting elegant spidery handwriting of his inheritance. There was nothing fundamentally incompatible with B Seven having been the author of those pencilled lines.

All the same, it was an oddity.

And in cases of sudden death, however natural, oddities have importance. When he first came in contact with B Seven, he was so divorced from his professional self, so detached from the world at large, that he had considered the matter as any other sleep-sodden civilian would. B Seven had been for him merely the young dead occupant of a whisky-sodden compartment who was being mauled about by a furiously impatient sleeping-car attendant. Now he became something quite different; he became The Subject of an Inquest. A professional matter; a matter bound by rules and regulations; a matter to be proceeded with circumspectly, with due decorum and by the book. And it occurred to Grant for the first time that his abstraction of that newspaper might be held, if orthodoxy must be pushed to its furthest point, to be a little irregular. It had been an entirely unintended abstraction, an accidental purloining. But it had, if one had to be analytical about it, been a removal of evidence.

While Grant was debating the matter, Laura came back from the kitchen and said, "Alan, I want you to do something for me."

She took her mending basket and brought it over to a chair beside him.

"Anything I can do."

"Pat is sticking in his toes about something that he has to do and I want you to talk him into it. You're his hero, and he will listen to you."

"It isn't about presenting a bouquet, by any chance?"

"How did you know? Has he talked about it to you already?"

"He just mentioned it this morning on the loch."

"You didn't take his side, did you?"

"With you in the background! No. I expressed the opinion that it was a great honour."

"Was he convinced?"

"No. He thinks the whole thing is 'havers.' "

"So it is. The hall has been in unofficial use for weeks. But the glen people spent a lot of money and energy on getting that thing put up, and it is only right that it should be opened with a 'splash.' "

"But does it have to be Pat who presents the bouquet?"

"Yes. If he doesn't do it, the MacFadyean's Willie will."

"Laura, you shock me."

"I wouldn't if you could see the MacFadyean's Willie. He looks like a frog with elephantiasis. And his socks are always falling down. It should be a little girl's business, but there is no female child of the right age in the glen. So it rests between Pat and the MacFadyean's Willie. And quite apart from Pat's looking nicer, it is right that someone from Clune should do it. And don't say 'Why?' and don't say I shock you. You just see what you can do to talk Pat into it."

"I'll try," Grant said, smiling at her. "Who is his Viscountess?"

"Lady Kentallen."

"The dowager?"

"The widow, you mean. There is only one, so far. Her boy isn't old enough yet to be married."

"How did you get her?"

"She was at school with me. At St. Louisa's."

"Oh: blackmail. The tyranny of auld lang syne."

"Tyranny nothing," said Laura. "She was glad to come and do the chore. She's a darling."

"The best way to bring Pat up to his bit would be to make her attractive in his eyes."

"She's ragingly attractive."

"I don't mean that way. I mean, make her good at something he admires."

"She's an expert with a fly," Laura said doubtfully, "but I don't know that Pat would find that very impressive. He just thinks that someone who can't fish is abnormal."

"I suppose you couldn't endow her with a few revolutionary tendencies."

"Revolutionary!" said Laura, her eye brightening. "Now that's an idea. Revolutionary. She used to be a little on the pink side. She did it 'to annoy Miles and Georgiana,' she used to say. They are her parents. She was never very serious about it; she was much too good-looking to need anything like that. But I might build something on that foundation. Yes. We might make her a revolutionary."

The quirks that women are reduced to! thought Grant, watching her needle flicker through the wool of the sock she was darning, and went back to considering his own problem. He was still considering it when he went to bed. But before he went to sleep, he decided that he would write to Bryce in the morning. It would be to all intents a letter reporting his arrival in these healthful surroundings and his hope to be better in less time than the doctor had given him, but in the course of it he would take the opportunity of putting himself in the right by passing the knowledge of the newspaper's presence on to those whom it might concern.

He slept the deep, uninterrupted sleep induced by fresh air and an unsullied conscience, and woke to an immense silence. The silence was not only out-of-doors; the house itself was in a trance. And Grant suddenly remembered that it was Sunday. There would be no post out of the glen today. He would have to go all the way to Scoone with his letter.

He asked Tommy at breakfast if he might borrow the car to go to Scoone to post an important letter, and Laura offered to drive him. As soon as breakfast was over, he went back to his room to compose the letter, and in the end was very pleased with it. He brought the matter of B Seven into the texture of it as neatly as an invisible mender fits an unbelonging piece to the over-all pattern. He had not been able to shake the memory of work from him as soon as he might, he said, because the first thing he had been confronted with at the end of the journey was a dead body. The body was being furiously shaken by an enraged sleeping-car attendant who thought that the man was just sleeping it off. However, it had been none of his business, thank Heaven. His only part in the affair had been to purloin unintentionally a newspaper from the compartment. He had found it among his own when he was having breakfast. It was a *Signal,* and he would have taken it for granted that it was his own property if it had not been that in the Stop-Press space someone had been pencilling a scribbled attempt at verse. The verse was in English and in English writing, and might not have been written by the dead man at all. He understood that the inquest was being held in London. If Bryce thought that it was of any importance, he might hand on the small item of information to the relevant authority.

He came downstairs again to find the Sabbath atmosphere shattered. The house rocked with war and rebellion. Pat had discovered that someone was going in to Scoone (which in his country eyes was even on a Sunday a metropolis of delectable variety) and he wanted to go too. His mother, on the other hand, was determined that he was going to Sunday school as usual.

"You ought to be very glad of the lift," she was saying, "instead of grumbling about not wanting to go."

Grant thought that "grumbling" was a highly inadequate word to describe the blazing opposition that lighted Pat like a torch. He throbbed with it, like a car at rest with the engine running.

"If we didn't happen to be going in to Scoone, you would have to walk to the church as usual," she reminded him.

"Huch, who ever minds walking! We have fine talks when we're walking, Duggie and me." Duggie was the shepherd's son. "It's wasting time at Sunday school when I might be going to Scoone that's a fact. It's not fair."

"Pat, I will not have you referring to Sunday school as a waste of time."

"You won't have me at all if you're not careful. I'll die of a decline."

"Oh. What would bring that on?"

"Lack of fresh air."

She began to laugh. "Pat, you're wonderful!" But it was always the wrong thing to laugh at Pat. He took himself as seriously as an animal does.

"All right, laugh!" he said bitterly. "You'll be going to church on Sundays to put wreaths on my grave, that's what you'll be doing on Sundays, not going into Scoone!"

"I shouldn't dream of doing anything so extravagant. A few dog-daisies now and then when I'm passing is as much as you'll get from me. Go and get your scarf; you'll need it."

"A gravat! It's March!"

"It's also cold. Get your scarf. It will help to keep off that decline."

"A lot you care about my decline, you and your daisies. A mean family the Grants always were. A poor mean lot. I'm very glad I'm a Rankin, and I'm very glad I don't have to wear their horrible red tartan." Pat's tattered green kilt was Macintyre, which went better with his red hair than the gay Grant. It had been part of Tommy's mother's web, and she, as a good Macintyre, had been glad to see her grandson in what she called a civilised cloth.

He stumped his way into the back of the car and sat there simmering, the despised "gravat" flung in a limp disavowed heap at the far end of the seat.

"Heathen aren't supposed to go to church," he offered, as they slipped down the sandy road to the gate, the loose stones spurting from under the tires.

"Who is heathen?" his mother asked, her mind on the road.

"I am. I'm a Mohammedan."

"Then you have great need to go to a Christian church and be converted. Open the gate, Pat."

"I've no wish to be converted. I'm fine as I am." He held the gate open for them and shut it behind them. "I disapprove of the Bible," he said, as he got in again.

"Then you can't be a good Mohammedan."

"What for no?"

"They have some of the Bible too."

"I bet they don't have David!"

"Don't you approve of David?" Grant asked.

"A poor soppy thing, dancing and singing like a lassie. There's not a soul in the Old Testament I'd trust to go to a sheep sale."

He sat erect in the middle of the back seat, too alive with rebellion to relax, his bleak eye watching the road ahead in absent-minded fury. And it occurred to Grant that he might equally have slumped in a corner and sulked. He was glad that this cousin of his was a rude and erect flame of resentment and not a small collapsed bundle of self-pity.

The injured heathen got out at the church, still rude and erect, and walked away, without a backward glance, to join the small group of children by the side door.

"Will he behave, now he is there?" Grant asked as Laura set the car in motion again.

"Oh, yes. He really likes it, you know. And of course Douglas will be there: his Jonathan. A day when he couldn't spend part of it laying down the law to Duggie would be a day wasted. He didn't really believe that I would let him come to Scoone instead. It was just a try-on."

"It was a very effective try-on."

"Yes. There's a lot of the actor in Pat."

They had gone another two miles before the thought of Pat faded from his mind. And then, quite suddenly, into the blank that Pat's departure left, came the realisation that he was in a car. That he was shut into a car. He ceased on the instant to be an adult watching, tolerant and amused, the unreasonable antics of a child, and became a child watching, gibbering and aghast, the hostile advance of giants.

He let down the window on his side to its fullest extent. "Let me know if you feel that too much," he said.

"You've been too long in London," she said.

"How?"

"Only people who live in towns are fresh-air fiends. Country people like a nice fug as a change from unlimited out-of-doors."

"I'll put it up, if you like," he said, although his mouth was stiff with effort as he said the words.

"No, of course not," she said, and began to talk about a car they had ordered.

So the old battle started. The old arguments, the old tricks, the old cajoling. The pointing out of the open windows, the reminding himself that it was only a car and could be stopped at any moment, the willing himself to consider a subject far removed from the present, the self-persuading that he was lucky to be alive at all. But the tide of his panic rose with a slow abominable menace. A black evil tide, scummy and revolting. Now it was round his chest, pressing and holding, so that he could hardly breathe. Now it was up to his throat, feeling round his windpipe, clutching his neck in a pincer embrace. In a moment it would be over his mouth.

"Lalla, stop!"

"Stop the car?" she asked, surprised.

"Yes."

She brought the car to a standstill, and he got out on trembling legs and hung over the dry-stone dyke sucking in great mouthfuls of the clean air.

"Are you feeling ill, Alan?" she asked anxiously.

"No, I just wanted to get out of the car."

"Oh," she said in a relieved tone. "Is that all!"

"Is that all?"

"Yes: claustrophobia. I was afraid you were ill."

"And you don't call that being ill?" he said bitterly.

"Of course not. I nearly died of terror once, when I was taken to see the Cheddar caves. I had never been in a cave before." She had switched off the motor and now she sat down on a roadside boulder with her back half-turned to him. "Except those rabbit burrows that we called caves in our youth." She held up her cigarette case to him. "I'd never been really underground before, and I didn't mind going in the least. I went all eager and delighted. I was a good half-mile from the entrance when it struck me. I sweated with terror. Do you have it often?"

"Yes."

"Do you know that you're the only person who still calls me Lalla sometimes? We are getting very old."

He looked round and down at her, the strain fading from his expression. "I didn't know you had any terrors other than rats."

"Oh, yes. I have a fine variety. Everyone has, I think. At least everyone who is not just a clod. I keep placid because I lead a placid life and collect adipose tissue. If I overworked the way you do, I'd be a raving maniac. I'd probably have claustrophobia *and* agoraphobia, and make medical history. One would have the enormous consolation of being something in the *Lancet,* of course."

He turned from leaning over the wall and sat down beside her. "Look," he said, and held out the shaking hand that held his cigarette for her to see.

"Poor Alan."

"Poor Alan, indeed," he agreed. "That came not from being half a mile underground in the dark, but from being a passenger in a car with wide-open windows in an open countryside on a fine Sunday in a free country."

"It didn't, of course."

"It didn't?"

"It came from four years of consistent overwork and an overgrown conscience. You always were a demon where conscience was concerned. Quite tiresome you could be. Would you rather have a spot of claustrophobia or a stroke?"

"A stroke?"

"If you work yourself half to death you have to pay in some manner or other. Would you rather pay in the more usual physical manner with high blood pressure or a strained heart? It's better to be scared of being shut into a car than to be pushed about in a bath-chair. At least you have time off from being scared. If you hate the thought of getting back into the car, by the way, I can go on to Scoone with your letter and pick you up on the way back."

"Oh, no, I'll go on."

"I thought it was better not to fight it?"

"Did *you* scream and yell half a mile underground in the Cheddar Gorge?"

"No. But I wasn't a pathological specimen suffering from overwork."

He smiled suddenly. "It's extraordinary how comforting it is to be called a pathological specimen. Or rather, to be called a pathological specimen in just those tones."

"Do you remember the day at Varese when it rained and we went to the museum and saw those specimens in bottles?"

"Yes; you were sick on the pavement outside."

"Well, you were sick when we had sheep's heart for lunch because you had watched it being stuffed," she said instantly.

"Lalla, darling," he said, beginning to laugh, "you haven't grown up at all."

"Well, it's nice that you can still laugh, even if it's only at me," she said, caught out in that flash of childhood rivalry. "Say when you want to go on."

"Now."

"Now? Are you sure?"

"Quite sure. Being called a pathological specimen has wonderfully curative qualities, I find."

"Well, next time don't wait until you are on the point of suffocation," she said matter-of-factly.

He did not know which he found more reassuring: her awareness that the thing was a sort of suffocation or her matter-of-fact acceptance of unreason.

# 4

IF GRANT HAD IMAGINED that his chief would be gratified either by the possibility of his earlier recovery or by his punctiliousness in the matter of the newspaper, he was wrong. Bryce was still antagonist rather than colleague. And his reply contained a right-and-left that was typically Bryce. Reading it, Grant thought that only Bryce could manage to have his cake and eat it so successfully. In the first paragraph he rebuked Grant for his unprofessional conduct in abstracting any article from the vicinity of sudden and unexplained death. In the second paragraph he was surprised that Grant should have thought of bothering a busy Department with any matter as trivial as that of the purloined paper, but supposed that no doubt his divorce from workaday surroundings had contributed to a lack of judgment and proportion. There was no third paragraph.

What came off the familiar thin office paper was a strong impression that he had been put, not in his place, but outside. What the letter really said was: "I can't imagine why you, Alan Grant, should be bothering us, either to report on your health or to take an interest in our business. We are not interested in the one and you have no concern with the other." He was an outsider. A renegade.

And it was only now, reading the snubbing letter and having the door banged in his face, that he became aware that beyond his conscientious need to put himself straight with the Department over the purloined paper had been the desire to hang on to B Seven. His letter, as well as an apology, had been a way to information. There was no longer hope of obtaining information from the Press. B Seven was not news. Every day people died in trains. There was nothing to interest the lieges in that. As far as the Press was concerned B Seven was dead twice over, once in fact and once as news. But he had wanted to know more about B Seven, and he had hoped, without knowing it, that his colleagues might be chatty on the subject.

He might have known Bryce better, he thought, tearing up the sheet of paper and dropping it into the wastepaper basket. However, there was always Sergeant Williams, thank Heaven; the faithful Williams. Williams would wonder why someone of his rank and experience should be interested in an unknown dead body seen once for a moment or two, but he would probably put it down to boredom. In any case there would be no lack of chat about Williams. So to Williams he wrote. Would Williams find out what the result of the inquest had been on a young man, Charles Martin, who had died on Thursday night a week ago on the night train to the Highlands, and anything else about the young man that might have transpired in the course of the inquiry? And kind regards to Mrs. Williams and Angela and Leonard.

And for two days he settled back in a sort of happy impatience to wait for Williams's reply. He inspected the unfishable Turlie, pool by pool; he caulked the boat at Lochan Dhu; he walked the hill in the company of Graham the shepherd with Tong and Zang more or less at heel; and he listened to Tommy's plan for a nine-hole private golf course between the house and the hillside. And on the third day he went homing at post time with an eagerness he had not known since he was nineteen and used to send his poems to magazines.

Nor was his blank unbelief when there was nothing for him any less poignant than it had been in those callow years.

He reminded himself that he was being unreasonable (the unforgivable sin, always, in Grant's estimation). The inquest had nothing to do with the Department. He did not even know which Division might have been landed with the job. Williams would have to find out. Williams had work of his own; twenty-four-hours-a-day work. It was unreasonable to expect him to drop everything to satisfy some holiday-making colleague's frivolous questions.

For two more days he waited, and then it came.

Williams hoped that Grant wasn't hankering after work. He was supposed to be having a rest, and everyone in the Department hoped that he was getting it (not everyone! thought Grant, remembering Bryce) and feeling the better for it. They missed him very badly. As to Charles Martin, there was no mystery about him. Or about his death, if that is what Grant had been thinking. He had hit the back of his head against the edge of the porcelain wash-hand basin, and although able to crawl around for a little on his hands and knees and eventually reach the bed, he had died from internal haemorrhage very shortly after falling over. The fact that he had fallen backwards at all was due to the amount of neat whisky he had consumed. Not enough to make him drunk but quite enough to make him muzzy, and the tilt of the coach as it changed direction had done the rest. There was no mystery, either, about the man himself. He had had the usual bundle of French identity papers in his possession, and his people were still living at his home address near Marseilles. They had not seen him for some years—he had left home after being in trouble for stabbing his girl in a fit of jealousy—but they had sent money to bury him so that he should not be buried in a pauper's grave.

This left Grant with an appetite whetted rather than assuaged.

He waited until, according to his reckoning, Williams would be happily settled down with his pipe and his paper, while Mrs. Williams mended and Angela and Leonard did their homework, and put in a personal call to him. There was always the chance that Williams was out pursuing the ill-doer through the devious ways of his inhabiting, but there was, too, the chance that he was at home.

He was at home.

When he had been duly thanked for his letter, Grant said: "You said his people sent money to bury him. Didn't anyone come to identify him?"

"No; they identified a photograph."

"A live photograph?"

"No, no. A photograph of the body."

"Didn't anyone turn up to identify him in London?"

"Not a soul, it seems."

"That's odd."

"Not so odd if he was a wide boy. Wide boys don't want trouble."

"Was there any suggestion that he was wide?"

"No, I don't think so."

"What was his profession?"

"Mechanic."

"Did he have a passport?"

"No. Just the usual papers. And letters."

"Oh, he had letters?"

"Yes; the usual odd two or three that people carry. One was from a girl saying she would wait for him. She's going to wait some time."

"Were the letters in French?"

"Yes."

"What money had he?"

"Wait a minute till I find my notes. Um-m-m. Twenty-two, ten, in mixed notes; eighteen and tuppence ha'penny in silver and copper."

"All English?"

"Yes."

"Between the lack of passport and the English currency, it looks as if he had been in England a good long time. I wonder why no one came to claim him."

"They may not know yet that he is dead. It didn't get much publicity."

"Didn't he have any address in Britain?"

"He had no address on him. The letters were not in envelopes: just in his wallet. His friends will probably turn up yet."

"Does anyone know where he was going? Or why?"

"No; seemingly not."

"What luggage had he?"

"An overnight case. Shirt, socks, pyjamas, and bedroom slippers. No laundry marks."

"*What?* Why? Were the things new?"

"No, oh, no." Williams sounded amused at Grant's overt suspicion. "Very well worn."

"Maker's name in the slippers?"

"No; those hand-made thick leather things you find in North African bazaars and in the Mediterranean ports."

"What else?"

"In the case? A New Testament in French, and a yellow paper-backed novel, also in French. Both well worn."

"Your three minutes are up," said the operator.

Grant had another three minutes, but he got no nearer an explanation of B Seven. Apart from the fact that he had no record, either in France (the stabbing had been merely a domestic incident, it seemed) or in Britain, nothing was known of him. It was indeed typical that the one positive thing about him should be a negation.

"By the way," Williams said, "when I was writing I quite forgot to answer your postscript."

"What postscript?" Grant asked, and then remembered that he had written as an afterthought:

"If you ever have nothing better to do you might ask the Special Branch if they are interested at all in a man called Archibald Brown. Scottish patriot. Ask for Ted Hanna and tell him I was asking."

"Oh, yes, of course. About the patriot. Did you have time to do anything about it? It wasn't important."

"Well, as it happened, I met your reference on a Whitehall bus, day before yesterday. He says he has nothing against your bird but they would very much like to know who the ravens are. Do you know what he was talking about?"

"I think I do," Grant said, amused. "I'll do my best to find out for them. Just as a piece of holiday homework, tell him."

"You keep your mind off your work, if you please, and get well enough to be back here before the place falls to pieces without you."

"The shoes he was wearing: where were *they* made?"

"Who was wearing? Oh. Yes. Karachi."

"*Where?*"

"Karachi."

"Yes, that's what I thought you said. He seems to have got around. No name on the fly-leaf of the Testament?"

"Don't think so. I don't think I made any note of that when I read the evidence. Just a minute. Oh, yes, I did. No name."

"And no one in 'missing persons' that fits him?"

"No. No one. No one even approximately like him, it seems. He isn't 'missing' from anywhere."

"Well, it was wonderful of you to go to all that trouble for me instead of telling me to go fish in my burn. I'll do as much for you some day."

"Are the fish in your burn biting?"

"There's hardly any burn, and the fish are cowering in the deepest recesses of the remaining pools. That is why I am reduced to taking an interest in cases that aren't worth a flicker of real interest in busy places like South-West One."

But he knew that that was not so. It was not boredom that had driven him to this interest in B Seven, this—he had almost said—alliance. He had a curious feeling of identification with B Seven. Not in the sense of being one, but in the sense of having an identity of interests. This, in view of the fact that he had seen him only once and knew nothing whatever about him, was highly unreasonable. Was it perhaps that he had thought of B Seven as also wrestling with demons? Had the feeling of personal interest, the championship, begun in that?

He had supposed that B Seven's Paradise had been oblivion. He had supposed that because of the whisky-sodden fug in the compartment. But the young man had not after all been sodden. He had not, indeed, been very drunk. Just tipsy. His backwards fall against the solid round bulk of the basin had been the kind of thing that might happen to anyone. His so strangely guarded Paradise had not after all been oblivion.

He caught his attention back to what Williams was saying.

"*What's* that?"

"I forgot to say that the sleeping-car attendant is of the opinion that Martin was seen off by someone at Euston."

"Why is this an afterthought?"

"Well, I gather that he wasn't much of a help anyway, the sleeping-car chap. He seemed to treat the whole thing as a personal insult, the sergeant who was there said."

Old Yoghourt seemed to have run very true to form.

"What *did* he say?"

"He said that when he walked through the corridor, at Euston, Martin had someone with him in the compartment. Another man. He didn't see the man because Martin was facing him and the door was half open, so that all he noticed was that Martin was talking to another man. They seemed very happy and friendly. They were talking about robbing a hotel."

"*What!*"

"You see what I mean? The coroner said 'What!' too. The railway chap said that they were talking about 'robbing the Caley,' and since no one could rob a football team it must have been a hotel. It seems that all the hotels in Scotland that are not called Waverley are called Caledonian. Popularly known as 'Caley.' They weren't serious about it, he said."

"And that was all he saw of the seer-off?"

"Yes, that was all."

"He mightn't have been a seer-off at all. He might have been just a friend who came across him on the train. Saw his name on the sleeper list, or noticed him in passing."

"Yes; except that you'd expect a friend to turn up again in the morning."

"Not necessarily. Especially if he was far down the train. And the removal of the body would have been so discreet that I doubt if any passengers knew that someone had died. The station was clear of passengers long before the ambulance arrived. I know, because the ambulance fuss was taking place when I had nearly finished breakfast."

"Yes. The sleeping-car chap said he took it for granted that the other man was a seer-off because he was standing in hat and coat. Mostly, he says, when people go coffee-housing along the train they take their hats off. It's the first thing they do, he says: throw their hat on a rack. When they get to their compartment, I mean."

"Talking of names on the sleeper list, how was the berth booked?"

"By phone; but he picked up the ticket himself. At least, it was picked up by a thin dark man. Booked a week in advance."

"All right. Go on about Yoghourt."

"About who?"

"About the sleeping-car attendant."

"Oh. Well. He said that when he came down the train collecting tickets, about twenty minutes out from Euston, Martin had gone to the lavatory, but his sleeper ticket and the outward half of his ticket to Scoone were lying ready on the little shelf below the mirror. He took them and marked them off in his book, and as he was passing the lavatory he knocked at the door and said, 'Are you in B Seven, sir?' Martin said Yes. The attendant said: 'I've taken your tickets, thank you, sir. Will you be wanting tea in the morning?' And Martin said, 'No, thank you; good night.' "

"So he had a return ticket."

"Yes. The return half was in his wallet."

"Well, it's all straightforward enough, it seems. Even the lack of anyone to make inquiries about him, or to claim his body, may be due to the fact that he was off on a trip and people didn't expect to hear from him."

"That and the lack of publicity. I don't suppose his people even bothered to put an announcement in an English paper; they would just announce it in their own local affair, where people knew him."

"What did the P.M. say?"

"Oh, the usual. Light meal about an hour before death, large quantity of whisky in stomach and a fair amount in the blood. Quite enough to make him tight."

"No suggestion that he was a soak?"

"Oh, no. No degeneration of any kind. Head and shoulder injuries at some earlier period, but otherwise good healthy specimen. Not to say tough."

"So he had some earlier injury?"

"Yes, but a long time ago. I mean, nothing to do with this. He had at some time had a fractured skull and a broken collar-bone. Would it be very bad-mannered or very indiscreet of me to ask why all this interest in a simple case?"

"So help me, Sergeant, if I knew I would tell you. I think I must be getting childish."

"It's more likely that you're just bored," Williams said sympathetically. "Me, I was brought up in the country and I was never a one for watching the grass grow. An over-rated place, the country. Everything's too far away. Once that burn of yours starts flowing, you'll forget about Mr. Martin. It's pouring stair-rods here, so you probably won't have long to wait for rain now."

It did not, in fact, rain that night in the Turlie valley, but something else happened. The cold bright stillness gave place to a light wind. The wind was soft and warm; the air hung damp and heavy between gusts; the earth was moist and slippery; and down from the high tops came the snow water, filling the river bed from bank to bank. And up the brown racing water came the fish, flashing silver in the light as they leaped over the broken ledges of rock and up the narrow sluicing current between the boulders. Pat took his precious invention from his fly case (where it had a special compartment of its own) and presented it to Grant with the formal benevolence of a headmaster hand-ing over a certificate. "You'll take care of it, won't you?" he said. "It took me a long time to make." The thing was, as his mother had said, a fearsome object. Grant thought that it was rather like something for a woman's hat; but he was aware that he was being singled out among men as the sole recipient worthy of such an honour and he accepted it with due gratification. He put it safely away in his own case and hoped that Pat would not supervise his efforts to the extent of making him use it. But each time he chose a new fly in the days that followed, he caught sight of the fearsome object and was warmed by his small cousin's approval of him.

He spent his days by the Turlie, happy and relaxed about the brown swirling water. The water was clear as beer and its foam froth-white; it filled his ears with music and his days with delight. The damp soft air smurred his tweed with fine dew, and water from the hazel twigs dripped down the back of his neck.

For nearly a week he thought fish, talked fish, and ate fish.

And then, one evening, on his pet pool below the swing bridge, he was startled out of his complacence.

He saw a man's face in the water.

There was time for his heart to come up into his mouth before he realised that the face was not under the surface of the water but at the back of his eyes. It was the dead white face with the reckless eyebrows.

He swore, and sent his Jock Scott singing viciously to the far side of the pool. He was finished with B Seven. He had grown interested in B Seven under a complete misunderstanding of the situation. He had thought that B Seven, too, had been hounded by demons. He had built up for himself an entirely fallacious picture of B Seven. The toper's Paradise in B Seven's compartment boiled down to an overturned whisky bottle. He was no longer interested in B Seven: a very ordinary young man, bursting with rude health to the point of toughness, who had had one over the eight on a night journey and ended his life in the highly undignified manner of falling backwards and then crawling about on his hands and knees until he stopped breathing.

"But he wrote those lines about Paradise," a voice in him said.

"He didn't," he said to the voice. "There's not the slightest evidence that he did any such thing."

"There's his face. No ordinary face. It was the face that you first succumbed to. Long before you began to think of his Paradise at all."

"I have *not* succumbed," he said. "In my job you take an automatic interest in people."

"Yes? You mean, if the occupant of that whisky-sodden compartment had been a fat commercial traveller with a moustache like a badly kept hedge and a face like a boiled pudding, you would still have been interested?"

"I might."

"You lying dishonest bastard. You were B Seven's champion the minute you saw his face and noticed the way that Yoghourt was mauling him about. You snatched him from Yoghourt's grip and straightened his jacket like a mother pulling a shawl over her baby."

"Shut up."

"You wanted to know about him not because you thought there was anything odd about his death but because, quite simply, you wanted to know about him. He was young and dead, and he had been reckless and alive. You wanted to know what he had been like when he was reckless and alive."

"All right, I wanted to know. I also want to know who is going to ride the Lincolnshire favourite, and what my shares are quoted at in today's market, and what June Kaye's next picture is going to be; but I'm not losing any sleep about any of them."

"No, and you don't see June Kaye's face between you and the water, either."

"I have no intention of seeing anyone's face between me and the river.

*Nothing* is going to come between me and the river. I came here to fish, and nothing is going to muck up that for me."

"B Seven came North to do something too. I wonder what it was?"

"How should I know?"

"It couldn't be fishing, anyhow."

"Why couldn't it?"

"No one who was going five or six hundred miles to fish would be without tackle of some kind. If he was as keen as that, he would at least have his own pet lures with him, even if he was going to be lent a rod."

"Yes."

"Perhaps his Paradise was Tir nan Og. You know, the Gaelic one. That would fit."

"How would it fit?"

"Tir nan Og is supposed to be away out to the west, beyond the outermost islands. The Land of the Young. The land of eternal youth, that's the Gaelic Paradise. And what 'guards the way' to it? Islands with singing sands, it seems. Islands with stones that stand up like men walking."

"And beasts that talk? Do you find them, too, in the Outer Isles?"

"You do."

"You do? What are they?"

"Seals."

"Oh, go away and leave me alone. I'm busy. I'm fishing."

"You may be fishing, but you're not catching a damned thing. Your Jock Scott might as well be stuck in your hat. Now you listen to me."

"I will *not* listen to you. All *right*, there are singing sands in the Islands! All *right*, there are walking stones! *All right*, there are gabby seals! It has nothing to do with me. And I don't suppose it had anything to do with B Seven."

"No? What was he going North for?"

"To bury a relation, to sleep with a woman, to climb a rock! How should I know? And why should I care?"

"He was going to stay at a Caledonian Hotel somewhere."

"He was not."

"How do *you* know where he was going to stay?"

"I don't. Nobody does."

"Why should one of them be all facetious about 'robbing the Caley' if he was going to stay at a Waverley?"

"If he was going to Cladda—and I'll bet there's no inn on Cladda called anything as reeking of the mainland as the Caledonian—if he was going to Cladda he would have gone via Glasgow and Oban."

"Not necessarily. It's just as short and just as comfortable via Scoone. He probably loathed Glasgow. A lot of people do. Why not ring up the Caledonian in Scoone when you go back to the house tonight and find out if a Charles Martin was expected there?"

"I shall do no such thing."

"If you slap the water like that, you'll frighten every fish in the river."
He went back to the house at supper time in a very bad mood. He had
caught nothing and had lost his peace.

And in the somnolent hush that filled the sitting-room when work was over
for the day and the children in bed, he caught his eye wandering from his
book to the telephone at the other end of the room. It stood on Tommy's
desk, provocative in its suggestion of latent power, in the infinite promise of
its silent presence. He had only to lift that receiver and he could speak to a
man on the Pacific coast of America, he could speak to a man in the wastes
of the Atlantic Ocean, he could speak to a man two miles above the earth.

He could speak to a man in the Caledonian Hotel in Scoone.

He resisted this thought, with growing annoyance, for an hour. Then Laura
went to get bed-time drinks, and Tommy went to let the dogs out, and Grant
reached the telephone in a dive that was nearer a rugby tackle than any civilised method of crossing a room.

He had lifted the receiver before he realised that he did not know the number. He put the receiver back in its cradle and felt that he had been saved.
He turned to go back to his book but picked up the telephone book instead.
He would have no peace until he had talked to the Caledonian in Scoone; it
was cheap enough to have peace at the cost of being a little silly.

"Scoone 1460 . . . Caledonian Hotel? Can you tell me: Did a Mr. Charles
Martin book accommodation with you any time in the last fortnight? . . .
Yes, thank you, I'll wait . . . No? No one of that name . . . Oh . . . Thank
you very much. So sorry to have bothered you."

And that was that, he thought, slamming the receiver down. That, as far
as he was concerned, was definitely the end of B Seven.

He drank his nice soothing bed-time drink, and went to bed, and lay wide
awake staring at the ceiling. He put the light out, and resorted to his own cure
for insomnia: pretending to himself that he had to stay awake. He had evolved
this long ago from the simple premise that human nature wants to do the
thing it is forbidden to do. And so far it had never failed him. He had only
to begin pretending that he was not allowed to go to sleep for his eyelids to
droop. The pretence eliminated in one move the greatest barrier to sleep: the
fear that one is not going to, and so left the beach clear for the invading tide.

Tonight his eyelids dropped as usual, but a jingle ran round and round in
his head like a rat in a cage:

> *The beasts that talk,*
> *The streams that stand,*
> *The stones that walk,*
> *The singing sand . . .*

What were the streams that stand? Was there something in the Islands that
corresponded to that?

Not frozen streams. There was little snow or frost in the Islands. Then, what? Streams that ran into the sand and stood still? No. Fanciful. Streams that stand. Streams that stand?

Perhaps a librarian might know. There must be a goodish public library in Scoone.

"I thought you weren't interested any more?" said the voice.

"You go to hell."

A mechanic, he was. What did that mean? *Mechanicien*. It involved an endless range of possibilities.

Whatever he did, he was successful enough to be able to travel first class on a British railway. Which in these days made one practically a millionaire. And he had spent all that money on what, to judge by his overnight case, was a flying visit.

A girl, perhaps? The girl who had promised to wait?

But she had been French.

A woman? No Englishman would go five hundred miles for a woman, but a Frenchman might. Especially a Frenchman who had knifed his girl for letting her glance stray.

> The beasts that talk
> The streams that stand . . .

Oh, God! Not again. Little Miss Muffet sat on a tuffet eating her curds and whey. Hickory, dickory, dock. Simple Simon met a pieman going to the fair; said Simple Simon to the pieman Let me taste your ware. Ride a cock horse to Banbury Cross— Your imagination had to be caught before you were fired by the need to write down a thing. You could, if your imagination was vivid, get to a stage when you were in bondage to an idea. When it became an *idée fixe*. You could become so enraptured by the pictured grace of a temple's flight of steps that you would work for years to earn the money and gain the leisure to take you there. In extreme cases it became a compulsion, and you dropped everything and went to the thing that had seduced you: a mountain, a green stone head in a museum, an uncharted river, a bit of sailcloth.

How far had B Seven's vision ridden him? Enough to send him searching? Or just enough to make him write it down?

Because he *had* written those pencilled words.

Of course he had written them.

They belonged to B Seven as much as his eyebrows did. As much as those schoolboy capital letters did.

"Those *English* capital letters?" said the voice, provocative.

"*Yes*, those English letters."

"But he was a native of Marseilles."

"He could have been educated in England, couldn't he?"

"In two shakes you'll be telling me that he wasn't a Frenchman at all."

"In two shakes I will."

But that, of course, was to enter the realm of fantasy. There was no mystery about B Seven. He had an identity, a home and people, a girl who was waiting for him. He was demonstrably a Frenchman, and the fact that he wrote English verse in English handwriting was entirely by the way.

"He probably went to school in Clapham," he said nastily to the voice, and fell instantly asleep.

## 5

IN THE MORNING he woke with rheumatism in his right shoulder. He lay considering this in slow amusement. There was no end to what your subconscious and your body could achieve between them. They would provide you with any alibi you wanted. A perfectly good honest alibi. He had known husbands who developed high temperatures and the symptoms of 'flu each time their wives were on the point of departure to visit relations. He had known women who were so tough that they could watch a razor fight unmoved and yet would pass out in the deadest of dead faints when asked an awkward question. ("Was the accused so persecuted by police cross-examination that she was unconscious for fifteen minutes?" "She fainted, certainly." "There was no question of a simulated faint, was there? The doctor says that he saw her at the material time and there was great difficulty in reviving her. And that collapse was a direct result of the police cross-examination to which she was being—" and so on.) Oh, yes. There was no limit to what your subconscious and your body could cook up together. And today they had cooked up something that would keep him off the river. His subconscious had wanted to go in to Scoone today and talk to the librarian at the public library. His subconscious had remembered, moreover, that it was market day and that Tommy would be taking the car into Scoone. So his subconscious had set to work on the eternally sycophantic body and between them they had made a tired shoulder muscle into an unworkable joint.

Very neat.

He got up and dressed, wincing each time he lifted an arm, and went down to cadge a lift from Tommy. Tommy was heart-broken at his disablement but delighted by his company, and they were so gay together, this warm spring morning, and Grant was so filled with the pleasure that ferreting out information always provided for him, that they were running through the outer suburbs of Scoone before he remembered that he was in a car. That he was shut into a car.

He was enormously gratified.

He promised to meet Tommy for lunch at the Caledonian, and went away to find the public library. But before he had gone far, a new idea struck him.

The *Flying Highlander* would have come clicking over the points at Scoone only a few hours ago. Every twenty-four hours, from year's end to year's end, the *Flying Highlander* made that night journey and came into Scoone in the morning. And since the train crews habitually stuck to the same run, alternating time on and time off, there was just the chance that one of the staff who had come into Scoone on the *Flying Highlander* this morning was Murdo Gallacher.

So he changed direction and went to the station instead.

"Were you on duty when the London Mail arrived this morning?" he asked a porter.

"No, but Lachie was," said the porter. He stretched his mouth into a line, let out a whistle that would have done credit to an engine, tilted his head back an inch to summon a distant colleague, and went back to reading the racing page of the *Clarion*.

Grant went to meet the slowly advancing Lachie and asked him the same question.

Yes, Lachie had been on duty.

"Can you tell me if Murdo Gallacher was one of the sleeping-car attendants?"

Lachie said that Yes, Old Sourpuss was on her.

Could Lachie say where Old Sourpuss could be found now?

Lachie glanced up at the station clock. It was after eleven.

Yes, Lachie could say where he would be. He would be in the Eagle Bar waiting for someone to stand him a drink.

So to the Eagle Bar at the back of Scoone Station Grant went, and found that Lachie had been, in the main, right. Yoghourt was indeed there, mooning over a half-pint. Grant ordered a whisky for himself and saw Yoghourt's ears prick.

"Good-morning," he said amiably to Yoghourt. "I've had some very good fishing since I saw you last." He was pleased to notice the hope grow on Yoghourt's face.

"I'm glad of that, sir, very glad," he said, pretending to remember Grant. "The Tay, is it?"

"No, the Turlie. By the way, what did your dead young man die of? The one I left you trying to waken." Antagonism began to wither the eagerness on Yoghourt's face. "Won't you join me?" Grant added. "A whisky?" Yoghourt relaxed.

After that it was easy. Yoghourt was still prickled with resentment at the inconvenience that he had been caused. He had even had to attend the inquest in his spare time. It was, Grant thought, as easy as dealing with a toddler who has just learned to run. It needed only a touch to steer him in any required direction.

Yoghourt had not only hated having to attend the inquest, he had hated the inquest and he had hated every single soul connected with the inquest. Between his hatred and two double whiskies he provided Grant with the most detailed account of everyone and everything. He was the best value for money that Grant had ever had. He had been "on" in the affair from first to last; from the first appearance of B Seven at Euston to the coroner's verdict. As a source of information he was pure horse's mouth, and he "gave" like a beer-tap.

"Had he travelled with you before?" Grant asked.

No, Yoghourt had never seen him before and was glad that he was never going to again.

This was where Grant's satisfaction suddenly changed to satiation. One more half-minute of Yoghourt and he would be sick. He pushed himself off the counter of the Eagle Bar and went to look for the public library.

The library was frightful beyond description: a monstrosity in liver-coloured stone; but after Yoghourt it seemed the fine flower of civilisation. The assistants were charming, and the librarian was a thin little piece of faded elegance with a tie no broader than the black silk ribbon of his eyeglasses. As an antidote to too much Murdo Gallacher, it could not have been better.

Little Mr. Tallisker was a Scot from Orkney—which, he pointed out, was not being a Scot at all—and he was both interested in and knowledgeable about the Islands. He knew all about the singing sands on Cladda. There were other alleged singing sands, too (every Island wanted to have what its neighbours had as soon as they heard about any new possession, whether it was a pier or a legend), but the Cladda ones were the original. They lay, like most of the Island sands, on the Atlantic side, facing the unbroken ocean, looking out to Tir nan Og. Which, as Mr. Grant might know, was the Gaelic heaven. The land of the eternally young. It was interesting, wasn't it, how each people evolved its own idea of Heaven? One as a feast of lovely women, one as forgetfulness, one as continuous music and no work, one as good hunting grounds. The Gaels, Mr. Tallisker thought, had had the loveliest idea. The land of youth.

What sang? Grant asked, interrupting the dissection of comparative bliss.

It was a moot point, Mr. Tallisker said. Indeed, you could have it either way. He had walked them himself. Endless miles of pure white sand by a brilliant sea. They did "sing" as one trod on them, but he himself held that "squeak" would be a better description. On the other hand, on any day that provided a steady wind—and such days were of no unusual occurrence in the Islands—the fine, almost invisible, surface sand was swept along the wide beaches so that they did in fact "sing."

From sand Grant led him to seals (the Islands were full of seal stories, it seemed; the translation of seals into men and vice versa; if they were to be believed half the population of the Islands had some seal blood in them) and from seals to walking stones, and on all Mr. Tallisker was interesting and informative. But on streams he fell down. Streams seemed to be the only things on Cladda that were exactly like their counterpart anywhere else. Except that they too often spread into little lochs or lost themselves in bog, the streams of Cladda were just streams; water in the process of finding its own level.

Well, thought Grant, going away to meet Tommy for lunch, that in a way was "standing." Running into standing water, into bog. B Seven might have used the word because he needed the rhyme. He had wanted something to rhyme with sand.

He listened with only half an ear to the talk of the two fellow sheep-farmers that Tommy brought to lunch, and envied them their untroubled eyes and their air of unlimited leisure. Nothing hounded these large *rangé* creatures. Their flocks were decimated every now and then by strokes of fate: great snowstorms or swift disease. But they themselves stayed quiet and sane, like the hills that bred them. Big slow men, full of little jokes and pleased with small things. Grant was very conscious that his obsession with B Seven was an unreasonable thing, abnormal; that it was part of his illness; that in his sober mind he would not have thought a second time about B Seven. He resented his obsession and clung to it. It was at once his bane and his refuge.

But he drove home with Tommy even more cheerful than when he had set out. There was practically nothing about the inquest on Charles Martin, French mechanic, that he did not now know. He was that much to the good. And that was a lot.

After supper that night he discarded the book on European politics which had shared with Tommy's telephone his interest on the previous evening and went hunting along the bookshelves for something about the Islands.

"Are you looking for anything in particular, Alan?" Laura asked, looking up from *The Times*.

"I'm looking for something about the Islands."

"The Hebrides?"

"Yes. I suppose there is a book about them."

"Hah!" said Laura, mock amused. "Is there a book about them! There's a whole literature, my dear. It's a distinction in Scotland not to have written a book about the Islands."

"Have you any of them?"

"We have practically all of them. Everyone who has ever come to stay here has brought one."

"Why didn't they take them away with them?"

"You'll see why when you have a taste of them. You'll find them on the bottom shelf. A whole row of them."

He began to go through the row, gutting the books with a swift, practised eye.

"Why this sudden interest in the Hebrides?" Laura asked.

"Those singing sands that Wee Archie talked about stuck in my mind."

"That must be the first time Wee Archie has ever said anything that stuck in someone's mind."

"I expect his mother remembers his first word," Tommy put in from behind the *Clarion*.

"It seems that Tir nan Og is just one jump west from the singing sands."

"So is America," said Laura. "Which is much nearer the Islanders' idea of Heaven than Tir nan Og is."

Grant, repeating Mr. Tallisker's speech on comparative heavens, said that the Gaels were the only race who visualised Heaven as a country of the young, which was endearing of them.

"They are the only known race who have no word for No," Laura said drily. "That is a much more revealing characteristic than their notions of eternity."

Grant came back to the fire with an armful of books and began to go through them at leisure.

"It is difficult to imagine a mind that has never evolved a word for No, isn't it?" Laura said musingly, and went back to *The Times*.

The books varied from the scientific, through the sentimental, to the purely fantastic. From kelp-burning to the saints and heroes. From bird-watching to soul's pilgrimages. They varied, too, from the admirable but dull to the unbelievably bad. It seemed that no one who had ever visited the Islands had refrained from writing about them. The bibliographies at the end of the soberer books would have done justice to the Roman Empire. On one thing all were agreed, however: the Islands were magic. The Islands were the last refuge of civilisation in a world gone mad. The Islands were beautiful beyond imagining, a world carpeted with wild flowers and bounded by a sea that broke in sapphire on silver beaches. A land of brilliant sunlight, of good-looking people and heart-searching music. Wild, lovely music handed down from the beginning of time, from an age when the gods were young. And if you wanted to go there, see MacBrayne's time-table on Page 3 of the Appendix.

The books lasted Grant very happily until bedtime. And while they drank their nightcaps, he said, "I'd like to have a look at the Islands."

"Make a plan for next year," Tommy said, agreeing. "There's quite good fishing on Lewis."

"No, I mean now."

"Go now!" Laura said. "I never heard anything so daft."

"Why? I can't fish until my shoulder is better, so I might as well go exploring."

"Your shoulder will be better in two days with my treatment."

"How does one get to Cladda?"

"From Oban, I should think," Tommy said.

"Alan Grant, don't be absurd. If you can't fish for a day or two, there are a hundred other things you can do instead of being bucketed about on a Minch crossing in March."

"Spring comes early to the Islands, they say."

"It doesn't to the Minch, believe me."

"You could fly, of course," Tommy said, considering the subject as he considered everything that was put in front of him, with a kind sobriety. "You could fly one day and come back the next, if you liked. It's quite a good service."

There was a little silence while Grant met his cousin's eye. She knew that he could not fly, and why.

"Give it up, Alan," she said, in a kinder tone. "There are much nicer things to do than being stood on one's head in the middle of the Minch in March. If you just want to get away from Clune for a bit, why don't you hire a car—there's a very good garage in Scoone—and go exploring on the mainland for a week or so? Now that the weather is soft, it will be getting green in the West."

"It isn't that I want to get away from Clune. Quite the contrary. If I could take Clune *en bloc* with me, I would. It is just that I have got bitten with the idea of those sands."

He saw Laura begin to consider the idea from a new angle, and he could follow her thought quite well. If this was what his sick mind wanted, then it would be wrong to try to dissuade him. The interest of a place he had never seen before should be an ideal counteraction to self-conscious brooding.

"Oh, well, what you want is a Bradshaw, I suppose. We do have one, but it's mostly used as a door-stop or a step for the top bookshelf, so it's a little out of date."

"As far as the services to the Outer Islands are concerned, it won't matter what the date of it is," said Tommy. "The Laws of the Medes and the Persians are not more unchangeable than MacBrayne's schedules. As someone has remarked, they don't exactly encroach on eternity but they very nearly outlast time."

So Grant found the Bradshaw and took it to bed with him.

And in the morning he borrowed a small case from Tommy, and packed into it the bare necessities of existence for a week or so. He had always had a passion for travelling light, and it always pleased him to be getting away by himself, even from people he loved (a trait that had done much to keep him single), and he caught himself whistling under his breath as he put the few things into the small space. He had not whistled to himself since the shadow of unreason had reached out and taken the sunlight from him.

He was going to be foot-loose again. Foot-loose: it was a beautiful thought.

Laura had promised to drive him into Scoone in time to catch the train to Oban, but Graham was late in coming back with the car from Moymore village, so that it was touch-and-go whether he caught the train at all. They made it with thirty seconds to spare, and a breathless Laura pushed a bundle of papers into the open window as the train pulled out, and gasped: "Enjoy yourself, my dear. Seasickness does wonders for the liver."

He sat, alone in the compartment, in a daze of contentment with the magazines unheeded on the seat beside him. He watched the bare empty landscape trundle by and grow slowly greener as they went west. He had no idea why he was going to Cladda. It was certainly not to gather information in the police sense. He was going—to find B Seven. That is as near as it could be put into words. He wanted to go and see the place which so nearly reproduced the landscape of the poem. He wondered, sunk in sleepy bliss, whether B Seven had ever talked to anyone about his Paradise. He remembered the writing and thought not. Those tightly arcaded *m*s and *n*s were too defensive to have been made by a talker. In any case, it didn't matter how many people he had talked to about the thing, since there was no way of making contact with them. He could hardly put an advertisement in the papers saying: Read this poem and tell me if you recognise it.

Or—why couldn't he?

His sleepiness fell from him while he considered this new angle.

He considered it all the way to Oban.

In Oban he went to a hotel, ordered a self-congratulatory drink, and while he consumed it he wrote to each of the London daily papers, enclosing a cheque and asking them to print an identical notice in their personal column. The notice said:

> The beasts that talk, the streams that stand, the stones that walk, the singing sand. . . . Anyone recognising please communicate with A. Grant, c/o P.O., Moymore, Comrieshire.

The only daily papers to which he did not send his appeal were the *Clarion* and *The Times*. He did not want Clune to think that he had taken leave of his senses altogether.

As he made his way along the front to the cockleshell in which he was due to brave the Minch, he thought: It will serve me right if someone writes to say that the thing is one of the best-known lines of some Xanadu concoction of Coleridge's, and that I must be illiterate not to have known it!

# 6

THE WALLPAPER CONSISTED of far too heavy roses hanging from a far too slender trellis-work, and the insecure character of the whole thing was increased by the fact that the paper not only hung away from the wall but moved about in the draught. It was not readily obvious where the draught came from because the small window was not only tightly shut but had patently been tightly shut since its manufacture and original insertion in the house structure about the beginning of the century. The little swing mirror on the chest of drawers lived up to its promise in the first respect but not in the second. It would swing with ease amounting to abandon through the whole circle of 360 degrees, but it did not reflect anything to any noticeable degree. A last year's cardboard calendar folded in four kept its gyratory talents in check, but nothing, of course, could be done to increase its powers of reflection.

Two of the four drawers in the chest were capable of being opened. The third would not open because it had lost its knob, and the fourth because it had lost the will. Above the black iron fireplace with its frill of red crinkled paper brown with age was an engraving of a partially clothed Venus comforting a quite unclothed Cupid. If the cold had not already eaten into his bones, Grant thought that the picture would have finished the process.

He looked from the little window down on the small harbour with its collection of fishing-boats, at the grey sea slapping drearily against the breakwater, and the grey rain beating on the cobbles, and he thought of the log fire in the sitting-room at Clune. He toyed with the idea of going to bed as the quickest way of getting warm, but a second glance at the bed dissuaded him. Its plate-like thinness was made even more plate-like by the meagre covering of a white honeycomb cotton cover. At the foot, a turkey-red cotton quilt suitable for a doll's perambulator was folded into an elaborate pattern. Above it brooded the finest collection of unmatching brass knobs that it had ever been Grant's fortune to meet.

Cladda Hotel. The gateway to Tir nan Og.

He went downstairs and poked the smoky fire in the sitting-room. Someone had banked the fire with the potato peelings from lunch, so his efforts were not very successful. Rage came to his rescue and he rang the bell with all his might. The wires jangled in a crazy dance somewhere in the walls, but no bell rang. He went out into the lobby where the wind was coming soughing in under the front door and shouted. Never, even in his best form on the "square," had he used his voice with so passionate a determination to produce results. A young female creature came from the back regions and stared at him. She had a face like a rather practical Madonna and legs the same length as her body.

"Wis yu bawling?" she asked.

"No, I wasn't bawling. That sound you heard was my teeth chattering. In my country a sitting-room fire is designed to give out heat, not to consume refuse."

She looked at him a little longer, as if translating his speech into a more understandable idiom, and then moved past him to look at the fire.

"*Oh, Dé*," she said, "that will never do. Stop you and I'll get you a bit of fire."

She went away and came back with what seemed to be most of the kitchen fire blazing on a shovel. Before he could remove some of the packed dross and vegetable matter from the grate, she had dumped the flaming mass on top of all.

"I'll be getting some tea to warm you," she said. "Mr. Todd is down at the pier seeing did the things come on the boat. He'll be back in no time at all."

She said it comfortingly, as if the presence of the proprietor would automatically be warming. Grant took it for granted that she was apologising for the absence of an official welcome to a guest.

He sat and watched the kitchen fire gradually lose heart as it became conscious of the bed of potato peelings on which it had been cast away. He did his best to rake out some of the damp black mass from underneath so as to provide an encouraging draught, but the thing merely settled down in a sad heap. He watched the glow fade until only little red worms of incandescence ran to and fro across the surface of the blackened coals as the passing wind sucked the air from the room into the chimney. He thought of putting on his waterproof and walking in the rain; walking in the rain could be a delightful thing. But the thought of hot tea held him where he was.

After nearly an hour of fire-watching, no tea had come. But "N. Todd, Prop.," came back from the harbour, accompanied by a boy in a navy-blue jersey pushing a wheelbarrow laden with large cardboard cartons, and came in to welcome his guest. They did not expect guests at this time of the year, he said; he thought when he had seen him come off the boat that he would be staying with someone on the island. Gathering songs, or something.

There was something in the way he said "gathering songs"—a detached tone bordering on comment—that made Grant sure that he was no native.

No, said Mr. Todd, when asked, he did not belong to the place. He had had a good little commercial hotel in the Lowlands, but this was more to his taste. And, seeing the surprise on his guest's face he added: "To tell you the truth, Mr. Grant, I was tired of counter-rappers. You know, the kind of chap who can't wait a minute. Out here no one ever thinks of rapping on a counter. Today, tomorrow, or next week is all the same to an Islander. It's a bit maddening now and then, when you want something done, but for most of the time it's fine and restful. My blood pressure's away down." He noticed the fire. "That's a poor sort of fire Katie-Ann's given you. You'd better come ben to my office and warm yourself."

At this moment Katie-Ann put her head in at the door and said that it had taken all this time to boil the kettle because the kitchen fire had gone out on her, and would Mr. Grant now think it a good thing to have his tea and his high tea at one and the same time. Grant did indeed think it a good thing, and as she went away to prepare this evening repast he asked his host for a drink.

"The magistrates took away the licence from my predecessor, and I haven't yet got it back. I'll get it back at the next Licensing Court. So I can't sell you a drink. There isn't a licence on the island. But if you'll come ben to my office, I'll be glad to stand you a whisky."

The office was a tiny place, tropical in its breathless heat. Grant savoured the oven atmosphere gratefully, and drank the bad whisky neat, as it was proffered. He took the indicated chair and stretched out his feet to the blaze.

"You're not an authority on the island, then," he said.

Mr. Todd grinned. "In one way I am," he said wickedly. "But probably not the way you mean it."

"To whom should I go to learn about the place?"

"Well, there's two authorities. Father Heslop and the Reverend Mr. MacKay. On the whole perhaps Father Heslop would be better."

"You think he is the more knowledgeable?"

"No; they're about fifty-fifty as far as that goes. But two-thirds of the islanders are R.C. If you go to the priest, you'll only have a third of the population against you, instead of two-thirds. Of course the Presbyterian third are much nastier customers to be up against, but if numbers count with you then you'd better see Father Heslop. Better see Father Heslop anyway. I'm a heathen myself, so I'm an outcast from both flocks; but Father Heslop is for a licence and Mr. MacKay dead against it." He grinned again and refilled Grant's glass.

"I take it the priest would rather see the stuff sold openly than drunk on the sly."

"That's it."

"Did you ever have a visitor called Charles Martin staying here?"

"Martin? No. Not in my time. But if you'd like to look through the visitors' book, it's on the table in the lobby."

"If a visitor doesn't stay at the hotel, where would he be likely to stay? In rooms?"

"No, no one lets rooms on the island. The houses are too small for that. They'd stay either with Father Heslop or at the manse."

By the time that Katie-Ann came to say that his tea was waiting on him in the sitting-room, the blood was flowing freely again through Grant's once-moribund body and he was hungry. He looked forward to his first meal in this "tiny oasis of civilisation in a barbarous world" (see *Dream Islands* by H. G. F. Pynche-Maxwell, Beal and Batter, 15/6). He rather hoped that it might not be either salmon or sea-trout, having had an elegant sufficiency of both in the last eight or nine days. He would not turn up his nose at a piece of grilled sea-trout if it happened to be that. Grilled with some local butter. But he hoped for lobster—the island was famous for its lobsters—and failing that some herring fresh from the sea, split, and fried after being dipped in oatmeal.

His first meal in the isles of delight consisted of a couple of bright orange kippers inadequately cured and liberally dyed in Aberdeen, bread made in Glasgow, oatcakes baked by a factory in Edinburgh and never toasted since, jam manufactured in Dundee, and butter made in Canada. The only local produce was a pallid, haggis-shaped mound of crowdie, a white crumbly by-product without smell or taste.

The sitting-room in unshaded lamplight was even less appetising than it had been in the grey light of afternoon, and Grant fled to his freezing little bedroom. He demanded two hot-water bottles and suggested to Katie-Ann that since he was the sole guest she should filch the quilts from every other bedroom in the house and dedicate them to his use. She did this with all her native Celt pleasure in the irregular, heaping his bed with borrowed luxury and suffocating with giggles.

He lay under the five meagre bits of wadding, topped off with his own coat and Burberry, and pretended that the whole thing was one good English eiderdown. As he grew warm, he became conscious of the cold stuffiness of the room. That was the last straw, and quite suddenly he began to laugh. He lay there and laughed as he had not laughed for nearly a year. Laughed till the tears came, laughed until he was so exhausted that he could no more, and lay spent and purged and happy under his fine variety of bedclothes.

Laughter must do untold things for one's endocrine glands, he thought, feeling the well-being flood through him in a life-giving tide. More especially, perhaps, when it is laughter at oneself. At the fine, glorious absurdity of oneself in relation to the world. To set out for the threshold of Tir nan Og and fetch up at the Cladda Hotel had an exquisite ridiculousness. If the Islands provided him with nothing but this, he would consider himself well rewarded.

He ceased to care that the room was airless and the covers insecure. He lay looking at the rose-heavy wallpaper and wished that he could show it to Laura. He remembered that he had not yet been transferred into that newly decorated bedroom at Clune which, up till now, had always been his. Was Laura expecting another visitor? Was it possible that her latest candidate for his affections was to be housed under the same roof? So far he had been happily free of female society; the evenings at Clune had been family evenings, peaceful and long-breathing. Had Laura been merely holding her hand until he was, so to speak, able to sit up and take notice? She had been suspiciously regretful that he was going to miss the opening of the new hall at Moymore. A ceremony that she would have in her normal mind not expected him to attend at all. Had she expected a guest for the opening? The bedroom could not be meant for Lady Kentallen, because she would come over from Angus and go back the same afternoon. Then for whom was the bedroom redecorated and kept empty?

He was still turning the small question over in his mind when he fell asleep. And it was only in the morning that it occurred to him that he had hated the closed window because it made the room stuffy and not because it was closed.

He washed in the two pints of tepid water that Katie-Ann brought him and went downstairs rejoicing. He felt on top of the world. He ate the Glasgow bread, still another day older this morning, and the Edinburgh oatcakes, and the Dundee jam, and the Canadian butter, together with some sausages from the English midlands, and enjoyed them. Having given up his expectation of primitive elegance, he was prepared to accept primitive existence.

He was gratified to find that in spite of cold wind and wet weather and thinly covered hard beds his rheumatism had entirely gone, being no longer needed by his subconscious to provide an alibi. The wind was still howling in the chimney and the water spouting up from the breakwater, but the rain had stopped. He put on his Burberry and tacked round the harbour front to the shop. There were only two places of business in the row of houses that fringed the harbour: a post-office and a provision merchant. The two between them supplied the island with all that it needed. The post-office was also a newsagent; and the provision merchant was a combination of grocer, iron-monger, chemist, draper, shoe-shop, tobacconist, china-merchant, and ship's chandler. Bolts of sprigged cotton for curtains or dresses lay on shelves along-side the biscuit tins, and hams hung from the roof among strings of locknit undergarments. Today, Grant noticed, there was also a large wooden tray of tuppenny buns baked, if the paper round the queen cakes was to be believed, in Oban. They were crumby and depressed-looking, as if they had been tumbled about in one of the cardboard cartons that were such an indispensable part of island life, and they smelled very faintly of paraffin, but he supposed that they made a change from the Glasgow bread.

In the shop were several men from the fishing-boats in the harbour and a little round man in a black raincoat who could be nothing but a priest. This was a fortunate thing. Even the Presbyterian third, he felt, could hardly hold against him a fortuitous meeting in a public store. He edged in beside His Reverence and waited with him while the fishermen were being served. After that it was plain sailing. The priest "picked him up" and he had five witnesses to it. Moreover, Father Heslop deftly included the proprietor, one Duncan Tavish, in the conversation, and, from the fact that Father Heslop called him Mr. Tavish and not Duncan, Grant deduced that the proprietor was not one of his flock. So he was very happily parcelled out among the islanders over the paraffiny buns and the margarine, and there would be no internecine war over the possession of his person.

He went out into the gale with Father Heslop and strolled home with him. Or rather they beat up against the wind together, staggering a few steps for-ward at a time, and shouting remarks to each other above the noise of their flapping garments. Grant had the advantage of his companion in that he wore no hat, but Father Heslop was not only lower on the ground but had a figure ideally streamlined for life in a gale. He had no angles anywhere.

It was good to go in from the blast to a warm turf fire and silence.

"Morag!" called Father Heslop, into the further end of the house, "Some tea for me and my friend here. And a scone maybe, like a good girl."

But Morag had not baked, any more than Katie-Ann had. They were given Marie biscuits, a little soft in the island dampness. But the tea was wonderful.

Because he knew that he was an object of curiosity to Father Heslop, as he was to everyone on the island, he said that he had been fishing with relations in Scotland, but had to stop owing to a bad shoulder. And because he had been bitten with the idea of the Islands, and more especially with the singing sands on Cladda, he had taken the chance of coming to see them, a chance he might never have presented to him again. He supposed that Father Heslop was well acquainted with the sands?

Oh, yes, of course Father Heslop knew the sands. He had been fifteen years on the island. They were on the west side of the island, facing the Atlantic. It was no distance across the island. Grant could walk there this afternoon.

"I would rather wait for fine weather. It would be better to see them in sunlight, wouldn't it?"

"At this time of year you might wait for weeks before you'd see them in sunlight."

"I thought spring came early to the Islands?"

"Oh, I think, myself, that's just an idea of the people who write books about them. This is my sixteenth spring on Cladda, and I have yet to catch one here before its time. The spring's an Islander too," he added with a little smile.

They talked of the weather, the winter gales (which made today, according to Father Heslop, a thing of zephyrs), the penetrating damp, the occasionally idyllic summer days.

Why had a place of so few attractions captured the imagination of so many people, Grant wanted to know.

Well, partly it was that they saw it only at high summer, and partly it was that those who came and were disappointed were reluctant to admit their disappointment either to themselves or the friends they had left behind. They compensated themselves by talking big. But it was Father Heslop's own theory that most people who came were unconsciously running away from life, and they found what their imaginations prepared for them. Through their eyes the Islands were beautiful.

Grant thought this over, and then asked him if he had ever known a Charles Martin, who had been interested in singing sands.

No; Father Heslop had never met a Charles Martin, as far as he could remember. Had he come to Cladda?

Grant did not know.

He went out into the blast, and was blown back to the hotel at an undignified trot, teetering on his toes like an elderly toper. The bare lobby at the hotel smelled of unidentifiable hot food and sang like a choir as the wind came shrieking in under the outside door. But they had managed a fire that looked like a fire, in the sitting-room. To the scream of wind in the passage and the yowling of wind in the chimney he ate beef from South America, carrots tinned in Lincolnshire, potatoes grown in Moray, milk pudding packaged in North London, and fruit bottled in the Vale of Evesham. Now that he was no longer conditioned to magic, he filled his stomach thankfully with what was put in front of him. If Cladda had denied him spiritual joy, it had provided him with a fine physical appetite.

"Don't you ever bake scones, Katie-Ann?" he said, when he was arranging the time of his high tea.

"Is it scones you'll be wanting?" she said surprised. "Indeed, yes, I'll bake you some. But we have baker's cakes for your tea. And biscuits and ginger-snaps. Would you rather be having scones than them?"

Remembering the "baker's cakes" Grant said enthusiastically that he would, he would indeed.

"Well, then," she said kindly, "of course I'll bake you a scone."

For an hour he walked, along a flat grey road through a flat grey desolation. To his right, distant in the mist, was a hill, the only visible height. The whole thing was as inspiring as the fens on a wet January day. Every now and then the wind on his left flank would send him spinning sideways off the road altogether, and he struggled back half amused, half irritated. At long distances odd cottages lay cowering close to the earth, blind and limpet-like, without any sign of human habitation. Some had stones slung from the roof by ropes to weight the structure against the wind's importunity. None of them had fence, outhouse, garden, or bush. It was living at its most primitive; inside four walls; everything under hatches and battened down.

And then, suddenly, the wind smelt salt.

And in less than half an hour he came on it. He came on it without warning, across a great waste of wet green grass that in summer-time must be starred with flowers. There had been no visible reason why the long levels of grassy land should not go on for ever to the horizon; it was all part of this flat grey endless world of bog. He had been prepared to go on walking to the horizon, so that he was startled to find that the horizon was ten miles out at sea. There it lay in front of him, the Atlantic; and if it was not beautiful it was, nevertheless, impressive in its sweep and simplicity. The green water, dirty and ragged, roared on to the beach and broke in a flash of white that was vicious. To right and left, as far as eye could see, were the long lines of breaking water and the pale sands. There was nothing else in all the world but the green torn sea and the sands.

He stood there looking at it, and remembering that the nearest land was America. Not since he had stood in the North African desert had he known the uncanny feeling that is born of unlimited space, the feeling of human diminution.

So sudden had been the presence of the sea, and its rage and extent so overwhelming, that he had hung there motionless for several moments before realising that here were the sands that had brought him to the fringe of the western world in March. These were the singing sands.

Nothing sang today but the wind and the Atlantic. Together they made a Wagnerian tumult that buffeted one almost as physically as did the gale and the spray. The whole world was one mad uproar of grey-green and white and wild noise.

He walked down over the fine white sand to the edge of the water, and let the tumult roar over him. At close quarters it had a senseless quality that dissolved his uncomfortable sense of diminution and made him feel human and superior. He turned his back on it almost contemptuously, as one would on a bad-mannered child who was making an exhibition of himself. He felt warm and alive and master of himself; admirably intelligent and gratifyingly sentient. He walked back up the sand, absurdly and extravagantly glad to be a human being and alive. The air that came off the land when he had turned his back on the salt sterile wind from the sea was gentle and warm. It was like opening the door of a house. He went on across the grassy levels without once looking back. The wind hounded him along the flat bogs, but it was no longer in his face and the salt was no longer in his nostrils. His nostrils were full of the good smell of damp earth, the smell of growing things.

He was happy.

As he came at last down the slope to the harbour, he looked up at the hill in the mist and decided that tomorrow he would climb it.

He came back to the hotel ravenous, and was gratified to be given no fewer than two items of local manufacture for his high tea. One was a plate of Katie-Ann's scones, and the other was "sleeshacks": a delicacy he had known of old. Sleeshacks were mashed potatoes fried in slices; and they certainly helped to make appetising the remains of cold beef from lunch which was the *pièce de résistance* of the meal. But as he ate his first course, he kept smelling something more evocative of those early Strathspey days than even sleeshacks could be. An aroma both sharp and subtle it was, floating and circling about his brain in a nostalgic tantalisation. It was not until he had put his knife into one of Katie-Ann's scones that he knew what it was. The scone was yellow with soda and quite uneatable. With a regretful salute to her for the memory (platefuls of yellow soda-laden scones laid out in the farmhouse kitchen table for the farm-hands' tea: Oh, Tir nan Og!), he buried two of Katie-Ann's scones under the glowing coals in the grate and made do with the Glasgow bread.

And that night he fell asleep without looking at the wallpaper and without remembering the closed window at all.

# 7

IN THE MORNING he ran into the Reverend Mr. MacKay in the post-office and felt that he was distributing his favours very successfully. Mr. MacKay was on his way down to the harbour to see if the crew of a Swedish fishing-boat that was lying there would like to come to church if they were still there the day after tomorrow. There was also, he understood, a Dutch vessel that might be presumed to be of a Presbyterian persuasion. If they showed signs of wanting to come, he would prepare a sermon in the English for them.

He condoled with Grant about the rough weather. It was early in the year for the Islands, but he supposed that one had to take holidays when one was given them.

"You'll be a schoolmaster, maybe, Mr. Grant."

No, Grant said, he was a Civil Servant. Which was his normal answer to questions about his profession. People were prepared to believe that Civil Servants were human beings; no one ever believed that a policeman was one. They were two-dimensional characters with silver buttons and a notebook.

"You'd be amazed, now, you that has not been here before, if you could see what the Islands are like in June, Mr. Grant. Not a cloud in the sky, day after day, and the air so hot that ye'll see it dancing before you. And the mirage as mad as ever it was in the desert."

"Were you in North Africa?"

Och, yes; Mr. MacKay had been in North Africa with the Jocks. "And believe me, Mr. Grant, I've seen odder things from my window up in the manse there than ever I did between Alamein and Tripoli. I've seen the lighthouse on the point there standing up in the air. Yes, half-way up the sky. I've seen the hill there change shape till it looked like a great mushroom. And as for the rocks by the sea, those great pillars of stone, they can turn light and transparent and move about as if they were walking through a set of the Lancers."

Grant considered this with interest, and ceased to listen to the rest of Mr. MacKay's discourse. As he parted from him alongside the *Ann Loefquist* of Goteborg, Mr. MacKay hoped that he was coming to the *ceilidh* tonight. All the island would be there and he would hear some fine singing.

When he asked his host about the *ceilidh* and where it was being held, Mr. Todd said that it would be the usual mixture of song and talk, that it would end up with the usual dance, and that it would be held in the only place on the island suitable for such a gathering—the Peregrine Hall.

"Why Peregrine?"

"That is the name of the lady who gave it. She used to come to the island in the summer and she was all for improving trade and making the islanders self-supporting, so she built a fine long hut with big windows and skylights so that they could weave in company and not be ruining their eyes over looms in tiny dark rooms. They should get together, she said, and have a Cladda mark for their tweed and make it sought-after, like Harris. She could have saved her breath and her bawbees, poor lady. No islander would walk a yard to work. They would rather go blind than move out of their own light. But the hut is very useful for island gatherings. Why don't you have a look in tonight when it gets going?"

Grant said that he would do that, and went away to spend the rest of the day climbing Cladda's solitary hill. There was no mist, although the wind was still moisture-laden, and as he went upward the seas opened under him, scattered with islands and streaked with the tides. Here and there a single line, unnaturally straight in that arrangement of nature, marked the track of a ship. From the top he had the whole Hebridean world at his feet. He sat there and considered it, the barren, water-logged universe, and it seemed to him the ultimate in desolation. A world half-emerged from chaos, formless and void. Looking down on Cladda itself, it was impossible to tell, so mixed were sea and land, whether one was looking at a land full of lochs or a sea full of islands. It was a place best left to the grey geese and the seals.

He was happy up there, however; watching the changing patterns on the sea floor, violet and grey and green; watching the sea birds soar to inspect him and the flutter of nesting plovers on the low ground. Thinking about Mr. MacKay's mirages and the stones that walked. Thinking, as he never ceased for any length of time to think, about B Seven. Here was B Seven's world, according to specification. The singing sands, the talking beasts, the walking stones, the streams that ceased to run. What had B Seven intended to do here? Just to come, as he himself had done, and look?

A flying dash, with an overnight case. That surely portended one of two things: a meeting or an inspection. Since no one had yet missed him, then it could not have been a rendezvous. Therefore it was an inspection. One could go to inspect many things: a house, a prospect, a painting. But if one was driven to write verse *en route*, then the verse was surely a pointer to the subject for inspection.

What had held B Seven in bondage to this bleak world? Had he been reading too many books by H. G. F. Pynche-Maxwell and his like? Had he forgotten that the silver sands and the wild flowers and the sapphire seas were strictly seasonal?

From the top of the hill at Cladda, Grant sent B Seven a salute and a blessing. But for B Seven he would not be sitting above this sodden world feeling like a king, newborn and self-owning. He was something more than B Seven's champion now: he was his debtor, his servant.

As he left the shelter he had found for himself, the wind caught him in the chest, and he leaned on it as he went downhill as he used to when he was a boy, so that it supported him and he could almost fall downhill in the most surprising manner and still be safe.

"How long do gales usually last in this part of the world?" he asked his host as they staggered through the darkness after supper towards the *ceilidh*.

"Three days is the minimum," Mr. Todd said, "but that doesn't happen often. Last winter it blew for a month on end. You got so used to the roar of it that if it died away for a moment you thought you'd gone deaf. You'd be better to fly back, when you go, than cross the Minch in this weather. Most people fly nowadays, even the old people who've never seen a train. They take aeroplanes for granted."

It occurred to Grant that he might indeed fly back; that if he waited another few days, if he had a little longer to grow accustomed to his new-found well-being, he might use the air journey as a test. It would be a pretty severe test, the severest he could subject himself to. To any claustrophobe the prospect of being boxed into a small space and hung helplessly in the air was sheer horror. If he faced it without wincing, and accomplished it without disaster, then he could pronounce himself cured. He would be a man again.

But he would wait a little; it was too early yet to ask himself the question.

The *ceilidh* had been in progress for some twenty minutes when they arrived, and they stood with the rest of the male population at the back. Only the women and the ancients occupied the chairs in the hall. Except for a row of male heads in the very front, where the Importances of the island sat (Duncan Tavish, the merchant, who was uncrowned king of Cladda, the two Churches, and some lesser lights), the male population lined the walls at the back and clustered round the entrance. It was an abnormally cosmopolitan gathering, Grant noticed, as the outsiders made way for them; both the Swedes and the Hollanders had come in force, and there were accents that belonged to the Aberdeenshire coast.

A girl was singing in a thin soprano. Her voice was sweet and true but without expression. It was like someone trying over an air on a flute. She was succeeded by a self-confident youngish man who received an ovation, on which he plumed himself so obviously that it was funny; one waited for him to bill his breast feathers like a bird. He was a great favourite, it seemed, with audiences of exiled Gaels on the mainland, and he spent more time being encored there than he did on his neglected croft. He sang a hearty ditty in a rough over-worked tenor and was cheered to the echo. It surprised Grant a little that he had never bothered to learn the rudiments of singing. He must, in his jaunts to the mainland, have met real singers, who had been taught how to use their voices; even in the case of someone so vain it was astonishing that he had not been moved to learn the basis of the art he professed.

Another woman sang another expressionless song, contralto, and a man recited a funny story. Except for the few phrases that he had learned from the old folk in Strathspey when he was a child, Grant understood no Gaelic, and he listened as he would have listened to an entertainment in Italian or Tamil. Except for the delight of the people themselves in the thing, it was a sufficiently dull affair. The songs were musically negligible; some of them deplorable. If this was the kind of thing that people came to the Hebrides to "gather," then they were hardly worth the gathering. The few inspired songs had, like all products of inspiration, gone over the world on their own wings. It was better that these feeble imitations should be left to die.

Throughout the concert there was a continuous coming and going among the men at the back of the hall, but Grant had been aware of it only as an obbligato until his arm was pressed and a voice said in his ear, "Could you be doing with a wee drop yourself, perhaps?" and he realised that Island hospitality was offering him a share of the scarcest commodity known to Island economy. Since it would have been ungracious to refuse, he thanked his benefactor and followed him out into the darkness. Against the lee wall of the meeting-place leaned a representative minority of the male population of Cladda in a contented silence. A flat two-gill bottle was thrust into his hands. *"Slainte!"* he said, and took a swig of it. A hand, guided by an eye more acclimatised to the dark than his own, took the bottle back from him and a voice wished him health in return. Then he followed his unknown friend back to the lighted hall. Presently he saw Mr. Todd being surreptitiously tapped on the arm, and Mr. Todd, too, went out into the darkness to be sustained with something out of the bottle. It could happen nowhere else, Grant thought. Unless in the States during prohibition. Not much wonder that the Scots were silly and arch and coy about whisky. (Except, of course, in Strathspey, where the stuff was made. In Strathspey they put the bottle in the middle of the table, as matter-of-factly as an Englishman would, if a little more proudly.) Not much wonder that they behaved as if there was something very dashing, not to say daring, about having a drink of whisky. The surprising, the knowing leer with which the ordinary Scot referred to his national drink could only come from inherited knowledge of prohibition: either the Kirk's or the Law's.

Warmed by his mouthful out of the flat bottle, he listened tolerantly to Duncan Tavish being confident and long-winded in Gaelic. He was introducing a guest who had come a long way to speak to them, a guest who needed no introduction from him or from anyone; whose own achievements spoke for themselves. (Nevertheless Duncan spoke for them at length.) Grant did not catch the Gaelic name of the guest, but he was aware that the renegades from outside came pressing in at the sound of the cheering that greeted Mr. Tavish's peroration. Either the speaker was the real interest of the evening or the whisky had given out.

He watched in idle curiosity the small figure detach itself from the front row, clamber up on to the platform with the aid of the piano, and stride into the middle of it.

It was Wee Archie.

Wee Archie looked even odder in Cladda than he had on Clune moor; his stature more inadequate, his cockatoo brightness more startling. The kilt was not the dress of the islands, and among all these sober-coloured males in their thick, stiff clothes he looked more than ever "a souvenir doll." Without his dashing bonnet with its sprouting greenery, he looked somehow undressed, like a policeman without his helmet. His hair was very scanty, and was drawn in thin strings across the top of his head to hide the bare patch. He was like something out of a not very expensive Christmas stocking.

However, there was no qualification to the welcome he was given. Apart from the Royal Family, in person and *in toto*, Grant could think of no one who could be guaranteed the equivalent of the reception that Wee Archie was now being accorded. Even discounting the effect of libations at the lee end, it was surprising. And the silence that succeeded it when he began to talk was flattering. Grant wished that he could see the faces. He remembered that Bella from Lewis had had no use for his back-door proselytising; and what Pat Rankin thought of him would not go through the post. But what did these Islanders, cut off from the world and from the variety that alone could teach a man to judge between this and that, what did these Islanders think of him? Here was the material of his dreams; innocent, acquisitive, self-conscious, egotistical. They could not be subverted to another rule, the Islanders, because no one had ever ruled them in any real sense. A Government was there, as far as the Islanders were concerned, to be milked of benefits and diddled out of its dues. But their separateness could be played upon to alienate sympathy; their opportunism could be sharpened by dangled benefits. In Cladda, Wee Archie was not the embarrassing nonentity he had been at Lochan Dhu; in Cladda he was a possible power. Cladda and all its attendant islands represented, in the ultimate reckoning, submarine bases, smuggling points, stepping-off places, watch-towers, airfields, patrol bases. What did the Islanders think of Gilleasbuig Mac-a'-Bruithainn and his creed? He wished that he could see the faces.

For half an hour Wee Archie spoke to them in his thin, angry voice, with passion and without pause, and they listened without a sound. And then Grant, casting a glance at the rows of seats in front of him, thought that they looked less full than they had been at the beginning of the evening. This was so unlikely that he took his attention from Archie to consider the matter. He caught a stealthy movement along the trough between Row 5 and Row 6 and followed it with his eye until it reached the end of the row. There it stood upright and materialised into the person of Katie-Ann. With no fuss at all Katie-Ann, still with demure eyes fixed on the speaker, faded backwards through the standing rows of males and disappeared into the outer air.

Grant watched a little longer and found that this melting process was continuous, both among the seated audience and among the males standing round the walls. The audience was melting away invisibly under Archie's very nose. This was so unusual—a country audience will always wait to the end however boring an entertainment—that Grant turned to Mr. Todd and whispered, "Why are they leaving?"

"They're going to watch the ballet."

"The *ballet?*"

"Television. It's their great treat. Everything else they see on television is just a version of something they've seen already. Plays, and singing, and what not. But ballet is something they've never seen before. They wouldn't miss ballet for anything or anyone. . . . What is so amusing about that?"

But Grant was not amused by Cladda's passion for ballet. He was enjoying Archie's so unlikely disarming. Poor Archie. Poor wee deluded Archie. He had been overthrown by an arabesque, foiled by an *entrechat,* defeated by a *plié.* It was fantastically appropriate.

"Have they gone for good?"

"Oh, no, they'll be back for the dance."

And back they were, in force. Every soul on the island was at the dance; the ancients sitting round, and the active taking the roof off with their wild yelling. It was less agile dancing than Grant was used to on the mainland, less graceful; for Highland dancing one needed the kilt, and the soft thonged shoes that made no sound on the floor and let a man dance like a flame among the sword points. The Island dancing had much of the Irish in it; much of the sad Irish immobility that left the dancing a matter of footwork only, and not an uprush of joy that filled a man to the last finger-tip of his up-flung hands. But if the dancing itself lacked art and gaiety, there was a fine wholesale merriment in its stamping performance. There was room, with some squeezing, for three eightsomes, and sooner or later everyone, including the Swedes and the Hollanders, were dragged into this orgy of exercise. A fiddle and a piano gave out the lovely floating rhythm (for that one needed a regimental band, thought Grant as he swung Katie-Ann into the arms of a delighted Swede; one needed that double drumbeat and pause; it might not be purist but it certainly was effective) and the hands of those at rest beat time. The wind howled along the skylights on the roof, the dancers yelled, the fiddle sawed, and the piano thumped, and a wonderful time was had by all.

Including Alan Grant.

He swayed home through the stinging lash of hail wielded by a pitiless southwester, and dropped into bed drunk with exercise and fresh air. It had been a delightful day.

It had also been a profitable one. He would have something to tell Ted Hanna when he got back to town. He knew now who Archie Brown's "ravens" were.

Tonight he did not look at the closed window with misgiving. Nor tonight did he forget it altogether. He looked at the closed window and was glad of it. He had absorbed the Island point of view that a window is there to keep out the weather.

He burrowed into his cotton-quilt nest, out of the wind and the weather, and fell into dreamless depths of sleep.

# 8

WEE ARCHIE DEPARTED next morning when "the boat" called, on his way to spread light throughout all the other dark places of the archipelago. He had been staying with the Reverend Mr. MacKay, it transpired; and Grant wondered what that blameless padre to a Highland regiment would think if he knew what he had been sheltering under his roof. Or was the Reverend Mr. MacKay, too, sick of Archie Brown's disease?

On the whole Grant thought not.

Mr. MacKay had all the authority that mortal man could crave; he had a satisfaction for his vanity every Sunday morning; he had seen the world, and life and death, and men's souls in relation to both, and he was not likely to hanker after esoteric glories. He had merely been host to a Scottish celebrity. For in a small country like Scotland Archie ranked as a celebrity, and Mr. MacKay was no doubt greatly pleased to entertain him.

So Grant had the island to himself, and for five days in the company of the whooping wind he quartered his bleak kingdom. It was rather like walking with a bad-mannered dog; a dog that rushes past you on narrow paths, leaps on you in ecstasy so that you are nearly knocked over, and drags you from the direction in which you want to go. He spent his evenings with his legs stretched out to the office fire listening to Mr. Todd's tales of pub-owning in the Lowlands. He ate enormously. He put on weight visibly. He slept as soon as his head touched the pillow, and he woke only when it was morning. And by the end of the fifth day he was ready to face a hundred air journeys rather than spend another twelve hours in the place.

So on the sixth morning he stood on the great flat of white sand waiting for the little plane to pick him up on its way back from Stornoway. And the small misgiving somewhere in the depths of him was nothing like the pervading apprehension with which he had expected to be filled at this moment. Mr. Todd stood with him, and beside them on the sand was his small case. Up on the grass, where the road ended, was the Cladda Hotel car, the only one on the island and the only one of its class anywhere in the world. They stood there, four tiny dark objects in the shining waste, watching the small bird-like thing in the sky drop down to them.

This, Grant thought, was as near to the original idea of flight as one was likely to get nowadays. As someone had pointed out, when man first dreamed of flying he had seen himself rising on his own silver wings into the blue empyrean, but it hadn't turned out at all like that. First he was trundled to a field, then he was shut in a box, then he was terrified, then he was sick, then he was in Paris. Being picked up from the sands on the sea-ward fringe of the world by a casual-alighting bird was as near as one would ever come to the free soaring of man's original vision.

The great bird idled up to them along the sand, and for a moment Grant panicked. It was, when all was said, a box. A tight-closed trap of a thing. But the casualness of everything loosened his rigid muscles almost as soon as they had stiffened. In the clinical order of an airport, shepherded and compelled, panic might have conquered. But here, on the open sand, with the pilot draped about the top step as he gossiped with Mr. Todd, and the crying of gulls and the smell of the sea, it was a thing one could take or leave. There was no compulsion to be afraid of.

So when the moment came he put his foot over the last step with nothing more than a slight heart-quickening. And before he could analyse his reaction to the closing door, a nearer interest caught his mind. In front of him, on the other side of the gangway, was Wee Archie.

Wee Archie looked as if he had just got out of bed, and as if he had done that getting-out in some hurry. His dishevelled splendour looked more than ever as if they were someone else's clothes altogether. He looked like a discarded armature with some studio props flung on top of it. He greeted Grant like an old friend, condescended to him about his ignorance of the Islands, recommended Gaelic to him as a language it would pay him to study, and went back to sleep. Grant sat and looked at him.

The little bastard, he thought. The vain, worthless little bastard.

Archie's mouth had fallen open, and the strands of black hair no longer covered the thin patch. The knees above the fat brilliant socks were more like anatomical specimens than any mechanism designed for the propulsion of a living being. They weren't knees; they were "the knee joint." The articulation of the fibula was particularly interesting.

The vain, vicious little bastard. He had had a profession that would give him his bread and butter, a profession that would have given him a certain standing, a profession that would have brought him spiritual reward. But that had not satisfied his egotistical soul. He had needed the limelight. And as long as he could strut in the light, he did not care who paid for the illumination.

Grant was still considering the fundamental part that vanity played in the make-up of the criminal when a geometrical pattern opened below him like a Japanese flower in water. He took his thoughts from psychological matters in order to consider this Euclidean phenomenon in a world of nature and found that they were circling the mainland airport. He had flown back from Cladda and had hardly been aware of it.

He climbed down on to the tarmac and wondered what would happen if he did a war-dance of joy there and then. He wanted to go whooping and prancing round the aerodrome like a child on his first hobby-horse. Instead he went to the telephone booths and asked Tommy if he could pick him up at the Caledonian in Scoone in about two hours. Tommy could and would.

The food at the airport restaurant tasted like Lucas-Carton, the Tour d'Argent, and La Crémaillière all rolled into one. The man at the next table was complaining bitterly about it. But he, of course, had not just been reborn after five months of hell and seven days of Katie-Ann.

Tommy's round kind face in the lounge of the Caledonian looked rounder and kinder than even Tommy's face had ever looked before.

There was no wind.

No wind at all.

It was a beautiful world.

What a frightful anticlimax it would be, he thought, if when he got into the car with Tommy the old horror overcame him. Perhaps the thing was just waiting there for him, licking its lips with anticipation.

But there was nothing in the car. Just himself and Tommy and the good relaxed atmosphere of their habitual intercourse. They drove away into the country, an appreciably greener country than it had been ten days ago, and the evening sun came out and sent long golden fingers of light across the calm fields.

"How did the Moymore ceremony come off?" he asked. "The bouquet presentation."

"Oh, heavens: that!" Tommy said, making motions as of a man mopping his forehead.

"Didn't he present it?"

"If letting her have it is presenting it, I suppose technically he presented it. He handed it over with a speech he had thought up himself."

"What kind of speech?"

"I think he had been rehearsing a sort of get-out for himself ever since we talked him into it by making Zoë Kentallen a rebel of some kind. Which was Laura's idea, by the way, not mine. Well, when she stooped to take the great bush of carnations from him—she's very tall—he held them out of her reach for a moment and said firmly, 'I'm only giving you this, mind, because you're a fellow-revolutionary.' She took it without batting an eyelid. She said: 'Yes, of course. How very kind of you,' although she hadn't an idea what he was talking about. She bowled him over, by the way."

"How?"

"In the good old female way. Pat is in the throes of his first infatuation."

Grant looked forward to seeing this phenomenon.

Clune lay very peaceful in its green hollow, and Grant looked at it as one coming home victorious from battle. The last time he had driven up that sandy road he had been a slave; now he was a free man. He had gone out to look for B Seven and had found himself.

Laura came out to meet him at the doorstep and said, "Alan, have you taken to a tipster's business on the side?"

"No. Why?"

"Or one of those Lonely Hearts columns, or something?"

"No."

"Because Mrs. Mair says there is a whole sackful of mail waiting for you at the post-office."

"Oh. How did Mrs. Mair know that the letters were for me?"

"She said you were the only A. Grant in the district. I take it you haven't advertised for a wife?"

"No, just for a bit of information," he said, going with her into the sitting-room.

The room in the early dusk was full of firelight and wavering shadows. He thought it was empty until he noticed that someone was sitting in the big wing-chair by the hearth. A woman, so long and slender that she seemed as fluid as the shadows and he had to look a second time to be sure that she was not in truth a shadow.

"Lady Kentallen," said Laura's voice behind him, in an introducing tone. "Zoë has come back to Clune for a few days' fishing."

The woman leant forward to shake hands with him and he saw that she was a girl.

"Mr. Grant," she said, greeting him. "Laura says that you like to be called Mr."

"Yes. Yes, I do. 'Inspector' has a grim sound in private life."

"And a little unreal, too," she said in her gentle voice. "Like something out of a detective story."

"Yes; people expect you to say, 'Where were you on the evening of the umpteenth inst.?'" How could this virginal creature be the mother of three sons, one of them nearly old enough to leave school? "Have you been having any luck on the river?"

"I had a nice grilse this morning. You are going to have it for supper."

She had the kind of beauty that allows a woman to part her hair in the middle and wear it smooth to her head. A dark small head on a long graceful neck.

He remembered suddenly about the newly decorated bedroom. So the fresh paint had been for Zoë Kentallen, and not for Laura's latest candidate for his interest. That was an enormous relief. It had been bad enough to have Laura's selections put under his nose, but to have had the latest one actually under the same roof would have been, to put it mildly, tiresome.

"The Oban train must have been in time for once," Laura said, remarking on his early arrival.

"Oh, he flew back," Tommy said, throwing another log on the fire. He said it casually, unaware that the fact had any importance.

Grant looked over at Laura and saw her face light with happiness. She turned her head to find him among the shadows and saw that he was looking at her, and smiled. Had it mattered so much to her then? Dear Lalla. Dear kind understanding Lalla.

They began to talk about the Islands. Tommy had a fine tale of a man whose hat blew off as he was boarding a boat in Barra and who found it waiting for him on the pier at Mallaig. Laura was funny about the impossibility of carrying on a conversation in a language that has no words for anything less than two hundred years old and supplied an imaginary account of a road accident. ("Blah-blah bicycle blah-blah S-bend blah-blah brakes blah-blah traction-engine blah-blah ambulance blah-blah stretcher blah-blah anaesthetic blah-blah private ward blah-blah temperature-chart blah-blah chrysanthemums freezias ranunculus narcissus carnations . . .") Zoë had stayed in the Islands as a child and was very knowledgeable about poaching salmon, an art she had been taught by local talent under the very nose of her host's gamekeeper.

Grant was pleased to find that the family atmosphere of Clune had been in no way disturbed by the presence of this guest. She seemed unaware of her beauty, and unexpectant of attention. He was not surprised that Pat had been "bowled over."

It was only when his bedroom door finally closed on him and he was alone that his mind went to the waiting sack of letters in the post-office at Moymore. A sack of them! Well, that was not unbearably surprising, after all. A life in the C.I.D. conditioned one to the existence of the letter-writer. There were people whose only interest in life was writing letters. To the newspapers, to authors, to strangers, to City Councils, to the police. It did not much matter to whom; the satisfaction of writing seemed to be all. Seven-eighths of that pile of letters would be the product of those whose hobby was writing letters.

But there was still the odd eighth.

What would the odd eighth have to say?

In the morning he watched the guest getting her tackle ready for the river and wished that he was going with her, but still more he wanted to go to the post-office at Moymore. She set off without fuss, self-sufficient and unobtrusive, and Grant, watching her walk down the path, thought that she was more like an adolescent boy than a prospective dowager. She was wearing very elegant trousers and a disreputable old lumber jacket, and he remarked to Tommy that she was one of the few women who looked really well in trousers.

"She's the only woman in the *world*," Tommy said, "who looks beautiful in waders."

So Grant went away to interview Mrs. Mair at Moymore. Mrs. Mair hoped that he had a secretary, and presented him with a paper-knife. It was a thin silver affair, very tarnished, with a thistle head made of amethyst. When he pointed out that the thing was hall-marked and of some value nowadays and that he could not accept expensive presents from strange women, she said:

"Mr. Grant, that thing has been in my shop for twenty-five years. It was made for the souvenir trade in the days when people could read. Now they just look and listen. You're the first person I've met in a quarter of a century that *needed* a paper-knife. Indeed, by the time you've slit open all the letters in that sack, you'll need more than a paper-knife, I'm thinking. Anyway it's the first and last time I'll ever have a sack of mail addressed to one person in this office and I'd like to mark the occasion. So you take the wee knife!"

He took it gratefully, hoisted the sack into the car, and went back to Clune.

"The bag's post-office property," she said after him, "so see you bring it back!"

He took the sack to his own room, polished the little knife until it shone with a pleased and grateful air as if glad to be noticed after all those years, emptied the bag on to the floor, and slipped the knife into the first letter to come to hand. The first letter asked him how he dared expose to the public gaze the words the writer had written, with such pain and heart-searching, in the spring of 1911, under the orders of her spirit guide Azul. It was like being publicly exhibited without clothes, to see her own precious lines so wantonly laid bare.

Thirteen other correspondents claimed to have written the lines (without spirit guidance) and asked what was in it for them. Five sent the completed poem—five different poems—and claimed that they were the author of it. Three accused him of blasphemy, and seven said he was plagiarising from Revelation. One said: "Thank you very much for an evening's entertainment, old boy, and how is the fishing on the Turlie this year?" One directed him to the Apocrypha, one to the Arabian Nights, one to Rider Haggard, one to Theosophy, one to Grand Canyon, and five to various parts of Central and South America. Nine sent him cures for alcoholism, and twenty-two sent him circulars about esoteric cults. Two suggested subscriptions to poetry magazines, and one offered to teach him to write salable verse. One said: "If you are the A. Grant I sat through the monsoon with at Bishenpur this is my present address." One said: "If you are the A. Grant I spent the night with in a rest hotel in Amalfi this is just to say hullo, and I wish my husband was as good." One sent him particulars of a Clan Grant association. Nine were obscene. Three were illegible.

There were one hundred and seventeen letters.

The one that gave him most pleasure was one that read: "I've fathomed your code, you bloody traitor, and I shall report you to the Special Branch."

Not one of them was of any help at all.

Oh, well. He had not really hoped. It had been a shot in the dark.

He had at least had some amusement out of it. Now he could settle down and fish until the end of his sick-leave. He wondered how long Zoë Kentallen was staying.

The guest had taken sandwiches with her and did not appear for lunch, but in the afternoon Grant took his rod and followed her down to the river. She had probably already fished the whole of the Clune water, but perhaps she did not know it as well as he did. She might be glad of some unobtrusive advice. Not, of course, that he was going down to the river for the sole purpose of talking to her. He was going to fish. But he would have to find out first which part of the water she herself was fishing. And he could hardly, having found her, pass with a casual wave of the hand.

He did not pass at all, of course. He sat on the bank watching her drop a Green Highlander above the big one that she had been pursuing with various lures for the last hour. "He just thumbs his nose at me," she said. "It has become a personal affair between us." She used her rod with the ease of someone who has fished since she was a child, almost absent-mindedly, as Laura did. It was very satisfying to watch.

He gaffed the fish for her an hour later, and they sat together on the grass and ate the rest of her sandwiches. She asked about his work, not as if it was a sensational matter, but as she might inquire about it if he had been an architect or an engine-driver; she told him about her three boys and what they were going to be. Her simplicity was indestructible, and her unselfconsciousness child-like in its completeness.

"Nigel will be sick when he hears that I have been fishing the Turlie," she said. She said it as a girl might say it of a schoolboy brother; and he deduced that this described with fair accuracy the relationship between herself and her sons.

There were hours yet of daylight, but neither of them made any move to go back to the river. They sat there looking down on the brown water and talked. Grant, out of his wide acquaintance, tried to think of an equivalent to her, and failed. None of the beautiful women he had seen in his time had had her fairy-princess quality, her air of timeless youth. A stray from Tir nan Og, he thought. It was surprising that she should, soberly considered, be the same age as Laura.

"Did you know Laura well at school?"

"Not bosom-friend well. I was terribly in awe of her, you see."

"In awe? Of Laura?"

"Yes. She was very clever, you know, and good at everything, and I never could add two and two."

Since part of his delight in her was the contrast between her Hans-Andersen-illustration quality and her practicality, he deduced that this was an exaggeration. But it was probably true that she had no—no branches to her, so to speak. No multitude of leaves to breathe the air of the world. The climate of her mind was uncritical. Her utterance had none of Laura's glancing comment, none of Laura's swift interest and dissection.

"We are very lucky, you and Laura and I, to have known the Highlands when we were children," she said, when they were talking of early fishing experiences. "That is what I should wish most for a child. To have a beautiful calf-country. When David—my husband—was killed they wanted me to sell Kentallen. We had never had much money, and the death duties took the margin that made the place workable. But I wanted to hang on to it at least until Nigel and Timmy and Charles are grown-up. They will hate losing it, but at least they will have had the years that matter in a beautiful country."

He looked at her, putting her tackle neatly away in its box with the sober care of a tidy child, and thought that the solution of her problem was surely remarriage. The West End that he knew so well was lousy with sleek men in shiny cars who could keep Kentallen with no more effort than they would keep a Japanese garden in one of the rooms that they called lounges. The difficulty was, he supposed, that in Zoë Kentallen's world money was neither an introduction nor an absolution.

The spring sunlight faded. The skies grew luminous. The hills went far away and lay down, as Laura had once said as a child, describing in eight easy words the whole look and atmosphere of an evening of settled weather when tomorrow is going to be a wonderful day.

"We ought to be getting back," Zoë said.

As he picked up their fishing things from the bank he thought that there had been more magic in this one afternoon on the Turlie than in all the much advertised Islands of the West.

"You love your work, don't you?" she said as they walked up the hill to Clune. "Laura told me that you could have retired years ago if you had wanted to."

"Yes," he said, a little surprised. "I suppose that I could have retired. My mother's sister left me a legacy. She married a man who did well in Australia and she had no children."

"What would you do if you retired?"

"I don't know. I have never even considered it."

# 9

BUT THAT NIGHT, going to sleep, he did consider it. Not as a prospect, but with speculation. What would it be like to retire? To retire while he was still young enough to begin something else? If he began something else what would it be? A sheep-farm like Tommy's? That would be a good life. But could he make a success of an entirely country existence? He doubted it. And if not, then what else could he do?

He played with this nice new toy until he fell asleep, and he took it to the river with him next morning. One of the really charming facets of the game was the thought of Bryce's face when he read his resignation. Bryce would not merely be short of staff for a week or two; he would find himself deprived for good and all of his most valued subordinate. It was a delicious thought.

He fished his favourite pool, below the swing bridge, and conducted delightful conversations with Bryce. Because, of course, there would be a conversation. He would give himself the ineffable delight of laying that written resignation on the desk in front of Bryce's nose; laying it there himself, in person. Then there would be some really satisfying chat, and he would walk out into the street a free man.

Free to do what?

To be himself, at the beck and call of nobody.

To do things he had always wanted to do and had had no time for. To mess about in small boats, for instance.

To get married, perhaps.

Yes, to get married. With leisure there would be time to share his life. Time to love and be loved.

This lasted him very happily for another hour.

About noon he became aware that he was not alone. He looked up and saw that a man was standing on the bridge watching him. He was standing only a few yards from the bank, and since the bridge was motionless he must have been there for some time. The bridge was the usual trough of wire floored with wooden slats, a structure so light that even the wind was capable of moving it. He was grateful to the stranger for not walking into the middle of the thing and swaying about there so that he distracted every fish in the neighbourhood.

He nodded to the man by way of expressing his approval.

"Your name Grant?" asked the man.

After the circumlocutions of a people so devious-minded that they had no word for No, it was pleasant to be asked a straight question in simple English.

"Yes," he said, and wondered a little. The man sounded as if he might be an American.

"You the guy who put that advertisement in the paper?"

There was no doubt about the nationality this time.

"Yes."

The man tipped his hat further back on his head and said in a resigned way, "Oh, well, I'm crazy too, I guess, or I wouldn't be here."

Grant began to reel in.

"Won't you come down, Mr.—"

The man moved off the bridge and came down the bank to him.

He was youngish, well-dressed, and pleasant-looking.

"My name is Cullen," he said. "Tad Cullen. I'm a flyer. I fly freight for OCAL. You know: Oriental Commercial Airlines Ltd."

It was said that all you needed to fly for OCAL was a certificate and no sign of leprosy. But that was an exaggeration. Indeed, it was a perversion. You had to be good to fly for OCAL. In the big shiny passenger lines, if you made a mistake you were on the carpet. In OCAL, if you made a mistake you were out on your ear. OCAL had an unlimited supply of personnel to draw upon. OCAL cared nothing for your grammar, your colour, your antecedents, your manners, your nationality, or your looks, as long as you could fly. You had to be able to fly. Grant looked at Mr. Cullen with a double interest.

"Look, Mr. Grant, I know that that thing, those words in the paper, I know they were just some kind of quotation that you wanted identified, or something like that. And of course I can't identify them. I was never any good at books. I haven't come here to be any use to you. Quite the opposite, I guess. But I've been very worried, and I thought even a long shot like this might be worth trying. You see, Bill used words like that one night when he was a bit high—Bill's my buddy—and I thought, maybe, it might be a place. I mean the description might be a place. Even if it is a quotation. I'm afraid I'm not making myself very clear."

Grant smiled a little and said No, not so far, but suppose they both sat down and straightened it out. "Am I to understand that you have come here looking for me?"

"Yes, I actually came last night. But the post-office place was shut, so I got a bed at the inn. Moymore, they call it. And then I went to the post-office this morning and asked them where I could find the A. Grant who had a lot of letters. I was sure you'd have had a lot, you see, after that advertisement. And they said Oh, yes, if it was Mr. Grant I wanted I would find him on the river somewhere. Well, I came down to look, and the only other person on the river was a lady, so I guessed you must be it. You see, it wasn't any good writing to you because I really hadn't anything that seemed worth putting on paper. I mean, it was just a daffy kind of hope. And you mightn't have bothered answering it anyway—when it had nothing to do with you, I mean." He paused a moment, and added in a half-hopeful, half-hoping-for-nothing tone, "It isn't a night-club, is it?"

"What isn't?" Grant asked, surprised.

"That place with talking beasts at the door. And the odd scenery. It sounded like a fun-fair place. You know: the kind of place where you go in a boat through tunnels in the dark and see ridiculous and frightening things unexpectedly. But Bill wouldn't be interested in a place like that. So I thought of a night-club. You know, one of those got up with oddities to impress the customers. That would be much more Bill's mixture. Especially in Paris. And it was in Paris that I was to meet him."

For the first time a gleam of light appeared.

"You mean that you were due to meet this Bill? And he didn't keep the appointment?"

"He didn't show up at all. And that's very unlike Bill. If Bill says he'll do a thing, or be in a place, or remember a thing, believe you me he'll deliver. That's why I'm so worried. And not a word of explanation. Not a message left at the hotel or anything. Of course, they may have forgotten to put down the message, hotels being what they are. But even if they did forget, there would have been some follow-up. I mean, when I didn't react, Bill would have telephoned again saying: What are you up to, you old so-and-so? Didn't you get my message? But there wasn't anything like that. It's funny, isn't it, that he would book a room and then not turn up to occupy it and not send a word in explanation?"

"Very strange indeed. Especially since you say your friend was a dependable type. But why were you interested in my advertisement? I mean, in connection with Bill? Bill—what, by the way?"

"Bill Kenrick. He's a flyer like me. With OCAL. We've been friends for a year or two now. The best friend I ever had, I don't mind saying. Well, it was like this, Mr. Grant. When he didn't turn up, and no one seemed to know anything about him or to have heard from him—and he had no people in England that I could write to—I thought about what other ways there were of communicating with people. Other than telephones and letters and telegrams and what not. And so I thought of what you call the Agony Column. You know, in the newspapers. So I got the Paris edition of the *Clarion*—the files, I mean, at their Paris office—and went through them, and there was nothing. And then I tried *The Times,* and there was nothing there either. This was after some time, of course, so I had to go back through the files, but there was nothing. I was going to give it up because I thought that that was all the English papers that had regular Paris editions, but someone said why didn't I try the *Morning News.* Well, I went to the *News,* and there didn't seem to be anything from Bill, but there was this thing of yours that rang a bell. If Bill hadn't been missing I don't suppose I would have thought twice about it, but having heard Bill gabble something along those lines made me notice it and be interested. Are you with me, as Bill says?"

"Entirely. Go on. When was it that Bill talked about the odd landscape?"

"He didn't talk about it at all. He just babbled one night when we were all a little drunk. Bill doesn't drink, Mr. Grant. I don't want you to get the wrong idea. I mean, drink as a habit. A few of the boys in our lot do, I admit, but they don't last long in OCAL. They don't last long anyway. That's why OCAL heaves them out. They don't mind them killing themselves, but it gets expensive in crates. But now and then we have a night out like other people. And it was on one of those nights out that Bill got going. We were all a little high so I don't remember anything in detail. I know we were drinking toasts and we were running out of subjects by that time. And we were taking it in turn to think up unlikely things to toast. You know, like 'The third daughter of the Lord Mayor of Bagdad,' or 'June Kaye's left little toe.' And Bill said, 'To Paradise!' and then gabbled a piece about talking beasts and singing sands and what not."

"Didn't anyone ask about this Paradise of his?"

"No. The next fellow was just waiting to get his word in. No one was paying any attention to anything. They'd just think Bill's toast pretty dull. I wouldn't have remembered it myself if I hadn't come across the words in the paper when my mind was full of Bill."

"And he never mentioned it again? Never talked about anything like that in his sober moments?"

"No. He isn't much of a talker at the best of times."

"You think, perhaps, if he was greatly interested in something he would keep it to himself?"

"Oh, yes, he does that; he does that. He's not close, you know; just a bit cagey. In most ways he's the most open guy you could imagine. Generous with his roll, and careless with his things, and willing to do anything for anyone. But in the things that—in personal things, if you know what I mean, he sort of shuts the door on you."

"Did he have a girl?"

"Not more than any of us can be said to have one. But that's a very good sample of what I mean. When the rest of us are out for an evening, we take what's going. But Bill will go off by himself to some other quarter of the town where he has picked something more to his fancy."

"What town?"

"Any town we happen to be in. Kuwait, Masquat, Quatif, Mukalla. Anything from Aden to Karachi, if it comes to that. Most of us fly scheduled routes, but some fly tramps. Take anything anywhere."

"What did—does Bill fly?"

"He's flown all sorts. But lately he's been flying between the Gulf and the South Coast."

"Arabia, you mean."

"Yes. It's a damned dreary route but Bill seemed to like it. Me, I think he was too long on it. If you're too long on one route, you get stale."

"Why do you think he was too long on it? Had he changed at all?"

Mr. Cullen hesitated. "Not exactly. He was just the old Bill, easy-going and nice. But he got so that he couldn't leave it behind him."

"Leave his work behind, you mean?"

"Yes. Most of us—all of us, in fact—drop work when we turn the bus over to the ground staff. We don't remember it until we say hullo to the mechanic in charge next morning. But Bill got so that he would pore over maps of the route as if he had never flown the hop before."

"Why this interest in the route, do you think?"

"Well, I did think maybe he was figuring out a way to avoid the bad weather areas. It did begin—the interest in maps, I mean—one time when he came in very late after being blown out of his way by one of those terrific hurricanes that come out of nowhere in that country. We had nearly given him up that time."

"Don't you fly above the weather?"

"On a long hop, of course. But when you're flying freight you have to come down at the oddest places. So you're always more or less at the mercy of the weather."

"I see. And you think Bill changed after that experience?"

"Well, I think it left a mark on him. I was there when he came in. In the plane, I mean. I was waiting for him, on the field. And he seemed to me a bit —concussed, if you get me."

"Suffering from shock."

"Yes. Still back there, if you know what I mean. Not really listening to what you said to him."

"And after that he began to study maps. To plan his route, you think."

"Yes. From then on it was in the forefront of his mind instead of being something that you drop with your working clothes. He even began to come in late as a habit. As if he went out of his way to look for an easier route."

He paused a moment, and then added in a quick warning tone, "Please understand, Mr. Grant, I'm not saying Bill has lost his nerve."

"No, of course not."

"Lost nerves don't take you that way at all, believe me. You get quite the opposite. You don't want to think of flying at all. You get short in the temper, and you drink too much and too early in the day, and you try to wangle short hops, and you go sick when there's nothing wrong with you. There's no mystery about lost nerve, Mr. Grant. It announces itself like a name on a marquee. There was nothing like that about Bill—and I don't think there ever will be. It was just that he couldn't leave the thing behind."

"It became an obsession with him."

"That's about it, I suppose."

"Did he have other interests?"

"He read books," Mr. Cullen said, in an apologetic way, as one confessing a peculiarity in a friend. "Even in that, it showed."

"How: showed?"

"I mean, instead of the books being the usual story affairs they'd as likely as not be about Arabia."

"Yes?" Grant said thoughtfully. Ever since this stranger had first mentioned Arabia, Grant had been altogether "with him." Arabia to all the world meant one thing: sand. And what was more, he realised that when he had had the feeling, that morning in the Scoone hotel, that "singing sands" did actually exist somewhere, it was with Arabia that he should have connected them. Somewhere in Arabia there were in fact sands that were alleged to sing.

"So I was glad when he took his leave earlier than he meant to," Mr. Cullen was saying. "We had planned to go together, and spend our leave in Paris. But he changed his mind and said he wanted a week or two in London first. He's English, you know. So we arranged to meet at the Hotel St. Jacques in Paris. He was to meet me there on the 4th of March."

"*When?*" said Grant, and was suddenly still. Mind and body still, like a pointer with the bird in sight; like a man with the target in his sights.

"The 4th of March. Why?"

Singing sands were anyone's interest. Men who fly for OCAL were two a penny. But the wide, vague, indefinite affair of Bill Kenrick who was obsessed with Southern Arabia and did not turn up to his appointments in Paris narrowed suddenly to one small focused point. To a date.

On the 4th of March, when Bill Kenrick should have turned up in Paris, the London Mail had come into Scoone bearing the dead body of a young man who was interested in singing sands. A young man with reckless eyebrows. A young man who, on looks, would have made a very likely flyer. Grant remembered that he had tried him, in imagination, on the bridge of a small ship; a fast small ship, hell in any kind of sea. He had looked well there. But he would look just as well at the controls of a plane.

"Why did Bill choose Paris?"

"Why does anyone choose Paris!"

"It wasn't because he was French?"

"Bill? No, Bill's English. Very English."

"Did you ever see his passport?"

"Not that I can remember. Why?"

"You don't think that he might have been French by birth?"

It wouldn't work out, anyway. The Frenchman was called Martin. Unless his English upbringing had made him want to adopt an English name?

"You don't happen to have a photograph of your friend, do you?"

But Mr. Cullen's attention was on something else. Grant turned to look, and found that Zoë was approaching them along the river bank. He looked at his watch.

"Hell!" he said. "And I promised to have the stove going!" He turned to his bag and fished the primus from it.

"Your wife?" asked Mr. Cullen, with that refreshing frankness. In the Islands it would have taken five minutes' conversation to have elicited that information from him.

"No. That's Lady Kentallen."

"Lady? A title?"

"Yes," Grant said, busy with the stove. "She is Viscountess Kentallen."

Mr. Cullen considered this in silence for a little.

"I suppose that's a sort of marked-down Countess."

"No. On the contrary. A very superior kind. Practically a Marchioness. Look, Mr. Cullen, let's postpone this matter of your friend for a little. It's a matter that interests me more than I can say, but—"

"Yes, of course. I'll go. When can I talk to you again about it?"

"Of course you will not go! You'll stay and have some food with us."

"You mean you want me to meet this Marchioness, this—what-you-may-call-it, Viscountess?"

"Why not? She is a very nice person to meet. One of the nicest persons I know."

"Yes?" Mr. Cullen looked with interest at the approaching Zoë. "She's certainly very nice to look at. I didn't know they came like that. Somehow I imagined all aristocrats had beaky noses."

"Specially provided for looking down, I take it."

"Something like that."

"I don't know how far back in English history one would have to go to find an aristocratic nose that was looked down. I doubt if you'd find one at all. The only place to find a looked-down nose is in the suburbs. In what is known as lower-middle-class circles."

Mr. Cullen looked puzzled. "But the aristocrats keep themselves to themselves and look down on the rest, don't they?"

"It has never been possible in England for any class to keep themselves to themselves, as you call it. They have been intermarrying at all levels for two thousand years. There never have been separate and distinct classes—or an aristocratic class at all in the sense that you mean it."

"I suppose nowadays things are evening up," Mr. Cullen suggested, faintly unbelieving.

"Oh, no. It has always been a fluid thing. Even our Royalty. Elizabeth the First was the grand-daughter of a Lord Mayor. And you'll find that Royalty's personal friends have no titles at all: I mean the people who are on calling-terms at Buckingham Palace. Whereas the bold bad baron who sits next you in an expensive restaurant probably started life as a platelayer on the railway. There *is* no keeping oneself to oneself in England, as far as class goes. It can't be done. It can only be done by Mrs. Jones who sniffs at her neighbour Mrs. Smith because Mr. Jones makes two pounds a week more than Mr. Smith."

He turned from the puzzled American to greet Zoë. "I'm truly sorry about the stove. I'm afraid I got it going too late to be ready. We were having a very interesting conversation. This is Mr. Cullen, who flies freight for Oriental Commercial Airlines."

Zoë shook hands, and asked him what kind of plane he flew.

From the tone of his voice when he told her, Grant deduced that Mr. Cullen thought that Zoë was merely taking a condescending interest. Condescension was what he would expect from an "aristocrat."

"They're very heavy in hand, aren't they?" Zoë remarked sympathetically. "My brother used to fly one when he was on the Australia run. He was always cursing it." She began to open the packets of food. "But now that he works in an office in Sydney he has a little runabout of his own. A Beamish Eight. A lovely thing. I used to fly it when he first bought it, before he took it to Australia. David—my husband—and I used to dream of having one too, but we could never afford it."

"But a Beamish Eight costs only four hundred," Mr. Cullen blurted.

Zoë licked her fingers, sticky from a leaking apple tart, and said, "Yes, I know, but we never had four hundred to spare."

Mr. Cullen, feeling himself being washed out to sea, sought some terra firma.

"I oughtn't to be eating your food this way," he said. "They'll have plenty for me back at the hotel. I really ought to go back."

"Oh, don't go," Zoë said with a simplicity so genuine that it penetrated even Mr. Cullen's defences. "There is enough for a platoon."

So to Grant's pleasure in more ways than one, Mr. Cullen stayed. And Zoë, unaware that she was providing the United States with a revised view of the genus English Aristocrat, ate like a hungry schoolboy and talked in her gentle voice to the stranger as if she had known him all her life. By the apple-tart stage, Mr. Cullen had ceased to be on his guard. By the time that they were handing round the chocolates that Laura had included, he had surrendered unconditionally.

They sat together in the spring sunshine, full-fed and content. Zoë lying back against the grassy bank with her feet crossed and her hands behind her head, her eyes closed against the sun; Grant with his mind busy with B Seven, and the material that Tad Cullen had brought him; Mr. Cullen himself perched on a rock looking down the river to the green civilised strath where the moors ended and the fields began.

"It's a fine little country, this," he said. "I like it. If you ever decide to fight for your freedom, count me in."

"Freedom?" said Zoë, opening her eyes. "Freedom from whom or what?"

"From England, of course."

Zoë looked helpless, but Grant began to laugh. "I think you must have been talking to a little black man in a kilt," he said.

"He had a kilt, yes, but he wasn't coloured," Mr. Cullen said.

"No, I meant black-haired. You've been talking to Archie Brown."

"Who is Archie Brown?" asked Zoë.

"He is the self-appointed saviour of Gaeldom, and our future Sovereign, Commissar, President, or what have you, when Scotland has freed herself from the murderous burden of the English yoke."

"Oh, yes, that man," Zoë said mildly, identifying Archie in her mind. "He is a little off his head, isn't he? Does he live around here?"

"He is staying at the hotel at Moymore, I understand. He has been doing missionary work on Mr. Cullen, it seems."

"Well," Mr. Cullen grinned a little sheepishly, "I did just wonder if he wasn't over-stating things a bit. I've met some Scots in my time and they didn't seem to me to be the kind of people to put up with the treatment Mr. Brown was describing. Indeed, if you'll forgive me, Mr. Grant, they always seemed to me the kind of people to get the best of whatever bargain was going."

"Did you ever hear the Union better described?" Grant said to Zoë.

"I never knew anything about the Union," Zoë said comfortably, "except that it took place in 1707."

"Was there a battle, then?" Mr. Cullen asked.

"No," Grant said. "Scotland stepped thankfully on to England's band-wagon, and fell heir to all the benefits. Colonies, Shakespeare, soap, solvency, and so forth."

"I hope Mr. Brown doesn't go lecture-touring in the States," Zoë said, half asleep.

"He will," Grant said. "He will. All vociferous minorities go lecture-touring in the States."

"It will give them very wrong ideas, won't it?" Zoë said mildly. Grant thought with what a blistering phrase Laura would have expressed the same idea. "They have the oddest ideas. When David and I were there, the year before he was killed, we were always being asked why we didn't stop taxing

Canada. When we said we had never taxed Canada they just looked at us as if we were telling lies. Not very good lies, either."

From Mr. Cullen's expression Grant deduced that he, too, had had "odd" ideas about Canadian taxation, but Zoë's eyes were closed. Grant wondered if Mr. Cullen realised that Zoë was quite unaware that he was an American; that it had not occurred to her to consider his accent, his nationality, his clothes or any personal thing about him. She had accepted him as he stood, as a person. He was just a flyer, like her brother; someone who had turned up in time to share their picnic and who was pleasant and interesting to talk to. It would not occur to her to pigeonhole him, to put him in any special category. If she was conscious at all of his narrow *as* she no doubt took him for a North-countryman.

He looked at her, half asleep there in the sun, and thought how beautiful she was. He looked across at Mr. Cullen and saw that he, too, was looking at Zoë Kentallen and thinking how beautiful she was. Their glances met and ran away from each other.

But Grant, who last night could imagine no greater felicity than to sit and look at Zoë Kentallen, was conscious now of a faint impatience with her, and this so shocked him that he took it out, in his self-analytical way, to examine it. What flaw could there be in this divinity? What imperfection in this princess from a fairy-tale?

"You know very well what's wrong," said that irreverent voice in him. "You want her to get the hell out of here so that you can find out about B Seven."

And for once he did not try to contradict the voice. He did in brutal fact wish that Zoë would "get the hell out of here." The Zoë whose very presence had made magic of yesterday afternoon was now an encumbrance. Tiny prickles of boredom chased each other up and down his spine. Lovely, simple, heavenly Zoë, do get a move on. Creature of delight and princess of my dreams, go away.

He was rehearsing phrases for taking his own departure, when she gave the abrupt half-sigh half-yawn of a child and said, "Well, there is a seven-pounder in the Cuddy Pool that must be finding life dull without me." And with her usual lack of fuss or chat she took her things and departed into the spring afternoon.

Mr. Cullen looked after her approvingly, and Grant waited for comment. But it seemed that Mr. Cullen, too, had been waiting for the departure of his "marked-down Countess." He watched her out of earshot and then said immediately:

"Mr. Grant, why did you ask me if I had a photograph of Bill? Does that mean that you think you know him?"

"No. No. But it would eliminate people who could not be Bill."

"Oh. Yes. Well, I haven't one in my pocket but I have one in my grip at the hotel. It isn't a very good one, but it would give you the general idea. Could I bring it to you some time?"

"No. I'll walk down to Moymore with you now."

"You will? You're certainly very kind, Mr. Grant. You think you've got a line on this thing? You haven't told me what those words were. That quotation or whatever it was. That's really what I came to ask you. What the talking-beasts thing was all about. If it was a place he was interested in, you see, he might have gone there, and I could go there too and cross his trail that way."

"You're very fond of this Bill, aren't you?"

"Well, we've been together quite a time, and though we're opposites in most ways we get along fine. Just fine. I wouldn't like anything to happen to Bill."

Grant changed the conversation and asked about Tad Cullen's own life. And while they walked down the glen to Moymore, he heard about the clean small town back in the States, and what a dull place it seemed to a boy who could fly, and how wonderful the East had seemed in the distance and how unexciting close up.

"Just Main Street with smells," Mr. Cullen said.

"What did you do in Paris during your long wait for Bill to turn up?"

"Oh, I helled around some. It wasn't much fun without Bill. I met a couple of fellows I'd known in India, and we went places together, but I was impatient all the time for Bill to be there. I let them go, after a bit, and went to look at some of the places in the tourist folders. Some of those old places are pretty nice. There was one place built right over the water—a castle, I mean—on stone arches, so that the river flowed underneath. That was fine. It would have done very well for the Countess. Is that the kind of place she lives in?"

"No," Grant said, thinking of the difference between Chenonceaux and Kentallen. "She lives in a grim flat grey house with tiny windows and poky rooms and narrow stairs and a front door as welcoming as the exit of a laundry chute. It has two little turrets on the fourth-storey level, next the roof, and in Scotland that makes it a castle."

"Sounds like a prison. Why does she stay?"

"A prison! No prison committee would consider it for a moment; questions would be asked in the House immediately about its lack of light, heating, sanitary conveniences, colour, beauty, space, and what not. She stays because she loves the place. I doubt if she can stay much longer, however. Death duties have been so heavy that she will have to sell."

"But will anyone buy it?"

"Not to live in. But some speculator will buy it, and cut down the woods. The lead on the roof would probably fetch something; and they'd have to take the roof off anyhow to avoid paying tax on the house."

"Hah! Dust-bowl stuff," remarked Mr. Cullen. "It hasn't a moat, by any chance?"

"No. Why?"

"I must see a moat before I go back to OCAL." And then, after a pause, "I'm really very worried about Bill, Mr. Grant."

"Yes, it is certainly very odd."

"That was nice of you," Mr. Cullen said unexpectedly.

"What was?"

"Not to say, 'Don't you worry, he'll turn up all right!' I can hardly keep my hands off people who say, 'Don't you worry, he'll turn up.' I could strangle them."

Moymore Hotel was a tiny version of Kentallen, without the turrets. But it was whitewashed and cheerful, and the trees behind it were coming into leaf. In the little flagged entrance-hall Mr. Cullen hesitated.

"In Britain I notice people don't ask you up to their hotel bedroom. Would you like to wait in the sitting-room, perhaps?"

"Oh, no; I'll come up. I don't think we have any feeling about hotel bedrooms. It is probably just that our hotel sitting-rooms are so near our bedrooms that there is no need to go up, and so we don't suggest it. When a public lounge is a day's journey from your own room, it is easier to take a guest with you, I suppose. That way you are at least in the same hemisphere."

Mr. Cullen had a front room, looking across the road to the fields and the river and the hills beyond. With his professional eye Grant noticed the log fire ready-laid in the hearth and the daffodils in the window: Moymore had standards. With his personal mind he was concerned for this Tad Cullen, who had interrupted his leave and come to the wilds of Caledonia to find the friend who meant so much to him. A foreboding that he could not shake off had grown in him with every step of the way to Moymore, and now it filled him to the point of nausea.

The young man took a letter-case from his travelling-bag and opened it on the dressing-table. It contained practically everything but the wherewithal for writing letters. Among the mess of papers, maps, travel folders, and what not, there were two leather articles: an address-book and a pocket-book. From the pocket-book he took some photographs and riffled through the feminine smiles until he found what he was looking for.

"Here it is. I'm afraid it isn't a very good one. It's just a snapshot, you see. It was taken when a crowd of us were at the beach."

Grant took the proffered piece of paper, almost reluctantly.

"That's—" Tad Cullen was beginning, lifting his arm to point.

"No, wait!" Grant said, stopping him. "Let me see if I—if I recognise anyone."

There were perhaps a dozen young men in the photograph, which had been taken on the verandah of some beach-house. They were clustered round the steps and draped over the rickety wooden railing in various stages of *déshabillé*. Grant swept a swift glance over their laughing faces and was conscious of a great relief. There was no one there that he had ever—

And then he saw the man on the bottom step.

He was sitting with his feet pushed away from him into the sand, his eyes screwed up against the sun and his chin tilted back a little as if he had been in the act of turning to say something to the men behind. It was just so that his head had been tilted back against the pillow in Compartment B Seven on the morning of the 4th of March.

"Well?"

"Is that your friend?" Grant said, pointing to the man on the bottom step.

"Yes, that's Bill. How did you know? Have you met him somewhere, then?"

"I—I'm inclined to think that I have. But of course, on that photograph, I could hardly swear to it."

"I don't want you to do any swearing. Just give me a general weather report. Just tell me roughly when and where you saw him and I'll track him down, don't you be in any doubt about it. Do you know where you met him? I mean, do you remember?"

"Oh, yes. I remember. I saw him in a compartment—a sleeping-berth compartment—of the London Mail when it was running into Scoone early in the morning of the 4th of March. That was the train I came north on."

"You mean Bill came *here?* To Scotland? What for?"

"I don't know."

"Didn't he tell you? Did you talk to him?"

"No. I couldn't."

"Why not?"

Grant put out his hand and pushed his companion gently backwards so that he sat down in the chair that was behind him.

"I couldn't because he was no longer alive."

There was a short silence.

"I'm truly sorry, Cullen. I wish I could pretend to you that it might not be Bill, but short of going into a witness-box on oath I am prepared to back my belief that it is."

After another little silence Cullen said: "Why was he dead? What happened to him?"

"He had had a fair load of whisky and he fell backwards against the solid porcelain wash-basin. It fractured his skull."

"Who said all this?"

"That was the finding of the coroner's court. In London."

"In London? Why in London?"

"Because he had died, according to the post-mortem, very shortly after leaving Euston. And by English law, a sudden death is investigated by a coroner and a jury."

"But all that's just—just supposition," Cullen said, beginning to come alive and be angry. "If he was alone, how can anyone tell what happened to him?"

"Because the English police are the most painstaking creatures as well as the most suspicious."

"Police? There were police in on this thing?"

"Oh, assuredly. The police do the investigating and report in public to the coroner and his jury. In this case there had been the most exhaustive examination and tests. They knew in the end almost to a mouthful how much neat whisky he had drunk, and at what intervals before his—his death."

"And that about his falling backwards—how could they know that?"

"They went prowling with microscopes. The oil and broken hair were still evident on the edge of the basin. And the skull injury was consistent with a backwards fall against just such an object."

Cullen calmed down at this, but he looked disorientated.

"How do you know all this?" he asked, vaguely; and then with growing suspicion, "How did you come to see him anyway?"

"When I was on my way out, I came across the sleeping-car attendant trying to rouse him. The man thought he was just sleeping it off, because the whisky bottle had rolled all over the floor and the compartment smelt as if he had been making a night of it."

This did not satisfy Cullen. "You mean that was the only time you saw him? Just for a moment, lying—lying dead there, and you could recognise him from a snapshot—a not very good snapshot—weeks later?"

"Yes. I was impressed by his face. Faces are my business, and in a way my hobby. I was interested in the way the slant of the eyebrows gave the face a reckless expression, even—even as it was, without any real expression whatever. And the interest was intensified in a way that was quite accidental."

"What was that?" Cullen was not giving an inch.

"When I was having breakfast, in the Station Hotel at Scoone, I found that I had picked up by accident a newspaper that had been tumbled off the berth when the attendant was trying to waken him, and in the Stop Press— the blank space, you know—someone had been pencilling some lines of verse. 'The beasts that talk, the streams that stand, the stones that walk, the singing sand—' then two blank lines, and then, 'that guard the way to Paradise.'"

"That was what you advertised about," Cullen said, his face growing momentarily blacker. "What was it to you that you went to the trouble of advertising about it?"

"I wanted to know where the lines came from if they were lines from some book. If they were lines in the process of being made into a poem, then I wanted to know what the subject was."

"Why? What should you care?"

"I had no choice in the matter. The thing ran round and round in my head. Do you know anyone called Charles Martin?"

"No, I don't. And don't change the subject."

"I'm not changing the subject, oddly enough. Do me the kindness to think of it seriously for a moment. Have you ever, at any time, heard of or known a Charles Martin?"

"I've told you, no! I don't have to think. And of course you're changing the subject! What has Charles Martin got to do with this?"

"According to the police, the man who was found dead in Compartment B Seven was a French mechanic called Charles Martin."

After a moment Cullen said: "Look, Mr. Grant, maybe I'm not very bright, but you're not making sense. What you're saying is that you saw Bill Kenrick lying dead in a compartment of a train, but he wasn't Bill Kenrick at all; he was a man called Martin."

"No, what I'm saying is that the police believe him to be a man called Martin."

"Well, I take it they have good grounds for their belief."

"Excellent grounds. He had letters, and identity papers. Even better, his people have identified him."

"They did! Then what have you been stringing me along for? There isn't any suggestion that that man was Bill! If the police are satisfied that the man was a Frenchman called Martin, why in thunder should you decide that he wasn't Martin at all but Bill Kenrick!"

"Because I'm the only person in the world who has seen both the man in B Seven and that snapshot." Grant nodded at the photograph where it lay on the dressing-table.

This gave Cullen pause. Then he said: "But that's a poor photograph. It can't convey much to someone who has never seen Bill."

"It may be a poor photograph in the sense that it is a mere snapshot, but it is a very good likeness indeed."

"Yes," Cullen said slowly, "it is."

"Consider three things, three facts. One: Charles Martin's people had not seen him for years, and then they saw only a dead face; if you are told that your son has died, and no one suggests that there is any doubt as to identity, you see the face you expected to see. Two: the man known as Charles Martin was found dead on a train on the same day as Bill Kenrick was due to join you in Paris. Three: in his compartment there was a pencilled jingle about talking beasts and singing sands, a subject that on your own showing had interested Bill Kenrick."

"Did you tell the police about the paper?"

"I tried to. They weren't interested. There was no mystery, you see. They knew who the man was, and how he died, and that was all that concerned them."

"It might have interested them that he was writing verse in English."

"Oh, no. There is no evidence that he wrote anything, or that the paper belonged to him at all. He may have picked it up somewhere."

"The whole thing's crazy," Cullen said, angry and bewildered.

"It's fantastic. But at the heart of all the whirling absurdity there is a small core of stillness."

"Yes?"

"Yes. There is one small clear space on which one can stand while taking one's bearings."

"What is that?"

"Your friend Bill Kenrick is missing. And out of a crowd of strange faces, I pick Bill Kenrick as a man I saw dead in a sleeping-compartment at Scoone on the morning of the 4th of March."

Cullen thought this over. "Yes," he said drearily, "I suppose that makes sense. I suppose it must be Bill. I suppose I knew all the time that something —something awful had happened. He would never have left me without word. He would have written or telephoned or something to say why he hadn't turned up on time. But what was he doing on a train to Scotland? What was he doing on a train anyhow?"

"How: anyhow?"

"If Bill wanted to go somewhere, he would fly. He wouldn't take a train."

"Lots of people take a night train because it saves time. You sleep and travel at the same time. The question is: why as Charles Martin?"

"I think it's a case for Scotland Yard."

"I don't think the Yard would thank us."

"I'm not asking for their thanks," Cullen said tartly. "I'm instructing them to find out what happened to my buddy."

"I still don't think they would be interested."

"They'd better be!"

"You have no evidence at all that Bill Kenrick didn't duck of his own accord; that he isn't having a good time on his own until it is time to go back to OCAL."

"But he was found dead in a railway compartment!" Cullen said in a voice that was nearly a howl.

"Oh, no. That was Charles Martin. About whom there is no mystery whatever."

"But you can identify Martin as Kenrick!"

"I can say, of course, that in my opinion that face in the snapshot is the face I saw in Compartment B Seven on the morning of March the 4th. Scotland Yard will say that I am entitled to my opinion, but that I am without doubt misled by a resemblance, since the man in Compartment B Seven is one Charles Martin, a mechanic, and a native of Marseilles, in the suburbs of which his parents still live."

"You're very smooth in the part of Scotland Yard, aren't you? All the same—"

"I ought to be. I've worked there for more years than I care to think about. I shall be going back there a week Monday, as soon as my holiday is over."

"You mean that *you* are Scotland Yard?"

"Not the whole of it. One of its minor props. Props in the support sense. I don't carry cards in my fishing clothes, but if you come up to my host's house with me he will vouch for my genuineness."

"Oh. No. No, of course I believe you, Mr.—er—"

"Inspector. But we'll stick to Mr., since I'm off duty."

"I'm sorry if I was fresh. It just didn't occur to me— You see, you don't expect to meet Scotland Yard in real life. It's just something you read about. You don't expect them to—to—"

"To go fishing."

"No, I guess you don't, at that. Only in books."

"Well, now that you have accepted me as genuine, and you know that my version of Scotland Yard's reaction is not only accurate but straight from the horse's mouth, what are we going to do?"

# 10

WHEN LAURA HEARD next morning that Grant intended to go in to Scoone instead of spending the day on the river, she was indignant.

"But I've just made up a wonderful luncheon for you and Zoë," she said. He was left with the impression that her dismay was rooted in some cause more valid than a miscalculated meal, but his mind was too busy with more important matters to analyse trivialities.

"There's a young American staying at Moymore who has come to ask my help about something. I thought that he might take my place on the river, if no one has any objection. He has fished quite a bit, he tells me. Perhaps Pat would like to show him the ropes."

Pat had come to breakfast in a state so radiant that the glow of it could be felt clear across the table. It was the first day of the Easter holidays. He looked with interest when he heard his cousin's suggestion. There were few things in life that he enjoyed so much as showing someone something.

"What's his name?" he asked.

"Tad Cullen."

"What's 'Tad'?"

"I don't know. Short for Theodore, perhaps."

"M-m-m," said Pat doubtfully.

"He's a flyer."

"Oh," said Pat, his brow clearing. "I thought maybe with a name like that he was a professor."

"No. He flies to and fro across Arabia."

"Arabia!" said Pat, rolling the r so that the mundane Scots breakfast table scintillated with reflections of the jewelled East. Between modern transport and ancient Bagdad, Tad Cullen seemed to have satisfactory credentials. Pat would "show him" with pleasure.

"Of course Zoë gets first choice of places to fish," Pat said.

If Grant had imagined that Pat's infatuation would take the form of blush-

ing silences and a mooning adoration, he was wrong. Pat's only sign of surrender was the constant interjection of "me and Zoë" into his conversation;
and it was to be observed that the personal pronoun still came first.

Grant borrowed the car after breakfast and went down to Moymore to
tell Tad Cullen that a small boy with red hair and a green kilt would be
waiting for him, with all appliances and means to boot, by the swing bridge
across the Turlie. He himself would be back from Scoone in time to join
them on the river some time in the afternoon, he hoped.

"I'd like to come with you, Mr. Grant," Cullen said. "Have you got a line
on this thing? Is that why you're going in to Scoone this morning?"

"No. It's to look for a line that I'm going in. There's not a thing you can
do just now, so you might as well have a day on the river."

"All right, Mr. Grant. You're the boss. What's your young friend's name?"

"Pat Rankin," Grant said, and drove away to Scoone.

He had spent most of last night lying awake with his eyes on the ceiling,
letting the patterns in his mind slip and fade into each other like trick camera
work in a film. Constantly the patterns materialised and broke and dissolved,
never the same for two moments together. He lay supine and let them dance
their endless slow interlacing; taking no part in their gyrations, as detached
as if they were a display of Northern Lights.

It was that way his mind worked best. It would also work the other way,
of course. Work very well. In problems involving a time-place sequence, for
instance. In matters where A was at a spot X at 5.30 P.M. on the umpteenth
inst., Grant's mind worked with the tidiness of a calculating machine. But in
an affair where motive was all, he sat back and let his mind loose on the
problem. Presently, if he left it alone, it would throw up the pattern that he
needed.

He still had no idea why Bill Kenrick had journeyed to the north of Scotland when he should have been travelling to Paris to meet his friend; still
less had he any idea why he should have been travelling with another man's
papers. But he was beginning to have an idea as to why Bill Kenrick developed his sudden interest in Arabia. Cullen, looking at the world from his
limited, flyer's point of view, had thought of that interest in terms of flying
routes. But Grant was sure that the interest had other origins. On Cullen's
own showing, Kenrick had exhibited none of the usual signs of "nerves." It
was unlikely that his obsession with the route he flew had anything to do
with weather in any of its forms. Somewhere, some time, on one of those
flights over that "damned dreary" route, Kenrick had found something that
interested him. And that interest had begun on an occasion when he had
been blown far off his course by one of the dust-storms that haunted the interior of Arabia. He had come back from that experience "concussed," "not
listening to what was said to him," "still back there."

So this morning Grant was going in to Scoone to find out what might possibly have interested Bill Kenrick in the interior of that bleak and stony im-

mensity, in the desert and forbidding half-continent that was Arabia. And for that, of course, he was going to Mr. Tallisker. Whether it was the rateable value of a cottage or the composition of lava that one wanted to be enlightened about, one went to Mr. Tallisker.

The public library in Scoone was deserted at that hour of the morning, and he found Mr. Tallisker having a doughnut and a cup of coffee. Grant thought the doughnut an endearingly childish and robust choice for a man who looked as though he lived on gaufrettes and China tea with lemon. Mr. Tallisker was delighted to see Grant, asked how his study of the Islands was progressing, listened with interest to Grant's heretic account of that Paradise, and was helpful about his new search. Arabia? Oh, yes, they had a whole shelf of books about the country. Almost as many people wrote books about Arabia as about the Hebrides. There was, too, if Mr. Tallisker might be permitted to say so, the same tendency to idealise the subject in its devotees.

"You think that, boiled down to plain fact, they are both just windy deserts."

Oh, no; not entirely. That was being a little—wholesale. Mr. Tallisker had had much happiness and beauty from the Islands. But the tendency to idealise a primitive people was perhaps the same in each case. And here was the shelf of books on the subject, and he would leave Mr. Grant to study them at his leisure.

The books were in a reference room, and there was no other reader there. The door closed on the silence and he was left with his search. He went through the row of books very much as he had gone through the row about the Hebrides in the sitting-room at Clune, gutting each book with a swift, practised eye. The range was much the same as it had been in the earlier case: all the way from the sentimentalists to the scientists. The only difference was that in this case some of the books were classics, as befitted a classic subject.

If Grant had had any last lingering doubt that the man in B Seven was Bill Kenrick, it went when he found that the desert part of south-eastern Arabia, the Empty Quarter, was called the Rub'al-Khali.

So that was what "robbing the Caley" had been!

After that he devoted his interest to the Empty Quarter, picking each book from the shelf, flipping through the pages on this one region, and putting it back again to go on to the next. And presently a phrase caught his eye: "Inhabited by monkeys." Monkeys, said his mind. Talking beasts. He turned the page back to see what the paragraph had been talking about.

It was talking about Wabar.

Wabar, it seemed, was the Atlantis of Arabia. The fabled city of Ad ibn Kin'ad. Somewhere in the time between legend and history it had been destroyed by fire for its sins. For it had been rich and sinful beyond the power of words to express. Its palaces had housed the most beautiful concubines and its stables the most perfect horses in the world, the one no less finely decked than the other. It stood in country so fertile that one had only to reach out a hand to pluck the fruits of the soil. There was infinite leisure to sin old sins and devise new ones. So destruction had come on the city. It had come in a night, with cleansing fire. And now Wabar, the fabled city, was a cluster of ruins guarded by the shifting sands, by cliffs of stone that forever changed place and form; and inhabited by a monkey race and by evil jinn. No one could approach the place because the jinn blew dust-storms in the faces of those who sought it.

That was Wabar.

And no one, it seemed, had ever found the ruins, although every Arabian explorer had looked for them, openly or secretly. Indeed, no two explorers agreed as to which part of Arabia the legend referred to. Grant went back through the various volumes, using the magic key, the word Wabar, and found that each authority had his own pet theory, and that the argued sites lay as far apart as Oman and the Yemen. None of the writers, he noticed, attempted to belittle or discount the legend as palliation of their failure; the story was universal in Arabia and constant in its form, and sentimentalist and scientist alike believed that it had its basis in fact. It had been every explorer's dream to be the discoverer of Wabar, but the sands and the jinn and the mirages had guarded it well.

"It is probable," wrote one of the greatest, "that when the fabled city is at last found it will be by no striving or calculation but by accident."

By accident.

By a flyer blown off his course by a dust-storm?

Was that what Bill Kenrick had seen when he came out of the solid brown cloud of sand that had blinded and buffeted him? Empty palaces in the sand? Was that what he had gone out of his way to look for—perhaps to look *at*— when he "began to come in late as a habit"?

He had said nothing after that first experience. And that, if what he had seen was a city in the sand, was understandable. He would have been teased about it: teased about mirages, and one over the eight, and what not. Even if any of the OCAL boys had ever heard the legend—and in so shifting, so easy-come a crowd it was unlikely—they would still have teased him about wish-fathered ideas. So Bill, who wrote those tight-closed *m*s and *n*s and was "just a bit cagey," said nothing and went back to have another look. Went back again and again. Either because he wanted to find the place he had seen, or to look at a place he had already pin-pointed.

He studied maps. He read books about Arabia. And then—

Then he decided to come to England.

He had arranged to go to Paris with Tad Cullen. But instead he wanted a little time by himself in England. He had no people in England. He had not been in England for years, and according to Cullen had never seemed home-sick for the place nor written to anyone there in any kind of regular cor-respondence. He had been brought up by an aunt when his parents were killed, and she too was now dead. He had never until then had any desire to go back to England.

Grant sat back and let the stillness fall round him. He could almost hear the dust coming to rest. Year after year the dust falling in the quiet. Like Wabar.

Bill Kenrick came to England. And about three weeks later, when he is due to meet his friend in Paris, he turns up in Scotland as Charles Martin.

Grant could imagine why he wanted to come to England, but why the masquerade? Why the flying visit to the North?

Whom was he going to visit as Charles Martin?

He could have paid that flying visit and still have met his friend in Paris on the appointed date if it had not been for the accident of his tipsy fall. He could have interviewed someone in the Highlands and then flown from Scoone to meet his friend at the Hotel St. Jacques for dinner.

But why as Charles Martin?

Grant put the books back on their shelf with an approving pat that he had never wasted on the Hebrides selection, and went to call on Mr. Tallisker in his little office. He had at least got his line on Kenrick. He knew how to cross his trail.

"Who would you say was the greatest authority on Arabia in England today?" he asked Mr. Tallisker.

Mr. Tallisker waved his beribboned pince-nez and smiled in a deprecating way. There were what might be termed a swarm of successors to Thomas and Philby and the other great names, he said, but he supposed that only Heron Lloyd ranked as a really great authority. It was possible that he, Mr. Tallisker, was prejudiced in Lloyd's favour because he was the only one of the crowd who wrote English that was literature, but it was true that apart from his gifts as a writer he had stature and integrity and a great reputation. He had done some spectacular journeys in the course of his various explorations, and had considerable standing among the Arabs.

Grant thanked Mr. Tallisker and went away to look up *Who's Who*. He wanted Heron Lloyd's address.

Then he went to have a meal; and instead of going to the Caledonian, which was convenient and sufficiently bestarred, he obeyed an obscure impulse and walked to the other side of the town so that he could eat where he had eaten breakfast with the shade of B Seven on that dark morning only a few weeks ago.

There was no half-lit gloom in the dining-room today; the place was starched and shining, silver, glass, and linen. There was even a shirt-front where a head waiter hovered. But there was also Mary, calm and comfortable and plump as she had been that morning. He remembered how in need of soothing and reassurance he had been, and could hardly believe that that tortured and exhausted creature could have been himself.

He sat down at the same table, near the screens in front of the service door, and Mary came to take his order and to ask how the fishing on the Turlie was these days.

"How did you know I was fishing the Turlie?"

"You were with Mr. Rankin when you came in for breakfast, off the train."

Off the train. He had come off the train after that night of conflict and suffering; that loathsome night. He had come off the train, leaving B Seven dead there with a casual glance and a passing moment of regret. But B Seven had paid back a hundred-fold that moment of easy compassion. B Seven had come with him and in the end had saved him. It was B Seven who had sent him to the Islands, on that mad, cold, blown search for nothing. In that strange absurd limbo he had done all those things that he could never have done elsewhere; he had laughed till the tears ran, he had danced, he had let himself be flung about like a leaf from one empty horizon to the next, he had sung, he had sat still and looked. And he had come back a whole man. He owed B Seven more than he could ever repay.

He thought about Bill Kenrick while he had his luncheon; the young man who had had no roots. Had he been lonely in his unattached life, or just free? And if free, was it a swallow's freedom, or an eagle's? A sun-seeking skimming, or a soaring lordliness?

At least he had had a trait that in all climes and ages has been both rare and endearing: he was the man of action who was also by instinct a poet. It was what distinguished him from the light-come crowds of OCAL employees who spun their airy patterns across the continents as unthinking as mosquitoes. It was what distinguished him from the milling five-o'clock crowds in a London railway station to whom adventure was half-a-crown each way. If the dead boy in B Seven had been neither a Sidney nor a Grenfell, he had at least been of their kind.

And for that Grant loved him.

He over-tipped Mary and went away to book two seats on the morning plane to London. He had still more than a week of holiday to come, and the Turlie still swarmed with fish, beautiful silver clean-run fighting fish, but he had other business. Since yesterday afternoon he had only one business: Bill Kenrick.

He had qualms about the air journey to London, but not very serious qualms. He could hardly recognise, when he looked back at him, the demon-ridden frightened creature who had stepped down on to Scoone platform from the London Mail less than a month ago. All that was left of that deplorable object was a slight fear of being afraid. The terror itself was no longer there.

He bought enough sweets for Patrick to keep him sick for three months on end, and drove back to the hills. He was afraid that the sweets were a little too elegant to please Patrick entirely—a little too "jessie-like" perhaps—since Pat's avowed favourites were something in Mrs. Mair's window labelled

Ogo-Pogo Eyes. But Laura would no doubt dole out the Scoone ones in drib-
lets anyway.

He halted the car above the river, half-way between Moymore and Scoone,
and went down across the moor to look for Tad Cullen. It was still early
afternoon, and he would not yet have finished his after-luncheon spell on the
river.

He had not yet begun it. As Grant came to the edge of the moor and
looked down at the river's immediate hollow, he saw below him in the mid-
distance a small group of three persons, idle and relaxed on the bank. Zoë
was propped in her favourite position against a rock, and on either side of
her, on a level with her crossed feet and gazing at her with an unwavering
attention, were her two followers: Pat Rankin and Tad Cullen. Looking at
them, amused and indulgent, Grant became aware that Bill Kenrick had done
him a final service for which he had not yet had credit. Bill Kenrick had
saved him from falling in love with Zoë Kentallen.

A few more hours would have done it. A few more hours in her uninterrupted company, and he would have been involved past recovery. Bill Kenrick had intervened just in time.

It was Pat who saw him first and came to meet him and bring him back to
the company as children and dogs do to those of whom they approve. Zoë
tilted her head back to watch him come and said: "You haven't missed anything, Mr. Grant. No one has had a nibble all day. Would you like to take my
rod for a little? Perhaps a change of rhythm will fetch them."

Grant said that he would like that very much, since his time for fishing was
running out.

"You have still a week to catch everything in the river," she said.

Grant wondered how she had known that. "No," he said, "I am going
back to London tomorrow morning," and for the first time saw Zoë react
to a stimulus as an adult would. The instant regret on her face was as vivid
as that on Pat's, but unlike Pat she controlled and removed it. She said in her
polite gentle voice how sorry she was, but her face no longer showed any
emotion. It was her fairy-tale face again, the Hans Andersen illustration.

Before he could consider the phenomenon, Tad Cullen said: "Can I come
back with you, Mr. Grant? To London."

"I meant you to. I've booked two seats on the morning plane."

In the end Grant took the rod that Tad Cullen was using—a spare one
from Clune—so that they could go downriver together and talk. But Zoë made
no motion to continue her fishing.

"I've had enough," she said, unjointing her rod. "I think I shall go back
to Clune and write some letters."

Pat stood irresolute, still like a friendly dog between two allegiances, and
then said, "I'm going back with Zoë."

He said it, Grant thought, almost as if he were championing her instead of
merely accompanying her; as if he had joined an Unfair-to-Zoë movement.

But since no one could ever think of being unfair to Zoë, his attitude was surely unnecessary.

From the rock where he sat with Tad Cullen to give him the news, he watched the two figures grow small across the moor, and wondered a little at that sudden withdrawal, at the dispirited air that hung about her progress. She looked like a discouraged child, tired and trailing homeward unexpectant. Perhaps the thought of David, her husband, had suddenly drowned her. That was the way with grief: it left you alone for months together until you thought that you were cured, and then without warning it blotted out the sunlight.

"But that wouldn't be much to get excited about, would it?" Tad Cullen was saying.

"What wouldn't?"

"This ancient city you're talking about. Would anyone get all that excited about it? I mean, about a few ruins. Ruins are two a nickel in the world nowadays."

"Not these, they aren't," Grant said, forgetting Zoë. "The man who found Wabar would make history."

"I thought when you said he had found something important, you were going to say munition works in the desert or something like that."

"Now that really *is* something that is two for a nickel!"

"What?"

"Secret munition plants. No one who found one of those would be a celebrity."

Tad's ears pricked. "A celebrity? You mean the man who found this place would be a celebrity?"

"I've already said so."

"No. You just said he would make history."

"True. Too true," Grant said. "The terms are not synonymous any more. Yes, he would be a celebrity. Tutankhamen's tomb would be nothing to it."

"And you think Bill will have gone to see this fellow, this Lloyd guy?"

"If not to him, then to someone else in that line. He wanted to talk to someone who would take what he had to tell as a serious matter; I mean, who would not just tease him about seeing things. And he wanted to meet someone who would be personally interested and excited by his news. Well, he would do just what I did. He would go to a museum, or a library, or perhaps even to one of the Information Departments, and find out who the best-known English explorer of Arabia happened to be. He would probably be given a choice, since librarians and curators are pedantic people and Information Departments subject to the law of libel, but Lloyd is head and shoulders above the others because he writes almost as well as he explores. He is the household word of the bunch, so to speak. So the chances are twenty to one that Bill would choose Lloyd."

"So we find out when and where he saw Lloyd and pick up his trail from there."

"Yes. We also find out whether he went to see Lloyd as Charles Martin or under his own name."

"Why would he go as Charles Martin?"

"Who knows? You said that he was a little cagey. He may have wanted to keep back his connection with OCAL. Are OCAL strict about their routes and schedules? It may be as simple as that."

Cullen sat in silence for a little, making a pattern in the turf with the butt of the fishing-rod. Then he said:

"Mr. Grant, don't think I'm being dramatic or—or sensational or silly, but you don't think, do you, that Bill could have been bumped off?"

"He could have been, of course. Murder does happen. Even clever murders. But the chances against it are very long."

"Why?"

"Well, for one thing it has passed a police investigation. In spite of all the detective stories to the contrary, the Criminal Investigation Department really is a highly efficient organisation. By far the most efficient organisation, if you'll accept a slightly prejudiced opinion, that exists in this country today— or in any other country, in any period."

"But the police have already been wrong about one thing."

"About his identity, you mean. Yes, but they can hardly be blamed for that."

"You mean, because the set-up was perfect. Well, what's to hinder the other set-up being as perfect as the Charles Martin one?"

"Nothing, of course. Clever murders, as I say, do happen. But it is much easier to forge an identity than to get away with murder. How do you think it was done? Someone came in and slugged him after the train left Euston, and arranged it to look like a fall?"

"Yes."

"But no one visited B Seven after the train left Euston. B Eight heard him come back shortly after the attendant had done his round, and close his door. After that there was no conversation."

"It doesn't need conversation to slug a man on the back of the head."

"No, but it does need opportunity. The chances against opening that door and finding the occupant in the right position for slugging him are astronomical. A sleeping-compartment is not an easy place to take a swing at anyone, even choosing your own time. Anyone with lethal intentions would have to come into the compartment: it couldn't be done from the corridor. It couldn't be done when the victim was in bed. And it couldn't be done with the victim facing you; and he would face round as soon as he was aware that there was someone in the compartment. Therefore it could only be done after preliminary conversation. And B Eight says there was no conversation or visiting. B Eight is the kind of woman who 'can't sleep on a train.' She makes up her mind about that beforehand, and every little sound and squeak and rattle is welcomed as a sign of her suffering. She is usually dead asleep and snoring by about half-past two; but long before that time Bill Kenrick was dead."

"Did she hear him fall?"

"She heard a 'thump,' it seems, and thought that he was taking down a suitcase. He had no suitcase, of course, that would make a thump in being handled. Did Bill speak French, by the way?"

"Well enough to get by."

"*Avec moi.*"

"Yes. About that. Why?"

"I just wondered. It looks as if he planned to spend a night somewhere."

"In Scotland, you mean?"

"Yes. The Testament and the French novel. And yet he didn't speak French."

"Perhaps the Scotch party didn't either."

"No. Scotch parties usually don't. But if he planned to spend a night somewhere, he couldn't meet you that day in Paris."

"Oh, being a day late wouldn't worry Bill. He could have sent me a wire on the 4th."

"Yes . . . I wish I could think of his reason for blacking himself all over."

"Blacking himself?"

"Yes. Dressing the part so completely. Why did he want someone to think that he was French?"

"I can't think why anyone would want anyone to think they were French," Mr. Cullen said. "What are you hoping from this Lloyd guy?"

"I'm hoping that it was Lloyd who saw him away at Euston. They were talking about the Rub'al-Khali, remember. What sounded to Old Yoghourt's ear—quite typically—as 'rob the Caley.' "

"Does this Lloyd live in London?"

"Yes. In Chelsea."

"I hope he's home."

"I hope so indeed. Now I am going to have a last hour with the Turlie, and if you can bear just to sit and think the problem over for a little then perhaps you would come back to supper at Clune and meet the Rankin family?"

"That would be fine," Tad said. "I haven't said good-bye to the Countess. I'm a convert to Countesses. Would you say that the Countess is typical of your aristocracy, Mr. Grant?"

"In the sense of having all the qualities of the type, she is indeed typical," Grant said, picking his way down the bank to the water.

He fished until the level light warned him that it was evening, but he caught nothing. This was a result that neither surprised nor disappointed him. His thoughts were elsewhere. He no longer saw Bill Kenrick's dead face in the swirling water, but Bill Kenrick's personality was all round him. Bill Kenrick possessed his mind.

He reeled in for the last time with a sigh, not for his empty bag or his farewell to the Turlie, but because he was no nearer to finding a reason why Bill Kenrick should have blacked himself all over.

"I'm glad I had this chance of seeing this island," Tad said as they walked up to Clune. "It's not a bit the way I imagined it."

From his tone Grant deduced that he had imagined it as a sort of Wabar, inhabited by monkeys and jinn.

"I wish it had been a happier way of seeing it," he said. "You must come back some day and fish in peace."

Tad grinned a little shamefacedly and rubbed his tumbled hair. "Oh, I guess it will always be Paris for me. Or Vienna, maybe. When you spend your days in Godforsaken little towns, you look forward to the bright lights."

"Well, we do have bright lights in London."

"Yes. Maybe I'll have another smack at London. London's all right."

Laura came to the door as they arrived and said, "Alan, what's this I hear about—" and then noticed his companion. "Oh. You must be Tad. Pat says you don't believe that there *are* any fish in the Turlie. How d'you do. I'm so glad you've come up. Go in and Pat will show you where to wash, and then come and join us in a drink before supper." She summoned Pat, who was hovering, and passed the visitor into his charge, blocking the way firmly on any advance by her cousin. When she had got rid of Mr. Cullen, she turned again to her charge. "Alan, you're *not* going back to town tomorrow?"

"But I'm cured, Lalla," he said, thinking that that was what disturbed her.

"Well, what if you are? There is still more than a week of your leave, and the Turlie better than it has been for seasons. You can't give up all that just to get some young man out of some hole that he's got himself into."

"Tad Cullen's not in any hole. I'm not being quixotic, if that is what you're thinking. I'm going away tomorrow because that is the thing I want to do." He was going to add, "I just can't wait to get away," but even with an intimate like Laura that might lead to misunderstanding.

"But we are all so happy, and things were—" She broke off. "Oh, well. Nothing I can say will make you change your mind. I ought to know that. Nothing has ever made you deviate by a hairsbreadth from any line that you once set your mind on. You've always been a damned Juggernaut."

"A damned horrible metaphor," he said. "Couldn't you make it a bullet or a bee-line or something equally undeviating but less destructive?"

She put her arm through his, friendly and a little amused. "But you are destructive, darling." And as he began a protest: "All in the very kindest and most lethal way imaginable. Come and have a drink. You look as if you could do with one."

# 11

EVEN THE UNDEVIATING Grant, of course, had his unsure moments.

"You fool!" said that inner voice, as he was climbing into the London plane at Scoone. "Giving up even a day of your precious leave to hunt will-o'-the-wisps."

"I'm not hunting any will-o'-the-wisps. I just want to know what happened to Bill Kenrick."

"And what is Bill Kenrick to you that you should give up even an hour of your free time for him?"

"I'm interested in him. If you want to know, I like him."

"You don't know a thing about him. You have made a god in your own image, and are busy worshipping it."

"I know quite a lot about him. I've listened to Tad Cullen."

"A prejudiced witness."

"A nice boy, which is more important. The Cullen boy had a wide choice of friends in an organisation like OCAL, and he chose Bill Kenrick."

"Lots of nice boys have chosen criminal friends."

"Come to that, I've known some nice criminals."

"Yeah? How many? And how many minutes of your leave would you give up to a criminal type?"

"Not thirty seconds. But the Kenrick boy is no criminal."

"A complete set of another man's papers isn't a particularly law-abiding thing to be carrying round, is it?"

"I'll find out about that presently. Meanwhile shut up and leave me alone."

"Huh! Stumped, aren't you!"

"Go away."

"Sticking your neck out for an unknown boy at your age!"

"Who's sticking his neck out?"

"You didn't have to do this plane journey at all. You could have gone back by train or by road. But no, you had to arrange to have yourself shut into a box. A box without a window or a door that will open. A box you can't escape from. A tight, silent, enclosed, sealed—"

"*Shut up!*"

"Huh! You're breathing short already! In about ten minutes the thing will hit you for six. You ought to have your head examined, Grant; you certainly ought to have your head examined."

"There is one part of my cranial equipment that is still in admirable working order."

"What is that?"

"My teeth."

"You planning to chew something? That's no cure."

"No. I plan to grit them."

And whether it was because he had thumbed his nose at the devil or whether it was that Bill Kenrick stood beside him all the way, Grant made the journey in peace. Tad Cullen slumped into the seat beside him and fell instantly asleep. Grant closed his eyes and let the patterns form in his mind and dissolve and fade and form anew.

Why had Bill Kenrick blacked himself all over?

Whom was he trying to fool?

Why had it been necessary to fool anyone?

As they were circling to land, Tad woke up and without looking out of the window began to pull up his tie and smooth his hair. Apparently some sixth sense in a flyer's brain kept tally of speed, distance, and angle, even when he was unconscious.

"Well," said Tad, "back to the lights of London and the old Westmorland."

"You don't have to go back to your hotel," Grant said. "I can give you a bed."

"That's very kind of you, Mr. Grant, and I appreciate it. But I don't have to put your wife—or—or whoever it is—"

"My housekeeper."

"I don't have to put your housekeeper out." He slapped his pocket. "I'm loaded."

"Even after—what was it?—a fortnight in Paris? I congratulate you."

"Oh, well. I don't think Paris is what it used to be. Or perhaps it was just that I missed Bill. Anyhow, I don't need to fuss anyone making beds for me, thanks all the same. And if you're going to be busy, you don't want me around. But you'll not shut me out of this thing, will you? You'll keep me 'with you,' as Bill says. Said, I mean."

"I will indeed, Tad; I will indeed. I put a fly on a line in a hotel in Oban and fished you out of the white population of the world. I'm certainly not going to throw you back now."

Tad grinned. "I suppose you know what you're talking about. When are you going to see this Lloyd guy?"

"This evening if he is at home. The worst of explorers is that if they are not exploring they are lecturing; so he may be anywhere between China and Peru. What startled you?"

"How did you know I was startled?"

"My dear Tad, your fresh and open countenance was never made for either poker or diplomacy."

"No, it was just that you chose two places that Bill always chose. He used to say that, 'From China to Peru.'"

"He did? He seems to have known his Johnson."

"Johnson?"

"Yes. Samuel Johnson. It's a quotation."

"Oh. Oh, I see." Tad looked faintly abashed.

"If you're still doubtful about me, Tad Cullen, you had better come along the Embankment with me now and let some of my colleagues vouch for me."

Mr. Cullen's fair skin went a deep red. "I'm sorry. Just for a moment there I— It did sound as if you had known Bill. You'll have to forgive me being suspicious, Mr. Grant. I'm all at sea, you know. I don't know a soul in this country. I just have to take people as they come. On face value, I mean. Of *course* I'm not doubtful about you. I'm too grateful to you to be able to find words to describe how grateful I am. You have to believe that."

"Of course I believe it. I was only teasing you, and I had no right to. It would be unintelligent of you not to be suspicious. Here is my address and telephone number. I'll telephone you as soon as I've seen Lloyd."

"You don't think I should come with you, perhaps?"

"No. I think a deputation of two would be a little excessive for so slight an occasion. What time will you be at the Westmorland tonight to take a phone call?"

"Mr. Grant, I'll be sitting with my hand on that thing until you call."

"Better eat some time. I'll call you at half-past eight."

"Okay. Half-past eight."

London was a misty grey with scarlet trimmings, and Grant looked at it with affection. Army nurses used to have that rig-out, that grey and scarlet. And in some ways London gave one the same sense of grace and power that went with that Sister's uniform. The dignity, the underlying kindness beneath the surface indifference, the respect-worthiness that compensated for the lack of pretty frills. He watched the red buses making the grey day beautiful, and blessed them. What a happy thing it was that London buses should be scarlet. In Scotland the buses were painted that most miserable of all colours: blue. A colour so miserable that it was a synonym for depression. But the English, God bless them, had had gayer ideas.

He found Mrs. Tinker turning out the spare bedroom. There was not the slightest need for anyone to turn out the spare bedroom, but Mrs. Tinker obtained the same pleasure from turning out a room that other people get from writing a symphony, or winning a cup at golf, or swimming the Channel. She belonged to that numerous species once succinctly described by Laura as "the kind of woman who washes her front doorstep every day and her hair every six weeks."

She came to the door of the spare bedroom when she heard the key in the lock, and said: "Well, now! And not a bite in the house! Why didn't you let me know you was comin' back from foreign parts before your time?"

"It's all right, Tink. I don't want a meal anyhow. I've just looked in to leave my luggage. Get in something and leave it for me when you go, so that there is something for me to eat tonight."

Mrs. Tinker went home every night, partly because she had to see to the evening meal of someone she referred to as "Tinker," and partly because Grant had always liked to have the flat to himself in the evenings. Grant had never seen Tinker, and Mrs. Tinker's only connection with him seemed to consist of this matter of an evening meal and some marriage lines. Her real life and interest was in 19 Tenby Court, S.W.1.

"Any telephones?" Grant asked, thumbing through the telephone pad.

"Miss Hallard telephoned to say ring her up and dine with her as soon as you were back."

"Oh. Did the new play go well? What were the notices like?"

"Stinkers."

"All of them?"

"Every one I seen, anyway."

In the days of her freedom, before Tinker, Mrs. Tinker had been a theatre dresser. Indeed, if it had not been for the ritual of the evening meal it was likely that she would still be dressing someone each evening in W.1 or W.C.2 instead of turning out spare bedrooms in S.W.1. Her interest in theatre matters was therefore that of an initiate.

"Have you seen the play?"

"Not me. It's one of them plays what means something else. You know. She keeps a china dog on the mantelpiece, but it isn't a china dog at all, it's 'er ex-husband; and 'e breaks the dog, the new boy-friend does, and she goes mad. Not *gets* mad, you know; *goes* mad. 'Ighbrow. But I suppose if you want to be a Dame you got to act 'ighbrow plays. What was you thinkin' of 'avin' for your supper?"

"I wasn't thinking."

"I could leave a nice bit of fish poachin' over some hot water for you."

"Not fish, if you love me. I've eaten enough fish in the last month to last me a lifetime. As long as it isn't fish or mutton, I don't mind what it is."

"Well, it's too late now to get any kidneys out of Mr. Bridges, but I'll see what I can do. You 'ad a good 'oliday?"

"A wonderful, wonderful holiday."

"That's good. You bin and put on a little weight, I'm glad to see. And you needn't slap your stomach in that doubtful way neither. A little bit of weight never 'urt no one. It don't do to be as thin as a rail. You don't 'ave no reserves."

She hung around while Grant changed into his best town suit, doling out bits of gossip as they happened to occur to her. Then he shooed her back to her piece of self-indulgence with the spare bedroom, dealt with the small businesses that had piled up in his absence, and went out into the calm of the early April evening. He went round to the garage, answered questions about his fishing, listened to three fishing stories that he had listened to before he set out for the Highlands a month ago, and reclaimed the little two-seater that he used when on his own business.

Number 5 Britt Lane took some finding. In the huddle of old houses all kinds of adaptation and conditioning had taken place. Stables had become cottages, kitchen wings had become houses, odd storeys had become maisonettes. Number 5 Britt Lane seemed to be just a number on a gate. The gate was in a brick wall, and its iron-studded oak seemed to Grant a little affected in so unpretentious a stretch of ordinary London brick. However, it was solid and in itself unexceptional, and it opened easily when asked to. It opened on to what had been a kitchen yard when Number 5 had been merely the back wing of a house in another street altogether. Now the yard was a small paved court with a fountain playing in the middle of it, and the one-time wing was a small flat stucco house of three storeys, painted cream with green window-sashes. As Grant crossed the little court to the doorway, he noticed that the paving was of tiles, some of them old and many of them beautiful. The fountain, too, was beautiful. He mentally applauded Heron Lloyd for not having replaced the plain London electric bell-push by some more aesthetic piece of fancy-work; it augured a good taste that the inappropriate gate had left open to question.

The interior of the house, too, had the Arab bareness and space without any suggestion that a piece of the East had been transported to London. Beyond the figure of the manservant who answered his ring, he could see the clean walls and the rich carpet; an idiom adapted, not a décor transposed. His respect for Heron Lloyd mounted.

The manservant appeared to be Arab, an Arab of the towns, plumpish, lively-eyed, and good-mannered. He listened to Grant's inquiry and asked in a gentle, too correct English if he had an appointment. Grant said no, but that he would not detain Mr. Lloyd more than a moment. Mr. Lloyd could be of some help in giving information connected with Arabia.

"If you will come in, please, and wait for a moment, I will ask."

He ushered Grant into a tiny room just inside the front door which, judging from its limited space and scanty furnishing, was used for the purpose of waiting. He supposed that someone like Heron Lloyd must be used to strangers appearing on his doorstep to claim his interest or help. Even perhaps just to ask for his autograph. A realisation that made his own intrusion less deplorable.

Mr. Lloyd had not debated his desirability very long, it seemed, for the man was back in a few moments.

"Will you come, please? Mr. Lloyd will be very happy to see you."

A formula, but such a pleasant formula. How good manners did cushion life, he thought as he followed the man up the narrow stairs and into the big room that occupied the whole of the first floor.

"Mr. Grant, *hadji*," said the man, standing aside to let him come. Grant caught the word and thought: That is the first piece of chi-chi. Englishmen don't make the pilgrimage to Mecca, surely.

Watching Heron Lloyd as he was made welcome, Grant wondered whether

he had first thought of going to desert Arabia because he looked like a desert
Arab, or whether he had come to look like a desert Arab after years in desert
Arabia. Lloyd was the Arab of the desert idealised to the $n$th. He was, Grant
thought with amusement, the Arab of the circulating libraries. It was across
the saddle of Arabs like Heron Lloyd that blameless matrons in the Crescents
and Drives and Avenues had been carried off to a fate worse than death.
The black eyes, the lean brown face, the white teeth, the whip-lash body, the
delicate hands, the graceful movements: it was all there, straight out of Page
Seventeen of Miss Tilly Tally's latest (two hundred and fifty-four thousand,
new printing next week). Grant had to remind himself forcibly that he must
not judge on looks.

For this man had done journeys that had made history in the world of
exploration, and had written about them in English which, even if a little lush
(Grant had bought a copy of his latest in Scoone yesterday afternoon) was
nevertheless recognisable as literature. Heron Lloyd was no parlour sheik.

Lloyd was wearing orthodox London clothes and a manner to match. If
one had never heard of him, one would accept him as a Londoner of the
well-to-do professional classes. One of the slightly more flamboyant classes,
perhaps; an actor, or conceivably a Harley Street consultant or a society
photographer; but a Londoner of the orthodox professions, when all was considered.

"Mr. Grant," he said, shaking hands. "Mahmoud says that I can be of
service to you."

His voice surprised Grant. It had no body and a faintly querulous tone
that had nothing to do with the sense of the words or their mood. He took
a box of cigarettes from the low coffee table and offered them. He did not
smoke himself, he said, because he had adopted Mohammedan customs during his long life in the East, but he could recommend the cigarettes if Grant
cared to try something that tasted a little out of the ordinary.

Grant took the cigarette, as he took every new experience and sensation,
with interest, and apologised for his intrusion. He wanted to know whether a
young man called Charles Martin had applied to him at any time within the
last year or so for information about Arabia.

"Charles Martin? No. No, I don't think so. Many people do come, of
course, to see me about one thing and another. And I cannot always remember their names afterwards. But I think I should remember anyone with that
simple name. You like that tobacco? I know the very half-acre where it is
grown. A beautiful place that has not changed since Alexander the Macedo-
nian passed that way." He smiled a little and added: "Except, of course, that
they have learned how to grow this weed. The weed, I understand, goes very
well with a not too dry sherry. Another of the grosser indulgences that I
avoid; but I shall have a fruit drink to keep you company."

Grant thought that the desert tradition of hospitality to the stranger must
come a little expensive in a London where you were a celebrity and all and

sundry were free to drop in. He noticed that the label on the bottle that Lloyd had picked up was a guarantee as well as an announcement. It seemed that Lloyd was neither a pauper nor a piker.

"Charles Martin was also known as Bill Kenrick," he said.

Lloyd lowered the glass which he was about to fill, and said:

"Kenrick! But he was here only the other day. Or rather, when I say only the other day, I mean a week or two ago. Quite lately, anyway. Why should he have an alias?"

"I don't know that myself. I am making inquiries about him on behalf of his friend. He was due to meet his friend in Paris at the beginning of March. On the 4th, to be exact. But he didn't turn up. We have discovered that he died as the result of an accident on the very day that he should have turned up in Paris."

Lloyd put the glass slowly down on to the table.

"So *that* is why he did not come back," he said in that querulous voice that did not mean to be querulous. "Poor boy. Poor boy."

"You had arranged to see him again?"

"Yes. I thought him charming and very intelligent. He was bitten with the desert—but perhaps you know that. He had ideas about exploring. A few young men still have. There are still the adventurers, even in this hedged and garnished world. Of which one must be glad. What happened to Kenrick? A car smash?"

"No. He had a fall on a train and fractured his skull."

"Poor wretch. Poor wretch. A pity. I could have supplied the jealous gods with a dozen more expendable in his place. An atrocious word: expendable. The expression of an idea that would not even have been conceivable a few years ago. So far have we progressed towards our ultimate barbarism. Why did you want to know if the Kenrick boy had come to see me?"

"We wanted to pick up his trail. When he died he was masquerading as Charles Martin, with a complete set of Charles Martin's papers. We want to know at what stage he began to be Charles Martin. We were almost certain that, being bitten by the desert, he would come to see some authority on the subject in London, and since you, sir, are the ultimate authority we began with you."

"I see. Well, it was most certainly as Kenrick, Bill Kenrick I think, that he came to see me. A dark young man, very attractive. Tough, too, in a nice way. I mean, good manners covering unknown possibilities. I found him delightful."

"Had he come to you with any definite plans? I mean, with a specific proposition?"

Lloyd smiled a little. "He came to me with one of the commonest of all the propositions that are habitually put to me. An expedition to the site of Wabar. Do you know about Wabar? It is the fabled city of Arabia. It is Arabia's 'cities of the plain.' How that pattern does repeat itself in legend. The human race feels eternally guilty when it is happy. We cannot even remark on our good health without touching wood or crossing our fingers or otherwise averting the gods' anger at mortal well-being. So Arabia has its Wabar: the city that was destroyed by fire because of its wealth and its sins."

"And Kenrick thought that he had discovered the site."

"He was sure of it. Poor boy, I hope that I was not short-tempered with him."

"You think that he was wrong, then?"

"Mr. Grant, the legend of Wabar exists from the Red Sea clear across Arabia to the Persian Gulf, and for almost every mile of that distance there is a different alleged site for the city."

"And you don't believe that perhaps someone might stumble on it by accident?"

"By accident?"

"Kenrick was a flyer. It is possible that he saw the place when blown off his course, isn't it?"

"Had he talked to his friend about it then?"

"No. He had talked to no one that I know of. That was my own deduction. What is to hinder the discovery being made that way?"

"Nothing, of course, nothing; if the place exists at all. I have said it is a legend almost universal throughout the world. But where stories of ruins have been tracked to their source the 'ruins' have always proved to be something else. Natural rock formation, mirage-cloud formation even. I think what poor Kenrick saw was the crater of a meteor. I have seen the place myself. A predecessor of mine discovered it when he was looking for Wabar. It is unbelievably like a place made with hands. The thrown-up earth makes pinnacles and jagged ruinous-looking heights. I think I have a photograph somewhere. You might like to see it: it is a unique affair." He got up and slid back a panel in the bare painted-wood wall, disclosing shelves of books all the way from floor to ceiling. "It is, perhaps mercifully, not every day a meteor of any size falls on the earth."

He picked a photograph album from one of the lower shelves, and came back across the room looking for the place in the collection. And Grant was seized without warning by a strange sense of familiarity, a feeling of having met Lloyd somewhere before.

He looked at the photograph that Lloyd laid before him. It was certainly an uncanny thing. An almost mocking pastiche of human achievement. But his mind was busy with that odd moment of recognition.

Was it just that he had seen Heron Lloyd's photograph somewhere? But if it had been that, if he had merely seen Lloyd's face as adjunct to some description of his exploits, then the sense of recognition would have come when he had first walked into the room and seen him. It was not so much a recognition as a sense of having known Lloyd somewhere else. In some other surroundings.

"You see?" Lloyd was saying. "Even on the ground, one has to go close up to it before one can be sure that the thing is not a collection of human dwellings. How much more misleading it must be from the air."

"Yes," agreed Grant, and did not believe it. For one very good reason. From the air the crater would have been plainly visible. From the air it would have looked exactly what it was: a circular hollow surrounded by the thrown-up earth. But he was not going to say that to Lloyd. Let Lloyd talk. He was growing very interested in Lloyd.

"That lies very close to the Kenrick boy's route across the desert, as described by himself, and I think that that is what he saw."

"Did he pin-point the place, do you know?"

"I don't know. I didn't ask him. But I should think he would. He struck me as being a very efficient and intelligent young man."

"You didn't ask him for details?"

"If someone told you, Mr. Grant, that he had discovered a holly tree growing in the middle of Piccadilly immediately opposite the In and Out, would you be interested? Or would you just think that you must be patient with him? I know the Empty Quarter as well as you know Piccadilly."

"Yes, of course. Then it was not you who saw him off at the station?"

"Mr. Grant, I never see *anyone* off. A combination of masochism and sadism that I have always deplored. Off where, by the way?"

"To Scoone."

"To the Highlands? I understood that he was longing for some gaiety. Why was he going to the Highlands?"

"We don't know. That is one of the things we are most anxious to find out. He said nothing to you that might provide a clue?"

"No. He did suggest finding other backing. I mean, when I had proved a broken reed. Perhaps he had found a backer, or hoped to find a backer, who lives up there. I can't think of any obvious one off-hand. There is Kinsey-Hewitt, of course. He has Scottish connections. But I think he is in Arabia at the moment."

Well, at least Lloyd had provided the first reasonable explanation of the flying visit north with an overnight case. To talk to a possible backer. He had found a backer at the last moment, when he was almost due to meet Tad Cullen in Paris, and had dashed north to see him. That fitted beautifully. They were getting on. But why as Charles Martin?

As if the thought had been transferred, Lloyd said: "By the way, if the Kenrick boy was travelling as Charles Martin, how has he been identified as Kenrick?"

"I travelled on that train to Scoone. I saw him when he was dead, and grew interested in some verse he had been scribbling."

"Scribbling? On what?"

"On a blank bit of an evening paper," Grant said, wondering why it should matter what Kenrick had been writing on.

"Oh."

"I was on holiday, with nothing else to do, so I amused myself with the clues provided."

"You played detective."

"Yes."

"What is your profession, Mr. Grant?"

"I'm a Civil Servant."

"Ah, I was going to suggest the Army." He smiled a little and picked up Grant's glass to refill it. "The more rarefied ranks, of course."

"G.S.O. 1?"

"No. An attaché, I think. Or Intelligence."

"I have done a spot of Intelligence during my Army career."

"So that is where you developed your taste for it. May I say, your flair."

"Thank you."

"Or had he Kenrick belongings that made the identification easy?"

"No. He was buried as Charles Martin."

Lloyd paused as he was setting the filled glass down and said: "That is so typical of the careless Scottish way of dealing with sudden death. They are always very smug about their lack of inquests. Myself, I think Scotland must be an ideal place in which to get away with murder. If ever I plan one, I shall lure my victim north of the Border."

"There was an inquest, as it happens. The accident took place shortly after the train left Euston."

"Oh." Lloyd thought this over and then said: "Don't you think that this should be reported to the police? I mean the fact that they have buried someone under a wrong name."

Grant was about to say, "The only proof we have that the dead Charles Martin was Kenrick is my identification of a not very good snapshot," but something stopped him. Instead he said, "We should like first to know why he had Charles Martin's papers."

"Ah, yes. I see. That of course is a sufficiently questionable matter. One doesn't acquire a man's papers without some—preliminaries. Does anyone know who Charles Martin is—or was?"

"Yes. The police were satisfied on that score. There was no mystery."

"The only mystery is how Kenrick came by his papers. I see why you are reluctant to go to official sources. What about this man who saw him off? At Euston. Could he have been Charles Martin?"

"He could, I suppose."

"The papers may merely have been lent. Kenrick somehow did not strike me as a—shall we say, nefarious type?"

"No. On all the evidence, he wasn't."

"It's a very curious business altogether. This accident that you say he had: I suppose there is no doubt that it was an accident? No suggestion of a quarrel?"

"No, it was just one of those things. A fall that might happen to anyone."

"Distressing. As I say, there are too few young men nowadays who have the combination of courage and intelligence. A great many come to me, indeed they travel great distances to see me—"

He went on talking, and Grant sat watching and listening.

Were there, in fact, so many who came? Lloyd seemed very pleased to sit and talk to a stranger. There was no suggestion that he had an engagement for the evening or guests coming to dinner. None of the convenient pauses that a host leaves in the conversation so that a casual guest may take his leave. Lloyd sat talking in that thin, complacent voice and admiring the hands that lay in his lap. He continually changed the position of the hands, not as a gesture to emphasise a phrase, but as one making a new arrangement of some decoration. Grant found this Narcissus-like preoccupation fascinating. He listened to the silence of the little house, shut away from the town and its traffic. In the biography in *Who's Who* there had been no mention of wife or children, possessions that the owners of both are habitually proud to mention; so the household no doubt consisted of Lloyd and his servants. Had he sufficient interests to compensate for that lack of human companionship?

He, Alan Grant, had a household just as bare of human warmth; but his life was so full of people that to come back to his empty flat was a luxury, a spiritual delight. Was Heron Lloyd's life full and satisfying?

Or did your true Narcissus ever need any company other than his own image?

He wondered how old the man was. Older than he seemed, certainly; he was the doyen of Arabian exploration. Fifty-five or more. Probably nearer sixty. He had not given his date of birth in the biography, so the chances were that he was nearly sixty. There could not be many years of hard-living left to him, even given his good physique and condition. What would he do with the remaining years? Spend them admiring his hands?

"The only true democracy in the world today," Lloyd was saying, "and it is being destroyed by the thing that we call civilisation."

And again Grant had the sense of familiarity, of recognition. Was it that he had met Lloyd before? Or was it that Lloyd reminded him of someone? If so, of whom?

He must get away and think about it. It was time that he took his leave anyhow.

"Did Kenrick tell you where he was staying?" he asked as he began to take his leave.

"No. We made no definite appointment to meet again, you understand. I asked him to come to see me again before he left London. When he did not come I believed that he was resentful, perhaps angry, at my lack of—sympathy, shall we say?"

"Yes, it must have been a blow to him. Well, I have taken up a great deal of your time, and you have been very forbearing. I am most grateful."

"I am very glad to have been of help. I am afraid it has not been very valuable help. If there is anything else that I can do in the matter, I hope very much that you will not hesitate to call on me."

"Well—there is one thing, but you have already been so kind that I hate to ask you. Especially since it is a little irrelevant."

"What is it?"

"May I perhaps borrow the photograph?"

"The photograph?"

"The photograph of the meteor crater. I notice that the print is slotted into your album, not pasted. I should like very much to show it to Kenrick's friend. I promise faithfully to return it. And in perfect—"

"But of course you may have the photograph. And don't bother to return it. I took the picture myself, and the negative is filed in the proper place. I can replace the print at any time with ease."

He manœuvred the print from its anchorage in the album, and handed it to Grant. He came downstairs with Grant and saw him to the door, talked a bit about the little courtyard when Grant admired it, and waited courteously until Grant had reached the gate before closing the door on him.

Grant opened the evening paper that was lying on the car cushions and laid the photograph carefully between its folds. Then he drove down to the river and along the Embankment.

The old place looked very much as usual, he thought, as the hideous pile loomed up in the dusk. And so, too, did the finger-print department once he got there. Cartwright was stubbing out a cigarette in the saucer of a half-drunk cup of cold tea and admiring his latest handiwork: a complete set of left-hand prints.

"Lovely, 'm?" he said, looking up as Grant's shadow fell across him. "These are going to hang Pinky Mason."

"Hadn't Pinky the price of a pair of gloves?"

"Huh! Pinky could have bought up Dent's. He just couldn't believe, clever little man Pinky, that the police would ever get round to thinking it anything but a suicide. Gloves are for smalltime trash, burglars and such, not for master-minds like Pinky. You been away?"

"Yes. I've been fishing in the Highlands. If you're not too busy, could you do something off the cuff for me?"

"Now?"

"Oh, no. Tomorrow would do."

Cartwright looked at the clock. "I've nothing to do till I meet my wife at the theatre. We're going to Marta Hallard's new play. So I can do it now, if you like. Is it a difficult job?"

"No. Dead easy. Just here, in the lower right-hand corner of this photograph, there is a beautiful thumb-print. And at the back I think you'll find a nice set of finger-tips. I want to check them with the files."

"All right. Will you wait?"

"I'm going to the library. I'll come back."

In the library he took down *Who's Who,* and looked up Kinsey-Hewitt. The paragraph on Kinsey-Hewitt was a very modest little affair compared with the half-column on Heron Lloyd. He was a much younger man, it seemed; married, with two children; and his address was a London one. The "Scottish connection" that Lloyd had mentioned seemed to consist in the fact that he was the younger son of some Kinsey-Hewitt who had a place in Fife.

Well, there was always the chance that he was now, or had been lately, in Scotland. Grant went to a telephone and called the London address. A woman with a pleasant voice answered, and said that her husband was not at home. No, he would not be at home for some time; he was in Arabia. He had been in Arabia since November and was not expected back until May at the earliest. Grant thanked her and hung up. It had not been to Kinsey-Hewitt that Bill Kenrick had gone. Tomorrow he would have to go through the various authorities on Arabia, one by one, and ask them the question.

He went back, after some coffee-housing with such friends as he happened to run into at that hour, to Cartwright.

"Got the photograph or am I too early?"

"I've not only got it but looked it up for you. The answer is No."

"No, I didn't really think there would be anything. I was just clearing decks. But thank you, all the same. I'll take the print with me. I thought the new Hallard show got awful notices."

"Did it? I never read 'em. Neither does Beryl. She just likes Marta Hallard. So do I, if it comes to that. Nice long legs. Good night."

"Good night, and thanks again."


# 12


"YOU DON'T SEEM awfully sweet on this guy," Tad Cullen said, when Grant had finished his story over the telephone.

"Don't I? Oh, well, perhaps it's just that he doesn't happen to be what we call my cup of tea. Look, Tad, you're quite sure that you have no idea, even in the back of your mind, where Bill could have been staying?"

"I haven't got a back to my mind. I have just a small, narrow space in front where I keep all that's useful to me. A few telephone numbers, and a prayer or two."

"Well, tomorrow I'd like you to do the round of the more obvious places, if you would."

"Yes, sure. I'll do anything. Anything you say."

"All right. Have you got a pen? Here's the list."

Grant gave him the names of twenty of the more likely places, going on
the assumption that a young man from the wide open spaces and the small
towns would look for a caravanserai that was both large and gay and not too
expensive. And just for good measure he added a couple of the best-known
expensive ones; young men with several months' back-pay were liable to be
extravagant.

"I don't think I'd bother with any more than that," he said.

"*Are* there any more?"

"If he didn't stay in one of these, then we're sunk, because if he didn't
stay in any of them we'd have to hunt every hotel in London to find him,
to say nothing of the boarding-houses."

"Okay. I'll start first thing in the morning. Mr. Grant, I'd like to tell you
how much I appreciate what you're doing for me. Giving up your time to
something that no one else could do; I mean, something the police wouldn't
touch. If it wasn't for you—"

"Listen, Tad. I'm not being benevolent. I'm being self-indulgent and typically nosey and I'm enjoying myself to the top of my bent. If I wasn't, believe
me I wouldn't be in London. I'd be going to sleep tonight in Clune. So good
night and sleep well. We'll crack this thing between us."

He hung up and went to see what Mrs. Tinker had left on the stove. It
seemed to be a sort of shepherd's pie. He carried it into the living-room and
ate it absent-mindedly, his thoughts still on Lloyd.

What was familiar about Lloyd?

He went back in his mind over the few moments before his first feeling
of recognition. What had Lloyd been doing? Pulling open the panel of the
book cupboard. Pulling it open with a gesture self-consciously graceful,
faintly exhibitionist. What was there in that to provoke a sense of familiarity?

And there was something even more curious.

Why had Lloyd said "On what?" when he had mentioned Kenrick's
scribbling?

That, surely, was a most unnatural reaction.

What exactly had he said to Lloyd? He had said that he became interested
in Kenrick because of some verses he had been scribbling. The normal come-
back to that was surely, "Verses?" The operative word in the sentence was
"verses." That he was scribbling was entirely by the way. And that anyone's
reaction to the information should be to say "On what?" was inexplicable.

Except that no human reaction was inexplicable.

It was Grant's experience that it was the irrelevant, the unconsidered words
in a statement that were important. Quite surprising and gratifying revelations
lay in the gap between an assertion and a *non sequitur*.

Why had Lloyd said "On what?"

He took the problem to bed with him, and fell asleep with it.

In the morning he began his hunt through the authorities on Arabia, and
finished it not at all astonished that it had produced no result. People who

explored Arabia as a hobby very seldom had money to back anything. They were, on the contrary, usually prospecting for backing themselves. The only chance had been that some one of them had proved interested to the point of being willing to share his backing. But none of them had ever heard of either Charles Martin or Bill Kenrick.

It was lunch-time before he finished, and he stood by the window waiting for Tad's call and wondering whether to go out to luncheon or to let Mrs. Tinker make him an omelette. It was another grey day, but there was a slight breeze and a smell of damp earth that was queerly countrified. A fine fishing day, he noted. He wished for a moment that he was walking down over the moor to the river instead of wrestling with the London telephone system. It wouldn't even have to be the river. He would settle for an afternoon on Lochan Dhu in a leaky boat with Pat for company.

He turned to his desk and began to clear up the mess of the morning's opened mail. He had stooped to throw the torn pages and the empty envelopes into the wastepaper basket, but he stopped with the action half spent.

It had come to him.

He knew now who it was that Heron Lloyd reminded him of.

It was Wee Archie.

This was so unexpected and so ridiculous that he sat down on the chair by his desk and began to laugh.

What had Wee Archie in common with that elegant and sophisticated creature who was Heron Lloyd?

Frustration? Of a surety not. The fact that he was an Auslander in the country of his devotion? No; too far-fetched. It was something nearer home than that.

For it *was* of Wee Archie that Lloyd had reminded him. He had no doubt of that now. He was experiencing that inimitable relief that comes when one has remembered a name that has eluded one.

Yes, it was Wee Archie.

But why?

What had that incongruous pair in common?

Their gestures? No. Their physique? No. Their voices? Was that it?

"Their vanity, you fool!" said that inner voice in him.

Yes; that was it. Their vanity. Their pathological vanity.

He sat very still, considering; he was not amused any longer.

Vanity. The first requisite in wrong-doing. The constant factor in the criminal mind.

Just supposing that—

The telephone at his elbow gave its sudden purr.

It was Tad. He had reached number eighteen, he said, and was now an old, old man but the blood of pioneers was in his veins and he was pursuing the search.

"Drop it for a little and come and eat with me somewhere."

"Oh, I've had my lunch. I had a couple of bananas and a milk shake in Leicester Square."

"Merciful Heaven!" said Grant.

"What's the matter with that?"

"Starch; that's what's the matter with it."

"A little starch is fine when you're ironed out. No luck your end?"

"No. If it was a backer he was going North to see, then the backer was merely some amateur who had money; not anyone actively engaged in Arabian exploration."

"Oh. Well. I'll be on my way. When shall I ring you next?"

"As soon as you come to the end of the list. I'll wait here for your call."

Grant decided to have the omelette, and while Mrs. Tinker prepared it he walked about his living-room letting his mind soar into speculation and pulling it down instantly to a common-sense level, so that it behaved like telegraph lines outside a railway compartment, continually soaring and continually caught back.

If only they had a starting-point. What if Tad came to the end of the likely hotels and still drew a blank? It was only a matter of days before he would have to go back to work. He stopped speculating on vanity and its possibilities and began to reckon how long it would take Tad to cover the remaining four hotels.

But before his omelette was half finished, Tad arrived in person. He was flushed and triumphant.

"I don't know how you ever thought of that dull little dump in connection with Bill," he said, "but you were right. That's where he stayed all right."

"And which is the dull little dump?"

"The Pentland. How did you think of that one?"

"It has an international reputation."

"*That* one has?"

"And English people go on going to it generation after generation."

"That's what it looks like!"

"So that is where Bill Kenrick stayed. I like him more than ever."

"Yeah," Tad said more quietly. And the flush of triumph died away. "I wish you'd known Bill. I sure wish you'd known him. They don't come any better than Bill."

"Sit down and have some coffee to settle your milk shake. Or would you like a drink?"

"No, thanks, I'll have coffee. It actually smells like coffee," he added in a surprised way. "Bill checked out on the 3rd. The 3rd of March."

"Did you ask about his luggage?"

"Sure. They weren't all that interested at first. But eventually they got out a ledger the size of the Judgement Book and said that Mr. Kenrick had left nothing either in the box-room or the safe."

"That means that he took them to a cloak-room—to a left-luggage office, that is—to be ready to his hand when he came back from Scotland. If he meant to fly when he came back, then I suppose he would leave them at Euston to be picked up on his way to the airport. If he meant to go by sea, then he may have taken them to Victoria before going to Euston. Did he like the sea?"

"So-so. He wasn't daffy about it. But he had a mania for ferries."

"Ferries?"

"Yes. Seems it began when he was a kid at a place called Pompey—know where that is?" Grant nodded. "And he spent all his time on a penny ferry."

"A ha'penny one, it used to be."

"Well, anyway."

"So the train-ferry might have had an interest for him, you think. Well, we can but try. But if he was going to be late in meeting you, I should think he would fly over. Would you know the cases if you saw them?"

"Oh, yes. Bill and I shared a Company bungalow. I helped pack them. In fact one of them's mine, if it comes to that. He just took the two of them. He said if we bought many things we could buy a suitcase to—" Tad's voice died away suddenly, and he buried his face in his coffee cup. It was a great flat bowl of a cup, willow-patterned in pink, which Marta Hallard had brought back from Sweden for Grant because he liked his coffee out of large cups; and it made a very good screen for emotion.

"We have no ticket to recover them with, you see. And I can't use any official means. But I know most of the men on duty at the big terminuses, and can probably wangle our way behind the scenes. It will be up to you to spot the cases. Was Bill a labeller by nature, would you say?"

"I expect he'd label things he was going to leave behind like that. Why, do you think, didn't he have the left-luggage ticket in his wallet?"

"I did think that someone else may have deposited those cases for him. The person who saw him off at Euston, for instance."

"The Martin guy?"

"It might be. If he had borrowed papers for this odd masquerade, he would have to return them. Perhaps Martin was going to meet him at the airport, or at Victoria, or wherever it was that he had planned to leave England from, with the cases and collect his own papers."

"Yeah. That makes sense. I suppose we couldn't Agony-advertise for this Martin?"

"I don't think that this Martin would be very willing to answer, having lent his papers for a piece of sharp practice and being now without identity."

"No. Perhaps you're right. He wasn't anyone who was staying at that hotel, anyway."

"How do you know that?" asked Grant, surprised.

"I looked through the book: the register. When I was identifying Bill's signature."

"You're wasted in OCAL, Tad. You should come to us."

But Tad was not listening. "You've no idea what a queer feeling it was to see Bill's writing suddenly like that, among all those strange names. It sort of stopped my breath."

Grant took Lloyd's picture of the crater "ruins" from his desk and brought it over to the table. "That is what Heron Lloyd thinks that Bill saw."

Tad looked at it with interest. "It sure is queer, isn't it? Just like ruined sky-scrapers. You know, until I saw Arabia I thought the United States invented sky-scrapers. But some of those old Arab towns are just the Empire State on a smaller scale. But you say it couldn't have been this that Bill saw."

"No. From the air it must be quite obvious what it is."

"Did you tell Lloyd that?"

"No. I just let him talk."

"Why do you dislike the guy so much?"

"I didn't say that I disliked him."

"You don't have to."

Grant hesitated, analysing, as always, just exactly what he did feel.

"I find vanity repellent. As a person I loathe it, and as a policeman I distrust it."

"It's a harmless sort of weakness," Tad said, with a tolerant lift of a shoulder.

"That is just where you are wrong. It is *the* utterly destructive quality. When you say vanity, you are thinking of the kind that admires itself in mirrors and buys things to deck itself out in. But that is merely personal conceit. Real vanity is something quite different. A matter not of person but of personality. Vanity says, 'I must have this because I am me.' It is a frightening thing because it is incurable. You can never convince Vanity that anyone else is of the slightest importance; he just doesn't understand what you are talking about. He will kill a person rather than be put to the inconvenience of doing a six months' stretch."

"But that's being insane."

"Not according to Vanity's reckoning. And certainly not in the medical sense. It is merely Vanity being logical. It is, as I said, a frightening trait, and the basis of all criminal personality. Criminals—true criminals, as opposed to the little man who cooks the accounts in an emergency or the man who kills his wife when he finds her in bed with a stranger—true criminals vary in looks and tastes and intelligence and method as widely as the rest of the world does, but they have one invariable characteristic, their pathological vanity."

Tad looked as though he were only half-listening because he was using this information on some private reference of his own. "Listen, Mr. Grant," he said. "Are you saying that this guy Lloyd isn't to be trusted?"

Grant thought that over.

"I wish I knew," he said at last. "I wish I knew."

"We-e-ll!" said Tad. "That sure puts a different look on things, doesn't it?"

"I've spent quite a long time this morning wondering whether I have seen so much of the vanity in criminals that I have begun to have a 'thing' about it; to distrust it unduly. On the face of it Heron Lloyd is irreproachable. He is more: he is admirable. He has a fine record behind him; he lives simply; he has excellent taste, which means a natural sense of proportion; and he has achieved enough surely to satisfy the most egotistical soul."

"But you think—there's something wrong somewhere."

"Do you remember a little man in the hotel at Moymore who did missionary work on you?"

"Persecuted Scotland! The little man in kilts."

"A kilt," said Grant automatically. "Well, for some reason Lloyd gives me the same feeling as Archie Brown. It's absurd, but it is very strong. They have the same—" He looked for a word.

"Smell," said Tad.

"Yes. That's about it. They have the same smell."

After a long silence Tad said: "Mr. Grant, are you still of the opinion that what happened to Bill was an accident?"

"Yes, because there is no evidence to the contrary. But I'm quite prepared to believe that it wasn't, if I can see any reason for it. Can you clean windows?"

"Can I what?"

"Clean windows."

"I could make a shot at it if really pushed, I suppose," Tad said, staring. "Why?"

"You may have to before this is over. Let us go and collect those suitcases. I'm hoping that all the information we want will be in those cases. I've just remembered that Bill booked that berth to Scoone a week in advance."

"Perhaps his backer in Scotland couldn't see him until the 4th."

"Perhaps. Anyhow, all his papers and personal things will be in one of the cases, and I'm hoping that it will include a diary."

"Bill wouldn't keep a diary!"

"Not that kind. The Meet-Jack-1.15-Call-for-Toots-7.30 kind."

"Oh, yes, that. Yes, I expect he'd have one of those if he was going touting round London for backing. Brother, that may be all we need!"

"That *will* be all we need. If it is there."

But nothing was there.

Nothing at all.

They began light-heartedly with the obvious places: Euston, the airport, Victoria; pleased with the formula that worked so well.

"Hullo, Inspector. What can I do for you today?"

"Well, you might be able to help my young friend from America."

"Yes? One for the three-thirty?"

"We've got one for the three-thirty. He wants to know whether his buddy left a couple of suitcases here. Do you mind if he has a look round? We don't want to move anything. Just to look."

"Well, that's something that's still free in this country, Inspector, believe it or not. Come behind, will you?"

So they came behind. Each time they came behind. And each time the tiered luggage looked back at them, contemptuous and withdrawn. As detached as only other people's belongings can look.

From the likely places they moved on to the mere possibles, sobered and apprehensive. They had hoped for a diary, for personal papers. Now they would settle for even a sight of the suitcases.

But there were no familiar cases on any of the shelves.

This so staggered Tad that Grant had difficulty in dragging him away from the later ports-of-call. He went round and round the filled racks in an unbelieving daze.

"They must be here," he kept saying. "They must be here."

But they were not there.

As they came out on to the street, baffled, after their last bet had gone down the drain, he said: "Inspector—I mean, Mr. Grant—where else is there that you would leave luggage after checking out of a hotel? Have you those personal lock-up places?"

"Only limited-period ones. For people who want to park a case for an hour or two while they do something."

"Well, where *are* Bill's things? Why aren't they in any of the obvious places?"

"I don't know. They may be with his girl."

"What girl?"

"I don't know. He was young and handsome and celibate; he would have a fairly wide choice."

"Yes, of course. That's maybe what he did with them. Which reminds me." His face lost its discontented, purposeless look. He glanced at his watch. It was nearly dinner-time. "I've got a date with that girl in the milk-bar." He caught Grant's eye and looked faintly abashed. "But I'll stand her up if you think I can be any good to you."

Grant sent him away to meet his milk-bar sweetie with a slight sense of relief. It was rather like having a mournful puppy around. He himself decided to postpone dinner for a little and go and see some of his Metropolitan friends.

He dropped into the Astwick Street Police Station and was greeted with the identical phrase that he had been listening to all the afternoon and evening: "Hullo, Inspector, what can we do for you?"

Grant said that they might tell him who was on the Britt Lane beat just now.

The man on the beat was P. C. Bithel, it seemed; and if the Inspector wanted to see him he was at this moment in the canteen having sausage-and-mashed. His number was 30.

Grant found Number Thirty at a table by himself at the far end of the room. A French grammar was propped up in front of him. Looking at him, sitting there unaware, Grant thought how London policemen had changed in type in the short space of a quarter-century. He himself, he knew, was a departure from type; a fact that had been of great use to him on various occasions. P. C. Bithel was a dark, slight boy from County Down with a mat sallow skin and a kind, reassuring drawl. Between the French grammar and the drawl, Grant felt that P. C. Bithel was headed for great things.

The boy began to get up when Grant had introduced himself, but Grant sat down and said: "There's one small thing you might do for me. I'd like to know who cleans the windows of 5 Britt Lane. You might make a few inquiries when—"

"Mr. Lloyd's place?" the boy said. "Richards does them."

Yes, indeed, and indeed P. C. Bithel had a future; he must keep his eye on P. C. Bithel.

"How do you know that?"

"I pass the time of day with him here and there on my beat. He stables his barrow and things in that mews further along Britt Lane."

He thanked the budding Superintendent and went away to find Richards. Richards, it seemed, lived above his barrow. He was a bachelor ex-serviceman with a short leg, a cat, a collection of china mugs, and a passion for darts. There was nothing that P. C. Bithel, not long from County Down, did not know about his London beat.

At the corner of Britt Lane was the Sun, where Richards played darts, and it was to the Sun that Grant went. This was to be an altogether informal arrangement and it demanded an informal launching. He did not know the Sun or its proprietor, but he had only to sit still and behave himself and presently he would be invited to play darts, and from that to having a quiet one with Richards was only a step.

It was a step that took a couple of hours, as it turned out; but eventually he had Richards to himself in a corner with a pint. He was debating with himself whether to produce his card and use his official credentials for unofficial business, or to make it an affair of one ex-serviceman obliging another for a small consideration, when Richards said:

"You don't seem to have put on any weight with the years, sir."

"Have I met you somewhere?" Grant asked, a little annoyed that he should have forgotten a face.

"Camberley. More years ago than I like to think about. And you needn't worry about forgetting me," he added, "because I doubt if you ever saw me. I was a cook. You still in the Army?"

"No, I'm a policeman."

"No kidding! Well, well. I'd have said you were a dead cert for C.I.G.S. I see now why you were so anxious to get me into a corner. And me thinking it was my way with a dart that won you!"

Grant laughed. "Yes, you can do something for me, but it isn't official business. Would you take a pupil tomorrow for a small consideration?"

"To do any special windows?" Richards asked, after a moment's thought.

"Number 5 Britt Lane."

"Ho!" said Richards, amused. *"I'd* pay *him* to do *them!"*

"Why?"

"That bastard is never pleased. There's no hanky-panky about this, is there?"

"Neither hanky nor panky. Nothing is going to be abstracted from the house, and nothing upset. I'll go bail for that. Indeed, if it will make you any happier, I'll put the contract in writing."

"I'll take your word for it, sir. And your man can have the privilege of doing Mr. Flipping Lloyd's windows for nothing." He lifted his mug. "Here's to the old eyes-right. What time will your pupil be coming along tomorrow?"

"Ten o'clock do?"

"Make it half-past. Your valentine goes out most mornings about eleven."

"That's very thoughtful of you."

"I'll get my early windows done and meet him at my place—3 Britt Mews— at half-past ten."

It·was no use trying to telephone Tad Cullen again tonight, so Grant left a message at the Westmorland asking him to come to the flat as soon as he had had breakfast in the morning.

Then he at last had dinner, and went thankfully to bed.

As he was falling asleep a voice in his head said, "Because he knew that there was nothing to write on."

"What?" he said, coming awake. "Who knew?"

"Lloyd. He said, 'On what?' "

"Yes. Well?"

"He said it because he was startled."

"He certainly sounded surprised."

"He was surprised because he knew that there was nothing to write on."

He lay thinking about it until he fell asleep.

# 13

TAD ARRIVED, VERY WASHED and shining, before Grant had finished breakfast. His soul was troubled, however, and he had to be coaxed out of a contrite mood ("Can't help feeling that I walked out on you, Mr. Grant") before he was any good to anyone. He cheered up at last when he found that there were definite plans for the day.

"You mean you were serious about window cleaning? I thought it was only a—a sort of figure of speech, maybe. You know, like, 'I'll be selling matches for a living if this goes on.' Why am I going to clean Lloyd's windows?"

"Because it is the only honest way of getting a foot inside the house. My colleagues can prove that you have no right to read a gas-meter, or test the electricity, or the telephone. But they cannot deny that you are a window-cleaner and are legally and professionally getting on with your job. Richards—your boss for today—says that Lloyd goes out nearly every day about eleven, and he is going to take you there when Lloyd has gone. He'll stay with you and work with you, of course, so that he can introduce you as his assistant who is learning the trade. That way you will be accepted without suspicion and left alone."

"So I'm left alone."

"On the desk in the big room that occupies most of the first floor there is an engagement book. A large, very expensive, red-leather affair. The desk is a table one—I mean that it doesn't shut—and it stands just inside the middle window."

"So?"

"I want to know Lloyd's engagements for the 3rd and 4th of March."

"You think maybe he travelled on that train, 'm?"

"I should like to be sure that he didn't, anyhow. If I know what his engagements were I can find out quite easily whether he kept them or not."

"Okay. That's quite easy. I'm looking forward to that window cleaning. I've always wondered what I could do when I get too old for flying. I might as well look into the window trade. To say nothing of looking into a few windows."

He went away, blithe and apparently forgetful that half an hour ago he was "lower than a worm's belly," and Grant looked round in his mind for any acquaintances that he and Heron Lloyd might have in common. He remembered that he had not yet rung up Marta Hallard to announce his return to town. It might be a little early in the day to break in on Marta's slumbers, but he would risk it.

"Oh, no," Marta said, "you didn't wake me. I'm half-way through my breakfast and having my daily dose of news. Every day I swear that never again will I read a daily paper, and every morning there is the blasted thing lying waiting for me to open it and every morning I open it. It upsets my digestive juices, and hardens my arteries, and my face falls with a thud and undoes five guineas' worth of Ayesha's ministrations in five minutes, but I have to have my daily dose of poison. How are you, my dear? Are you better?"

She listened to his answer without interrupting. One of Marta's more charming characteristics was her capacity for listening. With most of his other women friends silence meant that they were preparing their next speech and were merely waiting for the next appropriate moment to give utterance to it.

"Have supper with me tonight. I'll be alone," she said when she had heard about Clune and his recovered health.

"Make it early next week, can you? How is the play going?"

"Well, darling, it would be going a lot better if Ronnie would come up-stage now and then and talk to me instead of to the audience. He says it emphasises the detachment of the character to practically stamp on the floats and let the front stalls count his eyelashes, but I think myself it's just a hang-over from his music-hall days."

They discussed both Ronnie and the play for a little, and then Grant said: "Do you know Heron Lloyd, by the way?"

"The Arabia man? Not to say know; no. But I understand he's almost as much of a hogger as Ronnie."

"How?"

"Rory—my brother's boy—was mad to go exploring in Arabia—though why anyone should want to go exploring in Arabia I can't imagine—all dust and dates—anyway, Rory wanted to go with Heron Lloyd, but it seems that Lloyd travels only with Arabs. Rory, who is a nice child, says that that is be-cause Lloyd is so Arabian that he is *plus royaliste que le roi*, but I think myself—being a low-minded creature and a rogue and vagabond—that he is just suffering from Ronnie's trouble and wants the whole stage."

"What is Rory doing now?" Grant asked, skating away from Heron Lloyd.

"Oh, he's in Arabia. The other man took him. Kinsey-Hewitt. Oh, yes, Rory wouldn't be put off by a little thing like a snub. Can you make it Tuesday: the supper?"

Yes, he would make it Tuesday. Before Tuesday he would be back at work, and the matter of Bill Kenrick, who had come to England full of excitement about Arabia and had died as Charles Martin in a train going to the Highlands, would have to be put behind him. He had only a day or two more.

He went out to have a hair-cut, and to think in that relaxed hypnotic atmosphere of anything that they had left undone. Tad Cullen was lunching with his boss. "Richards won't accept anything for this," he had said to Tad, "so take him out to lunch and give him a thundering good one and I'll pay for it."

"I'll take him out all right and be glad to," Tad said, "but I'm damned if I'll let you pay for it. Bill Kenrick was my buddy, not yours."

So he sat in the warm, aromatic air of the barber's shop, half dive, half clinic, and tried to think of something that they could still do to find Bill Kenrick's suitcases. But it was the returning Tad who provided the suggestion.

Why, said Tad, not Agony-advertise for this girl.

"What girl?"

"The girl who has his luggage. *She* has no reason to be shy—unless she's been helping herself to the contents, which wouldn't be unknown. But Bill is a—was a better picker than that. Why don't we say in capital letters: 'BILL KENRICK'—to catch the eye, get it?—and then just, 'Any friend get in touch with Number what's-it.' Is there anything against that?"

No, Grant could think of nothing against that, but his eye was on the piece of paper that Tad was fishing from his pocket.

"Did you find the book?"

"Oh, yes. I had only to lean in and pick it up. That guy doesn't do any homework, it seems. It's the dullest list of engagements outside a prison. Not a gardenia from start to finish. And no good to us anyway."

"No good?"

"He was busy, it seems. Will I write out that advertisement for the papers?"

"Yes, do. There's paper in my desk."

"Which papers shall we send it to?"

"Write six, and we can address them later."

He looked down at Tad's child-like copy of the entries in Lloyd's engagement book. The entries for the 3rd and 4th of March. And as he read them the full absurdity of his suspicions came home to him. What was he thinking of? Was his mind still the too impressionable mind of a sick man? How could he ever have dreamed that Heron Lloyd could possibly have been moved to murder? Because that was what he had been thinking, wasn't it? That somehow, in some way that they could not guess, Lloyd had been responsible for Bill Kenrick's death.

He looked at the crucial entries, and thought that even if it were proved that Lloyd had not kept these particular engagements it would be fantastic to read into that absence any more than the normal explanation: that Lloyd had been indisposed or had changed his mind. On the night of the 3rd he had apparently attended a dinner. "Pioneer Society, Normandie, 7.15" the entry read. At 9.30 the following morning a Pathé Magazine film unit was due to arrive at 5 Britt Lane and make him into number something-or-other of their Celebrities at Home series. It would seem that Heron Lloyd had more important things to think of than an unknown flyer who claimed to have seen ruins in the sands of Arabia.

"But he said, 'On what?' " said that voice in him.

"All *right*, he said, 'On what?' A fine world it would be if one was going to be suspected, if one was going to be judged, by every unconsidered remark!"

The commissioner had once said to him: "You have the most priceless of all attributes for your job, and that is flair. But don't let it ride you, Grant. Don't let your imagination take hold. Keep it your servant."

He had been in danger of letting his flair bolt with him. He must take a pull on himself.

He would go back to where he was before he saw Lloyd. Back to the company of Bill Kenrick. Back from wild imaginings to fact. Hard, bare, uncompromising fact.

He looked across at Tad, nose to paper and pursuing his pen across the page with it as a terrier noses a spider across a floor.

"How was your milk-bar lady?"

"Oh, fine, fine," said Tad, absent-minded and not lifting his glance from his handiwork.

"Taking her out again?"

"Uh-huh. Meeting her tonight."

"Think she will do as a steady?"

"She might," Tad said, and then as he became aware of this unusual interest he looked up and said: "What's this all about?"

"I'm thinking of deserting you for a day or two, and I'd like to know that you won't be bored if left to your own devices."

"Oh. Oh, no; I'll be all right. It's time you took some time off to attend to your own affairs, I guess. After all, this is no trouble of yours. You've done far too much as it is."

"I'm not taking time off. I'm planning to fly over and see Charles Martin's people."

"People?"

"His family. They live just outside Marseilles."

Tad's face, which had looked blank for a moment, grew animated again. "What do you think you'll get from them?"

"I'm not doing any thinking. I'm just beginning from the other end. We've come to a blank wall where Bill Kenrick is concerned—unless his hypothetical girl-friend answers that advertisement, and that won't be for two days at the very least—so we'll try the Charles Martin end and see where we get from there."

"Fine. What about me coming with you?"

"I think not, Tad. I think you had better stay here and be O.C. the Press. See that all these are inserted and pick up any answers."

"You're the boss," Tad said in a resigned way. "But I sure would like to see Marseilles."

"It's not a bit the way you picture it," Grant said, amused.

"How do you know how I picture it?"

"I can imagine."

"Oh, well, I suppose I can sit on a stool and look at Daphne. What funny names girls have in this neck of the woods. It's a bit draughty, but I can count up the number of times people say thank you for doing other people service."

"If it's iniquity you're looking for, you'll find as much on a Leicester Square pavement as you will on the Cannebière."

"Maybe, but I like my iniquity with some ooh-la-la in it."

"Hasn't Daphne got any ooh-la-la?"

"No. Daphne's very la-di-da. I have an awful suspicion that she wears woollen underwear."

"She would need it in a milk-bar in Leicester Square in April. She sounds a nice girl."

"Oh, she's fine, fine. But don't you stay too long away, or the wolf in me will prove too strong and I'll take the first plane out to Marseilles to join you. When do you plan to go?"

"Tomorrow morning, if I can get a seat. Move over and let me reach the telephone. If I get an early-morning service I can, with a piece of luck, get back the following day. If not, then Friday at the latest. How did you get on with Richards?"

"Oh, we're great buddies. But I'm a bit disillusioned."

"About what?"

"About the possibilities of the trade."

"Doesn't it pay?"

"I expect it pays off in coin but not any other way, take it from me. All you can see from outside a window, believe it or not, is your own reflection in the glass. What are the names of those papers you want me to address these things to?"

Grant gave him the names of the six newspapers with the largest circulations, and sent him away with his blessing to employ his time as he saw fit until they met again.

"I certainly wish I was going with you," Tad said once more as he was leaving, and Grant wondered if seeing the South of France as one big honkytonk was any more absurd than seeing it as mimosa. Which was what it was to him.

"France!" said Mrs. Tinker. "When you've only just come back from foreign parts!"

"The Highlands may be foreign parts, but the South of France is merely an extension of England."

"It's a very expensive extension, I've 'eard. *Roonous*. When was you expectin' to be back? I got a loverly chicken from Carr's for you."

"The day after tomorrow, I hope. Friday at the latest."

"Oh, then it'll keep. Was you wantin' to be called earlier tomorrow mornin', then?"

"I'll be away before you come in, I think. So you can have a late morning tomorrow."

"A late mornin' wouldn't suit Tinker, it wouldn't. But I'll get me shoppin' done before I come in. Now you see and take care of yerself. No burning the candle at both ends and comin' back lookin' no better than when you went away to Scotland in the beginnin'. I 'ope it keeps fine for you!"

Fine indeed, Grant thought, looking down at the map of France next morning. From that height on this crystal morning it was not a thing of earth and water and crops. It was a small jewelled pattern set in a lapis-lazuli sea; a Fabergé creation. Not much wonder that flyers as a species had a detached attitude to the world. What had the world—its literature, its music, its philosophies, or its history—to do with a man who saw it habitually for the thing it was: a bit of Fabergé nonsense?

Marseilles, at close quarters, was no jeweller's creation. It was the usual noisy crowded place filled with impatient taxi-horns and the smell of stale coffee; that very French smell that haunts its houses with the ghosts of ten million coffee-brewings. But the sun shone, and the striped awnings flapped a little in the breeze from the Mediterranean, and the mimosa displayed its pale expensive yellow in prodigal masses. As a companion picture to the grey and scarlet of London it was, he thought, perfect. If he ever was rich he would commission one of the best artists in the world to put the two pictures on canvas for him; the chiaroscuro of London and bright positive blaze of Marseilles. Or perhaps two different artists. It was unlikely that the man who could convey the London of a grey day in April would also be able to paint the essence of Marseilles on a spring noon.

He stopped thinking about artists and ceased to find Marseilles either bright or positive when he found that the Martin family had left their suburb only the week before for parts unknown. Unknown, that was, to the neighbours. By the time that he had, with the help of the local authorities, discovered that "parts unknown" merely meant Toulon, a great deal of precious time had been wasted, and still more was wasted in journeying to Toulon and finding the Martins among its teeming inhabitants.

But in the end he found them and listened to the little they had to tell. Charles was a "bad boy," they said, with all the antagonism of the French for someone who has apostatised from that supreme god of the French idolatry, the Family. He had always been a wilful, headstrong creature and (crime of crimes in the French calendar) lazy. Bone-lazy. He had gone away five years ago after a small trouble over a girl—no, no, he had merely stabbed her—and had not bothered to write to them. They had had no news of him in all those years except that a friend had run into him in Port Said about three years ago. He was doing pavement deals in second-hand cars, the friend said. Buying up crocks and selling them after he had tinkered with them a little. He was a very good mechanic; he could have been a very successful man, with a garage of his own and people working for him, if he had not been so lazy. Bone-lazy. A laziness that was formidable. A laziness that was a disease. They had heard nothing more of him until they had been asked to identify his body.

Grant asked if they had a photograph of Charles.

Yes, they had several, but of course they were of Charles when he was much younger.

They showed him the photographs, and Grant saw why Bill Kenrick, dead, looked not too unlike the Charles Martin that his family had remembered. One thin dark man with marked eyebrows, hollowed cheeks, and straight dark hair looked very like any other similar young man when the individuality of life was quenched. They did not even have to have the same colour of eyes.

A parent receives a message saying: Your son is dead as the result of a regrettable accident; would you please identify him as your son and arrange for the burial. The bereaved parent is presented with his dead son's papers and belongings and is asked to identify the owner as his son. There is no question in his conditioned mind; he accepts what he sees, and what he sees is what he expected to see. It would not occur to him to say: Are this man's eyes blue or brown?

In the end, of course, it was Grant who submitted to questioning. Why was he interested in Charles? Had Charles after all left some money? Was it that Grant was looking for the legal heirs, perhaps?

No, Grant had promised to look Charles up on behalf of a friend who had known him on the Persian Gulf coast. No, he did not know what the friend wanted of him. He understood that there was some suggestion of a future partnership.

In the expressed opinion of the Martin family, the friend was lucky.

They gave him Armagnac and coffee and little biscuits with Bath-bun sugar on them, and asked him to come again if he was ever in Toulon.

On the doorstep he asked if they had possession of their son's papers. Only his personal ones, they said: his letters. The official ones they had not bothered with or thought about. They were no doubt still with the Marseilles police, who had first made contact with them when the accident happened.

So a little more time was wasted in making friends with the Marseilles officials; but this time Grant spent no energy on conscientiously unofficial methods. He produced his credentials and asked for a loan of the papers. He drank a *sirop,* and signed a receipt. And he caught the afternoon plane to London on Friday afternoon.

He had two more days. Or one day and a Sunday, to be accurate.

France was still a jewelled pattern as he flew back over it, but Britain seemed to have disappeared altogether. Beyond the familiar outline of the western European coast there was nothing but an ocean of haze. Very odd and incomplete the map looked without the familiar shape of that very individual island. Supposing there never had been that island: How different would the history of the world have been? It was a fascinating speculation. An all-Spanish America, one supposed. A French India; an India without a colour-bar and so racially intermarried that it had lost its identity. A Dutch South Africa ruled by a fanatic Church. Australia? Who would have discovered and colonised Australia? The Dutch from South Africa, or the Spaniards from America? It was immaterial, he supposed, since either race would in a generation have become tall, lean, tough, nasal, drawling, sceptical and indestructible.

They dropped into the ocean of cloud and found Britain again. A very mundane, muddy, and workaday place to have changed the history of a world. A steady drizzle soaked the land and the lieges. London was a water-colour of grey reflections with spots of vermilion oil paint where the buses plunged dripping through the haze.

All the lights were on in the finger-print department, although it was still daylight; and Cartwright was sitting just as he had last seen him—as he had always seen him—with a half-drunk cup of cold tea at his elbow, the saucer filled with cigarette butts.

"Something I can do for you this beautiful spring afternoon?" Cartwright said.

"Yes. There is one thing I want very much to know. Have you ever drunk the second half of a cup of tea?"

Cartwright considered this. "Come to think of it, I don't know that I ever have. Beryl usually takes my cup away and fills it up with fresh stuff. Something else off the cuff? Or is this just a social call?"

"Yes, something else. But you'll be *working* for me on Monday, so don't let your sense of benevolence get out of hand." He put Charles Martin's papers on the table. "When can you do these for me?"

"What is this? French identity papers. What are you getting into—or do you want to keep it to yourself?"

"I'm just having one last bet on a horse called Flair. If it comes off I'll tell you about it. I'll pick up the prints tomorrow morning."

He looked at the clock and reckoned that if Tad Cullen was "dating" Daphne, or any other female creature, tonight, he would at this moment be dolling himself up in his hotel room. He left Cartwright and went to a telephone where he could talk unheard.

"*We-e-ll!*" said Tad joyously, when he heard Grant's voice. "Where are you talking from? Are you back?"

"Yes, I'm back. I'm in London. Look, Tad, you say you've never known anyone called Charles Martin. But is it possible that you knew him under another name? Did you ever know a very good mechanic, very good with cars, who was French and looked a little like Bill?"

Tad thought this over.

"I don't think I've ever known any mechanic who was French. I've known a Swedish mechanic and a Greek mechanic, but neither of them was in the least like Bill. Why?"

"Because Martin worked in the Middle East. And it is just possible that Bill got those papers from him before he ever came to Britain at all. Martin may have sold them to him. He was—is: he may be living—a lazy creature and probably very hard-up at intervals. Out there, where no one bothers very much about credentials, he might have tried to cash them."

"Yes; he might. Someone else's papers are usually more valuable than your own out there. To have around, I mean. But why would *Bill* buy them? Bill never did anything on the side."

"Perhaps because he looked a little like Martin. I don't know. Anyhow, you yourself have never run into anyone like Martin in the Middle East?"

"Not anywhere, that I can think of. What did you get out of the Martins? Anything worth while?"

"I'm afraid not. They showed me photographs which made it clear how much he would look like Bill if he was not alive. Something that we knew already. And of course the fact that he had gone East to work. Any answers to the advertisement?"

"Five."

"*Five?*"

"All from fellows called Bill Kenrick."

"Oh. Asking what was in it for them?"

"You've got it."

"Not a word from anyone who knew him?"

"Not a peep. And nothing at the Charles Martin end either, it seems. We're sunk, aren't we?"

"Well—waterlogged, shall we say. We have one remaining asset."

"We have? What is that?"

"Time. We have forty-eight more hours."

"Mr. Grant, you're an optimist."

"You have to be in my business," Grant said, but he did not feel very optimistic. He felt flat and tired. He was within an ace of wishing that he had never heard of Bill Kenrick. Wishing that he had come down that corridor at Scoone just ten seconds later. In ten more seconds Yoghourt would have realised that the man was dead and would have shut the door and gone for help; and he, Grant, would have walked down that empty corridor and stepped down on to the platform unaware that there had ever existed a young man called Bill Kenrick. He would never have known that anyone had died on the train. He would have driven away with Tommy to the hills, and no words about singing sands would have disturbed his holiday. He would have fished in peace, and finished his holiday in peace.

In too much peace perhaps? With too much time to think about himself and his bondage to unreason. Too much time to take his own mental and spiritual pulse.

No, of course he was not sorry that he had heard of Bill Kenrick. He was Bill Kenrick's debtor as long as he lived, and if it took him till the end of his days he would find out what had changed Bill Kenrick into Charles Martin. But if only he could clear up this thing before he was swamped by that demanding life that was waiting for him on Monday.

He asked how Daphne was, and Tad said that as a female companion she had one enormous advantage over everyone he had ever known: she was pleased with very little. If you gave her a bunch of violets, she was as pleased as most girls are with orchids. It was Tad's considered opinion that she had never heard of orchids, and he, personally, had no intention of bringing them to her notice.

"She sounds the domestic type. You take care, Tad, or she'll be going back to the Middle East with you."

"Not while I'm conscious," Tad said. "No female is going back East with me. I'm not having any little woman round the house cluttering up *our* bungalow. I mean, my bun—I mean—" His voice died away.

The conversation became suddenly broken-backed, and Grant rang off after promising to call him as soon as he had anything to report or an idea to share.

He went out into the wet haze, bought himself an evening paper, and found a taxi to take him home. The paper was a *Signal*, and the sight of the familiar heading took him back to that breakfast at Scoone four weeks ago. He thought again how constant in kind the headlines were. The Cabinet row, the dead body of the blonde in Maida Vale, the Customs prosecution, the hold-up, the arrival of an American actor, the street accident. Even "PLANE CRASH IN ALPS" was common enough to rank as a constant.

"Yesterday evening the dwellers in the high valleys of Chamonix saw a rose of flame break out on the icy summit of Mont Blanc—"

The *Signal's* style was constant too.

The only thing waiting for him at 19 Tenby Court was a letter from Pat, which said:

Dear Alan, they say you must have marjuns but I think marjuns is havers. waste not want not. this is a fly I made for you. it was not done in time before you went. it may not be any good for those english rivers but you better have it anyway your affectionate cousin Patrick.

This production cheered Grant considerably, and while he ate his dinner he considered alternately the economy, in capitals as well as in margins, and the enclosed lure. The fly exceeded in originality even that remarkable affair which he had been lent at Clune. He decided to use it on the Severn on a day when fish would take a piece of red rubber hot-water bottle, so that he could write honestly to Pat and report that the Rankin fly had landed a big one.

The typical Scots insularity in "those english rivers" made him hope that Laura would not wait too long before sending Pat away to his English school. The quality of Scotchness was a highly concentrated essence, and should always be diluted. As an ingredient it was admirable; neat, it was as abominable as ammonia.

He stuck the fly above the calendar on his desk, so that he might go on being amused by its catholicity and warmed by his young cousin's devotion, and got thankfully into pyjamas and a dressing-gown. There was at least one consolation for being in town when he might still be in the country: he could get into a dressing-gown and put his feet on the fender in the sure and certain knowledge that no telephone call from Whitehall 1212 would intrude on his leisure.

But he had not had his feet up for twenty minutes when Whitehall 1212 was on the telephone.

It was Cartwright.

"Did I understand you to say that you had had a bet on Flair?" said Cartwright's voice.

"Yes. Why?"

"I don't know anything about it, but I have an idea that your horse has won," said Cartwright. He added, very silky and sweet like a Broadcasting Aunt, "*Good* night, sir," and hung up.

"Hey!" said Grant, and jiggled the telephone key. "*Hey!*"

But Cartwright had gone. And it would be no use trying to bring him to the telephone any more tonight. This amiable piece of teasing was Cartwright's come-back, his charge for doing a couple of buckshee jobs.

Grant went back to his Runyon, but he could no longer keep his attention on that strictly legit character, Judge Henry G. Blake. Blast Cartwright and his little jokes. Now he would have to go to the Yard first thing in the morning.

But in the morning he forgot all about Cartwright.

By eight o'clock in the morning Cartwright had sunk back into the great ocean of incidentals that bear us on from one day to the next, unremarkable in their plankton swarming.

The morning began as it always did, with the rattle of china and the voice of Mrs. Tinker as she set down his early-morning tea. This was the preliminary to four glorious minutes during which he lay still more asleep than awake and let his tea cool, so that Mrs. Tinker's voice came to him down a long tunnel that led to life and the daylight but need not yet be traversed.

"Just listen to it," Mrs. Tinker's voice said, referring apparently to the steady beat of the rain. "Stair rods, cats and dogs, reservoyers. Niagara also ran. Seems they've bin and found Shangri-la. I could do with a spot of Shangri-la myself this morning."

The word turned over in his sleepy mind like a weed in calm water. Shangri-la. Very soporific. Very soporific. Shangri-la. Some place in a film. In a novel. Some unspoiled Eden. Shut away from the world.

"According to this mornin's papers they never 'ave no rain at all there."

"Where?" he said, to show that he was awake.

"Arabia, so it seems."

He heard the door close and dropped a little further under the surface of things for the enjoyment of those four minutes. Arabia. Arabia. Another soporific. They had found Shangri-la in Arabia. They—

*Arabia!*

In one great whirl of blankets he came to the surface and reached for the papers. There were two, but it was the *Clarion* that came to his hand first because it was the *Clarion* whose headlines constituted Mrs. Tinker's daily dose of reading.

He did not have to search for it. It was there on the front page. It was the best front-page stuff that any newspaper had had since Crippen.

SHANGRI-LA REALLY EXISTS. SENSATIONAL DISCOVERY. HISTORIC FIND IN ARABIA.

He glanced over the hysterically excited paragraphs and discarded the paper impatiently for the more trustworthy *Morning News*. But the *Morning News* was almost as excited as the *Clarion*. KINSEY-HEWITT'S GREAT FIND, said the *Morning News*. ASTOUNDING NEWS FROM ARABIA.

"We print, with great pride, Paul Kinsey-Hewitt's own despatch," said the *Morning News*. "As our readers will see, his discovery had been vouched for by three R.A.F. planes sent to locate the place after Mr. Kinsey-Hewitt's arrival at Makallah." The *Morning News* had had a contract with Kinsey-Hewitt for a series of articles on his present journey, when that journey should be completed, and was now delirious with pleasure at its unexpected luck.

He skipped the *Morning News* on its own triumph and went on to the far soberer prose of the triumphant explorer himself:

We were in the Empty Quarter on scientific errands . . . no thought in our minds of human history either factual or legendary . . . a well-explored country . . . bare mountains that no one had ever considered climbing . . . a waste of time between one well and the next . . . in a land where water is life no one turns aside to climb precipitous heights . . . attention caught by a plane that came twice in five days and spent some time circling low above the mountains . . . occurred to us that some plane had crashed . . . possible rescue . . . conference . . . Rory Hallard and I to search while Daoud went on to the well at Zaruba and brought a load of water back to meet us . . . no entrance apparent . . . walls like the Garbh Coire on Braeriach . . . giving up . . . Rory . . . a track that even a goat would baulk at . . . two hours to the ridge . . . a valley of astounding beauty . . . green almost shocking . . . kind of tamarisk . . . crumbled architecture reminiscent of Greece rather than Arabia . . . colonnades . . . paved squares and streets . . . oddly metropolitan . . . in the position of a small island in an ocean of desert . . . strip cultivation . . . monkey god in stone . . . Wabar . . . volcanic convulsion . . . Wabar . . . Wabar . . .

The *Morning News* had inset a neat outline map of Arabia with crosses in the appropriate place.

Grant lay and stared at it.

So *that* was what Bill Kenrick had seen.

He had come out of the shouting heart of the storm, out of the whirling sand and the darkness, and looked down at that green valley lying among the rocks. Not much wonder that he had come back looking "concussed," looking as if his mind were "still back there." He had not quite believed it himself. He had gone back to search; to look for, and eventually look at, this place that appeared on no map. This—*this*—was his Paradise.

This was what he had been writing about on the blank space of an evening paper.

This was what he had come to England to—

To Heron Lloyd to—

To *Heron Lloyd!*

He flung the *News* away and leaped out of bed.

"Tink!" he called as he turned on the bath-water. "Tink, never mind breakfast. Get me some coffee."

"But you can't go out on a morning like this with just a cup of—"

"*Don't argue!* Get me some coffee!"

The water roared into the bath. The liar. The Goddamned smooth heartless limelight-hogging liar. The vain vicious murdering liar. How had he done it?

By God, he would see that he hanged for this.

"On what evidence?" said his inner voice, nasty-polite.

"You shut up! I'll get the evidence if I have to discover a whole new continent to find it! Poor boy! Poor boy!" said he, shaking his head over so sad a fate. "Sweet Christ, I'll hang for him myself if I can't kill him any other way!"

"Calm down, calm down. That's no mood to interview a suspect in."

"I'm not interviewing a suspect, blast your police mind. I'm going to tell Heron Lloyd what I think of him. I'm not a police-officer until after I've dealt personally with Lloyd."

"You can't hit a man of sixty."

"I'm not going to hit him. I'm going to half murder him. The ethics of hitting or not hitting don't enter into the matter at all."

"He may be worth hanging for but not worth being requested to resign for."

" 'I found him delightful,' said he, kind and patronising. The bastard. The smooth vain murdering bastard. The—"

From the wells of his experience he dredged up words to serve his need. But his anger went on consuming him like a furnace.

He flung out of the house after two mouthfuls of toast and three gulps of coffee, and went round to the garage at the double. It was too early to hope for a taxi; the quickest way was to use his car.

Would Lloyd have read the papers yet?

If he did not normally leave the house before eleven o'clock, then surely breakfast could not be until nine. He would like very much to be at 5 Britt Lane before Lloyd opened his morning paper. It would be sweet, consoling sweet, satisfying sweet, to watch Lloyd take the news. He had murdered to keep the secret his own, to ensure that the glory should be his, and now the secret was front-page news and the glory belonged to his rival. Oh, sweet Jesus, let him not have read about it yet.

He rang twice at 5 Britt Lane before his summons was answered, and then it was answered not by the amiable Mahmoud but by a large woman in felt slippers.

"Mr. Lloyd?" he asked.

"Oh, Mr. Lloyd's up in Cumberland for a day or two."

"Cumberland! When did he go to Cumberland?"

"Thursday afternoon."

"When do you expect him back?"

"Oh, they've just gone for a day or two."

"They? Mahmoud too?"

"Of course Mahmoud too. Mr. Lloyd he doesn't go anywhere without Mahmoud goes with him."

"I see. Can you give me his address?"

"I'd give it you if I had it. But they don't bother with re-addressing when they go for only a day or two. Will you leave a message? Or will you call back, perhaps? They'll like as not arrive back this afternoon."

No, he would not leave a message. He would come back. His name did not matter.

He felt like someone who has braked too suddenly and been hit in the wind. As he went out to his car, he remembered that Tad Cullen would read the story in a few minutes' time, if he had not read it already. He went back to the flat and was met in the lobby by a relieved Mrs. Tinker.

"Thank heaven you're back. That American boy's been on the phone and goin' on somethink awful. I can't make 'ead or tail of what 'e thinks 'e's talkin' about. Ravin' mad, 'e is. I says: 'Mr. Grant'll ring you,' I says, 'the minute 'e come in,' but 'e can't leave the phone alone. Just puts it down an' picks it up again. I bin running backwards and forwards between the sink and the phone like a—" The telephone rang. "There you are! There 'e is again!"

Grant picked up the receiver. It was indeed Tad, and he was all that Mrs. Tinker had said. He was incoherent with rage.

"But he lied!" he kept saying. "That guy lied. Of *course* Bill told him all that!"

"Yes, of course he did. Listen, Tad . . . listen . . . No, you can't go and beat him to a jelly . . . Yes, of course you can find his house for yourself; I don't doubt it, but . . . *Listen,* Tad! I've *been* to his house . . . Oh, yes, even at *this* hour of the morning. I read my papers earlier than you do . . . No, I didn't beat him up. I couldn't . . . No, not because I'm windy but because he's in Cumberland . . . Yes. Since Thursday . . . I don't know. I'll have to think about it. Give me until lunch-time. Do you trust my judgment on things in general? . . . Well, you'll have to trust it in this. I must have time to think . . . To think up some evidence, of course . . . It's customary . . . I'll tell my story to the Yard, of course, and of course they will believe me. I mean, my story of Bill's visit to Lloyd, and Lloyd's lies to me. But proving that Charles Martin was Bill Kenrick is quite a different matter. Until lunch-time I shall be writing out a statement for the Yard. Come about one o'clock and we can have lunch together. In the afternoon I must turn the whole thing over to the authorities."

He hated the thought. This was his own private fight. It had been his own private fight from the very beginning. From that moment when he had looked down through the open compartment door on to the dead face of an unknown boy. It was a thousand times more his private fight since his meeting with Lloyd.

He had begun to write, when he remembered that he had not yet picked up the papers he had left with Cartwright. He lifted the receiver, dialled the number, and asked for Cartwright's extension. Could Cartwright possibly find a messenger to send round with those papers? He, Grant, was frantically busy. It was Saturday, and he was clearing up before going back to work on Monday. He would be very grateful.

He went back to his writing, and became so absorbed that he was conscious only in a dim way that Mrs. Tinker had brought in the second post: the noon one. It was when he raised his glance from the paper to search his mind for a word, that his eye fell on the envelope she had laid beside him on the desk. It was a foolscap envelope, rather stiff and expensive, well-filled, and addressed in a thin, angular cramped hand that managed to be at once finicking and flamboyant.

Grant had never seen Heron Lloyd's handwriting. He recognised it instantly.

He put down his pen; cautiously, as if the strange letter was a bomb and any undue vibration might send it off.

He wiped his palms down the thighs of his trousers in a gesture he had not used since he was a child, the gesture of a small boy facing the incalculable, and put out his hand for the envelope.

It had been posted in London.

# 14

THE LETTER WAS DATED Thursday morning.

MY DEAR MR. GRANT,

Or should I say Inspector? Oh, yes, I know about that. It did not take me long to find out. My excellent Mahmoud is a better detective than any of your well-meaning amateurs on the Embankment. But I shall not give you your rank, because this is a social communication. I write to you as one unique human being to another worthy of his attention. Indeed, it is because you are the only Englishman who has ever moved me to even a momentary admiration that I present these facts to you and not to the Press.

And because, of course, I am sure of your interest.

I have this morning had a letter from my follower, Paul Kinsey-Hewitt, announcing his discovery in Arabia. The letter was sent from the *Morning News* office at his request, to anticipate the publication of the news tomorrow morning. A piece of courtesy for which I am grateful to him. It is ironic that it should have been the Kenrick youth who was responsible for bringing to him, too, the knowledge of the valley's existence. I saw a great deal of the Kenrick youth while he was in London and I could find nothing in him worthy of so great a destiny. He was a very commonplace young man. He spent his days flying a mechanical contraption mindlessly across deserts that men had conquered only with suffering and resolution. He was full of a plan whereby I should provide the transport and he should lead me to this find of his. But that of course was absurd. I have not lived my life and made a great name in the desert to be led to discovery by an instrument-watcher from the back streets of Portsmouth; to be a transport provider, a camel-hirer, for some other man's convenience. It was not to be thought of that a youth who by a climatic hazard, a geographical accident, had stumbled on one of the great discoveries of the world should be allowed to profit by it at the expense of men who had given their lives to exploration.

As far as I could judge, the young man's only virtue (why do you waste your interest on so dull a piece of human mass-production?) was a capacity for continence. In speech, of course; please don't misunderstand me. And it was important from my point of view that the tongue which he had held with so rare a continence should go on being unwagged.

Since he had arranged to meet another of his kind in Paris on the 4th (poor beautiful Lutetia, for ever raped by the barbarian), I had a little less than a fortnight to contrive this. I did not, in fact, need the fortnight. I could have achieved my end in two days if necessary.

I had once, when travelling to Scotland by night, stayed awake to write some letters and post them at Crewe when the train would reach its first stop. I had thought then, as I sat looking at the platform after getting rid of my letters, how easy it would be to leave the train unobserved. The attendant stepped out to receive late-joining passengers and then went away on affairs of his own. There was a long wait at a quite deserted platform while luggage was loaded into the distant vans. If one had managed to travel so far unaccounted for, one could step off the train and no one would ever know that one had been on it.

That memory was the first of the two props for my inspiration.

The second was my possession of Charles Martin's papers.

Charles Martin was my mechanic. He was the only European and the only technician (what an appropriately deplorable word!) ever employed by me. I engaged him for the least successful of my expeditions, the semi-mechanised one, because my Arabs (though learning rapidly, alas!)

were not skilful with machinery. He was a repellent creature, interested in nothing but internal combustion and the avoidance of his share of camp duties, and I was not sorry when he died in mid-desert. We had by that time found the vehicles a liability rather than a help and had decided to abandon them, so Martin had already outlived his usefulness. (No, I had nothing to do with his death; Heaven in this instance did its own scavenging.) No one asked for his papers, and since the journey was from coast to coast we never returned to the town in which I had engaged him. His papers lay in my baggage, a matter of no interest to me or to anyone else, and came back to England with me.

I remembered them when it was necessary to silence the Kenrick youth. Kenrick looked not too unlike Charles Martin.

It was Kenrick's plan to go back to his Carter-Paterson occupation in the East until such time as I should join him there, and we should then set out on our expedition together. He came to see me at Britt Lane very often, to discuss routes and plume himself on the prospect in front of him, and it amused me to see him sit there and babble his nonsense when I had so strange a translation prepared for him.

He had arranged to go to Paris by the night-ferry on the 3rd. He "collected" ferries, it seemed. He would go many miles out of his way to be punted across a stream which he could have crossed by a bridge a few yards from where he was standing. The Dover ferry was to be his two-hundredth, I think. When he told me that he had booked a berth on the train-ferry I telephoned, as soon as he had gone, and booked a berth to Scoone in the name of Charles Martin for the same night.

When I next saw him I suggested that since I was going to Scotland on the same evening on which he was leaving for Paris, he should leave his luggage (he had only two suitcases) in the cloak-room at Victoria, dine early with me at Britt Lane, and see me off at Euston.

He was always delighted to fall in with any suggestion that I was moved to put to him, and he agreed, as I knew he would, to this. We dined, on a rice and cutlets and apricots dish that Mahmoud has taught Mrs. Lucas to make (it needs long cooking so that the dish is impregnated with the flavour of the apricots), and Mahmoud drove us to Euston. At Euston I sent Kenrick to pick up my sleeper ticket while I went ahead. By the time Kenrick rejoined me, I had found my compartment and was waiting on the platform for his arrival. If by chance he wondered why I was travelling as Charles Martin I had the excuse of my fame to account for an incognito. But he made no comment.

I felt that the gods were on my side when I saw that the attendant was Old Yoghourt. You will not know Old Yoghourt. He has never in the whole course of his career been known to take an interest in any passenger whatever, his chief object when on duty being to retire to his own unsavoury compartment at the earliest possible moment and go to sleep there.

We had less than five minutes before the train was due to depart. We stood talking for a little with the door half closed, Kenrick facing the corridor. Presently he said that he had better get out, or he might be carried to the Highlands. I indicated my small overnight case, which was lying beside him on the bunk, and said: "If you open my case you'll find something in it for you. A keepsake till we meet again."

He bent over, with an almost childish eagerness, to unfasten the two locks. The position was perfect. I took from my pocket the most satisfactory weapon ever devised by man for the destruction of his unsuspecting enemy. Primitive man in desert countries had neither knife nor rifle, but he made the sand serve. A rag and a few handfuls of sand, and a skull would crack like an egg-shell; very neatly it would crack, without blood or fuss. He gave a small grunt and fell forward over the case. I shut and locked the door and looked to see if his nose was bleeding. It was not. I dragged him off the berth and bundled him under it. This was my only miscalculation. One half of the space under the berth was occupied by some permanent obstruction, and thin and slight as he was his knees could not be pushed back out of sight. I took off my own coat and flung it on the berth so that it hung over and hid his legs. As I arranged the folds in a manner at once concealing and suitably casual, the whistle went. I put the outward half of my ticket to Scoone, together with my sleeper ticket, on the small shelf below the mirror where Yoghourt would see it, and walked down the corridor to the lavatory. No one had interest for anything but the moment of leave-taking. I shut myself into the lavatory and waited.

About twenty minutes later I heard the successive closing of doors that meant that Yoghourt was making his rounds. When I heard him in the compartment next door, I began to wash, noisily. He tapped at the door a few moments later and asked if I were the passenger in B Seven. I said that I was. He announced that he had found my tickets and taken them. I heard him go through to the next coach and begin his door-slamming, and I walked back to B Seven and locked myself in.

After that I had three uninterrupted hours to make all perfect.

If you ever want to be sure of uninterrupted peace, my dear Mr. Grant, buy yourself a sleeper ticket to the North of Scotland. There is nowhere in this world where one is so safe from interruption as one is in a sleeping compartment once the attendant has done his round. Not even in the desert.

I retrieved Kenrick from below the bunk, rubbed his head on the edge of the wash-hand basin, and laid him on the bunk. An examination of his clothes showed a gratifying cosmopolitanism. His underclothes seemed to be dhobi-washed, his suit made in Hong Kong, and his shoes in Kara-chi. His watch was a cheap metal one with neither name nor initials.

I removed the contents of his pockets and substituted Charles Mar-tin's pocket-book and its contents.

He was still alive, but he stopped breathing as we were running through the yards at Rugby.

From then on I dressed the set, as they say in the theatre. And I don't think that I missed anything, did I, Mr. Grant? The details were perfect, even to the crushed hairs in the wash-hand basin and the dusty palms of his hands. In the case that I was leaving behind were old clothes of my own, well-worn and washed, and of a type that he was in the habit of wearing; and such Frenchness as I had been able to supply from my own store: a novel and a Testament. The case also, of course, contained the all-important bottle.

Kenrick had an extraordinarily hard head. I refer to the matter of drink, of course, not to the results of sand-bagging. I had plied him with whisky at dinner, and had offered him a stirrup-cup of such dimensions that any other man would have blenched at the prospect. He did indeed look at the half-tumbler of neat whisky a little doubtfully, but, as I have said, he was always anxious to please me and he drank it down without protest. He remained sober, or to all appearances sober. But both his blood and his stomach would be whisky-sodden when he died.

So was his compartment when I had finished with it. As the lights of Crewe began to go by, I put the final touch. I laid the half-full bottle on the floor and rolled it to and fro over the carpet. As the train slowed down I unlocked the door, shut it behind me, walked away down the train until I had several coaches between me and B Seven, stood looking in a casual, interested way at the traffic on the platform, stepped, still casual, down on to that platform and strolled along it. In hat and coat I did not look like a passenger, and no one took any notice of me.

I came back to London on the midnight train, arriving at Euston at half-past three, and was so exhilarated that I walked all the way home. I walked as if on air. I let myself in, and was sleeping peacefully when Mahmoud came to call me at seven-thirty and to remind me that I had an appointment to entertain Pathé representatives at half-past nine.

It was not until you called to see me that I knew about the scribbled words on the newspaper that had been in his coat pocket. I admit that I was for a moment dismayed that I should have overlooked anything at all, but I was instantly comforted by the venial nature of the slip. It did not in any way detract from nor endanger my unique achievement. I had let him keep his deplorable rag, as a piece of set-dressing. That it proved to have Kenrick's handwriting on it would not be of interest to authorities who had accepted the young man as Charles Martin.

The following evening, at the rush hour, I drove myself to Victoria and retrieved Kenrick's two cases from the cloak-room. I took them home, removed from them all maker's marks and easily identifiable articles, sewed them both up in canvas, and sent them with their contents to a refugee organisation in the Near East. If you ever want to get rid of anything, my dear Mr. Grant, do not burn it. Post it to a remote island in the South Seas.

Having seen to it that the admirably reticent tongue of the Kenrick youth would stay reticent, I looked forward to enjoying the fruits of my labours. Indeed, yesterday I had assurance of sufficient backing for my new expedition, and had planned to fly out next week. The letter from Kinsey-Hewitt this morning alters all that, of course. The fruits of my achievement have been taken from me. But no one can take from me the achievement itself. If I cannot be known as the discoverer of Wabar, I shall be known as the author of the only perfect murder ever perpetrated.

I cannot stay to be a candle-holder at Kinsey-Hewitt's triumph. And I am too old to have more triumphs of my own. But I *can* light a blaze that will make the candles on the Kinsey-Hewitt altar look small and pale and uninteresting. My funeral pyre will be a beacon to light all Europe, and my achievement in murder a tidal-wave that will sweep Kinsey-Hewitt and Wabar into the wastepaper baskets of the world's Press.

This evening, at dusk, I light my own pyre, on the highest slope of the highest mountain in Europe. Mahmoud does not know this. He thinks we are flying out to Athens. But he has been with me for many years and would be very unhappy without me. So I am taking him with me.

Good-bye, my dear Mr. Grant. It grieves me that someone of your intelligence should be wasting his talents in that rather stupid establishment on the Embankment. It was clever of you to discover that Charles Martin was not Charles Martin but someone called Kenrick, and I salute you. What you are not clever enough to discover is that he did not die by accident. What no one would ever be clever enough to discover is that I am the man who killed him.

Please take this letter as a mark of my esteem and *pour prendre congé*. Mrs. Lucas will post this on Friday morning.

H. C. HERON LLOYD

Grant became aware that Mrs. Tinker was showing Tad Cullen into the room, and that she must already have been in without his noticing because the envelope from the Yard was lying beside him on the desk.

"Well?" said Tad, his face still thunderous. "Where do we go from here?"

Grant pushed over the pages of Lloyd's letter for him to read.

"What's all this?"

"Read it."

Tad took the thing up doubtfully, looked for a signature, and then fell on the manuscript. Grant put his thumb in the envelope from Cartwright and broke it open.

When Tad had finished he looked up with a shocked face and stared at Grant. When at last he spoke, what he said was, "I feel dirty all over."

"Yes. It is an evil thing."

"Vanity."

"Yes."

"That's the crash that was in the evening papers last night. The crate in flames on Mont Blanc."

"Yes."

"So he would have got away with it after all."

"No."

"No? He had thought of everything, hadn't he?"

"They never think of everything."

"They?"

"Murderers. Lloyd forgot so obvious a thing as fingerprints."

"You mean he didn't do that job in gloves? I don't believe it!"

"Of course he did it in gloves. Nothing he touched in the compartment would have any print of his. What he forgot was that there was something in the compartment that he had handled before."

"What was that?"

"Charles Martin's papers, the Testament, and the French novel." Grant flipped them with his finger-tip where they lay on the desk. "They are covered with Lloyd's prints. They never think of everything."

# 15

"YOU LOOK LIKE a bridegroom," Sergeant Williams said in great satisfaction, pump-handling Grant on Monday morning.

"Well, I'd better go and have rice thrown at me, I suppose. How is the old man's rheumatism this morning?"

"Oh, fairly good, I think."

"What is he smoking? A pipe? Or cigarettes?"

"Oh, a pipe."

"Then I'd better go in while the barometer is still high."

In the passage he encountered Ted Hanna.

"How did you run into Archie Brown?" Hanna asked, when he had greeted him.

"He's writing a Gaelic epic in the hotel at the place where I was staying. And his 'ravens,' by the way, are foreign fishing-boats."

"Yes?" said Hanna, stiffening into interest. "How do you know?"

"They got together at a party. It was the old 'have-a-cigarette-no-no-keep-the-packet' routine."

"Sure it *wasn't* cigarettes?"

"Quite sure. I picked his pocket in the course of one Grand Chain and unpicked it next time round."

"Don't tell me you've been *country dancing!*"

"You'd be surprised at the things that I've been doing. I'm a little surprised myself."

"Your holiday seems to have done you good," Hanna said. "I've never seen you so on top of the world. You're positively purring."

"As they say in the far North, I wouldn't call the King my cousin," Grant said, and meant it.

He was happy not because of the report that he was going to give Bryce, not even because he was his own man again; he was happy because of something young Cullen had said to him at the airport that morning.

"Mr. Grant," Tad had said, standing very straight and solemn and making a formal little speech of leave-taking like a well-brought-up boy, "I want you to know that I'll never forget what you've done for me and Bill. You couldn't bring Bill back to me, but you've done something much more wonderful: you've made him immortal."

And indeed that was just what he had done. As long as books were written and history read, Bill Kenrick would live; and it was he, Alan Grant, who had done that. They had buried Bill Kenrick six feet deep in oblivion, but he, Alan Grant, had dug him up again and set him in his rightful place as the discoverer of Wabar.

He had paid back the debt he owed that dead boy in B Seven.

Bryce greeted him amiably, and said that he was looking well (which didn't count, because he had said that at their last interview) and suggested that he might go down to Hampshire in answer to an appeal from the Hampshire police which had just come in.

"Well, if it's all the same to you, sir, I'd like to get the Kenrick murder off my chest first."

"The what?"

"This is my written report on it," Grant said, laying in front of Bryce the neat bundle of quarto pages that was the product of his pleasant Sunday at home.

As he laid the thing down he remembered in a vague, surprised way that what he had planned to lay in front of Bryce was his resignation.

What odd notions occurred to one on holiday.

He was going to resign, and be a sheep farmer or something, and get married.

What an extraordinary idea. What a most extraordinary idea.

# A
# Shilling
# for
# Candles

# 1

IT WAS A LITTLE after seven on a summer morning, and William Potticary was taking his accustomed way over the short down grass of the cliff-top. Beyond his elbow, two hundred feet below, lay the Channel, very still and shining, like a milky opal. All roundabout him hung the bright air, empty as yet of larks. In all the sunlit world no sound except for the screaming of some sea-gulls on the distant beach; no human activity except for the small lonely figure of Potticary himself, square and dark and uncompromising. A million dewdrops sparkling on the virgin grass suggested a world new-come from its Creator's hand. Not to Potticary, of course. What the dew suggested to Potticary was that the ground fog of the early hours had not begun to disperse until well after sunrise. His subconscious noted the fact and tucked it away, while his conscious mind debated whether, having raised an appetite for breakfast, he should turn at the Gap and go back to the Coastguard Station, or whether, in view of the fineness of the morning, he should walk into Westover for the morning paper, and so hear about the latest murder two hours earlier than he would otherwise. Of course, what with wireless, the edge was off the morning paper, as you might say. But it was an objective. War or peace, a man had to have an objective. You couldn't go into Westover just to look at the front. And going back to breakfast with the paper under your arm made you feel fine, somehow. Yes, perhaps he would walk into the town.

The pace of his black, square-toed boots quickened slightly, their shining surface winking in the sunlight. Proper service, these boots were. One might have thought that Potticary, having spent his best years in brushing his boots to order, would have asserted his individuality, or expressed his personality, or otherwise shaken the dust of a meaningless discipline off his feet by leaving the dust on his boots. But no, Potticary, poor fool, brushed his boots for love of it. He probably had a slave mentality, but had never read enough for it to worry him. As for expressing one's personality, if you described the symptoms to him he would, of course, recognise them. But not by name. In the Service they call that "contrariness."

A sea-gull flashed suddenly above the cliff-top, and dropped screaming from sight to join its wheeling comrades below. A dreadful row these gulls were making. Potticary moved over to the cliff edge to see what jetsam the tide, now beginning to ebb, had left for them to quarrel over.

The white line of the gently creaming surf was broken by a patch of verdigris green. A bit of cloth. Baize, or something. Funny it should stay so bright a colour after being in the water so—

Potticary's blue eyes widened suddenly, his body becoming strangely still. Then the square black boots began to run. *Thud, thud, thud,* on the thick turf, like a heart beating. The Gap was two hundred yards away, but Potticary's time would not have disgraced a track performer. He clattered down the rough steps hewn in the chalk of the Gap, gasping; indignation welling through his excitement. That was what came of going into cold water before breakfast! Lunacy, so help him. Spoiling other people's breakfasts, too. Schaefer's best, except where ribs broken. Not likely to be ribs broken. Perhaps only a faint after all. Assure the patient in a loud voice that he is safe. Her arms and legs were as brown as the sand. That was why he had thought the green thing a piece of cloth. Lunacy, so help him. Who wanted cold water in the dawn unless they had to swim for it? He'd had to swim for it in his time. In that Red Sea port. Taking in a landing party to help the Arabs. Though why anyone wanted to help the lousy bastards— That was the time to swim. When you had to. Orange juice and thin toast, too. No stamina. Lunacy, so help him.

It was difficult going on the beach. The large white pebbles slid maliciously under his feet, and the rare patches of sand, being about tide level, were soft and yielding. But presently he was within the cloud of gulls, enveloped by their beating wings and their wild crying.

There was no need for Schaefer's, nor for any other method. He saw that at a glance. The girl was past all help. And Potticary, who had picked bodies unemotionally from the Red Sea surf, was strangely moved. It was all wrong that someone so young should be lying there when all the world was waking up to a brilliant day; when so much of life lay in front of her. A pretty girl, too, she must have been. Her hair had a dyed look, but the rest of her was all right.

A wave washed over her feet and sucked itself away, derisively, through the scarlet-tipped toes. Potticary, although the tide in another minute would be yards away, pulled the inanimate heap a little higher up the beach, beyond reach of the sea's impudence.

Then his mind turned to telephones. He looked around for some garment which the girl might have left behind when she went in to swim. But there seemed to be nothing. Perhaps she had left whatever she was wearing below high-water level and the tide had taken it. Or perhaps it wasn't here that she had gone into the water. Anyhow, there was nothing now with which to cover her body, and Potticary turned away and began his hurried plodding along the beach again, and so back to the Coastguard Station and the nearest telephone.

"Body on the beach," he said to Bill Gunter as he took the receiver from the hook and called the police.

Bill clicked his tongue against his front teeth, and jerked his head back. A gesture which expressed with eloquence and economy the tiresomeness of circumstances, the unreasonableness of human beings who get themselves drowned, and his own satisfaction in expecting the worst of life and being right. "If they want to commit suicide," he said in his subterranean voice, "why do they have to pick on us? Isn't there the whole of the south coast?"

"Not a suicide," Potticary gasped in the intervals of hulloing.

Bill took no notice of him. "Just because the fare to the south coast is more than to here! You'd think when a fellow was tired of life he'd stop being mean about the fare and bump himself off in style. But no! They take the cheapest ticket they can get and strew themselves over our doorstep!"

"Beachy Head get a lot," gasped the fair-minded Potticary. "Not a suicide, anyhow."

"Course it's a suicide. What do we have cliffs for? Bulwark of England? No. Just as a convenience to suicides. That makes four this year. And there'll be more when they get their income tax demands."

He paused, his ear caught by what Potticary was saying.

"—a girl. Well, a woman. In a bright green bathing-dress." (Potticary belonged to a generation which did not know swim-suits.) "Just south of the Gap. 'Bout a hundred yards. No, no one there. I had to come away to telephone. But I'm going back right away. Yes, I'll meet you there. Oh, hullo, Sergeant, is that you? Yes, not the best beginning of a day, but we're getting used to it. Oh, no, just a bathing fatality. Ambulance? Oh, yes, you can bring it practically to the Gap. The track goes off the main Westover road just past the third milestone, and finishes in those trees just inland from the Gap. All right, I'll be seeing you."

"How can you tell it's just a bathing fatality?" Bill said.

"She had a bathing-dress on, didn't you hear?"

"Nothing to hinder her putting on a bathing-dress to throw herself into the water. Make it look like accident."

"You can't throw yourself into the water this time of year. You land on the beach. And there isn't any doubt what you've done."

"Might have walked into the water till she drowned," said Bill, who was a last-ditcher by nature.

"Ye'? Might have died of an overdose of bull's-eyes," said Potticary, who approved of last-ditchery in Arabia but found it boring to live with.

# 2

THEY STOOD ROUND the body in a solemn little group: Potticary, Bill, the sergeant, a constable, and the two ambulance men. The younger ambulance man was worried about his stomach, and the possibility of its disgracing him, but the others had nothing but business in their minds.

"Know her?" the sergeant asked.

"No," said Potticary. "Never seen her before."

None of them had seen her before.

"Can't be from Westover. No one would come out from town with a perfectly good beach at their doors. Must have come from inland somewhere."

"Maybe she went into the water at Westover and was washed up here," the constable suggested.

"Not time for that," Potticary objected. "She hadn't been that long in the water. Must have been drowned hereabouts."

"Then how did she get here?" the sergeant asked.

"By car, of course," Bill said.

"And where is the car now?"

"Where everyone leaves their car: where the track ends at the trees."

"Yes?" said the sergeant. "Well, there's no car there."

The ambulance men agreed with him. They had come up that way with the police—the ambulance was waiting there now—but there was no sign of any other car.

"That's funny," Potticary said. "There's nowhere near enough to be inside walking distance. Not at this time in the morning."

"Shouldn't think she'd walk anyhow," the older ambulance man observed. "Expensive," he added, as they seemed to question him.

They considered the body for a moment in silence. Yes, the ambulance man was right; it was a body expensively cared for.

"And where are her clothes, anyhow?" The sergeant was worried.

Potticary explained his theory about the clothes; that she had left them below high-water mark and that they were now somewhere at sea.

"Yes, that's possible," said the sergeant. "But how did she get here?"

"Funny she should be bathing alone, isn't it?" ventured the young ambulance man, trying out his stomach.

"Nothing's funny, nowadays," Bill rumbled. "It's a wonder she wasn't playing jumping off the cliff with a glider. Swimming on an empty stomach, all alone, is just too ordinary. The young fools make me tired."

"Is that a bracelet round her ankle, or what?" the constable asked.

Yes, it was a bracelet. A chain of platinum links. Curious links, they were. Each one shaped like a C.

"Well," the sergeant straightened himself, "I suppose there's nothing to be done but to remove the body to the mortuary, and then find out who she is. Judging by appearances that shouldn't be difficult. Nothing 'lost, stolen or strayed' about that one."

"No," agreed the ambulance man. "The butler is probably telephoning the station now in great agitation."

"Yes." The sergeant was thoughtful. "I still wonder how she came here, and what—"

His eyes had lifted to the cliff face, and he paused.

"So! We have company!" he said.

They turned to see a man's figure on the cliff-top at the Gap. He was standing in an attitude of intense eagerness, watching them. As they turned towards him he did a swift right-about and disappeared.

"A bit early for strollers," the sergeant said. "And what's he running away for? We'd better have a talk with him."

But before he and the constable had moved more than a pace or two it became evident that the man, far from running away, had been merely making for the entrance to the Gap. His thin dark figure shot now from the mouth of the Gap and came towards them at a shambling run, slipping and stumbling, and giving the little group watching his advent an impression of craziness. They could hear the breath panting through his open mouth as he drew near, although the distance from the Gap was not long and he was young.

He stumbled into their compact circle without looking at them, pushing aside the two policemen who had unconsciously interposed their bulk between him and the body.

"Oh, yes, it is! Oh, it is, it is!" he cried, and without warning sat down and burst into loud tears.

Six flabbergasted men watched him in silence for a moment. Then the sergeant patted him kindly on the back and said, idiotically, "It's all right, son!"

But the young man only rocked himself to and fro and wept the more.

"Come on, come on," rallied the constable, coaxing. (Really, a dreadful exhibition on a nice bright morning.) "That won't do anyone any good, you know. Best pull yourself together—sir," he added, noting the quality of the handkerchief which the young man had produced.

"A relation of yours?" the sergeant enquired, his voice suitably modulated from its former businesslike pitch.

The young man shook his head.

"Oh, just a friend?"

"She was so good to me, so good!"

"Well, at least you'll be able to help us. We were beginning to wonder about her. You can tell us who she is."

"She's my—hostess."

"Yes, but I meant, what is her name?"

"I don't know."

"You—don't—know! Look here, sir, pull yourself together. You're the only one that can help us. You must know the name of the lady you were staying with."

"No, no; I don't."

"What did you call her, then?"

"Chris."

"Chris, what?"

"Just Chris."

"And what did she call you?"

"Robin."

"Is that your name?"

"Yes, my name's Robert Stannaway. No, Tisdall. It used to be Stannaway," he added, catching the sergeant's eye and feeling apparently that explanation was needed.

What the sergeant's eye said was, "God give me patience!" What his tongue said was, "It all sounds a bit strange to me, Mr.—er—"

"Tisdall."

"Tisdall. Can you tell me how the lady got here this morning?"

"Oh, yes. By car."

"By car, eh? Know what became of the car?"

"Yes. I stole it."

"You what?"

"I stole it. I've just brought it back. It was a swinish thing to do. I felt a cad so I came back. When I found she wasn't anywhere on the road, I thought I'd find her stamping about here. Then I saw you all standing round something—oh dear, oh dear!" He began to rock himself again.

"Where were you staying with this lady?" asked the sergeant, in exceedingly businesslike tones. "In Westover?"

"Oh, no. She has—had, I mean—oh dear!—a cottage. Briars, it's called. Just outside Medley."

" 'Bout a mile and a half inland," supplemented Potticary, as the sergeant, who was not a native, looked a question.

"Were you alone, or is there a staff there?"

"There's just a woman from the village—Mrs. Pitts—who comes in and cooks."

"I see."

There was a slight pause.

"All right, boys." The sergeant nodded to the ambulance men, and they bent to their work with the stretcher. The young man drew in his breath sharply and once more covered his face with his hands.

"To the mortuary, Sergeant?"

"Yes."

The man's hands came away from his face abruptly.

"Oh, no! Surely not! She had a home. Don't they take people home?"

"We can't take the body of an unknown woman to an uninhabited bungalow."

"It isn't a bungalow," the man automatically corrected. "No. No, I suppose not. But it seems dreadful—the mortuary. Oh, God in Heaven above!" he burst out, "why did this have to happen!"

"Davis," the sergeant said to the constable, "you go back with the others and report. I'm going over to—what is it?—Briars? with Mr. Tisdall."

The two ambulance men crunched their heavy way over the pebbles, followed by Potticary and Bill. The noise of their progress had become distant before the sergeant spoke again.

"I suppose it didn't occur to you to go swimming with your hostess?"

A spasm of something like embarrassment ran across Tisdall's face. He hesitated.

"No. I—not much in my line, I'm afraid: swimming before breakfast. I—I've always been a rabbit at games and things like that."

The sergeant nodded, noncommittal. "When did she leave for a swim?"

"I don't know. She told me last night that she was going to the Gap for a swim if she woke early. I woke early myself, but she was gone."

"I see. Well, Mr. Tisdall, if you've recovered I think we'll be getting along."

"Yes. Yes, certainly. I'm all right." He got to his feet and together and in silence they traversed the beach, climbed the steps at the Gap, and came on the car where Tisdall said he had left it: in the shade of the trees where the track ended. It was a beautiful car, if a little too opulent. A cream-coloured two-seater with a space between the seats and the hood for parcels, or, at a pinch, for an extra passenger. From this space, the sergeant, exploring, produced a woman's coat and a pair of the sheepskin boots popular with women at winter race-meetings.

"That's what she wore to go down to the beach. Just the coat and boots over her bathing things. There's a towel, too."

There was. The sergeant produced it: a brilliant object in green and orange.

"Funny she didn't take it to the beach with her," he said.

"She liked to dry herself in the sun usually."

"You seem to know a lot about the habits of a lady whose name you didn't know." The sergeant inserted himself into the second seat. "How long have you been living with her?"

"Staying with her," amended Tisdall, his voice for the first time showing an edge. "Get this straight, Sergeant, and it may save you a lot of bother: Chris was my hostess. Not anything else. We stayed in her cottage unchaperoned, but a regiment of servants couldn't have made our relations more correct. Does that strike you as so very peculiar?"

"Very," said the sergeant frankly. "What are these doing here?"

He was peering into a paper bag which held two rather jaded buns.

"Oh, I took these along for her to eat. They were all I could find. We always had a bun when we came out of the water when we were kids. I thought maybe she'd be glad of something."

The car was slipping down the steep track to the main Westover-Stonegate road. They crossed the high-road and entered a deep lane on the other side. A signpost said "Medley 1, Liddlestone 3."

"So you had no intention of stealing the car when you set off to follow her to the beach?"

"Certainly not!" Tisdall said, as indignantly as if it made a difference. "It didn't even cross my mind till I came up the hill and saw the car waiting there. Even now I can't believe I really did it. I've been a fool, but I've never done anything like that before."

"Was she in the sea then?"

"I don't know. I didn't go to look. If I had seen her even in the distance I couldn't have done it. I just slung the buns in and beat it. When I came to I was half-way to Canterbury. I just turned her round without stopping, and came straight back."

The sergeant made no comment.

"You still haven't told me how long you've been staying at the cottage?"

"Since Saturday midnight."

It was now Thursday.

"And you still ask me to believe that you don't know your hostess's last name?"

"No. It's a bit queer, I know. I thought so, myself, at first. I had a conventional upbringing. But she made it seem natural. After the first day we simply accepted each other. It was as if I had known her for years." As the sergeant said nothing, but sat radiating doubt as a stove radiates heat, he added with a hint of temper, "Why shouldn't I tell you her name if I knew it!"

"How should I know?" said the sergeant, unhelpfully. He considered out of the corner of his eye the young man's pale, if composed, face. He seemed to have recovered remarkably quickly from his exhibition of nerves and grief. Light-weights, these moderns. No real emotion about anything. Just hysteria. What they called love was just a barn-yard exercise; they thought anything else "sentimental." No discipline. No putting up with things. Every time something got difficult, they ran away. Not slapped enough in their youth. All this modern idea about giving children their own way. Look what it led to. Howling on the beach one minute and as cool as a cucumber the next.

And then the sergeant noticed the trembling of the too fine hands on the wheel. No, whatever else Robert Tisdall was he wasn't cool.

"This is the place?" the sergeant asked, as they slowed down by a hedged garden.

"This is the place."

It was a half-timbered cottage of about five rooms; shut in from the road by a seven-foot hedge of briar and honeysuckle, and dripping with roses. A godsend for Americans, week-enders, and photographers. The little windows yawned in the quiet, and the bright blue door stood hospitably open, disclosing in the shadow the gleam of a brass warming pan on the wall. The cottage had been "discovered."

As they walked up the brick path, a thin small woman appeared on the doorstep, brilliant in a white apron; her scanty hair drawn to a knob at the back of her head, and a round bird's-nest affair of black satin set insecurely at the very top of her arched, shining poll.

Tisdall lagged as he caught sight of her, so that the sergeant's large official elevation should announce trouble to her with the clarity of a sandwich board.

But Mrs. Pitts was a policeman's widow, and no apprehension showed on her tight little face. Buttons coming up the path meant for her a meal in demand; her mind acted accordingly.

"I've been making some griddle cakes for breakfast. It's going to be hot later on. Best to let the stove out. Tell Miss Robinson when she comes in, will you, sir?" Then, realising that buttons were a badge of office, "Don't tell me you've been driving without a license, sir!"

"Miss—Robinson, is it? has met with an accident," the sergeant said.

"The car! Oh, dear! She was always that reckless with it. Is she bad?"

"It wasn't the car. An accident in the water."

"Oh," she said slowly. "*That* bad!"

"How do you mean: that bad?"

"Accidents in the water only mean one thing."

"Yes," agreed the sergeant.

"Well, well," she said, sadly contemplative. Then, her manner changing abruptly, "And where were *you?*" she snapped, eyeing the drooping Tisdall as she eyed Saturday-night fish on a Westover fishmonger's slab. Her superficial deference to "gentry" had vanished in the presence of catastrophe. Tisdall appeared as the "bundle of uselessness" she had privately considered him.

The sergeant was interested but snubbing. "The gentleman wasn't there."

"He ought to have been there. He left just after her."

"How do you know that?"

"I saw him. I live in the cottage down the road."

"Do you know Miss Robinson's other address? I take it for granted this isn't her permanent home."

"No, of course it isn't. She only has this place for a month. It belongs to Owen Hughes." She paused, impressively, to let the importance of the name sink in. "But he's doing a film in Hollywood. About a Spanish count, it was to be, so he told me. He said he's done Italian counts and French counts and he thought it would be a new experience for him to be a Spanish count. Very nice, Mr. Hughes is. Not a bit spoilt in spite of all the fuss they make of him. You wouldn't believe it, but a girl came to me once and offered me five pounds if I'd give her the sheets he had slept in. What I gave her was a piece of my mind. But she wasn't a bit ashamed. Offered me twenty-five shillings for a pillow-slip. I don't know what the world is coming to, that I don't, what with—"

"What other address had Miss Robinson?"

"I don't know any of her addresses but this one."

"Didn't she write and tell you when she was coming?"

"Write! No! She sent telegrams. I suppose she could write, but I'll take my alfred davy she never did. About six telegrams a day used to go to the post office in Liddlestone. My Albert used to take them, mostly; between school. Some of them used three or four forms, they were that long."

"Do you know any of the people she had down here, then?"

"She didn't have any folks here. 'Cept Mr. Stannaway, that is."

"No one!"

"Not a one. Once—it was when I was showing her the trick of flushing the W.C.; you have to pull hard and then let go smart-like—once she said: 'Do you ever, Mrs. Pitts,' she said, 'get sick of the sight of people's faces?' I said I got a bit tired of some. She said: 'Not some, Mrs. Pitts. All of them. Just sick of people.' I said when I felt like that I took a dose of castor oil. She laughed and said it wasn't a bad idea. Only everyone should have one and what a good new world it would be in two days. 'Mussolini never thought of that one,' she said."

"Was it London she came from?"

"Yes. She went up just once or twice in the three weeks she's been here. Last time was last week-end, when she brought Mr. Stannaway back." Again her glance dismissed Tisdall as something less than human. "Doesn't *he* know her address?" she asked.

"No one does," the sergeant said. "I'll look through her papers and see what I can find."

Mrs. Pitts led the way into the living-room; cool, low-beamed, and smelling of sweetpeas.

"What have you done with her—with the body, I mean?" she asked.

"At the mortuary."

This seemed to bring home tragedy for the first time.

"Oh, deary me." She moved the end of her apron over a polished table, slowly. "And me making griddle cakes."

This was not a lament for wasted griddle cakes, but her salute to the strangeness of life.

"I expect you'll need breakfast," she said to Tisdall, softened by her unconscious recognition of the fact that the best are but puppets.

But Tisdall wanted no breakfast. He shook his head and turned away to the window, while the sergeant searched in the desk.

"I wouldn't mind one of those griddle cakes," the sergeant said, turning over papers.

"You won't get better in Kent, though it's me that's saying it. And perhaps Mr. Stannaway will swallow some tea."

She went away to the kitchen.

"So you didn't know her name was Robinson?" said the sergeant, glancing up.

"Mrs. Pitts always addressed her as 'miss.' And anyhow, did she look as if her name was Robinson?"

The sergeant, too, did not believe for a moment that her name was Robinson, so he let the subject drop.

Presently Tisdall said: "If you don't need me, I think I'll go into the garden. It—it's stuffy in here."

"All right. You won't forget I need the car to get back to Westover."

"I've told you. It was a sudden impulse. Anyhow, I couldn't very well steal it now and hope to get away with it."

Not so dumb, decided the sergeant. Quite a bit of temper, too. Not just a nonentity, by any means.

The desk was littered with magazines, newspapers, half finished cartons of cigarettes, bits of a jigsaw puzzle, a nail file and polish, patterns of silk, and a dozen more odds and ends; everything, in fact, except note paper. The only documents were bills from the local tradesmen, most of them receipted. If the woman had been untidy and unmethodical, she had at least had a streak of caution. The receipts might be crumpled and difficult to find if wanted, but they had never been thrown away.

The sergeant, soothed by the quiet of the early morning, the cheerful sounds of Mrs. Pitts making tea in the kitchen, and the prospect of griddle cakes to come, began as he worked at the desk to indulge in his one vice. He whistled. Very low and round and sweet, the sergeant's whistling was, but, still—whistling. "Sing to me sometimes" he warbled, not forgetting the grace notes, and his subconscious derived great satisfaction from the performance. His wife had once shown him a bit in the *Mail* that said that whistling was the sign of an empty mind. But it hadn't cured him.

And then, abruptly, the even tenor of the moment was shattered. Without warning there came a mock tattoo on the half open sitting-room door—*tum-te-ta-tum-tumta-TA!* A man's voice said, "So this is where you're hiding out!" The door was flung wide with a flourish and in the opening stood a short dark stranger.

"*We-e-ell,*" he said, making several syllables of it. He stood staring at the sergeant, amused and smiling broadly. "I thought you were Chris! What is the Force doing here? Been a burglary?"

"No, no burglary." The sergeant was trying to collect his thoughts.

"Don't tell me Chris has been throwing a wild party! I thought she gave that up years ago. They don't go with all those high-brow rôles."

"No, as a matter of fact, there's—"

"Where is she, anyway?" He raised his voice in a cheerful shout directed at the upper storey. "Yo-hoo! Chris. Come on down, you old so-and-so! Hiding out on me!" To the sergeant: "Gave us all the slip for nearly three weeks now. Too much Kleig, I guess. Gives them all the jitters sooner or later. But then, the last one was such a success they naturally want to cash in on it." He hummed a bar of "Sing to me sometimes," with mock solemnity. "That's why I thought you were Chris: you were whistling her song. Whistling darned good, too."

"Her—her song?" Presently, the sergeant hoped, a gleam of light would be vouchsafed him.

"Yes, her song. Who else's? You didn't think it was mine, my dear good chap, did you? Not on your life. I wrote the thing, sure. But that doesn't count. It's her song. And perhaps she didn't put it across! Eh? Wasn't that a performance?"

"I couldn't really say." If the man would stop talking, he might sort things out.

"Perhaps you haven't seen *Bars of Iron* yet?"

"No, I can't say I have."

"That's the worst of wireless and gramophone records and what not: they take all the pep out of a film. Probably by the time you hear Chris sing that song you'll be so sick of the sound of it that you'll retch at the *ad lib*. It's not fair to a film. All right for songwriters and that sort of cattle, but rough on a film, very rough. There ought to be some sort of agreement. Hey, Chris! Isn't she here, after all my trouble in catching up on her?" His face drooped like a disappointed baby's. "Having her walk in and find me isn't half such a good one as walking in on her. Do you think—"

"Just a minute, Mr.—er—I don't know your name."

"I'm Jay Harmer. Jason on the birth certificate. I wrote 'If it can't be in June.' You probably whistle that as—"

"Mr. Harmer. Do I understand that the lady who is—was—staying here is a film actress?"

"Is she a film actress!" Slow amazement deprived Mr. Harmer for once of speech. Then it began to dawn on him that he must have made a mistake. "Say, Chris *is* staying here, isn't she?"

"The lady's name is Chris, yes. But—well, perhaps you'll be able to help us. There's been some trouble—very unfortunate—and apparently she said her name was Robinson."

The man laughed in rich amusement. "Robinson! That's a good one. I always said she had no imagination. Couldn't write a gag. Did you believe she was a Robinson?"

"Well, no; it seemed unlikely."

"What did I tell you! Well, just to pay her out for treating me like bits on the cutting-room floor, I'm going to split on her. She'll probably put me in the ice-box for twenty-four hours, but it'll be worth it. I'm no gentleman, anyhow, so I won't damage myself in the telling. The lady's name, Sergeant, is Christine Clay."

"Christine Clay!" said the sergeant. His jaw slackened and dropped, quite beyond his control.

"Christine Clay!" breathed Mrs. Pitts, standing in the doorway, a forgotten tray of griddle cakes in her hands.

# 3

"Christine Clay! Christine Clay!" yelled the midday posters.

"Christine Clay!" screamed the headlines.

"Christine Clay!" chattered the wireless.

"Christine Clay!" said neighbour to neighbour.

All over the world people paused to speak the words. Christine Clay was drowned! And in all civilisation only one person said, "Who is Christine Clay?" —a bright young man at a Bloomsbury party. And he was merely being "bright."

All over the world things happened because one woman had lost her life. In California a man telephoned a summons to a girl in Greenwich Village. A Texas airplane pilot did an extra night flight carrying Clay films for rush showing. A New York firm cancelled an order. An Italian nobleman went bankrupt: he had hoped to sell her his yacht. A man in Philadelphia ate his first square meal in months, thanks to an "I knew her when" story. A woman in Le Touquet sang because now her chance had come. And in an English cathedral town a man thanked God on his knees.

The Press, becalmed in the doldrums of the silly season, leaped to movement at so unhoped-for a wind. The *Clarion* recalled Bart Bartholomew, their "descriptive" man, from a beauty contest in Brighton (much to Bart's thankfulness—he came back loudly wondering how butchers ate meat), and "Jammy" Hopkins, their "crime and passion" star, from a very dull and low-class poker killing in Bradford. (So far had the *Clarion* sunk.) News photographers deserted motor race tracks, reviews, society weddings, cricket, and the man who was going to Mars in a balloon, and swarmed like beetles over the cottage in Kent, the maisonette in South Street, and the furnished manor in Hampshire. That, having rented so charming a country retreat as this last, Christine Clay had yet run away to an unknown and inconvenient cottage without the knowledge of her friends made a very pleasant appendage to the main sensation of her death. Photographs of the manor (garden front, because of the yews) appeared labelled, "The place Christine Clay owned" (she had only rented it for the season, but there was no emotion in renting a place); and next these impressive pictures were placed photographs of the rose-embowered home of the people, with the caption, "The place she preferred."

Her press agent shed tears over that. Something like that *would* break when it was too late.

It might have been observed by any student of nature not too actively engaged in the consequences of it that Christine Clay's death, while it gave rise to pity, dismay, horror, regret, and half a dozen other emotions in varying degrees, yet seemed to move no one to grief. The only outburst of real feeling had been that hysterical crisis of Robert Tisdall's over her body. And who should say how much of that was self-pity? Christine was too international a figure to belong to anything so small as a "set." But among her immediate acquaintances dismay was the most marked reaction of the dreadful news. And not always that. Coyne, who was due to direct her third and final picture in England, might be at the point of despair, but Lejeune (late Tomkins), who had been engaged to play opposite her, was greatly relieved; a picture with Clay might be a feather in your cap but it was a jinx in your box-office. The Duchess of Trent, who had arranged a Clay luncheon which was to rehabilitate her as a hostess in the eyes of London, might be gnashing her teeth, but Lydia Keats was openly jubilant. She had prophesied the death, and even for a successful society seer that was a good guess. "Darling, how wonderful of you!" fluttered her friends. "Darling, how wonderful of you!" On and on. Until Lydia so lost her head with delight that she spent all her days going from one gathering to another so that she might make that delicious entrance all over again, hear them say: "Here's Lydia! Darling, how—" and bask in the radiance of their wonder. No, as far as anyone could see, no hearts were breaking because Christine Clay was no more. The world dusted off its blacks and hoped for invitations to the funeral.

# 4

BUT FIRST THERE was the inquest. And it was at the inquest that the first faint stirring of a much greater sensation began to appear. It was Jammy Hopkins who noted the quiver on the smooth surface. He had earned his nickname because of his glad cry of "Jam! Jam!" when a good story broke, and his philosophical reflection when times were thin that "all was jam that came to the rollers." Hopkins had an excellent nose for jam, and so it was that he stopped suddenly in the middle of analysing for Bartholomew's benefit the various sensation seekers crowding the little Kentish village hall. Stopped dead and stared. Because, between the fly-away hats of two bright sensationalists, he could see a man's calm face which was much more sensational than anything in that building.

"Seen something?" Bart asked.

"Have I seen something!" Hopkins slid from the end of the form, just as the coroner sat down and tapped for silence. "Keep my place," he whispered, and disappeared out of the building. He entered it again at the back door, expertly pushed his way to the place he wanted, and sat down. The man turned his head to view this gate-crasher.

"Morning, Inspector," said Hopkins.

The Inspector looked his disgust.

"I wouldn't do it if I didn't need the money," Hopkins said, *vox humana*. The coroner tapped again for silence, but the Inspector's face relaxed.

Presently, under cover of the bustle of Potticary's arrival to give evidence, Hopkins said, "What is Scotland Yard doing here, Inspector?"

"Looking on."

"I see. Just studying inquests as an institution. Crime slack these days?" As the Inspector showed no sign of being drawn: "Oh, have a heart, Inspector. What's in the wind? Is there something phoney about the death? Suspicions, eh? If you don't want to talk for publication I'm the original locked casket."

"You're the original camel-fly."

"Oh, well, look at the hides I have to get through!" This produced a grin and nothing else. "Look here. Just tell me one thing, Inspector. Is this inquest going to be adjourned?"

"I shouldn't be surprised."

"Thank you. That tells me everything," Hopkins said, half sarcastic, half serious, as he made his way out again. He prised Mrs. Pitts's Albert away from the wall where he clung limpet-like by the window, persuaded him that two shillings was better than a partial view of dull proceedings, and sent him to Liddlestone with a telegram which set the *Clarion* office buzzing. Then he went back to Bart.

"Something wrong," he said out of the corner of his mouth in answer to Bart's eyebrows. "The Yard's here. That's Grant, behind the scarlet hat. Inquest going to be adjourned. Spot the murderer!"

"Not here," Bart said, having considered the gathering.

"No," agreed Jammy. "Who's the chap in the flannel bags?"

"Boy friend."

"Thought the boy friend was Jay Harmer."

"Was. This one newer."

" 'Love nest killing'?"

"Wouldn't mind betting."

"Supposed to be cold, I thought?"

"Yes. So they say. Fooled them, seemingly. Good enough reason for murder, I should think."

The evidence was of the most formal kind—the finding and identification of the body—and as soon as that had been offered the coroner brought the proceedings to an end, and fixed no date for resumption.

Hopkins had decided that, the Clay death being apparently no accident, and Scotland Yard not being able so far to make any arrest, the person to cultivate was undoubtedly the man in the flannel bags. Tisdall, his name was. Bart said that every newspaper man in England had tried to interview him the previous day (Hopkins being then en route from the poker murder) but that he had been exceptionally tough. Called them ghouls, and vultures, and rats, and other things less easy of specification, and had altogether seemed unaware of the standing of the Press. No one was rude to the Press any more—not with impunity, that was.

But Hopkins had great faith in his power to seduce the human mind.

"Your name Tisdall, by any chance?" he asked casually, "finding" himself alongside the young man in the crowded procession to the door.

The man's face hardened into instant enmity.

"Yes, it is," he said aggressively.

"Not old Tom Tisdall's nephew?"

The face cleared swiftly.

"Yes. Did you know Uncle Tom?"

"A little," admitted Hopkins, no whit dismayed to find that there really was a Tom Tisdall.

"You seem to know about my giving up the Stannaway?"

"Yes, someone told me," Hopkins said, wondering if the Stannaway was a house, or what? "What are you doing now?"

By the time they had reached the door, Hopkins had established himself. "Can I give you a lift somewhere? Come and have lunch with me?"

A pip! In half an hour he'd have a front-page story. And this was the baby they said was difficult! No, there was no doubt of it: he, James Brooke Hopkins, was the greatest newspaper man in the business.

"Sorry, Mr. Hopkins," said Grant's pleasant voice at his shoulder. "I don't want to spoil your party, but Mr. Tisdall has an appointment with me." And, since Tisdall betrayed his astonishment and Hopkins his instant putting two and two together, he added, "We're hoping he can help us."

"I don't understand," Tisdall was beginning. And Hopkins, seeing that Tisdall was unaware of Grant's identity, rushed in with glad maliciousness.

"That is Scotland Yard," he said. "Inspector Grant. Never had an unsolved crime to his name."

"I hope you write my obituary," Grant said.

"I hope I do!" the journalist said, with fervour.

And then they noticed Tisdall. His face was like parchment, dry and old and expressionless. Only the pulse beating hard at his temple suggested a living being. Journalist and detective stood looking in mutual astonishment at so unexpected a result of Hopkins's announcement. And then, seeing the man's knees beginning to sag, Grant took him hastily by the arm.

"Here! Come and sit down. My car is just here."

He edged the apparently blind Tisdall through the dawdling, chattering crowd, and pushed him into the rear seat of a dark touring car.

"Westover," he said to the chauffeur, and got in beside Tisdall.

As they went at snail's pace towards the high-road, Grant saw Hopkins still standing where they had left him. That Jammy Hopkins should stay without moving for more than three consecutive minutes argued that he was being given furiously to think. From now on—the Inspector sighed—the camel-fly would be a bloodhound.

And the Inspector, too, had food for his wits. He had been called in the previous night by a worried County Constabulary who had no desire to make themselves ridiculous by making mountains out of molehills, but who found themselves unable to explain away satisfactorily one very small, very puzzling obstacle to their path. They had all viewed the obstacle, from the Chief Constable down to the sergeant who had taken charge on the beach, had been rude about each other's theories, and had in the end agreed on only one thing: that they wanted to push the responsibility on to someone else's shoulders. It was all very well to hang on to your own crime, and the kudos of a solution, when there *was* a crime. But to decide in cold blood to announce a crime, on the doubtful evidence of that common little object on the table; to risk, not the disgrace of failure, but the much worse slings of ridicule, was something they could not find it in their hearts to do. And so Grant had cancelled his seat at the Criterion and had journeyed down to Westover. He had inspected the stumbling block, listened with patience to their theories and with respect to the police surgeon's story, and had gone to bed in the small hours with a great desire to interview Robert Tisdall. And now here was Tisdall, beside him, still speechless and half fainting because he had been confronted without warning by Scotland Yard. Yes, there was a case; no doubt of it. Well, there couldn't be any questioning with Cork in the driving seat, so until they got back to Westover Tisdall might be left to recover. Grant took a flask from the car pocket and offered it to him. Tisdall took it shakily but made good use of it. Presently he apologised for his weakness.

"I don't know what went wrong. This affair has been an awful shock to me. I haven't been sleeping. Keep going over things in my mind. Or rather, my mind keeps doing it; I can't stop it. And then, at the inquest it seemed—I say, is something not right? I mean, was it not a simple drowning? Why did they postpone the end of the inquest?"

"There are one or two things that the police find puzzling."

"As what, for instance?"

"I think we won't discuss it until we get to Westover."

"Is anything I say to be used in evidence against me?" The smile was wry but the intention was good.

"You took the words out of my mouth," the Inspector said lightly, and silence fell between them.

By the time they reached the Chief Constable's room in the County Police offices, Tisdall was looking normal if a little worn. In fact, so normal did he look that when Grant said, "This is Mr. Tisdall," the Chief Constable, who was a genial soul except when someone jumped in his pocket out hunting, almost shook hands with him, but recollected himself before any harm was done.

"Howdyudo. Harrump!" He cleared his throat to give himself time. Couldn't do that, of course. My goodness, no. Fellow suspected of murder. Didn't look it, no, upon his soul he didn't. But there was no telling these days. The most charming people were—well, things he hadn't known till lately existed. Very sad. But couldn't shake hands, of course. No, definitely not. "Harrump! Fine morning! Bad for racing, of course. Going very hard. But good for the holiday makers. Mustn't be selfish in our pleasures. You a racing man? Going to Goodwood? Oh, well, perhaps— No. Well, I expect you and—and our friend here—" somehow one didn't want to rub in the fact of Grant's inspectorship. Nice-looking chap. Well brought up, and all that —"would like to talk in peace. I'm going to lunch. The Ship," he added, for Grant's benefit, in case the Inspector wanted him. "Not that the food's very good there, but it's a self-respecting house. Not like these Marine things. Like to get steak and potatoes without going through sun lounges for them." And the Chief Constable took himself out.

"A Freedy Lloyd part," Tisdall said.

Grant looked up appreciatively from pulling forward a chair.

"You're a theatre fan."

"I was a fan of most things."

Grant's mind focused on the peculiarity of the phrase. "Why 'was'?" he asked.

"Because I'm broke. You need money to be a fan."

"You won't forget that formula about 'anything you say,' will you?"

"No. Thanks. But it doesn't make any difference. I can only tell you the truth. If you draw wrong deductions from it then that's your fault, not mine."

"So it's I who am on trial. A nice point. I appreciate it. Well, try me out. I want to know how you were living in the same house with a woman whose name you didn't know? You did tell the County Police that, didn't you?"

"Yes. I expect it sounds incredible. Silly, too. But it's quite simple. You see, I was standing on the pavement opposite the Gaiety one night, very late, wondering what to do. I had fivepence in my pocket, and that was fivepence too much, because I had aimed at having nothing at all. And I was wondering whether to have a last go at spending the fivepence (there isn't much one can do with fivepence) or to cheat, and forget about the odd pennies. So—"

"Just a moment. You might explain to a dullard just why these five pennies should have been important."

"They were the end of a fortune, you see. Thirty thousand. I inherited it from my uncle. My mother's brother. My real name is Stannaway, but Uncle Tom asked that I should take his name with the money. I didn't mind. The Tisdalls were a much better lot than the Stannaways, anyhow. Stamina and ballast and all that. If I'd been a Tisdall I wouldn't be broke now, but I'm nearly all Stannaway. I've been the perfect fool, the complete Awful Warning. I was in an architect's office when I inherited the money, living in rooms and just making do; and it went to my head to have what seemed more than I could ever spend. I gave up my job and went to see all the places I'd wanted to see and never hoped to. New York and Hollywood and Budapest and Rome and Capri and God knows where else. I came back to London with about two thousand, meaning to bank it and get a job. It would have been easy enough two years before—I mean, to bank the money. I hadn't anyone to help spend it then. But in those two years I had gathered a lot of friends all over the world, and there were never less than a dozen of them in London at the same time. So I woke up one morning to find that I was down to my last hundred. It was a bit of a shock. Like cold water. I sat down and thought for the first time for two years. I had the choice of two things: sponging— you can live in luxury anywhere in the world's capitals for six months if you're a good sponger: I know; I supported dozens of that sort—and disappearing. Disappearing seemed easier. I could drop out quite easily. People would just say, 'Where's Bobby Tisdall these days?' and they'd just take it for granted that I was in some of the other corners of the world where their sort went, and that they'd run into me one of these days. I was supposed to be suffocatingly rich, you see, and it was easier to drop out and leave them thinking of me like that than to stay and be laughed at when the truth began to dawn on them. I paid my bills, and that left me with fifty-seven pounds. I thought I'd have one last gamble then, and see if I could pick up enough to start me off on the new level. So I had thirty pounds—fifteen each way; that's the bit of Tisdall in me—on Red Rowan in the Eclipse. He finished fifth. Twenty-odd pounds isn't enough to start anything except a barrow. There was nothing for it but tramping. I wasn't much put out at the thought of tramping—it would be a change—but you can't tramp with twenty-seven pounds in the bank, so I decided to blue it all in one grand last night. I promised myself that I'd finish up without a penny in my pocket. Then I'd pawn my evening things for some suitable clothes and hit the road. What I hadn't reckoned with was that you can't pawn things in the west-end on a Saturday midnight. And you can't take to the road in evening things without being conspicuous. So I was standing there, as I said, feeling resentful about these five pennies and wondering what I was to do about my clothes and a place to sleep. I was standing by the traffic lights at the Aldwych, just before you turn round into Lancaster Place, when a car was pulled up by the red lights. Chris was in it, alone—"

"Chris?"

"I didn't know her name, then. She looked at me for a little. The street was very quiet. Just us two. And we were so close that it seemed natural when she smiled and said, 'Take you anywhere, mister?' I said: 'Yes. Land's End.' She said: 'A bit off my route. Chatham, Faversham, Canterbury, and points east?' Well, it was one solution. I couldn't go on standing there, and I couldn't think of a water-tight tale that would get me a bed in a friend's house. Besides, I felt far away from all that crowd already. So I got in without thinking much about it. She was charming to me. I didn't tell her all I'm telling you, but she soon found out I was broke to the wide. I began to explain, but she said: 'All right, I don't want to know. Let's accept each other on face value. You're Robin and I'm Chris.' I'd told her my name was Robert Stannaway, and without knowing it she used my family pet name. The crowd called me Bobby. It was sort of comforting to hear someone call me Robin again."

"Why did you say your name was Stannaway?"

"I don't know. A sort of desire to get away from the fortune side of things. I hadn't been much ornament to the name, anyhow. And in my mind I always thought of myself as Stannaway."

"All right. Go on."

"There isn't much more to tell. She offered me hospitality. Told me she was alone, but that—well, that I'd be just a guest. I said wasn't she taking a chance. She said, 'Yes, but I've taken them all my life and it's worked out pretty well, so far.' It seemed an awkward arrangement to me, but it turned out just the opposite. She was right about it. It made things very easy, just accepting each other. In a way (it was queer, but it was like that) it was as if we had known each other for years. If we had had to start at scratch and work up, it would have taken us weeks to get to the same stage. We liked each other a lot. I don't mean sentimentally, although she was stunning to look at; I mean I thought her grand. I had no clothes for the next morning, but I spent that day in a bathing suit and a dressing-gown that someone had left. And on Monday Mrs. Pitts came in to my room and said, 'Your suit-case, sir,' and dumped a case I'd never seen before in the middle of the floor. It had a complete new outfit in it—tweed coat and flannels, socks, shirts, everything. From a place in Canterbury. The suit-case was old, and had a label with my name on it. She had even remembered my name. Well, I can't describe to you what I felt about these things. You see, it was the first time for years that anyone had *given* me anything. With the crowd it was take, take, all the time. 'Bobby'll pay.' 'Bobby'll lend his car.' They never thought of *me* at all. I don't think they ever stopped to look at me. Anyhow, those clothes sort of broke me up. I'd have died for her. She laughed when she saw me in them— they were reach-me-downs, of course, but they fitted quite well—and said:

'Not exactly Bruton Street, but they'll do. Don't say I can't size a man up.'
So we settled down to having a good time together, just lazing around, reading, talking, swimming, cooking when Mrs. Pitts wasn't there. I put out of
my head what was going to happen after. She had said that in about ten
days she'd have to leave the cottage. I tried to go after the first day, out of
politeness, but she wouldn't let me. And after that I didn't try. That's how
I came to be staying there, and that's how I didn't know her name." He
drew in his breath in a sharp sigh as he sat back. "Now I know how these
psycho-analysts make money. It's a long time since I enjoyed anything like
telling you all about myself."

Grant smiled involuntarily. There was an engaging childlikeness about the
boy.

Then he shook himself mentally, like a dog coming out of water.

Charm. The most insidious weapon in all the human armoury. And here
it was, being exploited under his nose. He considered the good-natured feck-
less face dispassionately. He had known at least one murderer who had had
that type of good looks; blue-eyed, amiable, harmless; and he had buried his
dismembered fiancée in an ash-pit. Tisdall's eyes were of that particular warm
opaque blue which Grant had noted so often in men to whom the society of
women was a necessity of existence. Mother's darlings had those eyes; so,
sometimes, had womanizers.

Well, presently he would check up on Tisdall. Meanwhile—

"Do you ask me to believe that in your four days together you had no
suspicion at all of Miss Clay's identity?" he asked, marking time until he
could bring Tisdall unsuspecting to the crucial matter.

"I suspected that she was an actress. Partly from things she said, but mostly
because there were such a lot of stage and film magazines in the house. I
asked her about it once, but she said: 'No names, no pack drill. It's a good
motto, Robin. Don't forget.' "

"I see. Did the outfit Miss Clay bought for you include an overcoat?"

"No. A mackintosh. I had a coat."

"You were wearing a coat over your evening things?"

"Yes. It had been drizzling when we set out for dinner—the crowd and I,
I mean."

"And you still have that coat?"

"No. It was stolen from the car one day when we were over at Dymchurch." His eyes grew alarmed suddenly. "Why? What has the coat got to
do with it?"

"Was it dark- or light-coloured?"

"Dark, of course. A sort of grey-black. Why?"

"Did you report its loss?"

"No, neither of us wanted attention called to us. What has it—"

"Just tell me about Thursday morning, will you?" The face opposite him

was steadily losing its ingenuousness and becoming wary and inimical again.
"I understand that you didn't go with Miss Clay to swim. Is that right?"

"Yes. But I awoke almost as soon as she had gone—"

"How do you know when she went if you were asleep?"

"Because it was still only six. She couldn't have been gone long. And Mrs.
Pitts said afterwards that I had followed down the road on her heels."

"I see. And in the hour and a half—roughly—between your getting up and
the finding of Miss Clay's body you walked to the Gap, stole the car, drove
it in the direction of Canterbury, regretted what you had done, came back,
and found that Miss Clay had been drowned. Is that a complete record of
your actions?"

"Yes, I think so."

"If you felt so grateful to Miss Clay, it was surely an extraordinary thing
to do."

"Extraordinary isn't the word at all. Even yet I can't believe I did it."

"You are quite sure that you didn't enter the water that morning?"

"Of course I'm sure. Why?"

"When was your last swim? Previous to Thursday morning, I mean?"

"Noon on Wednesday."

"And yet your swimming suit was soaking wet on Thursday morning."

"How do you know that! Yes, it was. But not with salt water. It had been
spread to dry on the roof below my window, and when I was dressing on
Thursday morning I noticed that the birds in the tree—an apple tree hangs
over that gable—had made too free with it. So I washed it in the water I had
been washing in."

"You didn't put it out to dry again, though, apparently?"

"After what happened the last time? No! I put it on the towel rail. For
God's sake, Inspector, tell me what all this has to do with Chris's death? Can't
you see that questions you can't see the reason of are torture? I've had about
all I can stand. The inquest this morning was the last straw. Everyone describing how they found her. Talking about 'the body,' when all the time it
was Chris. Chris! And now all this mystery and suspicion. If there was anything not straightforward about her drowning, what has my coat got to do
with it, anyway?"

"Because this was found entangled in her hair."

Grant opened a cardboard box on the table and exhibited a black button
of the kind used for men's coats. It had been torn from its proper place, the
worn threads of its attachment still forming a ragged "neck." And round the
neck, close to the button, was twined a thin strand of bright hair.

Tisdall was on his feet, both hands on the table edge, staring down at the
object.

"You think someone *drowned* her? I mean—like *that!* But that isn't mine.
There are thousands of buttons like that. What makes you think it is mine?"

"I don't think anything, Mr. Tisdall. I am only eliminating possibilities.

All I wanted you to do was to account for any garment owned by you which had buttons like that. You say you had one but that it was stolen."

Tisdall stared at the Inspector, his mouth opening and shutting helplessly.

The door breezed open, after the sketchiest of knocks, and in the middle of the floor stood a small, skinny child of sixteen in shabby tweeds, her dark head hatless and very untidy.

"Oh, sorry," she said. "I thought my father was here. Sorry."

Tisdall slumped to the floor with a crash.

Grant, who was sitting on the other side of the large table sprang to action, but the skinny child, with no sign of haste or dismay, was there first.

"Dear me!" she said, getting the slumped body under the shoulders from behind and turning it over.

Grant took a cushion from a chair.

"I shouldn't do that," she said. "You let their heads stay back unless it's apoplexy. And he's a bit young for that, isn't he?"

She was loosening collar and tie and shirt-band with the expert detachment of a cook paring pastry from a pie edge. Grant noticed that her sunburnt wrists were covered with small scars and scratches of varying age, and that they stuck too far out of her out-grown sleeves.

"You'll find brandy in the cupboard, I think. Father isn't allowed it, but he has no self-control."

Grant found the brandy and came back to find her slapping Tisdall's unconscious face with a light insistent *tapotement*.

"You seem to be good at this sort of thing," Grant said.

"Oh, I ran the Guides at school." She had a voice at once precise and friendly. "A *ve-*ry silly institution. But it varied the routine. That is the main thing, to vary the routine."

"Did you learn this from the Guides?" he asked, nodding at her occupation.

"Oh, no. They burn paper and smell salts and things. I learned this in Bradford Pete's dressing-room."

"Where?"

"You know. The welter-weight. I used to have great faith in Pete, but I think he's lost his speed lately. Don't you? At least, I *hope* it's his speed. He's coming to nicely." This last referred to Tisdall. "I think he'd swallow the brandy now."

While Grant was administering the brandy, she said: "Have you been giving him the third degree, or something? You're police, aren't you?"

"My dear young lady—I don't know your name?"

"Erica. I'm Erica Burgoyne."

"My dear Miss Burgoyne, as the Chief Constable's daughter you must be aware that the only people in Britain who are subjected to the third degree are the police."

"Well, what did he faint for? Is he guilty?"

"I don't know," Grant said, before he thought.

"I shouldn't think so." She was considering the now spluttering Tisdall. "He doesn't look capable of much." This with the same grave detachment as she used to everything she did.

"Don't let looks influence your judgment, Miss Burgoyne."

"I don't. Not the way you mean. Anyhow, he isn't at all my type. But it's quite right to judge on looks if you know enough. You wouldn't buy a washy chestnut narrow across the eyes, would you?"

This, thought Grant, is quite the most amazing conversation.

She was standing up now, her hands pushed into her jacket pockets so that the much-tried garment sagged to two bulging points. The tweed she wore was rubbed at the cuffs and covered all over with "pulled" ends of thread where briars had caught. Her skirt was too short and one stocking was violently twisted on its stick of leg. Only her shoes—scarred like her hands, but thick, well-shaped and expensive—betrayed the fact that she was not a charity child.

And then Grant's eyes went back to her face. Except her face. The calm sureness of that sallow little triangular visage was not bred in any charity school.

"There!" she said encouragingly, as Grant helped Tisdall to his feet and guided him into a chair. "You'll be all right. Have a little more of Father's brandy. It's a much better end for it than Father's arteries. I'm going now. Where is Father, do you know?" This to Grant.

"He has gone to lunch at The Ship."

"Thank you." Turning to the still dazed Tisdall, she said, "That shirt collar of yours is far too tight." As Grant moved to open the door for her, she said, "You haven't told me *your* name?"

"Grant. At your service." He gave her a little bow.

"I don't need anything just now, but I might some day." She considered him. Grant found himself hoping with a fervour which surprised him that he was not being placed in the same category as "washy chestnuts." "You're much more my type. I like people broad across the cheekbones. Good-bye, Mr. Grant."

"Who was that?" Tisdall asked, in the indifferent tones of the newly conscious.

"Colonel Burgoyne's daughter."

"She was right about my shirt."

"One of the reach-me-downs?"

"Yes. Am I being arrested?"

"Oh, no. Nothing like that."

"It mightn't be a bad idea."

"Oh? Why?"

"It would settle my immediate future. I left the cottage this morning and now I'm on the road."

"You mean you're serious about tramping."

"As soon as I have got suitable clothes."

"I'd rather you stayed where I could get information from you if I wanted."

"I see the point. But how?"

"What about that architect's office? Why not try for a job?"

"I'm never going back to an office. Not an architect's anyhow. I was shoved there only because I could draw."

"Do I understand that you consider yourself permanently incapacitated from earning your bread?"

"Phew! That's nasty. No, of course not. I'll have to work. But what kind of job am I fit for?"

"Two years of hitting the high spots must have educated you to something. Even if it is only driving a car."

There came a tentative tap at the door, and the sergeant put his head in.

"I'm very sorry indeed to disturb you, Inspector, but I'd like something from the Chief's files. It's rather urgent."

Permission given, he came in.

"This coast's lively in the season, sir," he said, as he ran through the files. "Positively continental. Here's the chef at the Marine—it's just outside the town, so it's our affair—the chef at the Marine's stabbed a waiter because he had dandruff, it seems. The waiter, I mean, sir. Chef on the way to prison and waiter on the way to hospital. They think maybe his lung's touched. Well, thank you, sir. Sorry to disturb you."

Grant eyed Tisdall, who was achieving the knot in his tie with a melancholy abstraction. Tisdall caught the look, appeared puzzled by it, and then, comprehension dawning, leaped into action.

"I say, Sergeant, have they a fellow to take the waiter's place, do you know?"

"That they haven't. Mr. Toselli—he's the manager—he's tearing his hair."

"Have you finished with me?" he asked Grant.

"For today," Grant said. "Good luck."

# 5

"No. No ARREST," said Grant to Superintendent Barker over the telephone in the early evening. "But I don't think there's any doubt about its being murder. The surgeon's sure of it. The button in her hair might be accident—although if you saw it you'd be convinced it wasn't—but her fingernails were broken with clawing at something. What was under the nails has gone to the analyst, but there wasn't much after an hour's immersion in salt water. . . . 'M? . . . Well, indications point one way certainly, but they cancel each other out, somehow. Going to be difficult, I think. I'm leaving Williams here on routine enquiry, and coming back to town tonight. I want to see her lawyer—Erskine. He arrived just in time for the inquest, and afterwards I had Tisdall on my hands so I missed him. Would you find out for me when I can talk to him tonight. They've fixed the funeral for Monday. Golders Green. Yes, cremation. I'd like to be there, I think. I'd like to look over the intimates. Yes, I may look in for a drink, but it depends how late I am. Thanks."

Grant hung up and went to join Williams for a high tea, it being too early for dinner and Williams having a passion for bacon and eggs garnished with large pieces of fried bread.

"Tomorrow being Sunday may hold up the button enquiries," Grant said as they sat down. "Well, what did Mrs. Pitts say?"

"She says she couldn't say whether he was wearing a coat or not. All she saw was the top of his head over her hedge as he went past. But whether he wore it or not doesn't much matter, because she says the coat habitually lay in the back of the car along with that coat that Miss Clay wore. She doesn't remember when she saw Tisdall's dark coat last. He wore it a fair amount, it seems. Mornings and evenings. He was a 'chilly mortal,' she said. Owing to his having come back from foreign parts, she thought. She hasn't much of an opinion of him."

"You mean she thinks he's a wrong 'un?"

"No. Just no account. You know, sir, has it occurred to you that it was a clever man who did this job?"

"Why?"

"Well, but for that button coming off no one would ever have suspected anything. She'd have been found drowned after going to bathe in the early morning—all quite natural. No footsteps, no weapon, no signs of violence. Very neat."

"Yes. It's neat."

"You don't sound very enthusiastic about it."

"It's the coat. If you were going to drown a woman in the sea, would you wear an overcoat to do it?"

"I don't know. 'Pends how I meant to drown her."

"How *would* you drown her?"

"Go swimming with her and keep her head under."

"You'd have scratches that way, ten to one. Evidence."

"Not me. I'd catch her by the heels in shallow water and upend her. Just stand there and hold her till she drowned."

"Williams! What resource. And what ferocity."

"Well, how would you do it, sir?"

"I hadn't thought of aquatic methods. I mightn't be able to swim, or I mightn't like early-morning dips, or I might want to make a quick get-away from a stretch of water containing a body. No, I think I'd stand on a rock in deep water, wait till she came to talk to me, grip her head and keep it under. The only part of me that she could scratch that way would be my hands. And I'd wear leather gloves. It takes only a few seconds before she is unconscious."

"Very nice, sir. But you couldn't use that method anywhere within miles of the Gap."

"Why not?"

"There aren't any rocks."

"No. Good man. But there are the equivalent. There are stone groynes."

"Yes. Yes, so there are! Think that was how it was done, sir?"

"Who knows? It's a theory. But the coat still worries me."

"I don't see why it need, sir. It was a misty morning, a bit chilly at six. Anyone might have worn a coat."

"Y-es," Grant said doubtfully, and let the matter drop, this being one of those unreasonable things which occasionally worried his otherwise logical mind (and had more than once been the means of bringing success to his efforts when his logic failed).

He gave Williams instructions for his further enquiries, when he himself should be in town. "I've just had another few minutes with Tisdall," he finished. "He has got himself a waiter's job at the Marine. I don't think he'll bolt, but you'd better plant a man. Sanger will do. That's Tisdall's car route on Thursday morning, according to himself." He handed a paper to the sergeant. "Check up on it. It was very early but someone may remember him. Did he wear a coat or not? That's the main thing. I think, myself, there's no doubt of his taking the car as he said. Though not for the reason he gave."

"I thought it a silly reason myself, when I read that statement. I just thought: 'Well, he might have made up a better one!' What's your theory, sir?"

"I think that when he had drowned her his one idea was to get away. With a car he could be at the other end of England, or out of the country, before they found her body! He drove away. And then something made him realise what a fool he was. Perhaps he missed the button from his cuff. Anyhow, he realised that he had only to stay where he was and look innocent. He got rid of the tell-tale coat—even if he hadn't missed the button the sleeve almost up to the elbow must have been soaking with salt water—came back to replace the car, found that the body had been discovered thanks to an incoming tide, and put on a very good act on the beach. It wouldn't have been difficult. The very thought of how nearly he had made a fool of himself would have been enough to make him burst into tears."

"So you think he did it?"

"I don't know. There seems to me to be a lack of motive. He was penniless and she was a liberal woman. There was every reason for keeping her alive. He was greatly interested in her, certainly. He says he wasn't in love with her, but we have only his word for it. I think he's telling the truth when he says there was nothing between them. He *may* have suffered from frustration, but if that were so he would be much more likely to beat her up. It was a queerly cold-blooded murder, Williams."

"It was certainly that, sir. Turns my stomach." Williams laid a large forkful of best Wiltshire lovingly on a pink tongue.

Grant smiled at him: the smile that made Grant's subordinates "work their fingers to the bone for him." He and Williams had worked together often, and always in amity and mutual admiration. Perhaps, in a large measure because Williams, bless him, coveted no one's shoes. He was much more the contented husband of a pretty and devoted wife than the ambitious detective-sergeant.

"I wish I hadn't missed her lawyer after the inquest. There's a lot I want to ask him, and heaven knows where he'll be for the week-end. I've asked the Yard for her dossier, but her lawyer would be much more helpful. Must find out whom her death benefits. It was a misfortune for Tisdall, but it must have been lucky for a lot of people. Being an American, I suppose her will's in the States somewhere. The Yard will know by the time I get up."

"Christine Clay was no American, sir!" Williams said in a well-I-*am*-surprised-at-you voice.

"No? What then?"

"Born in Nottingham."

"But everyone refers to her as an American."

"Can't help that. She was born in Nottingham and went to school there. They do say she worked in a lace factory, but no one knows the truth of that."

"I forgot you were a film fan, Williams. Tell me more."

"Well, of course, what I know is just by reading *Screenland* and *Photoplay* and magazines like that. A lot of what they write is hooey, but on the other hand they'll never stop at truth as long as it makes a good story. She wasn't fond of being interviewed. And she used to tell a different story each time. When someone pointed out that that wasn't what she had said last time, she said: 'But that's so dull! I've thought of a much better one.' No one ever knew where they were with her. Temperament, they called it, of course."

"And don't you call it that?" asked Grant, always sensitive to an inflexion.

"Well, I don't know. It always seemed to me more like—well, like protection, if you know what I mean. People can only get at you if they know what you're like—what matters to you. If you keep them guessing, they're the victims, not you."

"A girl who'd pushed her way from a lace factory in Nottingham to the top of the film world couldn't be very vulnerable."

"It's *because* she was from a lace factory that she was what-d'you-call-it. Every six months she was in a different social sphere, she went up at such a rate. That takes a lot of living up to—like a diver coming up from a long way below. You're continually adjusting yourself to the pressure. No, I think she needed a shell to get into, and keeping people guessing was her shell."

"So you were a Clay fan, Williams."

"Sure I was," said Williams in the appropriate idiom. His pink cheeks grew a shade pinker. He slapped marmalade with venom onto his slab of toast. "And before this affair's finished I'm going to put bracelets on the chap that did it. It's a comforting thought."

"Got any theories yourself?"

"Well, sir, if you don't mind my saying so, you've passed over the person with the obvious motive."

"Who?"

"Jason Harmer. What was he doing snooping round at half-past eight of a morning?"

"He'd come over from Sandwich. Spent the night at the pub there."

"So he said. Did the County people verify that?"

Grant consulted his notes.

"Perhaps they haven't. The statement was volunteered before they found the button, and so they weren't suspicious. And since then everyone has concentrated on Tisdall."

"Plenty of motive, Harmer has. Clay walks out on him, and he runs her to earth in a country cottage, alone with a man."

"Yes, very plausible. Well, you can add Harmer to your list of chores. Find out about his wardrobe. There's an S.O.S. out for a discarded coat. I hope it brings in something. A coat's a much easier clue than a button. Tisdall, by the way, says he sold his wardrobe complete (except for his evening things) to a man called—appropriately enough—Togger, but doesn't know where his place of business is. Is that the chap who used to be in Craven Road?"

"Yes, sir."

"Where is he now?"

"Westbourne Grove. The far end."

"Thanks. I don't doubt Tisdall's statement. But there's just a chance there's the duplicate of that button on another coat. It might lead us to something." He got to his feet. "Well, on with the job of making bricks without straw! And talking of that Israelitish occupation, here's a grand sample of it to flavour your third cup." He pulled from his pocket the afternoon edition of the *Sentinel,* the *Clarion's* evening representative, and laid it, with its staring headlines, "Was Clay's Death an Accident?" upward, by Williams's plate.

"Jammy Hopkins!" Williams said, with feeling, and flung sugar violently into his black tea.

# 6

MARTA HALLARD, as befitted a leading lady who alternated between the St. James's and the Haymarket, lived in the kind of apartment block which has deep carpet on the stairs and a cloistered hush in the corridors. Grant, climbing the stairs with weary feet, appreciated the carpet even while his other self wondered about the vacuum cleaning. The dim pink square of the lift had fled upwards as he came through the revolving door, and rather than wait for its return he was walking the two flights. The commissionaire had said that Marta was at home: had arrived about eleven from the theatre with several people. Grant regretted the people, but was determined that this day was not going to end without his obtaining some light on Christine Clay and her entourage. Barker had failed to find the lawyer, Erskine, for him; his man said he was suffering from the shock of the last three days and had gone into the country over Sunday; address unknown. ("Ever heard of a lawyer suffering from shock?" Barker had said.) So the matter which most interested Grant—the contents of Christine Clay's will—must wait until Monday. At the Yard he had read through the dossier—still, of course, incomplete—which they had gathered together in the last twelve hours. In all the five sheets of it Grant found only two things remarkable.

Her real name, it appeared, was Christina Gotobed.

And she had had no lovers.

No public ones, that is. Even in those crucial years when the little Broadway hoofer was blossoming into the song-and-dance star, she seemed to have had no patron. Nor yet when, tiring of song-and-dance pictures, her ambition had reached out to drama; her rocket had shot to the stars under its own power, it would seem. This could only mean one of two things: that she had remained virgin until her marriage at twenty-six (a state of affairs which Grant, who had a larger experience of life than of psychology textbooks, found quite possible) or that her favour was given only when her heart (or her fancy, according to whether you are sentimentalist or cynic) was touched. Four years ago Lord Edward Champneis (pronounced Chins), old Bude's fifth son, had met her in Hollywood, and in a month they were married. She was at that time shooting her first straight film, and it was generally agreed that she had "done well for herself" in her marriage. Two years later Lord Edward was "Christine Clay's husband."

He took it gracefully, it was reported; and the marriage had lasted. It had become a casual affair of mutual friendliness; partly owing to the demands of time and space that her profession made on Christine, and partly to the fact that Edward Champneis's main interest in life (after Christine) was to invade the uncomfortable interiors of ill-governed and inaccessible countries and then to write books about it. During the book-writing solstice he and Christine lived more or less under one roof, and were apparently very happy. The fact that Edward, although a fifth son, had nevertheless a large fortune of his own, inherited from his mother's brother (Bremer, the leather king), had done much to save the marriage from its most obvious dangers. And Edward's delighted pride in his wife did the rest.

Now, where in that life, as shown in the dossier, did a murder fit in? Grant asked himself, toiling up the padded stairs. Harmer? He had been her constant companion for the three months she had been in England. True, they had work in common (producers still liked to insert a song somewhere in the plot of Christine's films: the public felt cheated if they did not hear her sing), but the world which amuses itself had no doubt of their relations, whatever their colleagues thought. Or Tisdall? An ill-balanced boy, picked up in a moment of waywardness or generosity, at a time when he was reckless and without direction.

Well, he himself would find out more about Tisdall. Meanwhile he would find out about the Harmers of her life.

As he came to the top of the second flight, he heard the gentle sound of the lift closing, and he turned the corner to find Jammy Hopkins just taking his thumb from the bell-push.

"Well, well," said Jammy, "it's a party!"

"I hope you have an invitation."

"I hope you have a warrant. People shriek for their lawyer nowadays at the very sight of a policeman on the mat. Look, Inspector," he said hurriedly in a different voice, "let's not spoil each other's game. We both thought of Marta. Let's pool results. No need for crowding."

From which Grant deduced that Hopkins was doubtful of his reception. He followed Grant into the little hall without giving his name, and Grant, while appreciating the ingenuity, rebelled at providing a cloak for the Press.

"This gentleman is, I believe, from the *Clarion*," he said to the servant who had turned away to announce them.

"Oh!" she said, turning back and eyeing Hopkins without favour. "Miss Hallard is always very tired at night, and she has some friends with her at the moment—"

But luck saved Hopkins from any necessity for coercion. The double doors to the living-room stood open, and from the room beyond came welcome in high excited tones.

"Mr. Hopkins! How charming! Now *you* can tell us what all these midday editions were talking about. I didn't know you knew Mr. Hopkins, Marta darling!"

"Who'd have thought I'd ever be glad to hear that voice!" Jammy murmured to Grant as he moved forward to greet the speaker, and Grant turned to meet Marta Hallard, who had come from the room into the hall.

"Alan Grant!" she said, smiling at him. "Is this business or pleasure?"

"Both. Do me a favour. Don't tell these people who I am. Just talk as you were talking before I came. And if you can get rid of them fairly soon, I'd like to talk to you alone for a little."

"I'd do a lot more than that for you. Every time I tie these round my neck," she indicated a rope of pearls, "I remember you."

This was not because Grant had given her the pearls but because he had once recovered them for her.

"Come and meet the others. Who is your friend?"

"Not a friend. Hopkins of the *Clarion*."

"Oh. Now I understand Lydia's welcome. And they say professional people are publicity hounds!" She led Grant in, introducing people as they came. The first was Clement Clements, the society photographer, radiant in purple "tails" and a soft shirt of a pale butter colour. He had never heard of an Alan Grant, and made it perfectly clear. The second was a Captain Somebody, a nondescript and humble follower of Marta's, who clung to his glass of whisky and soda as being the only familiar object in an unknown terrain. The third was Judy Sellers, a sulky fair girl who played "dumb" blondes from year's end to year's end, and whose life was one long fight between her greed and her weight. And the fourth was that intimate of the stars, Miss Lydia Keats, who was now talking all over Jammy Hopkins and enjoying herself immensely.

"*Mr.* Grant?" Jammy said, nastily, as Grant was introduced.

"*Isn't* it 'Mr.'?" Lydia asked, her ears pricked, her eyes snapping with curiosity.

"No, it isn't!"

But Hopkins met Grant's eye and lacked the courage of his desire. It would be folly to make an enemy of a C.I.D. Inspector.

"He has one of those Greek titles, you know, but he's ashamed to own it. Got it for rescuing a Greek royalist's shirt from a Greek laundry."

"Don't pay any attention to him, Mr. Grant. He loves to hear himself talk. I know, you see. He has interviewed me so often. But he never listens to a word I say. Not his fault, of course. Aries people are often talkative. I knew the first time he crossed my threshold that he was April born. Now you, Mr. Grant, are a Leo person. Am I right? No, you don't need to tell me. I know. Even if I couldn't feel it—here—" she thumped her skinny chest, "you have all the stigmata."

"I hope they're not very deadly?" Grant asked, wondering how soon he could disengage himself from this harpy.

"Deadly! My dear Mr. Grant! Don't you know anything of astrology? To be born in Leo is to be a king. They are the favourites of the stars. Born to success, predestined to glory. They are the great ones of the world."

"And when does one have to be born to qualify for a Leo benefit?"

"Between the middle of July and the middle of August. I should say that you were born in the first weeks of August."

Grant hoped he didn't look as surprised as he felt. He had certainly been born on the 4th of August.

"Lydia's uncanny," Marta broke in, handing Grant a drink. "She did poor Christine Clay's horoscope about a year ago, you know, and foretold her death."

"And wasn't that a break!" drawled the Judy girl, poking among the sandwiches.

Lydia's thin face was convulsed with fury, and Marta hastened to pour oil. "You know that's not fair, Judy! It isn't the first time Lydia has been right. She warned Tony Pickin about an accident before he was smashed up. If he'd listened to her and taken a little more care, he'd have two legs today. And she told me about not accepting the Clynes's offer, and she—"

"Don't bother to defend me, Marta darling. The credit is not mine, in any case. I only read what is there. The stars don't lie. But one does not expect a Pisces person to have either the vision or the faith!"

"Seconds out of the ring," murmured Jammy, and hit the rim of his glass with his fingernail so that it made a light "ping."

But there was to be no fight. Clements provided a distraction.

"What I want to know," he drawled, "is not what Lydia found in the stars but what the police found at Westover."

"What I want to know is who did her in?" Judy said, taking a large bite of sandwich.

"Judy!" Marta protested.

"Oh, bunk!" said Judy. "You know we're all thinking the same thing. Going round the possibles. Personally I plump for Jason. Has anyone any advance on Jason?"

"Why Jason?" Clements asked.

"He's one of these smouldering types, all passion and hot baths."

"Smoulder! Jason!" Marta protested. "What nonsense! He simmers. Like a merry kettle." Grant glanced at her. So she was sticking up for Jason? How much did she like him? "Jason's much too volatile to smoulder."

"Anyhow," Clements said, "men who take hot baths don't commit murder. It's the cold-plungers who see red. They are possessed by a desire to get back on life for the suffering they have endured."

"I thought masochists were rarely sadists," Grant said.

"Whether or not, you can put Jason out of it," insisted Marta. "He wouldn't hurt a fly."

"Oh, wouldn't he," Judy said, and they all paused to look at her.

"What exactly does that mean?" Clements asked.

"Never mind. My bet's on Jason."

"And what was the motive?"

"She was running out, I suspect."

Marta interrupted sharply. "You know that's nonsense, Judy. You know quite well that there was nothing between them."

"I know nothing of the sort. He was never out of her sight."

"A bitch thinks all the world a bitch," murmured Jammy into Grant's ear.

"I suspect"—it was Lydia's turn to break into a growing squabble—"that Mr. Hopkins knows much more about it than we do. He's been down at Westover today for his paper."

Jammy was instantly the center of attraction. What did he think? What had the police got? Who did they think had done it? Were all these hints in the evening papers about her living with someone true?

Jammy enjoyed himself. He was suggestive about murderers, illuminating on murder, discursive about human nature, and libellously rude about the police and their methods, all with a pleased eye on the helpless Grant.

"They'll arrest the boy she was living with," he finished. "Take it from me. Tisdall's his name. Good-looking boy. He'll create a sensation in the dock."

"Tisdall?" they said, puzzled. "Never heard of him."

All but Judy Sellers.

Her mouth opened in dismay, stayed that way helplessly for a moment, and then shut tightly; and a blind came down over her face. Grant watched the display in surprised interest.

"I think it's utterly ridiculous," Marta was saying, scornfully. "Can you imagine Christine Clay in a furtive business like that! It's not in the part at all. I'd as soon—as soon—I'd as soon believe that Edward could commit a murder!"

There was a little laugh at that.

"And why not?" asked Judy Sellers. "He comes back to England to find his adored wife being unfaithful, and is overcome with passion."

"At six of a morning on a cold beach. Can't you see Edward!"

"Champneis didn't arrive in England till Thursday," offered Hopkins, "so that lets him out."

"I do think this is the most heartless and reprehensible conversation," Marta said. "Let's talk of something else."

"Yes, do," said Judy. "It's a profitless subject. Especially since *you*, of course, murdered her yourself."

"I!" Marta stood motionless in an aura of bewildered silence. Then the moment broke.

"Of course!" Clement said. "You wanted the part she was due to play in the new film! We'd forgotten that!"

"Well, if we're looking for motives, Clement, my sweet, you were raving mad with fury because she refused to be photographed by you. If I remember rightly, she said your works were like spilt gravy."

"Clement wouldn't drown her. He'd poison her," Judy said. "With a box of chocolates, Borgia-wise. No, come to think of it, Lejeune did it, in case he'd have to act with her. He's the virile type. His father was a butcher, and he probably inherited a callous mentality! Or how about Coyne? He would have killed her on the *Iron Bars* set, if no one had been looking." She apparently had forgotten about Jason.

"Will you all kindly stop this silly chatter!" Marta said, with angry emphasis. "I know that after three days a shock wears off. But Christine was a friend of ours, and it's disgusting to make a game of the death of a person we all liked."

"Hooey!" said Judy, rudely. She had consumed her fifth drink. "Not one of us cared a brass farthing for her. Most of us are tickled to death she's out of the way."

# 7

IN THE BRIGHT COOL of Monday morning Grant drove himself down Wigmore Street. It was still early and the street was quiet; Wigmore Street's clients do not stay in town for week-ends. The flower shops were making up Saturday's roses into Victorian posies where their errant petals could be gently corseted. The antique shops were moving that doubtful rug to the other side of the window out of the too questioning gaze of the morning sun. The little cafés were eating their own stale buns for their morning coffee and being pained and haughty with inconsiderates who asked for fresh scones. And the dress shops took Saturday's bargains out of the cupboard and restored the original prices.

Grant, who was en route to see Tisdall's tailor, was a little disgruntled at the perversity of things. If Tisdall's coat had been made by a London tailor it would have been a simple matter to have the button identified by them as one used by them for coats, and for Tisdall's coat in particular. That wouldn't clinch the matter but it would bring the clinching appreciably nearer. But Tisdall's coat had been made, of all places, in Los Angeles. "The coat I had," he explained, "was too heavy for that climate, so I got a new one."

Reasonable, but trying. If the coat had been made by a London firm of standing, one could walk into their shop at any time in the next fifty years and be told without fuss and with benevolent politeness (provided they knew who you were) what kind of buttons had been used. But who was to say whether a Los Angeles firm would know what buttons they put on a coat six months ago! Besides, the button in question was wanted here. It could not very well be sent to Los Angeles. The best one could do was to ask them to supply a sample of the buttons used. *If* they remembered!

Grant's main hope was that the coat itself would turn up. An abandoned coat which could be identified as Tisdall's, with one button missing, would be the perfect solution. Tisdall was wearing the coat when he drove away the car. That was Sergeant Williams's contribution to the cause of justice and due promotion. He had found a farmer who had seen the car at the Wedmarsh cross-roads a little after six on Thursday morning. About twenty past, he reckoned, but he hadn't a watch. Didn't need one. Tell the time any time of day, sun or no sun. He was driving sheep, and the car slowed down because of them. He was positive that the man driving was young and wore a dark coat. He didn't think he'd be able to identify the man, not on his oath, he wouldn't—but he had identified the car. It was the only car he had seen that morning.

Williams's other contribution had not been so happy. He reported that Jason Harmer had not stayed at the hotel he had given as his sleeping place at Sandwich. Had not stayed at Sandwich at all, in fact.

Grant had left his Sunday kidney and bacon untouched and had gone out without ado to interview Mr. Harmer. He found him in his pinkish flat at Devonshire House, covered in a purple silk dressing-gown, black stubble, and sheet music.

"It's not often I'm up at this hour," he offered, pushing sheets of scrawled paper off a chair to make room for Grant. "But I've been sort of upset about Chris. Very good friends, we were, Inspector. Some people found her difficult, but me, no. 'Cause why? D'you know why? 'Cause we both felt no-account and were afraid people'd find it out. Humans are awful bullies, you know. If you look and act like a million dollars they'll lick your boots. But you let them suspect that you don't think much of yourself and they're on you like ants on a dying wasp. I knew Chris was bluffing first time I set eyes on her. You can't tell me anything about bluffing. I bluffed my way into the States and I bluffed the publishers into printing my first song. They didn't find out about it till the song was a wow, and then they sort of thought it might be a good idea to forget about having one put over on them. Have a drink? Yes, it's a bit early. I don't usually myself till lunch time, but it's the next best thing to sleep. And I've got two songs to finish on contract. For—for—" his voice died away—"for Coyne's new film," he went on with a rush. "Ever tried writing a song without an idea in your head? No. No, I suppose you haven't. Well, it's just plain torture. And who's going to sing them anyhow? That Hallard dame can't sing. Did you hear Chris sing: 'Sing to me sometimes'?"

Grant had.

"Now that's what I call putting over a song. I've written better songs, I admit. But she made it sound like the best song that was ever written. What's the good of writing songs anyway, for that up-stage Hallard bird to make a mess of?"

He was moving about the room, picking up a pile of papers here only to set it down in an equally inappropriate place there. Grant watched him with interest. This was Marta's "merry kettle" and Judy's "smouldering type." To Grant he seemed neither. Just one of those rather ordinary specimens of humanity from some poor corner of Europe who believes he's being continually exploited and persecuted by his fellow men, self-pitying, ill-educated, emotional, and ruthless. Not good-looking, but attractive to women, no doubt. Grant remembered that two such widely differing types as Marta Hallard and Judy Sellers had found him remarkable; each reading her own meaning into his personality. He apparently had the ability to be all things to all men. He had been friendly to the disliked Marta, that was certain: Marta did not hotly defend indifferent worshippers at her shrine. He spent his life, that is to say, "putting on an act." He had admitted so much himself a moment ago. Was he putting on an act now? For Grant?

"I'm sorry to disturb you so early, but it was a matter of business. You know that we are investigating Miss Clay's death. And in the course of investigation it is necessary to check the movements of everyone who knew her, irrespective of persons or probabilities. Now, you told the sergeant of the County police force, when you talked to him on Thursday, that you had spent the night in a hotel at Sandwich. When this was checked in the ordinary course it was found that you hadn't stayed there."

Harmer fumbled among the music, without looking up.

"Where *did* you stay, Mr. Harmer?"

Harmer looked up with a small laugh. "You know," he said, "it's pretty funny at that! Charming gentleman calls in a perfectly friendly way about breakfast time, apologising for disturbing you and hopes he isn't going to be a trouble to you but he's an inspector of police and would you be so very kind as to give some information because last time your information wasn't as accurate as it might have been. It's lovely, that's what it is. And you get results with it, too. Perhaps they just break down and sob, on account of all the friendliness. Pie like mother made. What I'd like to know is if that method goes in Pimlico or if you keep it for Park Lane."

"What I would like to know is where you stayed last Wednesday night, Mr. Harmer."

"The Mr., too, I guess that's Park Lane as well. In fact, if you'd been talking to the Jason of ten years back, you'd have had me to the station and scared hell out of me just like the cops of any other country. They're all the same; dough worshippers."

"I haven't your experience of the world's police forces, I'm afraid, Mr. Harmer."

Harmer grinned. "Stung you! A limey's got to be plenty stung before he's rude-polite like that. Don't get me wrong, though, Inspector. There aren't any police brands on me. As for last Wednesday night, I spent it in my car."

"You mean you didn't go to bed at all?"

"That's what I mean."

"And where was the car?"

"In a lane with hedges as high as houses each side, parked on the grass verge. An awful lot of space goes to waste in England in these verges. The ones in that lane were about forty feet wide."

"And you say you slept in the car? Have you someone who can bear witness to that?"

"No. It wasn't that kind of park. I was just sleepy and lost and couldn't be bothered going any further."

"Lost! In the east of Kent!"

"Yes, anywhere in Kent, if it comes to that. Have you ever tried to find a village in England after dark? Night in the desert is nothing to it. You see a sign at last that says 'Whatsit two and a half miles' and you think: Good old Whatsit! Nearly there! Hurrah for England and signposts! And then half a mile on you come to a place where three ways fork, and there's a nice tidy signpost on the little bit of green in the middle and every blame one of that signpost's arms has got at least three names on it, but do you think one of them mentions Whatsit? Oh, no! That would make it far too easy! So you read 'em all several times and hope someone'll come past before you have to decide, but no one comes. Last person passed there a week last Tuesday. No houses; nothing but fields, and an advertisement for a circus that was there the previous April. So you take one of the three roads, and after passing two more signposts that don't take any notice of Whatsit, you come to one that says: 'Whatsit, six and three-quarters.' So you start off all over again, four miles to the bad, as it were, and it happens all over again. And again! And by the time Whatsit has done that on you half a dozen times, you don't care what happens as long as you can stop driving round corners and go to sleep. So I just stopped where I was and went to sleep. It was too late to drop in on Chris by that time, anyway."

"But not too late to get a bed at an inn."

"Not if you know where an inn is. 'Sides, judging by some of the inns I've seen here, I'd just as soon sleep in the car."

"You grow a heavy beard, I notice." Grant nodded at Harmer's unshaven chin.

"Yes. Have to shave twice a day, sometimes. If I'm going to be out late. Why?"

"You were shaved when you arrived at Miss Clay's cottage. How was that?"

"Carry my shaving things in the car. Have to, when you have a beard like mine."

"So you had no breakfast that morning?"

"No, I was planning to get breakfast from Chris. I don't eat breakfast anyway. Just coffee, or orange juice. Orange juice in England. My God, your coffee— What do you think they do to it? The women, I mean. It's—"

"Leaving the coffee aside for a moment, shall we come to the main point? Why did you tell the sergeant on duty that you had slept at Sandwich?"

The man's face changed subtly. Until then he had been answering at ease, automatically; the curves of his broad, normally good-natured face slack and amiable. Now the slackness went; the face grew wary, and—was it?—antagonistic.

"Because I felt there was something wrong, and I didn't want to be mixed up in it."

"That is very extraordinary, surely? I mean, that you should be conscious of evil before anyone knew that it existed."

"That's not so funny. They told me Chris was drowned. I knew Chris could swim like an eel. I knew that I had been out all night. And the sergeant was looking at me with a Who-are-you-and-what-are-you-doing-here expression?"

"But the sergeant had no idea that the drowning was more than an accident. He had no reason to look at you in that way."

Then he decided to drop the subject of Harmer's lie to the sergeant.

"How did you know, by the way, where to find Miss Clay? I understood that she kept her retreat a secret."

"Yes, she'd run away. Gave us all the run-around, in fact, including me. She was tired and not very pleased at the way her last picture had turned out. On the floor, I mean; it isn't released yet. Coyne didn't know how to take her. A bit in awe of her, and afraid at the same time she'd put one over on him. You know. If he'd called her 'kid' and 'chocolate' the way old Joe Myers used to back in the States, she'd have laughed and worked like a black for him. But Coyne's full of his own dignity, the 'big director' stuff, and so they didn't get on too good. So she was fed-up, and tired, and everyone wanted her to go to different places for holidays, and it seemed she couldn't make up her mind, and then one day we woke up and she wasn't there. Bundle—that's her housekeeper—said she didn't know where she was, but no letters were to be forwarded and she'd turn up again in a month, so no one was to worry. Well, for about a fortnight no one heard of her, and then last Tuesday I met Marta Hallard at a sherry party at Libby Seemon's—she's going into that new play of his—and she said that on Saturday she had run into Chris buying chocolates at a place in Baker Street—Chris never could resist chocolates between pictures!—and she tried to worm out of Chris where she was hiding out. But Chris wasn't giving anything away. At least she thought she wasn't. She said: 'Perhaps I'm never coming back. You know that old Roman who grew vegetables with his own hands and was so stuck on the result that he made the arrangement permanent. Well, yesterday I helped pull the first cherries for Covent Garden market and, believe me, getting the Academy award for a picture is nothing to it!' "

Harmer laughed under his breath. "I can hear her," he said, affectionately. "Well, I went straight from Seemon's to Covent Garden and found out where those cherries came from. An orchard at a place called Bird's Green. And on Wednesday morning bright and early Jason sets off for Bird's Green. That took a bit of finding, but I got there about three o'clock. Then I had to find the orchard and the people who were working in it on Friday. I expected to find Chris straight away, but it seemed that they didn't know her. They said that when they were picking, early on Friday morning, a lady passing in a car had stopped to watch and then asked if she might help. The old boy who owned the place said they didn't need paid help, but if she liked to amuse herself good and well. 'She were a good picker,' he said. 'Wouldn't mind paying her another time.' Then his grandson said he'd seen the lady—or thought he'd seen her—one day lately in the post office at Liddlestone—about six miles away. So I found Liddlestone, but the post office regular staff was 'home to her tea' and I had to wait till she came back. She said that the lady who sent 'all the telegrams'—seems they never saw so many telegrams in their lives as Chris sent—was living over at Medley. So I set out in the half-dark to find Medley, and ended by sleeping in a lane. And sleeping out or no sleeping out, that was a better piece of detective work than you're doing this morning, Inspector Grant!"

Grant grinned good-humouredly. "Yes? Well, I've nearly done." He got up to go. "I suppose you had a coat with you in the car?"

"Sure."

"What was it made of?"

"Brown tweed. Why?"

"Have you got it here?"

"Sure." He turned to a wardrobe, built in the passage where the sitting-room led into the bedroom, and pulled the sliding door open. "Have a look at my whole wardrobe. You're cleverer than I am if you can find the button."

"What button?" Grant asked, more quickly than he intended.

"It's always a button, isn't it?" Harmer said, the small pansy-brown eyes, alert under their lazy lids, smiling confidently into Grant's.

Grant found nothing of interest in the wardrobe. He had taken his leave not knowing how much to believe of Jason Harmer's story, but very sure that he had "nothing on him." The hopes of the police, so to speak, lay in Tisdall.

Now, as he pulled up by the curb in the cool bright morning, he remembered Jason's wardrobe, and smiled in his mind. Jason did not get his clothes from Stacey and Brackett. As he considered the dark, small, and shabby interior which was revealed to him as he opened the door, he could almost hear Jason laugh. The English! They'd had a business for a hundred and fifty years and this was all they could make of it. The original counters probably. Certainly the original lighting. But Grant's heart warmed. This was the England he knew and loved. Fashions might change, dynasties might fall, horses' shoes in the quiet street change to the crying of a thousand taxi-hooters, but Stacey and Brackett continued to make clothes with leisured efficiency for leisured and efficient gentlemen.

There was now neither a Stacey nor a Brackett, but Mr. Trimley—Mr. Stephen Trimley (as opposed to Mr. Robert and Mr. Thomas!)—saw Inspector Grant and was entirely at Inspector Grant's service. Yes, they had made clothes for Mr. Robert Tisdall. Yes, the clothes had included a dark coat for wear with evening things. No, that certainly was not a button from the coat in question. That was not a button they had ever put on any coat. It was not a class of button they were in the habit of using. If the Inspector would forgive Mr. Trimley (Mr. *Stephen* Trimley), the button in question was in his opinion of a very inferior make, and would not be used by any tailor of any standing. He would not be surprised, indeed, to find that the button was of foreign origin.

"American, perhaps?" suggested Grant.

Perhaps. Although to Mr. Trimley's eye it suggested the Continent. No, he certainly had no reason for such a surmise. Entirely instinctive. Probably wrong. And he hoped the Inspector would not put any weight on his opinion. He also hoped that there was no question of Mr. Tisdall being in trouble. A very charming young man, indeed. The Grammar schools—especially the older Grammar schools of the country—turned out a very fine type of boy. Better often, didn't the Inspector think so? than came from the minor public schools. There was a yeoman quality of permanence about Grammar-school families—generation after generation going to the same school—that was not matched outside the great public schools.

There being, in Grant's opinion, no yeoman quality of permanence whatever about young Tisdall, he forbore to argue, contenting himself by assuring Mr. Trimley that as far as he knew Mr. Tisdall was in no trouble up to date.

Mr. Trimley was glad to hear that. He was getting old, and his faith in the young generation which was growing up was too often sadly shaken. Perhaps every generation thought that the rising one lacked due standards of behaviour and spirit, but it did seem to him this one . . . Ah, well, he was growing old, and the tragedy of young lives weighed more heavily on him than it used to. This Monday morning was blackened for him, yes, entirely blackened, by the thought that all the brightness that was Christine Clay was at this hour being transformed into ashes. It would be many years, perhaps generations (Mr. Trimley's mind worked in generations: the result of having a hundred-and-fifty-year-old business) before her like would be seen again. She had quality, didn't the Inspector think so? Amazing quality. It was said that she had a very humble origin, but there must be breeding somewhere. Something like Christine Clay did not just happen in space, as it were. Nature must plan for it. He was not what is known, he believed, as a film fan, but there was no picture of Miss Clay's which he had not seen since his niece had taken him to view her first essay in a dramatic rôle. He had on that occasion entirely forgotten that he was in a cinema. He was dazed with delight. Surely if this new medium could produce material of this strength and richness one need not continue to regret Bernhardt and Duse.

Grant went out into the street, marvelling at the all-pervading genius of Christine Clay. The mind of all the world it seemed was in that building at Golders Green. A strange end for the little lace-hand from Nottingham.

Strange, too, for the world's idol. "And they put him in an oven just as if he were—" Oh, no, he mustn't think of that. Hateful. Why whould it be hateful? He didn't know. The suburbanity of it, he supposed. Sensible, and all that. And probably much less harrowing for everyone. But someone whose brilliance had flamed across the human firmament as Clay's had should have a hundred-foot pyre. Something spectacular. A Viking's funeral. Not ovens in the suburb. Oh, my God, he was growing morbid, if not sentimental. He pressed the starter, and swung into the traffic.

He had yesterday changed his mind about going to the Clay funeral. The Tisdall evidence progressing normally, he had seen no need to give himself a harrowing hour which he could avoid. But only now did he realise how very glad he was to have escaped it, and (being Grant) began instantly to wonder whether after all he should have gone. Whether his subconscious desire to get out of it had influenced his decision. He decided that it had not. There was no need for him now to study the psychology of unknown friends of Christine's. He had had a good cross-section of them at Marta's, and had learned very little, after all. The party had stubbornly refused to break up. Jammy had begun to talk again, hoping that they would dance to his piping. But Marta vetoed any more talk of Christine, and although they had come back to her several times, not even Jammy's genius for evocation could keep them on the subject. Lydia, who could never stay off her own subject for long, had read their palms, cheiromancy being a side-line of hers when horoscopes were not available (she had given a shrewd enough reading of Grant's character and had warned him about making a mistaken decision in the immediate future: "a nice safe thing to say to anyone," he had reflected) and it was not until one o'clock that the hostess had managed to shepherd them all to the door. Grant had lingered, not, curiously enough, because he had questions to ask her (the conversation had provided answers for him), but because she was anxious to question him. Was Scotland Yard called in to investigate Christine's death? What was wrong? What had they found? What did they suspect?

Grant had said that Yes, they had been called in (so much would by now be common property) but that so far there was only suspicion. She had wept a little, becomingly, with not too disastrous effect on the mascara, had treated him to a short appreciation of Christine as artist and woman. "A grand person. It must have taken tremendous character to overcome her initial disadvantages." She enumerated the disadvantages.

And Grant had gone out into the warm night with a sigh for human nature —and a shrug for the sigh.

But there were bright spots even in human nature. Grant edged in towards the curb, and came to a halt, his brown face glad and welcoming.

"Good morning!" he called to the little grey figure.

"Oh, good morning, Mr. Grant," Erica said, crossing the pavement to him. She gave him a brief little smile, but seemed pleased to see him; so much was apparent through her schoolboy matter-of-factness. She was dressed in her "town" clothes, he noticed; but they did not seem to be an improvement on her country ones. They were neat, certainly, but they had an unused look; and the grey suit she was wearing, although undoubtedly "good," was dowdy. Her hat had been got to match, and matched also in dowdiness.

"I didn't know you ever stayed in town."

"I don't. I came up to get a bridge."

"A *bridge?*"

"But it seems you can't get them by the yard. They have to be made to measure. So I've got to come up another day. All he did today was put a lot of clay in my mouth."

"Oh, the dentist. I see. I thought only old ladies had bridges."

"Well, you see, the silly thing he put in the last time doesn't hold. I'm always picking it out of bits of toffee. I lost a lot of side teeth when Flight fell with me at a post-and-rails last winter. I had a face like a turnip. So it had to be a bridge, he says."

"A mis-nomer, Flight."

"In one way. Not in another. He was nearly at the other end of Kent before they caught him."

"Where are you going now? Can I give you a lift anywhere?"

"I suppose you wouldn't like to show me Scotland Yard?"

"I would. Very much. But in twenty minutes I have an appointment with a lawyer in the Temple."

"Oh. In that case perhaps you would drop me in Cockspur Street. I have an errand to do for Nannie."

Yes, he thought, as she inserted herself beside him, it would be a Nannie. No mother had chosen those clothes. They were ordered from the tailor just as her school clothes had been. "One grey flannel suit and hat to match." In spite of her independence and her sureness of spirit, there was something forlorn about her, he felt.

"This is nice," she said. "They're not very high, but I hate walking in them."

"What are?"

"My shoes." She held up a foot and exhibited her very modest cuban heel. "Nannie thinks they are the right thing to wear in town, but I feel dreadful in them. Teetery."

"I expect one gets used to them in time. One must conform to the tabus of the tribe."

"Why must one?"

"Because an unquiet life is a greater misery than wearing the badge of conformity."

"Oh, well. I don't come to town often. I suppose you haven't time to have an ice with me?"

"I'm afraid not. Let's postpone it until I'm back in Westover, shall we?"

"Of course, you'll be back. I had forgotten that. I saw your victim yesterday," she added conversationally.

"My victim?"

"Yes, the man who fainted."

"You saw him! Where?"

"Father took me over to luncheon at the Marine."

"But I thought your father hated the Marine?"

"He does. He said he'd never seen such a set of poisonous bloaters in his life. I think 'bloaters' is a little strong. They weren't so very bad. And the melon was very good."

"Did your father tell you that Tisdall was waiting there?"

"No, the sergeant did. He doesn't look very professional. Mr. Tisdall, not the sergeant. Too friendly and interested. No professional waiter looks interested. Not really. And he forgot the spoons for the ices. But I expect you upset him pretty thoroughly the day before."

"*I* upset him!" Grant took a deep breath and expressed his hope that Erica was not going to let the plight of a good-looking young man play havoc with her heart.

"Oh no. Nothing like that. His nose is too long. Besides, I'm in love with Togare."

"Who is Togare?"

"The lion-tamer, of course." She turned to look at him doubtfully. "Do you *really* mean that you haven't heard of Togare?"

Grant was afraid that that was so.

"Don't you go to Olympia at Christmas? But you should! I'll get Mr. Mills to send you seats."

"Thank you. And how long have you been in love with this Togare?"

"Four years. I'm very faithful."

Grant admitted that she must be.

"Drop me at the Orient office, will you?" she said, in the same tone as she had announced her faithfulness. And Grant set her down by the yellow-funnelled liner.

"Going cruising?" he asked.

"Oh, no. I go round the offices collecting booklets for Nannie. She loves them. She's never been out of England because she's terrified of the sea, but she likes to sit in safety and imagine. I got her some marvellous mountain ones from the Austrian place in Regent Street in the spring. And she's very knowledgeable about the German spas. Good-bye. Thank you for the lift. How shall I know when you come to Westover? For the ice, I mean."

"I shall send you word through your father. Will that do?"

"Yes. Good-bye." And she disappeared into the office.

And Grant went on his way to meet Christine Clay's lawyer and Christine Clay's husband, feeling better.

# 8

IT WAS OBVIOUS at once why no one called Edward Champneis anything but Edward. He was a very tall, very dignified, very good-looking, and very orthodox person, with a manner of grave, if kindly, interest, and a rare but charming smile. Alongside the fretful movements of the fussy Mr. Erskine, his composure was like that of a liner suffering the administrations of a tug.

Grant had not met him before. Edward Champneis had arrived in London on Thursday afternoon, after nearly three months' absence, only to be greeted by the news of his wife's death. He had gone down immediately to Westover and identified the body, and on Friday he had interviewed the worried County Constabulary, puzzling over the button, and helped them to make up their minds that it was a case for the Yard. The thousand things waiting in town to be done as a result of his wife's death and his own long absence had sent him back to London just as Grant left it.

He looked very tired, now, but showed no emotion. Grant wondered under what circumstances this orthodox product of five hundred years of privilege and obligation would show emotion. And then, suddenly, as he drew the chair under him, it occurred to him that Edward Champneis was anything but orthodox. Had he conformed to the tribe, as his looks conformed, he would have married a second cousin, gone into the Service, looked after an estate, and read the *Morning Post*. But he had done none of those things. He had married an artist picked up at the other side of the world, he explored for fun, and he wrote books. There was something almost eerie in the thought that an exterior could be so utterly misleading.

"Lord Edward has, of course, seen the will," Erskine was saying. "He was, in fact, aware of its more important provisions some time ago, Lady Edward having acquainted him with her desires at the time the testament was made. There is, however, one surprise. But perhaps you would like to read the document for yourself."

He turned the impressive-looking sheet round on the table so that it faced Grant.

"Lady Edward had made two previous wills, both in the United States, but they were destroyed, on her instructions, by her American lawyers. She was anxious that her estate should be administered from England, for the stability of which she had a great admiration."

Christine had left nothing to her husband. "I leave no money to my husband, Edward Champneis, because he has always had, and always will have, more than he can spend, and because he has never greatly cared for money." Whatever he cared to keep of her personal possessions were to be his, however, except where legacies specifically provided otherwise. There were various bequests of money, in bulk or in annuities, to friends and dependents. To Bundle, her housekeeper and late dresser. To her Negro chauffeur. To Joe Myers, who had directed her greatest successes. To a bellhop in Chicago "to buy that gas station with." To nearly thirty people in all, in all parts of the globe and in all spheres of existence. But there was no mention of Jason Harmer.

Grant glanced at the date. Eighteen months ago. She had at that time probably not yet met Harmer.

The legacies, however generous, left the great bulk of her very large fortune untouched. And that fortune was left, surprisingly, not to any individual, but "for the preservation of the beauty of England." There was to be a trust, in which would be embodied the power to buy any beautiful building or space threatened by extinction and to provide for its upkeep.

That was Grant's third surprise. The fourth came at the end of the list of legacies. The last legacy of all read, "To my brother Herbert, a shilling for candles."

"A brother?" Grant said, and looked up enquiring.

"Lord Edward was unaware that Lady Edward had a brother until the will was read. Lady Edward's parents died many years ago, and there had been no mention of any surviving family except for herself."

"A shilling for candles. Does it convey anything to you, sir?" He turned to Champneis, who shook his head.

"A family feud, I expect. Perhaps something that happened when they were children. These are often the things one is most unforgiving about." He glanced towards the lawyer. "The thing I remember when I meet Alicia is always that she smashed my birds'-egg collection."

"But not *necessarily* a childhood quarrel," Grant said. "She must have known him much later."

"Bundle would be the person to ask. She dressed my wife from her early days in New York. But is it important? After all, the fellow was being dismissed with a shilling."

"It's important because it is the first sign of real enmity I have discovered among Miss Clay's relationships. One never knows what it might lead us to."

"The Inspector may not think it so important when he has seen this," Erskine said. "This, which I will give you to read, is the surprise I spoke of."

So the surprise had not been one of those in the will.

Grant took the paper from the lawyer's dry, slightly trembling hand. It was a sheet of the shiny, thick, cream-coloured note-paper to be obtained in village shops all over England, and on it was a letter from Christine Clay to her lawyer. The letter was headed "Briars, Medley, Kent," and contained instructions for a codicil to her will. She left her ranch in California, with all stock and implements, together with the sum of five thousand pounds, to one Robert Stannaway, late of Yeoman's Row, London.

"That," said the lawyer, "was written on Wednesday, as you see. And on Thursday morning—" He broke off, expressively.

"Is it legal?" Grant asked.

"I should not like to contest it. It is entirely handwritten and properly signed with her full name. The signature is witnessed by Margaret Pitts. The provision is perfectly clear, and the style eminently sane."

"No chance of a forgery?"

"Not the slightest. I know Lady Edward's hand very well—you will observe that it is peculiar and not easy to reproduce—and moreover I am very well acquainted with her style, which would be still more difficult to imitate."

"Well!" Grant read the letter again, hardly believing in its existence. "That alters everything. I must get back to Scotland Yard. This will probably mean an arrest before night." He stood up.

"I'll come with you," Champneis said.

"Very good, sir," Grant agreed automatically. "If I may, I'll telephone first to make sure that the Superintendent will be there."

And as he picked up the receiver, the looker-on in him said: Harmer was right. We do treat people variously. If the husband had been an insurance agent in Brixton, we wouldn't take it for granted that he could horn in on a Yard conference!

"Is Superintendent Barker in the Yard, do you know? . . . Oh . . . At half past? That's in about twenty minutes. Well, tell him that Inspector Grant has important information and wants a conference straight away. Yes, the Commissioner, too, if he's there."

He hung up.

"Thank you for helping us so greatly," he said, taking farewell of Erskine. "And by the way, if you unearth the brother, I should be glad to know."

And he and Champneis went down the dark, narrow stairs and out into the hot sunshine.

"Do you think," Champneis asked, pausing with one hand on the door of Grant's car, "there would be time for a drink? I feel the need of some stiffening. It's been a—a trying morning."

"Yes, certainly. It won't take us longer than ten minutes along the Embankment. Where would you like to go?"

"Well, my club is in Carlton House Terrace, but I don't want to meet people I know. The Savoy isn't much better—"

"There's a nice little pub up here," Grant said, and swung the car round. "Very quiet at this time. Cool, too."

As they turned the corner Grant caught sight of the news-sellers' posters. CLAY FUNERAL: UNPRECEDENTED SCENES. TEN WOMEN FAINT. LONDON'S FAREWELL TO CLAY. And (the *Sentinel*) CLAY'S LAST AUDIENCE.

Grant's foot came down on the accelerator.

"It was unbelievably ghastly," said the man beside him, quietly.

"Yes, I can imagine."

"Those women. I think the end of our greatness as a race must be very near. We came through the war well, but perhaps the effort was too great. It left us—epileptic. Great shocks do, sometimes." He was silent a moment, evidently seeing it all again in his mind's eye. "I've seen machine guns turned on troops in the open—in China—and rebelled against the slaughter. But I would have seen that sub-human mass of hysteria riddled this morning with more joy than I can describe to you. Not because it was—Chris, but because they made me ashamed of being human, of belonging to the same species."

"I had hoped that at that early hour there would be very little demonstration. I know the police were counting on that."

"We counted on it too. That is why we chose that hour. Now that I've seen with my own eyes, I know that nothing could have prevented it. The people are insane."

He paused, and gave an unamused laugh. "She never did like people much. It was because she found people—disappointing that she left her money as she did. Her fans this morning have vindicated her judgment."

The bar was all that Grant had promised, cool, quiet, and undemanding. No one took any notice of Champneis. Of the six men present three nodded to Grant and three looked wary. Champneis, observant even in his pain, said: "Where do *you* go when you want to be unrecognised?" and Grant smiled. "I've not found a place yet," he admitted. "I landed in Labrador from a friend's yacht once, and the man in the village store said, 'You wear your moustache shorter now, Sergeant.' After that I gave up expecting."

They talked of Labrador for a little, and then of Galeria, where Champneis had spent the last few months.

"I used to think Asia primitive, and some of the Indian tribes of South America, but the east of Europe has them all beaten. Except for the towns, Galeria is still in the primeval dark."

"I see they've mislaid their spectacular patriot," Grant said.

"Rimnik? Yes. He'll turn up again when his party is ready. That's the way they run the benighted country."

"How many parties are there?"

"About ten, I think, not counting subdivisions. There are at least twenty races in that boiling pot of a country, all of them clamouring for self-government, and all of them medieval in their outlook. It's a fascinating place. You should go there some day. The capital is their shop-window—as nearly a replica of every other capital as they can make it. Opera, trams, electric light, imposing railway station, cinemas—but twenty miles into the country you'll find bride-barter. Girls set in rows with their dowry at their feet, waiting to go to the highest bidder. I've seen an old country woman led raving mad out of a lift in one of the town buildings. She thought she was the victim of witchcraft. They had to take her to the asylum. Graft in the town and superstition in the country—and yet a place of infinite promise."

Grant let him talk, glad that for even a few minutes he might be able to forget the horror of the morning. His own thoughts were not in Galeria but in Westover. So he had done it, that good-looking emotionalist! He had screwed a ranch and five thousand out of his hostess and then made sure that he would not have to wait for it. Grant's own inclination to like the boy died an instant death. From now on Robert Tisdall would be no more to him than the bluebottle he swatted on the windowpane, a nuisance to be exterminated as quickly and with as little fuss as possible. If, away in the depths, he was sorry that the pleasant person who was the surface Tisdall did not exist, his main and overwhelming emotion was relief that the business was going to be cleared up so easily. There was little doubt of the result of the conference. They had evidence enough. And they would have more before it came to a trial.

Barker, his Superintendent, agreed with him, and so did the Commissioner. It was a clear enough case. The man is broke, homeless, and at his wit's end. He is picked up by a rich woman at the psychological moment. Four days later a will is made in his favour. On the following morning very early, the woman goes to swim. He follows her ten minutes later. When her body is found he has disappeared. He reappears with an unbelievable tale about stealing the car and bringing it back. A black button is found twisted in the dead woman's hair. The man's dark coat is missing. He says it was stolen two days before. But a man identifies him as wearing it that morning.

Yes, it was a good enough case. The opportunity, the motive, the clue.

The only person to protest against the issue of the warrant was, strangely enough, Edward Champneis.

"It's too pat, don't you think?" he said. "I mean, would any man in his senses commit the murder the very next morning?"

"You forget, Lord Edward," Barker said, "that but for the merest chance there would be no question of murder at all."

"And moreover, time was precious to him," Grant pointed out. "There were only a few days left. The tenancy of the cottage expired at the end of the month. He knew that. She might not go bathing again. The weather might break, or she might be seized with a desire to go inland. More especially she might not go swimming in the early morning again. It was an ideal setting: a lonely beach in the very early morning, with the mist just rising. Too perfect a chance to let go to waste."

Yes, it was a good case. Edward Champneis went back to the house in Regent's Park which he had inherited with the Bremer fortune, and which between his peregrinations he called home. And Grant went down to Westover with a warrant in his pocket.

# 9

IF THERE WAS one thing Toselli hated more than another it was the police. All his life he had been no poor hater, Toselli. As *commis* he had hated the maître d'hôtel, as maître d'hôtel he had hated the management, as the management he hated many things: the chef, wet weather, his wife, the head porter's moustache, clients who demanded to see him at breakfast time—oh, many things! But more than all he hated the police. They were bad for business and bad for the digestion. It stopped his digestive juices flowing just to see one of them walk in through the glass doors. It was bad enough to remember his annual bill for New Year "presents" to the local officers—thirty bottles of Scotch, thirty of gin, two dozen champagne, and six of liqueur brandy it had come to last year—but to suffer the invasion of officers not so far "looked after," and therefore callous to the brittle delicacy of hotel well-being—well, it was more than Toselli's abundant flesh and high-pressured blood could stand.

That is why he smiled so sweetly upon Grant—all his life Toselli's smile had been stretched across his rage, like a tight-rope spanning a chasm—and gave him one of the second-best cigars. Inspector Grant wanted to interview the new waiter, did he? But certainly! This was the waiter's hour off—between lunch and afternoon tea—but he should be sent for immediately.

"Stop!" said Grant. "You say the man is off duty? Do you know where he will be?"

"Very probably in his room. Waiters like to take the weight off their feet for a little, you understand."

"I'd like to see him there."

"But certainly. Tony!" Toselli called to a page passing the office door. "Take this gentleman up to the room of the new waiter."

"Thank you," Grant said. "You'll be here when I come down? I should like to talk to you."

"I shall be here." Toselli's tone expressed dramatic resignation. His smile deepened as he flung out his hands. "Last week it was a stabbing affair in the kitchen; this week it is—what? Theft? Affiliation?"

"I'll tell you all about it presently, Mr. Toselli."

"I shall be here." His smile became ferocious. "But not for long, no! I am going to buy one of those businesses where one puts sixpence into a slot and the meal comes out. Yes. There, but there, would be happiness."

"Even there, there are bent coins," Grant said as he followed Tony to the lift.

"Sanger, you come up with me," he said as they passed through the busy hall. "You can wait for us here, Williams. We'll bring him out this way. Much less fuss than through the servants' side. No one will notice anything. Car waiting?"

"Yes, sir."

Grant and Sanger went up in the lift. In those few seconds of sudden quiet and suspended action, Grant found time to wonder why he had not shown his warrant and told Toselli what he had come for. That would have been his normal course. Why was he so anxious to have the bird in his hand? Was it just the canniness of his Scots ancestry coming out, or was there a presentiment that— That what? He didn't know. He knew only that now that he was here he could not wait. Explanations could follow. He must have the man in his hands.

The soft sound of the lift in the silence was like the sound of the curtain going up.

At the very top of the colossal building which was the Westover Marine Hotel, were the quarters of those waiters who were resident: small single rooms set in a row close together under the roof. As the page put out a bony fist to knock on a door, Grant restrained him. "All right, thank you," he said, and page and liftman disappeared into the crowded and luxurious depths, leaving the two policemen on the deserted cocoanut-matted landing. It was very quiet up there.

Grant knocked.

Tisdall's indifferent voice bade him come in.

The room was so small that Grant's involuntary thought was that the cell that waited would be no great change. A bed on one side, a window on the other, and in the far wall two cupboard doors. On the bed lay Tisdall in his shirt sleeves, his shoes on the floor. A book lay open, face down, on the coverlet.

He had expected to see a colleague. That was obvious. At the sight of Grant his eyes widened, and as they travelled to Sanger, standing behind Grant in the doorway, realisation flooded them.

Before Grant could speak, he said, "You can't mean it!"

"Yes, I'm afraid we do," Grant said. He said his regulation piece of announcement and warning, Tisdall sitting with feet dangling on the bed's edge, not apparently listening.

When he had finished Tisdall said slowly: "I expect this is what death is like when you meet it. Sort of wildly unfair but inevitable."

"How were you so sure what we had come for?"

"It doesn't need two of you to ask about my health." His voice rose a little. "What I want to know is why you're doing it? What have you against me? You can't have proved that button was mine because it wasn't. Why don't you tell me what you have found so that I can explain away whatever it was? If you have new evidence you can surely ask me for an explanation. I have a right to know, haven't I? Whether I can explain or not?"

"There isn't anything you could explain away, Tisdall. You'd better get ready to come with us."

Tisdall got to his feet, his mind still entangled in the unbelievableness of what was happening to him. "I can't go in these things," he said, looking down at his waiter's dress. "Can I change?"

"Yes, you can change, and take some things with you." Grant's hands ran over his pockets in expert questioning, and came away empty. "But you'll have to do it with us here. Don't be too long about it, will you? You can wait there, Sanger," he added, and swung the door to, leaving Sanger outside. He himself moved over to lean against the window-sill. It was a long way to the ground, and Tisdall, in Grant's opinion, was the suicide type. Not enough guts to brazen a thing out. Not enough vanity, perhaps, to like the limelight at any price. Certainly the "everyone sorry when I'm dead" type.

Grant watched him now with minute attention. To an outsider he was a casual visitor, propped casually in the window while he indulged in casual conversation. In reality he was ready for instant emergency.

But there was no excitement. Tisdall pulled his suit-case from under the bed, and began with automatic method to change into his tweed and flannels. Grant felt that if the man carried poison, it would be somewhere in his working garments, and unconsciously relaxed a little as the waiter's dress was cast aside. There was going to be no trouble. The man was coming quietly.

"I needn't have worried as to how I was going to live," Tisdall was saying. "There seems to be a moral somewhere in this very immoral proceeding. What do I do about a lawyer, by the way, when I have no money and no friends?"

"One will be provided."

"Like a table napkin. I see."

He opened the cupboard nearest to Grant, and began to take things from their hangers and fold them into his case.

"At least you can tell me what my motive was?" he said presently, as if a new thought had struck him. "You can mistake buttons; you can even wish a button on to a coat that never had it; but you can't pin a motive where there couldn't be one!"

"So you had no motive?"

"Certainly not. Quite the opposite. What happened last Thursday morning was the worst thing that has ever happened to me in my life. I should have thought that was obvious even to an outsider."

"And of course you had not the faintest idea that Miss Clay had made a codicil to her will leaving you a ranch and a large sum of money."

Tisdall had been readjusting the folds of a garment. He stopped now, his hands still holding the cloth, but motionless, and stared at Grant.

"Chris did that!" he said. "No. No, I didn't know. How wonderful of her!"

And for a moment doubt stirred in Grant. That had been beautifully done. Timing, expression, action. No professional actor could have done it better.

But the doubt passed. He recrossed his legs, by way of shaking himself, re-called the charm and innocence of murderers he had known (Andrew Hamey, who specialised in marrying women and drowning them and who looked like a choir soloist, and others of even greater charm and iniquity) and then composed his mind to the peace of a detective who has got his man.

"So you've raked up the perfect motive. Poor Chris! She thought she was doing me such a good turn. Have I any defence at all, do you know?"

"That is not for me to say."

"I have a great respect for you, Inspector Grant. I think it probable that I shall be unavailingly protesting my innocence on the scaffold."

He pushed the nearer cupboard door to, and opened the further one. The door opened away from Grant, so that the interior of the cupboard was not visible. "But you disappoint me in one way. I thought you were a better psychologist, you know. When I was telling you the story of my life on Saturday morning, I really thought you were too good a judge to think that I could have done what you suspected me of. Now I find you're just a routine policeman."

Still keeping his hand on the door-knob, he bent down to the interior of the cupboard as if to take shoes from the floor of it.

There was the rasp of a key torn from its lock, the cupboard door swung shut, and even as Grant leaped the key turned on the inside.

"Tisdall!" he shouted. "Don't be a fool! Do you hear!" His mind raced over the antidotes for the various poisons. Oh, God, what a fool he had been! "Sanger! Help me to break this open. He's locked himself in."

The two men flung their combined weight on the door. It resisted their best efforts.

"Listen to me, Tisdall," Grant said between gasps, "poison is a fool's trick. We'll get you soon enough to give you an antidote, and all that will happen is that you'll suffer hell's pain for nothing. So think better of it!"

But still the door resisted them.

"Fire axe!" Grant said. "Saw it when we came up. On wall at the end of the passage. Quick!"

Sanger fled and in eight seconds was back with the axe.

As the first blow of it fell, a half-dressed and sleepy colleague of Tisdall's appeared from next door and announced, "You mek a noise like thet you hev the cops een!"

"Hey!" he added, seeing the axe in Sanger's grasp. "What the hell you theenk you do, eh?"

"Keep away, you fool! There's a man in that cupboard committing suicide."

"Suicide! Cupboard!" The waiter rubbed his black hair in perplexity, like a half-awakened child. "That is not a cupboard!"

*"Not a cupboard!"*

"No, that is the what you call eet—leetle back stairs. For fire, you know."

"God!" said Grant, and made for the door.

"Where does it come out—the stairway?" he called back to the waiter.

"In the passage to the front hall."

"Eight flights," Grant said to Sanger. "Lift's quicker, perhaps." He rang. "Williams will stop him if he tries to go out by the door," he said, searching for comfort.

"Williams has never seen him, sir. At least I don't think so."

Grant used words he had forgotten since he stopped campaigning in France.

"Does the man on duty at the back know him?"

"Oh, yes, sir. That's what he's there for, to stop him. But Sergeant Williams was just waiting for us."

Words failed Grant altogether.

The lift appeared.

Thirty seconds later they were in the hall.

The pleased expectancy on Williams's pink face told them the worst. Williams had certainly not intercepted anyone.

People were arriving, people were departing, people were going to tea in the restaurant, people were going to eat ices in the sun lounge, to drink in the bar, to meet other people and go to tea at Lyons—the hall of the Marine was American in the catholicity of its inhabitants. To make oneself noticeable in that assembly it would be necessary to stand on one's hands and proceed so.

Williams said that a young brown-haired man, without a hat and wearing a tweed jacket and flannels had gone out about five minutes previously. In fact, two of them had gone out.

"Two of them! You mean together!"

No, Williams meant that two separate men answering to that description had gone out in the last five minutes. If it came to that, here was another.

Yes, there was another. And watching him, Grant was filled with a despair that ran up from his feet like a wave hitting him and flooding his whole being. Yes, *indeed* there would be others. In Kent alone at this moment were ten thousand men whose description corresponded to Tisdall's.

Grant pulled himself together and turned to the ungrateful task of forming a police cordon.

# 10

THAT WAS THE biggest scoop of Jammy Hopkins's life. The other papers that evening appeared on the street with horrifying photographs of the mob at

Golders Green—Medusa-like heads, close-up, screaming into the camera: dishevelled Furies with streaming locks and open mouths clawing each other in an abandon of hate—and thought that they were doing rather well. Nothing, surely, was as important today as the Clay funeral. And their photographers had done them proud. They could afford to be pleased.

But not for nothing had Hopkins trailed Grant from Wigmore Street, to the Orient offices, and from the Orient offices to the Temple, and from the Temple to the Yard. Not for nothing had he cooled his heels round the corner while his paid henchman kept watch on the Yard and gave him the sign when Grant left. Not for nothing had he followed him all the way to Westover.

"CLAY MURDERED," announced the *Sentinel* posters. "CLAY MURDERED: ARREST!" And the crowds milled round the excited newsboys. And in the other offices there was tearing of hair, and much talk of sacking. In vain to point out to irate editors that Scotland Yard had said that when there was publishable news they should be told. What were they paid for, the editors would like to know? Sitting on their behinds waiting to be called up, and given official scraps of information? What did they think they were? Tote officials?

But Jammy was in high favour with the powers who signed his pay cheque. Jammy settled into residence at the Marine—much more palatially than Grant, who also had a bedroom there but was to spend most of his life in the immediate future at the police station—and gave thanks to the stars which ordained so spectacular an end for Christine Clay.

As for Grant, he was—as he had known he would be—snowed under with information. By Tuesday noon Tisdall had been seen in almost every corner of England and Wales, and by tea-time was beginning to be seen in Scotland. He had been observed fishing from a bridge over a Yorkshire stream and had pulled his hat suspiciously over his face when the informant had approached. He had been seen walking out of a cinema in Aberystwyth. He had rented a room in Lincoln and had left without paying. (He had quite often left without paying, Grant noticed.) He had asked to be taken on a boat at Lowestoft. (He had also asked to be taken on a boat at half a dozen other places. The number of young men who could not pay their landladies and who wanted to leave the country was distressing.) He was found dead on a moor near Penrith. (That occupied Grant the best part of the afternoon.) He was found intoxicated in a London alley. He had bought a hat in Hythe, Grantham, Lewes, Tonbridge, Dorchester, Ashford, Luton, Aylesbury, Leicester, Chatham, East Grinstead, and in four London shops. He had also bought a packet of safety-pins in Swan and Edgars. He had eaten a crab sandwich at a quick lunch counter in Argyll Street, two rolls and coffee in a Hastings bun shop, and bread and cheese in a Haywards's Heath inn. He had stolen every imaginable kind of article in every imaginable kind of place— including a decanter from a glass-and-china warehouse in Croydon. When asked what he supposed Tisdall wanted a decanter for, the informant said that it was a grand weapon.

Three telephones kept ringing like demented things, and by post, telegram, wireless, and personal appearance the information poured in. Nine-tenths of it quite useless, but all of it requiring a hearing: some of it requiring much investigation before its uselessness became apparent. Grant looked at the massed pile of reports, and his self-control deserted him for a little.

"It's a big price to pay for a moment's lack of wit," he said.

"Cheer up, sir," said Williams. "It might be worse."

"Might be worse! Would you tell me what occurrence would, in your opinion, augment the horror of the situation?"

"Oh, well, so far no nut has come to confess to the crime, and waste our time that way."

But the nut arrived next morning.

Grant looked up from inspecting a dew-drenched coat which had just been brought in, to see Williams closing the door mysteriously and mysteriously advancing on him.

"What is it, Williams?" he asked, his voice sharp with anticipation.

"The nut," Williams said.

"The what?"

"The person to make a confession, sir." Williams's tone held a shade of guilt now, as if he felt that by mentioning the thing yesterday he had brought the evil to pass.

Grant groaned.

"Not a bit the usual kind, sir. Quite interesting. Very smart."

"Outside or inside?"

"Oh, her clothes, I meant, sir."

"Her! Is it a woman?"

"Yes. A lady, sir."

"Bring her in." Rage ran over him in little prickles. How dare some sensation-mad female waste his time in order to satisfy her perverted and depraved appetite.

Williams swung the door back and ushered in a bright fashionable figure. It was Judy Sellers.

She said nothing, but came into the room with a sulky deliberation. Even in his surprise at seeing her, Grant thought how Borstal she was in spite of her *soigné* exterior. That air of resentment against the world in general and her own fate in particular was very familiar to him.

He pulled out a chair in silence. Grant could be very intimidating.

"All right, Sergeant," he said, "there won't be any need for you to stay." And then, to Judy as Williams went: "Don't you think this is a little unfair, Miss Sellers?"

"Unfair?"

"I am working twenty-three hours out of the twenty-four, on dreadfully important work, and you see fit to waste my time by treating us to a bogus confession."

"There's nothing bogus about it."

"It's so bogus that I have a good mind to dismiss you now, without another word."

She stayed his half-movement to the door. "You can't do that. I'll just go to another police station and confess and they'll send me on to you. I *did* it, you see!"

"Oh, no, you didn't."

"Why not?"

"For one thing, you weren't near the place."

"How do you know where I was?"

"You forget that in the course of conversation on Saturday night it was apparent that on Wednesday night you were at Miss Keats's house in Chelsea."

"I was only there for cocktails. I left early because Lydia was going to a party up the river."

"Even so, that makes it rather unlikely that you should be on a beach near Westover shortly after dawn next morning."

"It wouldn't be at all surprising if I were in the north of England next morning. I motored down if you want to know. You can enquire at my flat. The girl I live with will tell you that I didn't come home till lunch time on Thursday."

"That hardly proves that your activities were murderous."

"They were, though. I drove to the Gap, hid in the wood, and waited till she came to swim."

"You were, of course, wearing a man's coat?"

"Yes, though I don't know how you knew. It was cold driving, and I wore one of my brother's that was lying in the car."

"Did you wear the coat to go down to the beach?"

"Yes. It was dithering cold. I don't like bathing in the dawn."

"You went bathing!"

"Of course I did. I couldn't drown her from the shore, could I?"

"And you left the coat on the beach?"

"Oh, no," she said with elaborate sarcasm. "I went swimming in it!"

And Grant breathed again. For a moment he had had a fright.

"So you changed into swimming things, walked down to the beach with your brother's coat over you, and—then what?"

"She was a fair way out. I went in, swam up to her and drowned her."

"How?"

"She said, 'Hello, Judy.' I said, 'Hello.' I gave her a light tap on the chin. My brother taught me where to hit a person's chin, so as to addle them. Then I dived under her and pulled her through the water by the heels until she was drowned."

"Very neat," Grant said. "You've thought it all out, haven't you? Have you invented a motive for yourself, too?"

"Oh, I just didn't like her. I hated her, if you want to know. Her success and her looks and her self-sufficiency. She got in my hair until I couldn't bear it another day."

"I see. And will you explain why, having achieved the practically perfect murder, you should calmly come here and put a noose round your neck?"

"Because you've got someone for it."

"You mean because we've got Robert Tisdall. And that explains everything. And now having wasted some precious minutes of my time, you might recompense me and rehabilitate yourself at the same time, by telling me what you know of Tisdall."

"I don't know anything. Except that he would be the very last person in the world to commit a murder. For any reason."

"You knew him fairly well, then?"

"No. I hardly knew him at all."

"You weren't—friends?"

"No, nor lovers, if that's what you're trying to say. Bobby Tisdall didn't know I was alive, except to hand me a cocktail."

Grant's tone changed. "And yet you'd go even to this length to get him out of a jam?" he said, quite kindly.

She braced into resentment at the kindness. "If you'd committed a murder wouldn't you confess to save an innocent person?"

"Depends on how innocent I thought the police were. You underrate us, Miss Sellers."

"I think you're a lot of idiots. You've got a man who is innocent. You're busy hounding him to death. And you won't listen to a perfectly good confession when you get one."

"Well, you see, Miss Sellers, there are always things about a case that are known only to the police and are not to be learned from newspapers. The mistake you made was to get up your story from the newspaper accounts. There was one thing you didn't know. And one thing you forgot."

"What did I forget?"

"That no one knew where Christine Clay was staying."

"The murderer did."

"Yes. That is my point. And now—I'm very busy."

"So you don't believe a word I say."

"Oh, yes. Quite a lot of it. You were out all night on Wednesday, you probably went swimming, and you arrived back at lunch time on Thursday. But none of that makes you guilty of murder."

She got up, in her reluctant, indolent way, and produced her lipstick. "Well," she drawled between applications, "having failed in my little bid for publicity, I suppose I must go on playing blonde nit-wits for the rest of my life. It's good I bought a day-return."

"You don't fool me," Grant said, with a not too grim smile as he opened the door for her.

"All right, then, maybe you're right about that, and blast you anyhow," she burst out. "But you're wrong about his doing it. So wrong that your name will stink before this case is over."

And she brushed past an astonished Williams and two clerks, and disappeared.

"Well," said Williams, "that's the first. Humans are queer, aren't they, sir? You know, if we announced the fact that the coat we want has a button missing, there'd be people who would pull the button off their coats and bring it in. Just for fun. As if things weren't difficult enough without that. Not just the usual type, though, was she, sir?"

"No. What did you make of her, Williams?"

"Musical comedy. Looking for publicity to help her career. Hard as nails."

"All wrong. Legitimate stage. Hates her career. Soft-hearted to the point of self-sacrifice."

Williams looked a little crestfallen. "Of course, I didn't have a chance to talk to her," he reminded.

"No. On looks it was quite a good reading, Williams. I wish I could read this case as well." He sat down and ran his fingers through his hair. "What would you do, Williams, once you had got clear of the Marine?"

Williams understood that he was supposed to be Tisdall.

"I'd take a fairly crowded bus somewhere. First that came to hand. Get off with a crowd of others, and walk off as if I knew where I was going. In fact, wherever I went I'd look as if I knew where I was going."

"And then, what?"

"I'd probably have to take another bus to get out of townified parts."

"You'd get out of built-up areas, would you?"

"Sure!" said Williams, surprised.

"A man's much more conspicuous in open country."

"There are woods. In fact, some of the woods in this part of the world would hide a man indefinitely. And if a man got as far west as Ashdown Forest, well, it'd take about a hundred men to comb Ashdown properly."

Grant shook his head. "There's food. And lodging."

"Sleep out. It's warm weather."

"He's been out two nights now. If he has taken to the country he must be looking shop-worn by this time. But has he? Have you noticed that no one has reported him as buying a razor? There's just the chance that he's with friends. I wonder—" his eyes strayed to the chair where Judy had been sitting. "But no! She'd never risk as big a bluff as that. No need for it."

Williams wished to himself that Grant would go to the hotel and have some sleep. He was taking far too much to heart his failure to arrest Tisdall. Mistakes happened to the best of people, and everyone knew that Grant was all right. He had the Yard solid behind him. Why need he worry himself sick over something that might have happened to anyone? There were one or two crabbers, of course—people who wanted his job—but no one paid any attention to the like of them. Everyone knew what they were getting at. Grant was all right, and everyone knew it. It was silly of him to get so worked up over a little slip.

If a policeman's heart can be said to ache, then Williams's stout heart ached for his superior.

"You can get rid of this disgusting object," Grant said, indicating the coat. "It's twenty years old, at least, and hasn't had a button on it for the last ten. That's one thing that puzzles me, you know, Williams. He had it at the beach, and it was missing when he came back. He had to get rid of that coat somewhere along his route. It isn't a very extensive route, when all is said. And there wasn't time for him to go far off it. He'd be too anxious to get back and cover up his mistake in going away. And yet we haven't turned the coat up. Two duck ponds, both shallow, both well dragged. Three streams that wouldn't hide a penny and wouldn't float a paper boat. Ditches beaten, garden walls inspected on the wrong side, two copses scoured. Nothing! What did he do with it? What would you do with it?"

"Burn it."

"No time. It's damp too. Soaking wet, probably."

"Roll it small and stick it in the fork of a tree. Everyone looks on the ground for things."

"Williams, you're a born criminal. Tell Sanger your theory and ask him to make use of it this afternoon. I'd rather have that coat than have Tisdall. In fact, I've got to have that coat!"

"Talking of razors, you don't think maybe, he took his razor with him, sir?"

"I didn't think of it. Shouldn't think he had the presence of mind. But then I didn't think he'd have the nerve to bolt. I concentrated on suicide. Where are his things?"

"Sanger took them over here in the case. Everything he had."

"Just see if his razor is there? It's just as well to know whether he's shaved or not."

There was no razor.

"Well!" said Grant. "Who'd have thought it! 'You disappoint me, Inspector,' says he, quietly pocketing the razor, and arranging his get-away with the world's prize chump of a detective watching him. I'm all wrong about that lad, Sergeant. All wrong. I thought first, when I took him from the inquest that he was one of these hysterical, do-it-on-the-spur-of-the-moment creatures. Then, after I knew about the will, I changed my mind. Still thought him a 'poor thing,' though. And now I find he was planning a get-away under my very nose—and he brought it off! It isn't Tisdall who's a washout, it's me!"

"Cheer up, sir. Our luck is out at the moment. But you and I between us, and no one else, so help me, are going to put that cold-blooded brute where he belongs," Williams said fervently, not knowing that the person who was to be the means of bringing the murderer of Christine Clay to justice was a rather silly little woman in Kansas City who had never heard of any of them.

# 11

ERICA STOOD ON the brake and brought her disreputable little car to a standstill. She then backed it the necessary yards, and stopped again. She inspected with interest the sole of a man's boot, visible in the grass and gorse, and then considered the wide empty landscape and the mile-long straight of chalky lane with its borders of speedwell and thrift, shining in the sun.

"You can come out," she said. "There's no one in sight for miles."

The boot sole disappeared and a man's astonished face appeared in the bushes above it.

"That's a great relief to me," Erica observed. "I thought for a moment that you might be dead."

"How did you know it was me? I suppose you *did* know it was me?"

"Yes. There's a funny squiggle on the instep part of your sole where the price has been scored off. I noticed it when you were lying on the floor of Father's office."

"Oh, yes; that's who you are, of course. You're a very good detective."

"You're a very bad escaper. No one could have missed your foot."

"You didn't give me much time. I didn't hear your car till it was nearly on me."

"You must be deaf. She's one of the County jokes, poor Tinny. Like Lady Middleway's hat and old Mr. Dyne's shell-collection."

"Tinny?"

"Yes. She used to be Christina, but the inevitable happened. You couldn't *not* have heard her."

"I think perhaps I was asleep for a minute or two. I—I'm a bit short of sleep."

"Yes, I expect so. Are you hungry?"

"Is that just an academic question, or—or are you offering me food?"

Erica reached into the back of the car and produced half a dozen rolls, a glass of tongue, half a pound of butter, and four tomatoes.

"I've forgotten a tin-opener," she said, passing him the tongue, "but if you hit the tin lid hard with a flint it will make a hole." She split a roll with a pen knife produced from her pocket and began to butter it.

"Do you always carry food about with you?" he asked, doubtfully.

"Oh, always. I'm a very hungry person. Besides I'm often not home from morning till night. Here's the knife. Cut a hunk of the tongue and lay it on that." She gave him the buttered roll. "I want the knife back for the other roll."

He did as he was bidden, and she busied herself with the knife again, politely ignoring him so that he should not have to pretend to an indifference that would be difficult of achievement.

Presently he said, "I suppose you know that all this is very wrong?"

"Why is it wrong?"

"For one thing, you're aiding an escaped criminal, which is wrong in itself, and doubly wrong in your father's daughter. And for another—and this is much worse—if I were what they think me you'd be in the gravest danger at this minute. You shouldn't *do* things like that, you know."

"If you were a murderer it wouldn't help you much to commit another one just to keep me from saying I saw you."

"If you've committed one, I suspect you don't easily stop at another. You can only be hanged once. And so you don't think I did it?"

"I'm quite sure you didn't."

"What makes you so sure?"

"You're not capable of it."

"Thank you," he said gratefully.

"I didn't mean it that way."

"Oh! Oh, I see." A smile actually broke through. "Disconcerting but invigorating. George an ancestor of yours?"

"George? Oh. No. No, I can tell lies with the best."

"You'll have to tonight. Unless you are going to give me up."

"I don't suppose anyone will question me at all," she said, ignoring the latter half of his remark. "I don't think a beard becomes you, by the way."

"I don't like it myself. I took a razor with me but couldn't manage to do anything without soap and water. I suppose you haven't soap in the car?"

"I'm afraid not. I don't wash as often as I eat. But there's a frothy stuff in a bottle—Snowdrop, they call it—that I use to clean my hands when I change a wheel. Perhaps that would work." She got out the bottle from the car pocket. "You must be much cleverer than I thought you were, you know."

"Yes? How clever does that make me actually?"

"To get away from Inspector Grant. He's very good at his job, Father says."

"Yes, I think he probably is. If I didn't happen to have a horror of being shut up, I wouldn't have had the nerve to run. As it was, that half-hour was the most exciting thing that ever happened to me. I know now what living at top speed means. I used to think having money and doing what you liked—twenty different things a day—was living at speed. But I just didn't know anything about it."

"Was she nice, Christine Clay?"

He looked disconcerted. "You do jump about, don't you? Yes, she was a grand person." He forgot his food for a moment. "Do you know what she did? She left me her ranch in California because she knew I had no money and hated an office."

"Yes, I know."

"You know?"

"Yes, I've heard Father and the others discussing it."

"Oh. Oh, yes. . . . And you still believe I didn't do it? I must be very bargain counter in your eyes!"

"Was she very beautiful?"

"Haven't you ever seen her, then? On the screen, I mean?"

"No. I don't think so."

"Neither have I. Funny, isn't it? I suppose, roaming from place to place it's easy to miss pictures."

"I'm afraid I don't go to the cinema often. It's a long way to a good one from our place. Have some more tongue."

"She meant to do me such a good turn—Chris. Irony, isn't it? That her gift should be practically my death warrant."

"I suppose you have no idea who could have done it?"

"No. I didn't know any of her friends, you know. She just picked me up one night." He considered the schoolgirlish figure before him. "I suppose that sounds dreadful to you?"

"Oh, no. Not if you liked the look of each other. I judge a lot on looks."

"I can't help feeling that the police may be making a mistake—I mean, that it was just accident. If you'd seen the country that morning. Utterly deserted. No one going to be awake for at least another hour. It's almost incredible that someone should have been out for murder at that time and in that place. That button *might* be an accident, after all."

"If your coat turned up with the buttons on it, would that prove you had nothing to do with it?"

"Yes, I think so. That seemed to be all the evidence the police had." He smiled a little. "But you know more about it than I do."

"Where were you when you lost it—the coat, I mean?"

"We'd gone over to Dymchurch one day: Tuesday, it was. And we left the car to walk along the sea-wall for about half an hour. Our coats were always left lying in the back. I didn't miss mine till we stopped for petrol about half-way home, and I turned round to get the bag Chris had flung there when she got in." His face suddenly flamed scarlet, and Erica watched him in surprise and then in embarrassment. It was moments later before it occurred to her that the tacit admission that the woman was paying was more humiliating to him than any murder accusation. "The coat wasn't there then," he went on hurriedly, "so it could only have gone while we were walking."

"Gipsies?"

"I don't think so. I didn't see any. A casual passer-by, more likely."

"Is there anything to tell that the coat is yours? You'd have to prove it to the police, you know."

"My name is on the lining—one of those tailor's tags, you know."

"But if it was stolen that would be the first thing they'd take off."

"Yes. Yes I suppose so. There's another thing, though. There's a small burn on the right-hand side below the pocket, where someone held a cigarette against it."

"That's better, isn't it! That would settle it very nicely."

"*If* the coat were found!"

"Well, no one who stole a coat is likely to bring it to the police station just because the police want it. And the police are not looking for coats *on* people. They're looking for discarded ones. So far no one has done anything about getting *your* coat. On your behalf, I mean. To be evidence for you."

"Well, what can I do?"

"Give yourself up."

"What!"

"Give yourself up. Then they'll give you a lawyer and things. And it will be his business to look for the coat."

"I couldn't do that. I just couldn't, What's-Your-Name."

"Erica."

"Erica. The thought of having a key turned on me gives me the jitters."

"Claustrophobia?"

"Yes. I don't really mind closed spaces as long as I know that I can get out. Caves and things. But to have a key turned on me, and then to have nothing to do but sit and think of— I just couldn't do it."

"No, I suppose you couldn't, if you feel like that about it. It's a pity. It's much the most sensible way. What are you going to do now?"

"Sleep out again, I suppose. There's no rain coming."

"Haven't you any friends who'd look after you?"

"With a murder charge against me? No! You overrate human friendship." He paused a moment, and added, in a surprised voice: "No. No, perhaps you don't, at that. I've just not met the right kind before."

"Then we had better decide on a place where I can meet you tomorrow and bring you some more food. Here, if you like."

"No!"

"Where then?"

"I didn't mean that. I mean that you're not meeting me anywhere."

"Why not?"

"Because you'd be committing a felony, or whatever it is. I don't know what the penalty is, but you'd be a criminal. It can't be done."

"Well, you can't stop me dropping food out of the car, can you? There is no law against that, that I know of. It will just happen that a cheese and a loaf and some chocolates will fall out of the car into these bushes tomorrow morning. I must go now. The landscape looks deserted, but if you leave a car standing long enough someone always pops up to make enquiries."

She swept the refuse of the food into the car, and got in herself.

He made a movement to get to his feet.

"Don't be foolish," she said sharply. "Keep down."

He swivelled round on to his knees. "All right. You can't object to this position. And it expresses my feelings much better."

She shut the car door, and leaned over it.

"Nut or plain?"

"What?"

"The chocolate."

"Oh! The kind with raisins in it, please. Some day, Erica Burgoyne, I shall crown you with rubies and make you to walk on carpets rich as—"

But the sentence was lost in the roar of Tinny's departure.

# 12

"KINDNESS," SAID ERICA, to her father's head groom, "have you anything laid by?"

Kindness paused in his checking of the corn account, shot her a pale glance from a wrinkled old eye, and went on with his adding.

"Tuppence!" he said at length, in the tone one uses instead of a spit.

This referred to the account, and Erica waited. Kindness hated accounts.

"Enough to bury me decent," he said, having reached the top of the column again.

"You don't want to be buried yet a while. Could you lend me ten pounds, do you think?"

The old man paused in licking his stub of pencil, so that the lead made a purple stain on the exposed tip of his tongue.

"So that's the way it is!" he said. "What have you been doing now?"

"I haven't *been* doing anything. But there are some things I might want to do. And petrol is a dreadful price."

The mention of petrol was a bad break.

"Oh, the car, is it?" he said jealously. Kindness hated Tinny. "If it's the car you want it for, why don't you ask Hart?"

"Oh, I *couldn't*." Erica was almost shocked. "Hart is quite new." Hart being a newcomer with only eleven years' service.

Kindness looked mollified.

"It isn't anything shady," she assured him. "I would have got it from Father at dinner tonight; the money, I mean; but he has gone to Uncle William's for the night. And women are so inquisitive," she added after a pause.

This, which could only refer to Nannie, made up the ground she had lost over the petrol. Kindness hated Nannie.

"Ten pounds is a big bit out of my coffin," he said with a sideways jerk of the head.

"You won't need it before Saturday. I have eight pounds in the bank, but I don't want to waste time tomorrow morning going into Westover for it. Time is awfully precious just now. If anything happens to me, you're sure of eight pounds anyhow. And Father is good for the other two."

"And what made you come to Kindness?"

There was complacence in the tone, and anyone but Erica would have said: Because you are my oldest friend, because you have always helped me out of difficulties since I was three years old and first put my legs astride a pony, because you can keep my counsel and yours, because in spite of your cantankerousness you are an old darling.

But Erica said, "I just thought how much handier tea-caddies were than banks."

*"What's that!"*

"Oh, perhaps I shouldn't have said that. Your wife told me about that, one day I was having tea with her. It wasn't her fault, really. I saw the notes peering through the tea. A bit germy, I thought. For the tea, I mean. But an awfully good idea." As Kindness was still speechless. "Boiling water kills most things, anyhow. Besides," she said, bringing up as support what she should have used for attack, "who else could I go to?"

She reached over and took the stub of pencil from him, turned over a handbill of the local gymkhana which was lying on the saddle-room table, and wrote in school-girl characters on the back:

*I owe Bartholomew Kindness ten pounds. Erica Meir Burgoyne.*

"That will do until Saturday," she said. "My cheque book is finished, anyhow."

"I don't like you frittering away my brass handles all over Kent," Kindness grumbled.

"I think brass handles are very showy," Erica said. "You'd do much better to have wrought iron."

As they went through the gardens together towards his cottage and the tea-caddy, Erica said:

"About how many pawnbrokers are there in Kent?"

" 'Bout two thousand."

"Oh, dear!" said Erica. And let the conversation lapse.

But the two thousand pawnbrokers slept with her that night, and leaped awake before her waking eyes.

Two thousand! My hat!

But of course Kindness was just guessing. He probably had never pawned anything in his life. How could he know in the very least how many pawnbrokers there were in a county? Still, there was bound to be quite a number. Even in a well-to-do county like Kent. She had never noticed even one. But she supposed you wouldn't notice one unless you happened to be looking for it. Like mushrooms.

It was half-past six of a hot, still morning as she backed Tinny out of the garage, and no one was awake in the bland white house that smiled at her as she went. Tinny made a noise at any time, but the noise she made in the before-breakfast silence of a summer morning was obscene. And for the first time Erica was guilty of disloyalty in her feeling for Tinny. Exasperated she had been often; yes, furious; but it had always been the fury of possession, the anger one feels for someone so loved as to be part of oneself. Never in her indignation, never in the moments of her friends' laughter, had she ever been tempted to disown Tinny. Still less to give her up.

But now she thought quite calmly, I shall really have to get a new car. Erica was growing up.

Tinny expostulated her way through the quiet shining lanes, chuffing, snorting, and shaking, while Erica sat upright in the old-fashioned seat and ceased to think about her. Beside her was a box containing half a spring chicken, bread and butter, tomatoes, shortbread, and a bottle of milk. This— "Miss Erica's lunch"—was the Steynes housekeeper's unwitting contribution to the confounding of the Law. Beyond it, in a brown-paper parcel, was Erica's own subscription—a less delicate but more filling one than the housekeeper's —purchased at Mr.-Deeds-in-the-village. ("Eastindiaman and provision Merchant. All the Best in Season.") Mr. Deeds had provided pink and shining slices of jellied veal ("Do you really want it as thick as that, Miss Erica?") but he had not been able to supply a brand of chocolates with raisins in it. No demand for that, there wasn't.

It had not even crossed Erica's mind that she was tired, that there remained less than an hour before closing-time, and that a starving man might just as well have good solid lumps of plain chocolate as be indulged in his light preference for raisins. No; Erica—although she could not have told you about it—knew all about the importance of little things. Especially the importance of little things when one was unhappy. In the hot and dusty evening she had toured the neighbouring villages with a determination that grew with her lack of success. So that now, in the torn and gaping pocket of Tinny's near door, lay four half-pound slabs of chocolate with raisins in it; the whole stock of Mrs.-Higgs-at-Leytham, who at a quarter past seven had been persuaded to leave her high tea ("only for you I'd do it, Miss Burgoyne, not for another soul") and turn the enormous key in her small blistered door.

It was after seven before she had clamoured her way through sleeping Mallingford and entered the hot, shadeless country beyond. As she turned into the long straight of the chalky lane where her quick country-trained eyes had noticed that boot yesterday, she wished that Tisdall might have better cover than those gorse bushes. Not cover from the Law, but cover from the sky there was going to be at midday. A blazing day, it was going to be. Tisdall would need all of that bottle of milk and those tomatoes. She debated whether or not it would be a good move to transport the fugitive to other climes. Over to Charing, for instance. There were woods enough there to house an army in safety from sun and law. But Erica had never much liked woods, and had never felt particularly safe in one. It was better to be hot in gorse bushes and be able to see a long way away, than have strangers stumbling over you in the cool of thick trees. Besides, the Tisdall man might refuse the offer of a lift.

There is no doubt as to what the Tisdall man's answer would have been, but the proposition was never put to him. Either he was so dead asleep that not even the uproar of Tinny's advent could rouse him, or he was no longer in that piece of country. Erica went to the end of the mile-long straight, Tinny full out and making a noise like an express train, and came back to the spot where she had stopped yesterday. As she shut off the engine, the silence fell about her, absolute. Not even a lark sang, not a shadow stirred.

She waited there, quietly, not looking about her, her arms propped on the wheel in the attitude of one considering her future movements. There must be no expectancy in her appearance to arouse suspicion in the mind of stray countrymen. For twenty minutes she sat, relaxed and incurious. Then she stretched herself, made sure during the stretch that the lane was still unoccupied, and got out. If Tisdall had wanted to speak to her, he would have reached her before now. She took the two parcels and the chocolate and cached them where Tisdall had been lying yesterday. To these she added a packet of cigarettes produced from her own sagging pocket. Erica did not smoke herself—she had tried it, of course, had not much liked it, and with the logic that was her ruling characteristic had not persisted—and she did not know that Tisdall smoked. These, and the matches, were just "in case." Erica never did a job that was not thorough.

She climbed in again, pressed Tinny into life, and without a pause or backward glance headed down the lane, her face and thoughts turned to the far-off coast and Dymchurch.

It was Erica's very sound theory that no "local" had stolen that coat. She had lived all her life in a country community, and knew very well that a new black overcoat cannot make its appearance even on the meanest back without receiving a truly remarkable amount of attention. She knew, too, that your countryman is not versed in the ways of pawnshops, and that a coat lying in a car would not represent to him a possible cash value, as it would to someone "on the road." If he coveted it at all, it would be for possession; and the difficulty of explaining its appearance would result in his leaving it where it was. The coat, therefore, according to Erica's reasoning, had been taken by a "casual."

This made things at once easier and more difficult. A "casual" is a much more noticeable person than a "local," and so easier to identify. On the other hand, a "casual" is a movable object and difficult to track. In the week that

A SHILLING FOR CANDLES 217

had passed since the theft, that coat might have traversed most of Kent. It might now be——

Hunger gave wings to Erica's imagination. By the time she was in sight of Dymchurch she had, thanks to modern methods of hitchhiking and old-fashioned methods of stowing away, placed the coat on the back of a clerk in the office of the Mayor of Bordeaux. He was a little pale clerk with a delicate wife and puny baby, and Erica's heart was sore at the thought of having to take the coat from him, even for Tisdall.

At this point Erica decided that she must eat. Fasting was good for the imagination but bad for logic. She stepped on the brake at sight of The Rising Sun, "good pull-up for car men, open all night." It was a tin shed, set down by the roadside with the inconsequence of a matchbox, painted gamboge and violet, and set about with geraniums. The door was hospitably open, and the sound of voices floated out on the warm air.

In the tiny interior were two very large men. The proprietor was cutting very large slices from a very fresh loaf, and the other man was sipping very hot liquid from a very large mug with very great noise. At sight of Erica on the doorstep all these activities ceased abruptly.

"Good morning," said Erica into the silence.

"Morning, miss," said the proprietor. "Cup of tea, perhaps?"

"Well—" Erica looked round. "You haven't any bacon, by any chance?"

"Lovely bacon," said the owner promptly. "Melt in your mouth."

"I'll have a lot," said Erica happily.

"Egg with it, perhaps?"

"Three," said Erica.

The owner craned his neck to see out the door, and found that she really was alone.

"Come," he said. "That's something like. Nice to see a young girl that can appreciate her vittles these days. Have a seat, miss." He dusted an iron chair for her with the corner of his apron. "Bacon be ready in no time. Thick or thin?"

"Thick, please. Good morning." This to the other man, in more particular greeting, as she sat down and so definitely became a partner in this business of eating and drinking. "Is that your lorry out there? I have always wanted to drive one of those."

"Ye'? I've always wanted to be a tightrope walker."

"You're the wrong build," said Erica seriously. "Better stick to lorry driving." And the owner paused in his slicing of the bacon to laugh.

The lorry driver decided that sarcasm was wasted on so literal a mind. He relaxed into amiability.

"Oh, well; nice to have ladies' company for a change, eh, Bill?"

"Don't you have lots of it?" asked Erica. "I thought lorries were very popular." And before the astounded man could make up his mind whether this skinny child was being rude, provocative, or merely matter of fact, she went on, "Do you give lifts to tramps, ever, by the way?"

"Never!" said the driver promptly, glad to feel his feet on firm ground.

"That's a pity. I'm interested in tramps."

"Christian interest?" enquired Bill, turning the sizzling bacon in the pan.

"No. Literary."

"Well, now. You writing a book?"

"Not exactly. I'm gathering material for someone else. You must *see* a lot of tramps, even if you don't give them lifts," she persisted, to the driver.

"No time to see anyone when you're driving that there."

"Tell her about Harrogate Harry," prompted Bill, breaking eggs. "I saw him in your cab last week sometime."

"Never saw anyone in my cab, you didn't."

"Oh, come unstuck, will you? The little lady's all right. She's not the sort to go blabbing even if you did give an odd tramp a lift."

"Harrogate isn't a tramp."

"Who is he, then?" asked Erica.

"He's a china merchant. Travelling."

"Oh, I know. A blue-and-white bowl in exchange for a rabbit skin."

"No. Nothing like that. Mends teapot handles and such."

"Oh. Does he make much?" This for the sake of keeping the driver on the subject.

"Enough to be going on with. And he cadges an old coat or a pair of boots now and then."

Erica said nothing for a moment, and she wondered if the thumping of her heart was as audible to these two men as it was in her ears. An old coat, now and then. What should she say now? She could not say: Did he have a coat the day you saw him? That would be a complete give-away.

"He sounds interesting," she said, at last. "Mustard, please," to Bill. "I should like to meet him. But I suppose he is at the other end of the county by now. What day did you see him?"

"Lemme see. I picked him up outside Dymchurch and dropped him near Tonbridge. That was a week last Monday."

So it hadn't been Harrogate. What a pity! He had sounded so hopeful a subject, with his desire for coats and boots, his wandering ways, and his friendliness with lorry drivers who get a man away quickly from possibly unfriendly territory. Oh, well, it was no good imagining that it was going to be as easy as this had promised to be.

Bill set down the mustard by her plate. "Not Monday," he said. "Not that it makes any difference. But Jimmy was here unloading stores when you went by. Tuesday, it was."

Not that it made any difference! Erica took a great mouthful of eggs and bacon to quiet her singing heart.

For a little there was silence in The Rising Sun; partly because Erica had a masculine habit of silence while she ate, partly because she had not yet made up her mind what it would be both politic and productive to say next. She was startled into anxiety when the lorry driver thrust his mug away from him and rose to go.

"But you haven't told me about Harrogate What's-His-Name!"

"What is there to tell?"

"Well, a travelling china-mender must be chock full of interest. I *would* like to meet him and have a talk."

"He isn't much of a talker."

"I'd make it worth his while."

Bill laughed. "If you was to give Harrogate five bob, he'd talk his head off. And for ten he'll tell you how he found the south pole."

Erica turned to the more sympathetic one of the two.

"You know him? Does he have a home, do you know?"

"In winter he stays put, mostly, I think. But in summer he lives in a tent."

"Living with Queenie Webster somewhere near Pembury," put in the driver, who didn't like the shift of interest to Bill.

He put down some coppers on the scrubbed table and moved to the door.

"And if you're making it worth anyone's while, I'd square Queenie first if I was you."

"Thank you," said Erica. "I'll remember. Thank you for your help."

The genuine warmth of gratitude in her voice made him pause. He stood in the doorway considering her. "Tramps are a queer taste for a girl with a healthy appetite," he said, and went out to his lorry.

# 13

ERICA'S HEALTHY APPETITE extended to bread and marmalade and several cups of tea, but she absorbed little information with the nourishment. Bill, for all his willingness to give her anything she wanted, knew very little about Harrogate Harry. She had now to decide whether or not to leave a "warm" Dymchurch and follow the unknown and elusive Harry into the "cold" of the Tonbridge country.

"Are most tramps honest, would you say?" she asked as she was paying her bill.

"We-ll," said Bill, thinking it out, "honest up to the point of opportunity, if you know what I mean."

Erica knew. Not one tramp in fifty would refuse the gift of a coat lying unattended. And Harrogate Harry definitely liked to acquire coats and boots. And Harry had been in Dymchurch a week last Tuesday. Her job, therefore, was to follow the china-mender through the summer landscape until she caught up with him. If night overtook her in her search she must think of some really reassuring lie which could be telephoned to her father at Steynes to account for her absence. The need for lying caused her the first pang she had suffered so far in her self-appointed crusade; she had never needed to shut out her father from any ploy of hers. For the second time in a few hours her loyalty was divided. She had not noticed her disloyalty to Tinny; but this time she noticed and cared.

Oh, well, the day was young, and days just now were long. And Tinny might be a veteran but she was never sick or sorry. If luck held as it had begun she might still be back in her own bed at Steynes tonight. Back at Steynes—*with the coat!*

Her breath stopped at the very prospect.

She said good-bye to the admiring Bill, promised to recommend his break-fasts to all her friends, and set Tinny's nose west and north through the hot flowery country. The roads were blinding now in the glare of the sky, the horizons beginning to swim. Tinny sweltered stoutly through the green furnace, and was soon as comfortable as a frying-pan. In spite of her eager-ness Erica was forced every few miles to pause and open both doors while Tinny cooled. Yes, she really must get another car.

Near Kippings Cross, on the main Tonbridge road, she repeated as tactics what she had by accident found serviceable: she pulled up for lunch at a wayside hut. But this time luck was lacking in the service. The hut was kept by a jolly woman with a flow of conversation but no interest in tramps. She had all the normal woman's intolerance of a waster, and "didn't encourage vagrants." Erica ate sparingly and drank her bottled coffee, glad of the tem-porary shade; but presently she rose and went out to find a "better place." The "better" referring not to food but to possible information. With a self-control beyond praise she turned her eyes away from the endless tea-gardens, green and cool, with gay cloths gleaming like wet stones in the shadows. Not for her that luxury today. Tea-gardens knew nothing of tramps.

She turned down a lane to Goudhurst, and sought an inn. Inns had always china to mend, and now that she was in Harrogate's home country, so to speak, she would surely find someone who knew him.

She ate cold underdone beef and green salad in a room as beautiful as any at Steynes, and prayed that one, at least, of the dishes on her table, should be cracked. When the tinned fruit appeared in a broken china rose-bowl she nearly whooped aloud.

Yes, the waitress agreed, it was a pretty bowl. She didn't know if it was valuable or not, she was only there for the season (it being understood that the possible value of household goods could not interest anyone whose play-ground was the world). Yes, she supposed that someone local mended their china but she didn't know. Yes, she *could* ask, of course.

The landlord, asked who had mended the china bowl so beautifully, said that that particular bowl was bought just as it was, in a job lot of stuff over at Matfield Green. And anyhow it was so old a mend that the man that did it was probably dead by now. But if Erica wanted a man to mend her china, there was a good travelling man who came round now and then. Palmer, by name. He could put fifty pieces together when he was sober without showing a join. But you'd got to be sure he was sober.

Erica listened to the vices and virtues of Palmer, and asked if he was the only one in the district.

The only one the landlord knew. But you couldn't find a better than Harry.

"Harry?"

That was his name. Harrogate Harry they called him. No, the landlord did not know where he was to be found. Lived in a tent Brenchley way, so he understood. Not the kind of household that Erica had better visit alone, he thought he had better say. Harry was no example as a citizen.

Erica went out into the heat encouraged by the news that for days, sometimes weeks, together, Harry did not stir away from his temporary home. As soon as he made a little extra money, he sat back and drank it.

Well, if one is going to interview a china-mender one's first necessity is broken china. Erica drove into Tunbridge Wells, hoping that the great-aunt who lived sombrely in Claverly Park was sleeping off her forbidden pastry and not promenading under the lime trees, and in an antique shop spent some of Kindness's coffin money on a frivolous little porcelain figure of a dancer. She drove back to Pembury and in the afternoon quiet of a deep lane proceeded to drop the dancer with abandon on the running-board of the car. But the dancer was tough. Even when Erica took her firmly by the feet and tapped her on the jamb of the door, she remained whole. In the end, afraid that greater violence might shatter her completely, she snapped off an arm with her finger and thumb, and there was her passport to Harrogate Harry.

You cannot ask questions about a vague tramp who, you think, may have stolen a coat. But to look for a china-mender is quite a legitimate search, involving no surprise or suspicion in the minds of the questioned. It took Erica only ninety minutes to come face to face with Harrogate. It would have taken her less, but the tent was a long way from any made road; first up a cart track through woods, a track impassable even for the versatile Tinny, then across an open piece of gorse land with far views of the Medway valley, and into a second wood to a clearing at its further edge, where a stream ran down to a dark pool.

Erica wished that the tent had not been in a wood. From her earliest childhood she had been fearless by nature (the kind of child of whom older people say out hunting: Not a nerve in her body), but there was no denying that she didn't like woods. She liked to see a long way away. And though the stream ran bright and clear and merry in the sunlight, the pool in the hollow was still and deep and forbidding. One of those sudden, secret cups of black water more common in Sussex than in Kent.

As she came across the clearing carrying the little dancer in her hand, a dog rushed out at her, shattering the quiet with hysterical protest. And at the noise a woman came to the tent door and stood there watching Erica as she came. She was a very tall woman, broad-shouldered and straight, and Erica had the mad feeling that this long approach to her over an open floor should end in a curtsey.

"Good afternoon," she called, cheerfully, above the clamour of the dog. But the woman waited without moving. "I have a piece of china— Can't you make that dog be quiet?" She was face to face with her now, only the noise of the dog between them.

The woman lifted a foot to the animal's ribs, and the high yelling died into silence. The murmur of the stream came back.

Erica showed the broken porcelain figure.

"Harry!" called the woman, her black inquisitive eyes not leaving Erica. And Harry came to the tent door: a small weaselish man with bloodshot eyes, and evidently in the worst of tempers. "A job for you."

"I'm not working," said Harry, and spat.

"Oh. I'm sorry. I heard you were very good at mending things."

The woman took the figure and broken piece from Erica's hands. "He's working, all right," she said.

Harry spat again, and took the pieces. "Have you the money to pay?" he asked, angrily.

"How much will it be?"

"Two shillings."

"Two and six," said the woman.

"Oh, yes, I have that much."

He went back into the tent, and the woman stood in the way, so that Erica could neither follow nor see. Unconsciously she had, in imagining this moment, always placed herself inside the tent—with the coat folded up in the corner. Now she was not even to be allowed to see inside.

"He won't be long," Queenie said. "By the time you've cut a whistle from the ash tree, it'll be ready."

Erica's small sober face broke into one of its rare smiles. "You thought I couldn't do that, didn't you?" For the woman's phrase had been a flick in the face of a supposed town-dweller.

She cut the wood with her pocket-knife, shaped it, nicked it, and damped it in the stream, hoping that a preoccupation might disarm Queenie and her partner. She even hoped that the last processes of whistle-manufacture might be made in friendly company with the mending of china. But the moment she moved back to the tent, Queenie came from her desultory stick-gathering in the wood to stand guard. And Erica found her whistle finished and the mended figure in her hands, without being one whit wiser or richer than she was when she left the car in the road. She could have cried.

She produced her small purse (Erica hated a bag) and paid her half-crown, and the sight of the folded notes in the little back partition all waiting to do their work of rescue, drove her to desperation. Without any warning and without knowing she was going to say it, she asked the man:

"What did you do with the coat you took at Dymchurch?"

There was a moment of complete stillness, and Erica rushed on:

"I don't want to do anything about it. Prosecuting, or anything like that, I mean. But I do want that coat awfully bad. I'll buy it back from you if you still have it. Or if you've pawned it—"

"You're a nice one!" the man burst out. "Coming here to have a job of work done and then accusing a man of battle and blue murder. You be out of here before I lose my temper good and proper and crack you one on the side of the jaw. Impudent little —— with your loose tongue. I've a good mind to twist it out of your bloody head, and what's more I—"

The woman pushed him aside and stood over Erica, tall and intimidating. "What makes you think my man took a coat?"

"The coat he had when Jake, the lorry driver, gave him a lift a week last Tuesday was taken from a car at Dymchurch. We know that." She hoped the "we" sounded well. And she hoped she didn't sound as doubtful as she felt. They were both very innocent and indignant-looking. "But it isn't a matter of making a case. We only want the coat back. I'll give you a pound for it," she added, as they were about to break in on her again.

She saw their eyes change. And in spite of her predicament a great relief flooded her. The man was *the* man. They knew what coat she was talking about.

"And if you've pawned it, I'll give you ten shillings to tell me where."

"What do you get out of this?" the woman said. "What do *you* want with a man's coat?"

"I didn't say anything about it being a man's." Triumph ran through her like an electric shock.

"Oh, never mind!" Queenie dismissed with rough impatience any further pretence. "What is it to you?"

If she mentioned murder they would both panic, and deny with their last breath any knowledge of the coat. She knew well, thanks to her father's monologues, the petty offender's horror of major crime. They would go to almost any lengths to avoid being mixed up, even remotely, in a capital charge.

"It's to get Hart out of trouble," she said. "He shouldn't have left the car unattended. The owner is coming back tomorrow, and if the coat isn't found by then Hart will lose his job."

"Who's Art?" asked the woman. "Your brother?"

"No. Our chauffeur."

"Chauffeur!" Harry gave a high skirl of laughter that had little amusement in it. "That's a good one. I suppose you have two Rolls Royces and five Bentleys." His little red eyes ran over her worn and outgrown clothes.

"No. Just a Lanchester and my old Morris." As their disbelief penetrated: "My name is Erica Burgoyne. My father is Chief Constable."

"Ye'? My name is John D. Rockfeller, and my father was the Duke of Wellington."

Erica whipped up her short tweed skirt, gripped the elastic waistband of the gym knickers she wore summer and winter, and pushed the inner side of it towards him on an extended thumb.

"Can you read?" she said.

"Erica M. Burgoyne," read the astonished man, in red on a Cash's label.

"It's a great mistake to be too sceptical," she said, letting the elastic snap back into place.

"So you're doing it for a chauffeur, eh?" Harry leered at her, trying to get back his lost ground. "You're very concerned about a chauffeur, aren't you?"

"I'm desperately in love with him," Erica said, in the tone in which one says: "And a box of matches, please." At school theatricals Erica had always had charge of the curtains.

But it passed. Their minds were too full of speculation to be concerned with emotion.

"How much?" said the woman.

"For the coat?"

"No. For telling you where to find it."

"I told you, I'll give you ten shillings."

"Not enough."

"But how do I know you'll tell me the truth?"

"How do we know you're telling the truth?"

"All right, I'll give you a pound. I shall still have to buy it from the pawn-shop, you know."

"It isn't in a pawnshop," the man said. "I sold it to a stone-breaker."

"W-h-a-t!" cried Erica in a despairing wail. "Do I have to begin looking for someone else?"

"Oh, no need to look, no need at all. You hand over the cash, and I'll tell you where to find the bloke."

Erica took out a pound note and showed it to him. "Well?"

"He's working at the Five Wents cross-road, Paddock Wood way. And if he ain't there, he lives in a cottage in Capel. Near the church."

Erica held out the note. But the woman had seen the contents of the purse.

"Wait, Harry! She'll pay more." She moved between Erica and the path through the wood.

"I won't give you a penny more," Erica said incisively. Indignation overcame her awareness of the black pool, the silence, and her dislike of woods. "That's cheating."

The woman grabbed at her purse; but Erica had played lacrosse for her school only last winter. Queenie's eager hand, to her great astonishment, met not the purse but Erica's other arm, and came up and hit her own face with surprising violence. And Erica was round her stately bulk and running across the clearing, as she had swerved and run, half-bored, half-pleased, through many winter afternoons.

She heard them come after her, and wondered what they would do to her if they caught up with her. She wasn't afraid of the woman, but the man was small and light, and for all his drinking might be speedy. And he knew the path. In the shade of the trees, after the bright sunlight, she could hardly see a path at all. She wished she had said that someone was waiting for her in the car. It would have been—

Her foot caught in a root, and she rolled over and over.

She heard him coming thudding down the soft path, and as she sat up his face appeared, as it were swimming towards her, above the undergrowth. In a few seconds he would be on her. She had fallen heavily because she was still clutching something in either hand. She looked to see what she was holding. In one hand was the china figure; in the other her purse and—the whistle.

The whistle! She put it to her mouth and blew a sort of tattoo. Long and short, like a code. A signal.

At the sound the man stopped, only a few yards from her, doubtfully.

"Hart!" she called with all the force of her very good lungs. "Hart!" And whistled again.

"All right," said the man, "all right! You can have your —— Hart. Some day I'll tell your pa what's going on round his house. And I'll bet you pay me more than a few quid then, me lady!"

"Good-bye," said Erica. "Thank your wife from me for the whistle."

# 14

"AND OF COURSE, what *you* want, Inspector, is a rest. A little relaxation." The Chief Constable heaved himself into his raincoat. "Overworking yourself disgracefully. That never got a man anywhere. Except into his grave. Here it is Friday, and I dare swear you haven't had a night's sleep or a proper meal this week. Ridiculous! Mustn't take the thing to heart like that. Criminals have escaped before and will escape again."

"Not from me."

"Overdue, then. That's all I can say. Very overdue. Everyone makes mistakes. Who was to think a door in a bedroom was a fire-escape, anyhow?"

"I should have looked in the cupboards."

"Oh, my dear good sir—!"

"The first one opened towards me, so that I could see inside. And by the time he came to the second he had lulled me into—"

"I told you you were losing your sense of proportion! If you don't get away for a little, you'll be seeing cupboards everywhere. You'll be what your Sergeant Williams calls 'falling down on the job.' You are coming back to dinner with me. You needn't 'but' me! It's only twenty miles."

"But meanwhile something may—"

"We have a telephone. Erica said I was to bring you. Said something about ordering ices specially. You fond of ices? Anyhow, she said she had something to show you."

"Puppies?" Grant smiled.

"Don't know. Probably. Never a moment in the year, it seems to me, when there isn't a litter of sort at Steynes. Here is your excellent substitute. Good evening, Sergeant."

"Good evening, sir," said Williams, rosily pink from his high tea.

"I'm taking Inspector Grant home to dinner with me."

"Very glad, sir. It'll do the Inspector good to eat a proper meal."

"That's my telephone number, in case you want him."

Grant's smile broadened as he watched the spirit that won the empire in full blast. He was very tired. The week had been a long purgatory. The thought of sitting down to a meal in a quiet room among leisured people was like regaining some happier sphere of existence that he had known a long time ago and half-forgotten about. Automatically he put together the papers on the desk.

"To quote one of Sergeant Williams's favourite sayings: 'As a detective I'm a grand farmer.' Thank you, I'd like to come to dinner. Kind of Miss Erica to think of me." He reached for his hat.

"Thinks a lot of you, Erica. Not impressionable as a rule. But you are the big chief, it seems."

"I have a picturesque rival, I'm afraid."

"Oh, yes. Olympia. I remember. I don't know much about bringing up children, you know, Grant," he said as they went out to the car. "Erica's my only one. Her mother died when she was born, and I made her a sort of companion instead of letting her grow up in the nursery. Her old nurse and I were always having words about it. Great stickler for the *comme il faut* and all that, Nannie. Then she went to school. Must find your own level, that's all education is: learning to deal with people. She didn't like it, but she stuck it. A good plucked 'un, she is."

"I think she is a charming child," Grant said heartily, answering the "justifying" tone and the Colonel's worried look.

"That's just it, Grant, that's just it! She isn't a child any longer. She should be coming out. Going to dances. Staying with her aunts in town and meeting people. But she doesn't want to. Just stays at home and runs wild. Doesn't care for clothes or pretties or any of the things she should care about at her age. She's seventeen, you know. It worries me. She's taken to gadding about all over the place in that little car of hers. I don't know where she has been half the time. Not that she doesn't tell me if I ask. Always a truthful child. But it worries me."

"I don't think it need, sir. She'll make her own happiness. You'll see. It's rare to meet anyone of that age who has so sure a knowledge of what she wants."

"Hrrmp!" said the Colonel. "And gets it! George will be there for dinner," he added. "George Meir. Cousin of my wife's. Perhaps you know him? Nerve specialist."

"I know him well by reputation, but I've never met him."

"That's Erica's doing. Nice fellow, George, but a bit of a bore. Don't understand what he's talking about half the time. Reactions, and things. But Erica seems to understand the lingo. Good shot, though: George. Nice fellow!"

Sir George was a nice fellow. Grant liked him at sight, and noticing his narrow cheekbones, felt that some other attribute in him must weigh very strongly with Erica to overcome his physical characteristics. He was certainly a pleasant person, with neither the slight flamboyance nor the condescension so common in Wimpole Street. That he could commiserate with Grant on his non-success without making Grant want to hit him, was a test of his worth. Grant, in fact, turned to him in his sore state, as to someone who would understand. This was a man to whom human failure must be a very ordinary affair.

Colonel Burgoyne had forbidden mention of the Clay affair during dinner, but he might as well have bidden the tides cease. They were all talking Tisdall, Colonel included, before the fish had disappeared. All but Erica, who sat at the end of the table in her demure school-supper white dress, listening quietly. She had powdered her nose, but looked no more grown up than she did by day.

"We never picked up his trail at all," Grant said in answer to a question of Meir. "He just disappeared from the moment he left the hotel. Oh, there were dozens of accounts of men like him, of course. But they all led to nothing. We don't know a thing more than we did last Monday. He might have been sleeping out, the first three nights. But you know what last night was like. Torrents. Not even an animal could have stayed out in it. He must have found shelter somewhere, if he's still alive. It wasn't local, the storm. There are floods from here to the Tyne. And yet another whole day has gone past and not a hint of him."

"No chance of his escaping by sea?"

"Not likely. Curiously enough, not one criminal in a thousand escapes that way."

"So much for our island race!" laughed Meir. "The sea's the last thing they think of. You know, Inspector, I don't know if you know it, but you have made the man very vivid in the half-hour we've been talking. And there's something else you've made clear, I think; something you probably are not aware of yourself."

"What is that?"

"You were surprised in your heart of hearts that he had done it. Perhaps even sorry. You hadn't believed it."

"Yes, I think that's true. You'd have been sorry yourself, Sir George." Grant grinned. "He's very plausible. And he stuck to truth as far as it served him. As I told you, we've checked his statement from beginning to end. It's true as far as it can be checked. But that thin story about stealing the car! And losing his coat—the all-important coat!"

"Curiously enough, I don't think the stealing episode is as incredible as it sounds. His main thought for the past few weeks had been escape. Escape from the disgrace of his spent fortune, from the crowd (whom he seems to have begun to value at their proper worth), from the necessity of earning his living again (tramping was just as mad a notion, in the case of a boy with influential connections, as stealing a car: the escape motif again), and latterly escape from the equivocal situation at the cottage. He must have looked forward, you know, with subconscious dread to the leavetaking that was due in a day or two. He was in a highly emotional condition due to his self-disgust and self-questioning (at bottom what he wanted to escape from was himself). At a moment of low vitality (six in the morning) he is presented with the means of physical escape. A deserted country-side and abandoned car. He is possessed for the time being. When he recovers he is horrified, just as he says. He turns the car without having to think twice, and comes back at the best speed he can make. To his dying day he'll never understand what made him steal the car."

"Stealing will pretty soon not be a crime at all, what with all you specialists," the Colonel remarked with a sort of tart resignation.

"Not a bad theory, sir," Grant said to Meir. "Can you make the thin tale about the coat thicker too?"

"Truth is often terribly thin, don't you think?"

"Are you taking the view that the man may be innocent?"

"I had thought of it."

"Why?"

"I have an excellent opinion of your judgment."

"*My* judgment?"

"Yes. You were surprised the man had done it. That means that your first impression was clouded by circumstantial evidence."

"In fact, I'm logical as well as imaginative. Mercifully, since I'm a police officer. The evidence may be circumstantial but it is very satisfying and neat."

"Much too neat, don't you feel?"

"Lord Edward said that. But no policeman feels that evidence is too neat, Sir George."

"Poor Champneis!" the Colonel said. "Dreadful for him. Very devoted they were, I'm told. A nice fellow. Didn't know him, but knew the family in my young days. Nice people. Dreadful for them!"

"I travelled up from Dover with him on Thursday," Meir said. "I had come over from Calais—I've just come back from a medical conference in Vienna —and he joined the boat train with the usual Champneis lordliness at Dover. He seemed very happy to be back. Showed me some topazes he had brought from Galeria for his wife. They corresponded every day by telegram, it seemed. I found that more impressive than the topazes, if I must be frank. European telegrams being what they are."

"Just a moment, Sir George. Do you mean that Champneis hadn't come over on the boat from Calais?"

"No, oh, no. He came home by yacht. The *Petronel*. It belongs to his elder brother, but he lent it to Edward for the voyage back from Galeria. A charming little ship. She was lying in the harbour."

"Then when had Lord Edward arrived in Dover?"

"The night before, I believe. Too late to go up to town." He paused and looked quizzically at Grant. "Neither logic nor imagination will make Edward Champneis suspect."

"I realise that." Grant went on calmly to prise the stone from a peach, an operation he had suspended abruptly at Meir's phrase about Champneis joining the boat train. "It is of no importance. The police habit of checking up."

But his mind was full of surprise and conjecture. Champneis had distinctly let him understand that he had crossed from Calais on Thursday morning. Not in words but by implication. Grant had made some idle remark, something about the accommodation in the new steamers, and Champneis in his reply had implied that he had been on board that morning. Why? Edward Champneis was in Dover on Wednesday night, and was reluctant to have the fact known. Why? In the name of all that was logical, why?

Because an awkward pause had succeeded the revelation of Champneis's presence in England, Grant said lightly, "Miss Erica hasn't produced the puppies, or whatever it was I was to be shown."

To everyone's surprise Erica grew pink. This was so unheard-of a happening that all three men stared.

"It isn't puppies," she said. "It's something you wanted very much. But I'm terribly afraid you're not going to be happy about it."

"It sounds exciting," admitted Grant, wondering what the child had imagined he wanted. He hoped she hadn't brought him something. Hero-worship was all very well, but it was embarrassing to be given something in full view of the multitude. "Where is it?"

"It's in a parcel up in my room. I thought I'd wait till you had finished your port."

"Is it something you can bring into a dining-room?" her father asked.

"Oh, yes."

"Then Burt will fetch it."

"Oh, no!" she cried, arresting her father's hand on the bell. "I'll get it. I shan't be a minute."

She came back carrying a large brown-paper parcel, which her father said looked like a Salvation Army gift day. She unwrapped it and produced a man's coat, of a greyish black.

"That is the coat you wanted," she said. "But it has all its buttons."

Grant took the coat automatically, and examined it.

"Where in Heaven's name did you get that, Erica?" her father asked, astonished.

"I bought it for ten shillings from a stone-breaker at Paddock Wood. He gave a tramp five shillings for it, and thought it such a bargain that he didn't want to part with it. I had to have cold tea with him, and listen to what the Border Regiment did on the first of July, and see the bullet scar on his shin, before he would give up the coat. I was afraid to go away and leave him with it in case he sold it to someone else, or I couldn't find him again."

"What makes you think this is Tisdall's coat?" Grant asked.

"This," she said, and showed the cigarette burn. "He told me to look for that."

"Who did?"

"Mr. Tisdall!"

"Who?" said all three men at once.

"I met him by accident on Wednesday. And since then I've been searching for the coat. But it was great luck coming across it."

"You met him! Where?"

"In a lane near Mallingford."

"And you didn't report it?" Grant's voice was stern.

"No." Hers quavered just a little, and then went on equably. "You see, I didn't believe he had done it. And I really do like you a lot. I thought it would be better for you if he could be proved innocent before he was really arrested. Then you wouldn't have to set him free again. The papers would be awful about that."

There was a stunned silence for a moment.

Then Grant said, "And on Wednesday Tisdall told you to look for this." He held forward the burned piece, while the others crowded from their places to inspect.

"No sign of a replaced button," Meir observed. "Do you think it's the coat?"

"It may be. We can't try it on Tisdall, but perhaps Mrs. Pitts may be able to identify it."

"But—but," stammered the Colonel—"if it is the coat do you realise what it means?"

"Completely. It means beginning all over again."

His tired eyes, cold with disappointment, met Erica's kind grey ones, but he refused their sympathy. It was too early to think of Erica as his possible saviour. At the moment she was just someone who had thrown a wrench into the machinery.

"I shall have to get back," he said. "May I use your telephone?"

# 15

MRS. PITTS IDENTIFIED the coat. She had dried it at the kitchen fire one day when a thermos bottle of hot water had leaked on it. She had noticed the cigarette burn then.

Sergeant Williams, interviewing the farmer who had identified Tisdall's car, found that he was colour blind.

The truth stuck out with painful clarity. Tisdall had really lost his coat from the car on Tuesday. He had really driven away from the beach. He had not murdered Christine Clay.

By eleven that Friday evening Grant was faced with the fact that they were just where they were a week previously, when he had cancelled a theatre seat and come down to Westover. Worse still, they had hounded a man into flight and hiding, and they had wasted seven days on a dud investigation while the man they wanted made his escape.

Grant's mind was a welter of broken ends and unrelated facts.

Harmer. He came into the picture now, didn't he? They had checked his story as far as it went. He really had made enquiries from the owner of the cherry orchard, and from the post office at Liddlestone at the times he said. But after that, what? After that no one knew anything about his movements until he walked into the cottage at Medley, some time after eight the next morning.

There was—incredibly!—Edward Champneis, who had brought back topazes for his wife, but who, for some reason, was unwilling that his movements on that Wednesday night should be investigated. There could be no other reason for his desire to make Grant believe that he had arrived in England on Thursday morning. He had not come to England secretly. If you want to arrive secretly in a country, arriving in a populous harbour by yacht is not the way to do it. Harbour-master and customs' officials are a constitutionally inquisitive race. Therefore it was not the fact of his arrival that he wanted to hide, but the way in which he had occupied his time since. The more Grant thought about it, the queerer it became. Champneis was at Dover on Wednesday night. At six on Thursday morning his well-loved wife had met her death. And Champneis did not want his movements investigated. Very queer!

There was, too, the "shilling for candles." That, which had first caught his interest and had been put aside in favour of more obvious lines of enquiry, that would have to be looked into.

On Saturday morning the newspapers, beginning to be bored with a four-day-old man hunt, carried the glad news that the hunted man was innocent. "New information having come to police." It was confidently expected that Tisdall would present himself before nightfall, and in that hope reporters and photographers lingered round the County police station in Westover; with more optimism than logic, it would seem, since Tisdall was just as likely to present himself at a station miles away.

But Tisdall presented himself nowhere.

This caused a slight stirring of surprise in Grant's busy mind when he had a moment to remember Tisdall; but that was not often. He wondered why Tisdall hadn't enough sense to come in out of the wet. It had rained again on Friday night and it had been blowing a north-easter and raining all Saturday. One would have thought he would have been glad to see a police station. He was not being sheltered by any of his old friends, that was certain. They had all been shadowed very efficiently during the four days that he was "wanted." Grant concluded that Tisdall had not yet seen a newspaper, and dismissed the thing from his mind.

He had set the official machinery moving to discover the whereabouts of Christine Clay's brother; he had started a train of enquiries which had the object of proving that Jason Harmer had once had a dark coat which he had lately discarded and which had a missing button. And he himself took on the investigation of Lord Edward Champneis. He noticed with his usual self-awareness that he had no intention of going to Champneis and asking for an account of his movements on Wednesday night. It would be highly embarrassing, for one thing, if Champneis proved that he had slept peacefully in his bunk all night. Or at the Lord Warden. Or otherwise had a perfect alibi. For another—oh, well, there was no getting away from the fact; one didn't demand information from the son of a ducal house as one demanded it from a coster. A rotten world, no doubt, but one must conform.

Grant learned that the *Petronel* had gone round to Cowes, where her owner, Giles Champneis, would live in her for Cowes's week. On Sunday morning, therefore, Grant flew down to Gosport, and got a boat across the glittering Spithead to the island. What had been a white flurry of rain-whipped water yesterday was now a Mediterranean sea of the most beguiling blue. The English summer was being true to form.

Grant flung the Sunday papers on the seat beside him and prepared to enjoy the crossing. And then his eye caught the *Sunday Newsreel's* heading: The Truth About Clay's Early Life. And once more the case drew him into it. On the previous Sabbath, the *Sunday Wire* had had as its chief "middle" a tear-compelling article by that prince of newspaper men, Jammy Hopkins. The article had consisted of an interview with a Nottingham lace-hand, Miss Helen Cozens, who had, it appeared, been a contemporary of Christine Clay's in the factory. It had dealt touchingly with Chris's devotion to her family, her sunny disposition, her excellent work, the number of times Miss Helen Cozens had helped her in one way or another, and it had finished with a real Hopkins touch of get-togetherness. It had been the fate of one of these two friends, he pointed out, to climb to the stars, to give pleasure to millions, to irradiate the world. But there were other fates as glowing if less spectacular; and Helen Cozens, in her little two-room home, looking after a delicate mother, had had a destiny no less wonderful, no less worthy of the world's homage. It was a good article, and Jammy had been pleased with it.

Now the *Sunday Newsreel* appeared with an interview of its own. And it caused Grant the only smile he had enjoyed that week. Meg Hindler was the lady interviewed. Once a factory hand but now the mother of eight. And she wanted to know what the hell that God-damned old maid Nell Cozens thought she was talking about, and she hoped she might be struck down for her lies, and if her mother drank the lord knew it was no wonder with a nagging dyspeptic piece of acid like her daughter around, and everyone knew that Christina Gotobed was out of the factory and away from the town long before Nell Cozens put her crooked nose into the place at all.

It was not put just like that, but to anyone reading between the lines it was perfectly clear.

Meg really had known Christine. She was a quiet girl, she said, always trying to better herself. Not very popular with her contemporaries. Her father was dead and she lived with her mother and brother in a three-room tenement house. The brother was older, and was the mother's favourite. When Chris was seventeen the mother had died, and the family had disappeared from Nottingham. They did not belong to the town and had had no roots there, and no one had regretted them when they went. Least of all people who hadn't come into the town until years afterwards.

Grant wondered how Jammy would enjoy being taken for a ride by the imaginative Nell. So the elder brother had been the mother's favourite, had he? Grant wondered how much that meant. A shilling for candles. What family row had left such a mark that she should immortalise it in her will? Oh, well! Reporters thought they were clever, but the Yard had ways and means that were not open to the Press, however powerful. By the time he got back to-night, Christine Clay's early life would be on his desk in full detail. He discarded the *Wire* and turned to the other papers in the bundle. The *Sunday Telegraph* had a symposium—a very dignified and conveniently cheap method of filling a page. Everyone from the Archbishop of Canterbury to Jason Harmer had given their personal view of Christine Clay and her influence on her art. (The *Sunday Telegraph* liked influence and art. Even boxers never described punches to it: they explained their art.) The silly little paragraphs were all conventional, except Jason's, which had a violent sincerity beneath its sickly phrases. Marta Hallard was graceful about Clay's genius, and for once omitted to condone her lowly origin. The heir to a European throne extolled her beauty. A flying ace her courage. An ambassador her wit. It must have cost the *Telegraph* something in telephones.

Grant turned to the *Courier,* and found Miss Lydia Keats being informative all over the middle pages on the signs of the Zodiac. Lydia's stock had dropped a little in her own circles during the last week. It was felt that if she had foreseen the Clay end so clearly it was a little weak of her to overlook a small detail like murder. But in the public eye she was booming. There was no fraud about Lydia. She had stated in public, many months ago, what the stars foretold for Christine Clay, and the stars were right. And if there is anything the public loves it is a prophecy come true. They pushed their shuddering spines more firmly into the cushions and asked for more. And Lydia was giving it to them. In small type at the end of the article appeared the information that, thanks to the *Courier's* generosity, its readers might obtain horoscopes from the infallible Miss Keats at the cost of one shilling, coupon on the back page.

Grant tucked the smaller illustrateds under his arm, and prepared to get off the boat. He watched a sailor twisting a hawser round a bollard and wished that he had chosen a profession that dealt with things and not with people.

The *Petronel* was moored in the roads. Grant engaged a boatman and was rowed out to her. An elderly deckhand pushed a pipe into a pocket and prepared to receive them. Grant asked if Lord Giles were on board, happily aware that he was in Buckinghamshire. On hearing that he was not expected for a week, Grant looked suitably disappointed and asked if he might come on board: he had hoped that Giles would show him the craft. The man was pleased and garrulous. He was alone on board and had been very bored. It would be a pleasant diversion to show the good-looking friend of Lord Giles round the ship, and no doubt there would be a tip forthcoming. He did the honours with a detail that wearied Grant a little, but he was very informative. When Grant remarked on the splendid sleeping accommodation, the man said that Lord Giles wasn't one for ever sleeping ashore if he could help it. Never so happy as on salt water, Lord Giles wasn't.

"Lord Edward isn't so fond of it," Grant remarked, and the man chuckled.

"No, not Lord Edward, he wasn't. He was ashore the minute the dinghy could be swung out or a hawser slapped on a quay."

"I suppose he stayed with the Beechers the night you made Dover?"

The deckhand didn't rightly know where he slept. All he knew was that he didn't sleep on board. In fact, they hadn't seen him again. His hand luggage had been sent to the boat train and the rest had been sent to town after him. Because of the sad thing that happened to his lady, that was. Had Grant ever seen her? A film actress, she was. Very good, too. It was dreadful wasn't it, the things that happened in good families nowadays. Even murders. Changed days indeed.

"Oh, I don't know," Grant said. "The older families of England made a pastime of murder if my history books told the truth."

The man was so pleased with his tip that he offered to make cocoa for the visitor, but Grant wanted to get ashore so that he could talk to the Yard. On the way back he wondered just how Champneis had spent that night ashore. The most likely explanation was that he had stayed with friends. But if he had stayed with friends, why the desire to avoid attention? The more Grant thought of it the more out-of-character it was in the man to want to hide anything. Edward Champneis was a person who did what he wanted to in broad daylight and cared not a straw for opinions or consequences. Grant found it difficult to associate him in his mind with any furtive activity whatever. And that very thought led to a logical and rather staggering sequel. It was no petty thing that Champneis had to hide. Nothing but some matter of vast importance would have driven Champneis to prevarication. Grant could dismiss, therefore, any thought of a light love affair. Champneis had, in any case, a reputation that bordered on the austere. And if one dismissed a love affair what was left? What possible activity could a man of Champneis's stamp want to keep secret? Except murder!

Murder was just possible. If that calm security were once shattered, who knew what might flame out? He was a man who would both give and demand fidelity—and be unforgiving to the faithless. Supposing—! There was Harmer. Christine Clay's colleagues may have doubted that she and Harmer were lovers, but the *beau monde,* unused to the partnership of work, had no doubt. Had Champneis come to believe that? His and Christine's love for each other was an equable affair, but his pride would be a very real thing, fragile and passionate. Had he—? That was an idea! Had he driven over to the cottage that night? He was, after all, the only person who knew where she was: nearly all her telegrams had been to him. He was in Dover, and she was only an hour away. What more natural than that he should have motored over to surprise her? And if so—

A picture swam into Grant's mind. The cottage in the summer dark, the lit windows open to the night, so that every word, every movement almost, is audible outside. And in the rose-tangled mass of the garden a man standing, arrested by the voices. He stands there, quite silent, quite still, watching. Presently the lights go out. And in a little while the figure in the garden moves away. Where? To brood on his home-coming; on his cuckold state? To tramp the downs till morning? To see her come to the beach, unexpected, alone? To—

Grant shook himself and picked up the telephone receiver.

"Edward Champneis didn't spend the night of Wednesday on board," he said, when he had been connected. "I want to know where he did spend it. And don't forget, discretion is the better part. You may find that he spent it with the Warden of the Cinque Ports, or something equally orthodox, but I'll be surprised if he did. It would be a good idea if someone got friendly with his valet and went through his wardrobe for a dark coat. You know the strongest card we have is that no one outside the force knows about that button. The fact that we asked for any discarded coat that was found to be brought in doesn't convey much to anyone. The chances are ten to one, I think, that the coat is still with its owner. Keeping a coat, even with a missing button, is less conspicuous than getting rid of one. And that S.O.S. for the coat was only a police circular, anyhow, not a public appeal. So inspect the Champneis wardrobe. . . . No, I haven't got anything on him. . . . Yes, I know it is mad. But I'm not taking any more chances in this case. Only be discreet, for Heaven's sake. I'm in bad enough odour as it is. What is the news? Has Tisdall turned up? . . . Oh, well, I expect he will by night. He might give the Press a break. They're waiting breathless for him. How is the Clay dossier coming? . . . Oh. Has Vine come back from interviewing the dresser—What's-Her-Name? Bundle—yet? No? All right, I'm coming straight back to town."

As Grant hung up he shut his mind quickly on the thought that tried to jump in. Of *course* Tisdall was all right. What could happen to an adult in the English country-side in summer? Of course he was all right.

# 16

THE DOSSIER WAS filling up nicely. Henry Gotobed had been an estate carpenter near Long Eaton, and had married a laundry maid at the "big house." He had been killed in a threshing-mill accident, and—partly because his father and grandfather had been estate servants, partly because she was not strong enough to work—the widow had been given a small pension. The cottage at Long Eaton having to be vacated, she had brought her two children to Nottingham, where there was better hope of ultimate employment for them. The girl was then twelve and the boy fourteen. It had been curiously difficult to obtain information about them after that. Information other than the bare official record, that is to say. In the country, changes were slow, interests circumscribed, and memories long. But in the fluctuating life of the town, where a family stayed perhaps six months in a house and moved elsewhere, interest was superficial where it existed at all.

Meg Hindler, the *Newsreel's* protégée, had proved the only real help. She was an enormous, hearty, loud-voiced, good-natured woman, who cuffed her numerous brood with one hand and caressed with the other. She was still suffering a little from a Nell-Cozens phobia, but when she could be kept off the Cozens tack she was genuinely informative. She remembered the family not because there was anything memorable about them, but because she had lived with her own family across the landing from them, and had worked in the same factory as Chris, so that they sometimes came home together. She had liked Chris Gotobed in a mild way; didn't approve of her stuck-up ideas, of course; if you had to earn your living by working in a factory, then you had to earn your living by working in a factory, and why make a fuss about it? Not that Chris made a fuss, but she had a way of shaking the dust of the factory off her as if it was dirt. And she wore a hat always; a quite unnecessary piece of affectation. She had adored her mother, but her mother couldn't see anything in life but Herbert. A nasty piece of work, if ever there was one, Herbert. As slimy, sneaking, cadging, self-satisfied a piece of human trash as you'd meet in a month of Sundays. But Mrs. Gotobed thought he was the cat's whiskers. He was always making it difficult for Chris. Chris had once talked her mother into letting her have dancing lessons—though what you wanted dancing lessons for, Meg couldn't think: you'd only to watch the others hopping round for a little and you'd got the general idea: after that it was only practice—but when Herbert had heard about it he had quickly put a stop to anything like that. They couldn't afford it, he said—they never could afford anything unless Herbert wanted it—and, besides, dancing was a light thing, and the Lord wouldn't approve. Herbert always knew what the Lord would like. He not only stopped the dancing-lesson idea but he found some way of getting the money Chris had saved and that she had hoped her mother would make up to the required amount. He had pointed out how selfish it was of Chris to save money for her own ends when their mother was so poorly. He talked such a lot about their mother's bad health that Mrs. Gotobed began to feel very poorly indeed, and took to her bed. And Herbert helped eat the delicacies that Chris bought. And Herbert went with his mother for four days to Skegness because Chris couldn't leave the factory and it just happened that this was one of the numerous occasions when Herbert was without a job.

Yes, Meg had been helpful. She did not know what had become of the family, of course. Chris had left Nottingham the day after her mother's funeral, and because the rent was paid up to the end of the week Herbert had stayed on alone in the house for several days after. Meg remembered that because he had had one of his "meetings" in the house—he was always having meetings where he could hear the sound of his own voice—and the neighbours had to complain about the noise of the singing. As if there wasn't enough row always going on in a tenement without adding meetings to the din! What kind of meetings? Well, as far as she could remember he had begun with political harangues, but very soon took to religion; because it doesn't matter how you rave at your audience, when it's religion they don't throw things. She personally didn't think it mattered to him what he was talking about as long as he was the person who was talking. She never knew anyone who had a better opinion of himself with less cause than Herbert Gotobed.

No, she didn't know where Chris had gone, or whether Herbert knew her whereabouts. Knowing Herbert, she thought that Chris had probably gone without saying good-bye. She hadn't said good-bye to anyone, if it came to that. Meg's younger brother, Sydney—the one that was now in Australia—had

had a fancy for her, but she didn't give him any encouragement. Didn't have any beaux, Chris didn't. Funny, wasn't it, that she should have seen Christine Clay on the screen often and often, and never recognised Chris Gotobed. She had changed a lot, that she had. She'd heard that they made you over in Hollywood. Perhaps that was it. And of course it was a long time between seventeen and thirty. Look what a few years had done to her, come to think of it.

And Meg had laughed her ample laugh and revolved her ample figure for the detective's inspection, and had given him a cup of stewed tea and Rich Mixed Biscuits.

But the detective—who was the Sanger who had assisted at the non-arrest of Tisdall, and who was also a Clay fan—remembered that even in a city there are communities who have interests as narrow and memories as long as any village dwellers, and so he had come eventually to the little house in a suburb beyond the Trent where Miss Stammers lived with a toy Yorkshire terrier and the wireless. Both terrier and wireless had been given her on her retirement. She would never have had the initiative after thirty years of teaching at Beasley Road Elementary School to acquire either on her own behalf. School had been her life, and school still surrounded her. She remembered Christina Gotobed very clearly indeed. What did Mr. Sanger want to know about her? Not Mr.? A detective? Oh, dear! She did hope that there was nothing serious the matter. It was all a very long time ago, and of course she had not kept in touch with Christina. It was impossible to keep in touch with all one's pupils when one had as many as sixty in a class. But she had been an exceptionally promising child, exceptionally promising.

Sanger had asked if she was unaware that her exceptionally promising pupil was Christine Clay?

"Christine Clay? The film actress you mean? Dear me. Dear me!"

Sanger had thought the expression a little inadequate until he noticed her small eyes grow suddenly large with tears. She took off her pince-nez and wiped them away with a neatly folded square of handkerchief.

"So famous?" she murmured. "Poor child. Poor child."

Sanger reminded her of the reason for Christine's prominence in the news. But she seemed less occupied with the woman's cruel end than with the achievement of the child she had known.

"She was very ambitious, you know," she said. "That is how I remember her so well. She was not like the others: anxious to get away from school and become wage earners. That is what appeals to most elementary children, you know, Mr. Sanger: a weekly wage in their pockets and the means of getting out of their crowded homes. But Christina wanted to go to the secondary school. She actually won a scholarship—a 'free place,' they call it. But her people could not afford to let her take it. She came to me and cried about it. It was the only time I had known her to cry: she was not an emotional child. I asked her mother to come to see me. A pleasant enough woman, but without force of character. I couldn't persuade her. Weak people can be very stubborn.

It was a regret in my mind for years, that I had failed. I had great feeling for the child's ambition. I had been very ambitious once myself, and had— had to put my desire aside. I understood what Christina was going through. I lost sight of her when she left school. She went to work in the factory, I remember. They needed the money. There was a brother who was not earning. An unsympathetic character. And the mother's pension was small. But she made her career, after all. Poor child. Poor child!"

Sanger had asked, as he was taking his departure, how it was that she had missed the articles in the newspapers about Christine Clay's childhood.

She never saw Sunday newspapers, she said, and the daily paper was handed on to her a day late by her very kind neighbours, the Timpsons, and at present they were at the seaside, so that she was without news, except for the posters. Not that she missed the papers much. A matter of habit, didn't Mr. Sanger think? After three days without one, the desire to read a newspaper vanished. And really, one was happier without. Very depressing reading they made these days. In her little home she found it difficult to believe in so much violence and hatred.

Sanger had made further enquiries from many people about that unsympathetic character Herbert Gotobed. But hardly anyone remembered him. He had never stayed in a job for more than five months (the five months was his record: in an ironmonger's) and no one had been sorry to see him go. No one knew what had become of him.

But Vine, coming back from interviewing the one-time dresser, Bundle, in South Street, had brought news of him. Yes, Bundle had known there was a brother. The snapping brown eyes in the wizened face had snapped ferociously at the very mention of him. She had only seen him once, and she hoped she never saw him again. He had sent in a note to her lady one night in New York, to her dressing-room. It was the first dressing-room she had ever had to herself, the first show she had been billed in. *Let's Go!* it was. And she was a success. Bundle had dressed her as a chorus girl, along with nine others, but when her lady had gone up in the world she had taken Bundle with her. That's the sort her lady was: never forgot a friend. She had been talking and laughing till the note was brought in. But when she read that she was just like someone who was about to take a spoonful of ice-cream and noticed a beetle in it. When he came in she had said, "So *you*'ve turned up!" He said he'd come to warn her that she was bound for perdition, or something. She said, "Come to see what pickings there are, you mean." Bundle had never seen her so angry. She had just taken off her day make-up to put on her stage one, and there wasn't a spark of colour anywhere in her face. She had sent Bundle out of the room then, but there had been a grand row. Bundle, standing guard before the door—there were lots, even then, who thought they would like to meet her lady—couldn't help hearing some of it. In the end she had to go in because her lady was going to be late for her entrance if she didn't. The man had turned on her for interrupting, but her lady had said that she would give him in charge if he didn't go. He had gone then, and had never to her knowledge turned up again. But he had written. Letters came from him occasionally —Bundle recognised the writing—and he always seemed to know where they were, because the address was the correct one, not a forwarded affair. Her lady always had acute depression after a letter had come. Sometimes for two days or more. She had said once, "Hate is very *lowering,* isn't it, Bundle?" Bundle had never hated anyone except a cop who was habitually rude to her, but she had hated him plenty, and she agreed that hate was very weakening. Burned you up inside till there was nothing left.

And to Bundle's account of Christine's brother was added the report of the American police. Herbert Gotobed had entered the States about five years after his sister. He had worked for a short while as a sort of house man for a famous Boston divine who had been taken (in) by his manners and his piety. He had left the divine under some sort of cloud—the exact nature of the cloud was doubtful since the divine, either from Christian charity or more likely from a reluctance to have his bad judgment made public, had preferred no charges—and had disappeared from the ken of the police. It was supposed, however, that he was the man who, under the name of the Brother of God, had toured the States in the rôle of prophet, and had been, it was reported, both an emotional and financial success. He had been jailed in Kentucky for blasphemy, in Texas for fraud, in Missouri for creating a riot, in Arkansas for his own safety, and in Wyoming for seduction. In all detentions he had denied any connection with Herbert Gotobed. He had no name, he said, other than the Brother of God. When the police had pointed out that relation to the deity would not be considered by them an insuperable obstacle to deportation, he had taken the hint and had disappeared. The last that had been heard of him was that he had run a mission in the islands somewhere—Fiji, they thought—and had decamped with the funds to Australia.

"A charming person," Grant said, looking up from the dossier.

"That's our man, sir, never a doubt of it," Williams said.

"He certainly has all the stigmata: greed, enormous conceit, and lack of conscience. I rather hope he is our man. It would be doing the world a good turn to squash that slug. But why did he do it?"

"Hoped for money, perhaps."

"Hardly likely. He must have known only too well how she felt about him."

"I wouldn't put it past him to forge a will, sir."

"No, neither would I. But if he has a forged will, why hasn't he come forward? It will soon be a fortnight since her death. We haven't a thing to go on. We don't even know that he's in England."

"He's in England all right, sir. 'Member what her housekeeper said: that he always knew where she was? Clay had been more than three months in England. You bet he was here too."

"Yes. Yes, that's true. Australia? Let me see." He looked up the New York report again. "That's about two years ago. He'd be difficult to trace there, but if he came to England after Clay he shouldn't be difficult to trace. He can't keep his mouth shut. Anything quite so vocal must be noticeable."

"No letters from him among her things?"

"No, Lord Edward has been through everything. Tell me, Williams, on what provocation, for what imaginable reason, would a Champneis, in your opinion, tell a lie?"

"*Noblesse oblige,*" said Williams promptly.

Grant stared. "Quite right," he said at length. "I hadn't thought of that. Can't imagine what he could have been shielding, though."

# 17

So THE CANDLES weren't the kind you go to bed with, Grant thought, as the car sped along the Embankment that Monday afternoon en route for the Temple; they were the kind you put on altars. The Brother of God's tabernacle had been none of your bare mission tents. It had been hung with purple and fine linen and furnished with a shrine of great magnificence. And what had been merely an expression of Herbert's own love of the theatrical had in most cases (Kentucky was an exception) proved good business. A beauty-starved and theatrically-minded people had fallen hard—in hard cash.

Christine's shilling was the measure of her contempt. Her return, perhaps, for all those occasions when Herbert's Lord had seen fit to dèny her the small things her soul needed.

In the green subaqueous light of Mr. Erskine's small room beside the plane-tree, Grant put his proposition to the lawyer. They wanted to bring Herbert Gotobed to the surface, and this was the way to do it. It was quite orthodox, so the lawyer needn't mind doing it. Lord Edward had approved.

The lawyer hummed and hawed, not because he had any real objections but because it is a lawyer's business to consider remote contingencies, and a straightforward agreement to anything would be wildly unprofessional. In the end he agreed that it might be done.

Grant said: "Very well, I leave it to you. In tomorrow's papers, please," and went out wondering why the legal mind delighted in manufacturing trouble when there was so much ready-made in the world. There was plenty in poor Grant's mind at the moment. "Surrounded by trouble," as the spaewives said when they told your cards: that's what he was. Monday would soon be over and there was no sign that Robert Tisdall was in the world of men. The first low howl had come from the *Clarion* that morning, and by tomorrow the whole wolf pack would be on him. Where was Robert Tisdall? What were the police doing to find him? To do Grant justice the discomfort in his mind was less for the outcry that was imminent than for the welfare of Tisdall. He had genuinely believed for the last two days that Tisdall's non-appearance was due to lack of knowledge on Tisdall's part. It is not easy to see news-papers when one is on the run. But now doubt like a chill wind played through his thoughts. There was something wrong. Every newspaper poster in every village in England had read: TISDALL INNOCENT. HUNTED MAN IN-NOCENT. How could he have missed it? In every pub, railway carriage, bus, and house in the country the news had been the favourite subject of conversa-tion. And yet Tisdall was silent. No one had seen him since Erica drove away from him last Wednesday. On Thursday night the whole of England had been swamped by the worst storm for years, and it had rained and blown for two days afterwards. Tisdall had picked up the food left by Erica on Thursday, but not afterwards. The food she left on Friday was still there, a sodden pulp, on Saturday. Grant knew that Erica had spent all that Saturday scouring the country-side; she had quartered the country with the efficiency and persistence of a game dog, every barn, every shelter of any description, being subjected to search. Her very sound theory was that shelter he *must* have had on Thurs-day night—no human being could have survived such a storm—and since he had been in that chalky lane on Thursday morning to pick up the food she left, then he could not have gone far afield.

But her efforts had come to nothing. Today an organised gang of amateur searchers had undertaken the work—the police had no men to spare—but so far no news had come. And in Grant's mind was growing a slow fear that he tried with all his self-awareness to beat down. But it was like a moor fire. You whipped it to cinder only to see it run under the surface and break out ahead of you.

News from Dover was slow, too. The investigation was hampered beyond any but police patience by the necessity of (*a*) not offending the peerage, and (*b*) not frightening the bird: the first applying to a possibly innocent, the second to a possibly guilty. It was all very complicated. Watching Edward Champneis's calm face—he had eyebrows which gave a peculiar expression of repose—while he discussed with him the trapping of Herbert, Grant had sev-eral times forcibly to restrain himself from saying: "Where were you on Wednesday night?" What would Champneis do? Look a little puzzled, think a moment, and then say: "The night I arrived in Dover? I spent it with the So-and-sos at Such-and-Such." And then realisation of what the question en-tailed would dawn, and he would look incredulously at Grant, and Grant would feel the world's prize fool. More! In Edward Champneis's presence he felt that it was sheer insult to suggest that he might have been responsible for his wife's death. Away from him, that picture of the man in the garden, watch-ing the lighted house with the open windows, might swim up in his mind more often than he cared to admit. But in his presence, any such thought was fan-tastic. Until his men had accounted—or failed to account—for Champneis's movements that night, any direct enquiry must be shelved.

All he knew so far was that Champneis had stayed in none of the obvious places. The hotels and the family friends had both been drawn blank. The radius was now being extended. At any moment news might come that my lord had slept in a blameless four-poster and the county's best linen sheets, and Grant would be forced to admit that he had been mistaken when he imagined that Lord Edward was deliberately misleading him.

# 18

ON TUESDAY MORNING word came from Collins, the man who was investigating Champneis's wardrobe. Bywood, the valet, had proved "very sticky going," he reported. He didn't drink and he didn't smoke and there seemed to be no plane on which Collins could establish a mutual regard. But every man has his price, and Bywood's proved to be snuff. A very secret vice, it was. Lord Edward would dismiss him on the spot if he suspected such indulgence. (Lord Edward would probably have been highly pleased by anything so eighteenth century.) Collins had procured him "very special snuff," and had at last got within inspecting distance of the wardrobe. On his arrival in England—or rather, in London—Champneis had weeded out his wardrobe. The weeding out had included two coats, one dark and one camel-hair. Bywood had given the camel-hair one to his brother-in-law, a chorus-boy; the other he had sold to a dealer in London. Collins gave the name and address of the dealer.

Grant sent an officer down to the dealer, and as the officer went through the stock the dealer said: "That coat came from Lord Edward Champneis, the Duke of Bude's son. Nice bit of stuff."

It was a nice bit of stuff. And it had all its buttons; with no sign of replacements.

Grant sighed when the news came, not sure whether he was glad or sorry. But he still wanted to know where Champneis had spent the night.

And what the Press wanted to know was where Tisdall was. Every newspaper in Britain wanted to know. The C.I.D. were in worse trouble than they had been for many years. The *Clarion* openly called them murderers, and Grant, trying to get a line on a baffling case, was harassed by the fury of colleagues, the condolences of his friends, a worried Commissioner, and his own growing anxiety. In the middle of the morning Jammy Hopkins rang up to explain away his "middle" in the *Clarion*. It was "all in the way of business," and he knew his good friends at the Yard would understand. Grant was out, and it was Williams at the other end of the telephone. Williams was not in the mood for butter. He relieved his overburdened soul with a gusto which left Hopkins hoping that he had not irretrievably put himself in the wrong with the Yard. "As for hounding people to death," Williams finished, "you know very well that the Press do more hounding in a week than the Yard has since it was founded. And *all* your victims are innocent!"

"Oh, have a heart, Sergeant! You know we've got to deliver the goods. If we don't make it hot and strong, we'll be out on our ear. St. Martin's Crypt, or the Embankment. And you pushing people off the seats. We've got our jobs to keep just as much as—"

The sound of Williams's hang-up was eloquent. It was action and comment compressed into one little monosyllable. Jammy felt hardly used. He had enjoyed writing that article. He had in fact been full of righteous indignation as the scarifying phrases poured forth. When Jammy was writing his tongue came out of its habitual position in his cheek, and emotion flooded him. That the tongue went back when he had finished did not matter; the popular appeal of his article was secure; it was "from the heart"; and his salary went up by leaps and bounds.

But he was a little hurt that all his enemies-on-paper couldn't see just what a jape it was. He flung his hat with a disgusted gesture on to his right eyebrow and went out to lunch.

And less than five minutes away Grant was sitting in a dark corner, a huge cup of black coffee before him, his head propped in his hands. He was "telling it to himself in words of one syllable."

Christine Clay was living in secret. But the murderer knew where she was. That eliminated a lot of people.

Champneis knew.

Jason Harmer knew.

Herbert Gotobed almost certainly knew.

The murderer had worn a coat dark enough to be furnished with a black button and black sewing thread.

Champneis had such a coat, but there was no missing button.

Jason Harmer had no such coat, and had not lately worn any such coat.

No one knew what Herbert Gotobed wore.

The murderer had a motive so strong and of such duration that he could wait for his victim at six of a morning and deliberately drown her.

Champneis had a possible motive.

Jason Harmer had a possible motive if they had been lovers, but there was no proof of that.

Herbert Gotobed had no known motive but had almost certainly hated her.

On points Gotobed won. He knew where his sister was; he had the kind of record that was "headed for murder"; and he had been on bad terms with the victim.

Oh, well! By tomorrow Gotobed might have declared himself. Meanwhile he would drug himself with black coffee and try to keep his mind off the Press.

As he raised the cup to his lips, his eyes lighted on a man in the opposite corner. The man's cup was half empty, and he was watching Grant with amused and friendly eyes.

Grant smiled, and hit first. "Hiding that famous profile from the public gaze? Why don't you give your fans a break?"

"It's all break for them. A fan can't be wrong. You're being given a hell of a time, aren't you? What do they think the police are? Clairvoyants?"

Grant rolled the honey on his tongue and swallowed it.

"Some day," Owen Hughes said, "someone is going to screw Jammy Hopkins's head off his blasted shoulders. If my face wasn't insured for the sum total of the world's gold, I'd do it myself. He once said I was 'every girl's dream'!"

"And aren't you?"

"Have you seen my cottage lately?"

"No. I saw the photograph of the wreck in the paper one day."

"I don't mind telling you I wept when I got out of the car and saw it. I'd like to broadcast that photograph to the ends of the earth as a sample of what publicity can do. Fifty years ago a few people might have come a few miles to look at the place, and then gone home satisfied. They came in charabanc loads to see Briars. My lawyer tried to stop the running of the "trips," but there was nothing he could do. The County Police refused to keep a man there after the first few days. About ten thousand people have come in the last fortnight, and every one of the ten thousand has peered through the windows, stood on the plants and taken away a souvenir. There is hardly a scrap of hedge left—it used to be twelve feet high, a mass of roses—and the garden is a wilderness of trampled mud. I was rather attached to that garden. I didn't croon to the pansies, exactly, but I got a lot of kick out of planting things people gave me, and seeing them come up. Not a vestige left."

"Rotten luck! And no redress. Maddening for you. Perhaps by next year the plants will have taken heart again."

"Oh, I'm selling the place. It's haunted. Had you ever met Clay? No? She was grand. They don't make that kind in pairs."

"Do you know of anyone who would be likely to want to murder her, by any chance?"

Hughes smiled one of the smiles which made his fans grip the arms of their cinema seats. "I know lots who would gladly have murdered her on the spot. But only on the spot. The minute you cooled off, you'd cheerfully die for her. It's most unlikely death for Chris—the one that happened to her. Did you know that Lydia Keats prophesied it from her horoscope? She's a marvel, Lydia. She should have been drowned when she was a pup, but she really is a marvel. I sent her Marie Dacre's year, day, and minute of birth from Hollywood. Marie made me swear an oath before she divulged the awful truth of the year. Lydia hadn't the faintest notion whose horoscope she was doing, and it was marvellously accurate. She'd be a wow in Hollywood."

"She seems to be heading that way," Grant said dryly. "Do you like the place?"

"Oh, yes. It's restful." As Grant raised his eyebrows: "There are so many pebbles on the beach that you're practically anonymous."

"I thought they ran rubbernecking tours for Midwest fans."

"Oh, yes, they run motor-coaches down your street, but they don't tramp your flowers into the ground."

"If you were murdered they might."

"Not they. Murders are ten cents the dozen. Well, I must get along. Good luck. And God bless you. You've done me a power of good, so help me you have."

"I?"

"You've brought to my notice one profession that is worse than my own." He dropped some money on the table and picked up his hat. "They pray for judges on Sundays, but never a word for the police!"

He adjusted the hat at the angle which after much testing had been found by camera-men to be the most becoming, and strolled out, leaving Grant vaguely comforted.

# 19

THE PERSON WHO wasn't comforted was Jammy. The buoyant, the resilient, the hard-boiled but bouncing Jammy. He had eaten at his favourite pub (black coffee might be all very well for worried police officials and actors who had to think of their figure, but Jammy dealt only in other people's worries and remembered his figure only when his tailor measured him) and nothing during lunch had been right. The beef had been a shade too "done," the beer had been a shade too warm, the waiter had had hiccoughs, the potatoes were soapy, the cabinet pudding had tasted of baking soda, and they were out of his usual cigarettes. And so his feeling of being ill-used and misunderstood, instead of being charmed away by food and drink, had grown into an exasperation with the world in general. He looked sourly over his glass at his colleagues and contemporaries, laughing and talking over the coarse white cloths, and they, unused to a glower on his brow, paused in their traffic to tease him.

"What is it, Jammy? Pyorrhœa?"

"No. He's practising to be a dictator. You begin with the expression."
"No you don't," said a third. "You begin with the hair."
"And an arm movement. Arms are very important. Look at Napoleon.
Never been more than a corporal if he hadn't thought up that arm-on-chest
business. Pregnant, you know."

"If it's pregnant Jammy is, he'd better have the idea in the office, not
here. I don't think the child's going to be a pleasant sight."

Jammy consigned them all to perdition, and went out to find a tobacconist who kept his brand of cigarettes. What did the Yard want to take
it like that for? Everyone knew that what you wrote in a paper was just eye-
wash. When it wasn't bilge-water. If you stopped being dramatic over little
tuppenny no-account things, people might begin to suspect that they were no-
account, and then they'd stop buying papers. And where would the Press
barons, and Jammy, and a lot of innocent shareholders be then? You'd got
to provide emotions for all those moribund wage earners who were too tired
or too dumb to feel anything on their own behalf. If you couldn't freeze their
blood, then you could sell them a good sob or two. That story about Clay's
early days in the factory had been pure jam—even if that horse-faced dame
*had* led him up the garden about knowing Chris, blast her. But you couldn't
always rise to thrills or sobs, and if there was one emotion that the British
public loved to wallow in it was being righteously indignant. So he, Jammy,
had provided a wallow for them. The Yard knew quite well that tomorrow
all these indignant people wouldn't remember a thing about it, so what the
hell! What was there to get sore about? That "hounding innocents to death"
was just a phrase. Practically a cliché, it was. Nothing in that to make a
sensible person touchy. The Yard were feeling a bit thin in the skin, that was
what. They knew quite well that this shouldn't have been allowed to happen.
Far be it from him to crab another fellow's work, but some of that article
had been practically true, now he came to think of it. Not the "hounding
to death," of course. But some of the other bits. It really *was* something
amounting to a disgrace—oh, well, disgrace was a bit strong; but regrettable,
anyhow, that such a thing should occur in a force that thought it was efficient.
They were so very superior and keep-off-the-grass when times were good;
they couldn't expect sympathy when they made a bloomer. Now if they were
to let the Press in on the inside, the way they did in America, things like
that simply wouldn't happen. He, Jammy Hopkins, might be only a crime
reporter, but he knew just as much about crime and its detection as any
police force. If the "old man" were to give him leave, and the police the
use of their files, he would have the man who killed Clay inside prison walls—
and on the front page, of course—inside a week. Imagination, that's what
the Yard needed. And he had plenty of it. All he needed was a chance.

He bought his cigarettes, emptied them gloomily into the gold case his
provincial colleagues had given him when he left for London (it was whispered that the munificence was more the expression of thankfulness than of

devotion), and went gloomily back to the office. In the front entrance of that up-to-the-minute cathedral which is the headquarters of the *Clarion*, he encountered young Musker, one of the junior reporters, on his way out. He nodded briefly, and without stopping made the conventional greeting.

"Where you off to?"

"Lecture on stars," said Musker, with no great enthusiasm.

"Very interesting, astronomy," reproved Jammy.

"Not astronomy. Astrology." The boy was turning from the shade of the entrance into the sunlit street. "Woman called Pope or something."

"Pope!" Jammy stood arrested half-way to the lift door. "You don't mean Keats, do you?"

"Is it Keats?" Musker looked at a card again. "Yes, so it is. I knew it was a poet. Hey, what's the matter?" as Jammy caught him by the arm and dragged him back into the hall.

"Matter is you're not going to any astrology lecture," said Jammy, propelling him into the lift.

"Well!" said the astonished Musker. "For this relief much thanks, but why? You got a 'thing' about astrology?"

Jammy dragged him into an office and assaulted with his rapid speech the placid pink man behind the desk.

"But, Jammy," said the placid one when he could get a word in edgeways, "it was Blake's assignment. He was the obvious person for it: Doesn't he tell the world every week on Page 6 what is going to happen to it for the next seven days? It's his subject: astrology. What he didn't foresee was that his wife would have a baby this week instead of next. So I let him off and sent Musker instead."

"Musker!" said Jammy. "Say, don't you know that this is the woman who foretold Clay's death? The woman the *Courier* is running to give horoscopes at a shilling a time?"

"What of it?"

"What of it! Man, she's news!"

"She's the *Courier's* news. And about dead at that. I killed a story about her yesterday."

"All right, then, she's dead. But a lot of 'interesting' people must be interested in her at this moment. And the most interested of the lot is going to be the man who made her prophecy come true! For all we know she may have been responsible for giving him the idea; her and her prophecies. Keats may be dead, but her vicinity isn't. Not by a long chalk." He leaned forward and took the card that the Musker boy was still holding. "Find something for this nice boy to do this afternoon. He doesn't like astrology. See you later."

"But what about that story for—"

"All right, you'll have your story. And perhaps another one into the bargain!"

As Jammy was shot downwards in the lift he flicked the card in his hand with a reflective thumb. The Elwes Hall! Lydia was coming on!

"Know the best way to success, Pete?" he said to the liftman.

"All right, I'll buy," said Pete.

"Choose a good brand of hooey."

"You should know!" grinned Pete, and Jammy made a pass at him as he stepped through the doors. Pete had known him since—well, if not since his short-pants days, at least since his wrong-kind-of-collar days.

The Elwes Hall was in Wigmore Street: a nice neighbourhood; which had been responsible in no small measure for its success. Chamber music was much more attractive when one could combine it with tea at one's club and seeing about that frock at Debenham's. And the plump sopranos who were flattered at the hush that attended their *Lieder* never guessed at the crepe-versus-satin that filled their listeners' minds. It was a pleasant little place: small enough to be intimate, large enough not to be huddled. As Jammy made his way to a seat, he observed that it was filled with the most fashionable audience that he had seen at any gathering since the Beaushire-Curzon wedding. Not only was "smart" society present in bulk, but there was a blue-blooded leaven of what Jammy usually called "duchesses-up-for-the-day": of those long-shoed, long-nosed, long-pedigreed people who lived on their places and not on their wits. And sprinkled over the gathering, of course, were the cranks.

The cranks came not for the thrill, nor because Lydia's mother had been the third daughter of an improverished marquis, but because the Lion, the Bull, and the Crab were household pets of theirs, the houses of the Zodiac their spiritual home. There was no mistaking them: their pale eyes rested on the middle distance, their clothes looked like a bargain basement after a stay-in strike, and it seemed that they all wore the same string of six-penny beads round their thin necks.

Jammy refused the seat which had been reserved for the *Clarion* representative, and insisted on having one among the palms on the far side of the hall below the platform. This had been refused, with varying degrees of indignation, by both those who had come to see Lydia and those who had come to be seen. But Jammy belonged to neither of these. What Jammy had come to see was the audience. And the seat half buried in Messrs. Willoughby's decorations provided as good a view of the audience as anything but the platform itself could afford.

Next him was a shabby little man of thirty-five or so, who eyed Jammy as he sat down and presently leaned over until his rabbit-mouth was an inch from Jammy's ear, and breathed:

"Wonderful woman!"

This Jammy took to refer to Lydia.

"Wonderful," he agreed. "You know her?"

The shabby man ("Crank," said Jammy's mind, placing him) hesitated, and then said: "No. But I knew Christine Clay." And further converse was prevented by the arrival of Lydia and her chairman on the platform.

Lydia was at the best of times a poor speaker. She had a high thin voice, and when she became enthusiastic or excited her delivery was painfully like a very old gramophone record played on a very cheap gramophone. Jammy's attention soon wandered. He had heard Lydia on her favourite subject too often. His eyes began to quarter the crowded little hall. If *he* had bumped off Clay, and was still, thanks to the inadequacy of the police, both unsuspected and at large, would he or would he not come to see the woman who had prophesied for Clay the end he had brought about?

Jammy decided that, on the whole, he would. The Clay murderer was clever. That was admitted. And he must now be hugging himself over his cleverness. Thinking how superior a man of his calibre was to the ordinary rules that hedged common mortals. That was a common frame of mind in persons who achieved a planned murder. They had planned something forbidden, and had brought it off. It went to their heads like wine. They looked round for more "dares" to bring off, as children play "last across the road." This, this orthodox gathering of orthodox people in one of the most orthodox districts in London, was a perfect "dare." In every mind in that hall the thought of Christine's death was uppermost. It was not mentioned from the platform, of course; the dignities must be observed. The lecture was a simple lecture on astrology; its history and its meaning. But all these people—or nearly all—had come to the gathering because nearly a year ago Lydia had had that lucky brain wave about the manner of Christine Clay's death. Christine was almost as much part of the gathering as Lydia herself; the hall was full of her. Yes, it would give Jammy, hypothetical murderer, a great kick to be one of that audience.

He looked at the audience now, pluming himself on the imagination that had got him where he was; the imagination that Grant, poor dear idiot, could never aspire to. He wished he had brought Bartholomew along. Bart was much better informed where the society racket was concerned than he was. It was Bart's business to be descriptive: and at whatever was "descriptive"—weddings, motor racing, launches, or what not—the same faces from the racket turned up. Bart would have been useful.

But Jammy knew enough of those faces to keep him interested.

"On the other hand," said Lydia, "Capricorn people are often melancholic, doubtful of themselves, and perverse. On a lower plane still, they are gloomy, miserly and deceptive." But Jammy was not listening. In any case he did not know which of the signs had had the honour of assisting at his birth, and did not care. Lydia had several times told him that he was "typically, oh, but typically, Aries" but he never remembered. All hooey.

There was the Duchess of Trent in the third row. She, poor, silly, unhappy wretch, had the perfect alibi. She had been going to have a luncheon for Christine: a luncheon that would make her the most envied hostess in

London instead of a rather tiresome back-number; and Christine had gone and died on her.

Jammy's eye wandered, and paused at a good-looking dark face in the fourth row. Very familiar that face; as familiar as the head on a coin. Why? He didn't know the man; would swear he had never seen him in the flesh. And then it came to him. It was Gene Lejeune; the actor who had been engaged to play opposite Clay in her third and last picture in England: the picture she had never made. It was rumoured that Lejeune was glad that he would never have to make that picture; Clay's brilliance habitually made her men look like penny candles; but that was hardly a good reason for getting up at dawn to hold her head under water until she died. Jammy wasn't greatly interested in Lejeune. Next him was a fashion plate in black and white. Marta Hallard. Of course. Marta had been given the part that Clay had been scheduled to play. Marta was not in the Clay class, but holding up production was likely to prove expensive, and Marta had poise, sophistication, sufficient acting ability, sufficient personality, and what Coyne called "class." She was now Lejeune's leading woman. Or was he her leading man? It would be difficult to say which of these two was the "supporting" one. Neither of them was in the first flight. Considered simply as a partnership, it was likely to prove much more successful than the Clay-Lejeune one would have been. A step up—a big step up for Marta—and more chance to shine for Lejeune. Yes, Christine's death had been a lucky break for both of them.

He heard in his mind a girl's voice saying, "You, of course, murdered her yourself." Who had said that? Yes, that Judy girl who played dumb blondes. And she had said it about Marta. That Saturday night when he and Grant had met on the doorstep of Marta's flat and had been entertained by her. The Judy person had said it with that sulky air of defiance that she used to life's most trivial activities. And they had taken it as a joke. Someone else had laughed and agreed, supplying the motive: "Of course! You wanted that part for yourself!" And the conversation had flowed on in unbroken superficiality.

Well, ambition was one of the better known incentives to murder. It came, well up the list, just below passion and greed. But Marta Hallard was Marta Hallard. Murder and that brittle, insincere sophisticate were poles apart. She didn't even play murder well on the stage, now he came to think of it. She had always the air of saying at the back of her mind, "Too tiresome, all this earnestness." If she didn't find murder humourless, she would undoubtedly find it plebeian. No, he could imagine Marta being a murderee, but not a murderer.

He became aware that Marta was paying no attention whatever to Lydia. All her interest—and it was a fixed and whole-hearted interest—was centered on someone to her right in the row in front. Jammy's eyes followed the imaginary dotted line of her glance and came to rest, a little surprised, on a nondescript little man. Incredulous, he travelled the dotted line again. But the answer was still the small round-faced man with the sleepy expression. Now what could interest Marta Hallard in that very commercial exterior and that far from exciting—

And then Jammy remembered who that little man was. He was Jason Harmer, the song writer. One of Christine's best friends. Marta's "merry kettle." And, if women's judgment was to be accepted, anything but unexciting. In fact, that was the chap who was popularly supposed to have been Christine Clay's lover. Jammy's mind did the equivalent of a long, low whistle. Well, well, so that was Jay Harmer. He had never seen him off a song-cover until now. Queer taste women had, and no mistake.

Harmer was listening to Lydia with a rapt and childlike interest. Jammy wondered how anyone could remain unaware of so concentrated a battery of attention as Marta Hallard was directing on him. There he sat, short-necked and placid, while Marta's brilliant eyes bored into the side of his head. A lot of hooey, that about making people turn by just looking at them. And what, in any case, was the reason for Marta's secret interest? For secret it was. The brim of her hat hid her eyes from her escort, and she had taken it for granted that the eyes of everyone else were on the lecturer. Unconscious of being watched, she was letting her eyes have their fill of Harmer. Why?

Was it a "heart" interest—and if so, just how much of a heart interest? Or was it that, in spite of her companionship of him that night at her flat, she was seeing Jason Harmer as a possible murderer?

For nearly fifteen minutes Jammy watched them both, his mind full of speculation. Again and again his glance went over the crowded little hall and came back to them. Interest there was in plenty elsewhere, but not interest like this.

He remembered Marta's instant refutal of the suggestion that there was more than friendship between Harmer and Christine Clay. What did that mean? Was she interested in him herself? And how much? How much *would* Marta Hallard be interested? Enough to get rid of a rival?

He found himself wondering if Marta was a good swimmer, and pulled himself up. Fifteen minutes ago he had laughed at the very thought of Marta as a person passionate to the point of murder. The very idea had been ludicrous.

But that was before he had observed her interest—her strange consuming interest—in Jason. Supposing—just supposing; to pass the time while that woman made her boring way through the planets and back again—that Marta *was* in love with this Harmer fellow. That made Christine a double rival of hers, didn't it? Christine had been where Marta, for all her fashionable crust of superficiality and indifference, would have given her right hand to be: at the top of her professional tree. So often Marta had been within sight of that top, only to have the branch she relied on break and let her down. Certainly, and beyond any doubt, Marta wanted professional success. And certainly, for all her fair words, she had bitterly grudged the little factory hand from the Midlands her staggering, and as it seemed too easy, achievement. Five years ago Marta had been very nearly where she was now: famous, successful, financially sound, and with the top of the tree—that elusive, giddy top—somewhere in sight. It had been somewhere in sight for five years. And meanwhile an unknown dancer from a Broadway musical had sung, danced, and acted her way to canonisation.

It was no wonder if Marta's fair words where Christine was concerned were the merest lip-service. And supposing that Christine had not only the position she had thirsted after, but the man she desired? What then? Was that enough to make Marta Hallard hate to the point of murder?

Where was Marta when Christine was drowned? In Grosvenor Square, presumably. After all, she was playing in that thing at the St. James's. No, wait! At that Saturday night party something was said about her being away? What was it? What was it? She had said something about hard-working actresses, and Clement Clements had mocked, saying: "Hard-working, forsooth. And you've just had a week off to go dashing round the Continent!" She had said: "Not a week, Clement! Only four days. And an actress can presumably play with a broken spine but never with a gumboil."

Clement had said that the gumboil didn't prevent her having a grand time at Deauville. And she had said: "Not Deauville. Le Touquet."

Le Touquet. That was where she had been. And she had come back in time for the Saturday matinée. They had talked about the reception she had had, and the size of the "house," and the rage of her understudy. She had come back after four days at Le Touquet! She was in Le Touquet, just across the channel, when Christine died.

"If parents would only study their children's horoscopes with the same diligence that they use to study their diets," Lydia was saying, shrill as a sparrow and about as impressive, "the world would be a much happier place."

"Le Touquet! Le Touquet!" exulted Jammy's mind. Now he was getting somewhere! Marta Hallard was not only within reach of Christine on that fatal morning, but *she had the means to cover the distance easily*. Le Touquet had opened the doors of his memory. Clements and she and Jammy in that far corner by the cocktail cupboard, and she answering Clements's idle questions. She had flown over, it appeared, with someone in a private plane, and had come back by the same method. And the plane had been an amphibian!

On that misty morning a plane had landed either on the downs or on the sea, had stayed a little, and had gone again without having entered into the consciousness of any but one lonely swimmer. Jammy was so sure of it that he could see the thing come out of the fog like a great bird and drop on to the water.

Who had piloted that plane? Not Harmer. Harmer hadn't been out of England. That was why the police were taking such an interest in him. Harmer had been only too much on the spot. He had an alibi of sorts, but Jammy didn't know whether it was a good one or not. The police were so damned secretive. Well, he was on the track of something that the police, for all their vaunted efficiency, had missed. Marta was a friend of Grant's: it was natural that he should overlook her: he had never seen her look at Harmer, as Jammy was seeing her now; and he didn't know about that plane, Jammy would take his oath. And the plane made all the difference.

And if it was a case of a plane, then there were two in the business. The pilot, if not an accomplice, was certainly an accessory before the fact.

At this point Jammy mentally stopped to draw breath. He looked surprisedly along the well-dressed silent rows to the smart black-and-white figure in the middle distance. What connection had that familiar presence with the person his mind had drawn? There was the real Marta Hallard, her *soigné*, gracious, serene self. How had he let his mind make her into something so tortured, so desperate?

But she was still looking every now and then at Jason, her eyes resting longer on him than they did on Lydia. And there was something in that unguarded face that joined the real Marta to that shadowy one that his imagination had created. Whatever she might be, Marta Hallard was after all capable of strong feeling.

A patter like rain fell into Jammy's thoughts; the polite percussion of gloved hand on gloved hand. Lydia had apparently reached her peroration. Jammy sighed happily and felt for his hat. He wanted to get out into the air and think what his next move was to be. He hadn't been so excited since Old Man Willingdon had given him the exclusive story of how and why he had beaten his wife into pulp.

But there was going to be a question time, it would seem. Miss Keats, sipping water and smiling benevolently between sips, was waiting for the audience to collect its wits. Then some bold spirit began, and presently questions were raining round her. Some were amusing; and the audience, a little tired by the warm air, Lydia's voice, and the dullish lecture, laughed easily in relief. Presently the questions grew more intimate, and then—so inevitably that half the audience could see it coming—the query came:

Was it true that Miss Keats accurately foretold the manner of Christine Clay's death?

There was a shocked and eager silence. Lydia said, simply and with more dignity than she usually possessed, that it was true; that she had often foretold the future truly from a horoscope. She gave some instances.

Emboldened by the growing intimacy of the atmosphere, someone asked if she was helped in her reading of horoscopes by second-sight. She waited so long before answering that stillness fell back on the moving heads and hands; their eyes watched her expectantly.

"Yes," she said, at length. "Yes. It is not a matter that I like to discuss. But there are times when I have known, beyond reason, that a thing is so." She paused a moment, as if in doubt, and then took three steps forward to the edge of the platform with such impetuosity that it seemed that she meant to walk forward on to thin air. "And one thing I have known ever since I stepped on the platform. The murderer of Christine Clay is here in this hall."

It is said that ninety-nine people out of a hundred, receiving a telegram reading: *All is discovered: fly,* will snatch a toothbrush and make for the garage. Lydia's words were so unexpected, and their meaning when understood so horrifying, that there was a moment of blank silence. And then the rush began, like the first breath of a hurricane through palm trees. Above the rising babel, chairs shrieked like human beings as they were thrust out of the way. And the more they were thrust aside, the greater the chaos and the more frantic the anxiety of the escapers to reach the door. Not one in the crowd knew what they were escaping from. With most of them it began as a desire to escape from a tense situation; they belonged, as a class, to people who hate "awkwardness." But the difficulty of reaching the door through the scattered chairs and the densely packed crowd increased their natural desire to escape, into something like panic.

The chairman was saying something that was meant to be reassuring, to tide over the situation; but he was quite inaudible. Someone had gone to Lydia, and Jammy heard her say:

"What made me say that? Oh, what made me say that?"

He had moved forward to mount the platform, all the journalist in him tingling with anticipation. But as he laid his hand on the platform edge to vault, he recognised Lydia's escort. It was the fellow from the *Courier*. She was practically the *Courier's* property, he remembered. It was a million to one against his getting a word with her, and, at these odds, it wasn't worth the effort. There was better game, after all. When Lydia had made that incredible statement, Jammy, having abruptly pulled his own jaw into place, had turned to see how two people took the shock.

Marta had gone quite white, and a look of something like fury had come into her face. She had been one of the first to get to her feet, moving so abruptly that Lejeune was taken by surprise and had to fish his hat from under her heels. She had made for the door without a second glance at the platform or Lydia, but since she had had a seat in the front rows had become firmly wedged half-way down the hall, where confusion became worse confounded by someone having violent hysteria.

Jason Harmer, on the other hand, had not moved a muscle. He had gone on looking at Lydia with the same pleased interest during and after her staggering announcement as he had shown before. He had made no move to get up until people began to walk over him. Then he rose leisurely, helped a woman to climb over a chair that was blocking her path, patted his pocket to assure himself that something or other was there (his gloves probably), and turned to the door.

It took Jammy several minutes of scientific shoving to reach Marta, wedged in an alcove between two radiators.

"The silly fools!" she said viciously, when Jammy had reminded her who he

was. And she glared, with most un-Hallard-like lack of poise, at her fellow
beings.

"Nicer with an orchestra pit between, aren't they?"

Marta remembered that these were her public, and he could see her automatically pull herself together. But she was still what Jammy called "het up."

"Amazing business," he said, prompting. And in explanation: "Miss Keats."

"An utterly disgusting exhibition!"

"Disgusting?" said Jammy, at a loss.

"Why doesn't she turn cartwheels in the Strand?"

"You think this was just a publicity stunt?"

"What do you call it? A sign from Heaven?"

"But you said yourself, Miss Hallard, that night you were so kind as to
put up with me, that she isn't a quack. That she really—"

"Of course she isn't a quack! She has done some amazing horoscopes. But
that is a very different matter from this finding of murderers at a penny a time.
If Lydia doesn't take care," she said after a pause and with venom, "she will
end by being an Aimée McPherson!"

It occurred to Jammy that this was hardly the line he had expected Marta
to hand out. He didn't know what he had expected. But somehow it wasn't
this. Into the pause that his doubt made, she said in a new crisp tone:

"This isn't by any chance an interview, is it, Mr. Hopkins? Because if so,
please understand quite clearly that I have said none of these things."

"All right, Miss Hallard, you haven't said a word. Unless the police ask me,
of course," he added, smiling.

"I don't think the police are on speaking terms with you," she said. "And
now, if you will be so kind as to stand a little to your left, I think I can get past
you into that space over there."

She nodded to him, smiled a little, pushed her scented person past him into
the place of vantage, and was swallowed up in the crowd.

"Not a ha'penny change!" said Jammy to himself. And ruefully began to
push his way back to where he had last seen Jason Harmer. Dowagers cursed
him and debutantes glared, but half Jammy's life had been spent in getting
through crowds. He made a good job of it.

"And what do *you* think of this, Mr. Harmer?"

Jason eyed him in a good-humoured silence. "How much?" he said at last.

"How much what?"

"How much for my golden words?"

"A free copy of the paper."

Jason laughed, then his face grew sober. "Well, I think it has been a most
instructive afternoon. You believe in this star stuff?"

"Can't say I do."

"Me, I'm not so sure. There's a lot in that crack about more things in
heaven and earth whatever-it-is. I've seen some funny things happen in the

village where I was born. Witchcraft and that. No accounting for any of it by any natural means. Makes you wonder."

"Where was that?"

Jason looked suddenly startled for the first time that afternoon. "East of Europe," he said abruptly. And went on: "That Miss Keats, she's a wonder. Not a canny thing to have around the house, though. No, sir! Must spoil your chances of matrimony quite a bit to be able to see what's going to happen. To say nothing of what has been happening. Every man has a right to his alibis."

Was no one, thought Jammy in exasperation, going to take the expected line of country this afternoon! Perhaps if he pushed his way into Lydia's presence, she at least would behave according to the pattern he had marked out for her.

"You believe that Miss Keats was genuinely feeling the presence of evil when she made that statement?" he pursued hopefully.

"Sure, sure!" Jason looked a little surprised. "You don't make a fool of yourself that way unless you're pretty worked up."

"I noticed you weren't very surprised by the statement."

"I been in the States fifteen years. Nothing surprises me any more. Ever seen Holy Rollers? Ever seen Coney Island? Ever seen a tramp trying to sell a gold mine? Go west, young man, go west!"

"I'm going home to bed," said Jammy, and took his pushing way through the crowd.

But by the time he had reached the vestibule, he had recovered a little. He adjusted his collar and waited to see the crowd move past. Once outside the inner door, and breathing the secure air of Wigmore Street, they recovered from their fright and broke with one accord into excited speech.

But Jammy gleaned little from their unguarded chatter.

And then over their heads he saw a face that made him pause. A fair face with light lashes and the look of a rather kind terrier. He knew that man. His name was Sanger. And the last time he had seen him was sitting at a desk in Scotland Yard.

So Grant had had a little imagination after all!

Jammy flung his hat disgustedly on and went out to think things over.

# 20

GRANT HAD IMAGINATION, yes. But it was not Jammy's kind. It would never have occurred to him to waste the time of a perfectly good detective by sending him to look at an audience for two hours. Sanger was at the Elwes Hall because his job for the moment was to tail Jason Harmer.

He brought back an account of the afternoon's drama, and reported that Harmer had been, as far as he could see, quite unmoved. He, Jason, had been accosted by Hopkins from the *Clarion* directly afterwards; but Hopkins didn't seem to get very far with him.

"Yes?" said Grant, lifting an eyebrow. "If he's a match for Hopkins, we must begin to consider him again. Cleverer than I thought!" And Sanger grinned.

On Wednesday afternoon Mr. Erskine telephoned to say that the fish had bitten. What he said, of course, was that "the line of investigation suggested by Inspector Grant had, it would appear, proved unexpectedly successful," but what he meant was that the fish had risen. Would Grant come along as soon as he could to inspect a document which Mr. Erskine was anxious to show him?

Grant would! In twelve minutes he was in the little green-lighted room.

Erskine, his hand trembling a little more than usual, gave him a letter to read.

Sir,

    Having seen your advertisement saying that if Herbert Gotobed will call at your office he will hear of something to his advantage, I beg to state that I am unable to come personally but if you will communicate your news to me by letter to 5, Threadle Street, Canterbury, I will get the letter.

Yours faithfully,

Herbert Gotobed

"Canterbury!" Grant's eyes lighted. He handled the letter lovingly. The paper was cheap, and the ink poor. The style and the writing vaguely illiterate. Grant remembered Christine's letter with its easy sentences and its individual hand, and marvelled for the thousandth time at the mystery of breeding.

"Canterbury! It's almost too good to be true. An accommodation address. I wonder why? Is our Herbert 'wanted,' by any chance? The Yard certainly don't know him. Not by that name. Pity we haven't got a photograph of him."

"And what is our next move, Inspector?"

"You write saying that if he doesn't put in a personal appearance you have no guarantee that he is Herbert Gotobed, and that it is therefore necessary for him to come to your offices!"

"Yes. Yes, certainly. That would be quite in order."

As if it mattered a hoot whether it was in order, Grant thought. How did these fellows imagine criminals were caught? Not by wondering what would be in order, that was certain!

"If you post it straight away, it will be in Canterbury tonight. I'll go down tomorrow morning and be waiting for the bird when he arrives. May I use your telephone?"

He called the Yard and asked, "Are you sure that none of the list of 'wanted' men has a passion for preaching or otherwise indulging in theatricality?"

The Yard said no, only Holy Mike, and everyone in the force had known him for years. He was reported from Plymouth, by the way.

"How appropriate!" Grant said, and hung up. "Strange!" he said to Erskine. "If he isn't wanted, why lie low? If he has nothing on his conscience— no, he hasn't a conscience. I mean, if we have nothing on him, I should have thought the same lad would have been in your office by return of post. He'd do almost anything for money. Clay knew where to hurt him when she left him that shilling."

"Lady Edward was a shrewd judge of character. She had, I think, been brought up in a hard school, and that fact helped her to discriminate."

Grant asked if he had known her well.

"No, I regret to say, no. A very charming woman. A little impatient of orthodox form, but otherwise—"

Yes. Grant could almost hear her saying, "And in plain English what does that mean?" She, too, must have suffered from Mr. Erskine.

Grant took his leave, warned Williams to be ready to accompany him next morning to Canterbury, arranged for a substitute in the absence of them both, and went home and slept for ten hours. In the morning, very early, he and Williams left a London not yet awake and arrived in a Canterbury shrouded in the smoke of breakfast.

The accommodation address proved to be, as Grant had expected, a small newsagent in a side street. Grant considered it, and said: "I don't suppose our friend will show up this end of the day, but one never knows. You go across to the pub over the way, engage that room above the saloon door, and have breakfast sent up to you. Don't leave the window, and keep an eye on everyone who comes. I'm going inside. When I want you I'll sign from the shop window."

"Aren't you going to have breakfast, sir?"

"I've had it. You can order lunch for one o'clock, though. It doesn't look the kind of place that would have a chop in the house."

Grant lingered until he saw Williams come to the upper window. Then he turned into the small shop. A round bald man with a heavy black moustache was transferring cartons of cigarettes from a cardboard box to a glass case.

"Good morning. Are you Mr. Rickett?"

"That's me," Mr. Rickett said, with caution.

"I understand that you sometimes use these premises as an accommodation address?"

Mr. Rickett looked him over. His experienced eye asked, Customer or police? and decided correctly.

"And what if I do? Nothing wrong in that, is there?"

"Not a thing!" Grant answered cheerfully. "I wanted to know whether you knew a Mr. Herbert Gotobed?"

"This is a joke?"

"Certainly not. He gave your shop as an address for letters, and I wondered if you knew him."

"Not me. I don't take no interest in the people who has letters. They pay their fee when they come for them, and that finishes it as far as I am concerned."

"I see. Well, I want you to help me. I want you to let me stay in your shop until Mr. Gotobed comes to claim his letter. You have a letter for him?"

"Yes, I have a letter. It came last night. But— You police?"

"Scotland Yard." Grant showed his credentials.

"Yes. Well, I don't want no arrests on my premises. This is a respectable business, this is, even if I do a little on the side. I don't want no bad name hanging round my business."

Grant assured him that no arrest was contemplated. All he wanted was to meet Mr. Gotobed. He wanted information from him.

Oh, well, if that was all.

So Grant was established behind the little tower of cheap editions at the end of the counter, and found the morning passing not so slowly as he had feared. Humanity, even after all his years in the force, still had a lively interest in Grant's eyes—except in moments of depression—and interest proved plentiful. It was Williams, watching a very ordinary small-town street, who was bored. He welcomed the half-hour of conversation behind the books when Grant went to lunch, and went back reluctantly to the frowsy room above the saloon. The long summer afternoon, clouded and warm, wore away into a misty evening, and a too early dusk. The first lights appeared, very pale in the daylight.

"What time do you close?" Grant asked anxiously.

"Oh, tennish."

There was still plenty of time.

And then, about half-past nine, Grant became aware of a presence in the shop. There had been no warning of footsteps, no announcement at all except a swish of drapery. Grant looked up to see a man in monk's garb.

A high-pitched peevish voice said, "You have a letter addressed to Mr. Herbert—"

A light movement on Grant's part called attention to his presence.

Without a moment's pause the man turned and disappeared, leaving his sentence unfinished.

The apparition had been so unexpected, the disappearance so abrupt, that it was a second or two before mortal wits could cope with the situation. But Grant was out of the shop before the stranger was more than a few yards down the street. He saw the figure turn into an alley, and he ran. It was a little back-court of two-storey houses, all the doors open to the warm evening, and two transverse alleys leading out of it. The man had disappeared. He turned to find Williams, a little breathless, at his back.

"Good man!" he said. "But it isn't much use. You take that alley and I'll take this one. A monk of sorts!"

"I saw him!" Williams said, making off.

But it was no good. In ten minutes they met at the newsagent's, blank.

"Who was that?" Grant demanded of Mr. Rickett.

"Don't know. Never saw him before as far as I know."

"Is there a monastery here?"

"In Canterbury? No!"

"Well, in the district?"

"Not as I knows."

A woman behind them put down sixpence on the counter. "Goldflake," she said. "You looking for a monastery? There's that brotherhood place in Bligh Vennel. They're by way of being monks. Ropes round their middles and bare heads."

"Where is—what is it? Bligh Vennel?" Grant asked. "Far from here?"

"No. 'Bout two streets. Less as the crow flies, but that won't be much good to you in Canterbury. It's in the lanes behind the Cock and Pheasant. I'd show you myself, if Jim wasn't waiting for his smoke. A sixpenny packet, Mr. Rickett, please."

"After hours," said Mr. Rickett, gruffly, avoiding the detective's eye. The woman's confidence was a conviction in itself.

She looked surprised, and before she should commit herself further Grant pulled his own cigarette-case from his pocket. "Madame, they say a nation gets the laws it deserves. It is not in my weak power to obtain the sixpenny packet for you, but please let me repay your help by providing Jim's smoke." He poured his cigarettes into her astonished hands, and dismissed her, protesting.

"And now," he said to Rickett, "about this brotherhood or whatever it is. Do you know it?"

"No. There is such a thing, now I remember. But I don't know where they hang out. You heard what she said. Behind the Cock and Pheasant. Half the cranks in the world has branches here, if it comes to that. I'm shutting up now."

"I should," Grant said. "People wanting cigarettes are a nuisance."

Mr. Rickett growled.

"Come on, Williams. And remember, Rickett, not a word of this to anyone. You'll probably see us tomorrow."

Rickett was understood to say that if he never saw them again it would be too soon.

"This is a rum go, sir," Williams said, as they set off down the street. "What's the programme now?"

"I'm going to call on the brotherhood. I don't think you had better come along, Williams. Your good healthy Worcestershire face doesn't suggest any yearning after the life ascetic."

"You mean I look like a cop. I know, sir. It's worried me often. Bad for business. You don't know how I envy you your looks, sir. People think 'Army' the minute they see you. It's a great help always to be taken for Army."

"Considering all the dud cheques on Cox's, I find that surprising! No, I wasn't considering your looks, Williams, not that way. I was just talking 'thoughtless.' It's a one-man party, this. You'd better go back to the aspidistra and wait for me. Have a meal."

They found the place after some search. A row of first-storey windows looked down upon the alley, but the only opening on the ground floor was a narrow door, heavy and studded. The building apparently faced into a court or garden. There was neither plate nor inscription at the door to give information to the curious. But there was a bell.

Grant rang, and after a long pause there was the sound, faint through the heavy door, of footsteps on a stone floor. A small grill in the door shot back, and a man asked Grant's business.

Grant asked to see the principal.

"*Whom* do you wish to see?"

"The principal," said Grant firmly. He didn't know whether they called their Number One abbot or prior; principal seemed to him good enough.

"The Reverend Father does not give audience at this hour."

"Will you give the Reverend Father my card," Grant said, handing the little square through the grill, "and tell him that I shall be grateful if he would see me on a matter of importance."

"No worldly matter is of importance."

"The Reverend Father may decide differently when you have given him my card."

The grill shot back with an effect which might in a community less saintly have been described as snappish, and Grant was left in the darkening street. Williams saluted silently from some paces distance and turned away. The distant voices of children playing came clearly from adjoining streets, but there was no traffic in the alley. Williams's footsteps had faded out of hearing long before there was the sound of returning ones in the passage beyond the door. Then there was the creak of bolts being drawn and a key turned. (What did they shut out? Grant wondered. Life? Or were the bars to keep straying wills indoors?) The door was opened sufficiently to admit him, and the man bade him enter.

"Peace be with you and with all Christian souls and the blessing of the Lord God go with you now and for ever, amen," gabbled the man as he shot the bolts again and turned the key. If he had hummed a line of "Sing to me sometimes" the effect would have been exactly similar, Grant thought.

"The Reverend Father in his graciousness will see you," the man said, and led the way up the stone passage, his sandals slapping with a slovenly effect on the flags. He ushered Grant into a small white-washed room, bare except for a table, chairs, and a Crucifix, said "Peace be with you," and shut the door, leaving Grant alone. It was very chilly there, and Grant hoped that the Reverend Father would not discipline him by leaving him there too long.

But in less than five minutes the doorkeeper returned and with great impressiveness bowed in his principal. He uttered another of his gabbled benedictions and left the two men together. Grant had expected the fanatic type; he was confronted instead with the successful preacher; bland, entrenched, worldly.

"Can I help you, my son?"

"I think you have in your brotherhood a man of the name of Herbert Gotobed—"

"There is no one of that name here."

"I had not expected that that was the name he is known by in your community, but you are no doubt aware of the real names of the men who enter your order."

"The worldly name of a man is forgotten on the day he enters the door to become one of us."

"You asked if you could help me."

"I still wish to help you."

"I want to see Herbert Gotobed. I have news for him."

"I know of no one of that name. And there can be no 'news' for a man who has joined the Brotherhood of the Tree of Lebanon."

"Very well. You may not know the man as Gotobed. But the man I want to interview is one of your number. I have to ask that you will let me find him."

"Do you suggest that I should parade my community for your inspection?"

"No. You have some kind of service to which all the brothers come, haven't you?"

"Certainly."

"Let me be present at the service."

"It is a most unusual request."

"When is the next service?"

"In half an hour the midnight service begins."

"Then all I ask is a seat where I can see the faces of your community."

The Reverend Father was reluctant, and mentioned the inviolability of the holy house, but Grant's casually dropped phrases on the attractive but obsolete custom of sanctuary and the still-surviving magic of King's Writ, made him change his mind.

"By the way, will you tell me—I'm afraid I'm very ignorant of your rules and ways of life—do the members of your community have business in the town?"

"No. Only when charity demands it."

"Have the brothers no traffic with the world at all then?" Herbert was going to have a perfect alibi, if that were so!

"For twenty-four hours once every moon, a brother goes into the world. That is contrived lest the unspottedness of communal life should breed self-righteousness. For the twelve hours of the day he must help his fellow beings in such ways as are open to him. For the twelve hours of the night he must meditate in a place alone: in summer in some open place, in winter in some church."

"I see. And the twenty-four hours begin—when?"

"From a midnight to a midnight."

"Thank you."

# 21

THE SERVICE WAS HELD in a bare chapel, candle-lit and white-washed, very simple except for the magnificence of the altar at the East gable. Grant was surprised by the appearance of the altar. Poor the brothers might be, but there was wealth somewhere. The vessels on the white velvet cloth, and the Crucifix, might have been a pirate's loot from a Spanish American cathedral. He had found it difficult to associate the Herbert Gotobed he knew by reputation with this cloistered and poverty-struck existence. Being theatrical to no audience but oneself must soon pall. But the sight of that altar gave him pause. Herbert was perhaps running true to form after all.

Grant heard no word of the service. From his seat in the dim recess of a side window he could see all the faces of the participants; more than a score of them; and he found it a fascinating study. Some were cranks (one saw the same faces at "anti" meetings and folk-dance revivals), some fanatics (masochists looking for a modern hair shirt), some simple, some at odds with themselves and looking for peace, some at odds with the world and looking for sanctuary. Grant, looking them over with a lively interest, found his glance stayed as it came to one face. Now what had brought the owner of that face to a life of seclusion and self-denial? A round sallow face on a round ill-shaped head, the eyes small, the nose fleshy, the lower lip loose, so that it hung away from his teeth as he repeated the words of the service. All the others in that little chapel had been types that fitted easily into recognised niches in the everyday world: the principal to a bishopric, this one to a neurologist's waiting-room, this to a depot for unemployed. But where did that last one fit?

There was only one answer. In the dock.

"So that," said Grant's other self to him, "is Herbert Gotobed." He could not be sure, of course, until he had seen the man walk. That was all he had ever seen of him: his walk. But he was ready to stake much on his judgment. The best of judges were at fault sometimes—Gotobed might turn out to be that lean and harmless-looking individual in the front row—but he would be surprised if Gotobed were any but that unctuous creature with the loose lower lip.

As the men filed out after midnight, he had no more doubt. Gotobed had a peculiar walk, a gangling, shoulder-rotating progression which was quite his own.

Grant followed them out and then sought the Reverend Father. What was the name of the last man to leave the chapel?

That was Brother Aloysius.

And after a little persuasion Brother Aloysius was sent for.

As they waited Grant talked conventionally of the Order and its rules and learned that no member could own any worldly property or have communication for worldly purposes with human beings. Such trivial worldlinesses as newspapers were, of course, not even thought of. He also learned that the principal intended in about a month's time to take over a new Mission in Mexico, which they had built out of their funds, and that the privilege of electing his successor lay entirely with him.

A thought occurred to Grant.

"I don't want to be impertinent—please don't think this idle curiosity—but would you tell me whether you have decided in your mind on any particular person?"

"I have practically decided."

"May I know who it is?"

"I really do not know why I should tell to a stranger what I am not prepared to tell to the brothers of my own Order, but there is no reason to conceal it if I may trust your secrecy." Grant gave his word. "My successor is likely to be the man you have asked to see."

"But he is a newcomer!" Grant said before he thought.

"I am at a loss to know how you knew that," the Reverend Father said sharply. "It is true Brother Aloysius has been with us only a few months, but the qualities necessary for the priorship" (so he was a prior!) "are not developed with length of service."

Grant murmured agreement, and then asked which of their community had been on an errand in the streets this evening.

None of them, the prior said firmly; and the conversation was brought to an end by the entrance of the man Grant wanted.

He stood there passively, his hands folded within the wide sleeves of his dark-brown gown. Grant noticed that his feet were not sandalled but bare, and remembered that there had been no warning of his approach when he had presented himself in the newsagent's. The looker-on in Grant wondered whether it was an appearance of humility or the convenience of a noiseless tread which appealed so greatly to Herbert.

"This is Brother Aloysius," the prior said, and left them with a blessing, a much more poetic performance than the doorkeeper's.

"I am from Messrs. Erskine, Smythe, and Erskine, the lawyers in the Temple," Grant said. "You are Herbert Gotobed."

"I am Brother Aloysius."

"You were Herbert Gotobed."

"I never heard of him."

Grant considered him for a moment. "I'm sorry," he said. "We're looking for Gotobed about a legacy that has been left him."

"Yes? If he is a brother of this order, your news will be of little interest to him."

"If the legacy were big enough, he might realise that he could do far more for the cause of charity outside these walls than in them."

"Our oath is for life. Nothing that happens outside these walls is of interest to any member of our order."

"So you deny that you are Herbert Gotobed?"

Grant was conducting the conversation automatically. What his mind was occupied with, he found, was that the expression in the man's small pale eyes was hate. He had rarely seen such hate. But why hate? That was what his mind asked. It should be fear, surely?

Grant felt that to this man he was not a pursuer but someone who had butted in. The feeling stayed with him while he took his leave and all the way back to the hotel opposite the tobacconist's.

Williams was brooding over a cold meal he had caused to be set for his superior.

"Any news?" Grant asked.

"No, sir."

"No word of Tisdall? Have you telephoned?"

"Yes, I telephoned about twenty minutes ago. Not a word, sir."

Grant slapped some slices of ham between two pieces of bread. "Pity," he said. "I'd work much better if Tisdall were out of my mind. Come on. There isn't going to be much bed for us tonight."

"What is it, sir? Did you find him?"

"Yes, he's there all right. Denied he was Gotobed. They're not allowed to have any worldly transactions. That is why he was so shy in the shop. Didn't even wait to see who the second person behind the counter was: just fled at the very prospect of a watcher. That's what's worrying me, Williams. He seems much more occupied with not being chucked out of the order than with being run in for murder."

"But his running out of the shop might have been because he wanted to keep on in hiding. That monastery place is as good a hide-out as a murderer could wish for."

"Ye-s. Yes, but he's not frightened. He's angry. We're spoiling something for him."

They had been going quietly downstairs, Grant eating large mouthfuls of his improvised sandwich. As they approached the ground floor they were confronted by an enormous female who blocked their exit from the stairway. She had no poker in her hand, but the effect was the same.

"So that's what you are!" she said, with concentrated venom. "A couple of sneaking fly-by-nights. Come in here, as large as life, you do, and make me and my poor husband buy the best of everything for your meals—chops at tenpence each, and tongue at two-and-eightpence the pound, to say nothing of English tomatoes to suit your very particular tastes—and all we get for our expense and our trouble is a couple of empty rooms in the morning. I've a good mind to ring up the police and give you in charge—if it weren't for—"

"Oh, for God's sake!" Grant said angrily; and then began to laugh. He hung over the banisters laughing helplessly, while Williams talked to the angry hostess.

"Well, why didn't you say you were bobbies?" she said.

"We're *not* bobbies," Williams said, ferociously, and Grant laughed the more, and dragged him from the scene.

"Gilbertian!" he said, wiping his eyes. "Quite Gilbertian. Did me a lot of good. Now, listen. These monks, or whatever they esteem themselves, retire to their cells at midnight and don't move out of them till six. But Herbert gets in and out of that building more or less when he likes. I don't know how he works it: those first-floor windows are low enough to drop from but much too high to get back into, and he doesn't look like a gymnast. But get out he does. No one knew—or at least, the powers that be didn't know—he was out tonight. Well, I have a hunch that he's going walking again tonight, and I want to see where to."

"What makes you think so, sir?"

"Just instinct. If I were Herbert I'd have a base to conduct operations from. I walked round the block before I came back to the hotel. There are only two points where the monastery property abuts on the street. At the side where the door is; and at the very opposite side where the garden ends in a wall that looks fifteen feet high. There's a small gate there; iron and very solid. It's a long way from the living quarters, and I think our original side is the most helpful. But I want you to keep watch on the garden side, and tail anyone who comes out. I'll do the same on the door side. If nothing happens by six o'clock you can creep home and go to bed."

# 22

GRANT HAD BEEN WAITING for what seemed an eternity. The night was soft, with a damp air, and smelled pleasantly of green things and flowers. Somewhere there was a lime tree. There was no sky, only a thick misty dark above. Bells chimed every now and then, with aloof sweetness. In spite of himself, Grant found the peace of the night invading him; his mind grew blurred and incurious and he had to whip it to wakefulness.

And then, a few moments after half-past two had struck, something happened, and his mind leaped without any goading. He had heard no sound, but in the lane in front of the monastery there was movement. It was too dark to see a shape; all that happened was that the darkness moved, as a curtain might stir in a current of air. Someone was in the street.

Grant waited. The movement grew less, became more blurred, and ceased. Whoever was there had moved away from him. Grant slipped his unlaced boots from his feet and strung them across his shoulder; every step on a shod foot would be audible on a night like this. Silently he moved down the lane and past the high wall of the house. Out of its shadows the visibility was slightly better: he could see the movement in front of him again. He followed it with every sense alert; it was not only difficult to gauge his exact distance from it, but almost impossible to tell if it stopped for a moment. In the street beyond it was easier; the movement in the darkness became a form. A form retreating swiftly and effortlessly into the night. Grant set out to keep pace with it. Down the little streets of two-storey houses. Past small houses with small gardens. Past an occasional small paddock.

And then Grant felt gravel pavement under his stocking feet and cursed. The man was making for the country; for the outer suburbs at least.

For about twenty minutes Grant followed that half-seen figure through a dark and silent world. He did not know his surrounding; he had to follow the figure blindly. He did not know when a step came, or a declivity, or an obstacle. And a bad stumble might be fatal to the night's work. But as far as he could see, his quarry never hesitated. This was not a flight; it was a journey he had done often before.

Presently Grant could tell that they were in more or less open country. If there were houses they were built behind the original field hedges—a new suburb, probably. The hedges made it difficult to see the man he was following; their dark mass made a gloomy background for a moving figure. And then Grant suddenly found that he had lost him. Nothing moved in front of him any more. He stood still instantly. Was the man waiting for him? Or had he disappeared into an opening? Several times, when pebbles had slid under his own tread, he had wondered if the man suspected his presence. There had been as far as he could see no pause for reconnoitring in the man's progress. But now there was a complete absence of any movement at all.

Grant went forward step by step, and found himself level with an opening in the hedge. A gate. He wished passionately that he could use his torch. This blindfold moving through an unknown country was getting on his nerves. He decided to risk a guess that this was where the man had gone, and moved into the entrance. Immediately there was soft sand under his feet. He paused doubtfully. Was it only a sand-pit? What was the man planning? An attack?

Then he remembered that fine red sand which decorates the trim approaches to new villas, and breathed again. Reassured he moved forward, finding with one foot the cut edge of turf, and letting it lead him to the building which must be in front of him somewhere. It loomed quite suddenly in the darkness. A white-washed house of perhaps eight rooms. Its paleness made it slightly luminous even on so dark a night; and against its ghostly shimmer he saw the man again. He was standing still, and it seemed to Grant that he was looking back at him. He realised too late that he too was now standing where a wing of the house made a background for him. He dropped to his knees. And after a moment the man moved on and vanished round the corner of the house.

Grant made the best of his way to the corner and waited, pressed up against the wall. But there was no sound, no breathing, not a movement; the man had gone on; he was wasting time. He stepped round the corner. A soft wool substance smothered him, falling over his face and being drawn tightly about his neck. A split second before the folds closed on his throat, Grant got his fingers between the stuff and his flesh. He held on with all his might, and then, using the material as purchase, bent forward abruptly and felt the man's body come sliding over him, head first to the ground. The weight knocked Grant down, and the vile suffocating thing was still over his head, but his hands were free. He reached out for his opponent and felt with passionate gladness the restriction round his throat relax. He was still blind and suffocating, but he was in no immediate danger of being throttled. He was, in fact, doing his best to throttle the other man, if only he could find his throat. But the man was twisting like an eel, and using his knees with malicious art. This was not the first time that Herbert Gotobed had fought foul. Grant wished, hitting blindly and finding only seed-sown grass, that he could see for just thirty seconds. He let go the part of his assailant he happened to be holding—he was not sure whether it was a leg or an arm—and did his best to roll away. It was not successful, since the man had just as firm a grip of him. But he had time to reach into his pocket and close his fingers round his torch. His hand was prisoned there as he was rolled on to his back, but with all his might Grant hit with the free hand into the breath that was sobbing into his face. His knuckles hit bone and he heard the snap of teeth meeting. The man's full weight descended on him. He wrenched himself free from it, and dragged the torch from his pocket. Before he had got it out, the man was moving again. He had only rocked him. He flashed the torch on him, and before the light had reached his face the man leaped. Grant stepped aside and swung the weapon at him as he came. It missed him by a hairsbreadth and they went down together. Grant lacked stance for the reception of such a weight: all his attention had been on his own blow; he hit the ground with violence. In the dimness of the moment, when all his faculties were trying to summon his stunned body to its duty, he wondered detachedly how the man would kill him.

To his surprise he felt the weight of the man's body lift, something hit him across the side of the head, and he was aware, even while his ears sang, that the man had gone from his side.

He dragged himself to a sitting position; sitting, incidentally, on the stone he had been hit with (by its feel its proper place was a rockery), and was groping for his torch preparatory to following the man, when a woman's voice said out of the dark in a whisper:

"Is that you, Bert? Is anything wrong?"

Grant's hand lighted on the torch, and he got to his feet.

The light shone into eyes big and brown and soft as a deer's. But the rest of the face was not soft.

She drew in her breath as the light flashed, and made a movement backwards.

"Stay still," said Grant in a voice that brooked no disobedience, and the movement ceased.

"Don't talk so loud," she said urgently. "Who are you, anyway? I thought you were—a friend of mine."

"I'm a detective inspector—a policeman."

This statement, Grant had found, produced invariably one of two expressions: fear or wariness. Quite innocent people often showed the first; but the second was a give-away. It gave away the woman now.

Grant's light flashed on the house—a one-storey building with small attic rooms.

"Don't do that!" she hissed. "You'll waken her."

"Who is 'her'?"

"The old lady. My boss."

"You a maid here?"

"I'm the housekeeper."

"Just the two of you in the house?"

"Yes."

He indicated with his light the open window behind her. "Is that your room?"

"Yes."

"We'll go in there and talk."

"You can't come into the house. You can't do anything to me. I haven't done anything."

"Would you mind!" said Grant, in a tone that belied the meaning of the phrase.

"You can't come into the house without a warrant. I know!" She was standing against the window-sill now, defending her room.

"You don't need a warrant for murder," Grant said.

"Murder!" She stared at him. "What have I to do with murder?"

"Will you get in, please, and put on the light."

She did as she was bidden, climbing over the sill with the ease of practice. As the light clicked, Grant stepped over the sill and drew the curtains.

It was a very pleasant bedroom, with eiderdown on the bed and shaded light on the table.

"Who is your employer?" he asked.

She gave her employer's name, and admitted that she had been there only a few months.

"Where was your last reference from?"

"A place in Australia."

"And what relation are you to Herbert Gotobed?"

"Who's that?"

"Come, don't let's waste time, Miss— What name do you use, by the way?"

"I use my own name," she glared at him. "Rosa Freeson."

Grant tilted the lamp for a better view of her. He had never seen her before. "Herbert Gotobed came out here to see you tonight and you were waiting for him. You will save yourself a lot of trouble if you tell me all about it, now."

"I was waiting, if you must know, for Bert. He's the milk roundsman. You can't run me in for that. You can't blame me much, either. A girl has to have a little fun in a place like this."

"Yes?" He moved towards the built-in wardrobe. "Stay where you are," he said.

The wardrobe held nothing but women's clothes; rather too good for her position but none of them very new. Grant asked to see the contents of the chest of drawers, and she showed them sullenly. They were all quite normal. He asked where her boxes were.

"In the box room in the attic," she said.

"And what are the suit-cases under the bed?"

She looked ready to strike him.

"Let me see what is in these."

"You have no right! Show me your warrant. I won't open anything for you."

"If you have nothing to hide, you can't possibly object to my seeing what is inside."

"I've lost the key."

"You're making me very suspicious."

She produced the key from a string round her neck and pulled out the first suit-case. Grant, watching her, thought for the first time that she was not all white. Something in her movements, in the texture of her hair, was—what? Negro? Indian? And then he remembered the South Sea Mission which Herbert had run.

"How long since you left the Islands?" he asked conversationally.

"About—" She stopped, and finished immediately, "I don't know what you're talking about."

The first suit-case was empty. The second was full to the brim with men's clothes.

"Male impersonator?" asked Grant, who in spite of his swollen feet and aching head was beginning to feel happier. "Or just old-clothes dealer?"

"These are the clothes of my dead fiancé. I'll thank you not to be funny about them."

"Didn't your fiancé wear a coat?"

"Yes, but it was mussed up when he was killed."

"Oh? How was he killed?" Grant asked amiably, his hands running through the clothes.

"Motor accident."

"You disappoint me."

"Come again?"

"I'd expected a more imaginative end from you. What was your fiancé's name?"

"John Starboard."

"Starboard! That cancels out the motor accident."

"I suppose you know what you're talking about. I don't."

"It wasn't your fiancé's coat you kept in that now empty suit-case, by any chance?"

"It was not."

Grant's searching hand paused. He withdrew it holding a bundle of passports: four in all. One was a British one issued to Herbert Gotobed; one was an American one in the name of Alexander Byron Black; one a Spanish one, issued to a deaf-mute, one José Fernandez; and the fourth an American one for William Cairns Black and his wife. But the photographs were all of the same man: Herbert Gotobed; and the wife's photograph was that of Rosa Freeson.

"A collector, your fiancé. An expensive hobby, I've always understood." He put the passports into his pocket.

"You can't do that. They're not yours. I'll scream the house down. I will say you came in and attacked me. Look!" She pulled her wrap open and began to tear her nightdress.

"Scream as much as you like. Your old lady would be very interested in these passports. And if you have any designs on the old lady, by the way,

I should advise you to reconsider them. Now I shall retrieve my boots. They are lying somewhere in the garden. Though God alone knows if my feet will go into them. My advice to you, Mrs. Cairns Black, is to do nothing at all until you hear from me. We have nothing against *you*, so far, so don't begin putting ideas into our heads by doing anything you might regret."

# 23

GRANT MANAGED TO GET his boots on (by dint of thinking strenuously of something else, his childhood's recipe for painful moments), but after two or three steps hastily took them off again, and hobbled homeward as he had come: stocking-soled. It was not easy to find his way back, but he had an excellent bump of locality (it was said at the Yard that if you blindfolded Grant and turned him until he was dizzy he still knew where north was) and the general direction was clear enough to him. He stood in a doorway on the opposite side of the street and watched the officer on the beat go by, rather than ask a direction and have to explain himself. No member of the C.I.D. likes to appear before a borough policeman with his boots in his hands.

He wrote a note asking Williams to telephone the Yard when he came in at six and ask for any information they might have about a sect or order or what not called the Tree of Lebanon, and to waken him when the answer came. He then fell into bed, and slept dreamlessly, the passports under his pillow until Williams called him just before ten o'clock.

"News of Tisdall?" Grant said as his eyes opened.

But there was no news.

The Yard said that the Holy Order of the Tree of Lebanon had been founded by a rich bachelor in 1862, for the furtherance of the monastic life, he having been what was then known as jilted by the object of his affections. He himself had been the first prior, and all his wealth had been used to endow the foundation. The rule of poverty had been very strict, money being used only for charities approved by the prior of the moment, so that by the present day the order had the reputation of having a lot of money laid away. A prior was nominated by his predecessor, but a prior could be superseded at any moment by the unanimous vote of the brethren.

Grant drank the horrible coffee supplied by the establishment, and considered things. "That is what our Herbert wants: the priorship. He has the prior dancing on a stick. It's almost incredible that a man like the prior could be such a fool. But then! Think of the fools we've known, Williams."

"I'm thinking, sir," Williams said, eloquently.

"All those hard-headed self-made pieces of original conglomerate who fall for a few honeyed words from a confidence man in a hotel lobby! And of course Herbert has no ordinary gift of tongues. Perhaps he worked his churches in America as leaven to the prior's interest. Anyhow, he's the prior's fair-haired boy at the moment. With the prospect of having a fortune in his hands if he plays his cards rightly for the next few weeks. Not much wonder he was scared of getting in wrong. He wanted to know just how much his sister had left him, without compromising himself with his brethren. If she had left him enough to make it worth his while, he'd give up the monastic life. I shouldn't think it appeals greatly to him. Even with occasional visits to the villa."

"How long do you think he'd stay in any case, sir?"

"Till he had transferred enough hard cash to his own particular charities. Oh, well, these," he indicated the passports, "will be enough to frame a nice little indictment on, so that we can have him under our hands when we want him. The thing that disappoints me, Williams, is where is the murder in all this? I don't mean that he didn't do it. I've no doubt that he was having his twenty-four hours off at the time. But why did he do it? He came to England when he heard that she was coming. I think, judging by his woman's clothes, that he was possibly broke when he arrived. That was why he took to the Tree of Lebanon. But the possibilities of the Tree must have occurred to him pretty soon. Why kill his sister?"

"Went to see her and had a quarrel. The queer hour that's puzzled us all would be quite normal for him. Six o'clock would be just as usual as lunch time."

"Yes, that's true. I'm going now to find out from the Reverend Father whether Brother Aloysius was out of the monastery a fortnight yesterday. The Reverend Father would have sat on a very high horse yesterday, but he'll talk when he sees what his favourite looks like on these passports."

But the Reverend Father was not receiving callers. The little *guichet* displayed the sour face of the doorkeeper, who delivered his stolid message in answer to all Grant's questions, whether the phrase was relevant or not. Herbert's golden tongue had been at work. The guichet shut, and Grant was left helpless in the little lane. There was nothing for it but a warrant. He went slowly away, his feet still aching; admired the job Herbert had made of oiling the cellar entrance in the pavement, and climbed into his car. Yes, he had better get that warrant.

He went back to the hotel for his pyjamas, razor, and toothbrush (he had no intention of spending another night there) and was leaving a message for the sleeping Williams, when he was called to the telephone by the Yard.

Would he go to Dover? The man there wanted him. Something had turned up, it seemed.

He changed the message for Williams, threw his things into the car, found time to wonder why he over-tipped the frowsy virago for her inattendance, disgusting food, and deplorable cooking, and set out for Dover.

Something had turned up. That could only mean Champneis. Something out of the ordinary. If they had merely found where Champneis had spent the night, it would have been reported by telephone in the ordinary way. But—something had turned up.

Rimell, the detective in charge—a kind, melancholy-looking boy, whose greatest asset was his unlikeness to the popular conception of a detective—was waiting for Grant at the police-station door, and Grant drew him into the car. Rimell said that he had, after endless delving, unearthed an old fellow called Searle, a retired deckhand, who had been coming home from his granddaughter's engagement party about half-past twelve on the Wednesday night—or rather, the Thursday morning. He was alone, because very few people lived down the harbour way nowadays. They'd got ideas and lived up the hill in gimcrack villas you'd be afraid to sneeze in. He had stopped a minute or two when he had got to the sea level, to look at the harbour. It still made him feel fine to look at riding-lights at night. It was beginning to mist over, but it was still clear enough to see the outlines of everything. He knew the *Petronel* was coming in—had seen her through his glasses before he went to the party—and so he looked for her now, and saw her lying, not at the jetty, but out in the water at anchor. As he watched, a small motor-boat came out from her side and made for the shore, going slowly with a quiet *chug-chug* as if not anxious to call attention to itself. As it touched the jetty steps a man moved out of the shadows by the quay. A tall figure whom Searle identified as Lord Edward (he had seen him often and had in fact once served aboard a previous yacht of his brother's) appeared from the boat and said, "Is that you, Harmer?" and the smaller man had said, "It's me," and then, in a low tone, "Customs all right?" Lord Edward had said, "No trouble at all," and they had gone down into the motor-boat together and pushed off. The mist had come down quickly after that, blotting out the harbour. After about fifteen minutes Searle had gone on his way. But as he was going up the street, he heard a motor-boat leave the *Petronel*. Whether it came ashore or went out of the harbour he didn't know. He didn't think at the moment any of all this was of any importance.

"Great Heavens!" said Grant. "I can't believe it. There just—there just isn't one single thing in all the world that these two men have in common." (His subconscious added before he could stop it: Except a woman.) "They just don't touch anywhere. And yet they're as thick as thieves." He sat silent a little. "All right, Rimell. Good work. I'm going to have lunch and think this over."

"Yes, sir. May I give you a friendly piece of advice, sir?"

"If you must. It's a bad habit in subordinates."

"No black coffee, sir. I expect you had four cups for breakfast and nothing else."

Grant laughed. "Why should you worry?" he said, pressing the starter. "The more breakdowns, the quicker the promotion."

"I grudge the money for wreaths, sir."

But Grant was not smiling as he drove lunchwards. Christine Clay's husband and her reputed lover had midnight business together. That was strange enough. But that Edward Champneis, fifth son of the seventh Duke of Bude, and a reputable if unorthodox member of his race, should have underhand traffic with Jason Harmer, of Tin Pan Alley was definitely stranger. What was the common bond? Not murder. Grant refused to consider anything so *outré* as murder in couples. One or other might have wanted to murder her, but that they should have forgathered on the subject was unimaginable. The motor-boat had left the *Petronel* again, Searle said. Supposing only one of them had been in it? It was only a short distance north along the coast to the Gap at Westover; and Harmer had turned up at Clay's cottage two hours after her death. To drown Clay from a motor-boat was the ideal way. As good as his groyne theory, with escape both quicker and easier. The more he thought of the motor-boat, the more enamoured of the method he grew. They had checked the boats in the vicinity as a matter of routine at the time of the first investigation; but a motor-boat has a wide cruising radius. But— oh, well, just "but"! The theory was fantastic. Could one imagine Jason saying, "You lend me your boat and I'll drown your wife," or Champneis suggesting, "I'll lend you the boat if you'll do the work." These two had met for some other reason altogether. If murder had resulted, then it had been unplanned, incidental.

What then had they met for? Harmer had said something about Customs. It had been his first greeting. He had been anxious about it. Was Harmer a drug fiend?

There were two things against that. Harmer didn't look like an addict. And Champneis would never have supplied the stuff. Risk might be the breath of life to him, but that kind of risk would be very definitely out.

What, then, was to be kept from the eyes of the Customs? Tobacco? Jewels? Champneis had shown George Meir, next morning, the topazes he had brought back for Christine.

There was one thing against all of it. Smuggling Edward Champneis might descend to, as a ploy, a mere bit of excitement; but Grant could not see him smuggling for the benefit of Jay Harmer. One ran one's head continually against that. What had these two men in common? They had something. Their association proved it. But what? They were, as far as anyone knew, the merest acquaintances. Not even that. Champneis had almost certainly left England before Harmer had arrived, and Christine had not known Harmer until they worked together on these English pictures.

No digestive juices flowed in Grant's alimentary tracts during that lunch; his brain was working like an engine. The sweetbreads and green peas might as well have been thrown into the chef's waste bin. By the time coffee had arrived he was no nearer a solution. He wished he was one of these marvellous creatures of super-instinct and infallible judgment who adorned the pages of detective stories, and not just a hard-working, well-meaning, ordinarily intelligent Detective Inspector. As far as he could see, the obvious course was to interview one or other of these men. And the obvious one to interview was Harmer. Why? Oh, because he'd talk more easily. Oh, yes, all right, and because there was less chance of running into trouble! What it was to have someone inside you checking up your motives for everything you did or thought!

He refrained from his second cup of coffee, with a smile for the absent Rimell. Nice kid. He'd make a good detective some day.

He rang up Devonshire House, and asked if Mr. Harmer could make it convenient to see Alan Grant (no need to advertise his profession) this evening between tea and dinner.

He was told that Mr. Harmer was not in London. He had gone down to see Leni Primhofer, the continental star, who was staying at Whitecliffe. He was writing a song for her. No, he was not expected back that night. The address was Tall Hatch, Whitecliffe, and the telephone number Whitecliffe 3025.

Grant rang Whitecliffe 3025, and asked when Mr. Harmer could see him. Harmer was in the country motoring with Fräulein Primhofer and would not be back before dinner.

Whitecliffe is a continuation of Westover: a collection of plutocratic villas set on the cliff beyond the cries of trippers and the desecration of blown newspaper pages. Grant still had a room at the Marine, and so to Westover he went, and there Williams joined him. All he could do now was to wait for a warrant from the Yard and a visit from Harmer.

It was cocktail time when Harmer presented himself.

"Are you asking me to dinner, Inspector? If not, say you are and let the dinner be on me, will you; there's a good sport. Another hour of that woman and I shall be daffy. Loco. Nuts. I have known stars in my time, but holy mackerel! she takes the cake. You'd think with her English being on the sticky side that she'd let up now and then to think a bit. But no! Jabbers right along, with German to fill in, and bits of French dressing here and there to make it look nice. Waiter! What's yours, Inspector? Not drinking? Oh, come on! No? That's too bad. One gin and mixed, waiter. You don't need to climb on the wagon with a waist like that, Inspector. Don't say you're Prohibition from conviction!"

Grant disclaimed any crusading interest in the drink traffic.

"Well, what's the news? You have got news, haven't you?" He became serious, and looked earnestly, at Grant. "Something real turned up?"

"I just wanted to know what you were doing in Dover on that Wednesday night?"

"In Dover?"

"A fortnight last Wednesday."

"Someone been pulling your leg?"

"Listen, Mr. Harmer, your lack of frankness is complicating everything. It's keeping us from running down the man who killed Christine Clay. The whole business is cockeyed. You come clean about your movements on that Wednesday night, and half the irrelevant bits and pieces that are weighing the case down can be shorn off and thrown away. We can't see the outline of it with all the bits that are covering it up and hanging on to it. You want to help us get our man, don't you? Well, prove it!"

"I like you a lot, Inspector. I never thought I'd like a cop so much. But I told you already: I lost my way looking for Chris's cottage, and slept in the car."

"And if I bring witnesses to prove that you were in Dover after midnight?"

"I still slept in the car."

Grant was silent, disappointed. Now he would have to go to Champneis. Harmer's little brown eyes watched him with something like solicitude.

"You're not getting your sleep these days, Inspector. Heading for a breakdown. Change your mind and have a drink. Wonderful how a drink puts things in their place."

"If you didn't insist on sleeping in the car, I'd have a better chance of sleeping in my bed," Grant said angrily, and took his leave with less than his usual grace.

He wanted to get at Champneis before Jason Harmer had time to tell him that Grant had been making enquiries. The best way to do that was to telephone and ask Champneis to come down to Westover. Offer to send a police car for him at once. And if necessary keep Harmer talking until Champneis would have left town.

But Champneis had already left town. He was in Edinburgh addressing a polite gathering on "The Future of Galeria."

That settled it. Long before anyone could get to him, Harmer would have communicated with him either by telegram or telephone. Grant asked that both means of communication should be tapped, and went back to the lounge to find Jason still sitting over his drink.

"I know you don't like me, Inspector, but honest to God I like you, and honest to God that woman is a holy terror. Do you think you could sort of forget that we are famous-detective and worm-of-a-suspect, and eat together after all?"

Grant smiled, against his will. He had no objections.

Jason smiled too, a little knowingly. "But if you think by the end of dinner I won't have slept in that car, don't kid yourself."

In spite of himself, Grant enjoyed that meal. It was a good game: trying to trap Jason into some kind of admission. The food was good. And Jason was amusing.

Another telephone message came to say that Lord Edward was returning on the first train in the morning, and would be in London by tea-time. Grant could expect the warrant for Gotobed by the first post in the morning.

So Grant went to bed at the Marine, puzzled but not suicidal; at least there was a programme for the morrow. Jason too slept at the Marine, having declared his inability to face Leni any more that day.

# 24

THE KITCHEN OF THE MARINE was in the roof; the latest discovery of architects being that smells go upward. It had set out to be an all-electric kitchen, that being also in the recent creed of architects. But it was not in the creed of Henri, chef of chefs. Henri was a Provençal, and to cook by electricity, my God, it was a horror, but a horror! If God had meant us to cook by lightning, He would not have invented fire. So Henri had his stoves and his braziers. And so now, at three in the morning, a soft glow from the banked-up fires filled the enormous white room. Full of high lights, the room was: copper, silver, and enamel. (Not aluminium. Henri fainted at the mention of aluminium.) The door stood half open, and the fire made a quiet ticking now and then.

Presently the door moved. Was pushed a little further ajar. A man stood in the opening, apparently listening. He came in, silent as a shadow, and moved to the cutlery table. A knife gleamed in the dimness as he took it from the drawer. But he made no sound. From the table he moved to the wall where the keys hung on their little board, each on its appointed hook. Without fumbling he took the key he wanted. He hesitated as he was about to leave the room, and came back to the fire as if it fascinated him. His eyes in the light were bright and excited, his face shadowed.

By the hearth lay kindling wood for some morning fire. It had been spread on a newspaper to dry thoroughly. The man noticed it. He pushed the cut wood to one side and lifted the rest of the paper into the small square of firelight. For a moment he read, so still in that silent room that it might have been empty.

And suddenly all was changed. He leaped to his feet, ran to the electric button, and switched on the lights. Ran back to the paper and snatched it from its bed of sticks. He spread it on the table with shaking hands, patting it and smoothing it as if it were a live thing. Then he began to laugh. Softly and consumedly, drumming with his fists on the scrubbed wood. His laughter grew, beyond his control. He ran to the switch again and snapped on all the lights in the kitchen; one, two, three, four, five, six, seven, eight. A new thought possessed him. He ran out of the kitchen, along the tiled corridors, silent as a shadow. Down the dim stairs he sped, flight after flight, like a bat. And now he began to laugh again, in sobbing gusts. He shot into the darkness of the great lounge and across it to the green light of the reception desk. There was no one there. The night porter was on his rounds. The man turned a page of the registration book, and ran a wavering finger down it. Then he made off up the stairs again, silent except for his sobbing breath. In the service room on the second floor he took a master key from its hook, and ran to the door of Room 73. The door yielded, he put out his hand to the switch, and leaped on the man in the bed.

Grant struggled out of his dream of contraband, to defend himself against a maniac who was kneeling on his bed shaking him and repeating between sobs: "So you were wrong, and it's all right! You were wrong, and it's all right!"

"Tisdall!" said Grant. "My God, I'm glad to see you. Where have you been?"

"Among the cisterns."

"In the *Marine!* All the time?"

"Since Thursday night. How long is that? I just walked in at the service door late at night. Rain like stair rods. You could have walked the length of the town in your birthday suit, and there wouldn't have been anyone to see. I knew about the little attic place because I saw it when workmen were here one day. No one's ever there but workmen. I come out at night to get food from the larder. I expect someone's in trouble about that food. Or perhaps they never missed it? Do you think?"

His unnaturally bright eyes scanned Grant anxiously. He had begun to shiver. It did not need much guesswork to place his probable temperature.

Grant pushed him gently down to a sitting position on the bed, took a pair of pyjamas from the drawer, and handed them over.

"Here. Get into these and into bed at once. I suppose you were soaking when you arrived at the hotel?"

"Yes. My clothes weighed so much I could hardly walk. But it's dry up in the roof. Warm too. Too warm in the day-time. You have a n-n-nice taste in n-n-night wear." His teeth were chattering; reaction was flooding him.

Grant helped him with the pyjamas and covered him up. He rang for the porter and ordered hot soup and the presence of a doctor. Then he sat down at the telephone and told the good news to the Yard, Tisdall's over-bright eyes watching him, quizzically. When he had finished he came over to the bed and said: "I can't tell you how sorry I am about all this. I'd give a lot to undo it."

"Blankets!" said Tisdall. "Sheets! Pillows! Eiderdown! Gosh!" He grinned as far as his chattering teeth and his week's growth of beard would let him. "Say 'Now I Lay Me' for me," he said. And fell abruptly asleep.

# 25

IN THE MORNING, because the doctor said that "there was a certain congestion which in the subject's weakened condition might at any moment develop into pneumonia," Grant summoned Tisdall's Aunt Muriel, whom the Yard obligingly found, Tisdall having refused to consider the presence of any aunts. Williams was sent to Canterbury to arrest Brother Aloysius, and Grant planned to go back to town after lunch to interview Champneis. He had telephoned the good news of Tisdall's reappearance to Colonel Burgoyne, and the telephone had been answered by Erica.

"Oh, I'm so glad for you!" she said.

"For *me?*"

"Yes, it must have been awful for you."

And it was only then that Grant realised quite how awful it had been. That continual pushing down of an unnamed fear. What a nice child she was.

The nice child had sent over for the patient in the course of the morning a dozen fresh eggs taken from the Steynes nests that very hour. Grant thought how typical it was of her to send fresh eggs, and not the conventional flowers or fruit.

"I hope she didn't get into trouble for giving me food that time?" Tisdall asked. He always talked as if the occurrences of the last week were many years away; the days in the attic had been a lifetime to him.

"On the contrary. She saved your neck and my reputation. It was she who found your coat. No, I can't tell you about it now. You're supposed not to talk or be talked to."

But he had had to tell all about it. And had left Tisdall saying softly to himself, "Well!" Over and over again: "Well!" in a wondering tone.

The shadow of the Champneis interview had begun to loom over Grant. Supposing he said frankly: "Look here, both you and Jason Harmer went out of your way to lie to me about your movements on a certain night, and now I find that you were together at Dover. What were you doing?" What would the answer be? "My dear sir, I can't answer for Harmer's prevarications, but he was my guest on the *Petronel* and we spent the night fishing in our motor-boat." That would be a good alibi.

And still his mind dwelt on the contraband idea. What contraband was of interest to both Champneis and Harmer? And it didn't take a whole night to hand over even a whole cargo load of contraband. Yet neither of them had an alibi for that night. What had they done with the hours from midnight to breakfast?

He had felt, ever since Rimell's revelation at Dover, that if he could remember what Champneis had been talking about just before his fib about the day of his arrival, all would be clear to him.

He decided to go downstairs and have his hair cut before he left the Marine. He was to remember that hair-cut.

As he put out his hand to push the swing door open, he heard Champneis's voice in his mind, drawling a sentence.

So *that* was what he had been talking about!

Yes. Yes. Pictures ran together in Grant's mind to make a sequence that made sense. He turned from the saloon door to the telephone and called the Special Branch. He asked them half a dozen questions, and then went to have his hair cut, smiling fatuously. He knew now what he was going to say to Edward Champneis.

It was the busy time of the morning and all the chairs were full.

"Won't be a minute, sir," an anxious supervisor said. "Not a minute if you will wait."

Grant sat down by the wall and reached for a magazine from the pile on a shelf. The pile fell over; a well thumbed collection, most of them far from new. Because it had a frontispiece of Christine Clay, he picked up a copy of the *Silver Sheet,* an American cinema magazine, and idly turned over the pages. It was the usual bouquet. The "real truth" was told about someone for the fifty-second time, being a completely different real truth from all the other fifty-one real truths. A nit-wit blonde explained how she read new meaning into Shakespeare. Another told how she kept her figure. An actress who didn't know one end of a frying-pan from the other was photographed in her kitchen making griddle cakes. A he-man star said how grand he thought all the other he-man stars. Grant turned the pages more impatiently. He was on the point of exchanging the magazine for another when his attention was suddenly caught. He read through an article with growing interest. At the last paragraph he got to his feet, still holding the paper and staring at the page.

"Your turn now, sir," the barber said. "This chair, please."

But Grant took no notice.

"We're quite ready for you now, sir. Sorry you've been kept waiting."

Grant looked up at them, only half conscious of them.

"Can I have this?" he asked, indicating the magazine. "It's six months old. Thank you," and rushed out of the room.

They stared after him, and laughed a little, speculating as to what had taken his fancy.

"Found his affinity," someone suggested.

"Thought they were extinct, affinities," another countered.

"Found something to cure his corns."

"No, gone to consult his best friend."

And they laughed and forgot him.

Grant was in the telephone booth, and the impatient gentleman in the patent-leather shoes was beginning to wonder if he was ever coming out of it. He was talking to Owen Hughes, the cinema star. That was why the patent-leather gentleman didn't go upstairs to the numerous booths on the ground floor. He was hoping to hear some of the conversation. It was about whether someone had mentioned something in a letter to someone.

"You *did!*" Grant said. "Thanks! That's all I wanted to know. Keep it under your hat. That I asked, I mean."

Then he had asked for the Thames police, pulling the door tighter and so exasperating the waiting gentleman.

"Has 276 River Walk a motor-boat, do you know?"

There was a consultation at the other end.

Yes, 276 had a boat. Yes, very fast. Sea-going? Oh, yes, if necessary. Used it for fowling along the Essex flats, they thought. Used to navigation of the lower river, anyhow? Oh, yes.

Grant asked if they would have a boat ready for him in about an hour and a half, by which time he'd be in town, he hoped. He'd take it as a great favour.

Certainly, they would.

Grant telephoned to Barker—at which point the patent-leather gentleman gave it up—and asked that if Williams was back in town within the next ninety minutes he should meet Grant at Westminster Pier. If Williams was not back in time, then Sanger.

Grant took full advantage of the lunch-time lull in traffic, and in unrestricted areas excelled himself in the gentle art of speed with safety. He found Williams waiting for him, a little breathless, since he had that moment arrived from the Yard and sent the disappointed Sanger back. Williams had no intention of being out of anything, if he could help it. And the Superintendent had said that something exciting was due to break.

"Well, was the Reverend Father shocked?" Grant asked.

"Not as shocked as Brother Aloysius. He didn't for a moment imagine we'd got anything on him. By the way he behaved, I should think some other police forces must be anxious to catch up with him."

"I shouldn't wonder."

"Where are we going, sir?"

"Chelsea Reach. Beloved of painters and folk-dancers."

Williams looked benignly at his superior and noticed how much better he was looking now that the Tisdall boy had turned up.

The police boat drew in to the bank at 276 River Walk where a large greyish motor-boat was moored. The police boat edged gingerly nearer until only a foot separated the gunwales.

Grant stepped across. "Come with me, Williams. I want witnesses."

The cabin was locked. Grant glanced up at the house opposite and shook his head. "I'll have to risk it. I'm sure I'm right, anyhow."

While the river police stood by, he forced the lock and went in. It was a tidy, seamanlike cabin; everything was neat and ship-shape. Grant began to go through the lockers. In the one under the starboard bunk he found what he was looking for. An oilskin coat. Black. Bought in Cannes. With the button missing from the right cuff.

"You take that, Williams, and come up to the house with me."

The maid said that Miss Keats was in, and left them in a dining-room on the ground floor; a very austere and up-to-the-minute apartment.

"Looks more like a place to have your appendix out than to put roast beef into you," Williams observed.

But Grant said nothing.

Lydia came in, smiling, her bracelets jangling and her beads clashing.

"I'm sorry I couldn't take you upstairs, my dear Leo person, but I have some clients who mightn't understand that this is just a friendly visit."

"So you knew who I was, at Marta's?"

"Of course. You don't flatter my powers of divination, my dear Mr. Grant. Won't you present your friend?"

"This is Sergeant Williams."

She looked faintly disconcerted, Grant thought, but managed to be gracious to the sergeant. Then she saw what was under Williams's arm.

"What are you doing with my coat?" she asked sharply.

"Then it is your coat? The one in the locker of the boat?"

"Of course it is my coat! How dare you force my cabin! It is always kept locked."

"The lock will be repaired, Miss Keats. Meanwhile I regret to tell you that I must arrest you for the murder of Christine Clay at the Gap at Westover on Thursday morning, the 15th, and warn you that anything you say may be used in evidence against you."

Her face changed from her habitual expression of satisfaction to the convulsed fury he had seen when Judy Sellers had made light of her powers. "You can't arrest me," she said. "It is not in my stars. Who should know if not I? The stars have no secrets from me. The stars have predicted a glorious destiny for me. It is you, poor mistaken fool, who will go on stumbling and making mistakes. My sign is achievement. Whatever I will I can do. It is set there in the sky that it shall be so. Destiny. 'Some are born great'—that is true and the rest is lies. One is born great or is not great at all. I was born to achieve. To be a leader. To be looked up to by mankind—"

"Miss Keats, I should be grateful if you would prepare to come with us at once. Any clothes you want can be sent after you."

"Clothes? What for?"

"For use in prison."

"I don't understand. You can't put me in prison. It isn't in my stars. They said that what I wanted I could do."

"Everyone can do what they want if they want it enough. But no one with impunity. Will you send for your maid and explain to her? She will fetch your hat if you want it."

"I don't want it. I am not going with you. I am going to a party this afternoon at Marta's. She's got Christine's part, you know. In the new film. That's one good turn I did. It was all written a long time ago what we should do. It falls into place, like the cog things in a musical box, you know. Or perhaps you don't know. Are you musical? And from Marta's I'm going to Owen Hughes. After that we shall see. If you come back in the evening we can talk about it. Do you know Owen? A charming person. He had his appointed place too. If it hadn't been for Owen it would never have come into my head. No, I don't mean that. Great enterprises belong to great minds. They would happen in any case. But the releasing agent is often very small. Like electric light and the switch. I used that simile in a lecture in Scotland the other week. It went very well. Neat, don't you think? Will you have some sherry? I'm afraid I'm very remiss. It's the consciousness of these people upstairs waiting to be told."

"Told what?"

"About me, of course. No, about themselves. That is what they came for. I'm a little muddled. They want to know what destiny has in store for them. And only I can tell them. Only I, Lydia Keats—"

"May I use your telephone, Miss Keats?"

"Certainly. It is in the cupboard place in the hall. One of the new coloured kind. The telephone, not the cupboard. What was I saying?"

Grant said to Williams, "Ask them to send Reynolds round at once."

"Is that the painter? I shall be glad to meet him. He was born to greatness. It is not a matter of application, or mixing pigments, you know. It is having the matter in you. And that the stars arrange. You must let me do a horoscope for you. You are a Leo person. Very attractive people. Kingly born. I have been sorry sometimes that I was not August born. But Aries people are leaders. Talkative, too, I'm afraid." She giggled. "I do talk a lot they tell me. Chatterbox, they called me as a child—"

# 26

HALF AN HOUR later Reynolds, the police surgeon, gave the screaming, raving thing that had been Lydia Keats a morphine injection so that they might remove her to the station in some sort of decency.

Grant and Williams, standing in the door, watching the disappearing ambulance, found no words.

"Well," Grant said at length, pulling himself together, "I suppose I'd better get along and see Champneis."

"The people that made the laws of this country ought to be shot," Williams said with sudden venom.

Grant looked startled. "Capital punishment, you mean?"

"No! Closed hours."

"Oh, I see. There's a flask in my cupboard. You can help yourself."

"Thank you, sir. Don't take on, miss!" This to the sobbing maid in the background. "Things like that will happen."

"She was a very kind mistress to me," she said. "It hurts me to see her like that."

"Take care of that coat, Williams," Grant said as they went down the path to the car that had been sent for them, glad beyond speech to leave the house behind.

"Tell me, sir, how did you find out it was that woman of all people?"

Grant produced the pages he had torn from the magazine.

"I found that in a magazine in the barbershop at the Marine. You can read it for yourself."

It was an article written by some Midwest sob sister, who had been in New York for a vacation. New York was full of film stars who had either run out on their studies or were on their way back to them, and in New York also was Miss Lydia Keats. And the thing that most impressed the sob sister was not shaking hands with Grace Marvel, but the success of Miss Keats's prophecies. She had made three startling ones. She had prophesied that within three months Lyn Drake would have a serious accident; and everyone knew that Lyn Drake was still on his back. She had said that Millard Robinson would within a month lose a fortune by fire; and everyone knew how the reels of the new million-dollar film had been burned to a cinder. And her third statement prophesied the death by drowning of a woman star of the first magnitude, whose name, of course, she gave, but the sob sister equally of course could not reveal. "If this third prophecy, so circumstantial, so unequivocal, comes true, then Miss Keats is established as the possessor of one of the most uncanny talents in the world. All humanity will be besieging her. But don't go swimming with Miss Keats, little blonde star! The temptation might be too much for her!"

"Well, I'll be damned," said Williams, and was silent until Grant dropped him at the Yard.

"Tell the Superintendent I'll be in as soon as I've seen Lord Edward," Grant said, and was driven on to Regent's Park.

In an atmosphere of marble mantelpieces and sheepskin rugs he waited half an hour before Champneis arrived.

"How are you, Inspector? I hear from Binns that you've been waiting. Sorry to subject you to the furnishings longer than is vitally necessary. I hope

you drink tea? But if you don't there are what my uncle called 'cordials.'
A much nicer word than 'drinks,' don't you think? Have you news?"

"Yes, sir. I'm sorry to break in with it when you're just after a journey."

"It can't be worse than the drawing-room lecture of my great-aunt's yesterday. I only went for the old lady's sake, but I found that she thought I should
have cancelled it. It would have been more 'fitting.' So tell me the bad news."

Grant told him what had happened, and he listened gravely, the unusual
defensive flippancy gone.

"Is she insane?" he asked, when Grant had finished.

"Yes. Reynolds thinks so. It may be hysteria, but he thinks it's insanity.
Delusions of greatness, you know."

"Poor wretch. But how did she know where my wife was?"

"Owen Hughes told her in a letter from Hollywood. He forgot that it was
a secret that she had taken his cottage. He even mentioned the early-morning
swimming."

"So simple. I see. . . . Was she very expert with a motor-boat, then?"

"She had been practically brought up on one, it seems. Used the river constantly. No one would have thought of questioning her comings and goings.
She may have made that night journey down the river more than once before
the opportunity she was looking for turned up. Curious, but one never thinks
of the river as a high-road to anywhere. We had considered the possibility
of a motor-boat, naturally, but not a motor-boat from London. Not that it
would have helped us very much if it had. The man's coat she wore was
very misleading. Lots of women wear men's oilskins, yachting; but I don't
think it would have occurred to me."

There was a short silence.

Each man watched in his mind that boat's journey down the misty river,
out to the many-lighted estuary, and along the many-lighted coast. One little
town after another, from flaring dockyard lights among the flats to twinkling
villa lights among the cliffs, must have lit that progress. But later, there must
have been darkness; complete darkness and silence, as the summer fog
pressed down on the water. What had her thoughts been, in that time of
waiting? Alone, with time to reflect. And with no stars to remind her of her
greatness. Or was her madness even then so sure that she had no doubts?

And afterwards— Each man watched that too. The surprise. The friendly
greeting. Chris's green cap bobbing alongside the grey hull—the cap that had
never been found. The woman leaning over to talk to her. And then—

Grant remembered those broken nails on Christine's hands. It had not been
so easy, then.

"That finishes the case, sir, but it was really something else that brought
me to see you. Another case altogether."

"Yes? Here's tea. You needn't wait, Binns. Sugar, Inspector?"

"I want to know where you took Rimnik."

Champneis paused with the sugar poised. He looked both surprised and amused and—somehow—admiring.

"He is with friends of Harmer's, near Tunbridge Wells."

"May I have the exact address?"

Champneis gave it, and also gave Grant his tea. "Why do you want Rimnik?"

"Because he is in this country without a passport—thanks to you!"

"He *was*. The Office issued him a landing permit this morning. It took a lot of eloquence—Britain the lover of justice, the defender of the persecuted, the home of the righteous homeless: all that stuff—but it worked. Chests still swell in Whitehall, do you know? They were like a collection of pouter pigeons when I finished."

He looked at the Inspector's disapproving face. "I didn't know that that little business had been a worry to you."

"Worry!" Grant burst out. "It nearly ruined everything. You and Harmer both lying about what you had done that night—" He found that he was treading on delicate ground and pulled himself up.

But Champneis had understood. "I really am sorry, Inspector. Are you going to arrest me? Can one be arrested retrospectively, so to speak?"

"I don't think so. I shall have to enquire about it. It would give me great pleasure." Grant had recovered his temper.

"All right. Let's postpone the arrest. But tell me how you found out? I thought we'd been so clever."

"I might never have found out if it hadn't been for a good bit of work by a young officer—Rimell—at Dover."

"I must meet Rimell."

"He found that you and Harmer had met that night and had been worried about the Customs."

"Yes. Rimnik was in a cupboard in my cabin. It was an exciting half-hour. But the Customs and Harbour Masters are only human."

This Grant took to mean that they knocked off the Champneis pegs and lacked the nerve to knock on the bulkheads. "It was then I began to feel that if I could remember something you had said just before—you misled me about the time of your arrival in Dover, I would have the key to everything. And I remembered it! You said that Galeria's only hope was Rimnik, and that Rimnik would turn up again when his party was ready. But the big stumbling block was in seeing the connection between you and Harmer. It was so simple and so obvious I couldn't find it. You liked and admired one another immediately your wife introduced you. I must say he did a beautiful job of throwing dust in my eyes, putting on that resentful—underprivileged-classes act. I should have thought more about my recognition of your—"

"My what?"

"Unorthodoxy." Both men smiled. "Once I groped my way through that difficulty, the rest was easy. The Special Branch knew all about Rimnik's disappearance, his being refused a passport, and Britain's refusal to have him here. They even knew that he was supposed to be in England, but had no confirmation of it. So the motor-boat came ashore a second time?"

"That night, you mean? Yes. Harmer drove us over to his friend's place. He has guts; he was scared stiff, I think, but he went through with it. I see Tisdall has turned up," he said as Grant rose to go. "That must be an enormous relief to you. Is he ill?"

"No. He has a chill, and he's overwrought, of course. But I hope he's going to be all right."

"In the midday edition I bought at York, I read a harrowing description of his sufferings. Knowing the Press, I believed with confidence that not a word of it was true."

"Not a word. That was just Jammy Hopkins."

"Who is Jammy Hopkins?"

"Who is—" Words failed the Inspector. He looked enviously at Champneis. "Now I know," he said, "why men go out into the waste places of the earth!"

# 27

HERBERT GOTOBED LEFT England about a month later on his way to explain to the inquisitive police of Nashville, Tennessee, what he had done with the two thousand dollars old Mrs. Kinsley had given him to build a church with.

And on the day that he sailed—although neither party knew of the other's activities—Erica had a dinner-party at Steynes, "to take the taste of the last one away" as she said bluntly to Grant, when she invited him. The only addition to the original personnel was Robin Tisdall, and Grant found himself ridiculously relieved to find that her small nose was still as casually powdered, and her frock still as childish as on the first occasion. He was afraid that contact with anyone as good-looking and ill-used as Robin Tisdall would have bred a self-awareness that would be the end of her girlhood. But it seemed as if nothing could make Erica self-conscious. She treated Tisdall with the same grave matter-of-factness she had used when she had told him that his shirt collar was too tight. Grant saw Sir George's eyes going from one to the other in glad amusement. Their glances met, and moved by a common impulse the two men raised their glasses in a small gesture of mutual congratulation.

"Are you drinking a toast?" Erica asked. "I'll give you one. To Robin's success in California!"

They drank it with a will.

"If you don't like the ranch," Erica said, "wait till I am twenty-one and I'll buy it from you."

"Would you like that sort of life?" His tone was eager.

"Of course I should." She turned to Grant, beginning to say something.

"You'll have to come out and see it long before you're twenty-one," Robin persisted.

"Yes, that would be nice." She was sincere but inattentive. "Mr. Grant," (for some reason she never called him Inspector) "if I get those tickets from Mr. Mills myself will you come with me to the Circus at Christmas?"

She was very faintly pink, as if she had asked a forward thing. A phenomenon in Erica, who was forward by nature and never knew it.

"Of course I will," Grant said, "with the greatest pleasure."

"All right," she said. "That's a promise." She lifted her glass. "To Olympia, at Christmas!"

"To Olympia at Christmas!" Grant said.

# The
# Daughter
# of
# Time

# 1

GRANT LAY ON his high white cot and stared at the ceiling. Stared at it with loathing. He knew by heart every last minute crack on its nice clean surface. He had made maps of the ceiling and gone exploring on them; rivers, islands, and continents. He had made guessing games of it and discovered hidden objects; faces, birds, and fishes. He had made mathematical calculations of it and rediscovered his childhood; theorems, angles, and triangles. There was practically nothing else he could do but look at it. He hated the sight of it.

He had suggested to The Midget that she might turn his bed around a little so that he could have a new patch of ceiling to explore. But it seemed that that would spoil the symmetry of the room, and in hospitals symmetry ranked just a short head behind cleanliness and a whole length in front of Godliness. Anything out of the parallel was hospital profanity. Why didn't he read? she asked. Why didn't he go on reading some of those expensive brand-new novels that his friends kept on bringing him?

"There are far too many people born into the world, and far too many words written. Millions and millions of them pouring from the presses every minute. It's a horrible thought."

"You sound constipated," said The Midget.

The Midget was Nurse Ingham, and she was in sober fact a very nice five-feet-two, with everything in just proportion. Grant called her The Midget to compensate himself for being bossed around by a piece of Dresden china which he could pick up in one hand. When he was on his feet, that is to say. It was not only that she told him what he might or might not do, but she dealt with his six-feet-odd with an off-hand case that Grant found humiliating. Weights meant nothing, apparently, to The Midget. She tossed mattresses around with the absent-minded grace of a plate spinner. When she was off duty he was attended to by The Amazon, a goddess with arms like the limb of a beech tree. The Amazon was Nurse Darroll, who came from Gloucestershire and was homesick each daffodil season. (The Midget came from Lytham St. Anne's, and there was no daffodil nonsense about her.) She had large soft hands and large soft cow's eyes and she always looked very sorry for you, but the slightest physical exertion set her breathing like a suction-pump. On the whole Grant found it even more humiliating to be treated as a dead weight than to be treated as if he were no weight at all.

Grant was bed-borne, and a charge on The Midget and The Amazon, because he had fallen through a trap-door. This, of course, was the absolute in humiliation; compared with which the heavings of The Amazon and the light slingings of The Midget were a mere corollary. To fall through a trap-door was the ultimate in absurdity; pantomimic, bathetic, grotesque. At the moment of his disappearance from the normal level of perambulation he had been in hot pursuit of Benny Skoll, and the fact that Benny had careered round the next corner slap into the arms of Sergeant Williams provided the one small crumb of comfort in an intolerable situation.

Benny was now "away" for three years, which was very satisfactory for the lieges, but Benny would get time off for good behaviour. In hospitals there was no time off for good behaviour.

Grant stopped staring at the ceiling, and slid his eyes sideways at the pile of books on his bedside table; the gay expensive pile that The Midget had been urging on his attention. The top one, with the pretty picture of Valetta in unlikely pink, was Lavinia Fitch's annual account of a blameless heroine's tribulations. In view of the representation of the Grand Harbour on the cover, the present Valerie or Angela or Cecile or Denise must be a naval wife. He had opened the book only to read the kind message that Lavinia had written inside.

*The Sweat and the Furrow* was Silas Weekley being earthy and spade-conscious all over seven hundred pages. The situation, to judge from the first paragraph, had not materially changed since Silas's last book: mother lying-in with her eleventh upstairs, father laid-out after his ninth downstairs, eldest son lying to the Government in the cow-shed, eldest daughter lying with her lover in the hay-loft, everyone else lying low in the barn. The rain dripped from the thatch, and the manure steamed in the midden. Silas never omitted the manure. It was not Silas's fault that its steam provided the only up-rising element in the picture. If Silas could have discovered a brand of steam that steamed downwards, Silas would have introduced it.

Under the harsh shadows and highlights of Silas's jacket was an elegant affair of Edwardian curlicues and Baroque nonsense, entitled *Bells on Her Toes*. Which was Rupert Rouge being arch about vice. Rupert Rouge always seduced you into laughter for the first three pages. About Page Three you noticed that Rupert had learned from that very arch (but of course not vicious) creature George Bernard Shaw that the easiest way to sound witty was to use that cheap and convenient method, the paradox. After that you could see the jokes coming three sentences away.

The thing with a red gun-flash across a night-green cover was Oscar Oakley's latest. Toughs talking out of the corners of their mouths in synthetic American that had neither the wit nor the pungency of the real thing. Blondes, chromium bars, breakneck chases. Very remarkably bunk.

*The Case of the Missing Tin-Opener,* by John James Mark, had three errors of procedure in the first two pages, and had at least provided Grant with a pleasant five minutes while he composed an imaginary letter to its author.

He could not remember what the thin blue book at the bottom of the pile was. Something earnest and statistical, he thought. Tsetse flies, or calories, or sex behaviour, or something.

Even in that, you knew what to expect on the next page. Did no one, any more, no one in all this wide world, change their record now and then? Was everyone nowadays thirled to a formula? Authors today wrote so much to a pattern that their public expected it. The public talked about "a new Silas Weekley" or "a new Lavinia Fitch" exactly as they talked about "a new brick" or "a new hair-brush." They never said "a new book by" whoever it might be. Their interest was not in the book but in its newness. They knew quite well what the book would be like.

It might be a good thing, Grant thought as he turned his nauseated gaze away from the motley pile, if all the presses of the world were stopped for a generation. There ought to be a literary moratorium. Some Superman ought to invent a ray that would stop them all simultaneously. Then people wouldn't send you a lot of fool nonsense when you were flat on your back, and bossy bits of Meissen wouldn't expect you to read them.

He heard the door open, but did not stir himself to look. He had turned his face to the wall, literally and metaphorically.

He heard someone come across to his bed, and closed his eyes against possible conversation. He wanted neither Gloucestershire sympathy nor Lancashire briskness just now. In the succeeding pause a faint enticement, a nostalgic breath of all the fields of Grasse, teased his nostrils and swam about his brain. He savoured it and considered. The Midget smelt of lavender dusting powder, and The Amazon of soap and iodoform. What was floating expensively about his nostrils was *L'Enclos Numéro Cinq.* Only one person of his acquaintance used L'Enclos Number Five. Marta Hallard.

He opened an eye and squinted up at her. She had evidently bent over to see if he was asleep, and was now standing in an irresolute way—if anything Marta did could be said to be irresolute—with her attention on the heap of all too obviously virgin publications on the table. In one arm she was carrying two new books, and in the other a great sheaf of white lilac. He wondered whether she had chosen white lilac because it was her idea of the proper floral offering for winter (it adorned her dressing-room at the theatre from December to March), or whether she had taken it because it would not detract from her black-and-white chic. She was wearing a new hat and her usual pearls; the pearls which he had once been the means of recovering for her. She looked very handsome, very Parisian, and blessedly unhospital-like.

"Did I waken you, Alan?"

"No. I wasn't asleep."

"I seem to be bringing the proverbial coals," she said, dropping the two books alongside their despised brethren. "I hope you will find these more interesting than you seem to have found that lot. Didn't you even try a little teensy taste of our Lavinia?"

"I can't read anything."

"Are you in pain?"

"Agony. But it's neither my leg nor my back."

"What then?"

"It's what my cousin Laura calls 'the prickles of boredom.' "

"Poor Alan. And how right your Laura is." She picked a bunch of narcissi out of a glass that was much too large for them, dropped them with one of her best gestures into the wash-basin, and proceeded to substitute the lilac. "One would expect boredom to be a great yawning emotion, but it isn't, of course. It's a small niggling thing."

"Small nothing. Niggling nothing. It's like being beaten with nettles."

"Why don't you take up something?"

"Improve the shining hour?"

"Improve your mind. To say nothing of your soul and your temper. You might study one of the philosophies. Yoga, or something like that. But I suppose an analytical mind is not the best kind to bring to the consideration of the abstract."

"I did think of going back to algebra. I have an idea that I never did algebra justice, at school. But I've done so much geometry on that damned ceiling that I'm a little off mathematics."

"Well, I suppose it is no use suggesting jig-saws to someone in your position. How about cross-words? I could get you a book of them, if you like."

"God forbid."

"You could invent them, of course. I have heard that that is more fun than solving them."

"Perhaps. But a dictionary weighs several pounds. Besides, I always did hate looking up something in a reference book."

"Do you play chess? I don't remember. How about chess problems? White to play and mate in three moves, or something like that."

"My only interest in chess is pictorial."

"Pictorial?"

"Very decorative things, knights and pawns and what not. Very elegant."

"Charming. I *could* bring you along a set to play with. All right, no chess. You could do some academic investigating. That's a sort of mathematics. Finding a solution to an unsolved problem."

"Crime, you mean? I know all the case-histories by heart. And there is nothing more that can be done about any of them. Certainly not by someone who is flat on his back."

"I didn't mean something out of the files at the Yard. I meant something more—what's the word?—something classic. Something that has puzzled the world for ages."

"As what, for instance?"

"Say, the casket letters."

"Oh, *not* Mary Queen of Scots!"

"Why not?" asked Marta, who like all actresses saw Mary Stuart through a haze of white veils.

"I could be interested in a bad woman but never in a silly one."

"*Silly?*" said Marta in her best lower-register Electra voice.

"*Very* silly."

"Oh, Alan, how can you!"

"If she had worn another kind of headdress no one would ever have bothered about her. It's that cap that seduces people."

"You think she would have loved less greatly in a sunbonnet?"

"She never loved greatly at all, in any kind of bonnet."

Marta looked as scandalised as a lifetime in the theatre and an hour of careful make-up allowed her to.

"Why do you think that?"

"Mary Stuart was six feet tall. Nearly all out-size women are sexually cold. Ask any doctor."

And as he said it he wondered why, in all the years since Marta had first adopted him as a spare escort when she needed one, it had not occurred to him to wonder whether her notorious level-headedness about men had something to do with her inches. But Marta had not drawn any parallels; her mind was still on her favourite queen.

"At least she was a martyr. You'll have to allow her that."

"Martyr to what?"

"Her religion."

"The only thing she was a martyr to was rheumatism. She married Darnley without the Pope's dispensation, and Bothwell by Protestant rites."

"In a moment you'll be telling me she wasn't a prisoner!"

"The trouble with you is that you think of her in a little room at the top of a castle, with bars on the window and a faithful old attendant to share her prayers with her. In actual fact she had a personal household of sixty persons. She complained bitterly when it was reduced to a beggarly thirty, and nearly died of chagrin when it was reduced to two male secretaries, several women, an embroiderer, and a cook or two. And Elizabeth had to pay for all that out of her own purse. For twenty years she paid, and for twenty years Mary Stuart hawked the crown of Scotland round Europe to anyone who would start a revolution and put her back on the throne that she had lost; or, alternatively, on the one Elizabeth was sitting on."

He looked at Marta and found that she was smiling.

"Are they a little better now?" she asked.

"Are what better?"

"The prickles."

He laughed.

"Yes. For a whole minute I had forgotten about them. That is at least one good thing to put down to Mary Stuart's account!"

"How do you know so much about Mary?"

"I did an essay about her in my last year at school."

"And didn't like her, I take it."

"Didn't like what I found out about her."

"You don't think her tragic, then."

"Oh, yes, very. But not tragic in any of the ways that popular belief makes her tragic. Her tragedy was that she was born a queen with the outlook of a suburban housewife. Scoring off Mrs. Tudor in the next street is harmless and amusing; it may lead you into unwarrantable indulgence in hire-purchase, but it affects only yourself. When you use the same technique on kingdoms the result is disastrous. If you are willing to put a country of ten million people in pawn in order to score off a royal rival, then you end by being a friendless failure." He lay thinking about it for a little. "She would have been a wild success as a mistress at a girl's school."

"Beast!"

"I meant it nicely. The staff would have liked her, and all the little girls would have adored her. That is what I meant about her being tragic."

"Ah well. No casket letters, it seems. What else is there? The Man in the Iron Mask."

"I can't remember who that was, but I couldn't be interested in anyone who was being coy behind some tin-plate. I couldn't be interested in anyone at all unless I could see his face."

"Ah, yes. I forgot your passion for faces. The Borgias had wonderful faces. I should think they would provide a little mystery or two for you to dabble in if you looked them up. Or there was Perkin Warbeck, of course. Imposture is always fascinating. Was he or wasn't he? A lovely game. The balance can never come down wholly on one side or the other. You push it over and up it comes again, like one of those weighted toys."

The door opened and Mrs. Tinker's homely face appeared in the aperture surmounted by her still more homely and historic hat. Mrs. Tinker had worn the same hat since first she began to "do" for Grant, and he could not imagine her in any other. That she did possess another one he knew, because it went with something that she referred to as "me blue." Her "blue" was an occasional affair, in both senses, and never appeared at 19 Tenby Court. It was worn with a ritualistic awareness, and having been worn it was used in the event as a yardstick by which to judge the proceedings. ("Did you enjoy it, Tink? What was it like?" "Not worth putting on me blue for.") She had worn it to Princess Elizabeth's wedding, and to various other royal functions, and had indeed figured in it for two flashing seconds in a newsreel shot of the Duchess of Kent cutting a ribbon, but to Grant it was a mere report; a criterion of the social worth of an occasion. A thing was or was not worth putting on "me blue" for.

"I 'eard you 'ad a visitor," said Mrs. Tinker, "and I was all set to go away again when I thought the voice sounded familiar like, and I says to meself: 'It's only Miss Hallard,' I says, so I come in."

She was carrying various paper bags and a small tight bunch of anemones. She greeted Marta as woman to woman, having been in her time a dresser and having therefore no exaggerated reverence for the goddesses of the theatre world, and looked askance at the beautiful arrangement of lilac sprays that had blossomed under Marta's ministrations. Marta did not see the glance but she saw the little bunch of anemones and took over the situation as if it were something already rehearsed.

"I squander my vagabond's hire on white lilac for you, and then Mrs. Tinker puts my nose out of joint by bringing you the Lilies of the Field."

"Lilies?" said Mrs. Tinker, doubtfully.

"Those are the Solomon in all his glory things. The ones that toiled not neither did they spin."

Mrs. Tinker went to church only for weddings and christenings, but she belonged to a generation that had been sent to Sunday school. She looked with a new interest at the little handful of glory incased by her woollen glove.

"Well, now. I never knew that. Makes more sense that way, don't it? I always pictured them arums. Fields and fields of arums. Awful expensive, you know, but a bit depressing. So they was coloured? Well, why can't they say so? What do they have to call them lilies for?"

And they went on to talk about translation, and how misleading Holy Writ could be ("I always wondered what bread on the waters was," Mrs. Tinker said) and the awkward moment was over.

While they were still busy with the Bible, The Midget came in with extra flower vases. Grant noticed that the vases were designed to hold white lilac and not anemones. They were tribute to Marta; a passport to further communing. But Marta never bothered about women unless she had an immediate use for them; her tact with Mrs. Tinker had been mere *savoir faire;* a conditioned reflex. So The Midget was reduced to being functional instead of social. She collected the discarded narcissi from the wash-basin and meekly put them back into a vase. The Midget being meek was the most beautiful sight that had gladdened Grant's eyes for a long time.

"Well," Marta said, having finished her arrangement of the lilac and placed the result where he could see it, "I shall leave Mrs. Tinker to feed you all the titbits out of those paper bags. It couldn't be, could it, Mrs. Tinker darling, that one of those bags contains any of your wonderful bachelor's buttons?"

Mrs. Tinker glowed.

"You'd like one or two maybe? Fresh outa me oven?"

"Well, of course I shall have to do penance for it afterwards—those little rich cakes are death on the waist—but just give me a couple to put in my bag for my tea at the theatre."

She chose two with a flattering deliberation ("I like them a little brown at the edges"), dropped them into her handbag, and said: "Well, au revoir, Alan. I shall look in, in a day or two, and start you on a sock. There is nothing so soothing, I understand, as knitting. Isn't that so, nurse?"

"Oh, yes, indeed. A lot of my gentlemen patients take to knitting. They find it whiles away the time very nicely."

Marta blew him a kiss from the door and was gone, followed by the respectful Midget.

"I'd be surprised if that hussy is any better than she ought to be," Mrs. Tinker said, beginning to open the paper bags. She was not referring to Marta.

# 2

BUT WHEN MARTA came back two days later it was not with knitting needles and wool. She breezed in, very dashing in a Cossack hat worn at a casual rake that must have taken her several minutes at her mirror, just after lunch.

"I haven't come to stay, my dear. I'm on my way to the theatre. It's matinée day, God help me. Tea trays and morons. And we've all got to the frightful stage when the lines have ceased to have any meaning at all for us. I don't think this play is ever coming off. It's going to be like those New York ones that run by the decade instead of by the year. It's too frightening. One's mind just won't stay on the thing. Geoffrey dried up in the middle of the second act last night. His eyes nearly popped out of his head. I thought for a moment he was having a stroke. He said afterwards that he had no recollection of anything that happened between his entrance and the point where he came to and found himself half-way through the act."

"A black-out, you mean?"

"No. Oh, no. Just being an automaton. Saying the lines and doing the business and thinking of something else all the time."

"If all reports are true that's no unusual matter where actors are concerned."

"Oh, in moderation, no. Johnny Garson can tell you how much paper there is in the house what time he is sobbing his heart out on someone's lap. But that's different from being 'away' for half an act. Do you realise that Geoffrey had turned his son out of the house, quarrelled with his mistress, and accused his wife of having an *affaire* with his best friend all without being aware of it?"

"What *was* he aware of?"

"He says he had decided to lease his Park Lane flat to Dolly Dacre and buy that Charles the Second house at Richmond that the Latimers are giving up because he has got that Governor's appointment. He had thought about the lack of bathrooms and decided that the little upstairs room with the eighteenth-century Chinese paper would make a very good one. They could remove the beautiful paper and use it to decorate that dull little room downstairs at the back. It's full of Victorian panelling, the dull little room. He had also reviewed the drainage, wondered if he had enough money to take the old tiling off and replace it, and speculated as to what kind of cooking range they had in the kitchen. He had just decided to get rid of the shrubbery at the gate when he found himself face to face with me, on a stage, in the presence of nine hundred and eighty-seven people, in the middle of a speech. Do you wonder that his eyes popped? I see that you have managed to read at least one of the books I brought you—if the rumpled jacket is any criterion."

"Yes. The mountain one. It was a godsend. I lay for hours looking at the pictures. Nothing puts things in perspective as quickly as a mountain."

"The stars are better, I find."

"Oh, *no*. The stars merely reduce one to the status of an amoeba. The stars take the last vestige of human pride, the last spark of confidence, from one. But a snow mountain is a nice human-size yardstick. I lay and looked at Everest and thanked God that I wasn't climbing those slopes. A hospital bed was a haven of warmth and rest and security by comparison, and The Midget and The Amazon two of the highest achievements of civilisation."

"Ah, well, here are some more pictures for you."

Marta up-ended the quarto envelope she was carrying, and spilled a collection of paper sheets over his chest.

"What is this?"

"Faces," said Marta, delightedly. "Dozens of faces for you. Men, women, and children. All sorts, conditions, and sizes."

He picked a sheet off his chest and looked at it. It was an engraving of a fifteenth-century portrait. A woman.

"Who is this?"

"Lucrezia Borgia. Isn't she a duck?"

"Perhaps, but are you suggesting that there was any mystery about her?"

"Oh, yes. No one has ever decided whether she was her brother's tool or his accomplice."

He discarded Lucrezia, and picked up a second sheet. This proved to be the portrait of a small boy in late-eighteenth-century clothes, and under it in faint capitals was printed the words: Louis XVII.

"Now there's a *beautiful* mystery for you," Marta said. "The Dauphin. Did he escape or did he die in captivity?"

"Where did you get all these?"

"I routed James out of his cubby-hole at the Victoria and Albert, and made him take me to a print shop. I knew he would know about that sort of thing, and I'm sure he has nothing to interest him at the V. and A."

It was so like Marta to take it for granted that a Civil Servant, because he happened also to be a playwright and an authority on portraits, should be willing to leave his work and delve about in print shops for her pleasure.

He turned up the photograph of an Elizabethan portrait. A man in velvet and pearls. He turned the back to see who this might be and found that it was the Earl of Leicester.

"So that is Elizabeth's Robin," he said. "I don't think I ever saw a portrait of him before."

Marta looked down on the virile fleshy face and said: "It occurs to me for the first time that one of the major tragedies of history is that the best painters didn't paint you till you were past your best. Robin must have been quite a man. They say Henry the Eighth was dazzling as a young man, but what is he now? Something on a playing card. Nowadays we *know* what Tennyson was like before he grew that frightful beard. I must fly. I'm late as it is. I've been lunching at the Blague, and so many people came up to talk that I couldn't get away as early as I meant to."

"I hope your host was impressed," Grant said, with a glance at the hat.

"Oh, yes. She knows about hats. She took one look and said 'Jacques Tous, I take it.'"

"She!" said Grant surprised.

"Yes. Madeleine March. And it was I who was giving her luncheon. Don't look so astonished: it isn't tactful. I'm hoping, if you must know, that she'll write me that play about Lady Blessington. But there was such a to-ing and fro-ing that I had no chance to make any impression on her. However, I gave her a wonderful meal. Which reminds me that Tony Bittmaker was entertaining a party of seven. Magnums galore. How do you imagine he keeps going?"

"Lack of evidence," Grant said, and she laughed and went away.

In the silence he went back to considering Elizabeth's Robin. What mystery was there about Robin?

Oh, yes. Amy Robsart, of course.

Well, he wasn't interested in Amy Robsart. He didn't care how she had fallen down stairs, or why.

But he spent a very happy afternoon with the rest of the faces. Long before he had entered the Force he had taken a delight in faces, and in his years at the Yard that interest had proved both a private entertainment and a professional advantage. He had once in his early days dropped in with his Superintendent at an identification parade. It was not his case, and they were both there on other business, but they lingered in the background and watched while a man and a woman, separately, walked down the line of twelve nondescript men, looking for the one they hoped to recognise.

"Which is Chummy, do you know?" the Super had whispered to him.

"I don't know," Grant had said, "but I can guess."

"You can? Which do you make it?"

"The third from the left."

"What is the charge?"

"I don't know. Don't know anything about it."

His chief had cast him an amused glance. But when both the man and the woman had failed to identify anyone and had gone away, and the line broke into a chattering group, hitching collars and settling ties preparatory to going back to the street and the world of everyday from which they had been summoned to assist the Law, the one who did not move was the third man from the left. The third man from the left waited submissively for his escort and was led to his cell again.

"Strewth!" the Superintendent had said. "One chance out of twelve, and you made it. That was good going. He picked your man out of the bunch," he said in explanation to the local Inspector.

"Did you know him?" the Inspector said, a little surprised. "He's never been in trouble before, as far as we know."

"No, I never saw him before. I don't even know what the charge is."

"Then what made you pick him?"

Grant had hesitated, analysing for the first time his process of selection. It had not been a matter of reasoning. He had not said: "That man's face has this characteristic or that characteristic, therefore he is the accused person." His choice had been almost instinctive; the reason was in his subconscious. At last, having delved into his subconscious, he blurted: "He was the only one of the twelve with no lines on his face."

They had laughed at that. But Grant, once he had pulled the thing into the light, saw how his instinct had worked and recognised the reasoning behind it. "It sounds silly, but it isn't," he said. "The only adult entirely without face lines is the idiot."

"Freeman's no idiot, take it from me," the Inspector broke in. "A very wide-awake boy he is, believe me."

"I didn't mean that. I mean that the idiot is irresponsible. The idiot is the standard of irresponsibility. All those twelve men in that parade were thirty-ish, but only one had an irresponsible face. So I picked him at once."

After that it had become a mild joke at the Yard that Grant could "pick them at sight." And the Assistant Commissioner had once said teasingly: "Don't tell me that you believe that there is such a thing as a criminal face, Inspector."

But Grant had said no, he wasn't as simple as that. "If there was only one kind of crime, sir, it might be possible; but crimes being as wide as human nature, if a policeman started to put faces into categories he would be sunk. You can tell what the normal run of over-sexed women look like by a walk down Bond Street any day between five and six, and yet the most notorious nymphomaniac in London looks like a cold saint."

"Not so saintly of late; she's drinking too much these days," the A.C. had said, identifying the lady without difficulty; and the conversation had gone on to other things.

But Grant's interest in faces had remained and enlarged until it became a conscious study. A matter of case records and comparisons. It was, as he had said, not possible to put faces into any kind of category, but it was possible to characterise individual faces. In a reprint of a famous trial, for instance, where photographs of the principal actors in the case were displayed for the public's interest, there was never any doubt as to which was the accused and which the judge. Occasionally, one of the counsel might on looks have changed places with the prisoner in the dock—counsel were after all a mere cross-section of humanity, as liable to passion and greed as the rest of the world, but a judge had a special quality; an integrity and a detachment. So, even without a wig, one did not confuse him with the man in the dock, who had had neither integrity nor detachment.

Marta's James, having been dragged from his "cubby-hole," had evidently enjoyed himself, and a fine selection of offenders, or their victims, kept Grant entertained until The Midget brought his tea. As he tidied the sheets together to put them away in his locker his hand came in contact with one that had slipped off his chest and had lain all the afternoon unnoticed on the counterpane. He picked it up and looked at it.

It was the portrait of a man. A man dressed in the velvet cap and slashed doublet of the late fifteenth century. A man about thirty-five or thirty-six years old, lean and clean shaven. He wore a rich jewelled collar, and was in the act of putting a ring on the little finger of his right hand. But he was not looking at the ring. He was looking off into space.

Of all the portraits Grant had seen this afternoon this was the most individual. It was as if the artist had striven to put on canvas something that his talent was not sufficient to translate into paint. The expression in the eyes—that most arresting and individual expression—had defeated him. So had the mouth: he had not known how to make lips so thin and so wide look mobile, so the mouth was wooden and a failure. What he had best succeeded in was the bone structure of the face: the strong cheekbones, the hollows below them, the chin too large for strength.

Grant paused in the act of turning the thing over, to consider the face a moment longer. A judge? A soldier? A prince? Someone used to great responsibility, and responsible in his authority. Someone too conscientious. A worrier; perhaps a perfectionist. A man at ease in a large design, but anxious over details. A candidate for gastric ulcer. Someone, too, who had suffered ill-health as a child. He had that incommunicable, that indescribable look that childhood suffering leaves behind it; less positive than the look on a cripple's face, but as inescapable. This the artist had both understood and translated into terms of paint. The slight fullness of the lower eyelid, like a child that has slept too heavily; the texture of the skin; the old-man look in a young face.

He turned the portrait over to look for a caption.

On the back was printed: *Richard the Third. From the portrait in the National Portrait Gallery. Artist Unknown.*

Richard the Third.

So that was who it was. Richard the Third. Crouchback. The monster of nursery stories. The destroyer of innocence. A synonym for villainy.

He turned the paper over and looked again. Was that what the artist had tried to convey when he had painted those eyes? Had what he had seen in those eyes been the look of a man haunted?

He lay a long time looking at that face; at those extraordinary eyes. They were long eyes, set close under the brows; the brows slightly drawn in that worried, over-conscientious frown. At first glance they appeared to be peering; but as one looked one found that they were in fact withdrawn, almost absent-minded.

When The Midget came back for his tray he was still staring at the portrait. Nothing like this had come his way for years. It made La Giaconda look like a poster.

The Midget examined his virgin teacup, put a practised hand against the teapot's tepid cheek, and pouted. She had better things to do, she conveyed, than bring him trays for him to ignore.

He pushed the portrait at her.

What did she think of it? If that man were her patient what would be her verdict?

"Liver," she said crisply, and bore away the tray in heel-tapping protest, all starch and blond curls.

But the surgeon, strolling in against her draught, kindly and casual, had other views. He looked at the portrait, as invited, and said after a moment's interested scrutiny:

"Poliomyelitis."

"Infantile paralysis?" Grant said; and remembered all of a sudden that Richard III had a withered arm.

"Who is it?" the surgeon asked.

"Richard the Third."

"Really? That's interesting."

"Did you know that he had a withered arm?"

"Had he? I didn't remember that. I thought he was a hunchback."

"So he was."

"What I do remember is that he was born with a full set of teeth and ate live frogs. Well, my diagnosis seems to be abnormally accurate."

"Uncanny. What made you choose polio?"

"I don't quite know, now that you ask me to be definitive. Just the look of the face, I suppose. It's the look one sees on the face of a crippled child.

If he was born hunchbacked that probably accounts for it and not polio. I notice the artist has left out the hump."

"Yes. Court painters have to have a modicum of tact. It wasn't until Cromwell that sitters asked for 'warts and all.' "

"If you ask me," the surgeon said, absent-mindedly considering the splint on Grant's leg, "Cromwell started that inverted snobbery from which we are all suffering today. 'I'm a plain man, I am; no nonsense about *me.*' And no manners, grace, or generosity, either." He pinched Grant's toe with detached interest. "It's a raging disease. A horrible perversion. In some parts of the States, I understand, it's as much as a man's political life is worth to go to some constituencies with his tie tied and his coat on. That's being stuffed-shirt. The beau ideal is to be one of the boys. That's looking very healthy," he added, referring to Grant's big toe, and came back of his own accord to the portrait lying on the counterpane.

"Interesting," he said, "that about the polio. Perhaps it really was polio, and that accounts for the shrunken arm." He went on considering it, making no movement to go. "Interesting, anyhow. Portrait of a murderer. Does he run to type, would you say?"

"There isn't a murder type. People murder for too many different reasons. But I can't remember any murderer, either in my own experience, or in case-histories, who resembled him."

"Of course he was *hors concours* in his class, wasn't he? He couldn't have known the meaning of scruple."

"No."

"I once saw Olivier play him. The most dazzling exhibition of sheer evil, it was. Always on the verge of toppling over into the grotesque, and never doing it."

"When I showed you the portrait," Grant said, "before you knew who it was, did you think of villainy?"

"No," said the surgeon, "no, I thought of illness."

"It's odd, isn't it? I didn't think of villainy either. And now that I know who it is, now that I've read the name on the back, I can't think of it as anything but villainous."

"I suppose villainy, like beauty, is in the eye of the beholder. Well, I'll look in again towards the end of the week. No pain to speak of now?"

And he went away, kindly and casual as he had come.

It was only after he had given the portrait further puzzled consideration (it piqued him to have mistaken one of the most notorious murderers of all time for a judge; to have transferred a subject from the dock to the bench was a shocking piece of ineptitude) that it occurred to Grant that the portrait had been provided as the illustration to a piece of detection.

What mystery was there about Richard III?

And then he remembered. Richard had murdered his two boy nephews, but no one knew how. They had merely disappeared. They had disappeared, if he remembered rightly, while Richard was away from London. Richard had sent someone to do the deed. But the mystery of the children's actual fate had never been solved. Two skeletons had turned up—under some stairs?—in Charles II's day, and had been buried. It was taken for granted that the skeletons were the remains of the young princes, but nothing had ever been proved.

It was shocking how little history remained with one after a good education. All he knew about Richard III was that he was the younger brother of Edward IV. That Edward was a blond six-footer with remarkable good looks and a still more remarkable way with women; and that Richard was a hunchback who usurped the throne on his brother's death in place of the boy heir, and arranged the death of that heir and his small brother to save himself any further trouble. He also knew that Richard had died at the battle of Bosworth yelling for a horse, and that he was the last of his line. The last Plantagenet.

Every schoolboy turned over the final page of Richard III with relief, because now at last the Wars of the Roses were over and they could get on to the Tudors, who were dull but easy to follow.

When The Midget came to tidy him up for the night Grant said: "You don't happen to have a history book, by any chance, do you?"

"A history book? No. What would I be doing with a history book." It was not a question, so Grant did not try to provide an answer. His silence seemed to fret her.

"If you really want a history book," she said presently, "you could ask Nurse Darroll when she brings your supper. She has all her school books on a shelf in her room and it's quite possible she has a history among them."

How like The Amazon to keep her school books! he thought. She was still homesick for school as she was homesick for Gloucestershire every time the daffodils bloomed. When she lumbered into the room, bearing his cheese pudding and stewed rhubarb, he looked at her with a tolerance that bordered on the benevolent. She ceased to be a large female who breathed like a suction-pump and became a potential dispenser of delight.

Oh yes, she had a history book, she said. Indeed, she rather thought that she had two. She had kept all her school books because she had loved school.

It was on the tip of Grant's tongue to ask her if she had kept her dolls, but he stopped himself in time.

"And of course I loved history," she said. "It was my favourite subject. Richard the Lionheart was my hero."

"An intolerable bounder," Grant said.

"Oh, no!" she said, looking wounded.

"A hyperthyroid type," Grant said pitilessly. "Rocketing to and fro about the earth like a badly made firework. Are you going off duty now?"

"Whenever I've finished my trays."

"Could you find that book for me tonight?"

"You're supposed to be going to sleep, not staying awake over history books."

"I might as well read some history as look at the ceiling—which is the alternative. Will you get it for me?"

"I don't think I could go all the way up to the Nurses' Block and back again tonight for someone who is rude about the Lionheart."

"All right," he said. "I'm not the stuff that martyrs are made of. As far as I'm concerned Coeur-de-Lion is the pattern of chivalry, the chevalier *sans peur et sans reproche,* a faultless commander and a triple D.S.O. Now will you get the book?"

"It seems to me you've sore need to read a little history," she said, smoothing a mitred sheet-corner with a large admiring hand, "so I'll bring you the book when I come past. I'm going out to the pictures anyhow."

It was nearly an hour before she reappeared, immense in a camel-hair coat. The room lights had been put out and she materialised into the light of his reading-lamp like some kindly genie.

"I was hoping you'd be asleep," she said. "I don't really think you should start on these tonight."

"If there is anything that is likely to put me to sleep," he said, "it would be an English history book. So you can hold hands with a clear conscience."

"I'm going with Nurse Burrows."

"You can still hold hands."

"I've no patience with you," she said patiently and faded backwards into the gloom.

She had brought two books.

One was the kind of history book known as a Historical Reader. It bore the same relation to history as Stories from the Bible bears to Holy Writ. Canute rebuked his courtiers on the shore, Alfred burned the cakes, Raleigh spread his cloak for Elizabeth, Nelson took leave of Hardy in his cabin on the *Victory,* all in nice clear large print and one-sentence paragraphs. To each episode went one full-page illustration.

There was something curiously touching in the fact that The Amazon should treasure this childish literature. He turned to the fly-leaf to see if her name was there. On the fly-leaf was written:

> Ella Darroll,
> Form III
> Newbridge High School
> Newbridge,
> Gloucestershire.
> England
> Europe,
> The World
> The Universe.

This was surrounded by a fine selection of coloured transfers.

Did all children do that, he wondered? Write their names like that, and spend their time in class making transfers? He certainly had. And the sight of those squares of bright primitive colour brought back his childhood as nothing had for many years. He had forgotten the excitement of transfers. That wonderfully satisfying moment when you began the peeling-off and saw that it was coming perfectly. The adult world held few such gratifications. A clean smacking drive at golf, perhaps, was the nearest. Or the moment when your line tightened and you knew that the fish had struck.

The little book pleased him so much that he went through it at his leisure, solemnly reading each childish story. This, after all, was the history that every adult remembered. This was what remained in their minds when tonnage and poundage, and ship money, and Laud's Liturgy, and the Rye House Plot, and the Triennial Acts, and all the long muddle of schism and shindy, treaty and treason, had faded from their consciousness.

The Richard III story, when he came to it, was called *The Princes in the Tower*, and it seemed that young Ella had found the Princes a poor substitute for Coeur-de-Lion, since she had filled every small O throughout the tale with neat pencil shading. The two golden-haired boys who played together in the sunbeam from the barred window in the accompanying picture had each been provided with a pair of anachronistic spectacles, and on the blank back of the picture-page someone had been playing Noughts and Crosses. As far as young Ella was concerned the Princes were a dead loss.

And yet it was a sufficiently arresting little story. Macabre enough to delight any child's heart. The innocent children; the wicked uncle. The classic ingredients in a tale of classic simplicity.

It had also a moral. It was the perfect cautionary tale.

But the King won no profit from this wicked deed. The people of England were shocked by his cold-blooded cruelty and decided that they would no longer have him for King. They sent for a distant cousin of Richard's, Henry Tudor, who was living in France, to come and be crowned King in his stead. Richard died bravely in the battle which resulted, but he had made his name hated throughout the country and many deserted him to fight for his rival.

Well, it was neat but not gaudy. Reporting at its simplest.

He turned to the second book.

The second book was the School History proper. The two thousand years of England's story were neatly parcelled into compartments for ready reference. The compartments, as usual, were reigns. It was no wonder that one pinned a personality to a reign, forgetful that that personality had known and lived under other kings. One put them in pigeon-holes automatically. Pepys: Charles II. Shakespeare: Elizabeth. Marlborough: Queen Anne. It never crossed one's mind that someone who had seen Queen Elizabeth could also have seen George I. One had been conditioned to the reign idea from childhood.

However it did simplify things when you were just a policeman with a game leg and a concussed spine hunting up some information on dead and gone royalties to keep yourself from going crazy.

He was surprised to find the reign of Richard III so short. To have made oneself one of the best-known rulers in all those two thousand years of England's history, and to have had only two years to do it in, surely augured a towering personality. If Richard had not made friends he had certainly influenced people.

The history book, too, thought that he had personality.

Richard was a man of great ability, but quite unscrupulous as to his means. He boldly claimed the crown on the absurd grounds that his brother's marriage with Elizabeth Woodville had been illegal and the children of it illegitimate. He was accepted by the people, who dreaded a minority, and began his reign by making a progress through the south, where he was well received. During this progress, however, the two young Princes who were living in the Tower, disappeared, and were believed to have been murdered. A serious rebellion followed, which Richard put down with great ferocity. In order to recover some of his lost popularity he held a Parliament, which passed useful statutes against Benevolences, Maintenance, and Livery.

But a second rebellion followed. This took the form of an invasion, with French troops, by the head of the Lancaster branch, Henry Tudor. He encountered Richard at Bosworth, near Leicester, where the treachery of the Stanleys gave the day to Henry. Richard was killed in battle, fighting courageously, leaving behind him a name hardly less infamous than that of John.

What on earth were Benevolences, Maintenance, and Livery?

And how did the English like having the succession decided for them by French troops?

But, of course, in the days of the Roses, France was still a sort of semi-detached part of England; a country much less foreign to an Englishman than Ireland was. A fifteenth-century Englishman went to France as a matter of course; but to Ireland only under protest.

He lay and thought about that England. The England over which the Wars of the Roses had been fought. A green, green England; with not a chimney-stack from Cumberland to Cornwall. An England still unhedged, with great forests alive with game, and wide marshes thick with wild-fowl. An England with the same small group of dwellings repeated every few miles in endless permutation: castle, church, and cottages; monastery, church, and cottages; manor, church, and cottages. The strips of cultivation round the cluster of dwellings, and beyond that the greenness. The unbroken greenness. The deep-rutted lanes that ran from group to group, mired to bog in the winter and white with dust in the summer; decorated with wild roses or red with hawthorn as the seasons came and went.

For thirty years, over this green uncrowded land, the Wars of the Roses had been fought. But it had been more of a blood feud than a war. A Montague and Capulet affair; of no great concern to the average Englishman. No one pushed in at your door to demand whether you were York or Lancaster and to hale you off to a concentration camp if your answer proved to be the wrong one for the occasion. It was a small concentrated war; almost a private party. They fought a battle in your lower meadow, and turned your kitchen into a dressing-station, and then moved off somewhere or other to fight a battle somewhere else, and a few weeks later you would hear what had happened at that battle, and you would have a family row about the result because your wife was probably Lancaster and you were perhaps York, and it was all rather like following rival football teams. No one persecuted you for being a Lancastrian or a Yorkist, any more than you would be persecuted for being an Arsenal fan or a Chelsea follower.

He was still thinking of that green England when he fell asleep.

And he was not a whit wiser about the two young Princes and their fate.

# 3

"Can't you find something more cheerful to look at than that thing?" The Midget asked next morning, referring to the Richard portrait which Grant had propped up against the pile of books on his bed-side table.

"You don't find it an interesting face?"

"Interesting! It gives me the willies. A proper Dismal Desmond."

"According to the history books he was a man of great ability."

"So was Bluebeard."

"And considerable popularity, it would seem."

"So was Bluebeard."

"A very fine soldier, too," Grant said wickedly, and waited. "No Bluebeard offers?"

"What do you want to look at that face for? Who was he anyway?"

"Richard the Third."

"Oh, well, I ask you!"

"You mean that's what you expected him to look like."

"Exactly."

"Why?"

"A murdering brute, wasn't he?"

"You seem to know your history."

"Everyone knows that. Did away with his two little nephews, poor brats. Had them smothered."

"Smothered?" said Grant, interested. "I didn't know that."

"Smothered with pillows." She banged his own pillows with a fragile vigorous fist, and replaced them with speed and precision.

"Why smothering? Why not poison?" Grant inquired.

"Don't ask me. I didn't arrange it."

"Who said they were smothered?"

"My history book at school said it."

"Yes, but whom was the history book quoting?"

"Quoting? It wasn't quoting anything. It was just giving facts."

"Who smothered them, did it say?"

"A man called Tyrrel. Didn't you do any history, at school?"

"I attended history lessons. It is not the same thing. Who was Tyrrel?"

"I haven't the remotest. A friend of Richard's."

"How did anyone know it was Tyrrel?"

"He confessed."

*"Confessed?"*

"After he had been found guilty, of course. Before he was hanged."

"You mean that this Tyrrel was actually hanged for the murder of the two Princes?"

"Yes, of course. Shall I take that dreary face away and put up something gayer? There were quite a lot of nice faces in that bundle Miss Hallard brought you yesterday."

"I'm not interested in nice faces. I'm interested only in dreary ones; in 'murdering brutes' who are 'men of great ability.' "

"Well, there's no accounting for tastes," said The Midget inevitably. "And *I* don't have to look at it, thank goodness. But in my humble estimation it's enough to prevent bones knitting, so help me it is."

"Well, if my fracture doesn't mend you can put it down to Richard III's account. Another little item on that account won't be noticed, it seems to me."

He must ask Marta when next she looked in if she too knew about this Tyrrel. Her general knowledge was not very great, but she had been educated very expensively at a highly approved school and perhaps some of it had stuck.

But the first visitor to penetrate from the outside world proved to be Sergeant Williams; large and pink and scrubbed-looking; and for a little Grant forgot about battles long ago and considered wide boys alive today. Williams sat planted on the small hard visitors' chair, his knees apart and his pale blue eyes blinking like a contented cat's in the light from the window, and Grant regarded him with affection. It was pleasant to talk shop again; to use that elliptical, allusive speech that one uses only with another of one's trade. It was pleasant to hear the professional gossip, to talk professional politics; to learn who was on the mat and who was on the skids.

"The Super sent his regards," Williams said as he got up to go, "and said if there was anything he could do for you to let him know." His eyes, no longer dazzled by the light, went to the photograph propped against the books. He leant his head sideways at it. "Who's the bloke?"

Grant was just about to tell him when it occurred to him that here was a fellow policeman. A man as used, professionally, to faces as he was himself. Someone to whom faces were of daily importance.

"Portrait of a man by an unknown fifteenth-century painter," he said. "What do you make of it?"

"I don't know the first thing about painting."

"I didn't mean that. I meant what do you make of the subject?"

"Oh. Oh, I see." Williams bent forward and drew his bland brows into a travesty of concentration. "How do you mean: make of it?"

"Well, where would you place him? In the dock or on the bench?"

Williams considered for a moment, and then said with confidence: "Oh, on the bench."

"You would?"

"Certainly. Why? Wouldn't you?"

"Yes. But the odd thing is that we're both wrong. He belongs in the dock."

"You surprise me," Williams said, peering again. "Do you know who he was, then?"

"Yes. Richard the Third."

Williams whistled.

"So that's who it is, is it! Well, well. The Princes in the Tower, and all that. The original Wicked Uncle. I suppose, once you know, you can see it, but off-hand it wouldn't occur to you. I mean, that he was a crook. He's the spit of old Halsbury, come to think of it, and if Halsbury had a fault at all it was that he was too soft with the bastards in the dock. He used to lean over backwards to give them the benefit in his summing-up."

"Do you know how the Princes were murdered?"

"I don't know a thing about Richard III except that his mother was two years conceiving him."

"What! Where did you get that tale?"

"In my school history, I suppose."

"You must have gone to a very remarkable school. Conception was not mentioned in any history book of mine. That is what made Shakespeare and the Bible so refreshing as lessons; the facts of life were always turning up. Did you ever hear of a man called Tyrrel?"

"Yes; he was a con. man on the P. & O. boats. Drowned in the *Egypt*."

"No; I mean, in history."

"I tell you, I never knew any history except 1066 and 1603."

"What happened in 1603?" Grant asked, his mind still on Tyrrel.

"We had the Scots tied to our tails for good."

"Better than having them at our throats every five minutes. Tyrrel is said to be the man who put the boys out of the way."

"The nephews? No, it doesn't ring a bell. Well, I must be getting along. Anything I can do for you?"

"Did you say you were going to Charing Cross Road?"

"To the Phoenix, yes."

"You could do something for me."

"What is that?"

"Go into one of the bookshops and buy me a History of England. An adult one. And a Life of Richard III, if you can find one."

"Sure, I'll do that."

As he was going out he encountered The Amazon, and looked startled to find anything as large as himself in nurse's uniform. He murmured a good-morning in an abashed way, cast a questioning glance at Grant, and faded into the corridor.

The Amazon said that she was supposed to be giving Number Four her blanket bath but that she had to look in to see if he was convinced.

"Convinced?"

About the nobility of Richard Coeur-de-Lion.

"I haven't got round to Richard the First yet. But keep Number Four waiting a few moments longer and tell me what you know about Richard III."

"Ah, those poor lambs!" she said, her great cow's eyes soft with pity.

"Who?"

"Those two precious little boys. It used to be my nightmare when I was a kiddie. That someone would come and put a pillow over my face when I was asleep."

"Is that how it was done: the murder?"

"Oh, yes. Didn't you know? Sir James Tyrrel rode back to London when the court was at Warwick, and told Dighton and Forrest to kill them, and then they buried them at the foot of some stairs under a great mound of stones."

"But it doesn't say that in the book you lent me."

"Oh, that book is just history-for-exams, if you know what I mean. You don't get really interesting history in swot books like that."

"And where did you get the juicy gossip about Tyrrel, may one ask?"

"It isn't gossip," she said, hurt. "You'll find it in Sir Thomas More's history of his time. And you can't find a more respected or trustworthy person in the whole of history than Sir Thomas More, now can you?"

"No. It would be bad manners to contradict Sir Thomas."

"Well, that's what Sir Thomas says, and, after all, he was alive then and knew all those people to talk to."

"Dighton and Forrest?"

"No, of course not. But Richard, and the poor Queen, and those."

"The Queen? Richard's Queen?"

"Yes."

"Why 'poor'?"

"He led her an awful life. They say he poisoned her. He wanted to marry his niece."

"Why?"

"Because she was the heir to the throne."

"I see. He got rid of the two boys, and then wanted to marry their eldest sister."

"Yes. He couldn't marry either of the boys, you see."

"No, I suppose even Richard the Third never thought of that one."

"So he wanted to marry Elizabeth so as to feel safer on the throne. Actually, of course, she married his successor. She was Queen Elizabeth's grandmother. It always used to please me that Elizabeth was a little bit Plantagenet. I never was very fond of the Tudor side. Now I must go, or Matron will be here on her round before I have Number Four tidied up."

"That would be the end of the world."

"It would be the end of *me*," she said, and went away.

Grant took the book she had left him off the pile again, and tried to make head or tail of the Wars of the Roses. He failed. Armies marched and countermarched. York and Lancaster succeeded each other as victors in a bewildering repetition. It was as meaningless as watching a crowd of dodgem cars bumping and whirling at a fair.

But it seemed to him that the whole trouble was implicit, the germ of it sown, nearly a hundred years earlier, when the direct line was broken by the deposition of Richard II. He knew all about that because he had in his youth seen *Richard of Bordeaux* at the New Theatre; four times he had seen it. For three generations the usurping Lancasters had ruled England: Richard of Bordeaux's Henry unhappily but with fair efficiency, Shakespeare's Prince Hal with Agincourt for glory and the stake for zeal, and his son in half-witted muddle and failure. It was no wonder if men hankered after the legitimate line again, as they watched poor Henry VI's inept friends frittering away the victories in France while Henry nursed his new foundation of Eton and besought the ladies at court to cover up their bosoms.

All three Lancasters had had an unlovely fanaticism which contrasted sharply with the liberalism of the Court which had died with Richard II. Richard's live-and-let-live methods had given place, almost overnight, to the burning of heretics. For three generations heretics had burned. It was no wonder if a less public fire of discontent had begun to smoulder in the heart of the man in the street.

Especially since there, before their eyes, was the Duke of York. Able, sensible, influential, gifted, a great prince in his own right, and by blood the heir of Richard II. They might not desire that York should take the place of poor silly Henry, but they did wish that he would take over the running of the country and clean up the mess.

York tried it, and died in battle for his pains, and his family spent much time in exile or sanctuary as a result.

But when the tumult and the shouting was all over, there on the throne of England was the son who had fought alongside him in that struggle, and the country settled back happily under that tall, flaxen, wenching, exceedingly beautiful but most remarkably shrewd young man, Edward IV.

And that was as near as Grant would ever come to understanding the Wars of the Roses.

He looked up from his book to find Matron standing in the middle of the room.

"I did knock," she said, "but you were lost in your book."

She stood there, slender and remote; as elegant in her way as Marta was; her white-cuffed hands clasped loosely in front of her narrow waist; her white veil spreading itself in imperishable dignity; her only ornament the small silver badge of her diploma. Grant wondered if there was anywhere in this world a more unshakable poise than that achieved by the matron of a great hospital.

"I've taken to history," he said. "Rather late in the day."

"An admirable choice," she said. "It puts things in perspective." Her eye lighted on the portrait and she said: "Are you York or Lancaster?"

"So you recognise the portrait."

"Oh, yes. When I was a probationer I used to spend a lot of time in the National. I had very little money and very sore feet, and it was warm in the Gallery and quiet and it had plenty of seats." She smiled a very little, looking back from her present consequence to that young, tired, earnest creature she had been. "I liked the Portrait Gallery best because it gave one the same sense of proportion that reading history does. All those Importances who had made such a to-do over so much in their day. All just names. Just canvas and paint. I saw a lot of that portrait in those days." Her attention went back to the picture. "A most unhappy creature," she said.

"My surgeon thinks it is poliomyelitis."

"Polio?" She considered it. "Perhaps. I hadn't thought of it before. But to me it has always seemed to be intense unhappiness. It is the most desperately unhappy face that I have ever encountered—and I have encountered a great many."

"You think it was painted later than the murder, then?"

"Oh, yes. Obviously. He is not a type that would do anything lightly. A man of that calibre. He must have been well aware of how—heinous the crime was."

"You think he belonged to the type who can't live with themselves any more."

"What a good description! Yes. The kind who want something badly, and then discover that the price they have paid for it is too high."

"So you don't think he was an out-and-out villain?"

"No; oh, no. Villains don't suffer, and that face is full of the most dreadful pain."

They considered the portrait in silence for a moment or two.

"It must have seemed like retribution, you know. Losing his only boy so soon after. And his wife's death. Being stripped of his own personal world in so short a time. It must have seemed like Divine justice."

"Would he care about his wife?"

"She was his cousin, and they had known each other from childhood. So whether he loved her or not, she must have been a companion for him. When you sit on a throne I suspect that companionship is a rare blessing. Now I must go and see how my hospital is getting on. I have not even asked the question that I came to ask. Which was how you felt this morning. But it is a very healthy sign that you have interest to spare for a man dead these four hundred years."

She had not moved from the position in which he had first caught sight of her. Now she smiled her faint, withdrawn smile, and with her hands still clasped lightly in front of her belt-buckle moved towards the door. She had a transcendental repose. Like a nun. Like a queen.

# 4

IT WAS AFTER LUNCHEON before Sergeant Williams reappeared, breathless, bearing two fat volumes.

"You should have left them with the porter," Grant said. "I didn't mean you to come sweating up here with them."

"I had to come up and explain. I had only time to go to one shop, but it's the biggest in the street. That's the best history of England they have in stock. It's the best there is anywhere, they say." He laid down a severe-looking sage-green tome, with an air of taking no responsibility for it. "They had no separate history of Richard III. I mean, no life of him. But they gave me this." This was a gay affair with a coat of arms on the wrapper. It was called *The Rose of Raby*.

"What is this?"

"She was his mother, it seems. The Rose in question, I mean. I can't wait: I'm due at the Yard in five minutes from now and the Super will flay me alive if I'm late. Sorry I couldn't do better. I'll look in again, first time I'm passing, and if these are no good I'll see what else I can get."

Grant was grateful and said so.

To the sound of Williams' brisk departing footsteps he began his inspection of the "best history of England there is." It turned out to be what is known as a "constitutional" history; a sober compilation lightened with improving illustrations. An illumination from the Luttrell Psalter decorated the husbandry of the fourteenth century, and a contemporary map of London bisected the Great Fire. Kings and queens were mentioned only incidentally. Tanner's Constitutional History was concerned only with social progress and political evolution; with the Black Death, and the invention of printing, and the use of gunpowder, and the formation of the Trade Guilds, and so forth. But here and there Mr. Tanner was forced, by a horrid germaneness, to mention a king or his relations. And one such germaneness occurred in connection with the invention of printing.

A man called Caxton came out of the Weald of Kent as draper's apprentice to a future Lord Mayor of London, and then went to Bruges with the twenty marks his master left him in his will. And when, in the dreary autumn rain of the Low Countries, two young refugees from England fetched up on those low shores, in very low water, it was the successful merchant from the Weald of Kent who gave them succour. The refugees were Edward IV and his brother Richard; and when in the turn of the wheel Edward came back to rule England, Caxton came too, and the first books printed in England were printed for Edward IV and written by Edward's brother-in-law.

He turned the pages and marvelled how dull information is deprived of personality. The sorrows of humanity are no one's sorrows, as newspaper readers long ago found out. A *frisson* of horror may go down one's spine at wholesale destruction but one's heart stays unmoved. A thousand people drowned in floods in China are news: a solitary child drowned in a pond is tragedy. So Mr. Tanner's account of the progress of the English race was admirable but unexciting. But here and there where he could not avoid the personal his narrative flowered into a more immediate interest. In extracts from the Pastons' letters, for instance. The Pastons had a habit of sandwiching scraps of history between orders for salad oil and inquiries as to how Clement was doing at Cambridge. And between two of those domesticities appeared the small item that the two little York boys, George and Richard, were living in the Pastons' London lodgings, and that their brother Edward came every day to see them.

Surely, thought Grant, dropping the book for a moment on the counterpane and staring up at the now invisible ceiling, surely never before can anyone have come to the throne of England with so personal an experience of the ordinary man's life as Edward IV and his brother Richard. And perhaps only Charles II after them. And Charles, even in poverty and flight, had always been a King's son; a man apart. The two little boys who were living in the Pastons' lodgings were merely the babies of the York family. Of no particular importance at the best of times, and at the moment when the Paston letter was written without a home and possibly without a future.

Grant reached for The Amazon's history book to find out what Edward was about in London at that date, and learned that he was collecting an army. "London was always Yorkist in temper, and men flocked with enthusiasm to the banner of the youthful Edward," said the history book.

And yet young Edward, aged eighteen, idol of a capital city and on the way to the first of his victories, found time to come every day to see his small brothers.

Was it now, Grant wondered, that the remarkable devotion of Richard to his elder brother was born. An unwavering life-long devotion that the history books not only did not deny but actually used in order to point the moral. "Up to the moment of his brother's death Richard had been in all vicissitudes his loyal and faithful helpmeet, but the opportunity of a crown proved too much for him." Or in the simpler words of the Historical Reader: "He had been a good brother to Edward but when he saw that he might become King greed hardened his heart."

Grant took a sideways look at the portrait and decided that the Historical Reader was off the beam. Whatever had hardened Richard's heart to the point of murder had not been greed. Or did the Historical Reader mean greed for power? Probably. Probably.

But surely Richard must have had all the power that mortal man could wish. He was the King's brother, and rich. Was that short step further so important that he could murder his brother's children to achieve it?

It was an odd set-up altogether.

He was still mulling it over in his mind when Mrs. Tinker came in with fresh pyjamas for him and her daily précis of the newspaper headlines. Mrs. Tinker never read past the third headline of a report unless it happened to be a murder, in which case she read every word and bought an evening paper for herself on the way home to cook Tinker's supper.

Today the gentle burble of her comment on a Yorkshire arsenic-and-exhumation case flowed over him unbroken until she caught sight of the morning paper lying in its virgin condition alongside the books on the table. This brought her to a sudden halt.

"You not feelin' so good today?" she asked in a concerned way.

"I'm fine, Tink, fine. Why?"

"You 'aven't as much as opened your paper. That's 'ow my sister's gel started her decline. Not takin' no notice of what was in the paper."

"Don't you worry. I'm on the up-grade. Even my temper has improved. I forgot about the paper because I've been reading history stories. Ever heard of the Princes in the Tower?"

"*Everyone's* 'eard of the Princes in the Tower."

"And do you know how they met their end?"

"Course I do. He put a pillow on their faces when they was asleep."

"Who did?"

"Their wicked uncle. Richard the Third. You didn't ought to think of things like that when you're poorly. You ought to be reading something nice and cheerful."

"Are you in a hurry to get home, Tink, or could you go round by St. Martin's Lane for me?"

"No, I've plenty of time. Is it Miss Hallard? She won't be at the theatre till six-about."

"No, I know. But you might leave a note for her and she'll get it when she comes in."

He reached for his scribbling pad and pencil and wrote:

"For the love of Mike find me a copy of Thomas More's history of Richard III."

He tore off the page, folded it and scribbled Marta's name on it.

"You can give it to old Saxton at the stage-door. He'll see that she gets it."

"If I can get near the stage-door what with the stools for the queue," Mrs. Tinker said; in comment rather than in truth. "That thing's going to run for ever."

She put the folded paper carefully away in the cheap pseudo-leather handbag with the shabby edges that was as much a part of her as her hat. Grant had, Christmas by Christmas, provided her with a new bag; each of them a work of art in the best tradition of English leather-working, an article so admirable in design and so perfect in execution that Marta Hallard might have carried it to luncheon at the Blague. But that was the last he had ever seen of any of them. Since Mrs. Tinker regarded a pawnshop as one degree more disgraceful than prison, he absolved her from any suspicion of cashing in on her presents. He deduced that the handbags were safely laid away in a drawer somewhere, still wrapped up in the original tissue paper. Perhaps she took them out to show people sometimes, sometimes perhaps just to gloat over; or perhaps the knowledge that they were there enriched her, as the knowledge of "something put by for my funeral" might enrich another. Next Christmas he was going to open this shabby sack of hers, this perennial satchel à toute faire, and put something in the money compartment. She would fritter it away, of course, in small unimportances; so that in the end she would not know what she had done with it; but perhaps a series of small satisfactions scattered like sequins over the texture of everyday life was of greater worth than the academic satisfaction of owning a collection of fine objects at the back of a drawer.

When she had gone creaking away, in a shoes-and-corset concerto, he went back to Mr. Tanner and tried to improve his mind by acquiring some of Mr. Tanner's interest in the human race. But he found it an effort. Neither by nature nor by profession was he interested in mankind in the large. His bias, native and acquired, was towards the personal. He waded through Mr. Tanner's statistics and longed for a king in an oak tree, or a broom tied to a mast-head, or a Highlander hanging on to a trooper's stirrup in a charge. But at least he had the satisfaction of learning that the Englishman of the fifteenth century "drank water only as a penance." The English labourer of Richard III's day was, it seemed, the admiration of the continent. Mr. Tanner quoted a contemporary, writing in France.

The King of France will allow no one to use salt, but what is bought of himself at his own arbitrary price. The troops pay for nothing, and treat the people barbarously if they are not satisfied. All growers of vines must give a fourth to the King. All the towns must pay the King great yearly sums for his men-at-arms. The peasants live in great hardship and misery. They wear no woollens. Their clothing consists of little short jerkins of sackcloth, no trowse but from the knees up, and legs exposed and naked. The women all go barefoot. The people eat no meat, except the fat of bacon in their soup. Nor are the gentry much better off. If an accusation is brought against them they are examined in private, and perhaps never more heard of.

In England it is very different. No one can abide in another man's house without his leave. The King cannot put on taxes, nor alter the laws, nor make new ones. The English never drink water except for penance. They eat all sorts of flesh and fish. They are clothed throughout in good woollens, and are provided with all sorts of household goods. An Englishman cannot be sued except before the ordinary judge.

And it seemed to Grant that if you were very hard up and wanted to go to see what your Lizzie's first-born looked like it must have been reassuring to know that there was shelter and a hand-out at every religious house, instead of wondering how you were going to raise the train fare. That green England he had fallen asleep with last night had a lot to be said for it.

He thumbed through the pages on the fifteenth century, looking for personal items; for individual reports that might, in their single vividness, illumine the scene for him as a "spot" lights the desired part of a stage. But the story was distressingly devoted to the general. According to Mr. Tanner, Richard III's only Parliament was the most liberal and progressive within record; and he regretted, did the worthy Mr. Tanner, that his private crimes should have militated against his patent desire for the common weal. And that seemed to be all that Mr. Tanner had to say about Richard III. Except for the Pastons, chatting indestructibly through the centuries, there was a dearth of human beings in this record of humanity.

He let the book slide off his chest, and searched with his hand until he found *The Rose of Raby.*

THE *Rose of Raby* proved to be fiction; but it was at least easier to hold than Tanner's Constitutional History of England. It was, moreover, the almost-respectable form of historical fiction which is merely history-with-conversation, so to speak. An imaginative biography rather than an imagined story. Evelyn Payne-Ellis, whoever she might be, had provided portraits and a family tree, and had made no attempt, it seemed, to what he and his cousin Laura used to call in their childhood "write forsoothly." There were no "by our Ladys," no "nathelesses" or "varlets." It was an honest affair according to its lights.

And its lights were more illuminating than Mr. Tanner.

Much more illuminating.

It was Grant's belief that if you could not find out about a man, the next best way to arrive at an estimate of him was to find out about his mother.

So until Marta could provide him with the sainted and infallible Thomas More's personal account of Richard, he would do very happily with Cicely Nevill, Duchess of York.

He glanced at the family tree, and thought that if the two York brothers, Edward and Richard, were, as kings, unique in their experience of ordinary life they were no less unique in their Englishness. He looked at their breeding and marvelled. Nevill, Fitzalan, Percy, Holland, Mortimer, Clifford and Audley, as well as Plantagenet. Queen Elizabeth (who made it her boast) was all English; if one counted the Welsh streak as English. But among all the half-bred monarchs who had graced the throne between the Conquest and Farmer George—half-French, half-Spanish, half-Danish, half-Dutch, half-Portuguese—Edward IV and Richard III were remarkable in their home-bred quality.

They were also, he noted, as royally bred on their mother's side as on their father's. Cicely Nevill's grandfather was John of Gaunt, the first of the Lancasters; third son of Edward III. Her husband's two grandfathers were two other sons of Edward III. So three of Edward III's five sons had contributed to the making of the two York brothers.

"To be a Nevill" said Miss Payne-Ellis "was to be of some importance since they were great landowners. To be a Nevill was almost certainly to be handsome, since they were a good-looking family. To be a Nevill was to have personality, since they excelled in displays of both character and temperament. To unite all three Nevill gifts, in their finest quality, in one person was the good fortune of Cicely Nevill, who was the sole Rose of the north long before that north was forced to choose between White Roses and Red."

It was Miss Payne-Ellis's contention that the marriage with Richard Plantagenet, Duke of York, was a love match. Grant received this theory with a scepticism bordering on scorn until he noticed the results of that marriage. To have a yearly addition to the family was not, in the fifteenth century, evidence of anything but fertility. And the long family produced by Cicely Nevill to her charming husband augured nothing nearer love than cohabitation. But in a time when the wife's rôle was to stay meekly at home and see to her still-room, Cicely Nevill's constant travellings about in her husband's company were surely remarkable enough to suggest an abnormal pleasure in that company. The extent and constancy of that travel was witnessed to by the birthplaces of her children. Anne, her first, was born at Fotheringhay, the family home in Northamptonshire. Henry, who died as a baby, at Hatfield. Edward at Rouen, where the Duke was on active service. Edmund and Elizabeth also at Rouen. Margaret at Fotheringhay. John, who died young, at Neath in Wales. George in Dublin (and could it be, wondered Grant, that that accounted for the almost Irish perverseness of the ineffable George?). Richard at Fotheringhay.

Cicely Nevill had not sat at home in Northamptonshire waiting for her lord and master to visit her when it seemed good to him. She had accompanied him about the world of their inhabiting. There was a strong presumption in favour of Miss Payne-Ellis's theory. At the very canniest reckoning it was patently a very successful marriage.

Which perhaps accounted for the family devotion of those daily visits of Edward to his small brothers in the Pastons' lodgings. The York family, even before its tribulations, was a united one.

This was borne out unexpectedly when, spurting the pages from under his thumb, he came on a letter. It was a letter from the two elder boys, Edward and Edmund, to their father. The boys were at Ludlow Castle, undergoing their education, and on a Saturday in Easter week, taking advantage of a courier who was going back, they burst out in loud complaint of their tutor and his "odiousness" and begged their father to listen to the tale of the courier, William Smyth, who was fully charged with the details of their oppression. This S.O.S. was introduced and ended in respectful padding, the formality of which was a little marred by their pointing out that it was nice of him to send the clothes but that he had forgotten their breviary.

The conscientious Miss Payne-Ellis had given the reference for this letter (one of the Cotton manuscripts, it appeared) and he thumbed more slowly, in search of more. Factual evidence was a policeman's meat.

He could not find any, but he came on a family tableau which held him for a moment.

The Duchess moved out into the thin sharp sunlight of a London December morning, and stood on the steps to watch them go: her husband, her brother, and her son. Dirk and his nephews brought the horses into the courtyard, scattering the pigeons and the fussing sparrows from the cobbles. She watched her husband mount, equable and deliberate as always, and thought that for all the emotion he showed he might be riding down to Fotheringhay to look at some new rams instead of setting out on a campaign. Salisbury, her brother, was being Nevill and temperamental; a little conscious of the occasion and living up to it. She looked at them both and smiled in her mind at them. But it was Edmund who caught at her heart. Edmund at seventeen, very slender, very untried, very vulnerable. Flushed with pride and excitement at this setting-out to his first campaigning. She wanted to say to her husband: "Take care of Edmund," but she could not do that. Her husband would not understand; and Edmund, if he were to suspect, would be furious. If Edward, only a year older, was commanding an army of his own on the borders of Wales at this very minute, then he, Edmund, was more than old enough to see a war at first-hand.

She glanced behind her at the three younger children who had come out in her wake; Margaret and George, the two solid fair ones, and behind them, a pace in the rear as always, her changeling baby, Richard; his dark brows and brown hair making him look like a visitor. Good-natured untidy Margaret watched with all the moist-eyed emotion of fourteen; George in a passionate envy and wild rebellion that he was only eleven and of no consequence in this martial moment. Thin little Richard showed no excitement at all, but his mother thought that he vibrated like a softly tapped drum.

The three horses moved out of the courtyard in a clatter of slipping hooves and jingling accoutrements, to join the servants waiting for them in the roadway, and the children called and danced and waved them out of the gate.

And Cicely, who in her time had seen so many men, and so many of her family, go off to war, went back to the house with an unaccustomed weight at her bosom. Which of them, said the voice in her unwilling mind, which of them was it who was not coming back?

Her imagination did not compass anything so horrible as the fact that none of them was coming back again. That she would never see any one of them again.

That before the year was ended her husband's severed head, crowned for insult with a paper crown, would be nailed above the Micklegate Bar in York, and the heads of her brother and her son on the two other gates.

Well, that might be fiction, but it was an illuminating glimpse of Richard. The dark one in a blond family. The one who "looked like a visitor." The "changeling."

He abandoned Cicely Nevill for the moment, and went hunting through the book for her son Richard. But Miss Payne-Ellis seemed not to be greatly interested in Richard. He was merely the tail-end of the family. The magnificent young creature who flourished at the other end was more to her taste. Edward was much to the fore. With his Nevill cousin Warwick, Salisbury's son, he won the battle of Towton, and, with the memory of Lancastrian ferocity still fresh and his father's head still nailed to the Micklegate Bar, gave evidence of that tolerance that was to be characteristic of him. There was quarter at Towton for all who asked. He was crowned King of England in Westminster Abbey (and two small boys, home from exile in Utrecht, were created respectively Duke of Clarence and Duke of Gloucester). And he buried his father and his brother Edmund with great magnificence in the church at Fotheringhay (though it was Richard, aged thirteen, who convoyed that sad procession from Yorkshire, through the bright glory of five July days, to Northamptonshire; nearly six years after he had stood on the steps of Baynard's Castle in London to watch them ride away).

It was not until Edward had been King for some time that Miss Payne-Ellis allowed Richard to come back into the story. He was then being educated with his Nevill cousins at Middleham, in Yorkshire.

As Richard rode into the shadow of the keep, out of the broad sunlight and flying winds of Wensleydale, it seemed to him that there was an atmosphere of strangeness about the place. The guards were talking in loud excitement in the gatehouse and seemed abashed at his presence. From their sudden silence he rode on into a silent court that should have been bustling with activity at this hour of the day. It would soon be supper time, and both habit and hunger brought all the inhabitants of Middleham home from their various occupations, as they were bringing him back from his hawking, for the evening meal. This hush, this desertion, was unusual. He walked his horse to the stables, but there was no one there to give it to. As he unsaddled he noticed a hard-ridden bay in the next stall; a horse that did not belong to Middleham; a horse so tired that he had not eaten up and his head hung in a despondent beaten way between his knees.

Richard wiped his horse down and rugged him, brought him some hay and fresh water, and left him; wondering about that beaten horse and the uncanny silence. As he paused in the doorway he could hear voices in the distance of the great hall; and debated whether he should go there and investigate before going upstairs to his own quarters. As he hesitated a voice from the stairs above him said: "Z-z-zt!"

He looked up to see his cousin Anne's head peering over the banisters, her two long fair plaits hanging down like bell-ropes.

"Richard!" she said, half whispering. "Have you heard?"

"Is something wrong?" he asked. "What is it?"

As he moved up to her she grabbed his hand and dragged him upwards towards their schoolroom in the roof.

"But what is it?" he asked, leaning back in protest against her urgency. "What has happened? Is it something so awful that you can't tell me here!"

She swept him into the schoolroom and shut the door.

"It's Edward!"

"Edward? Is he ill?"

"No! *Scandal!*"

"Oh," said Richard, relieved. Scandal and Edward were never far apart. "What is it? Has he a new mistress?"

"Much worse than that! Oh, much, *much* worse. He's married."

"Married?" said Richard, so unbelieving that he sounded calm. "He can't be."

"But he is. The news came from London an hour ago."

"He can't be married," Richard insisted. "For a King marriage is a long affair. A matter of contracts, and agreements. A matter for Parliament, even, I think. What made you think he had got married?"

"I don't *think,*" Anne said, out of patience at this sober reception of her broadside. "The whole family is raging together in the Great Hall over the affair."

"Anne! have you been listening at the door?"

"Oh, don't be so righteous. I didn't have to listen very hard, anyhow. You could hear them on the other side of the river. He has married Lady Grey!"

"Who is Lady Grey? Lady Grey of Groby?"

"Yes."

"But he can't. She has two children and she's quite old."

"She is five years older than Edward, and she is wonderfully beautiful —so I overhear."

"When did this happen?"

"They've been married five months. They got married in secret down in Northamptonshire."

"But I thought he was going to marry the King of France's sister."

"So," said Anne in a tone full of meaning, "did my father."

"Yes; yes, it makes things very awkward for him, doesn't it; after all the negotiating."

"According to the messenger from London he is throwing fits. It isn't only the making him look a fool. It seems she has cohorts of relations and he hates every one of them."

"Edward must be possessed." In Richard's hero-worshipping eyes everything Edward did had always been right. This folly, this undeniable, this inexcusable folly, could come only from possession.

"It will break my mother's heart," he said. He thought of his mother's courage when his father and Edmund had been killed, and the Lancastrian army was almost at the gates of London. She had not wept nor wrapped herself in protective veils of self-pity. She had arranged that he and George should go to Utrecht, as if she were arranging for them to go away to school. They might never see each other again, but she had busied herself about warm clothes for their winter voyage across the Channel with a calm and dry-eyed practicality.

How would she bear this; this further blow? This destructive folly. This shattering foolishness.

"Yes," said Anne, softening. "Poor Aunt Cicely. It is monstrous of Edward to hurt everyone so. Monstrous."

But Edward was still the infallible. If Edward had done wrong it was because he was ill, or possessed, or bewitched. Edward still had Richard's allegiance; his heart-whole and worshipping allegiance.

Nor in after years was that allegiance—an adult allegiance of recognition and acceptance—ever less than heart-whole.

And then the story went on to Cicely Nevill's tribulation, and her efforts to bring some kind of order into the relations between her son Edward, half-pleased, half-ashamed, and her nephew Warwick, wholly furious. There was also a long description of that indestructibly virtuous beauty with the famous "gilt" hair, who had succeeded where more complaisant beauties had failed; and of her enthroning at Reading Abbey (led to the throne by a silently protesting Warwick, who could not but note the large array of Woodvilles, come to see their sister Elizabeth acknowledged Queen of England).

The next time Richard turned up in the tale he was setting out from Lynn without a penny in his pocket, in a Dutch vessel that happened to be in the harbour when it was needed. Along with him was his brother Edward, Edward's friend Lord Hastings, and a few followers. None of them had anything except what they stood up in, and after some argument the ship's captain agreed to accept Edward's fur-lined cape as fare.

Warwick had finally decided that the Woodville clan was more than he could stomach. He had helped to put his cousin Edward on the throne of England; he could just as easily unseat him. For the achievement of this he had the help of the whole Nevill brood; and, incredibly, the active assistance of the ineffable George. Who had decided that falling heir to half the lands of Montague, Nevill, and Beauchamp, by marrying Warwick's other daughter Isabel, was a better bet than being loyal to his brother Edward. In eleven days Warwick was master of a surprised England, and Edward and Richard were squelching through the October mud between Alkmaar and The Hague.

From then on, Richard was always in the background of the story. Through that dreary winter in Bruges. Staying with Margaret in Burgundy—for that kind moist-eyed Margaret who had stood on the steps of Baynard's Castle with himself and George to watch their father ride away was now the very new Duchess of Burgundy. Margaret, kind Margaret, was saddened and dismayed—as many people in future were to be saddened and dismayed—by George's inexplicable conduct, and set herself to missionary work what time she got together funds for her two more admirable brothers.

Not even Miss Payne-Ellis's interest in the magnificent Edward allowed her to conceal that the real work of outfitting the ships hired with Margaret's money was done by Richard; a Richard not yet eighteen. And when Edward with an absurd handful of followers found himself once more camped in an English meadow, facing George with an army, it was Richard who went over to George's camp and talked the Margaret-weakened George into alliance again and so left the road to London open to them.

Not, Grant thought, that this last was any great achievement. George could obviously be talked into anything. He was the born missionee.

# 6

HE HAD NOT NEARLY exhausted *The Rose of Raby* and the illicit joys of fiction when, next morning about eleven, a parcel arrived from Marta containing the more respectable entertainment of history as recorded by the sainted Sir Thomas.

With the book was a note in Marta's large sprawling writing on Marta's stiff expensive notepaper.

> Have to send this instead of bringing it. Frantically busy. Think I have got M.M. to the sticking point re Blessington. No T. More in any of the bookshops, so tried Public Library. Can't think why one never thinks of Public Libraries. Probably because books expected to be soupy. Think this looks quite clean and unsoupy. You get fourteen days. Sounds like a sentence rather than a loan. Hope this interest in Crouchback means that the prickles are less nettlish. Till soon.
>
> > Marta.

The book did indeed look clean and unsoupy, if a little elderly. But after the light going of *The Rose* its print looked unexciting and its solid paragraphs forbidding. Nevertheless he attacked it with interest. This was, after all, where Richard III was concerned, "the horse's mouth."

He came to the surface an hour later, vaguely puzzled and ill at ease. It was not that the matter surprised him; the facts were very much what he had expected them to be. It was that this was not how he had expected Sir Thomas to write.

> He took ill rest at nights, lay long waking and musing; sore wearied with care and watch, he slumbered rather than slept. So was his restless

heart continually tossed and tumbled with the tedious impression and stormy remembrance of his most abominable deeds.

That was all right. But when he added that "this he had from such as were secret with his chamberers" one was suddenly repelled. An aroma of back-stair gossip and servants' spying came off the page. So that one's sympathy tilted before one was aware of it from the smug commentator to the tortured creature sleepless on his bed. The murderer seemed of greater stature than the man who was writing of him.

Which was all wrong.

Grant was conscious too of the same unease that filled him when he listened to a witness telling a perfect story that he knew to be flawed somewhere.

And that was very puzzling indeed. What could possibly be wrong with the personal account of a man revered for his integrity as Thomas More had been revered for four centuries?

The Richard who appeared in More's account was, Grant thought, one that Matron would have recognised. A man highly-strung and capable of both great evil and great suffering. "He was never quiet in his mind, never thought himself secure. His eyes whirled about, his body was privily fenced, his hand ever on his dagger, his countenance and manner like one always ready to strike again."

And of course there was the dramatic, not to say hysterical, scene that Grant remembered from his schooldays; that every schoolboy probably remembered. The council scene in the Tower before he laid claim to the crown. Richard's sudden challenge to Hastings as to what was the proper fate for a man who plotted the death of the Protector of the Kingdom. The insane claim that Edward's wife and Edward's mistress (Jane Shore) were responsible for his withered arm by their sorcery. The smiting of the table in his rage, which was the signal for his armed satellites to burst in and arrest Lord Hastings, Lord Stanley, and John Morton, Bishop of Ely. The rushing of Hastings down into the courtyard and his beheading on a handy log of wood after bare time to confess himself to the first priest who could be found.

That was certainly the picture of a man who would act first—in fury, in fear, in revenge—and repent afterwards.

But it seemed that he was capable of more calculated iniquity. He caused a sermon to be preached by a certain Dr. Shaw, brother of the Lord Mayor, at Paul's Cross, on June 22, on the text: "Bastard slips shall take no root." Wherein Dr. Shaw maintained that both Edward and George were sons of the Duchess of York by some unknown man, and that Richard was the only legitimate son of the Duke and Duchess of York.

This was so unlikely, so inherently absurd, that Grant went back and read it over again. But it still said the same thing. That Richard had traduced

his mother, in public and for his own material advantage, with an unbelievable infamy.

Well, Sir Thomas More said it. And if anyone should know it would be
Thomas More. And if anyone should know how to pick and choose between
the credibilities in the reporting of a story it ought to be Thomas More,
Lord Chancellor of England.

Richard's mother, said Sir Thomas, complained bitterly of the slander with
which her son had smirched her. Understandably, on the whole, Grant
thought.

As for Dr. Shaw, he was overcome with remorse. So much so that "within
a few days he withered and consumed away."

Had a stroke, probably, Grant considered. And little wonder. To have
stood up and told that tale to a London crowd must have taken some nerve.

Sir Thomas's account of the Princes in the Tower was the same as The
Amazon's, but Sir Thomas's version was more detailed. Richard had suggested
to Robert Brackenbury, Constable of the Tower, that it might be a good
thing if the Princes disappeared, but Brackenbury would have no part in
such an act. Richard therefore waited until he was at Warwick, during his
progress through England after his coronation, and then sent Tyrrel to London with orders that he was to receive the keys of the Tower for one night.
During that night two ruffians, Dighton and Forrest, one a groom and one
a warder, smothered the two boys.

At this point The Midget came in with his lunch and removed the book
from his grasp; and while he forked the shepherd's pie from plate to mouth
he considered again the face of the man in the dock. The faithful and
patient small brother who had turned into a monster.

When The Midget came back for his tray he said: "Did you know that
Richard III was a very popular person in his day? Before he came to the
throne, I mean."

The Midget cast a baleful glance at the picture.

"Always was a snake in the grass, if you ask me. Smooth, that's what he
was: smooth. Biding his time."

Biding his time for what? he wondered, as she tapped away down the corridor. He could not have known that his brother Edward would die unexpectedly at the early age of forty. He could not have foreseen (even after a
childhood shared with him in uncommon intimacy) that George's on-goings
would end in attainder and the debarring of his two children from the succession. There seemed little point in "biding one's time" if there was nothing to
bide for. The indestructibly virtuous beauty with the gilt hair had, except for
her incurable nepotism, proved an admirable Queen and had provided Edward with a large brood of healthy children, including two boys. The whole
of that brood, together with George and his son and daughter, stood between
Richard and the throne. It was surely unlikely that a man busy with the ad-

ministration of the North of England, or campaigning (with dazzling success) against the Scots, would have much spare interest in being "smooth."

What then had changed him so fundamentally in so short a time?

Grant reached for *The Rose of Raby* to see what Miss Payne-Ellis had had to say about the unhappy metamorphosis of Cicely Nevill's youngest son. But that wily author had burked the issue. She had wanted the book to be a happy one, and to have carried it to its logical conclusion would have made it unredeemed tragedy. She had therefore wound it up with a fine resounding major chord by making her last chapter the coming-out of young Elizabeth, Edward's eldest child. This avoided both the tragedy of Elizabeth's young brothers and the defeat and death of Richard in battle.

So the book ended with a Palace party, and a flushed and happy young Elizabeth, very magnificent in a new white dress and her first pearls, dancing the soles out of her slippers like the princesses in the fairy-tale. Richard and Anne, and their delicate little son, had come up from Middleham for the occasion. But neither George nor Isabel was there. Isabel had died in childbirth years ago, obscurely and as far as George was concerned unmourned. George too had died obscurely, but with that perverseness that was so peculiarly George's, had by that very obscurity won for himself imperishable fame.

George's life had been a progression from one spectacular piece of spiritual extravagance to the next. Each time, his family must have said: Well, that at last is the summit of frightfulness; even George cannot think of anything more fantastic than that. And each time George had surprised them. There was no limit to George's antic capacity.

The seed was perhaps sown when, during his first backsliding in the company of his father-in-law, Warwick had created him heir to the poor crazy puppet-King, Henry VI, whom Warwick had dumped back on the throne to spite his cousin Edward. Both Warwick's hopes of seeing his daughter a Queen and George's royal pretensions had gone down the drain on that night when Richard had gone over to the Lancastrian camp and talked to George. But the taste of importance had perhaps proved too much for a natural sweet-tooth. In the years to come the family were always heading George off from unexpected vagaries, or rescuing him from his latest caper.

When Isabel died he had been certain that she had been poisoned by her waiting woman, and that his baby son had been poisoned by another. Edward, thinking the affair important enough to be tried before a London court, sent down a writ; only to find that George had tried them both at a petty sessions of his own magistrates and hanged them. The furious Edward, by way of rapping him over the knuckles, had two members of George's household tried for treason; but instead of taking the hint George declared that this was just judicial murder, and went about saying so in loud tones and a fine blaze of *lèse-majesté*.

Then he decided that he wanted to marry the richest heiress in Europe; who was Margaret's step-daughter, young Mary of Burgundy. Kind Margaret thought that it would be nice to have her brother in Burgundy, but Edward had arranged to back Maximilian of Austria's suit, and George was a continual embarrassment.

When the Burgundy intrigue came to nothing, the family hoped for a little peace. After all, George owned half the Nevill lands and had no need to marry again either for fortune or children. But George had a new scheme for marrying Margaret, the sister of James III of Scotland.

At last his *folie de grandeur* graduated from secret negotiation undertaken on his own behalf with foreign courts to open display of the Lancastrian act of Parliament which had declared him heir to the throne after Henry VI. This, inevitably, landed him before another Parliament, and a much less amenable one.

The trial was chiefly remarkable for a flaming and wordy row between the two brothers, Edward and George, but when the expected attainder was passed, there was a pause. Depriving George of his standing was one thing: desirable and indeed necessary. But executing him was something else again.

As the days went by without sentence being carried out, the Commons sent a reminder. And next day it was announced that George, Duke of Clarence, had died in the Tower.

"Drowned in a butt of malmsey," said London. And what was merely a Cockney's comment on a drunkard's end passed into history and made the undeserving George immortal.

So George was not at that party at Westminster, and the emphasis in Miss Payne-Ellis's final chapter was not on Cicely Nevill as the mother of sons, but on Cicely Nevill the grandmother of a fine brood. George might have died discredited, on a dried-leaf heap of worn-out friendships, but his son, young Warwick, was a fine upstanding boy, and little Margaret at ten was already showing signs of the traditional Nevill beauty. Edmund, dead in battle at seventeen, might seem a wanton waste of young life, but there to balance it was the delicate baby whom she had never thought to rear; and he had a son to follow him. Richard in his twenties still looked as though one could break him in two, but he was as tough as a heather root, and perhaps his fragile-looking son would grow up to be as resilient. As for Edward, her tall blond Edward, his beauty might be blurring into grossness and his amiability into sloth, but his two small sons and his five girls had all the character and good looks of their combined ancestry.

As a grandmother she could look on that crowd of children with a personal pride, and as a Princess of England she could look on them with assurance. The crown was safe in the York line for generations to come.

If anyone, looking in a crystal ball at that party, had told Cicely Nevill that in four years not only the York line but the whole Plantagenet dynasty would have gone for ever, she would have held it to be either madness or treason.

But what Miss Payne-Ellis had not sought to gloss over was the prevalence of the Woodville clan in a Nevill-Plantagenet gathering.

She looked round the room and wished that her daughter-in-law Elizabeth had been blessed either with a less generous heart or with fewer relations. The Woodville match had turned out far more happily than anyone had dared to hope; Elizabeth had been an admirable wife; but the by-products had not been so fortunate. It was perhaps inevitable that the governorship of the two boys should have gone to her eldest brother; and Rivers, if a little *nouveau riche* in his liking for display and a little too obviously ambitious, was a cultured creature and an admirable person to have the boys in charge during their school-room days at Ludlow. But as for the rest: four brothers, seven sisters, and two sons by her first husband, were really too many by half to have brought into the marriage market in her wake.

Cicely looked across the laughing mêlée of the children's blind-man's-buff to the grown-ups standing round the supper table. Anne Woodville married to the Earl of Essex's heir. Eleanor Woodville married to the Earl of Kent's heir. Margaret Woodville married to the Earl of Arundel's heir. Katherine Woodville married to the Duke of Buckingham. Jacquette Woodville to Lord Strange. Mary Woodville to Lord Herbert's heir. And John Woodville, disgracefully, to the Dowager of Norfolk who was old enough to be his grandmother. It was good that new blood should strengthen the old families—new blood had always seeped in—but it was not good that it should come suddenly and in a flood from one particular source. It was like a fever in the political blood of the country; a foreign introduction, difficult to be assimilated. Unwise and regrettable.

However. There were long years ahead in which that influx could be assimilated. This new sudden power in the body politic would cease to be so concentrated, would spread out, would settle down, would cease to be dangerous and upsetting. Edward for all his amiability had a shrewd common sense; he would keep the country on an even keel as he had kept it for nearly twenty years. No one had run England with a more despotic power or a lighter hand than her acute, lazy, woman-loving Edward.

It would be all right eventually.

She was about to rise and join them in their discussion of sweetmeats —they must not think that she was being critical or aloof—when her granddaughter Elizabeth came breathless and laughing out of the scrimmage and swept into the seat beside her.

"I am much too old for this sort of thing," she said between her gasps, "and it is ruinous to one's clothes. Do you like my dress, grandmother? I had to coax it out of Father. He said my old tawny satin would do. The one I had when Aunt Margaret came from Burgundy to visit us. That is the worst of having a father who notices what women wear. He knows too much about one's wardrobe. Did you hear that the Dauphin has jilted me? Father is in a pet, but I am so happy. I lighted ten candles to St. Catherine. It took all I had left of my allowance. I don't want to leave England. I want never to leave England ever. Can you arrange that for me, grandmother?"

Cicely smiled and said that she would try.

"Old Ankaret, who tells fortunes, says that I am to be a Queen. But since there is no prince to marry me I do not see how that may be." She paused, and added in a smaller voice: "She said Queen of England. But I expect she was just a little tipsy. She is very fond of hippocras."

It was unfair, not to say inartistic, of Miss Payne-Ellis to hint at Elizabeth's future as the wife of Henry VII if as author she was not prepared to face the unpleasantness that lay between. To presuppose in her readers a knowledge of Elizabeth's marriage to the first Tudor king was also to presuppose their awareness of her brothers' murder. So that a dark reminding shadow fell across the festive scene with which she had chosen to end her story.

But on the whole, Grant thought, she had made a good enough job of the story, judging by what he had read of it. He might even go back sometime and read the bits he had skipped.

# 7

GRANT HAD SWITCHED OFF his bedside light that night, and was half asleep, when a voice in his mind said, "But Thomas More was Henry the Eighth."

This brought him wide awake. He flicked the light on again.

What the voice had meant, of course, was not that Thomas More and Henry the Eighth were one and the same person, but that, in that business of putting personalities into pigeon-holes according to reigns, Thomas More belonged to the reign of Henry the Eighth.

Grant lay looking at the pool of light that his lamp threw on the ceiling, and reckoned. If Thomas More was Henry VIII's Chancellor, then he must have lived through the whole of Henry VII's long reign as well as Richard III's. There was something wrong somewhere.

He reached for More's *History of Richard III*. It had as preface a short life of More which he had not bothered to read. Now he turned to it to find out how More could have been both Richard III's historian and Henry VIII's Chancellor. How old was More when Richard succeeded?

He was five.

When that dramatic council scene had taken place at the Tower, Thomas More had been five years old. He had been only eight when Richard died at Bosworth.

Everything in that history had been hearsay.

And if there was one word that a policeman loathed more than another it was hearsay. Especially when applied to evidence.

He was so disgusted that he flung the precious book on to the floor before he remembered that it was the property of a Public Library and his only by grace and for fourteen days.

More had never known Richard III at all. He had indeed grown up under a Tudor administration. That book was the Bible of the whole historical world on the subject of Richard III—it was from that account that Holinshed had taken his material, and from that that Shakespeare had written his—and except that More believed what he wrote to be true it was of no more value than what the soldier said. It was what his cousin Laura called "snow on their boots." A "gospel-true" event seen by someone other than the teller. That More had a critical mind and an admirable integrity did not make the story acceptable evidence. A great many otherwise admirable minds had accepted that story of the Russian troops passing through Britain. Grant had dealt too long with the human intelligence to accept as truth someone's report of someone's report of what that someone remembered to have seen or been told.

He was disgusted.

At the first opportunity he must get an actual contemporary account of the events of Richard's short reign. The Public Library could have Sir Thomas More back tomorrow and be damned to their fourteen days. The fact that Sir Thomas was a martyr and a Great Mind did not cut any ice at all with him, Alan Grant. He, Alan Grant, had known Great Minds so uncritical that they would believe a story that would make a con. man blush for shame. He had known a great scientist who was convinced that a piece of butter muslin was his great-aunt Sophia because an illiterate medium from the back streets of Plymouth told him so. He had known a great authority on the Human Mind and Its Evolution who had been taken for all he had by an incurable knave because he "judged for himself and not on police stories." As far as he, Alan Grant, was concerned there was nothing so uncritical or so damn-silly as your Great Mind. As far as he, Alan Grant, was concerned Thomas More was washed out, cancelled, deleted; and he, Alan Grant, was beginning from scratch again tomorrow morning.

He was still illogically fuming when he fell asleep and he woke fuming.

"Do you know that your Sir Thomas More knew nothing about Richard III at all?" he said, accusing, to The Amazon the moment her large person appeared in the doorway.

She looked startled, not at his news but at his ferocity. Her eyes looked as if they might brim with tears at another rough word.

"But of *course* he knew!" she protested. "He *lived* then."

"He was eight when Richard died," Grant said, relentless. "And all he knew was what he had been told. Like me. Like you. Like Will Rogers of blessed memory. There is nothing hallowed at all about Sir Thomas More's history of Richard III. It's a damned piece of hearsay and a swindle."

"Aren't you feeling so well this morning?" she asked anxiously. "Do you think you've got a temperature?"

"I don't know about a temperature, but my blood pressure's away up."

"Oh dear, dear," she said, taking this literally. "And you were doing so very well. Nurse Ingham will be so distressed. She has been boasting about your good recovery."

That The Midget should have found him a subject for boasting was a new idea to Grant, but it was not one that gave him any gratification. He resolved to have a temperature in earnest if he could manage it, just to score off The Midget.

But the morning visit of Marta distracted him from this experiment in the power of mind over matter.

Marta, it seemed, was pluming herself on his mental health very much as The Midget was pluming herself on his physical improvement. She was delighted that her pokings-about with James in the print shop had been so effective.

"Have you decided on Perkin Warbeck, then?" she asked.

"No. Not Warbeck. Tell me: what made you bring me a portrait of Richard III? There's no mystery about Richard, is there?"

"No. I suppose we took it as illustration to the Warbeck story. No, wait a moment. I remember. James turned it up and said: 'If he's mad about faces, there's one for him!' He said: 'That's the most notorious murderer in history, and yet his face is in my estimation the face of a saint.' "

"A saint!" Grant said; and then remembered something. " 'Over-conscientious,' " he said.

"What?"

"Nothing. I was just remembering my first impressions of it. Is that how it seemed to you: the face of a saint?"

She looked across at the picture, propped up against the pile of books. "I can't see it against the light," she said, and picked it up for a closer scrutiny.

He was suddenly reminded that to Marta, as to Sergeant Williams, faces were a professional matter. The slant of an eyebrow, the set of a mouth, was just as much an evidence of character to Marta as to Williams. Indeed she actually made herself faces to match the characters she played.

"Nurse Ingham thinks he's dreary. Nurse Darroll thinks he's a horror. My surgeon thinks he's a polio victim. Sergeant Williams thinks he's a born judge. Matron thinks he's a soul in torment."

Marta said nothing for a little. Then she said: "It's odd, you know. When you first look at it you think it a mean, suspicious face. Even cantankerous. But when you look at it a little longer you find that it isn't like that at all. It is quite calm. It is really quite a gentle face. Perhaps that is what James meant by being saint-like."

"No. No, I don't think so. What he meant was the subservience to conscience."

"Whatever it is, it *is a face,* isn't it! Not just a collection of organs for seeing, breathing, and eating with. A wonderful face. With very little alteration, you know, it might be a portrait of Lorenzo the Magnificent."

"You don't suppose that it *is* Lorenzo and that we're considering the wrong man altogether?"

"Of course not. Why should you think that?"

"Because nothing in the face fits the facts of history. And pictures have got shuffled before now."

"Oh, yes, of course they have. But that is Richard all right. The original—or what is supposed to be the original—is at Windsor Castle. James told me. It is included in Henry VIII's inventory, so it has been there for four hundred years or so. And there are duplicates at Hatfield and Albury."

"It's Richard," Grant said resignedly. "I just don't know anything about faces. Do you know anyone at the B.M.?"

"At the British Museum?" Marta asked, her attention still on the portrait. "No, I don't think so. Not that I can think of at the moment. I went there once to look at some Egyptian jewellery, when I was playing Cleopatra with Geoffrey—did you ever see Geoffrey's Antony? it was superlatively genteel—but the place frightens me rather. Such a garnering of the ages. It made me feel the way the stars make you feel: small and no-account. What do you want of the B.M.?"

"I wanted some information about history written in Richard III's day. Contemporary accounts."

"Isn't the sainted Sir Thomas any good, then?"

"The sainted Sir Thomas is nothing but an old gossip," Grant said with venom. He had taken a wild dislike to the much-admired More.

"Oh, dear. And the nice man at the Library seemed so reverent about him. The Gospel of Richard III according to St. Thomas More, and all that."

"Gospel nothing," Grant said rudely. "He was writing down in a Tudor England what someone had told him about events that happened in a Plantagenet England when he himself was five."

"Five years old?"

"Yes."

"Oh, dear. Not exactly the horse's mouth."

"Not even straight from the course. Come to think of it, it's as reliable as a bookie's tips would be. He's on the wrong side of the rails altogether. If he was a Tudor servant he was on the laying side where Richard III was concerned."

"Yes. Yes, I suppose so. What do you want to find out about Richard, when there is no mystery to investigate?"

"I want to know what made him tick. That is a more profound mystery than anything I have come up against of late. What changed him almost overnight? Up to the moment of his brother's death he seems to have been entirely admirable. And devoted to his brother."

"I suppose the supreme honour must always be a temptation."

"He was Regent until the boy came of age. Protector of England. With his previous history, you would think that would have been enough for him. You would have thought, indeed, that it would have been very much his cup of tea: guardian of both Edward's son and the kingdom."

"Perhaps the brat was unbearable, and Richard longed to 'larn' him. Isn't it odd how we never think of victims as anything but white innocents. Like Joseph in the Bible. I'm sure he was a quite intolerable young man, actually, and long overdue for that pushing into the pit. Perhaps young Edward was just sitting up and begging to be quietly put down."

"There were two of them," Grant reminded her.

"Yes, of course. Of course there isn't an explanation. It was the ultimate barbarism. Poor little woolly lambs! Oh!"

"What was the 'Oh' for?"

"I've just thought of something. Woolly lambs made me think of it."

"Well?"

"No, I won't tell you in case it doesn't come off. I must fly."

"Have you charmed Madeleine March into agreeing to write the play?"

"Well, she hasn't actually signed a contract yet, but I think she is sold on the idea. Au revoir, my dear. I shall look in soon again."

She went away, sped on her way by a blushing Amazon, and Grant did not remember anything about woolly lambs until the woolly lamb actually turned up in his room next evening. The woolly lamb was wearing horn-rimmed spectacles, which in some odd way emphasised the resemblance instead of detracting from it. Grant had been dozing, more at peace with the world than he had been for some time; history was, as Matron had pointed out, an excellent way of acquiring a sense of perspective. The tap at his door was so tentative that he had decided that he had imagined it. Taps on hospital doors are not apt to be tentative. But something made him say: "Come in!" and there in the opening was something that was so unmistakably Marta's woolly lamb that Grant laughed aloud before he could stop himself.

The young man looked abashed, smiled nervously, propped the spectacles on his nose with a long thin forefinger, cleared his throat, and said:

"Mr. Grant? My name is Carradine. Brent Carradine. I hope I haven't disturbed you when you were resting."

"No, no. Come in, Mr. Carradine. I am delighted to see you."

"Marta—Miss Hallard, that is—sent me. She said I could be of some help to you."

"Did she say how? Do sit down. You'll find a chair over there behind the door. Bring it over."

He was a tall boy, hatless, with soft fair curls crowning a high forehead and a much too big tweed coat hanging unfastened round him in negligent folds, American-wise. Indeed, it was obvious that he was in fact American. He brought over the chair, planted himself on it with the coat spread round him like some royal robe and looked at Grant with kind brown eyes whose luminous charm not even the horn-rims could dim.

"Marta—Miss Hallard, that is—said that you wanted something looked up."

"And are you a looker-upper?"

"I'm doing research, here in London. Historical research, I mean. And she said something about your wanting something in that line. She knows I work at the B.M. most mornings. I'd be very pleased, Mr. Grant, to do anything I can to help you."

"That's very kind of you; very kind indeed. What is it that you are working on? Your research, I mean."

"The Peasants' Revolt."

"Oh, Richard II."

"Yes."

"Are you interested in social conditions?"

The young man grinned suddenly in a very unstudent-like way and said: "No, I'm interested in staying in England."

"And can't you stay in England without doing research?"

"Not very easily. I've got to have an alibi. My pop thinks I should go into the family business. It's furniture. Wholesale furniture. You order it by mail. Out of a book. Don't misunderstand me, Mr. Grant: it's very good furniture. Lasts for ever. It's just that I can't take much interest in furnishing-units."

"And, short of Polar exploration, the British Museum was the best hideaway you could think of."

"Well, it's warm. And I really do like history. I majored in it. And—well, Mr. Grant, if you really want to know, I just had to follow Atlanta Shergold to England. She's the dumb blonde in Marta's—I mean, in Miss Hallard's play. I mean she *plays* the dumb blonde. She's not at all dumb, Atlanta."

"No, indeed. A very gifted young woman indeed."

"You've seen her?"

"I shouldn't think there is anyone in London who hasn't seen her."

"No, I suppose not. It does go on and on, doesn't it? We didn't think—Atlanta and me—that it would run for more than a few weeks, so we just waved each other goodbye and said: See you at the beginning of the month! It was when we found that it was going on indefinitely that I just had to find an excuse to come to England."

"Wasn't Atlanta sufficient excuse?"

"Not for my pop! The family are very snooty about Atlanta, but Pop is the worst of the bunch. When he can bring himself to mention her he refers to her as 'that young actress acquaintance of yours.' You see, Pop is Carradine the Third, and Atlanta's father is very much Shergold the First. A little grocery store on Main Street, as a matter of fact. And the salt of the earth, in case you're interested. And of course Atlanta hadn't really done very much, back in the States. I mean, on the stage. This is her first big success. That is why she didn't want to break her contract and come back home. As a matter of fact it'll be quite a fight to get her back home at all. She says we never appreciated her."

"So you took to research."

"I had to think of something that I could do only in London, you see. And I had done some research at college. So the B.M. seemed to be what you call my cup of tea. I could enjoy myself and yet show my father that I was really working, both at the same time."

"Yes. It's as nice an alibi as ever I met with. Why the Peasants' Revolt, by the way?"

"Well, it's an interesting time. And I thought it would please Pop."

"Is *he* interested in social reform, then?"

"No, but he hates kings."

"Carradine the Third?"

"Yes, it's a laugh, isn't it? I wouldn't put it past him to have a crown in one of his safe deposit boxes. I bet he takes out the parcel every now and then and sneaks over to Grand Central and tries it on in the men's washroom. I'm afraid I'm tiring you, Mr. Grant; gabbing on about my own affairs like this. I didn't come for that. I came to——"

"Whatever you came for, you're manna straight from heaven. So relax, if you're not in a hurry."

"I'm never in a hurry," the young man said, unfolding his legs and laying them out in front of him. As he did it his feet, at the far extremity of his long limbs, touched the bedside table and shook the portrait of Richard III from its precarious position, so that it dropped to the floor.

"Oh, pardon me! That was careless of me. I haven't really got used to the length of my legs yet. You'd think a fellow would be used to his growth by twenty-two, wouldn't you?" He picked up the photograph, dusted it carefully with the cuff of his sleeve, and looked at it with interest. "Richardus III. Ang. Rex.," he read aloud.

"You're the first person to have noticed that background writing," Grant said.

"Well, I suppose it isn't visible unless you look into it. You're the first person I ever met who had a king for a pin-up."

"No beauty, is he?"

"I don't know," said the boy slowly. "It's not a bad face, as faces go. I had a prof. at college who looked rather like him. He lived on bismuth and glasses of milk so he had a slightly jaundiced outlook on life, but he was the kindest creature imaginable. Is it about Richard that you wanted information?"

"Yes. Nothing very abstruse or difficult. Just to know what the contemporary authority is."

"Well, that should be easy enough. It isn't very far from my own time. I mean my research period. Indeed, the modern authority for Richard II—Sir Cuthbert Oliphant—stretches over both. Have you read Oliphant?" Grant said that he had read nothing but school books and Sir Thomas More.

"More? Henry VIII's Chancellor?"

"Yes."

"I take it that that was a bit of special pleading!"

"It read to me more like a party pamphlet," Grant said, realising for the first time that that was the taste that had been left in his mouth. It had not read like a statesman's account; it had read like a party throw-away.

No, it had read like a columnist. Like a columnist who got his information below-stairs.

"Do you know anything about Richard III?"

"Nothing except that he croaked his nephews, and offered his kingdom for a horse. And that he had two stooges known as the Cat and the Rat."

"What!"

"You know: 'The Cat, the Rat, and Lovel Our Dog, Rule all England under a Hog.' "

"Yes, of course. I'd forgotten that. What does it mean, do you know?"

"No, I've no idea. I don't know that period very well. How did you get interested in Richard III?"

"Marta suggested that I should do some academic investigating, since I can't do any practical investigating for some time to come. And because I find faces interesting she brought me portraits of all the principals. Principals in the various mysteries she suggested, I mean. Richard got in more or less by accident, but he proved the biggest mystery of the lot."

"He did? In what way?"

"He is the author of the most revolting crime in history, and he has the face of a great judge; a great administrator. Moreover he was by all accounts an abnormally civilised and well-living creature. He actually *was* a good administrator, by the way. He governed the North of England and did it excellently. He was a good staff officer and a good soldier. And nothing is known against his private life. His brother, perhaps you know, was—bar Charles II— our most wench-ridden royal product."

"Edward IV. Yes, I know. A six-foot hunk of male beauty. Perhaps Richard suffered from a resentment at the contrast. And that accounts for his willingness to blot out his brother's seed."

This was something that Grant had not thought of.

"You're suggesting that Richard had a suppressed hate for his brother?"

"Why suppressed?"

"Because even his worst detractors admit that he was devoted to Edward. They were together in everything from the time that Richard was twelve or thirteen. The other brother was no good to anyone. George."

"Who was George?"

"The Duke of Clarence."

"Oh. Him! Butt-of-malmsey Clarence."

"That's the one. So there were just the two of them—Edward and Richard I mean. And there was a ten-year gap in their ages. Just the right difference for hero worship."

"If I were a hunchback," young Carradine said musingly, "I sure would hate a brother who took my credit and my women and my place in the sun."

"It's possible," Grant said after an interval. "It's the best explanation I've come on so far."

"It mightn't have been an overt thing at all, you know. It mightn't have even been a conscious thing. It may just have all boiled up in him when he saw the chance of a crown. He may have said—I mean his blood may have said: 'Here's my chance! All those years of fetching and carrying and standing one pace in the rear, and no thanks for them. Here's where I take my pay. Here's where I settle accounts.' "

Grant noticed that by sheer chance Carradine had used the same imagined description of Richard as Miss Payne-Ellis. Standing one pace in the rear. That is how the novelist had seen him, standing with the fair, solid Margaret and George, on the steps of Baynard's Castle watching their father go away to war. One pace in the rear, "as usual."

"That's very interesting, though, what you say about Richard being apparently a good sort up to the time of the crime," Carradine said, propping one leg of his horn-rims with a long forefinger in his characteristic gesture. "Makes him more of a person. That Shakespeare version of him, you know, that's just a caricature. Not a man at all. I'll be very pleased to do any investigating you want, Mr. Grant. It'll make a nice change from the peasants."

"The Cat and the Rat instead of John Ball and Wat Tyler."

"That's it."

"Well, it's very nice of you. I'd be glad of anything you can rake up. But at the moment all I pine for is a contemporary account of events. They must have been country-rocking events. I want to read a contemporary's account of them. Not what someone heard-tell about events that happened when he was five, and under another régime altogether."

"I'll find out who the contemporary historian is. Fabyan, perhaps. Or is he Henry VII? Anyway, I'll find out. And meanwhile perhaps you'd like a look at Oliphant. He's the modern authority on the period, or so I understand."

Grant said that he would be delighted to take a look at Sir Cuthbert.

"I'll drop him in when I'm passing tomorrow—I suppose it'll be all right if I leave him in the office for you?—and as soon as I find out about the contemporary writers I'll be in with the news. That suit you?"

Grant said that that was perfect.

Young Carradine went suddenly shy, reminding Grant of the woolly lamb which he had quite forgotten in the interest of this new approach to Richard.

He said goodnight in a quiet smothered way, and ambled out of the room followed by the sweeping skirts of his topcoat.

Grant thought that, the Carradine fortune apart, Atlanta Shergold looked like being on a good thing.

# 8

"WELL," SAID MARTA when she came again, "what did you think of my woolly lamb?"

"It was *very* kind of you to find him for me."

"I didn't have to find him. He's continually underfoot. He practically lives at the theatre. He must have seen *To Sea in a Bowl* five hundred times; when he isn't in Atlanta's dressing-room he's in front. I wish they'd get married, and then we might see less of him. They're not even living together, you know. It's all pure idyll." She dropped her "actress" voice for a moment and said: "They're rather sweet together. In some ways they are more like twins than lovers. They have that utter trust in each other; that dependence on the other half to make a proper whole. And they never have rows—or even quarrels, that I can see. An idyll, as I said. Was it Brent who brought you this?"

She poked the solid bulk of Oliphant with a doubtful finger.

"Yes, he left it with the porter for me."

"It looks very indigestible."

"A bit unappetising, let us say. It is quite easily digested once you have swallowed it. History for the student. Set out in detailed fact."

"Ugh!"

"At least I've discovered where the revered and sainted Sir Thomas More got his account of Richard."

"Yes? Where?"

"From one John Morton."

"Never heard of him."

"Neither did I, but that's our ignorance."

"Who was he?"

"He was Henry VII's Archbishop of Canterbury. And Richard's bitterest enemy."

If Marta had been capable of whistling, she would have whistled in comment.

"So *that* was the horse's mouth!" she said.

"That was the horse's mouth. And it is on that account of Richard that all the later ones were built. It is on that story that Holinshed fashioned his history, and on that story that Shakespeare fashioned his character."

"So it is the version of someone who hated Richard. I didn't know that. Why did the sainted Sir Thomas report Morton rather than someone else?"

"Whoever he reported, it would be a Tudor version. But he reported Morton, it seems, because he had been in Morton's household as a boy. And of course Morton had been very much 'on in the act,' so it was natural to write down the version of an eyewitness whose account he could have at first hand."

Marta poked her finger at Oliphant again. "Does your dull fat historian acknowledge that it is a biassed version?"

"Oliphant? Only by implication. He is, to be honest, in a sad muddle himself about Richard. On the same page he says that he was an admirable administrator and general, with an excellent reputation, staid and good-living, very popular by contrast with the Woodville upstarts (the Queen's relations) and that he was 'perfectly unscrupulous and ready to wade through any depth of bloodshed to the crown which lay within his grasp.' On one page he says grudgingly: 'There are reasons for supposing that he was not destitute of a conscience' and then on a later page reports More's picture of a man so tormented by his own deed that he could not sleep. And so on."

"Does your dull fat Oliphant prefer his roses red, then?"

"Oh, I don't think so. I don't think he is consciously Lancastrian. Though now that I think of it he *is* very tolerant of Henry VII's usurpation. I can't remember his saying anywhere, brutally, that Henry hadn't a vestige of a shadow of a claim to the throne."

"Who put him there, then? Henry, I mean."

"The Lancastrian remnant and the upstart Woodvilles, backed, I suppose, by a country revolted by the boys' murder. Apparently anyone with a spice of Lancastrian blood in their veins would do. Henry himself was canny enough to put 'conquest' first in his claim to the throne, and his Lancaster blood second. 'De jure belli et de jure Lancastriae.' His mother was the heir of an illegitimate son of the third son of Edward III."

"All I know about Henry VII is that he was fantastically rich and fantastically mean. Do you know the lovely Kipling story about his knighting the craftsman not for having done beautiful work but for having saved him the cost of some scroll-work?"

"With a rusty sword from behind the arras. You must be one of the few women who know their Kipling."

"Oh, I'm a very remarkable woman in many ways. So you are no nearer finding out about Richard's personality than you were?"

"No. I'm as completely bewildered as Sir Cuthbert Oliphant, bless his heart. The only difference between us is that I know I'm bewildered and he doesn't seem to be aware of it."

"Have you seen much of my woolly lamb?"

"I've seen nothing of him since his first visit, and that's three days ago. I'm beginning to wonder whether he has repented of his promise."

"Oh, no. I'm sure not. Faithfulness is his banner and creed."

"Like Richard."

"Richard?"

"His motto was: 'Loyaulté me lie.' Loyalty binds me."

There was a tentative tap at the door, and in answer to Grant's invitation, Brent Carradine appeared, hung around with topcoat as usual.

"Oh! I seem to be butting in. I didn't know you were here, Miss Hallard. I met the Statue of Liberty in the corridor there, and she seemed to think you were alone, Mr. Grant."

Grant identified the Statue of Liberty without difficulty. Marta said that she was in the act of going, and that in any case Brent was a much more welcome visitor than she was nowadays. She would leave them in peace to pursue their search for the soul of a murderer.

When he had bowed her politely to the door Brent came back and sat himself down in the visitor's chair with exactly the same air that an Englishman wears when he sits down to his port after the women have left the table. Grant wondered if even the female-ridden American felt a subconscious relief at settling down to a stag party. In answer to Brent's inquiry as to how he was getting on with Oliphant, he said he found Sir Cuthbert admirably lucid.

"I've discovered who the Cat and the Rat were, incidentally. They were entirely respectable knights of the realm: William Catesby and Richard Ratcliffe. Catesby was Speaker of the House of Commons, and Ratcliffe was one of the Commissioners of Peace with Scotland. It's odd how the very sound of words makes a political jingle vicious. The Hog of course was Richard's badge. The White Boar. Do you frequent our English pubs?"

"Sure. They're one of the things I think you do better than us."

"You forgive us our plumbing for the sake of the beer at the Boar."

"I wouldn't go as far as to say I forgive it. I discount it, shall we say?"

"Magnanimous of you. Well, there's something else you've got to discount. That theory of yours that Richard hated his brother because of the contrast between his beauty and Richard's hunchbacked state. According to Sir Cuthbert, the hunchback is a myth. So is the withered arm. It appears that he had no visible deformity. At least none that mattered. His left shoulder was lower than his right, that was all. Did you find out who the contemporary historian is?"

"There isn't one."

"None at *all?*"

"Not in the sense that you mean it. There *were* writers who were contemporaries of Richard, but they wrote after his death. For the Tudors. Which puts them out of court. There is a monkish chronicle in Latin somewhere that is contemporary, but I haven't been able to get hold of it yet. One thing I have discovered though: that account of Richard III is called Sir Thomas More's not because he wrote it but because the manuscript was found among his papers. It was an unfinished copy of an account that appears elsewhere in finished form."

"Well!" Grant considered this with interest. "You mean it was More's own manuscript copy?"

"Yes. In his own writing. Made when he was about thirty-five. In those days, before printing was general, manuscript copies of books were the usual thing."

"Yes. So, if the information came from John Morton, as it did, it is just as likely that the thing was written by Morton."

"Yes."

"Which would certainly account for the—the lack of sensibility. A climber like Morton wouldn't be at all abashed by back-stairs gossip. Do you know about Morton?"

"No."

"He was a lawyer turned churchman, and the greatest pluralist on record. He chose the Lancastrian side and stayed with it until it was clear that Edward IV was home and dried. Then he made his peace with the York side and Edward made him Bishop of Ely. And vicar of God knows how many parishes besides. But after Richard's accession he backed first the Woodvilles and then Henry Tudor and ended up with a cardinal's hat as Henry VII's Archbishop of——"

"Wait a minute!" said the boy, amused. "Of *course* I know Morton. He was Morton of 'Morton's Fork.' 'You can't be spending much so how about something for the King; you're spending such a lot you must be very rich so how about something for the King.' "

"Yes. That's Morton. Henry's best thumb-screw. And I've just thought of a reason why he might have a personal hatred for Richard long before the murder of the boys."

"Yes?"

"Edward took a large bribe from Louis XI to make a dishonourable peace in France. Richard was very angry about that—it really was a disgraceful affair—and washed his hands of the business. Which included refusing a large cash offer. But Morton was very much in favour both of the deal and the cash. Indeed he took a pension from Louis. A very nice pension it was. Two thousand crowns a year. I don't suppose Richard's outspoken comments went down very well, even with good gold for a chaser."

"No. I guess not."

"And of course there would be no preferment for Morton under the straight-laced Richard as there had been under the easy-going Edward. So he would have taken the Woodville side, even if there had been no murder."

"About that murder——" the boy said; and paused.

"Yes?"

"About that murder—the murder of those two boys—isn't it odd that no one talks of it?"

"How do you mean: no one talks of it?"

"These last three days I've been going through contemporary papers: letters and what not. And no one mentions them at all."

"Perhaps they were afraid to. It was a time when it paid to be discreet."

"Yes; but I'll tell you something even odder. You know that Henry brought a Bill of Attainder against Richard, after Bosworth. Before Parliament, I mean. Well, he accuses Richard of cruelty and tyranny but doesn't even mention the murder."

"What!" said Grant, startled.

"Yes, you may well look startled."

"Are you sure?"

"Quite sure."

"But Henry got possession of the Tower immediately on his arrival in London after Bosworth. If the boys were missing it is incredible that he should not publish the fact immediately. It was the trump card in his hand." He lay in surprised silence for a little. The sparrows on the window-sill quarrelled loudly. "I can't make sense of it," he said. "What possible explanation can there be for his omission to make capital out of the fact that the boys were missing?"

Brent shifted his long legs to a more comfortable position. "There is only one explanation," he said. "And that is that the boys weren't missing."

There was a still longer silence this time, while they stared at each other.

"Oh, no, it's nonsense," Grant said. "There must be some obvious explanation that we are failing to see."

"As what, for instance?"

"I don't know. I haven't had time to think."

"I've had nearly three days to think, and I still haven't thought up a reason that will fit. *Nothing* will fit the facts except the conclusion that the boys were alive when Henry took over the Tower. It was a completely unscrupulous Act of Attainder; it accused Richard's followers—the loyal followers of an anointed King fighting against an invader—of treason. Every accusation that Henry could possibly make with any hope of getting away with it was put into that Bill. And the very worst he could accuse Richard of was the usual cruelty and tyranny. The boys aren't even mentioned."

"It's fantastic."

"It's unbelievable. But it is fact."

"What it means is that there was *no contemporary accusation at all.*"

"That's about it."

"But—but wait a minute. Tyrrel was *hanged* for the murder. He actually confessed to it before he died. Wait a minute." He reached for Oliphant and sped through the pages looking for the place. "There's a full account of it here somewhere. There was no mystery about it. Even the Statue of Liberty knew about it."

"*Who?*"

"The nurse you met in the corridor. It was Tyrrel who committed the murder and he was found guilty and confessed before his death."

"Was that when Henry took over in London, then?"

"Wait a moment. Here it is." He skimmed down the paragraph. "No, it was in 1502." He realised all of a sudden what he had just said, and repeated in a new, bewildered tone: "In—1502."

"But—but—but that was——"

"Yes. Nearly twenty years afterwards."

Brent fumbled for his cigarette case, took it out, and then put it hastily away again.

"Smoke if you like," Grant said. "It's a good stiff drink I need. I don't think my brain can be working very well. I feel the way I used to feel as a child when I was blindfolded and whirled round before beginning a blindman's-buff game."

"Yes," said Carradine. He took out a cigarette and lighted it. "Completely in the dark, and more than a little dizzy."

He sat staring at the sparrows.

"Forty million school books can't be wrong," Grant said after a little.

"Can't they?"

"Well, can they!"

"I used to think so, but I'm not so sure nowadays."

"Aren't you being a little sudden in your scepticism?"

"Oh, it wasn't this that shook me."

"What then?"

"A little affair called the Boston Massacre. Ever heard of it?"

"Of course."

"Well, I discovered quite by accident, when I was looking up something at college, that the Boston Massacre consisted of a mob throwing stones at a sentry. The total casualties were four. I was brought up on the Boston Massacre, Mr. Grant. My twenty-eight inch chest used to swell at the very memory of it. My good red spinach-laden blood used to seethe at the thought of helpless civilians mowed down by the fire of British troops. You can't imagine what a shock it was to find that all it added up to in actual fact was a brawl that wouldn't get more than local reporting in a clash between police and strikers in any American lock-out."

As Grant made no reply to this, he squinted his eyes against the light to see how Grant was taking it. But Grant was staring at the ceiling as if he were watching patterns forming there.

"That's partly why I like to research so much," Carradine volunteered; and settled back to staring at the sparrows.

Presently Grant put his hand out, wordlessly, and Carradine gave him a cigarette and lighted it for him.

They smoked in silence.

It was Grant who interrupted the sparrows' performance.

"Tonypandy," he said.

"How's that?"

But Grant was still far away.

"After all, I've seen the thing at work in my own day, haven't I?" he said, not to Carradine but to the ceiling. "It's Tonypandy."

"And what in heck is Tonypandy?" Brent asked. "It sounds like a patent medicine. Does your child get out of sorts? Does the little face get flushed, the temper short, and the limbs easily tired? Give the little one Tonypandy, and see the radiant results." And then, as Grant made no answer: "All right, then; keep your Tonypandy. I wouldn't have it as a gift."

"Tonypandy," Grant said, still in that sleep-walking voice, "is a place in the South of Wales."

"I knew it was some kind of physic."

"If you go to South Wales you will hear that, in 1910, the Government used troops to shoot down Welsh miners who were striking for their rights. You'll probably hear that Winston Churchill, who was Home Secretary at the time, was responsible. South Wales, you will be told, will never forget Tonypandy!"

Carradine had dropped his flippant air.

"And it wasn't a bit like that?"

"The actual facts are these. The rougher section of the Rhondda valley crowd had got quite out of hand. Shops were being looted and property destroyed. The Chief Constable of Glamorgan sent a request to the Home Office for troops to protect the lieges. If a Chief Constable thinks a situation serious enough to ask for the help of the military a Home Secretary has very little choice in the matter. But Churchill was so horrified at the possibility of the troops coming face to face with a crowd of rioters and having to fire on them, that he stopped the movement of the troops and sent instead a body of plain, solid Metropolitan Police, armed with nothing but their rolled-up mackintoshes. The troops were kept in reserve, and all contact with the rioters was made by unarmed London police. The only bloodshed in the whole affair was a bloody nose or two. The Home Secretary was severely criticised in the House of Commons incidentally for his 'unprecedented intervention.' That was Tonypandy. That is the shooting down by troops that Wales will never forget."

"Yes," Carradine said, considering. "Yes. It's almost a parallel to the Boston affair. Someone blowing up a simple affair to huge proportions for a political end."

"The point is not that it is a parallel. The point is that *every single man* who was there knows that the story is nonsense, and yet it has never been contradicted. It will never be overtaken now. It is a completely untrue story grown to legend while the men who knew it to be untrue looked on and said nothing."

"Yes. That's very interesting; very. History as it is made."

"Yes. History."

"Give me research. After all, the truth of anything at all doesn't lie in someone's account of it. It lies in all the small facts of the time. An advertisement in a paper. The sale of a house. The price of a ring."

Grant went on looking at the ceiling, and the sparrows' clamour came back into the room.

"What amuses you?" Grant said, turning his head at last and catching the expression on his visitor's face.

"This is the first time I've seen you look like a policeman."

"I'm feeling like a policeman. I'm *thinking* like a policeman. I'm asking myself the question that every policeman asks in every case of murder: Who benefits? And for the first time it occurs to me that the glib theory that Richard got rid of the boys to make himself safer on the throne is so much nonsense. Supposing he had got rid of the boys. There were still the boys' five sisters between him and the throne. To say nothing of George's two: the boy and girl. George's son and daughter were barred by their father's attainder; but I take it that an attainder can be reversed, or annulled, or something. If Richard's claim was shaky, all those lives stood between him and safety."

"And did they all survive him?"

"I don't know. But I shall make it my business to find out. The boys' eldest sister certainly did because she became Queen of England as Henry's wife."

"Look, Mr. Grant, let's you and I start at the very beginning of this thing. Without history books, or modern versions, or anyone's opinion about anything. Truth isn't in accounts but in account books."

"A neat phrase," Grant said, complimentary. "Does it mean anything?"

"It means everything. The real history is written in forms not meant as history. In Wardrobe accounts, in Privy Purse expenses, in personal letters, in estate books. If someone, say, insists that Lady Whoosit never had a child, and you find in the account book the entry: 'For the son born to my lady on Michaelmas eve: five yards of blue ribbon, fourpence halfpenny' it's a reasonably fair deduction that my lady had a son on Michaelmas eve."

"Yes. I see. All right, where do we begin?"

"You're the investigator. I'm only the looker-upper."

"Research Worker."

"Thanks. What do you want to know?"

"Well, for a start, it would be useful, not to say enlightening, to know how the principals in the case reacted to Edward's death. Edward IV, I mean. Edward died unexpectedly, and his death must have caught everyone on the hop. I'd like to know how the people concerned reacted."

"That's straightforward and easy. I take it you mean what they did and not what they thought."

"Yes, of course."

"Only historians tell you what they thought. Research workers stick to what they did."

"What they did is all I want to know. I've always been a believer in the old saw that actions speak louder than words."

"Incidentally, what does the sainted Sir Thomas say that Richard did when he heard that his brother was dead?" Brent wanted to know.

"The sainted Sir Thomas (alias John Morton) says that Richard got busy being charming to the Queen and persuading her not to send a large body-guard to escort the boy prince from Ludlow; meanwhile cooking up a plot to kidnap the boy on his way to London."

"According to the sainted More, then, Richard meant from the very first to supplant the boy."

"Oh, yes."

"Well, we shall find out, at least, who was where and doing what, whether we can deduce their intentions or not."

"That's what I want. Exactly."

"Policeman," jibed the boy. " 'Where were you at five P.M. on the night of the fifteenth inst.?' "

"It works," Grant assured him. "It works."

"Well, I'll go away and work too. I'll be in again as soon as I have got the information you want. I'm very grateful to you, Mr. Grant. This is a lot better than the Peasants."

He floated away into the gathering dusk of the winter afternoon, his train-like coat giving an academic sweep and dignity to his thin young figure.

Grant switched on his lamp, and examined the pattern it made on the ceiling as if he had never seen it before.

It was a unique and engaging problem that the boy had dropped so casually into his lap. As unexpected as it was baffling.

What possible reason could there be for that lack of contemporary accusation?

Henry had not even needed proof that Richard was himself responsible. The boys were in Richard's care. If they were not to be found when the Tower was taken over, then that was far finer, thicker mud to throw at his dead rival than the routine accusations of cruelty and tyranny.

Grant ate his supper without for one moment being conscious either of its taste or its nature.

It was only when The Amazon, taking away his tray, said kindly: "Come now, that's a very good sign. Both rissoles all eaten up to the last crumb!" that he became aware that he had partaken of a meal.

For another hour he watched the lamp-pattern on the ceiling, going over the thing in his mind; going round and round it looking for some small crack that might indicate a way into the heart of the matter.

In the end he withdrew his attention altogether from the problem. Which was his habit when a conundrum proved too round and smooth and solid for immediate solution. If he slept on the proposition it might, tomorrow, show a facet that he had missed.

He looked for something that might stop his mind from harking back to that Act of Attainder, and saw the pile of letters waiting to be acknowledged. Kind, well-wishing letters from all sorts of people; including a few old lags. The really likable old lags were an outmoded type, growing fewer and fewer daily. Their place had been taken by brash young thugs with not a spark of humanity in their egocentric souls, as illiterate as puppies and as pitiless as a circular saw. The old professional burglar was apt to be as individual as the member of any other profession, and as little vicious. Quiet little domestic men, interested in family holidays and the children's tonsils; or odd bachelors devoted to cage-birds, or second-hand bookshops, or complicated and infallible betting systems. Old-fashioned types.

No modern thug would write to say that he was sorry that a "busy" was laid aside. No such idea would ever cross a modern thug's mind.

Writing a letter when lying on one's back is a laborious business, and Grant shied away from it. But the top envelope on the pile bore the writing of his cousin Laura, and Laura would become anxious if she had no answer at all from him. Laura and he had shared summer holidays as children, and had been a little in love with each other all through one Highland summer, and that made a bond between them that had never been broken. He had better send Laura a note to say that he was alive.

He read her letter again, smiling a little; and the waters of the Turlie sounded in his ears and slid under his eyes, and he could smell the sweet cold smell of a Highland moor in winter, and he forgot for a little that he was a hospital patient and that life was sordid and boring and claustrophobic.

Pat sends what would be his love if he were a little older or just a little younger. Being nine, he says: "Tell Alan I was asking for him," and has a fly of his own invention waiting to be presented to you when you come on sick-leave. He is a little in disgrace at the moment in school, having learned for the first time that the Scots sold Charles the First to the English and having decided that he can no longer belong to such a nation. He is therefore, I understand, conducting a one-man protest strike against all things Scottish, and will learn no history, sing no song, nor memorise any geography pertaining to so deplorable a country. He announced going to bed last night that he has decided to apply for Norwegian citizenship.

Grant took his letter pad from the table and wrote in pencil:

Dearest Laura,

Would you be unbearably surprised to learn that the Princes in the Tower survived Richard III?

As ever

Alan.

P.S. I am nearly well again.

# 9

"Do you know that the Bill attainting Richard III before Parliament didn't mention the murder of the Princes in the Tower?" Grant asked the surgeon next morning.

"Really?" said the surgeon. "That's odd, isn't it?"

"Extremely odd. Can you think of an explanation?"

"Probably trying to minimise the scandal. For the sake of the family."

"He wasn't succeeded by one of his family. He was the last of his line. His successor was the first Tudor. Henry VII."

"Yes, of course. I'd forgotten. I was never any good at history. I used to use the history period to do my home algebra. They don't manage to make history very interesting in schools. Perhaps more portraits might help." He glanced up at the Richard portrait and went back to his professional inspection. "That is looking very nice and healthy, I'm glad to say. No pain to speak of now?"

And he went away, kindly and casual. He was interested in faces because they were part of his trade, but history was just something that he used for other purposes; something that he set aside in favour of algebra under the desk. He had living bodies in his care, and the future in his hands; he had no thought to spare for problems academic.

Matron, too, had more immediate worries. She listened politely while he put his difficulty to her, but he had the impression that she might say: "I should see the almoner about it if I were you." It was not her affair. She looked down from her regal eminence at the great hive below her buzzing with activity, all of it urgent and important; she could hardly be expected to focus her gaze on something more than four hundred years away.

He wanted to say: "But you of all people should be interested in what can happen to royalty; in the frailness of your reputation's worth. Tomorrow a whisper may destroy you." But he was already guiltily conscious that to hinder a Matron with irrelevances was to lengthen her already lengthy morning round without reason or excuse.

The Midget did not know what an Attainder was, and made it clear that she did not care.

"It's becoming an obsession with you, that thing," she said, leaning her head at the portrait. "It's not healthy. Why don't you read some of those nice books?"

Even Marta, to whose visit he had looked forward so that he could put this odd, new proposition to her and see her reaction, even Marta was too full of wrath with Madeleine March to pay any attention to him.

"After practically promising me that she would write it! After all our get-together and my plans for when this endless thing finally comes to an end. I had even talked to Jacques about clothes! And now she decides that she must write one of her awful little detective stories. She says she must write it while it is fresh—whatever that is."

He listened to Marta's grieving with sympathy—good plays were the scarcest commodity in the world and good playwrights worth their weight in platinum—but it was like watching something through a window. The fifteenth century was more actual to him this morning than any on-goings in Shaftesbury Avenue.

"I don't suppose it will take her long to write her detective book," he said comfortingly.

"Oh, no. She does them in six weeks or so. But now that she's off the chain how do I know that I'll ever get her on again? Tony Savilla wants her to write a Marlborough play for him, and you know what Tony is when he sets his heart on something. He'd talk the pigeons off the Admiralty Arch."

She came back to the Attainder problem, briefly, before she took her leave.

"There's sure to be some explanation, my dear," she said from the door.

Of *course* there's an explanation, he wanted to shout after her, but what is it? The thing is against all likelihood and sense. Historians say that the murder caused a great revulsion of feeling against Richard, that he was hated for the crime by the common people of England, and that was why they welcomed a stranger in his place. And yet when the tale of his wrongdoing is placed before Parliament there is no mention of the crime.

Richard was dead when that complaint was drawn up, and his followers in flight or exile; his enemies were free to bring against him any charge they could think of. And they *had not thought of that spectacular murder*.

Why?

The country was reputedly ringing with the scandal of the boys' disappearance. The very recent scandal. And when his enemies collected his alleged offences against morality and the State they had not included Richard's most spectacular piece of infamy.

Why?

Henry needed every small featherweight of advantage in the precarious newness of his accession. He was unknown to the country at large and he had no right by blood to be where he was. But he hadn't used the overwhelming advantage that Richard's published crime would have given him.

Why?

He was succeeding a man of great reputation, known personally to the people from the Marches of Wales to the Scots border, a man universally liked and admired until the disappearance of his nephews. And yet he omitted to use the one real advantage he had against Richard, the unforgivable, the abhorred thing.

Why?

Only The Amazon seemed concerned about the oddity that was engaging

his mind; and she not out of any feeling for Richard but because her conscientious soul was distressed at any possibility of mistake. The Amazon would
go all the way down the corridor and back again to tear off a page in a loose-
leaf calendar that someone had forgotten to remove. But her instinct to be
worried was less strong than her instinct to comfort.

"You don't need to worry about it," she said, soothing. "There'll be some
quite simple explanation that you haven't thought of. It'll come to you sometime when you're thinking of something else altogether. That's usually how
I remember where something I've mislaid is. I'll be putting the kettle on in
the pantry, or counting the sterile dressings as Sister doles them out, and suddenly I'll think: 'Goodness, I left it in my Burberry pocket.' Whatever the
thing was, I mean. So you don't have to worry about it."

Sergeant Williams was in the wilds of Essex helping the local constabulary
to decide who had hit an old shop-keeper over the head with a brass scale-
weight and left her dead among the shoelaces and liquorice all-sorts, so there
was no help from the Yard.

There was no help from anyone until young Carradine turned up again
three days later. Grant thought that his normal insouciance had a deeper tinge
than usual; there was almost an air of self-congratulation about him. Being
a well-brought-up child he inquired politely about Grant's physical progress,
and having been reassured on that point he pulled some notes out of the capa-
cious pocket of his coat and beamed through his horn-rims at his colleague.

"I wouldn't have the sainted More as a present," he observed pleasantly.

"You're not being offered him. There are no takers."

"He's way off the beam. Way off."

"I suspected as much. Let us have the facts. Can you begin on the day
Edward died?"

"Sure. Edward died on April the 9th 1483. In London. I mean, in Westminster; which wasn't the same thing then. The Queen and the daughters
were living there, *and* the younger boy, I think. The young Prince was doing
lessons at Ludlow Castle in charge of the Queen's brother, Lord Rivers. The
Queen's relations are very much to the fore, did you know? The place is just
lousy with Woodvilles."

"Yes, I know. Go on. Where was Richard?"

"On the Scottish border."

"What!"

"Yes, I said: on the Scottish border. Caught away off base. But does he
yell for a horse and go posting off to London? He does not."

"What did he do?"

"He arranged for a requiem mass at York, to which all the nobility of the
North were summoned, and in his presence they took an oath of loyalty to
the young Prince."

"Interesting," Grant said dryly. "What did Rivers do? The Queen's
brother?"

"On the 24th of April he set out with the Prince for London. With two thousand men and a large supply of arms."

"What did he want the arms for?"

"Don't ask me. I'm only a research worker. Dorset, the elder of the Queen's two sons by her first marriage, took over both the arsenal and the treasure in the Tower and began to fit up ships to command the Channel. And Council orders were issued *in the name of Rivers and Dorset*—'avunculus Regis' and 'frater Regis uterinus' respectively—with no mention of Richard. Which was decidedly off-colour when you remember—if you ever knew—that in his will Edward had appointed Richard guardian of the boy and Protector of the Kingdom in case of any minority. Richard alone, mind you, without a colleague."

"Yes, that is in character, at least. He must always have had complete faith in Richard. Both as a person and as an administrator. Did Richard come south with a young army too?"

"No. He came with six hundred gentlemen of the North, all in deep mourning. He arrived at Northampton on April the 29th. He had apparently expected to join up with the Ludlow crowd there; but that is report and you have only a historian's word for it. But the Ludlow procession—Rivers and the young Prince—had gone on to Stoney Stratford without waiting for him. The person who actually met him at Northampton was the Duke of Buckingham with three hundred men. Do you know Buckingham?"

"We have a nodding acquaintance. He was a friend of Edward's."

"Yes. He arrived post haste from London."

"With the news of what was going on."

"It's a fair deduction. He wouldn't bring three hundred men just to express his condolences. Anyhow a Council was held there and then—he had all the human material for a proper Council in his own train and Buckingham's, and Rivers and his three aides were arrested and sent to the North, while Richard went on with the young Prince to London. They arrived in London on the 4th of May."

"Well, that is very nice and clear. And what is clearest of all is that, considering time and distances, the sainted More's account of his writing sweet letters to the Queen to induce her to send only a small escort for the boy is nonsense."

"Bunk."

"Indeed, Richard did just what one would expect him to do. He must of course have known the provisions of Edward's will. What his actions suggest is just what one would expect them to suggest; his own sorrow and his care for the boy. A requiem mass and an oath of allegiance."

"Yes."

"Where does the break in this orthodox pattern come? I mean: in Richard's behaviour."

"Oh, not for a long time. When he arrived in London he found that the

Queen, the younger boy, the daughters, and her first-marriage son, Dorset, had all bolted into sanctuary at Westminster. But apart from that things seem to have been normal."

"Did he take the boy to the Tower?"

Carradine riffled through his notes. "I don't remember. Perhaps I didn't get that. I was only—Oh, yes, here it is. No, he took the boy to the Bishop's Palace in St. Paul's Churchyard, and he himself went to stay with his mother at Baynard's Castle. Do you know where that was? I don't."

"Yes. It was the York's town house. It stood on the bank of the river just a little way west of St. Paul's."

"Oh. Well, he stayed there until June the 5th, when his wife arrived from the North and they went to stay in a house called Crosby Place."

"It is still called Crosby Place. It has been moved to Chelsea, and the window Richard put into it may not still be there—I haven't seen it lately—but the building is there."

"It is?" Carradine said, delighted. "I'll go and see it right away. It's a very domestic tale when you think of it, isn't it? Staying with his mother until his wife gets to town, and then moving in with her. Was Crosby Place theirs, then?"

"Richard had leased it, I think. It belonged to one of the Aldermen of London. So there is no suggestion of opposition to his Protectorship, or of change of plans, when he arrived in London."

"Oh, no. He was acknowledged Protector before he ever arrived in London."

"How do you know that?"

"In the Patent Rolls he is called Protector on two occasions—let me see—April 21st (that's less than a fortnight after Edward's death) and May the 2nd (that's two days before he arrived in London at all)."

"All right; I'm sold. And no fuss? No hint of trouble?"

"Not that I can find. On the 5th of June he gave detailed orders for the boy's coronation on the 22nd. He even had letters of summons sent out to the forty squires who would be made knights of the Bath. It seems it was the custom for the King to knight them on the occasion of his coronation."

"The 5th," Grant said musingly. "And he fixed the coronation for the 22nd. He wasn't leaving himself much time for a switch-over."

"No. There's even a record of the order for the boy's coronation clothes."

"And then what?"

"Well," Carradine said, apologetic, "that's as far as I've got. Something happened at a Council—on the 8th of June, I think—but the contemporary account is in the *Mémoires* of Philippe de Comines and I haven't been able to get hold of a copy so far. But someone has promised to let me see a copy of Mandrot's 1901 printing of it tomorrow. It seems that the Bishop of Bath broke some news to the Council on June the 8th. Do you know the Bishop of Bath? His name was Stillington."

"Never heard of him."

"He was a Fellow of All Souls, whatever that is, and a Canon of York, whatever *that* may be."

"Both learned and respectable, it appears."

"Well, we'll see."

"Have you turned up any contemporary historians—other than Comines?"

"Not any, so far, who wrote before Richard's death. Comines has a French bias but not a Tudor one, so he's more trustworthy than an Englishman writing about Richard under the Tudors would be. But I've got a lovely sample for you of how history is made. I found it when I was looking up the contemporary writers. You know that one of the things they tell about Richard III is that he killed Henry VI's only son in cold blood after the battle of Tewkesbury? Well, believe it or not, that story is made up out of whole cloth. You can trace it from the very time it was first told. It's the perfect answer to people who say there's no smoke without fire. Believe me, this smoke was made by rubbing two pieces of dry stick together."

"But Richard was just a boy at the time of Tewkesbury."

"He was eighteen, I think. And a very bonny fighter by all contemporary accounts. They were the same age, Henry's son and Richard. Well, *all* the contemporary accounts, of whatever complexion, are unanimous in saying that he was killed during the battle. Then the fun begins."

Carradine fluttered through his notes impatiently.

"Goldarn it, what did I do with it? Ah. Here we are. Now. Fabyan, writing for Henry VII, says that the boy was captured and brought before Edward IV, was struck in the face by Edward with his gauntlet and immediately slain by the King's servants. Nice? But Polydore Virgil goes one better. He says that the murder was done in person by George, Duke of Clarence, Richard, Duke of Gloucester, and William, Lord Hastings. Hall adds Dorset to the murderers. But that didn't satisfy Holinshed: Holinshed reports that it was Richard, Duke of Gloucester, who struck the first blow. How do you like that? Best quality Tonypandy, isn't it?"

"Pure Tonypandy. A dramatic story with not a word of truth in it. If you can bear to listen to a few sentences of the sainted More, I'll give you another sample of how history is made."

"The sainted More makes me sick at the stomach but I'll listen."

Grant looked for the paragraph he wanted, and read:

> Some wise men also ween that his drift [that is, Richard's drift] covertly conveyed, lacked not in helping forth his brother Clarence to his death; which he resisted openly, howbeit somewhat, as men deemed, more faintly than he that were heartily minded to his weal. And they who deem thus think that he, long time in King Edward's life, forethought to be King in case that the King his brother (whose life he looked that evil diet should shorten) should happen to decease (as indeed

he did) while his children were young. And they deem that for this intent he was glad of his brother Clarence's death, whose life must needs have hindered him so intending whether the same Clarence had kept true to his nephew the young King or enterprised to be King himself. But of all this point there is no certainty, and whoso divineth upon conjectures may as well shoot too far as too short.

"The mean, burbling, insinuating old bastard," said Carradine sweetly.

"Were you clever enough to pick out the one positive statement in all that speculation?"

"Oh, yes."

"You spotted it? That was smart of you. I had to read it three times before I got the one unqualified fact."

"That Richard protested openly against his brother George being put to death."

"Yes."

"Of course, with all that 'men say' stuff," Carradine observed, "the impression that is left is just the opposite. I told you, I wouldn't have the sainted More as a present."

"I think we ought to remember that it is John Morton's account and not the sainted More's."

"The sainted More sounds better. Besides, he liked the thing well enough to be copying it out."

Grant, the one-time soldier, lay thinking of the expert handling of that very sticky situation at Northampton.

"It was neat of him to mop up Rivers' two thousand without any open clash."

"I expect they preferred the King's brother to the Queen's brother, if they were faced with it."

"Yes. And of course a fighting man has a better chance with troops than a man who writes books."

"Did Rivers write books?"

"He wrote the first book printed in England. Very cultured, he was."

"Huh. It doesn't seem to have taught him not to try conclusions with a man who was a brigadier at eighteen and general before he was twenty-five. That's one thing that has surprised me, you know."

"Richard's qualities as a soldier?"

"No, his youth. I'd always thought of him as a middle-aged grouch. He was only thirty-two when he was killed at Bosworth."

"Tell me: when Richard took over the boy's guardianship, at Stoney Stratford, did he make a clean sweep of the Ludlow crowd? I mean, was the boy separated from all the people he had been growing up with?"

"Oh, no. His tutor, Dr. Alcock, came on to London with him, for one."

"So there was no panic clearing-out of everyone who might be on the Woodville side; everyone who might influence the boy against him."

"Seems not. Just the four arrests."

"Yes. A very neat, discriminating operation altogether. I felicitate Richard Plantagenet."

"I'm positively beginning to like the guy. Well, I'm going along now to look at Crosby Place. I'm tickled pink at the thought of actually looking at a place he lived in. And tomorrow I'll have that copy of Comines, and let you know what he says about events in England in 1483, and what Robert Stillington, Bishop of Bath, told the Council in June of that year."

# 10

WHAT STILLINGTON TOLD the Council on that summer day in 1483 was, Grant learned, that he had married Edward IV to Lady Eleanor Butler, a daughter of the first Earl of Shrewsbury, before Edward married Elizabeth Woodville.

"Why had he kept it to himself so long?" he asked when he had digested the news.

"Edward had commanded him to keep it secret. Naturally."

"Edward seems to have made a habit of secret marriages," Grant said dryly.

"Well, it must have been difficult for him, you know, when he came up against unassailable virtue. There was nothing for it but marriage. And he was so used to getting his own way with women—what with his looks and his crown—that he couldn't have taken very resignedly to frustration."

"Yes. That was the pattern of the Woodville marriage. The indestructibly virtuous beauty with the gilt hair, and the secret wedding. So Edward had used the same formula on a previous occasion, if Stillington's story was true. Was it true?"

"Well, in Edward's time, it seems, he was in turn both Privy Seal and Lord Chancellor, and he had been an ambassador to Brittany. So Edward either owed him something or liked him. And he, on his part, had no reason to cook up anything against Edward. Supposing he was the cooking sort."

"No, I suppose not."

"Anyway, the thing was put to Parliament so we don't have to take just Stillington's word for it."

"To Parliament!"

"Sure. Everything was open and above board. There was a very long meeting of the Lords at Westminster on the 9th. Stillington brought in his evidence and his witnesses, and a report was prepared to put before Parliament when it assembled on the 25th. On the 10th Richard sent a letter to the city of York asking for troops to protect and support him."

"Ha! Trouble at last."

"Yes. On the 11th he sent a similar letter to his cousin Lord Nevill. So the danger was real."

"It must have been real. A man who dealt so economically with that unexpected and very nasty situation at Northampton wouldn't be one to lose his head at a threat."

"On the 20th he went with a small body of retainers to the Tower—did you know that the Tower was the royal residence in London, and not a prison at all?"

"Yes, I knew that. It got its prison meaning only because nowadays being sent to the Tower has one meaning only. And of course because, being the royal castle in London, and the only strong keep, offenders were sent there for safe keeping in the days before we had His Majesty's Prisons. What did Richard go to the Tower for?"

"He went to interrupt a meeting of the conspirators, and arrested Lord Hastings, Lord Stanley, and one John Morton, Bishop of Ely."

"I thought we would arrive at John Morton sooner or later!"

"A proclamation was issued, giving details of the plot to murder Richard, but apparently no copy now exists. Only one of the conspirators was beheaded, and that one, oddly enough, seems to have been an old friend of both Edward and Richard. Lord Hastings."

"Yes, according to the sainted More he was rushed down to the courtyard and beheaded on the nearest log."

"Rushed nothing," said Carradine disgustedly. "He was beheaded a week later. There's a contemporary letter about it that gives the date. Moreover, Richard couldn't have done it out of sheer vindictiveness, because he granted Hastings' forfeited estates to his widow, and restored the children's right of succession to them—which they had automatically lost."

"No, the death of Hastings must have been inevitable," said Grant, who was thumbing through More's *Richard III*. "Even the sainted More says: 'Undoubtedly the Protector loved him well, and was loth to have lost him.' What happened to Stanley and to John Morton?"

"Stanley was pardoned—What are you groaning about?"

"Poor Richard. That was his death warrant."

"Death warrant? How could pardoning Stanley be his death warrant?"

"Because it was Stanley's sudden decision to go over to the other side that lost Richard the battle of Bosworth."

"You don't say."

"Odd to think that if Richard had seen to it that Stanley went to the block like his much-loved Hastings, he would have won the battle of Bosworth, there would never have been any Tudors, and the hunchbacked monster that appears in Tudor tradition would never have been invented. On his previous showing he would probably have had the best and most enlightened reign in history. What was done to Morton?"

"Nothing."

"Another mistake."

"Or at least nothing to signify. He was put into gentlemanly detention under the care of Buckingham. The people who did go to the block were the heads of the conspiracy that Richard had arrested at Northampton: Rivers and Co. And Jane Shore was sentenced to do penance."

"Jane Shore? What on earth has she got to do with the case? I thought she was Edward's mistress?"

"So she was. But Hastings inherited her from Edward, it seems. Or rather—let me see—Dorset did. And she was go-between between the Hastings side of the conspiracy and the Woodville side. One of Richard's letters existing today is about her. About Jane Shore."

"What about her?"

"His Solicitor-General wanted to marry her; when he was King, I mean."

"And he agreed?"

"He agreed. It's a lovely letter. More in sorrow than in anger—with a kind of twinkle in it."

" 'Lord, what fools these mortals be!' "

"That's it exactly."

"No vindictiveness there, either, it seems."

"No. Quite the opposite. You know, I know it isn't my business to think or draw deductions—I'm just the Research Worker—but it does strike me that Richard's ambition was to put an end to the York-Lancaster fight once and for all."

"What makes you think that?"

"Well, I've been looking at his coronation lists. It was the best-attended coronation on record, incidentally. You can't help being struck by the fact that practically nobody stayed away. Lancaster *or* York."

"Including the weather-cock Stanley, I suppose."

"I suppose so. I don't know them well enough to remember them individually."

"Perhaps you're right about his wanting a final end to the York-Lancaster feud. Perhaps his lenience with Stanley was due to that very thing."

"Was Stanley a Lancastrian, then?"

"No, but he was married to an abnormally rabid one. His wife was Margaret Beaufort, and the Beauforts were the reverse side, so to speak—the illegitimate side—of the Lancaster family. Not that her by-blow side worried her. *Or* her son."

"Who was her son?"

"Henry VII."

Carradine whistled, long and low.

"You actually mean to say that Lady Stanley was Henry's mother."

"She was. By her first husband Edmund Tudor."

"But—but Lady Stanley had a place of honour at Richard's coronation. She carried the Queen's train. I noticed that because I thought it quaint. Carrying the train, I mean. In our country we don't carry trains. It's an honour, I take it."

"It's a thundering great honour. Poor Richard. Poor Richard. It didn't work."

"What didn't?"

"Magnanimity." He lay thinking about it while Carradine shuffled through his notes. "So Parliament accepted the evidence of Stillington."

"They did more. They incorporated it into an Act, giving Richard the title to the crown. It was called Titulus Regius."

"For a holy man of God, Stillington wasn't cutting a very glorious figure. But I suppose that to have talked sooner would have been to compass his own ruin."

"You're a bit hard on him, aren't you? There wasn't any need to talk sooner. No harm was being done anyone."

"What about Lady Eleanor Butler?"

"She died in a convent. She's buried in the Church of the White Carmelites at Norwich, in case you're interested. As long as Edward was alive no wrong was being done anyone. But when it came to the question of succession, then he *had* to talk, whatever kind of figure he cut."

"Yes. Of course you're right. So the children were proclaimed illegitimate, in open Parliament. And Richard was crowned. With all the nobility of England in attendance. Was the Queen still in sanctuary?"

"Yes. But she had let the younger boy join his brother."

"When was that?"

Carradine searched through his notes. "On June the 16th. I've put: 'At the request of the Archbishop of Canterbury. Both boys living at the Tower.'"

"That was after the news had broken. The news that they were illegitimate."

"Yes." He tidied his notes into some kind of neatness and put them away in the enormous pocket. "That seems to be all, to date. But here's the pay-off." He gathered his train from either side of him on to his knees with a gesture that both Marta and King Richard might have envied. "You know that Act, that Titulus Regius."

"Yes; what about it?"

"Well, when Henry VII came to the throne he ordered that the Act should be repealed, without being read. He ordered that the Act itself should be destroyed, and forbade any copies to be kept. Anyone who kept a copy was to be fined and imprisoned during his pleasure."

Grant stared in great astonishment.

*"Henry VII!"* he said. "Why? What possible difference could it make to him?"

"I haven't a glimmer of an idea. But I mean to find out before I'm much older. Meanwhile, here is something to keep you amused till the Statue of Liberty brings your British tea."

He dropped a paper on to Grant's chest.

"What is this?" Grant said, looking at the torn-out page of a note-book.

"It's that letter of Richard's about Jane Shore. I'll be seeing you."

Left alone by himself in the quiet, Grant turned over the page and read.

The contrast between the sprawling childish handwriting and the formal phrases of Richard's imagining was piquant in the extreme. But what neither the untidy modern script nor the dignified phrases could destroy was the flavour of the letter. The bouquet of good humour that came up from the page as a bouquet comes up from a good-humoured wine. Translated into modern terms it said:

> I hear to my great astonishment that Tom Lynom wants to marry Will Shore's wife. Apparently he is infatuated with her, and is quite determined about it. Do, my dear Bishop, send for him and see if you can talk some sense into his silly head. If you can't, and if there is no bar to their marriage from the Church's point of view, then I agree to it, but tell him to postpone the marriage till I am back in London. Meanwhile this will suffice to secure her release, on surety for her good behaviour, and I suggest that you hand her over for the time being to the care of her father, or anyone else who seems good to you.

It was certainly, as young Carradine had said, "more in sorrow than in anger." Indeed, considering that it was written about a woman who had done him a deadly wrong, its kindness and good temper were remarkable. And this was a case where no personal advantage could come to him from magnanimity. The broad-mindedness that had sought for a York-Lancaster peace might not have been disinterested; it would have been enormously to his advantage to have a united country to rule. But this letter to the Bishop of Lincoln was a small private matter, and the release of Jane Shore of no importance to anyone but the infatuated Tom Lynom. Richard had nothing to gain by his generosity. His instinct to see a friend happy was apparently greater than his instinct for revenge.

Indeed, his instinct for revenge seemed to be lacking to a degree that would be surprising in any red-blooded male, and quite astonishing in the case of that reputed monster Richard III.

# 11

THE LETTER LASTED Grant very nicely until The Amazon brought his tea. He listened to the twentieth-century sparrows on his window-sill and marvelled that he should be reading phrases that formed in a man's mind more than four hundred years ago. What a fantastic idea it would have seemed to Richard that anyone would be reading that short, intimate letter about Shore's wife, and wondering about him, four hundred years afterwards.

"There's a letter for you, now isn't that nice?" The Amazon said, coming in with his two pieces of bread-and-butter and a rock bun.

Grant took his eyes from the uncompromising healthiness of the rock bun and saw that the letter was from Laura.

He opened it with pleasure.

Dear Alan [said Laura]

Nothing (repeat: nothing) would surprise me about history. Scotland has large monuments to two women martyrs drowned for their faith, in spite of the fact that they weren't drowned at all and neither was a martyr anyway. They were convicted of treason—fifth column work for the projected invasion from Holland, I think. Anyhow on a purely civil charge. They were reprieved *on their own petition* by the Privy Council, and the reprieve is in the Privy Council Register to this day.

This, of course, hasn't daunted the Scottish collectors of martyrs, and the tale of their sad end, complete with heart-rending dialogue, is to be found in every Scottish bookcase. Entirely different dialogue in each collection. And the gravestone of one of the women, in Wigtown churchyard, reads:

> Murdered for owning Christ supreme
> Head of his Church, and no more crime
> But her not owning Prelacy
> And not abjuring Presbytry
> Within the sea tied to a stake
> She suffered for Christ Jesus sake.

They are even a subject for fine Presbyterian sermons, I understand—though on that point I speak from hearsay. And tourists come and shake their heads over the monuments with their moving inscriptions, and a very profitable time is had by all.

All this in spite of the fact that the original collector of the material, canvassing the Wigtown district only forty years after the supposed martyrdom and at the height of the Presbyterian triumph, complains that "many deny that this happened"; and couldn't find any eyewitnesses at all.

It is very good news that you are convalescent, and a great relief to us all. If you manage it well your sick leave can coincide with the spring run. The water is very low at the moment, but by the time you are better it should be deep enough to please both the fish and you.

Love from us all,<br>Laura.

P.S. It's an odd thing but when you tell someone the true facts of a mythical tale they are indignant not with the teller but with you. They don't *want* to have their ideas upset. It rouses some vague uneasiness in them, I think, and they resent it. So they reject it and refuse to think about it. If they were merely indifferent it would be natural and understandable. But it is much stronger than that, much more positive. They are annoyed.

Very odd, isn't it?

*More* Tonypandy, he thought.

He began to wonder just how much of the school book which up to now had represented British history for him was Tonypandy.

He went back, now that he knew a few facts, to read the sainted More again. To see how the relevant passages sounded now.

If, when he had read them merely by the light of his own critical mind, they had seemed to him curiously tattling, and in places absurd, they now read plain abominable. He was what Laura's small Pat was in the habit of calling "scunnered." And he was also puzzled.

This was Morton's account. Morton the eyewitness, the participant. Morton must have known with minute accuracy what took place between the beginning and end of June that year. And yet there was no mention of Lady Eleanor Butler; no mention of Titulus Regius. According to Morton, Richard's case had been that Edward was previously married to his mistress Elizabeth Lucy. But Elizabeth Lucy, Morton pointed out, had denied that she was ever married to the King.

Why did Morton set up a ninepin just to knock it down again?

Why the substitution of Elizabeth Lucy for Eleanor Butler?

Because he could deny with truth that Lucy was ever married to the King, but could not do the same in the case of Eleanor Butler?

Surely the presumption was that it was very important to someone or other that Richard's claim that the children were illegitimate should be shown to be untenable.

And since Morton—in the handwriting of the sainted More—was writing for Henry VII, then that someone was presumably Henry VII. The Henry VII who had destroyed Titulus Regius and forbidden anyone to keep a copy.

Something Carradine had said came back into Grant's mind.

Henry had caused the Act to be repealed *without being read*.

It was so important to Henry that the contents of the Act should not be brought to mind that he had specially provided for its unquoted destruction.

Why should it be of such importance to Henry VII?

How could it matter to *Henry* what Richard's rights were? It was not as if he could say: Richard's claim was a trumped-up one, therefore mine is good. Whatever wretched small claim Henry Tudor might have was a Lancastrian one, and the heirs of York did not enter into the matter.

Then why should it have been of such paramount importance to Henry that the contents of Titulus Regius should be forgotten?

Why hide away Eleanor Butler, and bring in in her place a mistress whom no one ever suggested was married to the King?

This problem lasted Grant very happily till just before supper; when the porter came in with a note for him.

"The front hall says that young American friend of yours left this for you," the porter said, handing him a folded sheet of paper.

"Thank you," said Grant. "What do you know about Richard the Third?"

"Is there a prize?"

"What for?"

"The quiz."

"No, just the satisfaction of intellectual curiosity. What *do* you know about Richard III?"

"He was the first multiple murderer."

"Multiple? I thought it was two nephews?"

"No, oh, no. I don't know much history but I do know that. Murdered his brother, and his cousin, and the poor old King in the Tower, and then finished off with his little nephews. A wholesale performer."

Grant considered this.

"If I told you that he never murdered anyone at all, what would you say?"

"I'd say that you're perfectly entitled to your opinion. Some people believe the earth is flat. Some people believe the world is going to end in A.D. 2000. Some people believe that it began less than five thousand years ago. You'll hear far funnier things than that at Marble Arch of a Sunday."

"So you wouldn't even entertain the idea for a moment?"

"I find it entertaining all right, but not what you might call very plausible, shall we say? But don't let me stand in your way. Try it out on a better bombing range. You take it to Marble Arch one Sunday, and I'll bet you'll find followers aplenty. Maybe start a movement."

He made a gay sketchy half-salute with his hand and went away humming to himself; secure and impervious.

So help me, Grant thought, I'm not far off it. If I get any deeper into this thing I *will* be standing on a soapbox at Marble Arch.

He unfolded the message from Carradine, and read: "You said that you wanted to know whether the other heirs to the throne survived Richard. As well as the boys, I mean. I forgot to say: would you make out a list of them for me, so that I can look them up. I think it's going to be important."

Well, if the world in general went on its humming way, brisk and uncaring, at least he had young America on his side.

He put aside the sainted More, with its Sunday-paper accounts of hysterical scenes and wild accusations, and reached for the sober student's account of history so that he might catalogue the possible rivals to Richard III in the English succession.

And as he put down More-Morton, he was reminded of something.

That hysterical scene during the Council in the Tower which was reported by More, that frantic outburst on Richard's part against the sorcery that had withered his arm, had been against Jane Shore.

The contrast between the reported scene, pointless and repellent even to a disinterested reader, and the kind, tolerant, almost casual air of the letter that Richard had actually written about her, was staggering.

So help me, he thought again, if I had to choose between the man who wrote that account and the man who wrote that letter I'd take the man who wrote the letter, whatever either of them had done besides.

The thought of Morton made him postpone his listing of the York heirs until he had found out what eventually became of John Morton. It seemed that, having used his leisure as Buckingham's guest to organise a joint Wood-ville-Lancastrian effort (in which Henry Tudor would bring ships and troops from France and Dorset and the rest of the Woodville tribe would meet him with what English malcontents they could induce to follow them), he es-caped to his old hunting ground in the Ely district, and from there to the continent. And did not come back until he came in the wake of a Henry who had won both Bosworth and a crown; being himself on the way to Canter-bury and a cardinal's hat and immortality as Morton of "Morton's Fork." Almost the only thing that any schoolboy remembered about his master Henry VII.

For the rest of the evening Grant pottered happily through the history books, collecting heirs.

There was no lack of them. Edward's five, George's boy and girl. And if these were discounted, the first through illegitimacy and the second through attainder, there was another possible: his elder sister Elizabeth's boy. Eliza-beth was Duchess of Suffolk, and her son was John de la Pole, Earl of Lincoln.

There was, too, in the family, a boy whose existence Grant had not sus-pected. It appeared that the delicate child at Middleham was not Richard's only son. He had a love-child; a boy called John. John of Gloucester. A boy of no importance in rank, but acknowledged and living in the household. It was an age when a bend sinister was accepted without grief. Indeed the Conqueror had made it fashionable. And conquerors from then on had advertised its lack of disadvantage. By way of compensation, perhaps.

Grant made himself a little *aide-mémoire*.

| EDWARD | ELIZABETH | GEORGE | RICHARD |
|---|---|---|---|
| Edward, Prince of Wales | John de la Pole, Earl of Lincoln | Edward, Earl of Warwick | John of Gloucester |
| Richard, Duke of York | | Margaret, Countess of Salisbury | |
| Elizabeth | | | |
| Cicely | | | |
| Anne | | | |
| Katherine | | | |
| Bridget | | | |

He copied it out again for young Carradine's use, wondering how it could ever have occurred to anyone, Richard most of all, that the elimination of Edward's two boys would have kept him safe from rebellion. The place was what young Carradine would call just lousy with heirs. Swarming with focuses (or was it foci?) for disaffection.

It was brought home to him for the first time not only what a useless thing the murder of the boys would have been, but what a *silly* thing.

And if there was anything that Richard of Gloucester was not, beyond a shadow of a shadow of a doubt, it was silly.

He looked up Oliphant to see what Oliphant had to say on this obvious crack in the story.

"It is strange," said Oliphant, "that Richard does not seem to have published any version of their deaths."

It was more than strange: it was incomprehensible.

If Richard had wanted to murder his brother's sons then he most certainly would have done it expertly. They would have died of a fever, and their bodies would have been exposed to the public gaze as royal bodies habitually were, so that all men would know that they were in fact departed from this life.

No one can say that a man is incapable of murder—after long years on the Embankment Grant knew that only too well—but one can be sure to within one degree of the absolute when a man is incapable of silliness.

Oliphant had no doubts about the murder, nevertheless. Richard according to Oliphant was Richard the Monster. Perhaps when an historian was covering a field as large as the Middle Ages and the Renaissance he had no time to stop and analyse detail. Oliphant accepted the sainted More, even while he paused in flight to wonder at an oddity here and there. Not seeing that the oddities ate away at the very foundations of his theory.

Having Oliphant in his hand, he went on with Oliphant. On through the triumphal progress through England after the coronation. Oxford, Gloucester,

Worcester, Warwick. No dissentient voice was recorded on that tour. Only a chorus of blessing and thanksgiving. A rejoicing that good government was to be the order of the day for a lifetime to come. That, after all, Edward's sudden death had not condemned them to years of faction and a new civil struggle over the person of his son.

And yet it was during this triumph, this unanimous acclamation, this universal hosanna, that (according to Oliphant, riding in the pocket of the sainted More) Richard sent Tyrrel back to London to make away with the boys who were doing lessons in the Tower. Between July 7th and 15th. At Warwick. In the very summer of his safety, in the heart of the York country on the border of Wales, he planned the destruction of two discredited children.

It was a highly unlikely story.

He began to wonder whether historians were possessed of minds any more commonsensical than those Great Minds he had encountered, who had been so credulous.

He must find out without delay why, if Tyrrel did that job in 1485, he wasn't brought to book until twenty years afterwards. Where had he been in the meantime?

But Richard's summer was like an April day. Full of a promise that came to nothing. In the autumn he had to face that Woodville-Lancastrian invasion which Morton had cooked up before leaving these shores himself. The Lancastrian part of the affair did Morton proud: they came with a fleet of French ships and a French army. But the Woodville side could provide nothing better than sporadic little gatherings in widely separated centres: Guildford, Salisbury, Maidstone, Newbury, Exeter, and Brecon. The English wanted no part of Henry Tudor, whom they did not know, nor any part of the Woodvilles, whom they knew only too well. Even the English weather would have none of them. And Dorset's hope of seeing his half-sister Elizabeth Queen of England as Henry Tudor's wife was washed away in Severn floods. Henry tried to land in the West, but found Devon and Cornwall up in indignant arms at the idea. He therefore sailed away to France again, to wait for a luckier day. And Dorset went to join in the growing crowd of Woodville exiles hanging round the French court.

So Morton's plan was washed away in autumn rain and English indifference, and Richard could be at peace for a little; but with the spring came a grief that nothing could wash away. The death of his son.

"The King is said to have shown signs of desperate grief; he was not such an unnatural monster as to be destitute of the feeling of a father," said the historian.

Nor of a husband, it seemed. The same marks of suffering were reported of him less than a year later, when Anne died.

And after that there was nothing but the waiting for the renewal of the invasion that had failed; the keeping of England in a state of defence, and the anxiety that that drain on the Exchequer brought him.

He had done what good he could. He had given his name to a model Parliament. He had made peace at last with Scotland and arranged a marriage between his niece and James III's son. He had tried very hard for a peace with France, but had failed. At the French court was Henry Tudor, and Henry Tudor was France's white-headed boy. It would be only a matter of time before Henry landed in England, this time with better backing.

Grant suddenly remembered Lady Stanley, that ardent Lancastrian mother of Henry. What part had Lady Stanley had in that autumn invasion that had put paid to Richard's summer?

He hunted through the solid print until he found it.

Lady Stanley had been found guilty of treasonable correspondence with her son.

But again Richard had proved too lenient for his own good, it seemed. Her estates were forfeit, but they were handed over to her husband. And so was Lady Stanley. For safe keeping. The bitter joke being that Stanley had almost certainly been as knowledgeable about the invasion as his wife.

Truly, the monster was not running according to form.

As Grant was falling asleep a voice said in his mind: "If the boys were murdered in July, and the Woodville-Lancastrian invasion took place in October, why didn't they use the murder of the children as a rallying call?"

The invasion had, of course, been planned before there was any question of murder; it was a full-dress affair of fifteen ships and five thousand mercenaries and must have taken a long time to prepare. But by the time of the rising the rumours of Richard's infamy must have been widespread if there were any rumours at all. Why had they not gone shouting his crime through England, so that the horror of it brought men flocking to their cause?

# 12

"Cool off, cool off," he said to himself when he woke next morning, "you're beginning to be partisan. That's no way to conduct an investigation."

So, by way of moral discipline, he became prosecutor.

Supposing that the Butler story was a frame-up. A story concocted with Stillington's help. Supposing that both Lords and Commons were willing to be hoodwinked in the hope of stable Government to come.

Did that bring one any nearer the murder of the two boys?

It didn't, did it?

If the story was false, the person to be got rid of was Stillington. Lady

Eleanor had died in her convent long ago, so was not there to blow Titulus Regius to pieces any time she had a mind. But Stillington could. And Stillington evidently showed no difficulty in going on living. He survived the man he had put on the throne.

The sudden jar in the proceedings, the abrupt break in the pattern of the coronation preparation, was either wonderful stage-managing or just what one would expect if the thunderclap of Stillington's confession descended on unprepared ears. Richard was—what? Eleven? Twelve?—when the Butler contract was signed and witnessed; it was unlikely that he knew anything of it.

If the Butler story was an invention to oblige Richard, then Richard must have rewarded Stillington. But there was no sign of Stillington's being obliged with a cardinal's hat, or preferment, or office.

But the surest evidence that the Butler story was true lay in Henry VII's urgent need to destroy it. If it were false, then all he had to do to discredit Richard was to bring it into the open and make Stillington eat his words. Instead he hushed it up.

At this point Grant realised with disgust that he was back on the Defence side again. He decided to give it up. He would take to Lavinia Fitch, or Rupert Rouge, or some other of the fashionable authors lying in such expensive neglect on his table, and forget Richard Plantagenet until such time as young Carradine appeared to renew the inquisition.

He put the family-tree sketch of Cicely Nevill's grandchildren into an envelope and addressed it to Carradine, and gave it to The Midget to post. Then he turned down the portrait that was leaning against the books, so that he should not be seduced by that face which Sergeant Williams had placed, without hesitation, on the bench, and reached for Silas Weekley's *The Sweat and the Furrow.* Thereafter he went from Silas's seamy wrestlings to Lavinia's tea-cups, and from Lavinia's tea-cups to Rupert's cavortings in the *coulisses,* with a growing dissatisfaction, until Brent Carradine once more turned up in his life.

Carradine regarded him anxiously and said: "You don't look so bright as last time I saw you, Mr. Grant. You not doing so well?"

"Not where Richard is concerned, I'm not," Grant said. "But I've got a new piece of Tonypandy for you."

And he handed him Laura's letter about the drowned women who were never drowned.

Carradine read it with a delight that grew on him like slow sunlight coming out, until eventually he glowed.

"My, but that's wonderful. That's very superior, first growth, dyed-in-the-wool Tonypandy, isn't it? Lovely, lovely. You didn't know about this before? And you a Scotsman?"

"I'm only a Scot once removed," Grant pointed out. "No; I knew that none of these Covenanters died 'for their Faith,' of course; but I didn't know that one of them—or rather, two of them—hadn't died at all."

"They didn't die for their Faith?" Carradine repeated, bewildered. "D'you mean that the *whole thing's* Tonypandy?"

Grant laughed. "I suppose it is," he said, surprised. "I never thought about it before. I've known so long that the 'martyrs' were no more martyrs than that thug who is going to his death for killing that old shop-keeper in Essex, that I've ceased to think about it. No one in Scotland went to his death for anything but civil crime."

"But I thought they were very holy people—the Covenanters, I mean."

"You've been looking at nineteenth-century pictures of conventicles. The reverent little gathering in the heather listening to the preacher; young rapt faces, and white hair blowing in the winds of God. The Covenanters were the exact equivalent of the I.R.A. in Ireland. A small irreconcilable minority, and as bloodthirsty a crowd as ever disgraced a Christian nation. If you went to church on Sunday instead of to a conventicle, you were liable to wake on Monday and find your barn burned or your horses hamstrung. If you were more open in your disapproval you were shot. The men who shot Archbishop Sharp in his daughter's presence, in broad daylight on a road in Fife, were the heroes of the movement. 'Men of courage and zeal for the cause of God,' according to their admiring followers. They lived safe and swaggering among their Covenanting fans in the West for years. It was a 'preacher of the gospel' who shot Bishop Honeyman in an Edinburgh street. And they shot the old parish priest of Carsphairn on his own doorstep."

"It does sound like Ireland, doesn't it?" Carradine said.

"They were actually worse than the I.R.A. because there was a fifth column element in it. They were financed from Holland, and their arms came from Holland. There was nothing forlorn about their movement, you know. They expected to take over the Government any day, and rule Scotland. All their preaching was pure sedition. The most violent incitement to crime you could imagine. No modern Government could afford to be so patient with such a menace as the Government of the time were. The Covenanters were continually being offered amnesties."

"Well, well. And I thought they were fighting for freedom to worship God their own way."

"No one ever stopped them from worshipping God any way they pleased. What they were out to do was to impose their method of church government not only on Scotland but on England, believe it or not. You should read the Covenant some day. Freedom of worship was not to be allowed to anyone according to the Covenanting creed—except the Covenanters, of course."

"And all those gravestones and monuments that tourists go to see——"

"All Tonypandy. If you ever read on a gravestone that John Whosit 'suffered death for his adherence to the Word of God and Scotland's Covenanted work of Reformation,' with a touching little verse underneath about 'dust sacrificed to tyranny,' you can be sure that the said John Whosit was found guilty before a properly constituted court, of a civil crime punishable by death and that his death had nothing whatever to do with the Word of God." He laughed a little under his breath. "It's the final irony, you know, that a group whose name was anathema to the rest of Scotland in their own time should have been elevated into the position of saints and martyrs."

"I wouldn't wonder if it wasn't onomatopoeic," Carradine said thoughtfully.

"What?"

"Like the Cat and the Rat, you know."

"What are you talking about?"

" 'Member you said, about that Cat and Rat lampoon, that rhyme, that the sound of it made it an offence?"

"Yes; made it venomous."

"Well, the word dragoon does the same thing. I take it that the dragoons were just the policemen of the time."

"Yes. Mounted infantry."

"Well, to me—and I suspect to every other person reading about it—dragoons sound dreadful. They've come to mean something that they never were."

"Yes, I see. *Force majeure* in being. Actually the Government had only a tiny handful of men to police an enormous area, so the odds were all on the Covenanters' side. In more ways than one. A dragoon (read policeman) couldn't arrest anyone without a warrant (he couldn't stable his horse without the owner's permission, if it comes to that), but there was nothing to hinder a Covenanter lying snug in the heather and picking off dragoons at his leisure. Which they did, of course. And now there's a whole literature about the poor ill-used saint in the heather with his pistol; and the dragoon who died in the course of his duty is a Monster."

"Like Richard."

"Like Richard. How have you been getting on with our own particular Tonypandy?"

"Well, I still haven't managed to find out why Henry was so anxious to hush up that Act as well as repeal it. The thing *was* hushed-up and for years it was forgotten, until the original draft turned up, just by chance, in the Tower records. It was printed in 1611. Speed printed the full text of it in his *History of Great Britain*."

"Oh. So there's no question at all about Titulus Regius. Richard succeeded as the Act says, and the sainted More's account is nonsense. There never was an Elizabeth Lucy in the matter."

"Lucy? Who's Elizabeth Lucy?"

"Oh, I forgot. You weren't on in that act. According to the sainted More, Richard claimed that Edward was married to one of his mistresses, one Elizabeth Lucy."

The disgusted look that the mention of the sainted More always caused on young Carradine's mild face made him look almost nauseated.

"That's nonsense."

"So the sainted More smugly pointed out."

"Why did they want to hide Eleanor Butler?" Carradine said, seeing the point.

"Because she really had married Edward, and the children really were illegitimate. And if the children really were illegitimate, by the way, then no one could rise in their favour and they were no danger to Richard. Have you noticed that the Woodville-Lancastrian invasion was in Henry's favour, and not in the boys'—although Dorset was their half-brother? And that was before any rumours of their non-existence could have reached him. As far as the leaders of the Dorset-Morton rebellion were concerned the boys were of no account. They were backing Henry. That way, Dorset would have a brother-in-law on the throne of England, and the Queen would be his half-sister. Which would be a nice reversal of form for a penniless fugitive."

"Yes. Yes, that's a point, all right; that about Dorset not fighting to restore his half-brother. If there had been a chance at all that England would have accepted the boy, he surely would have backed the boy. I'll tell you another interesting thing I found. The Queen and her daughters came out of sanctuary quite soon. It's your talking about her son Dorset that reminded me. She not only came out of sanctuary but settled down as if nothing had happened. Her daughters went to festivities at the Palace. And do you know what the pay-off is?"

"No."

"That was *after the Princes had been 'murdered.'* Yes, and I'll tell you something else. With her two boys done to death by their wicked uncle, she writes to her other son, in France—Dorset—and asks him to come home and make his peace with Richard, who will treat him well."

There was silence.

There were no sparrows to talk today. Only the soft sound of the rain against the window.

"No comment," Carradine said at last.

"You know," Grant said, "from the police point of view there is no case against Richard at all. And I mean that literally. It isn't that the case isn't good enough. Good enough to bring into court, I mean. There, quite literally, isn't any case against him at all."

"I'll say there isn't. Especially when I tell you that every single one of those people whose names you sent me were alive and prosperous, and *free,* when Richard was killed at Bosworth. They were not only free, they were very well cared for. Edward's children not only danced at the Palace, they had pensions. He appointed one of the crowd his heir when his own boy died."

"Which one?"

"George's boy."

"So he meant to reverse the attainder on his brother's children."

"Yes. He had protested about his being condemned, if you remember."

"According to even the sainted More, he did. So all the heirs to the throne of England were going about their business, free and unfettered, during the reign of Richard III, the Monster."

"They were more. They were part of the general scheme of things. I mean, part of the family and the general economy of the realm. I've been reading a collection of York records by a man Davies. Records of the town of York, I mean; not the family. Both young Warwick—George's son—and his cousin, young Lincoln, were members of the Council. The town addressed a letter to them. In 1485, that was. What's more, Richard knighted young Warwick at the same time as he knighted his own son, at a splendid 'do' at York." He paused a long moment, and then blurted out: "Mr. Grant, do you want to write a book about this?"

"A book!" Grant said, astonished. "God forbid. Why?"

"Because I should like to write one. It would make a much better book than the Peasants."

"Write away."

"You see, I'd like to have something to show my father. Pop thinks I'm no good because I can't take an interest in furniture, and marketing, and graphs of sales. If he could actually handle a book that I had written he might believe that I wasn't so hopeless a bet after all. In fact, I wouldn't put it past him to begin to boast about me for a change."

Grant looked at him with benevolence.

"I forgot to ask you what you thought of Crosby Place," he said.

"Oh, fine, fine. If Carradine the Third ever sees it he'll want to take it back with him and rebuild it in the Adirondacks somewhere."

"If you write that book about Richard, he most certainly will. He'll feel like a part-owner. What are you going to call it?"

"The book?"

"Yes."

"I'm going to borrow a phrase from Henry Ford, and call it *History Is the Bunk*."

"Excellent."

"However, I'll have a lot more reading to do and a lot more research, before I can start writing."

"Most assuredly you have. You haven't arrived yet at the real question."

"What is that?"

"Who *did* murder the boys."

"Yes, of course."

"If the boys were alive when Henry took over the Tower what happened to them?"

"Yes. I'll get on to that. I still want to know why it was so important to Henry to hush up the contents of Titulus Regius."

He got up to go, and then noticed the portrait that was lying on its face on the table. He reached over and restored the photograph to its original place, propping it with a concerned care against the pile of books.

"You stay there," he said to the painted Richard. "I'm going to put you back where you belong."

As he went out of the door, Grant said:

"I've just thought of a piece of history which is *not* Tonypandy."

"Yes?" said Carradine, lingering.

"The massacre of Glencoe."

"That really did happen?"

"That really did happen. And—Brent!"

Brent put his head back inside the door.

"Yes?"

"The man who gave the order for it was an ardent Covenanter."

# 13

CARRADINE HAD NOT been gone more than twenty minutes when Marta appeared, laden with flowers, books, candy, and goodwill. She found Grant deep in the fifteenth century as reported by Sir Cuthbert Oliphant. He greeted her with an absent-mindedness to which she was not accustomed.

"If your two sons had been murdered by your brother-in-law, would you take a handsome pension from him?"

"I take it that the question is rhetorical," Marta said, putting down her sheaf of flowers and looking round to see which of the already occupied vases would best suit their type.

"Honestly, I think historians are all mad. Listen to this:

The conduct of the Queen-Dowager is hard to explain; whether she feared to be taken from sanctuary by force, or whether she was merely tired of her forlorn existence at Westminster, and had resolved to be reconciled to the murder of her sons out of mere callous apathy, seems uncertain.

"Merciful Heaven!" said Marta, pausing with a delft jar in one hand and a glass cylinder in the other, and looking at him in wild surmise.

"Do you think historians really *listen* to what they are saying?"

"Who was the said Queen-Dowager?"

"Elizabeth Woodville. Edward IV's wife."

"Oh, yes. I played her once. It was a 'bit.' In a play about Warwick the Kingmaker."

"Of course I'm only a policeman," Grant said. "Perhaps I never moved in the right circles. It may be that I've met only nice people. Where would one have to go to meet a woman who became matey with the murderer of her two boys?"

"Greece, I should think," Marta said. *"Ancient* Greece."

"I can't remember a sample even there."

"Or a lunatic asylum, perhaps. Was there any sign of idiocy about Elizabeth Woodville?"

"Not that anyone ever noticed. And she was Queen for twenty years or so."

"Of course the thing is farce, I hope you see," Marta said, going on with her flower arranging. "Not tragedy at all. 'Yes, I know he did kill Edward and little Richard, but he really is a rather charming creature and it is so bad for my rheumatism living in rooms with a north light.' "

Grant laughed, and his good temper came back.

"Yes, of course. It's the height of absurdity. It belongs to Ruthless Rhymes, not to sober history. That is why historians surprise me. They seem to have no talent for the *likeliness* of any situation. They see history like a peep-show; with two-dimensional figures against a distant background."

"Perhaps when you are grubbing about with tattered records you haven't time to learn about people. I don't mean about the people in the records, but just about People. Flesh and blood. And how they react to circumstances."

"How would you play her?" Grant asked, remembering that the understanding of motive was Marta's trade.

"Play who?"

"The woman who came out of sanctuary and made friends with her children's murderer for seven hundred marks per annum and the right to go to parties at the Palace."

"I couldn't. There is no such woman outside Euripides or a delinquent's home. One could only play her as a rag. She'd make a very good burlesque, now I think of it. A take-off of poetic tragedy. The blank verse kind. I must try it sometime. For a charity matinée, or something. I hope you don't hate mimosa. It's odd, considering how long I've known you, how little I know of your likes and dislikes. Who invented the woman who became buddies with her sons' murderer?"

"No one invented her. Elizabeth Woodville did come out of sanctuary, and did accept a pension from Richard. The pension was not only granted, it was paid. Her daughters went to parties at the Palace and she wrote to her other son—her first-marriage son—to come home from France and make his peace with Richard. Oliphant's only suggestion as to the reason for this is that she was either frightened of being dragged out of sanctuary (did you ever know of anyone who was dragged out of sanctuary? The man who did that would be excommunicated—and Richard was a very good son of Holy Church) or that she was bored with sanctuary life."

"And what is your theory about so odd a proceeding?"

"The obvious explanation is that the boys were alive and well. No one at that time ever suggested otherwise."

Marta considered the sprays of mimosa. "Yes, of course. You said that there was no accusation in that Bill of Attainder. After Richard's death, I mean." Her eyes went from the mimosa to the portrait on the table and then to Grant. "You think, then, you really soberly think, as a policeman, that Richard didn't have anything to do with the boys' deaths."

"I'm quite sure that they were alive and well when Henry took over the Tower on his arrival in London. There is *nothing* that would explain his omission to make a scandal of it if the boys were missing. Can you think of anything?"

"No. No, of course not. It is quite inexplicable. I have always taken it for granted that there was a terrific scandal about it. That it would be one of the main accusations against Richard. You and my woolly lamb seem to be having a lovely time with history. When I suggested a little investigation to pass the time and stop the prickles I had no idea that I was contributing to the rewriting of history. Which reminds me, Atlanta Shergold is gunning for you."

"For me? I've never even met her."

"Nevertheless she is looking for you with a gun. She says that Brent's attitude to the B.M. has become the attitude of an addict to his drug. She can't drag him away from it. If she takes him away from it physically, he spends the time harking back to it in his mind; so that she mightn't exist as far as he is concerned. He has even stopped sitting through *To Sea in a Bowl*. Do you see much of him?"

"He was here a few minutes before you came. But I don't expect to hear from him again for some days to come."

But in that he was wrong.

Just before supper-time the porter appeared with a telegram.

Grant put his thumb under the dainty Post Office lick on the flap and extracted two sheets of telegram. The telegram was from Brent.

Hell and damnation an awful thing has happened (stop) you know that chronicle in Latin I talked about (stop) the chronicle written by the monk at Croyland Abbey (stop) well I've just seen it and the rumour is there the rumour about the boys being dead (stop) the thing is written before Richard's death so we are sunk aren't we and I specially am sunk and that fine book of mine will never be written (stop) is anyone allowed to commit suicide in your river or is it reserved for the British

Brent

Into the silence the voice of the porter said: "It's reply-paid, sir. Do you want to send an answer?"

"What? Oh. No. Not right away. I'll send it down presently."

"Very good, sir," said the porter looking respectfully at the two sheets of

telegram—in the porter's family a telegram was confined to one sheet only—
and went away, not humming this time.

Grant considered the news conveyed with such transatlantic extravagance
in the matter of telegraphic communication. He read the thing again.

"Croyland," he said, considering. Why did that ring a bell? No one had
mentioned Croyland so far in this case. Carradine had talked merely of a
monkish chronicle somewhere.

He had been too often, in his professional life, faced with a fact that apparently destroyed his whole case to be dismayed now. He reacted as he
would have reacted in a professional investigation. He took out the upsetting
small fact and looked at it. Calmly. Dispassionately. With none of poor Carradine's wild dismay.

"Croyland," he said again. Croyland was somewhere in Cambridgeshire.
Or was it Norfolk? Somewhere on the borders there, in the flat country.

The Midget came in with his supper, and propped the flat bowl-like plate
where he could eat from it with a modicum of comfort, but he was not aware
of her.

"Can you reach your pudding easily from there?" she asked. And as he
did not answer: "Mr. Grant, can you reach your pudding if I leave it on the
edge there?"

"*Ely!*" he shouted at her.

"What?"

"Ely," he said; softly, to the ceiling.

"Mr. Grant, aren't you feeling well?"

He became conscious of The Midget's well-powdered and concerned little
face as it intruded between him and the familiar cracks.

"I'm fine, fine. Better than I've ever been in my life. Wait just a moment,
there's a good girl, and send a telegram down for me. Give me my writing-
pad. I can't reach it with that mess of rice pudding in the way."

She gave him the pad and pencil, and on the reply-paid form he wrote:

Can you find me a similar rumour in France at about the same date?
                                                                    Grant

After that he ate his supper with a good appetite, and settled down to a
good night's sleep. He was floating in that delicious half-way stage on the
way to unconsciousness when he became aware that someone was leaning
over to inspect him. He opened his eyes to see who it might be, and looked
straight into the anxious yearning brown irises of The Amazon, looking larger
and more cowlike than ever in the soft lamplight. She was holding in her
hand a yellow envelope.

"I didn't quite know what to do," she said. "I didn't want to disturb you
and yet I didn't know whether it mightn't be important. A telegram, you
know. You never can tell. And if you didn't have it tonight it would mean a
whole twelve hours' delay. Nurse Ingham has gone off duty, so there was no

one to ask till Nurse Briggs comes on at ten. I hope I haven't wakened you up. But you weren't really asleep, were you?"

Grant assured her that she had done the right thing and she let out a sigh that nearly blew the portrait of Richard over. She stood by while he read the telegram, with an air of being ready to support him in any evil news that it might contain. To The Amazon all telegrams conveyed evil tidings.

The telegram was from Carradine.

It said: "You mean you want repeat want that there should be another repeat another accusation questionmark—Brent."

Grant took the reply-paid form and wrote: "Yes. Preferably in France."

Then he said to The Amazon: "You can turn out the light, I think. I'm going to sleep until seven tomorrow morning."

He fell asleep wondering how long it would be before he saw Carradine again, and what the odds were against that much desired instance of a second rumour.

But it was not so long after all until Carradine turned up again, and he turned up looking anything but suicidal. Indeed he seemed in some queer way to have broadened out. His coat seemed less of an appendage and more of a garment. He beamed at Grant.

"Mr. Grant, you're a wonder. Do they have more like you at Scotland Yard? Or do you rate special?"

Grant looked at him almost unbelieving. "Don't tell me you've turned up a French instance!"

"Didn't you want me to?"

"Yes. But I hardly dared hope for it. The odds against seemed tremendous. What form did the rumour take in France? A chronicle? A letter?"

"No. Something much more surprising. Something much more dismaying, actually. It seems that the Chancellor of France, in a speech to the States-General at Tours, spoke of the rumour. Indeed he was quite eloquent about it. In a way, his eloquence was the one scrap of comfort I could find in the situation."

"Why?"

"Well, it sounded more to my mind like a Senator being hasty about someone who had brought in a measure his own people back home wouldn't like. More like politics than State, if you know what I mean."

"You should be at the Yard, Brent. What did the Chancellor say?"

"Well, it's in French and my French isn't very good so perhaps you'd better read it for yourself."

He handed over a sheet of his childish writing and Grant read:

Regardez, je vous prie, les événements qui après la mort du roi Edouard sont arrivés dans ce pays. Contemplez ses enfants, déjà grands et braves, massacrés impunément, et la couronne transportée à l'assassin par la faveur des peuples.

" 'Ce pays,' " said Grant. "Then he was in full flood against England. He even suggests that it was with the will of the English people that the boys were 'massacred.' We are being held up as a barbarous race."

"Yes. That's what I meant. It's a Congressman scoring a point. Actually, the French Regency sent an embassy to Richard that same year—about six months later—so they had probably found that the rumour wasn't true. Richard signed a safe-conduct for their visit. He wouldn't have done that if they had been still slanging him as a murdering untouchable."

"No. Can you give me the dates of the two libels?"

"Sure. I have them here. The monk at Croyland wrote about events in the late summer of 1483. He says that there was a rumour that the boys had been put to death but no one knew how. The nasty slap in the meeting of the States-General was in January 1484."

"Perfect," said Grant.

"*Why* did you want there to have been another instance of rumour?"

"As a cross-check. Do you know where Croyland is?"

"Yes. In the Fen country."

"In the Fen country. Near Ely. And it was in the Fen country that Morton was hiding out after his escape from Buckingham's charge."

"Morton! Yes, of course."

"If Morton was the carrier, then there had to be another outbreak on the Continent, when he moved on there. Morton escaped from England in the autumn of 1483, and the rumour appears promptly in January 1484. Croyland is a very isolated place, incidentally; it would be an ideal place for a fugitive bishop to hide out till he could arrange transport abroad."

"Morton!" said Carradine again, rolling the name over on his tongue. "Wherever there's hanky-panky in this business you stub your toe against Morton."

"So you've noticed that too."

"He was the heart of that conspiracy to murder Richard before he could be crowned, he was in the back of the rebellion against Richard once he *was* crowned, and his trail to the Continent is sticky as a snail's with—with subversion."

"We-ll, the snail part is mere deduction. It wouldn't stand up in court. But there's no peradventure about his activities once he was across the channel. He settled down to a whole-time job of subversion. He and a buddy of his called Christopher Urswick worked like beavers in Henry's interest; 'sending preuie letters and cloked messengers' to England to stir up hostility to Richard."

"Yes? I don't know as much as you about what stands up in court and what won't but it seems to me that that snail's trail is a very allowable deduction—if you'll allow me. I don't suppose Morton waited till he was overseas before beginning his undermining."

"No. No, of course he didn't. It was life and death to Morton that Richard should go. Unless Richard went, John Morton's career was over. He was finished. It wasn't even that there would be no preferment for him now. There would be nothing. He would be stripped of his numerous livings and be reduced to his plain priest's frock. He, John Morton. Who had been within touching distance of an archbishopric. But if he could help Henry Tudor to a throne then he might still become not only Archbishop of Canterbury but a Cardinal besides. Oh, yes; it was desperately, overwhelmingly important to Morton that Richard should not have the governing of England."

"Well," said Brent, "he was the right man for a job of subversion. I don't suppose he knew what a scruple was. A little rumour like infanticide must have been child's play to him."

"There's always the odd chance that he believed it, of course," Grant said, his habit of weighing evidence overcoming even his dislike of Morton.

"Believed that the boys were murdered?"

"Yes. It may have been someone else's invention. After all, the country must have been swarming with Lancastrian tales, part mere ill-will, part propaganda. He may have been merely passing on the latest sample."

"Huh! I wouldn't put it past him to be paving the way for their future murder," Brent said tartly.

Grant laughed. "I wouldn't, at that," he said. "What else did you get from your monk at Croyland?"

"A little comfort, too. I found after I had written that panic wire to you that he wasn't at all to be taken as gospel. He just put down what gossip came his way from the outer world. He says, for instance, that Richard had a second coronation, at York; and that of course just isn't true. If he can be wrong about a big, known, fact like a coronation, then he's not to be trusted as a reporter. But he *did* know about Titulus Regius, by the way. He recorded the whole tenor of it, including Lady Eleanor."

"That's interesting. Even a monk at Croyland had heard who Edward was supposed to have been married to."

"Yes. The sainted More must have dreamed up Elizabeth Lucy a good deal later."

"To say nothing of the unspeakable story that Richard based his claim on his mother's shame."

"What?"

"He says that Richard caused a sermon to be preached claiming that Edward and George were his mother's sons by some other father, and that he, Richard, was the only legitimate son and therefore the only true heir."

"The sainted More might have thought up a more convincing one," young Carradine said dryly.

"Yes. Especially when Richard was living in his mother's house at the time of the libel!"

"So he was. I'd forgotten that. I don't have a proper police brain. That's very neat, what you say about Morton being the carrier of the rumour. But suppose the rumour turns up somewhere else, even yet."

"It's possible, of course. But I'm willing to lay you fifties to any amount that it won't. I don't for one moment believe that there was any general rumour that the boys were missing."

"Why not?"

"For a reason that I hold to be unanswerable. If there had been any general uneasiness, any obviously subversive rumours or action, Richard would have taken immediate steps to checkmate them. When the rumour went round, later, that he was proposing to marry his niece Elizabeth—the boys' eldest sister—he was on to it like a hawk. He not only sent letters to the various towns denying the rumour in no uncertain terms, he was so furious (and evidently thought it of such importance that he should not be traduced) that he summoned the 'heid yins' of London to the biggest hall he could find (so that he could get them all in at one time) and told them face to face what he thought about the affair."

"Yes. Of course you're right. Richard would have made a public denial of the rumour if the rumour was general. After all, it was a much more horrifying one than the one that he was going to marry his niece."

"Yes; actually you could get a dispensation to marry your niece in those days. Perhaps you still can, for all I know. That's not my department at the Yard. What is certain is that if Richard went to such length to contradict the marriage rumour then he most certainly would have gone to much greater lengths to put a stop to the murder one, if it had existed. The conclusion is inevitable: there *was* no general rumour of disappearance or foul play where the boys were concerned."

"Just a thin little trickle between the Fens and France."

"Just a thin little trickle between the Fens and France. Nothing in the picture suggests any worry about the boys. I mean: in a police investigation you look for any abnormalities in behaviour among the suspects in a crime. Why did X, who always goes to the movies on a Thursday night, decide on that night of all nights not to go? Why did Y take a return half as usual and very unusually not use it? That sort of thing. But in the short time between Richard's succession and his death everyone behaves quite normally. The boys' mother comes out of sanctuary and makes her peace with Richard. The girls resume their court life. The boys are presumably still doing the lessons that their father's death had interrupted. Their young cousins have a place on the Council and are of sufficient importance for the town of York to be addressing letters to them. It's all quite a normal, peaceful scene, with everyone going about their ordinary business, and no suggestion anywhere that a spectacular and unnecessary murder has just taken place in the family."

"It looks as if I might write that book after all, Mr. Grant."

"Most certainly you will write it. You have not only Richard to rescue from calumny; you have to clear Elizabeth Woodville of the imputation of condoning her sons' murder for seven hundred merks a year and perks."

"I can't write the book and leave it in the air like that, of course. I'll *have* to have at least a theory as to what became of the boys."

"You will."

Carradine's mild gaze came away from the small woolly clouds over the Thames and considered Grant with a question in it.

"Why that tone?" he asked. "Why are you looking like a cat with cream?"

"Well, I've been proceeding along police lines. During those empty days while I was waiting for you to turn up again."

"Police lines?"

"Yes. Who benefits, and all that. We've discovered that it wouldn't be a pin's-worth of advantage to Richard that the boys should die. So we go on looking round to see whom, in that case, it *would* benefit. And this is where Titulus Regius comes in."

"What has Titulus Regius got to do with the murder?"

"Henry VII married the boys' eldest sister. Elizabeth."

"Yes."

"By way of reconciling the Yorkists to his occupation of the throne."

"Yes."

"By repealing Titulus Regius, he made her legitimate."

"Sure."

"But by making the children legitimate he automatically made the two boys heir to the throne before her. In fact, by repealing Titulus Regius he made the elder of the two King of England."

Carradine made a little clicking sound with his tongue. His eyes behind their horn-rims were glowing with pleasure.

"So," said Grant, "I propose that we proceed with investigation along those lines."

"Sure. What do you want?"

"I want to know a lot more about that confession of Tyrrel's. But first, and most of all, I'd like to know how the people concerned acted. What happened to them; not what anyone reported of anyone. Just as we did in the case of Richard's succession after Edward's unexpected death."

"Fine. What do you want to know?"

"I want to know what became of all the York heirs that Richard left so alive and well and prosperous. Every single one of them. Can you do that for me?"

"Sure. That's elementary."

"And I could bear to know more about Tyrrel. About the man himself, I mean. Who he was, and what he had done."

"I'll do that." Carradine got up with such an on-with-the-charge air that for one moment Grant thought that he was actually going to button his coat. "Mr. Grant, I'm so grateful to you for all this—this——"

"This fun and games?"

"When you're on your feet again, I'll—I'll—I'll take you round the Tower of London."

"Make it Greenwich-and-back by boat. Our island Race have a passion for the nautical."

"How long do they reckon it will be before you're out of bed, do you know?"

"I'll probably be up before you come back with the news about the heirs and Tyrrel."

# 14

GRANT WAS NOT, as it happened, out of bed when Carradine came again, but he was sitting up.

"You can't imagine," he said to Brent, "how fascinating the opposite wall looks, after the ceiling. And how small and queer the world looks right way up."

He was touched by Carradine's obvious pleasure in this progress and it was some time before they got down to business. It was Grant who had to say: "Well, how did the York heirs make out under Henry VII?"

"Oh, yes," said the boy, pulling out his usual wad of notes and drawing up a chair by hooking his right toe in the crossbar. He sat down on the chair. "Where shall I begin?"

"Well, about Elizabeth we know. He married her, and she was Queen of England until she died and he made a bid for the mad Juana of Spain."

"Yes. She was married to Henry in the spring of 1486—in January, rather; five months after Bosworth—and she died in the spring of 1503."

"Seventeen years. Poor Elizabeth. With Henry it must have seemed like seventy. He was what is euphemistically referred to as 'unuxorious.' Let us go on down the family. Edward's children, I mean. Fate of the two boys unknown. What happened to Cicely?"

"She was married to his old uncle Lord Welles, and sent away to live in Lincolnshire. Anne and Katherine, who were children, were married when they were old enough to good Lancastrians. Bridget, the youngest, became a nun at Dartford."

"Orthodox enough, so far. Who comes next? George's boy."

"Yes. Young Warwick. Shut up for life in the Tower, and executed for allegedly planning to escape."

"So. And George's daughter? Margaret."

"She became the Countess of Salisbury. Her execution by Henry VIII on a trumped-up charge is apparently the classic sample of judicial murder."

"Elizabeth's son? The alternative heir?"

"John de la Pole. He went to live with his aunt in Burgundy until——"

"To live with Margaret, Richard's sister."

"Yes. He died in the Simnel rising. But he had a younger brother that you didn't put in that list. He was executed by Henry VIII. He had surrendered to Henry VII under a safe-conduct, so Henry, I suppose, thought that it might break his luck to ignore that. In any case he had about used up his quota. Henry VIII took no chances. He didn't stop at De la Pole. There were four more that you missed out of that list. Exeter, Surrey, Buckingham, and Montague. He got rid of the lot."

"And Richard's son? John? The bastard one."

"Henry VII granted him a pension of £20 a year, but he was the first of the lot to go."

"On what charge?"

"On having been suspected of receiving an invitation to go to Ireland."

"You're joking."

"I'm not. Ireland was the focus of loyalist rebellion. The York family were very popular in Ireland, and to get an invitation from that direction was as good as a death warrant in Henry's eyes. Though I can't think why even Henry would have bothered about young John. 'An active, well-disposed boy,' he was, by the way, according to the 'Foedera.'"

"His claim was better than Henry's," Grant said, very tart. "He was the illegitimate only son of a King. Henry was the great-grandson of an illegitimate son of a younger son of a King."

There was silence for some time.

Then Carradine, out of the silence, said: "Yes."

"Yes to what?"

"To what you are thinking."

"It does look like it, doesn't it? They're the only two who are missing from the list."

There was another silence.

"They were all judicial murders," Grant said presently. "Murders under the form of law. But you can't bring a capital charge against a pair of children."

"No," agreed Carradine, and went on watching the sparrows. "No, it would have to be done some other way. After all, they were the important ones."

"The vital ones."

"How do we start?"

"As we did with Richard's succession. Find out where everyone was in the first months of Henry's reign and what they were doing. Say the first year of his reign. There will be a break in the pattern somewhere, just as there was a break in the preparations for the boy's coronation."

"Right."

"Did you find out anything about Tyrrel? Who he was?"

"Yes. He wasn't at all what I had imagined. I'd imagined him as a sort of hanger-on; hadn't you?"

"Yes, I think I did. Wasn't he?"

"No. He was a person of importance. He was Sir James Tyrrel of Gipping. He had been on various—committees, I suppose you'd call them, for Edward IV. And he was created a Knight Banneret, whatever that is, at the siege of Berwick. And he did well for himself under Richard, though I can't find that he was at the battle of Bosworth. A lot of people came too late for the battle —did you know?—so I don't suppose that means anything particular. Anyhow, he wasn't that lackey-on-the-make person that I'd always pictured."

"That's interesting. How did he make out under Henry VII?"

"Well, that's the *really* interesting thing. For such a very good and successful servant of the York family, he seems to have fairly blossomed under Henry. Henry appointed him Constable of Guisnes. Then he was sent as ambassador to Rome. He was one of the Commissioners for negotiating the Treaty of Etaples. And Henry gave him a grant for life of the revenues of some lands in Wales, but made him exchange them for revenues of the county of Guisnes of equal value—I can't think why."

"I can," said Grant.

"You can?"

"Has it struck you that all his honours and his commissions are outside England? Even the reward of land revenues."

"Yes, so they are. What does that convey to you?"

"Nothing at the moment. Perhaps he just found Guisnes better for his bronchial catarrh. It is possible to read too much into historical transactions. Like Shakespeare's plays, they are capable of almost endless interpretations. How long did this honeymoon with Henry VII last?"

"Oh, quite a long time. Everything was just grand until 1502."

"What happened in 1502?"

"Henry heard that he had been ready to help one of the York crowd in the Tower to escape to Germany. He sent the whole garrison of Calais to besiege the castle at Guisnes. That wasn't quick enough for him, so he sent his Lord Privy Seal—know what that is?"

Grant nodded.

"Sent his Lord Privy Seal—what names you English have dreamed up for your Elks officials—to offer him safe conduct if he would come aboard a ship at Calais and confer with the Chancellor of the Exchequer."

"Don't tell me."

"I don't need to, do I? He finished up in a dungeon in the Tower. And was beheaded 'in great haste and without trial' on May 6, 1502."

"And what about his confession?"

"There wasn't one."

"What!"

"Don't look at me like that. I'm not responsible."

"But I thought he confessed to the murder of the boys."

"Yes, according to various accounts. But they are accounts of a confession, not—not a transcript, if you see what I mean."

"You mean, Henry didn't publish a confession?"

"No. His paid historian, Polydore Virgil, gave an account of how the murder was done. After Tyrrel was dead."

"But if Tyrrel confessed that he murdered the boys at Richard's instigation, why wasn't he charged with the crime and publicly tried for it?"

"I can't imagine."

"Let me get this straight. Nothing was heard of Tyrrel's confession until Tyrrel was dead."

"No."

"Tyrrel confesses that way back in 1483, nearly twenty years ago, he pelted up to London from Warwick, got the keys of the Tower from the Constable— I forget his name——"

"Brackenbury. Sir Robert Brackenbury."

"Yes. Got the keys of the Tower from Sir Robert Brackenbury for one night, murdered the boys, handed back the keys, and reported back to Richard. He confesses this, and so puts an end to what must have been a much canvassed mystery, and yet nothing public is done with him."

"Not a thing."

"I'd hate to go into court with a story like that."

"I wouldn't even consider it, myself. It's as phoney a tale as ever I heard."

"Didn't they even bring Brackenbury in to affirm or deny the story of the keys being handed over?"

"Brackenbury was killed at Bosworth."

"So he was conveniently dead too, was he?" He lay and thought about it. "You know, if Brackenbury died at Bosworth, then we have one more small piece of evidence on our side."

"How? What?"

"If that had really happened; I mean: if the keys were handed over for a night on Richard's order, then a lot of junior officials at the Tower must have been aware of it. It is quite inconceivable that one or other of them wouldn't be ready to tell the tale to Henry when he took over the Tower. Especially if the boys were missing. Brackenbury was dead. Richard was dead. The next in command at the Tower would be expected to produce the boys. When they weren't producible, he *must* have said: 'The Constable handed over the keys, one night, and since then the boys have not been seen.' There would have been the most ruthless hue and cry after the man who had been given the keys. He would have been Exhibit A in the case against Richard, and to produce him would have been a feather in Henry's cap."

"Not only that, but Tyrrel was too well known to the people at the Tower to have passed unrecognised. In the small London of that day he must have been quite a well-known figure."

"Yes. If that story were true Tyrrel would have been tried and executed for the boys' murder, openly, in 1485. He had no one to protect him." He reached for his cigarettes. "So what we're left with is that Henry executed Tyrrel in 1502, and then announced by way of his tame historians that Tyrrel had confessed that twenty years before he had murdered the Princes."

"Yes."

"And he didn't offer, anywhere, at any time, any reason for not trying Tyrrel for this atrocious thing he had confessed."

"No. Not as far as I can make out. He was sideways as a crab, you know. He never went straight at anything, even murder. It had to be covered up to look like something else. He waited years to find some sort of legal excuse that would camouflage a murder. He had a mind like a corkscrew. Do you know what his first official action as Henry VII was?"

"No."

"To execute some of the men fighting for Richard at Bosworth *on a charge of treason*. And do you know how he managed to make it legally treason? By dating his reign from the day before Bosworth. A mind that was capable of a piece of sharp practice of that calibre was capable of anything." He took the cigarette that Grant was offering him. "But he didn't get away with it," he added, with sober joy. "Oh, no, he didn't get away with it. The English, bless them, drew the line at that. They told him where he got off."

"How?"

"They presented him, in that nice polite English way, with an Act of Parliament that said that no one serving the Sovereign Lord of the land for the time being should be convicted of treason or suffer either forfeiture or imprisonment, and they made him consent to it. That's terribly English, that ruthless politeness. No yelling in the street or throwing stones because they didn't like his little bit of cheating. Just a nice polite reasonable Act for him to swallow and like it. I bet he did a slow burn about that one. Well, I must be on my way. It's sure nice to see you sitting up and taking notice. We'll be having that trip to Greenwich in no time at all, I see. What's at Greenwich?"

"Some very fine architecture and a fine stretch of muddy river."

"That all?"

"And some good pubs."

"We're going to Greenwich."

When he had gone Grant slid down in bed and smoked one cigarette after another while he considered the tale of those heirs of York who had prospered under Richard III, and gone to their graves under Henry VII.

Some of them may have "asked for it." Carradine's report had, after all, been a précis; innocent of qualification, insusceptible to half-tones. But it was surely a thundering great coincidence that *all* the lives who stood between the Tudors and the throne had been cut short so conveniently.

He looked, with no great enthusiasm, at the book that young Carradine had brought him. It was called *The Life and Reign of Richard III*, by someone James Gairdner. Carradine had assured him that he would find Dr. Gairdner well worth his while. Dr. Gairdner was, according to Brent, "a scream."

The book did not appear to Grant to be markedly hilarious, but anything about Richard was better than something about anyone else, so he began to glance through it, and presently he became aware just what Brent had meant by saying that the good doctor was "a scream." Dr. Gairdner obstinately believed Richard to be a murderer, but since he was a writer honest, learned, and according to his lights impartial, it was not in him to suppress facts. The spectacle of Dr. Gairdner trying to make his facts fit his theory was the most entertaining thing in gymnastics that Grant had witnessed for some time.

Dr. Gairdner acknowledged with no apparent sense of incongruity Richard's great wisdom, his generosity, his courage, his ability, his charm, his popularity, and the trust that he inspired even in his beaten enemies; and in the same breath reported his vile slander of his mother and his slaughter of two helpless children. Tradition says, said the worthy Doctor; and solemnly reported the horrible tradition and subscribed to it. There was nothing mean or paltry in his character, according to the Doctor—but he was a murderer of innocent children. Even his enemies had confidence in his justice—but he murdered his own nephews. His integrity was remarkable—but he killed for gain.

As a contortionist Dr. Gairdner was the original boneless wonder. More than ever Grant wondered with what part of their brains historians reasoned. It was certainly by no process of reasoning known to ordinary mortals that they arrived at their conclusions. Nowhere in life, had he met any human being remotely resembling either Dr. Gairdner's Richard or Oliphant's Elizabeth Woodville.

Perhaps there was something in Laura's theory that human nature found it difficult to give up preconceived beliefs. That there was some vague inward opposition to, and resentment of, a reversal of accepted fact. Certainly Dr. Gairdner dragged like a frightened child on the hand that was pulling him towards the inevitable.

That charming men of great integrity had committed murder in their day Grant knew only too well. But not that kind of murder and not for that kind of reason. The kind of man whom Dr. Gairdner had drawn in his *Life and Reign of Richard III* would commit murder only when his own personal life had been *bouleversé* by some earthquake. He would murder his wife for unfaithfulness suddenly discovered, perhaps. Or kill the partner whose secret speculation had ruined their firm and the future of his children. Whatever murder he committed would be the result of acute emotion, it would never be planned; and it would never be a base murder.

One could not say: Because Richard possessed this quality and that, therefore he was incapable of murder. But one could say: Because Richard possessed these qualities, therefore he is incapable of this murder.

It would have been a silly murder, that murder of the boy Princes; and Richard was a remarkably able man. It was base beyond description; and he was a man of great integrity. It was callous; and he was noted for his warm-heartedness.

One could go through the catalogue of his acknowledged virtues, and find that each of them, individually, made his part in the murder unlikely in the extreme. Taken together they amounted to a wall of impossibility that towered into fantasy.

# 15

"THERE WAS ONE person you forgot to ask for," Carradine said, breezing in, very gay, some days later. "In your list of kind inquiries."

"Hullo. Who was that?"

"Stillington."

"Of course! The worthy Bishop of Bath. If Henry hated Titulus Regius, as a witness of Richard's integrity and his own wife's illegitimacy, he must still more have disliked the presence of its instigator. What happened to old Stillington? Judicial murder?"

"Apparently the old boy wouldn't play."

"Wouldn't play what?"

"Henry's pet game. Out goes he. Either he was a wily old bird, or he was too innocent to see the snare at all. It's my belief—if a mere Research Worker is entitled to a belief—that he was so innocent that no agent provocateur could provoke him to anything. Not anything that could be made a capital charge, anyhow."

"Are you telling me that he defeated Henry?"

"No. Oh, no. No one ever defeated Henry. Henry put him on a charge and conveniently forgot to release him. And never home came he. Who was that? Mary on the sands of Dee?"

"You're very bright this morning, not to say exhilarated."

"Don't say it in that suspicious tone. They're not open yet. This effervescence that you observe in me is intellectual carbonisation. Spiritual rejoicing. An entirely cerebral scintillation."

"Well? Sit down and cough up. What is so good? I take it that something is?"

"Good is hardly the proper word. It's beautiful, perfectly-holy beautiful."

"I think you *have* been drinking."

"I couldn't drink this morning if I tried. I'm bung full, full up to the gullet's edge, with satisfaction."

"I take it you found that break in the pattern we were looking for."

"Yes, I found it, but it was later than we had thought. Later in time, I mean. Further on. In the first months everyone did what you would expect them to do. Henry took over—not a word about the boys—and cleaned up, got married to the boys' sister. Got his own attainder reversed by a parliament of his own attainted followers—no mention of the boys—and got an act of attainder through against Richard and his loyal subjects whose service was so neatly made treason by that one day's ante-dating. That brought a fine heap of forfeited estates into the kitty in one go. The Croyland monk was terribly scandalised, by the way, at Henry's sharp practice in the matter of treason. 'O God,' he says, 'what security are our kings to have henceforth in the day of battle if their loyal followers may in defeat be deprived of life, fortune, and inheritance?' "

"He reckoned without his countrymen."

"Yes. He might have known that the English would get round to that matter sooner or later. Perhaps he was an alien. Anyhow, everything went on just as you would expect things to go with Henry in charge. He succeeded in August of 1485, and married Elizabeth in the following January. Elizabeth had her first child at Winchester, and her mother was there with her and was present at the baptism. That was in September 1486. Then she came back to London—the Queen Dowager, I mean—in the autumn. And in February—hold on to everything—in February she was shut up in a convent for the rest of her life."

"*Elizabeth Woodville?*" Grant said, in the greatest astonishment. This was the very last thing he had expected.

"Yes. Elizabeth Woodville. The boys' mother."

"How do you know that she didn't go voluntarily?" Grant asked, when he had thought of it for a little. "It was not an uncommon thing for great ladies who were tired of court life to retire into an Order. It was not a severe existence, you know. Indeed, I have an idea it was fairly comfortable for rich women."

"Henry stripped her of everything she owned, and ordered her into the nunnery at Bermondsey. And that, by the way, *did* create a sensation. There was 'much wondering,' it appears."

"I'm not surprised. What an extraordinary thing. Did he give a reason?"

"Yes."

"What did he say he was ruining her for?"

"For being nice to Richard."

"Are you serious?"

"Sure."

"Is that the official wording?"

"No. That's the version of Henry's pet historian."

"Virgil?"

"Yes. The actual order of council that shut her up said it was 'for various considerations.' "

"Are you quoting?" asked Grant, incredulous.

"I'm quoting. That's what it said: 'For various considerations.' "

After a moment Grant said: "He had no talent for excuses, had he? In his place I would have thought up six better ones."

"Either he couldn't be bothered or he thought other people very credulous. Mark you, her niceness to Richard didn't worry him until eighteen months after he succeeded Richard. Up till then everything had apparently been smooth as milk. He had even given her presents, manors and what not, when he succeeded Richard."

"What was his real reason? Have you any suggestion?"

"Well, I've another little item that may give you ideas. It certainly gave me one hell of a big idea."

"Go on."

"In June of that year——"

"Which year?"

"The first year of Elizabeth's marriage. 1486. The year when she was married in January and had Prince Arthur at Winchester in September, with her mother dancing attendance."

"All right. Yes."

"In June of that year, Sir James Tyrrel received a general pardon. On the 16th June."

"But that means very little, you know. It was quite a usual thing. At the end of a period of service. Or on setting out on a new one. It merely meant that you were quit of anything that anyone might think of raking up against you afterwards."

"Yes, I know. I know that. The first pardon isn't the surprising one."

"The *first* pardon? Was there a second one?"

"Yes. That's the pay-off. There was a second general pardon to Sir James exactly a month later. To be exact on the 16th July, 1486."

"Yes," Grant said, thinking it over. "That really is extraordinary."

"It's highly unusual, anyway. I asked an old boy who works next to me at the B.M.—he does historical research and he's been a wonderful help to me I don't mind telling you—and he said he had never come across another instance. I showed him the two entries—in the *Memorials of Henry VII*—and he mooned over them like a lover."

Grant said, considering: "On the 16th June, Tyrrel is given a general pardon. On the 16th July he is given a second general pardon. In November or thereabouts the boys' mother comes back to town. And in February she is immured for life."

"Suggestive?"

"Very."

"You think he did it? Tyrrel."

"It could be. It's very suggestive, isn't it, that when we find the break in the normal pattern that we've been looking for, Tyrrel is there, on the spot, with a most unconscionable break in his own pattern. When did the rumour that the boys were missing first become general? I mean, something to be talked openly about."

"Quite early in Henry's reign, it would seem."

"Yes; it fits. It would certainly explain the thing that has puzzled us from the beginning in this affair."

"What do you mean?"

"It would explain why there was no fuss when the boys disappeared. It's always been a puzzling thing, even to people who thought that Richard did it. Indeed, when you come to think of it it would be impossible for Richard to get away with it. There was a large, and very active, and very powerful opposition party in Richard's day, and he left them all free and scattered up and down the country to carry on as they liked. He had all the Woodville-Lancaster crowd to deal with if the boys had gone missing. But where interference or undue curiosity was concerned Henry was sitting pretty. Henry had got *his* opposition party safely in jail. The only possible danger was his mother-in-law, and at the very moment when she becomes capable of being a prying nuisance she too is put under hatches and battened down."

"Yes. Wouldn't you think that there was *something* she could have done? When she found that she was being prevented from getting news of the boys."

"She may never have known that they were missing. He may just have said: 'It is my wish that you should not see them. I think you are a bad influence on them: you who came out of sanctuary and let your daughters go to that man's parties!' "

"Yes, that's so, of course. He didn't have to wait until she actually became suspicious. The whole thing might have been one move. 'You're a bad woman, and a bad mother; I am sending you into a convent to save your soul and your children from the contamination of your presence.' "

"Yes. And where the rest of England were concerned, he was as safe as any murderer ever could be. After his happy thought about the 'treason' accusation, no one was going to stick his neck out by inquiring particularly about the boys' health. Everyone must have been walking on eggs as it was. No one knowing what Henry might think of next to make into a retrospective offence that would send their lives into limbo and their estates into Henry's kitty. No, it was no time to be overcurious about anything that didn't directly concern oneself. Not that it would be easy, in any case, to satisfy one's curiosity."

"With the boys living at the Tower, you mean."

"With the boys living in a Tower officialled by Henry's men. There was none of Richard's get-together live-and-let-live attitude about Henry. No York-Lancaster alliance for Henry. The people at the Tower would be Henry's men."

"Yes. Of course they would. Did you know that Henry was the first English King to have a bodyguard? I wonder what he told his wife about her brothers."

"Yes. That would be interesting to know. He may even have told her the truth."

"*Henry!* Never! It would cost Henry a spiritual struggle, Mr. Grant, to acknowledge that two and two were four. I tell you, he was a crab; he never went straight at anything."

"If he were sadist he could tell her with impunity, you know. There was practically nothing she could do about it. Even if she wanted to. She mightn't have wanted to all that much. She had just produced an heir to the throne of England and was getting ready to produce another. She might not have the spare interest for a crusade; especially a crusade that would knock the ground from under her own feet."

"He wasn't a sadist, Henry," young Carradine said sadly. Sad at having to grant Henry even a negative virtue. "In a way he was just the opposite. He didn't enjoy murder at all. He had to pretty it up before he could bear the thought of it. Dress it up in legal ribbons. If you think that Henry got a kick out of boasting to Elizabeth in bed about what he had done with her brothers, I think you're wrong."

"Yes, probably," Grant said. And lay thinking about Henry. "I've just thought of the right adjective for Henry," he said presently. "Shabby. He was a shabby creature."

"Yes. Even his hair was thin and scanty."

"I didn't mean it physically."

"I know you didn't."

"Everything that he did was shabby. Come to think of it, 'Morton's Fork' is the shabbiest piece of revenue-raising in history. But it wasn't only his greed for money. Everything about him is shabby, isn't it?"

"Yes. Dr. Gairdner wouldn't have any trouble in making *his* actions fit his character. How did you get on with the Doctor?"

"A fascinating study. But for the grace of God I think the worthy Doctor might have made a living as a criminal."

"Because he cheated?"

"Because he didn't cheat. He was as honest as the day. He just couldn't reason from B to C."

"All right, I'll buy."

"Everyone can reason from A to B—even a child. And most adults can reason from B to C. But a lot can't. Most criminals can't. You may not believe it—I know it's an awful come-down from the popular conception of the criminal as a dashing and cute character—but the criminal mind is an essentially silly one. You can't imagine how silly sometimes. You'd have to experience it to believe their lack of reasoning powers. They arrive at B, but they're quite incapable of making the jump to C. They'll lay two completely incompatible things side by side and contemplate them with the most unquestioning content. You can't make them see that they can't have both, any more than you can make a man of no taste see that bits of plywood nailed on to a gable to simulate Tudor beams are impossible. Have you started your own book?"

"Well—I've made a sort of tentative beginning. I know the way I *want* to write it. I mean the form. I hope you won't mind."

"Why should I mind?"

"I want to write it the way it happened. You know; about my coming to see you, and our starting the Richard thing quite casually and not knowing what we were getting into, and how we stuck to things that actually happened and not what someone reported afterwards about it, and how we looked for the break in the normal pattern that would indicate where the mischief was, like bubbles coming up from a diver way below, and that sort of thing."

"I think it's a grand idea."

"You do?"

"I do indeed."

"Well, that's fine, then. I'll get on with it. I'm going to do some research on Henry, just as garnish. I'd like to be able to put their actual records side by side, you see. So that people can compare them for themselves. Did you know that Henry invented the Star Chamber?"

"Was it Henry? I'd forgotten that. Morton's Fork and the Star Chamber. The classic sample of sharp practice, and the classic sample of tyranny. You're not going to have any difficulty in differentiating the rival portraits, are you? Morton's Fork and the Star Chamber make a nice contrast to the granting of the right to bail, and the prevention of the intimidation of juries."

"Was that Richard's Parliament? Golly, what a lot of reading I have to do. Atlanta's not speaking to me. She hates your marrow. She says I'm about as much use to a girl as last year's *Vogue*. But honestly, Mr. Grant, this is the first time in my life that anything exciting has happened to me. Important, I mean. Not exciting meaning exciting. Atlanta's exciting. She's all the excitement I ever want. But neither of us is important, the way I mean important—if you can understand what I mean."

"Yes, I understand. You've found something worth doing."

"That's it. I've found something worth doing. And it's me that's doing it; that's what's wonderful about it. Me. Mrs. Carradine's little boy. I come over here with Atlanta, with no idea about anything but using that research gag as an alibi. I walked into the B.M. to get me some dope to keep Pop quiet, and I walk out with a mission. Doesn't that shake you!" He eyed Grant in a considering way. "You're quite sure, Mr. Grant, that you don't want to write this book yourself? After all, it's quite a thing to do."

"I shall *never* write a book," Grant said firmly. "Not even *My Twenty Years at the Yard*."

"What! Not even your autobiography?"

"Not even my autobiography. It is my considered opinion that far too many books are written as it is."

"But this is one that must be written," Carradine said, looking slightly hurt.

"Of course it is. This one must be written. Tell me: there's something I forgot to ask you. How soon after that double pardon did Tyrrel get that appointment in France? How soon after his supposed service to Henry in July 1486 did he become Constable of the Castle of Guisnes?"

Carradine stopped looking hurt and looked as malicious as it was possible for his kind woolly-lamb face to look.

"I was wondering when you were going to ask that," he said. "I was going to throw it at you on my way out if you forgot to ask. The answer is: almost right away."

"So. Another appropriate little pebble in the mosaic. I wonder whether the constableship just happened to be vacant, or whether it was a French appointment because Henry wanted him out of England."

"I bet it was the other way about, and it was Tyrrel who wanted to get out of England. If I were being ruled by Henry VII, I'd sure prefer to be ruled by remote control. Especially if I had done a secret job for Henry that might make it convenient for Henry if I didn't live to too venerable an age."

"Yes, perhaps you're right. He didn't only go abroad, he stayed abroad—as we have already observed. Interesting."

"He wasn't the only one who stayed abroad. John Dighton did too. I couldn't find out who all the people who were supposed to be involved in the murder actually were. All the Tudor accounts are different, I suppose you know. Indeed most of them are so different that they contradict each other flat. Henry's pet historian, Polydore Virgil, says the deed was done when Richard was at York. According to the sainted More it was during an earlier trip altogether, when Richard was at Warwick. And the personnel changes with each account. So that it's difficult to sort them out. I don't know who Will Slater was—Black Will to you, and another piece of onomatopoesis—or Miles Forest. But there *was* a John Dighton. Grafton says he lived for long at Calais 'no less disdained than pointed at' and died there in great misery. How they relished a good moral, didn't they? The Victorians had nothing on them."

"If Dighton was destitute it doesn't look as if he had done any job for Henry. What was he by trade?"

"Well, if it's the same John Dighton, he was a priest, and he was anything but destitute. He was living very comfortably on the proceeds of a sinecure. Henry gave a John Dighton the living of Fulbeck, near Grantham—that's in Lincolnshire—on the 2nd of May, 1487."

"Well, well," Grant said, drawling. "1487. And he, too, lives abroad and in comfort."

"Uh-huh. Lovely, isn't it?"

"It's beautiful. And does anyone explain how the much-pointed-at Dighton wasn't haled home by the scruff of his neck to hang for regicide?"

"Oh, no. Nothing like that. Tudor historians didn't any of them think from B to C."

Grant laughed. "I see you're being educated."

"Sure. I'm not only learning history. I'm sitting at the feet of Scotland Yard on the subject of the human mind. Well, that will be about all for now. If you feel strong enough I'll read you the first two chapters of the book next time I come." He paused and said: "Would you mind, Mr. Grant, if I dedicated it to you?"

"I think you had better dedicate it to Carradine the Third," Grant said lightly.

But Carradine apparently did not feel it to be a light matter.

"I don't use soft soap as a dedication," he said, with a hint of stiffness.

"Oh, not soft soap," Grant said in haste. "A matter of policy merely."

"I'd never have started on this thing if it hadn't been for you, Mr. Grant," Carradine said, standing in the middle of the floor all formal and emotional and American and surrounded by the sweeping folds of his topcoat, "and I should like to make due acknowledgement of my indebtedness."

"I should be delighted, of course," murmured Grant, and the royal figure in the middle of the floor relaxed to boyhood again and the awkward moment was over. Carradine went away joyous and light-footed as he had come, looking thirty pounds heavier and twelve inches more round the chest than he had done three weeks ago.

And Grant took out the new knowledge that had been given him, hung it on the opposite wall, and stared at it.

# 16

SHE HAD BEEN SHUT away from the world; that indestructibly virtuous beauty with the gilt hair.

Why gilt, he wondered for the first time. Silver-gilt probably; she had been radiantly fair. A pity that the word blonde had degenerated to the point where it had almost a secondary meaning.

She had been walled up to end her days where she could be no trouble to anyone. An eddy of trouble had moved with her all through her life. Her marriage to Edward had rocked England. She had been the passive means of Warwick's ruin. Her kindnesses to her family had built a whole new party in England and had prevented Richard's peaceful succession. Bosworth was implicit in that scanty little ceremony in the wilds of Northamptonshire when she became Edward's wife. But no one seemed to have borne her malice. Even the sinned-against Richard had forgiven her her relations' enormities. No one—until Henry came.

She had disappeared into obscurity. Elizabeth Woodville. The Queen Dowager who was mother of the Queen of England. The mother of the Princes in the Tower; who had lived free and prosperous under Richard III.

That was an ugly break in the pattern, wasn't it?

He took his mind away from personal histories and began to think police-fashion. It was time he tidied up his case. Put it shipshape for presenting. It would help the boy with his book, and better still it would clear his own mind. It would be down in black and white where he could see it.

He reached for his writing-pad and pen, and made a neat entry:

*CASE:* Disappearance of two boys (Edward, Prince of Wales; Richard, Duke of York) from the Tower of London, 1485 or thereabouts.

He wondered whether it would be better to do the two suspects in parallel columns or successively. Perhaps it was better to finish with Richard first. So he made another neat headline; and began on his summing-up:

## RICHARD III

*Previous Record:*

Good. Has excellent record in public service, and good reputation in private life. Salient characteristic as indicated by his actions: good sense.

*In the matter of the presumed crime:*

(*a*) He did not stand to benefit; there were nine other heirs to the house of York, including three males.

(*b*) There is no contemporary accusation.

(*c*) The boys' mother continued on friendly terms with him until his death, and her daughters attended Palace festivities.

(*d*) He showed no fear of the other heirs of York, providing generously for their upkeep and granting all of them their royal state.

(*e*) His own right to the crown was unassailable, approved by Act of Parliament and public acclamation; the boys were out of the succession and of no danger to him.

(*f*) If he had been nervous about disaffection then the person to have got rid of was not the two boys, but the person who really was next in succession to him: young Warwick. Whom he publicly created his heir when his own son died.

## HENRY VII

*Previous Record:*

An adventurer, living at foreign courts. Son of an ambitious mother. Nothing known against his private life. No public office or employment. Salient characteristic as indicated by his actions: subtlety.

*In the matter of the presumed crime:*

(*a*) It was of great importance to him that the boys should not continue to live. By repealing the Act acknowledging the children's illegitimacy, he made the elder boy King of England, and the youngest boy the next heir.

(*b*) In the Act which he brought before Parliament for the attainting of Richard he accused Richard of the conventional tyranny and cruelty but made no mention of the two young Princes. The conclusion is inevitable that at that time the two boys were alive and their whereabouts known.

(*c*) The boys' mother was deprived of her living and consigned to a nunnery eighteen months after his succession.

(*d*) He took immediate steps to secure the persons of all the other heirs to the crown, and kept them in close arrest until he could with the minimum of scandal get rid of them.

(*e*) He had no right whatever to the throne. Since the death of Richard, young Warwick was *de jure* King of England.

It occurred to Grant for the first time, as he wrote it out, that it had been within Richard's power to legitimise his bastard son John, and foist him on the nation. There was no lack of precedent for such a course. After all, the whole Beaufort clan (including Henry's mother) were the descendants not only of an illegitimate union but of a double adultery. There was nothing to hinder Richard from legitimising that "active and well-disposed" boy who lived in recognised state in his household. It was surely the measure of Richard that no such course had apparently crossed his mind. He had appointed as his heir his brother's boy. Even in the destitution of his own grief, good sense was his ruling characteristic. Good sense and family feeling. No base-born son, however active and well-disposed, was going to sit in the Plantagenets' seat while his brother's son was there to occupy it.

It was remarkable how that atmosphere of family feeling permeated the whole story. All the way from Cicely's journeyings about in her husband's company to her son's free acknowledgement of his brother George's boy as his heir.

And it occurred to him too for the first time in full force just how that family atmosphere strengthened the case for Richard's innocence. The boys whom he was supposed to have put down as he would put down twin foals were Edward's sons; children he must have known personally and well. To Henry, on the other hand, they were mere symbols. Obstacles on a path. He may never even have set eyes on them. All questions of character apart, the choice between the two men as suspects might almost be decided on that alone.

It was wonderfully clearing to the head to see it neat and tidy as (*a*), (*b*), and (*c*). He had not noticed before how doubly suspect was Henry's behaviour over Titulus Regius. If, as Henry had insisted, Richard's claim was absurd, then surely the obvious thing to do was to have the thing reread in public and demonstrate its falsity. But he did no such thing. He went to endless pains to obliterate even the memory of it. The conclusion was inevitable that Richard's title to the crown as shown in Titulus Regius was unassailable.

# 17

ON THE AFTERNOON when Carradine reappeared in the room at the hospital Grant had walked to the window and back again, and was so cock-a-hoop about it that The Midget was moved to remind him that it was a thing that a child of eighteen months could do. But nothing could subdue Grant today.

"Thought you'd have me here for months, didn't you?" he crowed.

"We are very glad to see you better so quickly," she said primly; and added: "We are, of course, very glad, too, to have your bed."

And she clicked away down the corridor, all blond curls and starch.

Grant lay on his bed and looked at his little prison room with something approaching benevolence. Neither a man who has stood at the Pole nor a man who has stood on Everest has anything on a man who has stood at a window after weeks of being merely twelve stones of destitution. Or so Grant felt.

Tomorrow he was going home. Going home to be cosseted by Mrs. Tinker. He would have to spend half of each day in bed and he would be able to walk only with the aid of sticks, but he would be his own man again. At the bidding of no one. In tutelage to no half-pint piece of efficiency, yearned over by no lump of out-sized benevolence.

It was a glorious prospect.

He had already unloaded his hallelujahs all over Sergeant Williams, who had looked in on the completion of his chore in Essex, and he was now yearning for Marta to drop in so that he could peacock in front of her in his new-found manhood.

"How did you get on with the history books?" Williams had asked.

"Couldn't be better. I've proved them all wrong."

Williams had grinned. "I expect there's a law against that," he said. "MI 5 won't like it. Treason or lèse-majesté or something like that it might turn out to be. You never know nowadays. I'd be careful if I was you."

"I'll never again believe anything I read in a history book, as long as I live, so help me."

"You'll have to make exceptions," Williams pointed out with Williams' dogged reasonableness. "Queen Victoria was true, and I suppose Julius Caesar did invade Britain. And there's 1066."

"I'm beginning to have the gravest doubts about 1066. I see you've tied up the Essex job. What is Chummy like?"

"A thorough little bastard. Been treated soft all his life since he started stealing change from his Ma at the age of nine. A good belting at the age of twelve might have saved his life. Now he'll hang before the almond blossom's out. It's going to be an early spring. I've been working every evening in the garden this last few days, now that the days are drawing out. You'll be glad to sniff fresh air again."

And he had gone away, rosy and sane and balanced, as befitted a man who was belted for his good in his youth.

So Grant was longing for some other visitor from the outside world that he was so soon to be a part of again, and he was delighted when the familiar tentative tap came on his door.

"Come in, Brent!" he called, joyfully.

And Brent came in.

But it was not the Brent who had last gone out.

Gone was the jubilation. Gone was his newly acquired breadth.

He was no longer Carradine the pioneer, the blazer of trails.

He was just a thin boy in a very long, very large overcoat. He looked young, and shocked, and bereaved.

Grant watched him in dismay as he crossed the room with his listless unco-ordinated walk. There was no bundle of paper sticking out of his mail-sack of a pocket today.

Oh, well, thought Grant philosophically; it had been fun while it lasted. There was bound to be a snag somewhere. One couldn't do serious research in that lighthearted amateur way and hope to prove anything by it. One wouldn't expect an amateur to walk into the Yard and solve a case that had defeated the pros; so why should he have thought himself smarter than the historians. He had wanted to prove to himself that he was right in his face-reading of the portrait; he had wanted to blot out the shame of having put a criminal on the bench instead of in the dock. But he would have to accept his mistake, and like it. Perhaps he had asked for it. Perhaps, in his heart of hearts, he had been growing a little pleased with himself about his eye for faces.

"Hullo, Mr. Grant."

"Hullo, Brent."

Actually it was worse for the boy. He was at the age when he expected miracles to happen. He was still at the age when he was surprised that a balloon should burst.

"You look saddish," he said cheerfully to the boy. "Something came unstuck?"

"Everything."

Carradine sat down on the chair and stared at the window.

"Don't these damned sparrows get you down?" he asked, fretfully.

"What is it? Have you discovered that there was a general rumour about the boys before Richard's death, after all?"

"Oh, much worse than that."

"Oh. Something in print? A letter?"

"No, it isn't that sort of thing at all. It's something much worse. Something quite—quite fundamental. I don't know how to tell you." He glowered at the quarrelling sparrows. "These damned birds. I'll never write that book now, Mr. Grant."

"Why not, Brent?"

"Because it isn't news to anyone. Everyone has known all about those things all along."

"Known? About what?"

"About Richard not having killed the boys at all, and all that."

"They've *known*? Since when!"

"Oh, hundreds and hundreds of years."

"Pull yourself together, chum. It's only four hundred years altogether since the thing happened."

"I know. But it doesn't make any difference. People have known about Richard's not doing it for hundreds and hundreds——"

"Will you stop that keening and talk sense. When did this—this rehabilitation first begin?"

"Begin? Oh, at the first available moment."

"When was that?"

"As soon as the Tudors were gone and it was safe to talk."

"In Stuart times, you mean?"

"Yes, I suppose—yes. A man Buck wrote a vindication in the seventeenth century. And Horace Walpole in the eighteenth. And someone called Markham in the nineteenth."

"And who in the twentieth?"

"No one that I know of."

"Then what's wrong with your doing it?"

"But it won't be the same, don't you see? It won't be a great discovery!" He said it in capitals. A Great Discovery.

Grant smiled at him. "Oh, come! You can't expect to pick Great Discoveries off bushes. If you can't be a pioneer what's wrong with leading a crusade?"

"A crusade?"

"Certainly."

"Against what?"

"Tonypandy."

The boy's face lost its blankness. It looked suddenly amused, like someone who has just seen a joke.

"It's the damnedest silliest name, isn't it!" he remarked.

"If people have been pointing out for three hundred and fifty years that

Richard didn't murder his nephews and a school book can still say, in words of one syllable and without qualification, that he did, then it seems to me that Tonypandy has a long lead on you. It's time you got busy."

"But what can *I* do when people like Walpole and those have failed?"

"There's that old saying about constant water and its effect on stone."

"Mr. Grant, right now I feel an awfully feeble little trickle."

"You look it, I must say. I've never seen such self-pity. That's no mood to start bucking the British public in. You'll be giving enough weight away as it is."

"Because I've not written a book before, you mean?"

"No, that doesn't matter at all. Most people's first books are their best anyway; it's the one they wanted most to write. No, I meant that all the people who've never read a history book since they left school will feel themselves qualified to pontificate about what you've written. They'll accuse you of whitewashing Richard: 'whitewashing' has a derogatory sound that 'rehabilitation' hasn't, so they'll call it whitewashing. A few will look up the *Britannica,* and feel themselves competent to go a little further in the matter. These will slay you instead of flaying you. And the serious historians won't even bother to notice you."

"By God, I'll make them notice me!" Carradine said.

"Come! That sounds a little more like the spirit that won the Empire."

"We haven't got an Empire," Carradine reminded him.

"Oh, yes, you have," Grant said equably. "The only difference between ours and yours is that you acquired yours, economically, in the one latitude, while we got ours in bits all over the world. Had you written any of the book before the awful knowledge of its unoriginality hit you?"

"Yes, I'd done two chapters."

"What have you done with them? You haven't thrown them away, have you?"

"No. I nearly did. I nearly threw them in the fire."

"What stopped you?"

"It was an electric fire." Carradine stretched out his long legs in a relaxing movement and began to laugh. "Brother, I feel better already. I can't wait to land the British public one in the kisser with a few home truths. Carradine the First is just raging in my blood."

"A very virulent fever, it sounds."

"He was the most ruthless old blackguard that ever felled timber. He started as a logger and ended up with a Renaissance castle, two yachts, and a private car. Railroad car, you know. It had green silk curtains with bobbles on them and inlay woodwork that had to be seen to be believed. It has been popularly supposed, not least by Carradine the Third, that the Carradine blood was growing thin. But right now I'm all Carradine the First. I know just how the old boy felt when he wanted to buy a particular forest and someone said that he couldn't have it. Brother, I'm going to town."

"That's nice," Grant said, mildly. "I was looking forward to that dedication." He took his writing-pad from the table and held it out. "I've been doing a policeman's summing-up. Perhaps it may help you when you come to your peroration."

Carradine took it and looked at it with respect.

"Tear it off and take it with you. I've finished with it."

"I suppose in a week or two you'll be too busy with real investigations to care about a—an academic one," Carradine said, a little wistfully.

"I'll never enjoy one more than I've enjoyed this," Grant said, with truth. He glanced sideways at the portrait which was still propped against the books. "I was more dashed than you would believe when you came in all despondent, and I thought it had come to pieces." He looked back at the portrait and said: "Marta thinks he is a little like Lorenzo the Magnificent. Her friend James thinks it is the face of a saint. My surgeon thinks it is the face of a cripple. Sergeant Williams thinks he looks like a great judge. But I think, perhaps, Matron comes nearest the heart of the matter."

"What does she say?"

"She says it is a face full of the most dreadful suffering."

"Yes. Yes, I suppose it is. And would you wonder, after all?"

"No. No, there was little he was spared. Those last two years of his life must have happened with the suddenness and weight of an avalanche. Everything had been going along so nicely. England on an even keel at last. The civil war fading out of mind, a good firm government to keep things peaceful and a good brisk trade to keep things prosperous. It must have seemed a good outlook, looking out from Middleham across Wensleydale. And in two short years—his wife, his son, and his peace."

"I know one thing he was spared."

"What?"

"The knowledge that his name was to be a hissing and a byword down the centuries."

"Yes. That would have been the final heart-break. Do you know what I personally find *the* convincing thing in the case for Richard's innocence of any design for usurpation?"

"No. What?"

"The fact that he had to send for those troops from the North when Stillington broke his news. If he had had any fore-knowledge of what Stillington was going to say, or even any plans to concoct a story with Stillington's help, he would have brought those troops with him. If not to London then to the Home Counties where they would be handy. That he had to send urgently first to York and then to his Nevill cousins for men is proof that Stillington's confession took him entirely unawares."

"Yes. He came up with his train of gentlemen, expecting to take over the Regency. He met the news of the Woodville trouble when he came to Northampton, but that didn't rattle him. He mopped up the Woodville two thousand and went on to London as if nothing had happened. There was still nothing but an orthodox Coronation in front of him as far as he knew. It wasn't until Stillington confessed to the council that he sends for troops of his own. And he has to send all the way to the North of England at a critical moment. Yes, you're right, of course. He was taken aback." He propped the leg of his spectacles with a forefinger in the old tentative gesture, and proffered a companion piece. "Know what I find the convincing thing in the case for Henry's guilt?"

"What?"

"The mystery."

"Mystery?"

"The mysteriousness. The hush-hush. The hole-and-corner stuff."

"Because it is in character, you mean?"

"No, no; nothing as subtle as that. Don't you see: Richard had no need of any mystery; but Henry's whole case depended on the boys' end being mysterious. No one has ever been able to think up a reason for such a hole-and-corner method as Richard was supposed to have used. It was a quite mad way to do it. He couldn't hope to get away with it. Sooner or later he was going to have to account for the boys not being there. As far as he knew he had a long reign in front of him. No one has ever been able to think why he should have chosen so difficult and dangerous a way when he had so many simpler methods at hand. He had only to have the boys suffocated, and let them lie in state while the whole of London walked by and wept over two young things dead before their time of fever. That is the way he *would* have done it, too. Goodness, *the whole point* of Richard's killing the boys was to prevent any rising in their favour, and to get any benefit from the murder the fact of their deaths would *have* to be made public, and as soon as possible. It would defeat the whole plan if people didn't *know* that they were dead. But Henry, now. Henry *had* to find a way to push them out of sight. Henry *had* to be mysterious. Henry *had* to hide the facts of when and how they died. *Henry's whole case* depended on no one's knowing what exactly happened to the boys."

"It did indeed, Brent; it did indeed," Grant said, smiling at counsel's eager young face. "You ought to be at the Yard, Mr. Carradine!"

Brent laughed.

"I'll stick to Tonypandy," he said. "I bet there's a lot more of it that we don't know about. I bet history books are just riddled with it."

"You'd better take Sir Cuthbert Oliphant with you, by the way." Grant took the fat respectable-looking volume from his locker. "Historians should be compelled to take a course in psychology before they are allowed to write."

"Huh. That wouldn't do anything for them. A man who is interested in what makes people tick doesn't write history. He writes novels, or becomes an alienist, or a magistrate——"

"Or a confidence man."

"Or a confidence man. Or a fortune-teller. A man who understands about people hasn't any yen to write history. History is toy soldiers."

"Oh, come. Aren't you being a little severe? It's a very learned and erudite——"

"Oh, I didn't mean it that way. I mean: it's moving little figures about on a flat surface. It's half-way to mathematics, when you come to think about it."

"Then if it's mathematics they've no right to drag in backstairs gossip," Grant said, suddenly vicious. The memory of the sainted More continued to upset him. He thumbed through the fat respectable Sir Cuthbert in a farewell review. As he came to the final pages the progress of the paper from under his thumb slackened, and presently stopped.

"Odd," he said, "how willing they are to grant a man the quality of courage in battle. They have only tradition to go on, and yet not one of them questions it. Not one of them, in fact, fails to stress it."

"It was an enemy's tribute," Carradine reminded him. "The tradition began with a ballad written by the other side."

"Yes. By a man of the Stanleys. 'Then a knight to King Richard gan say.' It's here somewhere." He turned over a leaf or two, until he found what he was looking for. "It was 'good Sir William Harrington,' it seems. The knight in question.

"There may no man their strokes abide, the Stanleys dints they be so
    strong [the treacherous bastards!]
Ye may come back at another tide, methinks ye tarry here too long,
Your horse at your hand is ready, another day you may worship win
And come to reign with royalty, and wear your crown and be our king.
'Nay, give me my battle-axe in my hand, set the crown of England on my
    head so high.
For by Him that made both sea and land, King of England this day I
    will die.
One foot I will never flee whilst the breath is my breast within.'
As he said so did it be—if he lost his life he died a King."

" 'Set the crown of England on my head,' " said Carradine, musing. "That was the crown that was found in a hawthorn bush afterwards."

"Yes. Set aside for plunder probably."

"I used to picture it one of those high plush things that King George got crowned in, but it seems it was just a gold circlet."

"Yes. It could be worn outside the battle helmet."

"Gosh," said Carradine with sudden feeling, "I sure would have hated to wear that crown if I had been Henry! I sure would have hated it!" He was silent for a little, and then he said: "Do you know what the town of York wrote—wrote in their records, you know—about the battle of Bosworth?"

"No."

"They wrote: 'This day was our good King Richard piteously slain and murdered; to the great heaviness of this city.' "

The chatter of the sparrows was loud in the quiet.

"Hardly the obituary of a hated usurper," Grant said at last, very dry.

"No," said Carradine. "No. 'To the great heaviness of this city,' " he repeated slowly, rolling the phrase over in his mind. "They cared so much about it that even with a new régime in the offing and the future not to be guessed at they put down in black and white in the town record their opinion that it was murder and their sorrow at it."

"Perhaps they had just heard about the indignities perpetrated on the King's dead body and were feeling a little sick."

"Yes. Yes. You don't like to think of a man you've known and admired flung stripped and dangling across a pony like a dead animal."

"One wouldn't like to think of even an enemy so. But sensibility is not a quality that one would look for among the Henry-Morton crowd."

"Huh. Morton!" said Brent, spitting out the word as if it were a bad taste. "No one was 'heavy' when Morton died, believe me. Know what the Chronicler wrote of him? The London one, I mean. He wrote: 'In our time was no man like to be compared with him in all things; albeit that he lived not without the great disdain and hatred of the Commons of this land.' "

Grant turned to look at the portrait which had kept him company through so many days and nights.

"You know," he said, "for all his success and his Cardinal's hat I think Morton was the loser in that fight with Richard III. In spite of his defeat and his long traducing, Richard came off the better of these two. He was loved in his day."

"That's no bad epitaph," the boy said soberly.

"No. Not at all a bad epitaph," Grant said, shutting Oliphant for the last time. "Not many men would ask for a better." He handed over the book to its owner. "Few men have earned so much," he said.

When Carradine had gone Grant began to sort out the things on his table, preparatory to his homegoing on the morrow. The unread fashionable novels could go to the hospital library to gladden other hearts than his. But he would keep the book with the mountain pictures. And he must remember to give The Amazon back her two history books. He looked them out so that he could give them to her when she brought in his supper. And he read again, for the first time since he began his search for the truth about Richard, the school-book tale of his villainy. There it was, in unequivocal black and white, the infamous story. Without a perhaps or a peradventure. Without a qualification or a question.

As he was about to shut the senior of the two educators his eye fell on the beginning of Henry VII's reign, and he read: "It was the settled and considered policy of the Tudors to rid themselves of all rivals to the throne, more especially those heirs of York who remained alive on the succession of Henry

VII. In this they were successful, although it was left to Henry VIII to get rid of the last of them."

He stared at this bald announcement. This placid acceptance of wholesale murder. This simple acknowledgement of a process of family elimination.

Richard III had been credited with the elimination of two nephews, and his name was a synonym for evil. But Henry VII, whose "settled and considered policy" was to eliminate a whole family, was regarded as a shrewd and far-seeing monarch. Not very lovable perhaps, but constructive and painstaking, and very successful withal.

Grant gave up. History was something that he would never understand.

The values of historians differed so radically from any values with which he was acquainted that he could never hope to meet them on any common ground. He would go back to the Yard, where murderers were murderers and what went for Cox went equally for Box.

He put the two books tidily together and when The Amazon came in with his mince and stewed prunes he handed them over with a neat little speech of gratitude. He really was very grateful to The Amazon. If she had not kept her school books he might never have started on the road that led to his knowledge of Richard Plantagenet.

She looked confused by his kindness, and he wondered if he had been such a bear in his illness that she expected nothing but carping from him. It was a humiliating thought.

"We'll miss you, you know," she said, and her big eyes looked as if they might brim with tears. "We've grown used to having you here. We've even got used to *that*." And she moved an elbow in the direction of the portrait.

A thought stirred in him.

"Will you do something for me?" he asked.

"Of course. Anything I can do."

"Will you take that photograph to the window and look at it in a good light as long as it takes to count a pulse?"

"Yes, of course, if you want me to. But why?"

"Never mind why. You just do it to please me. I'll time you."

She took up the portrait and moved into the light of the window.

He watched the second-hand of his watch.

He gave her forty-five seconds and then said: "Well?" And as there was no immediate answer he said again: "Well?"

"Funny," she said. "When you look at it for a little it's really quite a nice face, isn't it?"

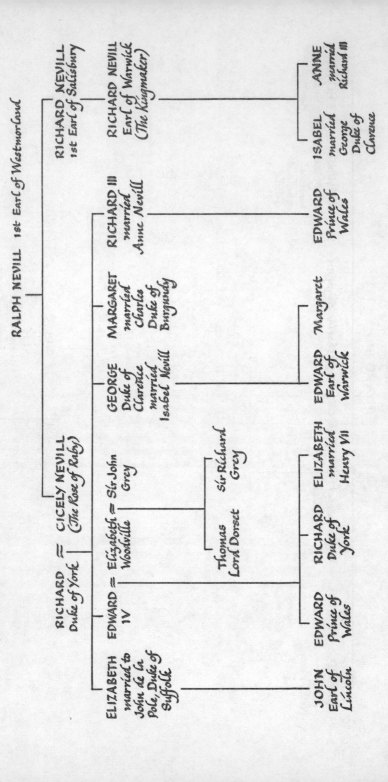

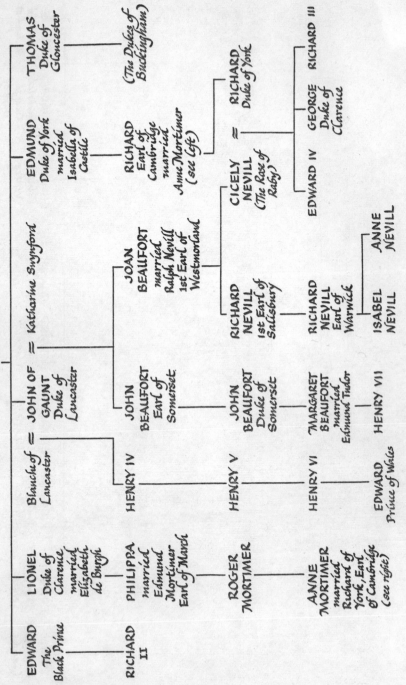